SKULDUGGERY PLEASANT
LAST STAND OF DEAD MEN

SKULDUGGERY PLEASANT
LAST STAND OF DEAD MEN

DEREK LANDY

HarperCollins *Children's Books*

First published in Great Britain by
HarperCollins *Children's Books* in 2013
First published in this edition in the
United States of America by HarperCollins *Children's Books* in 2019
HarperCollins *Children's Books* is a division of HarperCollins*Publishers* Ltd,
HarperCollins Publishers
1 London Bridge Street
London SE1 9GF

The HarperCollins website address is:
www.harpercollins.co.uk

Skulduggery Pleasant rests his weary bones on the web at:
www.skulduggerypleasant.com

Derek Landy blogs under duress at
www.dereklandy.blogspot.com

18 19 20 21 22 LSCC 10 9 8 7 6 5 4 3 2 1

ISBN 978–0–00–826642–4

Derek Landy asserts the moral right to be identified as the author of the work.

Printed and bound in the United States of America by LSC Communications

Find out more about HarperCollins and the environment at
www.harpercollins.co.uk/green

This book is dedicated to you.

Whether you are a Minion or a Skuttlebug or just, you know, a normal person, it's because of you that I get to do what I love and laughingly call it work.

I know some of you by name and some of you by sight (and some of you by smell, but let's not get into that) but there are still countless others I have never met, and to all of you I say thank you for your support, your passion, and your lunacy.

Now please, for the love of whatever god you pray to, leave me alone.

FIVE YEARS AGO

The camp was dark and quiet, and the Warlocks slept. Up on the hill, watching them, a man with golden eyes pulled the collar of his coat tighter in a vain attempt to stave off the cold. His fingers and toes were already numb. His teeth were starting to chatter. How many times had he been in similar circumstances, enduring discomfort while he waited for the perfect time to strike? More than he could remember, that was for sure. It was worth it, of course. It was always worth it.

There was movement behind him, but he didn't turn. He recognised the footsteps. "I didn't think you were coming."

The old man stopped beside him, cupped his hands and blew into them to warm them. "I had visitors," he said. His voice was rough. Words scraped from his throat. "The Skeleton Detective and a girl. She has old blood in her. Ancient blood, I reckon. She's dangerous."

"She's thirteen years old. She's a child."

"She won't stay a child. A few more years and she'll be a threat, you mark my words."

"Consider them marked," said the man with the golden eyes. What had Madame Mist said about the Torment? Once upon a

1

time, he'd been formidable, he'd been dangerous, but he was an old man now, a good blade that had lost its edge. Maybe she was right.

"These plans of yours," the Torment said, "the plans you've made with my fellow Children of the Spider. These are good plans. They will suffice."

"You're onboard, then? What changed your mind?"

The Torment's lined faced was half hidden by the long grey hair and all that beard, but he didn't look like a dulled blade any more. He looked suddenly sharp. "My visitors. Their arrogance has stirred me from my apathy. The mortals they protect have run this world long enough. It's past time we took over."

"I'm so glad to hear it," said the man with the golden eyes. "In that case, there are some Warlocks down there in need of killing, if you're in the mood...?"

The man with the golden eyes approached the camp from the south, the Torment beside him, while the mercenaries closed in from all around. Mortals, in dark military clothing. Heavily armed. Not a sound was made, and yet one of the Warlocks stirred, woke, sat up, looked out into the night, a night that was suddenly lit up by the bright flashes of gunfire.

The three Warlocks leaped up, caught in the crossfire. Notoriously hard to kill, even they couldn't survive the relentless barrage of bullets. Light spilled from every wound as they jerked and fell and stumbled, and then the light faded and they toppled.

Silence followed, broken only by empty magazines being replaced.

The Torment put his gun away. He didn't like using mortal weapons. He didn't like having to work by their side. But he was going to like what came next.

The mercenaries walked into camp, made sure that the Warlocks were really dead.

"You three," said the man with the golden eyes, "take the jeep and go. I'll be in touch to arrange payment."

Three mercenaries faded into the darkness. The other two stayed close, waiting for orders.

The Torment grabbed the taller one's head, twisted till the neck broke. The smaller one stumbled back, going for his weapon, but the Torment took it from him and used it to beat him to death.

While the mercenary was being killed, the man with the golden eyes surveyed the scene. The other Warlocks would return to find their brothers slaughtered, and they would find the bodies of two of the soldiers who did it. Mortal soldiers, wearing no uniform, with no insignias or identification.

"Why did you let the others live?" the Torment asked when he was done. "They can identify us."

That was half right. The other mercenaries could identify the Torment, but the man with the golden eyes was already fading from their memories. "For this to work, they need to be able to boast about their missions. The three I let go have the biggest mouths. Their boasts will eventually reach the right ears."

The Torment scowled. "There is a faster way to do this."

"No," said the man with the golden eyes. "We're not ready yet. But we will be. Soon."

THREE MONTHS AGO

If its estimations were correct – and of course they were correct, they were never wrong – then the Engineer was going to make it. From the instant that warning *ping* had sounded in its head, it had had exactly four weeks to implement the shutdown procedure before catastrophe became somewhat inevitable. It used the caveat 'somewhat' because of course nothing was inevitable, not really. There were always hidden clauses to every eventuality. This the Engineer had learned in its travels, in what it called 'life experience'. That the Engineer was not, technically, alive, mattered not. It existed, and it had sentience, and as such it had life experience. Moving on...

If it had been where it was supposed to be when the *ping* had sounded, the four-week countdown would have mattered not one jot. Unfortunately, the Engineer was not where it was supposed to be. A regrettable unfolding of events, to be sure. The Engineer felt most bad about that. Not that it was the Engineer's fault. No one could possibly lay the blame at the Engineer's mechanical feet. Had it not stood guard for almost three decades? Had it not fulfilled its duty for the most part? Was it really the fault of the Engineer that its advanced programming, a wonderful mixture of technology and magic, enabled it to experience the human phenomenon of 'boredom'? Was it really the fault of the Engineer that it had decided to go for a walk, or that when the *ping* sounded, when the Engineer was finally needed to leap into action, instead of being right there, ready to help, it was on a beach in Italy looking for unusual shells?

No, the Engineer thought not.

It was making good time now, though. The magical symbols carved into its metal body erased it from the memories of mortals the instant they saw it, allowing the Engineer to travel in broad daylight, through busy city streets. The Engineer smiled (internally, for of course it had no mouth). It was feeling good. It was feeling optimistic. Moving at its current speed, it would arrive back in Ireland in plenty of time to shut everything down before a series of overloads and power loops inevitably led to a sequence of events which would, in turn, eventually lead to the probable destruction of the world. The Engineer wasn't worried.

And then the truck hit it.

War is the business of barbarians.
　　　—Napoleon Bonaparte

1

THE WITCHES

The sky was clear and the stars were bright and Gracious had fallen asleep on the grass. Donegan nudged him and he murmured and came round.

"You were supposed to be keeping an eye on the place," Donegan said.

"I was," Gracious yawned.

"You were asleep."

"I was resting my eyes."

"You were snoring."

"I was exercising my lungs."

"Get up."

Grumbling, he got to his feet and stretched. He didn't have to stretch very far. He wasn't that tall. Still, what Gracious O'Callahan lacked in height he made up for in muscle and cool hair. "Hi, Valkyrie," he said.

"Hi, Gracious."

"So is this your first time meeting a witch?"

She nodded.

"You'll do fine, don't worry. Witches are more afraid of you than you are of them."

"I thought that was bees."

9

He blinked. "You might be right. Yes, you *are* right. Bees are fine, witches are horrible. Always get those two mixed up." He was wearing baggy jeans and a faded *Star Wars* T-shirt. Valkyrie imagined that he had a special nerd room at home where he kept all of his weird clothes that referenced old movies, and she imagined him standing in the middle of that room for hours, slowly rotating on the spot, an unsettling smile on his face. By contrast, Donegan Bane, a tall and slender Englishman, favoured sports coats and narrow ties with his skinny jeans.

He glared at Gracious. "I can't believe you fell asleep."

"I *didn't* fall asleep."

"Then do you know if she's home or not?"

"I haven't a clue," Gracious admitted. "I fell asleep."

Valkyrie had first met them only a few months earlier, but she felt she knew them well enough by now to know that, if given the opportunity, they would stand on this hill and bicker for hours. So she turned and walked down to the cottage, and after a moment they followed her.

They arrived at the door and Donegan knocked three times. They waited and the door was opened by a frowning girl.

"Hello," Donegan said with a smile she didn't return.

"Do you know what time it is?" the girl asked. Valkyrie judged her to be around her age, maybe seventeen or eighteen. She had pale skin and full lips and luxuriant red hair that framed her face.

"Why no," Donegan replied as if it were a game. "What time is it?"

She scowled. "What do you want?"

"My name is Donegan Bane and this is my colleague Gracious O'Callahan – we're Monster Hunters. We're here with our associate Valkyrie Cain, and we were wondering if your grandmother was home."

"You're Monster Hunters?"

"Indeed we are. You've probably heard of us. Writers of *Monster*

Hunting for Beginners, *The Definitive Study of Were-Creatures*, and *The Passions of Greta Grey*, our first work of romantic fiction."

"And you want my grandmother?"

"If your grandmother is Dubhóg Ni Broin, yes."

"Are you going to kill her?"

"I'm sorry? Oh, no! No, nothing like that. We just want to talk to her."

"So you're not going to kill her?"

"No," Donegan said with a laugh. "I assure you, she's quite safe."

The girl's eyes narrowed. "How do I know I can trust you?"

"We came here unarmed," Donegan said cheerfully, and Gracious looked at him.

"You're unarmed?" he asked, surprised.

"Yes," Donegan said. "Aren't you?"

"Well, I suppose so. Apart from my gun."

Donegan glared at him. "What? Why did you bring a gun? I told you to come unarmed."

"I thought you were joking."

"Why would I be joking?"

"I don't know, I thought that's what made it funny."

Donegan looked like he might strangle his partner, but then forced the smile back on his face and turned once again to the girl.

"I'm sorry, miss, I didn't catch your name...?"

"Misery," the girl answered, suspicious.

"Misery, it's a pleasure to meet you. My friend here has many problems; he's quite bright in his own way, but likes taking guns to inappropriate places. Let me assure you that we mean your grandmother no harm. We just want to talk to her."

"Why?"

Valkyrie stepped forward before either of the Monster Hunters could make the situation worse. "We're looking for a friend of ours. Maybe you've seen him? Tall? Skinny? Wears nice suits?

Also he's a skeleton? His name's Skulduggery Pleasant and he's wandered off on his own and we think your gran might know where he is."

"Why would my grandmother know that?"

"Because he came to see her, and that's the last we heard of him."

"We don't have much to do with sorcerers," Misery said. "They don't like us and we don't like them. I don't recall seeing your friend, either. What did you say he was? A zombie? A mummy?"

"A skeleton."

"A skeleton, yeah. No, haven't seen one of those in ages."

"I think you're lying," Valkyrie said.

Misery smiled coldly. "What if I am? What are you going to do about it?"

"Whatever I have to."

"Ah, there it is, the arrogance that my grandmother is always talking about. And what kind of sorcerer are you, then? Let me guess. Standing here, dressed all in black... Are they armoured clothes you're wearing? They are, aren't they? And that big ugly ring on your finger – that's from that death magic thing, isn't it? Necromancy? But you... you're my age. You're too young to have had the Surge. You're probably still experimenting with your little sorcerer disciplines, like a good little girl. So I'd say you're an Elemental. I'm right, amn't I? See, witches don't have disciplines. Real magic isn't about choosing one thing over the other. Real magic is about opening yourself up to everything."

"Yeah," said Valkyrie. "That's really interesting. Is your granny home? Could we talk to her?"

"She's home," said Misery. "She's busy, though."

"Doing what?"

"Witchy things."

"Could we come in?"

"Nope."

"We're coming in, with or without your permission."

"I'd like to see you try."

"No, you really wouldn't."

"I think," Gracious said quickly, "that the wrong foot has been gotten off of. Misery, you seem to me to be a lovely girl, and I sense a sort of kindness in your eyes which reminds me of a newborn fawn, or the noble hedgehog. We've been looking for your grandmother for days now, and yesterday our dear friend Skulduggery went missing. We're very worried, as you can imagine, and some of us, without naming any names, might be a little more short-tempered than usual."

"I'm not short-tempered," said Valkyrie.

"Then how did you know I was referring to you?"

"Because you pointed."

"Getting back to the subject at hand, Misery, we would really appreciate it if you'd let us in. Please?"

Misery looked at him, but didn't respond.

"Um," said Gracious, "hello?"

"Quiet," she said, "I'm thinking." She chewed a plump lip, then sighed. "I don't really get along with my grandmother. She's stuck in her ways and... I look at her and she's all withered and stuff and I don't want to end up like that, you know? I don't want to live in a cottage in the middle of nowhere for the rest of my life. I want to live in the city. I want to wear high-heeled shoes every once in a while and do things that don't all revolve around being a witch."

Gracious nodded. "I understand and sympathise with everything you've just said, apart from the bit about the high-heeled shoes, which I wouldn't know about."

"Can you promise me you're not going to hurt her?" Misery asked.

Valkyrie frowned. "Why would we hurt her?"

"Because she has your friend trapped in the cellar."

Valkyrie stepped through the doorway. "He'd better be OK."

Misery held up her hands. "He's fine, he's fine. From what I can hear they're just talking. If you can promise me you won't hurt her, I'll show you how to get down there. Deal?"

"I'll defend myself," Valkyrie said. "If she attacks me, I'll defend myself. But... we promise to go easy on her if it's at all possible."

"That's really the best deal you're going to get," Gracious added, a little apologetically.

"Fine," said Misery, after a moment's consideration. "Come on in. Wipe your feet."

The cottage was dark and weird and smelled funny, like boiled cabbage and wet dog. Valkyrie could see why Misery didn't like living here. She couldn't see a TV or even a radio. It was lit by oil lamps, and there was a brazier in the corner. In the winter, she imagined this place would get very cold.

Misery pulled back a rug and lifted a heavy trapdoor. She put her finger to her lips, and Valkyrie nodded.

The cellar was bigger than she'd expected, but about as gloomy. Valkyrie and the Monster Hunters walked down the stone steps, then crept through the tunnel towards a flickering light, following the sound of Skulduggery's voice and another, a woman's. The nearer they got, the more distinct the words became.

"—see what this has got to do with me," said the woman. "I'm just an old witch living out her life with an ungrateful granddaughter. What would I know about the affairs of Warlocks?"

Valkyrie peered round the corner. Dubhóg Ni Broin looked remarkably like the witches in fairy tales. She was old and small and stooped, with tangled grey hair and a long chin with a wart on it – an actual *wart*. She was wearing a black shawl over a shapeless black dress but, disappointingly, no pointy hat. Still, Valkyrie wouldn't have wanted her to slip *fully* into caricature. That would have been silly.

Facing Dubhóg, his back to Valkyrie, Skulduggery Pleasant stood in a chalk circle. She knew enough about symbols and sigil magic by now to know that the circle was binding his powers, but there were other symbols there she didn't recognise. Seeing as how he didn't just step out of the circle, though, she guessed they were there to keep him in place.

"Witches and Warlocks get along like a house on fire," he said. He was wearing the grey suit he'd been in the last time she'd seen him. His hat was on the table in the corner, and the lamplight flickered off his skull. "You shop at the same stores, use the same recipes... If anyone would have heard what the Warlocks are up to, it'd be a witch."

"Maybe those *other* witches," Dubhóg said, somewhat resentfully. "Maybe the Maidens or those Brides of Blood Tears with their exposed bellies and their veils and their long legs... Is my belly exposed, Mr Skeleton? Am I wearing a veil? Are my legs long and shapely?"

"Uh," said Skulduggery.

"There are different sorts of witches and Warlocks," Dubhóg continued, "just like there are different sorts of sorcerers. There are male witches and female witches, just as there are male Warlocks and female Warlocks. There are all kinds. But we keep to ourselves. The business of others does not interest us."

"But the business of others *does* interest *me*," Skulduggery said. "I've been hearing rumours, Dubhóg. Disquieting rumours. I just thought you might be able to allay my fears."

"And that is why you attacked me?"

"I merely knocked on your front door."

"Then you attacked my *door*." Dubhóg squinted at him. "You think you're so clever, don't you? With your Sanctuaries and your rules. You think everyone should be like you. Well, I'm not like you. Witches aren't like you. Warlocks aren't like you. Why would we want to be? You live your lives restricted by rules. Even your magic is restricted. Sorcerers treat magic like science. It's disgusting and unnatural. It twists what true magic is all about."

"Control is important."

"Why? Why is it important? Magic should be allowed to flourish in whichever form it takes."

15

"That way madness lies."

"For the weak-minded, perhaps."

"Tell me what Charivari is up to."

"I wouldn't know," said Dubhóg. "I've never met the man. Why would you think I know anything about any of this?"

"A little over a year ago, you were seen talking to a Warlock who went on to try to kill me and my associate."

"A year? How can I be expected to remember that far back? I'm eight hundred years old. I get confused about the little things – who said what, who did what, who tried to kill who... My days are devoted to my granddaughter and my nights are spent making multiple trips to the toilet. I don't have time for anyone's grand schemes."

"So Charivari has a grand scheme?"

Dubhóg frowned. "I didn't say that."

"Actually, you sort of did."

"Oh, I see," said Dubhóg. "You're one of those, are you? You like to play around with words to try and get the better of me. Well, it's not going to work. With age comes wisdom, you ever hear that?"

"I did, but I've found that wisdom has a cut-off point of around one hundred and twenty years. Once you reach that, you're really as wise as you're going to get."

"Well, I'm wise enough to say nothing more on the subject."

"So you *know* more on the subject."

"I didn't say that."

"Again, you implied that you did. The Warlock you spoke to had been hired by the Necromancers to kill us – he said he owed them a special favour. Why?"

Dubhóg shrugged. "Why does anyone do anything?"

"What did the Necromancers do for the Warlocks? Did they give them something? They did? What was it – an item, an object, a person? Was it a thing, was it information, was it—? It was information? OK."

Dubhóg stepped back, horrified. "What are you doing? Are you reading my mind? No one can read my mind. Witches' minds cannot be read."

"I'm not reading your mind," Skulduggery said. "I'm reading your face. What information did the Necromancers give them? A strategy? A place? A name?"

Dubhóg screamed and covered her face with her hands.

"A name, then," Skulduggery said.

"You don't know that!" Dubhóg cried. "I have my face covered!"

"So that's what the Warlock wanted from the Necromancers, but what did he want from you? This will go easier for you if you just tell me what I want to know."

"Never!"

While Dubhóg reeled dramatically with her face covered, Valkyrie stepped out from hiding and approached the circle. Skulduggery gave her a little wave. She could have wet her finger and smudged the chalk, but instead she decided to put all those hours of practice to good use. Crouching by the edge of the circle, she put her hand flat on the ground and pushed her magic into the concrete until she was almost part of it, until she was cold and hard just like it was. And then she wrenched her hand to the side and the ground cracked, splitting one of the lines of chalk.

Dubhóg whirled at the noise, and stared at Valkyrie as Skulduggery stepped out of the circle. "How did you get in? Did you harm my granddaughter?"

"She's fine," Valkyrie said, straightening up.

"If you hurt her..."

"We didn't."

Dubhóg's face contorted in fury. "*You will pay!*"

"I told you," Valkyrie said, frowning, "we didn't hurt—"

But it was too late.

Dubhóg flew into the air, the space around her crackling with

17

an energy that made her long hair stand on end. She hovered there, looking like an electrocuted cartoon character, her face twisted in anger. Gracious leaped at her, and a stream of sizzling light caught him in the chest and sent him hurtling backwards. Donegan rushed in, his hands lighting up, but Dubhóg caught the energy stream he sent her way and responded with another one of her own. The air rushed in around Valkyrie and she shot towards Dubhóg, the shadows bunching round her fist. Dubhóg grabbed her by the throat, her grip strong, and Valkyrie clicked her fingers, summoning a ball of flame into her hand, and prepared to ram it into the witch's face.

"Granny," Misery called. "Granny, stop that. Gran. *NANA!*"

The battle froze, and Dubhóg looked round. "Misery? You're OK?"

"They didn't hurt me, Nana," Misery said, somewhat crossly. "Now put her down before you embarrass me even more."

Dubhóg drifted to the ground and let go of Valkyrie, who stepped back, rubbing her throat.

"Terribly sorry," Dubhóg said, her hair returning to normal, that ferocious power leaving her as quickly as it had arrived.

"That's quite all right," Skulduggery said, walking forward. "We all make mistakes, isn't that right? No harm done."

In the corner, Gracious moaned.

"Tell them what they want to know," Misery said, "then come upstairs. I'll put the kettle on."

Misery turned, walked away, and Dubhóg cleared her throat and smiled at Skulduggery.

"I'm a constant source of embarrassment to her," she explained. "I can't do anything right, really. All I want to do is protect her from the everyday cruelties of life, but I always do something wrong. I say the wrong thing, or I attack the wrong people..."

"Kids," Skulduggery said, sympathising.

"She'll miss me when I'm gone," Dubhóg said.

"So, the Warlock..."

18

"Oh, yes, him. I don't know what information the Necromancers gave him. He mentioned he'd been talking to one of them, a man with a ridiculous name."

"Bison Dragonclaw," said Valkyrie.

"Dragonclaw, yes," said Dubhóg. "That was it."

"And why did he come to see you in the first place?" Skulduggery asked.

"He thought I'd be able to convince my sisters to join with Charivari. But we Crones use magic differently from even other witches – it doesn't keep us so young. We are old women, and so I told him no."

"Join Charivari to do what? What are the Warlocks planning?"

"War," said Dubhóg. "They're planning on going to war."

2

BACK IN ROARHAVEN

Ghastly Bespoke returned to Roarhaven with a sense of overwhelming dread. It wasn't danger he dreaded, or battle, or confrontation or arguments. It was meetings. It was endless, monotonous meetings.

The last few days he'd spent at his old shop in Dublin, working on various items of clothing. Repairing, modifying, making from scratch. He had been content there. Happy. Alone with this thoughts, alone with the needle and thread, with the fabrics, his mind had been allowed to settle, and it had been wonderful.

But his vacation was over, and here he was, being driven back into the squalid, bleak little town of Roarhaven and all that anxiety he'd left behind was quickly building up again inside his chest. They drove through Main Street, drawing a few cold glances from the townspeople. There was a single, sad little tree planted in a square of earth on the pavement. For as long as he'd been here, he had never seen it with leaves. Here they were in August and it was just as thin and skeletal as it had been in winter. It wasn't dead, though. It was as if the town were keeping it alive purely to prolong its torture.

They approached the dark, stagnant lake and the squat building that rested beside it, all grey and concrete and uninspiring. The

Administrator, Tipstaff, was waiting for him as he thanked the driver and got out of the car.

"Elder Bespoke, welcome back. The meeting is about to start."

Ghastly frowned at him. "It's not scheduled till two. They arrived early?"

"In their words, they are 'eager to negotiate'."

Ghastly walked out of the warm sun into the chill Sanctuary, Tipstaff beside him. "Who's here?"

"Elder Illori Reticent of the English Sanctuary plus two associates, an Elemental and an Energy-Thrower."

"That's all?"

"We've been tracking them since they flew in this morning, and we've been keeping an eye on all known foreign sorcerers in the country. It would appear that these three are the only ones in the vicinity. Elder Bespoke?"

Tipstaff held a door open and Ghastly grumbled, but went inside. In here, his robe was waiting. He pulled it on, checked himself in the mirror. His shirt, his waistcoat, his tie, his trousers, all those clothes he'd made himself, all of them were covered up by this robe. His physique, honed by countless hours of punching bags and punching people, was rendered irrelevant by this shapeless curtain he now wore. The only thing that wasn't covered up was the one thing he'd spent his life trying to draw attention away from – the perfectly symmetrical scars that covered his entire head.

Tipstaff brushed a speck of lint from Ghastly's shoulder, and nodded approvingly. "This way, sir."

Ghastly could have walked to the conference room blindfolded, but he let Tipstaff take the lead. There was Ghastly's way of doing things and there was the proper way of doing things, and if there was one thing Tipstaff liked, it was procedure.

They reached a set of double doors guarded by two Cleavers. At Tipstaff's nod, the warriors in grey banged their scythes on the floor in perfect unison and the doors opened. Tipstaff stood to one side as Ghastly walked in.

Grand Mage Erskine Ravel sat at the round table and scratched at his neck. The robes could be particularly itchy against bare skin, which was why Ghastly had lined his with silk. He hadn't offered to line Ravel's, though. He found it quietly amusing to watch his friend suffer.

Beside Ravel sat Madame Mist, her face covered by that black veil she always wore. He'd often wondered if her features were as unsightly as his own, but decided that no, the veil was probably some piece of tradition that the Children of the Spider had chosen to keep alive.

Across from Ravel and Mist, Illori Reticent sat patiently. A pretty woman with a beautiful mind, Illori's smile grew warm when she saw him.

"Elder Bespoke," she said, rising to meet him, "so good to see you again."

"Elder Reticent," said Ghastly, shaking her hand. "Sorry I'm late."

"You're not late, we're early, which in some circumstances can be twice as rude as being late."

Ghastly glanced at the man and woman standing behind her, their backs to the wall and their expressions vacant. "You only came with two bodyguards, I see."

"Of course," Illori said, smiling innocently. "I'm not in any danger, am I? I am among friends, yes?"

"Indeed you are," said Ghastly, smiling back at her. "It's nice that you remember. So many of your fellow mages seem to have forgotten that fact."

"Well, they're not here, and I am, so I have been granted the honour of speaking for the whole of the Supreme Council. And I have some things I'd like to discuss with you."

"Then let's get started," Ghastly said, and took up his place at Ravel's side.

Illori looked at them all before speaking again. "The Irish Sanctuary has been at the forefront of the battle against oppression

22

and tyranny for the last six hundred years, ever since Mevolent's rise to power. We recognise that, and we appreciate that. Until recently, your Council of Elders was the most respected Council of any territory in living memory."

Ravel nodded. "Until recently."

"That's no secret, surely. The death of Eachan Meritorious was a great loss to us all, but for Ireland it signalled the beginning of a rapid slide into uncertainty, aided no doubt when Thurid Guild's brief time as Grand Mage ended with his imprisonment. Again and again, the Irish Sanctuary has been battered by enemies from without and within."

"And again and again we have triumphed," said Ghastly.

"Indeed you have," said Illori, "thanks to some exemplary work by your operatives. But your Sanctuary has been weakened. When the next attack comes, you may not be strong enough to prevail. So I have come to you with a solution, should you be agreeable."

"This'll be interesting," Ravel muttered.

"Before the Sanctuaries, there were communities. Each of these communities was ruled by twelve village Elders. Each of these twelve would oversee a different aspect of village life, but, when the time came to make important decisions, all twelve votes were counted equally."

"We know our own history," said Ravel. "We also know that when the Sanctuaries were established, the unwieldy twelve was cut down to a more practical three. Even the communities that are around today haven't kept up with the old ways."

"Even so," Illori said, "lessons can be learned. We propose the establishment of a supporting Council of nine – five mages of our choosing, four of yours – to help you in the running of your affairs. This would leave you with a majority of seven to five, and it would mean you had more sorcerers, more Cleavers, and more resources. Your Sanctuary would remain under your full control and it would be returned to its former strength."

Ravel looked at her. "I'm curious as to why you think we would possibly say yes to this."

"Because it's a fair proposal. You retain full control—"

"We retain full control now," said Mist. "Why would we change?"

"Because the current situation is not acceptable."

"To you," said Ravel.

"To us, yes," said Illori. "There are members of the Supreme Council who view you as dangerous and reckless and they continually call for action against you. Every mage paying attention is expecting war to break out at any moment. Why would you risk hostilities if the situation can be resolved amicably?"

"There's not going to be a supporting Council, Elder Reticent."

"Why not?"

"Because the Supreme Council does not tell us what to do."

Illori shook her head. "Is that what this is? A matter of pride? You won't accept our terms because you don't like being told what to do? Pride is wasted breath, Grand Mage Ravel. Pride is you putting your own petty concerns over the well-being of every sorcerer in your Sanctuary. More than that, it's putting your petty concerns over the well-being of every mortal around the world. If war breaks out, it's going to be so much harder to keep our activities off the news channels. If that happens, it's on your heads. But we can avoid it all if you'd just listen to reason."

"The Supreme Council has no right to dictate to other Sanctuaries how to conduct their business," said Mist. "In fact, the Supreme Council itself may even be an illegal organisation."

"Ridiculous."

"We have our people looking into it," Mist said.

"Don't bother," said Illori. "We've already had our own experts combing through the literature. There is no ancient rule or obscure law that says Sanctuaries cannot join forces to combat a significant threat. It's what we did against Mevolent, after all."

"We are a significant threat, are we?" asked Ravel.

"You might be," Illori answered, then shook her head. "Listen, I didn't come here to threaten you. We are standing on the precipice and the Supreme Council isn't going to back away. They're angry and they're frightened, and the more they think about this, the more angry and frightened they become. They're hurtling towards war and you're the only ones who can stop them."

"By agreeing to their demands."

"Yes."

"We're not going to do that, Illori."

"Do you *want* war, Erskine? Do you actually *want* to fight? How many of us do you want to kill?"

"If you're looking to calm things down, calm down those making all the noise. We will not be intimidated and we will not be bullied."

Illori laughed without humour. "You keep painting yourselves as the aggrieved, like you were just minding your own business and then the Supreme Council came along and tried to steal your lunch money. You are at fault, Erskine. Your Sanctuary is weak. You've made mistakes. We are not the bad guys here. We have gone out of our way to treat you with respect. We released Dexter Vex and his little group of thieves, didn't we?"

"What does that have to do with us?" asked Ghastly. "Vex's little group of thieves, as you call it, consisted of three Irishmen, an Englishman, an American and an African. It was an international group affiliated with no particular Sanctuary, who sought approval from no one before embarking on their mission."

"An international group that was led by Dexter Vex and Saracen Rue," Illori said, "two of your fellow Dead Men. They may not have told you what they were planning, but where would they have brought the God-Killer weapons had they succeeded in stealing them, except back to you?"

"Vex wanted them stockpiled in order to fight Darquesse."

"A more suspicious mind than mine might wonder if Darquesse was merely the excuse he needed."

"All of this is a moot point," Ravel said. "Tanith Low and her band of criminals got to the God-Killers before Vex and she had them destroyed."

"And you had her," said Mist. "Briefly."

"What was that?" Illori asked.

"You arrested her," said Mist. "The woman who assassinated Grand Mage Strom. You arrested her, chained her up, and she escaped."

"What's your point?"

"There are those who say Strom's assassination was the breaking point," said Mist. "It was his death that has propelled us to the verge of war. He was assassinated here, of course, in this very building. For this, you blame us, even though Tanith Low is a Londoner. But when you finally arrest Miss Low, when you have the chance to punish the killer herself for the crime she committed... she mysteriously escapes."

"Are you saying we let that happen?"

"It has allowed you to refocus your blame on us, has it not?"

"I haven't heard anything so stupid in a long time," said Illori, "and I've heard a lot of stupid things lately. We don't know how she escaped or who helped her. The investigation is ongoing. There are those in the Supreme Council, by the way, who think this Sanctuary had something to do with it."

"Of course they do," Ravel said, sounding tired.

"They believe both Vex's group and Tanith Low's gang were taking orders from you," Illori said. "Two teams going after the same prizes, independent of each other – doubling the chances of success."

"Well," said Ghastly, "it's nice to see the Supreme Council thinks we're so badly co-ordinated as to organise something as incredibly inept as that."

"Illori, go home," Ravel said gently. "Tell them you approached us with this proposal and we politely declined. Tell the Supreme Council that, before he died, Grand Mage Strom agreed that

26

their interference was not necessary. He would have recommended no further action if Tanith Low hadn't killed him. You and your colleagues have nothing to fear from us."

"But that's not strictly true, is it?" Illori asked. "You have the Accelerator. We've heard what it can do. Bernard Sult witnessed its potential. He saw the levels to which it can boost a sorcerer's power. If you so wanted, you could boost the magic of every one of your mages and you could send them against us. Our superior numbers would mean nothing against power like that."

"That's not something we're planning on doing."

"Then dismantle it. I'm sure that would go a long way to placating the Supreme Council."

Ravel shook his head. "The Accelerator is powering a specially-built prison cell – the only cell in existence capable of holding someone of Darquesse's strength. We need it active."

"Then give it to us as a gesture of good faith."

"As a gesture of naivety, you mean. We're not giving you the Accelerator. We're not dismantling it. We're not turning it off. We're not even sure if it *can* be turned off. If that makes the Supreme Council nervous, then that is unfortunate. Please make it clear to your colleagues that we do not intend to use the Accelerator against them as part of any pre-emptive strike." Ravel sat forward. "If, however, the Supreme Council launches any kind of attack against us or our operatives, and if we feel significantly threatened, then using the Accelerator to even the odds is always an option."

"They're not going to be pleased to hear that."

"Illori, at this point? I really don't give a damn."

3

THE BIG DAY

Desmond Edgley threw back his head and sang, "Happy birthday to you, happy birthday to you, you look like a monkey, and you smell like one, too!" and laughed like a drain as Valkyrie blew out her candles. It had been the same lyrics every year since she was old enough to know what a monkey was. She had grown up and matured. Her father had not.

Her mum and baby sister clapped and Valkyrie sat back down, grinning. Faint trails of smoke rose, twisting, from eighteen candles, and were quickly dispersed by her mother's waving hand.

"Did you make a wish?" her dad asked.

She nodded. "World peace."

He made a face. "Really? World peace? Not a jetpack? I would have wished for a jetpack."

"You always wish for a jetpack," her mum said, cutting the cake. "Have you got one yet?"

"No," he said, "but you need to use up a lot of wishes to get something like a jetpack. On my next birthday, I'll have wished for it forty times. Forty. I'll *have* to get one then. Imagine it, Steph – I'll be the only dad in town with his own jetpack..."

"Yeah," she said slowly, "I'll be ever so proud..."

Her mum passed out the plates, then stood and tapped her fork against a glass. "I'd like to make a toast, before we begin."

"Toast," said Alice.

"Thank you, Alice. Today is a big day for our little Stephanie. It's been a big week, actually, with the exam results and the college offers. We've always been proud of you, and now we're delighted beyond belief that the rest of the world will be able to see you the way we see you – as a strong, intelligent, beautiful young woman who can do whatever she puts her mind to."

"Toast," Alice said wisely.

"You've been in our lives for eighteen years," her mum continued, "and you have brightened every single day. You've brought joy and laughter to this house, even when times were tough."

Her dad leaned in. "It is *not* easy being married to me."

"And today is also the day that Gordon's estate passes into your name. You are now the sole custodian of his books, the owner of his house, and the spender of his money. And even though you've known that this was coming since you were twelve years old, you never slackened off. You never took anything for granted. You finished school, you got excellent results, and you made sure you faced the future on your own terms. We couldn't be prouder of you, honey."

Before her mum could start crying, Valkyrie's dad stood up. He cleared his throat, pondered a bit, and then began. "It is no secret that I always wanted a son."

Valkyrie howled with laughter and her mum threw a napkin at her husband, who waited until things had calmed down before continuing. "I thought that having a daughter would mean there'd be pink everywhere and I'd have to take her to ballet lessons and when she was old enough to have a boyfriend I'd be really weird around him. Thankfully, none of this turned out to be the case."

Valkyrie blinked. "You were extraordinarily weird around Fletcher."

"No, you're misremembering. I was cool."

"You kept touching his hair."

"I have no recollection of that ever happening."

"Des," her mum said, "you were really, really weird to that boy."

"Can I be allowed to finish my speech? Can I? Thank you. So, to recap, I never wanted daughters. But when Stephanie was born I looked into her big eyes and I was so overcome by both her cuteness and the baby fumes that I decided to let bygones be bygones, and start over. It was a noble and selfless act by me, but you were only two days old so you're probably too young to remember it."

"Probably," said Valkyrie.

"And now look at me!" her dad said. "Eighteen years on and I have two daughters, and the smaller one can barely walk in a straight line, let alone do ballet. What age are you, Alice? Four? Five?"

"Eighteen months," said Valkyrie's mum.

"Eighteen months and what have you to show for it? Do you even have a job? Do you? You're a burden on this family. A burden, I say."

"Toast," Alice responded, and squealed as her dad scooped her up and did his face-hugger walk round the kitchen.

"I'm pretty sure that when that speech started it was about you," Valkyrie's mum said, "but then he kind of got distracted. Des. Des, don't you think it's time to give Steph her birthday present?"

"Present!" Alice yelled, as her dad held her over his shoulder by one ankle.

"Fair enough, wifey. I suppose it can't be put off any longer. Steph, now that you have large sums of money, you can of course buy one of these brand-new if you so wanted. But I like to think that a second-hand one, bought by your parents, would have a sentimental value that you just wouldn't be able to get in a—"

Valkyrie sat up straight. "You got me a car?"

"I didn't say that."

She stood. "Oh my God, you got me a car?"

"Again, I didn't say that. It might not be a car. It might be a drum kit."

"Is it a drum kit?"

"No. It's a car."

"Toast!" Alice yelped.

"Ah, yes, sorry," Valkyrie's dad said, setting his youngest daughter back on the ground. She wobbled and fell over and started laughing.

"You are so dumb," her dad murmured.

Valkyrie ran to the front door, yanked it open, and froze. There, in the driveway, was a gleaming Ford Fiesta. And it was orange.

She'd been in an orange car before. One of Skulduggery's spare cars had been orange. But this... this...

She couldn't help herself. "It looks like an Oompa-Loompa," she blurted.

"Do you not like it?" her mum asked at her shoulder.

"I asked for the colour specially," her dad said. "The salesman said it wasn't a good idea, but I thought it might be extra safe and there was a possibility it could glow in the dark. It doesn't, though." He sounded dejected. "If you want a different colour, we can take it back. I mean, the salesman will probably laugh at me, but that's OK. He was laughing enough when I drove off in it."

Valkyrie walked up to the car, traced her fingertips along the side. The interior was dark green. Just like an Oompa-Loompa's hair. She looked back at her parents.

"You got me a car. You got me a *car*."

Her mum dangled the keys. "Do you like it?"

"I love it!"

Valkyrie caught the keys and slipped in behind the wheel. Her car had a very nice dashboard, and a very nice smell, and her car was very clean. She adjusted her rear-view mirror in her car and slid her seat back in her car and it was her car. It wasn't the Bentley and apart from the colour it wasn't very flashy, but it was *her* car. "You are the Oompa-Loompa," she said, patting the dash, "and I love you."

She put on Pixie Lott as she got ready, sang along as she danced round her bedroom, doing the hip-grinding thing in the mirror whenever the chorus popped up. The white dress tonight, she reckoned, laying it out on the bed. Tight, white and strapless – her dad was going to have a fit when he saw it. But this was her night, and she was going out with her friends, and she was going to wear whatever the hell she wanted. She was eighteen, after all.

As she sang into the hairbrush, she realised that she was actually looking forward to spending time with Hannah and the others. A girls' night out – the first girls' night out since school had ended. It was going to be fun. The fact that she had butterflies struck her as weird, though, until she tried to remember whether or not she'd actually met all of her friends, or if some were friends the reflection had made and then simply transferred the memory to Valkyrie's mind. She laughed at the oddness of her life, and then her phone rang and she paused the music.

"Happy birthday," Skulduggery said.

"Thank you," she grinned. "Guess what my parents got me."

"An orange car."

Her grin faded. "How did you know?"

"I'm looking at it."

"You're outside?"

"We got a call. You're not doing anything, are you?"

She looked at her dress, at her shoes, and felt the butterflies slowly stop fluttering. "No," she said, "not doing anything. I'll be out in a minute."

She hung up, and sighed. Then she tapped the mirror in her wardrobe and her reflection stepped out.

"I know," Valkyrie said. "You don't have to say it. I know."

"You deserve a different kind of fun," the reflection said.

Valkyrie pulled on her black trousers, hunted around for some socks, and grabbed her boots. "It's fine. Most of them are your friends anyway. I've never talked to them. What would I even say?"

"You're really going to use that excuse?"

"I'm going to use whatever excuse I have to. Where's my black top?"

"I put it in the wash."

"It was clean."

"It had blood on it."

"Yeah, but not mine."

The reflection held up a spaghetti-strap T-shirt.

"That's pink," said Valkyrie.

The reflection pulled it on. "It looks cute on you."

Valkyrie raised an eyebrow. "It *does* look cute on me. Wow. I look hot in that. Where did I get it?"

"I bought it last week," the reflection said, giving a twirl.

"OK, you've convinced me."

The reflection threw it to her and Valkyrie put it on, then zipped up her jacket.

"Do me a favour, OK?" said Valkyrie. "Have a good time tonight."

"I'll do my very best," said the reflection, and smiled. "You try to do the same."

Valkyrie opened the window. "I'll be with Skulduggery," she said. "No trying involved."

She slipped out as Pixie Lott started playing again, and she jumped.

Right before they reached the hotel, Skulduggery's gloved fingers pressed the symbols on his collarbones, and a face flowed up over his skull.

Valkyrie raised an eyebrow. "Not bad."

"You like this one?"

"It suits you. Can you keep it on file, or something?"

He smiled. "Every time I activate the façade, the result is random, you know that."

"Yeah, but you've had it for a few years now. It might be time to start thinking about settling down with something a little more permanent."

"Are you trying to make me normal?"

"Heaven forbid," she said, widening her eyes in mock horror. He opened the door for her, followed her through. They walked into the lobby, passed the reception desk and went straight to the elevators. Skulduggery slipped a black card into the slot, and pressed the button for the penthouse. The doors slid closed.

"So..." said Valkyrie.

"So."

"It's my eighteenth."

"Yes it is."

"The big one eight. I'm an adult now. Technically."

"Technically."

"It's an important birthday."

"Well, you're doing fine so far."

She laughed. "Did you... y'know... Did you get me a present?"

Skulduggery looked at her. "Did you want me to get you a present?"

Her smile dropped. "Of course."

The elevator stopped with a *ping*, and the doors opened. She was the first out, walking quickly.

"I see," he said, following her. "Do you have any suggestions?"

"I think you know me well enough by now to figure it out for yourself."

"You're mad at me."

"No I'm not."

"Despite my handsome face, you are."

She stopped before they reached the penthouse and turned.

"Yes, I'm mad at you. People buy presents for people who are important to them. After all this time, I didn't think I had to *tell* you to buy me a present."

"And I didn't think I had to buy you a present to prove that you're important to me."

"Well... I mean... you don't, but... but that's not the point. It's not about proving it, it's about showing it."

"And a gift is an accurate measurement? Your parents got you a car. Does this mean you are as important to them as a car is? Do they love you a car's worth?"

"Of course not. A birthday present is a token gift."

"A token gift is like an empty gesture – devoid of any kind of value."

"It's a nice thing to do!"

"Oh," Skulduggery said. "OK. I understand. I'll get you a present, then."

"Thank you." She turned back, and knocked on the door. "Who are we here to see?"

"An old friend of yours," Skulduggery said, and for the first time she noticed the edge to his voice.

She didn't have time to question him further. The doors opened as one and Solomon Wreath smiled at her.

"Hello, Valkyrie," he said.

Before she knew what she was doing, she was giving him a hug. "Solomon! What are you doing here? I thought you were off having adventures."

"I can't have adventures in my home country every once in a while? This is where the real action is, after all. Come in, come in. Skulduggery, I suppose you can join us."

"You're too kind," Skulduggery muttered, following them inside and closing the doors behind him.

The penthouse was huge and extravagant, though Valkyrie had been in bigger and more extravagant when she dated Fletcher. Back then, he'd spend his nights in whatever penthouse suite was available around the world, and all for free. Such were the advantages of being a Teleporter, she supposed, though these days all that had changed. Now he had a nice, normal girlfriend and he was living in his own apartment in Australia. He was almost settled. It was kind of scary.

She glanced back at Skulduggery, who had already let his false face melt away. He took off his hat and didn't say anything as Wreath came back with a small box, wrapped up in a bow.

"Happy birthday," Wreath said.

Valkyrie's eyes widened. "You got me a present?"

"Of course," Wreath said, almost laughing at her surprise. "You were my best student in all my years in the Necromancer Temple. No one took to it quite like you did, and although we may have hit a few bumps along the way—"

"Like you trying to kill billions of people," Skulduggery said.

"—you have always been my favourite," Wreath finished, ignoring him. "Open it. I think you'll like it."

Valkyrie pulled the bow apart and the wrapping opened like a gently blooming flower. There was a wooden box within, and she opened the lid and raised an eyebrow. "It's, uh, it's an exact copy of my ring."

"Not exact," said Wreath. "Inside, it is different indeed. When students begin their training, they are given objects like the ring you have now – good, strong, sturdy, capable of wielding an impressive amount of power. But after their Surge, they need something stronger, something to handle a lot more power."

"But I haven't had my Surge yet."

Wreath smiled. "I know, and yet you need an upgrade already. In this, as in so many other ways, you are exceptional, Valkyrie. Your ring, please?"

He held out his hand. She glanced at Skulduggery, then slid it from her finger and passed it over. As Wreath walked out of the room for a moment, she took the new one from the box, put it on.

Wreath returned, carrying a hammer. "Now for the fun part," he said, and put Valkyrie's ring on the table and smashed it. A wave of shadows exploded from the flying shards, twisted in the air and went straight for the ring on her finger. The ring sucked them in eagerly, turning cold, and Valkyrie gasped.

"Do you feel it?" Wreath asked. "Do you feel that power?"

"Wow," she said, regaining control of herself. "I do. Wow. That's... that's..."

"That's Necromancy."

It was startling. It was distracting. It was amazing. "Thank you," she said.

Wreath shrugged. "Turning eighteen is a big day for anyone. But I am well aware that you did not come to see me for gifts and hugs."

"Oh, yeah," she said, getting her mind back on track. "Why *are* we here to see you?"

"Your unusually silent partner here has been in touch. It seems you've been investigating the events surrounding that Warlock trying to kill you last year."

"He told us he was doing you Necromancers a favour," Skulduggery said. "It was in exchange for information. A name."

"First of all," said Wreath, "I was kept out of that particular loop. It was not my idea to include the Warlocks in any of our sordid schemes, because I am neither stupid nor deranged. That was all Craven, by way of that idiot Dragonclaw."

"So what did Dragonclaw tell the Warlock?" Valkyrie asked.

"Please," Wreath said, "take a seat. What do you know about the Warlocks?"

Valkyrie settled herself on the couch, the ring sending slivers of sensation dancing up and down her arm. "Just the, uh, you know, the usual stuff. They're not... wow, this ring is cool... they're not like the rest of us. They have their own culture, their own traditions, their own type of magic..."

Wreath nodded. "A type of magic that, quite frankly, we don't understand. And all of that is fine because there aren't very many of them and they keep to themselves. Or at least they did."

"What's happened?"

"Someone's been attacking them," Wreath said. "Provoking the Warlocks is not a wise move at the best of times, but there seems to be a group of people who are determined to do just that. In the past five years, dozens of Warlocks have been killed. They've been isolated from the others, hunted down, and executed. Now there is only a handful left."

Valkyrie frowned. "The one who attacked us, he said they're growing stronger every day."

Wreath smiled. "Warlocks are known for never showing weakness. It's what I like about them."

"So what name did he want from Dragonclaw?"

"An associate of mine, Baritone, actually one of the Necromancers who were killed during the battle at Aranmore, was travelling through France a year or so before he died and happened to come across a group of mortals in a bar who were boasting of a job well done. Naturally, he pretended to be a mere mortal just like they were and, from what he gathered, they were ex-Special Forces, funded by secret government money and directed to—"

"Wait," Skulduggery said. "You're talking about Department X."

"Who are they?" Valkyrie asked.

"They don't exist," Skulduggery said. "There have always been rumours of mortal governments forming death squads to go out and exterminate sorcerers. Department X was supposedly a British and Irish joint task force, shrouded in mystery and conspiracy. Except, as I said, they don't exist. Any time someone in power starts to ask questions, we send people like Geoffrey Scrutinous in to convince them they're being silly."

"That may be so," said Wreath, "but these mortals admitted to Baritone that they had just taken out, in their words, the most dangerous targets they'd ever hunted. They told Baritone he

38

wouldn't believe the whole story if he heard it – they said the targets they killed bled *light*. Sound familiar?"

"Sounds like Warlocks," said Valkyrie.

"And that's all Dragonclaw gave the Warlock in question?" Skulduggery pressed. "A sorcerer's urban legend?"

Wreath shrugged. "It's the only juicy little titbit concerning the Warlocks that we possess. I can't imagine what else it could have been. Obviously, word got out that we knew something and Charivari sent his little friend to investigate."

"And there's nothing else we should know?"

"Nothing else of value. The only other item of interest was that one of the soldiers mentioned their orders had been given by an old man with a long grey beard and another man he couldn't identify."

Valkyrie ignored the ring, and frowned. "What, he didn't know him?"

"No," said Wreath. "Baritone was under the impression that the soldier couldn't even *remember* him."

"All of this," Skulduggery said, "strikes me as something you could have told me over the phone."

Wreath laughed. "Now that is very true, Skulduggery. However, we don't like each other very much, so I wasn't about to tell you anything. And how else was I going to see my favourite student on her special day without popping up uninvited outside her window? Such behaviour strikes me as being vaguely unhealthy, wouldn't you agree?"

"A visit from you strikes me as *very* unhealthy," Skulduggery said.

Valkyrie got to her feet. "I'm going to cut this short before you start hitting each other. Solomon, thank you for your help and thank you so much for the present – it was really nice of you."

"My pleasure," he said, coming forward and kissing her cheek. "Happy birthday again."

Skulduggery put on his hat and walked out. Valkyrie caught

up with him at the elevator, right before the doors slid closed. They started their descent.

"What do you think it all means?" she asked.

Skulduggery didn't respond.

She sighed. "Are you sulking?"

"Me? No. I don't sulk."

"You sound like you're sulking."

"I'm just waiting for the violent urges to subside."

"Why don't you like Solomon? He's really not that bad."

"I've known him a lot longer than you have."

"Fine. Be like that. So this mystery man giving orders, the one who couldn't be remembered... We've been hearing that a lot lately."

Skulduggery activated his façade as they reached the ground floor. The face was plain, the expression grim. They walked to the exit. "Three years ago, Davina Marr was enlisted to destroy the Sanctuary in Dublin by a man she couldn't remember clearly. A similar man turns up *five* years ago and is revealed to be behind some Warlock killings. Sean Mackin, that lovable teenage psychopath, was released from his Sanctuary cell three *months* ago by a man he can't quite remember. It would appear that this is the same man, and he has a significant connection to Roarhaven." They left the hotel, walked to the Bentley.

"So..." said Valkyrie. "Department X is killing Warlocks, except Department X doesn't exist. But if the Warlocks think it *does* exist, then... what does that mean? Are they going to go after mortals in revenge? How does framing ordinary people help our mystery man achieve whatever it is he wants to achieve?"

"I don't know. But practically every mage in Roarhaven believes that sorcerers should be running the world."

"So that's his plan? To get the Warlocks to kill some mortals? That's kind of a stupid plan. I mean, as soon as we find the Warlocks, we're going to stop them, right?"

"Unless there's a war on to distract us."

40

"You think the mystery man has something to do with what's happening with the Supreme Council?"

"I don't like coincidences, Valkyrie. They're ugly and annoying." He glanced at her. "How do you like your ring?"

She couldn't help it. She beamed. "It is *awesome.*"

4

THE SECRET
ORIGIN OF...

It wasn't easy, being a woman in a man's world.

It was even less easy to be a man in a woman in a man's world. And who says it's a man's world anyway? Such outdated notions of sexism had no place in the mind of Vaurien Scapegrace. Not any more. Not since the... mistake.

Once he had been the Killer Supreme. Then the Zombie King. Then a head in a jar. That was probably the low point. But he'd been given a chance, an opportunity to turn it all around. He'd been shown a body, a perfect physical specimen, and he knew that this empty vessel would be the ideal place for his transplanted brain to rest. He could live again. He *would* live again. He would be a living, breathing man once more. No rotting flesh for him. No decomposition. No ridicule. He would have respect. Finally, he would have respect.

Instead, his brain got put into the body of a woman, and his idiot zombie sidekick got the body of the tall, handsome man with all those muscles.

Life had sucked when Scapegrace was alive. Then death sucked. And now life was sucking all over again.

Living in a new body was hard, but living in a woman's body was even harder. Every time he spoke, he heard a voice that wasn't his, and for the first few weeks he kept looking round to check if there were someone else in the room. He didn't even know how to walk without looking stupid. And then there was the whole trauma of looking into the mirror and seeing a face that was not his own.

It was a pretty face, he wasn't denying that. The woman had been very attractive. Early twenties, with auburn hair and green eyes. Six feet tall and in excellent physical condition. If Scapegrace had met her in other circumstances, he liked to think he would have swept her off her feet. Or he'd have considered it, at the very least. She would probably have laughed at him if he'd tried. Women this attractive usually did.

He frowned. Where was he going with this train of thought? He had no idea.

He looked at his reflection as he frowned. The woman even looked good when she did that. Or rather, he did. He even looked good when he did that. It was all very confusing.

"Are you looking at your reflection in that blade?"

Scapegrace whirled, the sword held out in front of him. The old man who had spoken stood there with his hands pressed together like he was praying. Grandmaster Ping was the kind of old that you just didn't see a whole lot of any more. He was a small Chinese man with a grey wispy beard that sprouted from his chin like a trail of hairy smoke. His skin was like parchment paper that had been crumpled up, tossed in a bin, then taken out and half-heartedly flattened. It was full of wrinkles, basically. Ping was dressed in what he called the traditional robes of his ancestors, but Scapegrace was fairly certain that the bathrobe was new.

"You must be ready at all times," Ping said in that heavy Chinese accent. "How can you see your enemies clearly when you cannot even take your eyes off yourself?"

Scapegrace didn't answer. He was pretty sure that was a rhetorical question.

Ping's hands moved like flowing water, and he stepped back into a deep fighting stance. "Come," he said. "Attack me."

"But you don't have a sword," Scapegrace said.

Ping smiled. "That does not mean I am unarmed."

Scapegrace let out a yell and ran forward, slashing his sword at the air, and then he leaped, spun, landed and twisted his ankle. He cried out, dropped the sword as he stumbled to one knee in front of Ping, who looked down at him and punched him on the nose.

"Ow!" Scapegrace yelled.

Ping brought his hands together again, and he bowed. "Ask yourself, my student, how did I beat you?"

"You hit my nose!"

"Exactly. If you can hit your opponent's nose more than he can hit yours, you too will taste victory."

"I'm bleeding!"

"You might need a tissue."

Thrasher came forward, a box of tissues in his big, stupid, masculine hands. Scapegrace yanked a handful free and held them to his face as he glared at Ping. "When will I be ready?"

"Soon, my student."

"You keep saying that. How soon is soon?"

"Soon is when the moment passes," Ping answered.

Scapegrace was certain that made no actual sense, but he knew better than to press it. Thrasher helped him to his feet. The idiot's new body was all muscle and chiselled jawline – a chiselled jawline that should have been Scapegrace's own.

"You seem frustrated," Ping said.

"Of course I'm frustrated," said Scapegrace. "I have one way of gaining the respect of the people who have mocked me all my life – to become the greatest warrior the world has ever seen. You were supposed to teach me the deadly arts, but all you do is hit me when I fall down."

"I see," said Ping. "You do not think you are learning, is that

44

it? Tell me something, my student. Have you ever seen *The Karate Kid*? The original, starring Ralph Macchio, not the remake, starring the son of Will Smith. Have you seen it?"

"Of course."

"In that movie, Daniel-san does not believe he is learning, either, does he? And yet Mr Miyagi is teaching him without him even being aware of it. That is sort of what I am doing."

"So what am I learning?"

"When the time comes, you will know."

Scapegrace narrowed his eyes. "In that movie, Mr Miyagi has Daniel doing all these mundane tasks like painting the fence and waxing the car, then later Daniel does the same moves and finds out it's karate. You have me doing all of these fighting moves... if I find out later that what you're actually doing is teaching me how to paint fences and wax cars, I'm not paying you, you understand?"

Ping chortled. "Very funny, you are, Miss Scapegrace."

"Mr!" Scapegrace roared. "I am a man!"

"Of course," Ping said, bowing. "Of course you are. Our lessons begin again in the morning." And with that, he stepped backwards into the shadows, and silence settled like autumn leaves falling from the trees.

Thrasher peered closer. "Are you still there?"

From the shadows, the aforementioned silence. Then, "No."

"You are," said Thrasher. "I can see you."

Scapegrace could see Ping, too, but he didn't say anything as the wise old grandmaster shuffled sideways until he reached the doorway, then went down on his hands and knees and crawled out. A few seconds later, the back door opened and closed. Thrasher murmured something.

Scapegrace glared. "What? What did you say?"

Thrasher sighed. "I just don't see why you have to become a warrior, Master. Why put yourself in harm's way? We have healthy new bodies and new lives to live and, OK, your body might not be ideal, but who cares about what we look like? It's who we are inside that counts."

"Tell me something – when Nye was putting your brain in that head, are you sure he didn't drop any on the floor?"

"Oh, Master, please don't be mean."

"Don't be mean? *Don't be mean?* You're an idiot! My new body isn't 'ideal'? It's not even the same gender as my old one! Do you know what it's like to be one gender trapped in another gender's body?"

"I... I might," said Thrasher.

"You have no idea! Look at you! You're an Adonis! You walk down the street and people stare in admiration! But when I walk down the street..."

"Well, maybe if you started wearing underwear..."

"*Underwear?*" Scapegrace screeched. "*Underwear?* You think *that's* the solution? Everything I wear is either too tight or too loose! I have pains in my back, did you know that? Do you know how hard it is to even stand upright in this body? How do women do it?"

Thrasher cleared his throat. "Well, sir, not all women are as... physically impressive as you are."

Scapegrace narrowed his eyes. "Don't you be getting any ideas."

"Sir?"

"I've seen the way you look at me."

Thrasher looked horrified. "Master, no! I assure you, I do not find your present body to be attractive in the slightest!"

"Oh, really? You think you could do better?" Scapegrace sagged, turned away. "What am I saying? Of course you could do better. Look at you. You could have any woman you want."

"But I don't *want* any woman, Master."

"You say that now..."

"I'll say that until the end of time, sir. I'm yours."

Scapegrace turned slowly, looked Thrasher in the eyes. "What do you mean?"

"Uh," said Thrasher.

"That was an odd thing to say."

"Was it?"

"Very."

"Oh."

"Very odd."

"We could ignore it, if you want."

Scapegrace looked at him. Thrasher was acting weird. Even weirder than usual. He appeared to be blushing, for God's sake. Scapegrace frowned. "What was I saying before?"

"Becoming a warrior, Master."

"Yes. Soon, I will unlock the secrets of the deadly arts and I will become the greatest warrior the world has ever known."

Thrasher looked at him. "Why?"

"Why what?"

"Why become a great warrior? What are you going to do afterwards?"

Scapegrace sneered. "You ask an awful lot of questions."

"I just... I was just wondering what—"

"I don't pay you to wonder."

"You don't pay me at all."

"I am a sorcerer, Thrasher. Among the many things that separate us, that is but one. There is no magic in you, but in me? Magic seethes within me. And now that I'm no longer a zombie, I can feel it again. It is reawakening."

"What kind of magic is it? I've always wanted to ask."

"But you haven't asked, have you? Not until right now. Why is that, I wonder? Is your new body giving you confidence, Thrasher?"

"What? No, Master!"

"Is it filling you with self-worth? With self-respect?"

"Never! I swear to you!"

"Because if I find out it is..."

Thrasher fell to his knees. "Master, I hate my new body. I do.

Granted, it's perfect in every physical way, but it's... it's not the body you attacked and killed on that warm September afternoon, those few short years ago. It's not the body you bit. It's not the body that came back, that opened its eyes and saw you, gazing at it..."

"This is getting weird again," Scapegrace muttered.

Thrasher stood up. He was so tall and good-looking it was stupid. "Master," he said, "we've been through a lot, you and I, and if I could switch bodies with you I would. I really would. Maybe then you could see me the way I see you."

Scapegrace tried to ponder that one and quickly gave up.

"You are the only important thing in my life," Thrasher continued, "and I... sir, I..."

"This conversation is boring me," Scapegrace announced. "Take out the rubbish bins."

Thrasher sagged. "Yes, Master."

While Thrasher trudged out with the bins, Scapegrace picked up his fallen sword and returned it to its sheath. Back in olden times, a Samurai would never put his sword away until the blade had tasted blood. But that was the olden times, back when they didn't understand things like basic hygiene. These days, Scapegrace was sure, a Samurai would much rather break this nonsensical little rule than risk a variety of unfortunate infections.

He heard a scream and, before he knew what he was doing, Scapegrace was running for the door, his sword once more in his hand.

Thrasher was struggling with something in the gloom behind the pub, his back jammed up against the wall while he tried to keep the creature at bay. It was big, as big as a Doberman but with longer hair, and it had a snout and sharp teeth and it snarled and snapped and Thrasher squealed.

"Hey!" Scapegrace shouted, because he could think of nothing else.

The creature turned its head, its eyes flashing. From this angle, the face almost looked human. Then it leaped at Scapegrace and Scapegrace slipped on fallen bits of rubbish and the creature impaled itself on the sword as he fell.

Scapegrace blinked as the creature gave a last rattling breath before it died. He pushed it off him and got to his feet.

Thrasher looked up at him. "Master!"

"What?"

"You saved me!"

"No I didn't."

"You rescued me!"

"It was an accident."

"You saved my life!"

"I didn't do it on purpose."

Thrasher bounded to his feet. He was so happy he looked like he was about to cry. "Master, you have no idea how much this means to me. I am a pathetic mortal, not worthy of being saved—"

"I know."

"—and yet you saved me anyway. You risked your life, which is vastly more important than mine—"

"Vastly."

"—and you rushed into danger, into the jaws of death... I don't know what to say. I don't have the words to... Oh, sir, forgive me, I may cry."

"Well, do it somewhere else," Scapegrace said, scowling. "What the hell is that thing anyway? Some kind of dog?"

Thrasher was too busy crying to answer.

Scapegrace pressed his foot against the creature's body, rolled it into the light. "That's no dog," he said. "It looks like a monkey and a dog fell in love and had babies and this is the ugly one they didn't want." He crouched down. "Maybe it's an alien. Maybe we're being invaded by aliens."

"Oh, I hope not, sir," Thrasher sobbed.

"Shut up. Look at that face. It's definitely an alien. Maybe. It's not from here, that's for sure."

Thrasher sniffled. "Maybe it's from an alternate dimension."

"From a what?"

"An alternate dimension, Master. You know, like the one Valkyrie Cain was pulled into."

Scapegrace stood up. "What the hell are you blubbing about?"

"Last April, sir, when we were waiting for these bodies, there was all this drama going on with Valkyrie being in a parallel dimension and this gentleman called Argeddion running around and... you missed all of this?"

"I was a head in a jar," Scapegrace said. "I had other things on my mind."

"Yes, sir, of course. But maybe this creature is from an alternate dimension just like that one. Maybe someone shunted back and brought that with them accidentally."

"Shunted?"

"That's what they call it, sir. The Shunter who caused all the trouble for Valkyrie was a man called Silas Nadir."

"Nadir," Scapegrace said. "Where have I heard that name before?"

"From what I gathered, he is a rather notorious serial killer, sir."

Scapegrace's eyes widened. "A serial killer? Where is he now? Did they catch him?"

"I'm afraid not, sir. He escaped the cells and—"

"He was in the Sanctuary?" Scapegrace interrupted. "So he escaped the cells, disappeared, and a few months later there's a... thingy..."

"Shunter."

"... Shunter, active in Roarhaven?"

Thrasher paled. "Oh, sir. You don't... you don't think he's still here, do you?"

Scapegrace turned away from him, eyes on the street. "I know the criminal mind, Thrasher. I know the mind of a murderer. Once upon a time, I was the Killer Supreme. I was the Zombie

King. But I have changed my ways since then. I will now channel my inner darkness into *fighting* evil, not *being* evil, in an epic tale of redemption and quiet dignity. And if there is one thing I know, if there is one thing of which I am certain, it is that Silas Nadir has never left Roarhaven, and this town needs a protector. Which makes it two things I know."

"Should we call Skulduggery?"

"No. We should call me."

"You?"

"This town cries out for a hero."

"You?"

"Let Pleasant and Cain save them from obvious threats. Let them stand in the spotlight. I will stand in the shadows. I will fight in darkness."

"You'll need a torch, sir," said Thrasher, rushing over to stand beside him. "Please – let me hold that torch."

"You can be my sidekick."

"Oh, yes, sir."

"I will be this town's champion, its unsung hero, its Dark and Stormy Knight."

"Yes, sir!" Thrasher squealed, clapping his hands.

Scapegrace narrowed his eyes. He could practically smell the evil. "We'll need masks."

5

UNFAIR ADVANTAGE

If it hadn't been for his mother, Ghastly reckoned he'd have taken to running instead of boxing. The bare-knuckle champion of her age, she had taught him everything she knew as he was growing up. To the taunts that followed him wherever he went, to the bullying that came soon after, his fists were his responses. They were the only words he needed.

He'd valued every moment he spent with her when she was alive, and he cherished every memory he had of her when she was gone. Along with his father, she was responsible for the man he became, for the man he was now. A fighter.

But fighting takes its toll. It took its toll on his mother. She'd entered into a fight she hadn't a hope of winning. And all this fighting, all this arguing and confrontation and playing politics, it was taking a toll on Ghastly now, too. He'd needed his few days off. He'd needed a lot more.

He wondered sometimes what person he would have been if he had chosen running instead of boxing. He could have run from the bullies, then, instead of turning and fighting them. He could have left their taunts far behind. He could have tuned the world out and just focused on his breathing and the rhythm – not of fists on leather, but of feet on track. If he'd been a runner, would he have fought in the war? Would he have become a Dead Man? Would he have lost a year of his life as a blank, unthinking statue? Would he have lost Tanith Low to a Remnant, and then lost her again to a killer?

Ghastly put his head down and ran.

The Sanctuary had so many long, winding corridors in its depths that he could run here for an hour and not see one other person. That's the way he liked it. Up there, where the corridors were brighter and warmer, he was Ghastly Bespoke the Elder, who had to wear that damn robe and appear respectable at all times. Down here, he was Ghastly Bespoke, the scarred tailor, the man who put on a tracksuit to go running and could sweat and push himself as hard as he damn well wanted.

He ran until he wasn't thinking of the Supreme Council. He ran until he wasn't thinking of the Warlocks. He ran and ran and tried to outrun the idea of Tanith Low and Billy-Ray Sanguine, but it caught up with him, ran alongside, and he lost his rhythm and his feet became clumsy and he slowed to a graceless stop.

He stood there, bent over, hands on his knees, sucking in air, and then he straightened, controlled his breathing, started walking. He shook out his arms and legs with each stride. No one would miss him for another twenty minutes or so. Plenty of time to cool down, shower, and pull on that stupid... robe...

He stopped, waiting for the air around him to settle. Once it had fallen back to its natural pattern, he concentrated on the currents and the draughts against his skin, and felt something else, a slight nudging, almost too gentle to notice. Someone was reading the air, keeping track of him. Someone skilled.

Raising his hands, Ghastly formed a vacuum, roughly the size of his own body, and pressed it outwards. Staying very, very still, he sent it rippling down the corridor at walking pace. The gentle nudging moved away from him, following the human-sized disruption. Once the Elemental, whoever he was, was satisfied that the threat had passed, he withdrew his probing little tentacles of awareness.

Ghastly took the stairs slowly down, both hands out to subdue the ripples he was making in the air and to prevent the sounds of his footsteps from travelling. In Ireland, running shoes were called runners. In Britain, trainers. In America, sneakers. The American term was the most sinister, in his opinion, but definitely most appropriate for this situation. At the bottom of the stairs there was a man, standing with his back to him. Now it was Ghastly's turn to read his surroundings, but he made sure to do it at an even gentler level than the Elemental had managed. Slowly, he used the air to reach past this man with the silenced pistol in a shoulder holster, then round the corner, and down the corridor. He ignored the open spaces he passed, the doorways, and focused on who was standing in the corridor itself. One person, halfway down. Big. Probably male. Another one, at the end, moving around. Fidgeting. Nervous.

Well, OK then.

Ghastly stepped up and wrapped his right arm round the Elemental's throat, gripped the bicep of his other arm and pressed his left hand against the back of the man's head. All of this in an instant. All of this before the man could even make a sound, let alone react physically.

Ghastly pulled him back away from the wall so that he couldn't kick out, make a noise to alert his friends. The man didn't go for his gun. He didn't even try to use magic. He just panicked and grabbed Ghastly's arm and tried to pull it away. But of course he couldn't, and all Ghastly had to do was tighten up and a moment later the man was unconscious.

Ghastly laid him on the ground. Nothing in his pockets. No ID. No money. Nothing. Ghastly took the pistol, removed the silencer and moved to the corner. He knelt and peeked round.

The big man in the middle of the corridor was looking into the Accelerator Room, the only room that had a light on. Plenty of activity in there, it seemed. Beyond him, at the junction at the other end of the corridor, a second man couldn't seem to stand still. He had a sub-machine gun on a strap hanging from his shoulder. Like the Elemental's, it too was silenced. Ghastly stood, stuck the pistol into the pocket of his tracksuit, and stepped into the corridor.

The Big Man was at the midway point, roughly fifty metres away. The Fidgeter was at the end. That meant a hundred-metre dash with two opponents to dispatch without alerting anyone inside the Accelerator Room. Ghastly tried to stop the grin from spreading, but failed miserably.

He gripped the air around him, and broke into a run. He dived forward, brought his hands in and out in front, shot down the corridor like a bullet. The Big Man turned and Ghastly took him off his feet, one hand clamped to his mouth and the other arm wrapped round him, and he piled on the speed. The Fidgeter didn't even get to look round before the Big Man's head cracked against his. Both men went down and Ghastly twisted away from them, found himself hurtling towards the far wall. He brought the air in, formed a cushion, bounced off and stumbled only a little when he landed. His first thought was that he had just come close to smashing every bone in his body. His second thought was not to mention that part to Skulduggery, or else the flying lessons would start to concentrate on how to stop instead of how to go faster.

As he knelt by the men, his eyes were on the Accelerator Room door. No one ran out. No one shouted an alarm. His luck was holding. He checked that both men were unconscious, then took the sub-machine gun, made sure it was loaded and ready to fire, and crept back up the corridor. He could hear voices now, snippets of what was being said. Three different people, two male, one female. American accents. One voice he recognised – the one issuing the orders.

He reached the Accelerator Room, and peered in. The man

in charge was hidden by the Accelerator itself. The other was tall and thin and Ghastly didn't know who he was. He'd seen the young woman before, though. She was a Necromancer. What was her name? Adrasdos, or something? He'd seen her with Vex, decades ago, back when everything was nice and friendly between Sanctuaries. She was attaching something to the right side of the Accelerator while the thin man did the same on the other side. They had duffel bags open all around them. Explosives. The man in charge stepped into view, trailing wires behind him. Bernard Sult.

"Nobody move," said Ghastly.

Naturally, they moved. They spun in shock, but managed to hold still when they saw the gun pointed at them. That was wise.

"Put it down," said Ghastly, stepping inside. "All of it. Very slowly, very gently, put it all down on the floor. You, too, Bernard. We wouldn't want any of this to go off, now would we?"

Sult's face was tight, but he obeyed, and rested the loop of wires at his feet. He straightened, hands up, and the other two did the same. They were all armed with silenced pistols. Ghastly raised his free hand and those pistols floated from their holsters to land gently behind him.

"You kill anyone getting in here?" Ghastly asked.

"We had to render one or two of your people unconscious," said Sult, "but we don't take lives if we can help it."

"Terrorists with principles," said Ghastly. "I like it."

"*You're* the terrorists," said Adrasdos, glaring at him with fire in her eyes. "*You're* the ones terrorising the world with your casual ineptitude and gross indifference to—"

"Adrasdos," said Sult, "don't bother. Elder Bespoke has heard it all before and he remains unmoved."

Ghastly gave a little shrug. "So what's the plan here, Bernard? Destroy the Accelerator and vanish before anyone knows you paid us a visit? You weren't even going to say hi, after everything we've been through? You were there when we joined forces to take down Argeddion's psycho teenagers. Doesn't that mean anything to you?"

"No, Elder Bespoke, it doesn't, because I was also here when you allowed Grand Mage Strom to be decapitated in his own quarters."

"By an English mage."

"By your would-be girlfriend."

"Who is possessed by a Remnant. And yet you lot still manage to blame that on us."

"Oh, it's not just that, Elder Bespoke. It's also the fact that you had falsely imprisoned the Grand Mage to keep him from reporting your mistakes back to the Supreme Council. These are not the actions of Elders who can be trusted to run the most volatile country in the world."

"Mistakes were made, I freely admit that. But no laws were violated. No rules were broken. But this... Breaking into a foreign Sanctuary, assaulting Sanctuary operatives, attempting to destroy Sanctuary equipment... Adrasdos, I know you don't like the word, but these are acts of terrorism. And you're all under arrest."

"I'm afraid we can't allow that to happen," said Sult. "And we can't allow anyone to find out we were here. We're going to have to kill you, Elder Bespoke."

Ghastly gave him a little smile. "I'd like to see you try."

Adrasdos and the thin man rushed him. Ghastly waved his hand and Adrasdos crashed into the wall, but the thin man was too close. Ghastly pulled the trigger. The bullets riddled the thin man's shirt, but bounced off his skin, and a single push sent Ghastly hurtling back into the corridor. He hit the wall, fell to the floor, left the gun there as he scrambled up. He ducked under the thin man's punch, and sent a left hook to the body in return. As expected, it was like hitting a boulder. He dodged a wild swipe and curled his fingers, felt the air forming battering rams around his knuckles, and when he punched again he sent a column of air into the thin man's jaw.

The thin man staggered.

Ghastly hit him again, and again, those battering rams crunching into the thin man's ribs enough times to make him cover up, and then Ghastly went for the head. The thin man was too used to being the strongest person in the room. He'd never bothered to learn to fight. Ghastly went for the chin and then punched at the knee, and while the thin man was trying to work out what the hell was happening he snapped his palms against the air and the space between them rippled, and the thin man flew backwards.

Ghastly reached for the fallen sub-machine gun, but a shadow lashed at him, curled round his wrist and yanked him off his feet. He rolled, glimpsed Adrasdos running at him, shadows pouring from something she was holding. He lunged at her and they went down. She cracked an elbow into his nose and his vision went blurry. He found her right hand, keeping the weapon away from him as they rolled. He couldn't even see what it was. It looked like a knife handle.

Adrasdos wriggled out from underneath him, went to kick him as she got to her feet, but he grabbed her foot, held it as he stood. The shadows writhed round the knife handle, grouping together to form a machete. She swung and he stumbled, letting go of her, barely dodging the black blade. The more shadows that writhed, the longer the blade got, and it nicked his shoulder and cut his arm and it was going to end up in his head if he didn't stop this. She swung and he stepped in, trapped her arm under his and fired a right cross into her jaw. She collapsed, the blade of shadows melting away as the handle skittered across the floor.

Sult was pressing the last of the explosives against the Accelerator when Ghastly returned to the room.

"Not one more step," the American said, holding out a grey box. His thumb rested against the silver switch. "There are enough explosives in this room to take out this machine five times over. You do *not* want to make me twitch."

Ghastly kept his hands down by his sides. "We haven't even completed our study of the Accelerator," he said. "We know it supercharges sorcerers, we know it's a source of energy, but we don't know how to properly harness it yet. We don't know what else it can do. And you want to destroy it?"

"I admit this sounds incredibly childish," said Sult, "but if *we* can't have it, then you can't, either. It's too unpredictable. And, let's face it, the supercharged sorcerer aspect would give you an unfair advantage if hostilities were to give way to all-out war."

Ghastly laughed. "Practically every Sanctuary in the world, apart from those in Africa and Australia, is on your side – and you want to talk to *me* about unfair advantages? We're outnumbered so greatly that it's not even worth calculating."

"This is very true," said Sult. "So let the Supreme Council come in. Form a partnership. You can still run your country as normal, for the most part. We'll just be here to ensure that you're making the right decisions."

"I seem to remember that we've had this discussion before. It didn't work out for either of us."

"Sadly, I must agree with you there."

"If you flick that switch, you could start a war."

"Only if they have proof it was me."

"Still plan to kill me, do you? You brought four sorcerers with you and they all have concussions. I'd say your plans are foiled – unless, of course, you're planning on doing it yourself...?"

Sult smiled, and laid the grey box on the floor. "I've been looking forward to this."

"Me, too," said Ghastly, and took the gun from his pocket and fired. He hit Sult twice in the chest and Sult dropped.

The grey box floated to Ghastly's free hand, but before he closed his fingers around it he glanced at the silenced pistols at his feet, the ones he'd taken from their holsters. Only two of them. But there were three when he'd—

The bullet hit him in the shoulder and Ghastly spun, stumbled, fell, the grey box falling. The harsh whisper of the missing silenced pistol accompanied another bullet that whistled by his ear and now Ghastly was returning fire, his gun barking loudly in the confined space of the room. Sult dived for cover and Ghastly scurried backwards, firing all the time. Sult kept moving. Ghastly ran out of bullets and Sult popped up and the gun shot from Ghastly's hand into Sult's face. Sult staggered, blood pumping from the cut on his forehead.

Ghastly used the air to launch himself across the room. They collided. Sult threw an elbow and brought his gun up. Ghastly grabbed his wrist and the gun barrel, twisted the gun from Sult's grip and slammed it into his face. Sult punched Ghastly's shoulder, and the pain from the bullet wound lanced through him. He dropped the gun and almost sank to his knees. Sult hit his shoulder again and the world darkened, and then an elbow hurtled towards him and the dark world tilted and spun. The ground bounced into his side and he rolled against it, pushed away from it, everything moving too fast with the sound muted.

Sult hit him, again and again. Ghastly's left arm went numb. His right was OK, so he threw it, caught Sult just as he was coming in with another shot. It wasn't perfect but it'd do. Ghastly fired another into the ribs, but felt the body armour beneath Sult's shirt. Now Sult was pushing against him, tangling his legs, and they fell with Sult on top. The blood from his forehead splashed on to Ghastly's cheek. Two punches came down, but Ghastly moved his head just like his mother had taught him all those years ago. One of the punches clipped his ear. The other missed altogether, hit the ground instead. Sult cursed in pain, pulled his hand back, and Ghastly heaved him sideways.

They wrestled there for a moment. Ghastly hung on and didn't let go. Again, just like his mother had taught him.

When you're rocked, hang on for dear life until you can see straight. Then let go and let him have it.

Ghastly pushed Sult away and they got to their feet at the same time. The world spun, but it wasn't nearly as bad as it had been. Keeping his left arm tight to his side, Ghastly whipped out a right jab, followed it with another, feinted with a third and went low with a hook that lifted Sult. Gasping, Sult backed off, his knees shaky, holding his hands out to ward off Ghastly as he closed in.

Sult came to a stop by stepping on the grey box. His heel crunched down on the silver switch. There was a small device attached to the explosives on the Accelerator. It beeped.

Sult's eyes widened.

The device beeped again and again and faster and faster and now it was one long continuous beep and Ghastly reached out with the air and yanked Sult off his feet. The moment Sult passed him, Ghastly pressed both hands against the air to form a shield and then the room was filled with fire and thunder and the shockwave hit the shield and Ghastly was launched backwards into the corridor. Sult hit the wall and Ghastly hit Sult and they collapsed in a tangle and Ghastly sprawled to a stop.

Eyes blinking. Eyes. Blinking.

Alarms. Shouts.

Alarms.

Hands gripping him, pulling him up, Ghastly sitting now, smoke everywhere. People and Cleavers. Ravel, in front of him, shaking him, speaking words.

"—hear me? Ghastly? Can you hear me? I need a doctor over here! My friend's a vegetable!"

Ghastly felt his mouth twitch into a smile.

"Oh, good," said Ravel. "He's not completely gone. Where's all this blood coming from? Ah, he's been shot. Of course he has. Typical."

Doctor Synecdoche hurried over, knelt by him, pressed

something against his wound. "Elder Bespoke," she said, "can you hear me? Can you tell me what day it is?"

"I don't know," Ghastly mumbled, "I'm sorry..."

"We need to get him to my lab as quickly as possible," said Synecdoche. "He needs a CAT scan and a—"

Ghastly shook his head. "No, I mean, I don't actually know what day it is. It was easier keeping track of days when I had my shop, but ever since I became an Elder..."

"The days become a blur," finished Ravel, nodding. "He's OK, Doc. I've seen him walk away from bigger traumas than this. Help me get him standing."

"I really don't think that's a good idea, Grand Mage," said Synecdoche. "He could still be suffering from—"

Ravel sighed, grabbed Ghastly's right arm and pulled him to his feet. "See?" he said while Synecdoche quietly freaked out. "Not a bother on him. Although you should probably call round to see him later for some private consultation."

Ghastly did his best to smile at her. "Doctor, thank you, I'll make my way to the Medical Wing in a moment. Maybe you could treat some of our prisoners while you're here?"

"Of course, Elder Bespoke," she said, and was immediately lost in the crowd of Sanctuary personnel.

"She likes you," Ravel whispered.

"Do not start," Ghastly responded. He turned as Sult was hauled to his feet by a pair of Cleavers, his hands shackled behind his back.

"Bernard Sult," said Ravel. "I take it you're responsible for this mess?"

Sult glared at them both. "I have Level 4 mindguards in place. We all do. Your Sensitives will get nothing from us."

"We don't really need anything," said Ravel. "The fact that you've been caught red-handed trying to destroy Sanctuary property will be enough of an embarrassment to the Supreme Council, believe me."

The defiance in Sult's eyes diminished somewhat. "What do you mean," he said, "*trying* to destroy?"

Ghastly frowned, too. "The Accelerator is salvageable after a blast like that?"

"See for yourselves," Ravel said.

Ghastly limped to the doorway and Sult came after him, his arms held by the Cleavers. Sanctuary Elementals worked to clear the acrid smoke from the room. The Accelerator stood tall and proud where it had always been. A little scorched, maybe, but definitely in one piece. One of the Elementals placed a hand to the scorch mark and wiped it clean. Just a little soot. Astonishing.

"When they built it," Ravel said from behind them, "they built it to last."

6

STARK REALITIES

To see such a thing as shock register on the face of the most beautiful woman in the world was a rare treat, and Valkyrie found herself enjoying it more than she really should have. China Sorrows' pale blue eyes were wide and her perfect lips were parted. Her hair, black as sin and just as luxuriant, was longer than Valkyrie remembered. She wore a bathrobe, silk, tied with a sash.

"Hi," said Valkyrie.

China looked at her for a few more moments. "Hello, Valkyrie," she said at last, composure quietly regained. "I must admit, I didn't expect to see you on my doorstep. To what do I owe the pleasure?"

"I've been meaning to stop by. You told me about this place ages ago, mentioned all the horses. It's beautiful around here."

"My refuge," said China. "I run to my country house to lick my wounds and bathe in self-pity. Is that... is that your car?"

Valkyrie glanced back at the Oompa-Loompa. "Yep. Isn't she beautiful?"

"She is remarkably orange. Would you like to come in?"

China stepped to one side, and Valkyrie passed through. A marble staircase swept from a marble floor. Dark paintings in

Gothic frames hung from the walls. Twisted sculptures sat on bone-white plinths. Through the windows the old stone yard was in full view, with the horses in their stables and, beyond them, the fields and meadows and the forest that bordered the land.

China led her into a large room with a rich carpet and a floor-to-ceiling bookcase that took up an entire wall. There was an old-fashioned writing desk that Valkyrie barely got a glance at before China closed the lid, and at China's invitation Valkyrie dutifully sat.

"Can I get you anything?" China asked. "Tea or coffee?"

"I'm fine, thank you."

China sat in the armchair opposite and crossed her legs. Her feet were bare. "What can I do for you?" she asked, but Valkyrie wasn't ready to answer that. Not yet.

"Impressive bookcase," she said instead. "Not as impressive as the library, but..."

"But then I have far fewer books," finished China. "Rebuilding my collection will take time, I'm afraid. Rebuilding it completely will be impossible – some of the works lost were truly one of a kind. Irreplaceable. The truly valuable books, of course, were kept here and not in the library, so that is a blessing, I suppose."

"Are you going to reopen?"

"I think not. As I said, I've been feeling very sorry for myself. My library was frequented by many patrons whom I viewed as loyal – and yet, when Eliza Scorn burned it to the ground, not one of them came to my aid. Don't get me wrong, Valkyrie – I am quite used to being a pariah. I just didn't think it would happen again quite so soon."

"So you're not joking, then? You really have been spending all this time feeling sorry for yourself?"

A smile, as sad as it was faint. "Not *all* this time. I spent a few days recovering from my injuries. The physical wounds healed and left not a bruise. The injury I suffered to my pride, however...

well. Once I was back on my feet, I had nothing but revenge in mind, so I began preparing."

"And what happened?"

"Eliza is nothing if not thorough. My holdings in America, in Switzerland, in Italy... all destroyed. My employees, the ones who haven't died in terribly suspicious accidents, are missing. The mortal men and women who tend to my horses are the only ones left unharmed. I am alone, Valkyrie. Without allies, without friends."

"I'm... I'm sorry."

"Nonsense. This is exactly how it should be. Nothing less than what I deserve after the things I've done."

"What about your assistant? The man with the bow tie?"

"Dead, the poor man. Strangled."

"Oh, China..."

China waved her hand dismissively. "I am allowed to pity myself, Valkyrie. You are not. So tell me how you have been."

"You don't know?"

"These days I only hear whispers about the impending war between the Sanctuaries – nothing fun. My sources and informants now report to Eliza and her Church of the Faceless. I have been deprived."

Valkyrie gave a little shrug. "Well, I'm doing grand. I'm doing OK. So is Skulduggery. We visited an alternate reality, did you hear that?"

China raised an eyebrow. "When was this?"

"Just a few months ago, around the beginning of May."

"Weren't you dealing with Argeddion back then?"

"This was part of it."

"You *have* been busy. What was it like, this alternate reality?"

"Horrible," said Valkyrie. "Mevolent is still alive over there, and from what I saw he basically rules the world. Mortals are slaves. Serpine's still alive, too. So was Vengeous – until he died."

China sat forward. "Oh, you lucky thing. That must have been astonishing."

"We met you over there."

China clapped her hands and laughed with delight. "Another me! Tell me, what was I like?"

"You led the Resistance."

"I did? Me? I'm sorry, I'm one of the heroes over there?"

"You were," said Valkyrie. "Kind of. You betrayed us a few times, and then you died."

China's face fell, and she sat back. "Typical. Who killed me?"

"Serpine."

"That sneaky little toerag." She went quiet for a moment, then looked up. "My brother?"

Valkyrie shook her head. "Mevolent had killed him a long time ago."

"Dead in both dimensions, then. That's unfortunate. How did Skulduggery handle talking to me?"

"Honestly? He was fine. He got on with the job."

"And what is his attitude towards me? This me, I mean. Not that me."

"His attitude towards you is... unknown. We don't talk about you much. He doesn't insult you, if that's what you're worried about."

"Insults are one of the lesser things to worry me, my dear. So are you going to tell why you've visited, or are we going to keep skipping around it?"

"Oh, yes, of course. We're after a guy that nobody can quite remember. They don't remember his name, his face, anything about who he is. Do you know anyone who could make you forget who they were?"

"I know a few Sensitives who could dislodge some things in your memory if given enough time."

"No, I get the feeling this is an instant thing. Like, you're talking to him and then you walk away and you can't quite remember who he was."

"Interesting," said China. "There is a German mage, a Sensitive again, whom you forget the moment you lose sight of her. Myosotis Terra."

"Never heard of her."

"The only other thing I can think of is a type of amethyst crystal with certain psychic properties. I'm sure if treated correctly it could induce that level of amnesia. I'd need my books to make sure but, unfortunately, I no longer have them."

"So it's not a discipline of magic, then? Anyone who holds that crystal could be the person we're looking for?"

"I'm afraid so."

Valkyrie sagged. "Wonderful. Any ideas where a person might find such a crystal?"

"Most of them have been locked carefully away. There used to be one in the Repository of the old Sanctuary, if I remember correctly. It might even have survived the relocation to Roarhaven."

"I see. Well, thank you, China. That's very helpful."

"Oh, think nothing of it," China said, smiling. "Now then, what's the real reason you're here?"

"Sorry? What do you...?"

At China's raised eyebrow, Valkyrie faltered, then took a deep breath, and settled back. "I need advice."

"On what subject?"

"My future."

China waited for Valkyrie to continue.

"My parents expect me to go to college. I did really well in the exams – or rather, my reflection did really well – and now I have all these offers from places I don't want to go to. I thought once school was over I wouldn't have to run around like this any more. I have everything that Gordon left me so I don't *have* to do anything, but then my folks are going to think I'm just taking the easy way out."

China nodded. "And you've come to me because obviously I know your parents really well."

Valkyrie had to smile. "I came to you because Skulduggery's being weird about it. I don't think he wants to influence me one way or the other."

"That's probably wise. Where you go from here should be your decision and yours alone."

"But this is what I want," Valkyrie said. "I want to keep working for the Sanctuary and doing everything we've been doing. This is where I belong. But at the same time, I don't want to end up like every other sorcerer."

"And how do we end up?"

"Isolated. I don't want to cut myself off from ordinary people. I don't see why I should have to."

China smiled sadly. "It's inevitable, I'm afraid."

"I don't accept that."

"They have a name for it these days. They have a name for *everything* these days. They call it Second Lifetime Syndrome, and it happens when a sorcerer watches her family and friends age and die around her. You'll latch on to other mages from that moment on, because what's the point of going through all that pain again? Valkyrie, there are some stark realities you have to face. You're going to look the way you do for the next eighty years. In two hundred years, you'll look twenty-five. You won't be able to form attachments to mortals. They will start to notice something is different about you when they're lined and saggy and you're still young and perky. You're going to have to say goodbye to your parents before they start to ask questions."

"Or I... I could just tell them."

The smile left China's lips. "That is never advisable."

"Why not? They wouldn't tell anyone."

"Your job as a sorcerer is to protect them from the truth, not share it with them to make your life easier."

"I can't just walk away from them. They're my parents. They'd come looking for me. And what about Alice? I can't just abandon her."

"You fake your own death."

"No," Valkyrie said. "No way, I'm not doing that to them."

"You don't have to do it today, Valkyrie. But you will have to do it."

"What's wrong with telling them? I'd make them understand and they'd keep the secret."

"Is that why you're really here? You're trying this out on me first before mentioning it to Skulduggery? He'll react the same way. If you tell your family the truth, you'll torture them. Their mortal lives will be shattered. They'll jump at every shadow. They'll grasp at religion or superstition to fill the sudden void they'll create for themselves. I've seen it happen. You will change who they are because you're too selfish to live without them."

"Not if I do it right."

"And that's not even taking into account how worried they'll be about you," China continued. "Every hour that passes when they don't hear from you is another possible death. You fight monsters, Valkyrie. Some in human form, and some not. Are you going to tell them about vampires? Are you? Will you tell them about Caelan? Will you tell them about the things you've done?"

Valkyrie's phone beeped. Grateful for the interruption, she took it out, read from the screen, and frowned.

"Something wrong?" China asked.

"Bernard Sult's been arrested at Roarhaven," Valkyrie said.

"The Supreme Council will not be pleased."

Valkyrie stood. "I have to go."

"Of course. Duty calls." China walked her to the door. "I'm sorry I couldn't give you the answers you were hoping for."

"There's still a way to do it right," Valkyrie said. "I just have to figure it out."

"Many have tried. Practically every sorcerer alive has been in your shoes."

70

"What about you?"

China smiled. "You forget. I was born into a family that worshipped the Faceless Ones. I hated mortals before I'd even taken my first breath. Sometimes that kind of dysfunction can work in your favour. Drive safely, Valkyrie. And happy birthday."

7

SARACEN

It took Valkyrie a little over two hours to get to Roarhaven. Knowing the route from the passenger seat was one thing – being able to remember every turn from behind the wheel was quite another. Added to that, there were no signs for the town, and the road that led to it was hidden from the prying eyes of the public. Aside from people who knew the way, only the very determined or the very lost could ever hope to stumble upon it. In the end, Valkyrie gave in to how lost she was, and fifteen minutes later she was pulling up outside the Sanctuary.

There were Cleavers in the streets, which was a rare sight to see. The townspeople stayed away from all the fuss, scowling at Sanctuary personnel from their doorways and behind their curtains. Valkyrie was let through without being searched, and she found Ieni, a young mage from Cork, arguing with an older sorcerer. He was called away and Ieni turned to Valkyrie as she approached.

"You all right?" Valkyrie asked.

"They're saying this is my fault," Ieni said, her eyes glistening. "I was at my post and someone came up behind me and... They're saying it's my fault Sult got in. But I'm not the only one they got."

"You'll be fine," Valkyrie said. "Everyone's just confused right now. What was Sult trying to do?"

"They set off explosives on the Accelerator. It wasn't damaged, though. Elder Bespoke took them down."

"Right," the older sorcerer said, striding back to Ieni, "you can consider yourself under investigation, you hear me? I can't believe anyone could be as incompetent as you claim to be, which leads me to believe that you were working with the enemy."

"No," Ieni said, her eyes widening, "I swear I wasn't."

Valkyrie was about to interject when a man in a good suit stepped out of the room beside them.

"Leave the girl alone," he said, making the order sound like a suggestion. He wasn't quite as tall as Valkyrie and he was carrying a few extra pounds around the midsection, but his smile was easy and his vibe was laid-back. "She got taken unawares by professionals. It happens to the best of us."

The mage glared. "I don't know who you are, but I'm fairly certain that this is none of your business."

"You don't know who I am?" the man said. "Really? I know who you are, Mr Dacanay. Newly-appointed sheriff of Roarhaven, am I right? You even have a little badge and ID card that you're suddenly embarrassed about, tucked away in your pocket there."

Dacanay loomed over him. "I don't like psychics picking through my head."

"Good thing I'm not a psychic, then. My name is Saracen Rue. I know things." At the mention of Saracen's name, Dacanay backed down considerably. "I know, for example, that you're going to walk away from this conversation within the next five seconds. Four... three... two..."

Dacanay scowled, turned to Ieni. "I'll be watching you."

As he stormed off, Saracen leaned in. "He might be the law in Roarhaven, but not in the Sanctuary. You don't have to worry about him."

"Thank you," Ieni said.

"Did you have a doctor look you over? That probably wouldn't be a bad idea."

Ieni nodded and hurried away, and Saracen turned to Valkyrie, stepped back to look her up and down, and smiled. "Valkyrie Cain. You are exactly what I expected."

She raised an eyebrow. "Is that good or bad?"

"Good," he said, shaking her hand. "It's great to finally meet you. Come on, everyone's meeting in the conference room."

"Is Ghastly OK?" she asked as they started walking.

"He's fine," said Saracen. "A headache and a few mild burns. Hey, well done on saving the world that time."

"Which time was that?"

Saracen laughed. "Take your pick. I haven't been home in years – this morning was the first time I'd set foot on Irish soil in the last decade – but I've heard so much about you."

"Likewise," Valkyrie said. "Although Skulduggery never mentioned what discipline you studied."

Saracen's smile turned to a grin. "I know things."

"But you said you're not a psychic."

"You don't have to be a Sensitive to know things."

"So... that's your magic? Knowing things is your power?"

"Knowing things is a *result* of my power."

"OK. No offence, but that vagueness is really annoying."

"I know. Dexter has been trying to figure out what I can do for over three hundred and fifty years. Seeing the annoyance in his eyes is just about the most hilarious thing I've ever experienced."

"Does *anyone* know what your power is?"

"Erskine," said Saracen. "About twenty years before the war with Mevolent ended, I was poisoned. I was dying. I was on my sickbed and Erskine was the only friend I had in the place, and in a moment of weakness I told him what I could do."

"But you survived."

"The next morning I started to recover. Dexter likes to say that it was the burden of this secret that was killing me, and only when I told someone was that burden lifted. I think that's the reason we're still friends. He wants to be around if I ever get sick again."

"And do you know... everything?"

"Not even close," Saracen said. "After you."

The Cleavers opened the doors for them and they joined Skulduggery and the Elders just as Tipstaff was handing Ravel a note. Valkyrie looked at Ghastly. He caught her eye and winked, and she smiled.

Ravel took a moment to read the note, then looked up. "All right, then," he said, "before we get on to Bernard Sult and what this means, I have to ask Skulduggery and Valkyrie if Tyren Lament or any of his sorcerers ever mentioned anything about the Engineer?"

Valkyrie frowned. "What engineer?"

"*The* Engineer," said Ravel. "The Sensitives were able to get a few snippets of information out of the mind of one of Sult's people before the psychic block went up. The Supreme Council has been doing a little research into the Accelerator, it seems, and they came across a mention of this 'Engineer'."

"So who is he?" Skulduggery asked.

"Not who – what. It's a machine. Apparently it's the only way to deactivate the Accelerator."

"And where is it?"

"No one knows. It wandered off."

"How can it wander off? It's a machine."

"It's humanoid, has an independent brain and is most likely sentient in a—"

Valkyrie's eyes bulged. "It's a *robot*?"

"Well... yes."

Excitement bubbled inside her. "There's a robot out there? That is so cool! Can it transform into anything?"

Ravel hesitated. "No."

"Really?" Valkyrie said, suddenly disappointed. "Wow. You'd

think if someone went to the trouble of building a robot, they'd at least make one that transforms."

"Yes," said Ravel slowly, "that was my first thought, too. Anyway, it was supposed to stay with the Accelerator, but obviously it wandered off. I can only assume that when the Supreme Council couldn't find it, they decided to cut out the middleman, plant a few bombs and just hope for the best. Luckily for us, Ghastly was on hand to save the day."

"Ghastly's my hero," said Saracen.

"But before I interrupted them," Ghastly said, ignoring Saracen, "Sult did manage to transmit an energy reading to the American Sanctuary. If the Accelerator and the Engineer were built together, and we have every reason to believe they were, then the energy reading of one could theoretically be used to track down the other."

"What does all this matter?" Valkyrie asked. "We're not going to use the Accelerator anyway, right?"

"The Supreme Council doesn't know that," said Ghastly. "All they know is that we have a weapon that we could deploy at any time. It's our nuclear deterrent: it stops them from doing anything too stupid. But if we no longer have the option of supercharging our sorcerers..."

"They're free to be as stupid as they like."

"Sadly, yes."

Skulduggery looked back to Ravel. "What has been their reaction to Sult's arrest?"

Ravel gave a shrug of exasperation. "The Supreme Council is demanding Sult's release, as you can expect. The interesting thing is that they haven't even attempted to lie about what he was doing here."

"So they don't think they owe anyone an explanation," Skulduggery said. "Then they've already decided on war – now they're just waiting for the instigating moment."

Ravel sat heavily into his chair. "It would appear so. In response to our refusal to release him, they're rounding up Irish mages all over the world, accusing them of spying and putting them in shackles. We'll use whatever contacts and resources we can to smuggle our people back to us, but we don't have a number yet on how many have been taken. And there's something you all should know – Dexter Vex was one of the first arrested."

"Do we know anything further?" asked Saracen.

"Only that he didn't resist, which is probably a good thing."

"And what are we doing about foreign agents on Irish soil?" Ghastly asked.

Ravel hesitated. "We're asking them to leave, and we're making sure they do. We can't afford to be as brash as the Supreme Council. If their sorcerers, people we know and have fought beside, see how respectfully we're treating them despite Sult's attack, then maybe they'll have second thoughts about the part they're playing in all this."

"Weakness," said Madame Mist.

Ravel looked at her. "Excuse me?"

"You're worried about being rude, and so we tiptoe where we should stride. Our enemies will see this as a weakness."

"They are not our enemies."

"Of course they are. Friends become enemies in times of war. If we enter into this with timid hearts, we will be crushed. We must stride, we must bellow, we must be merciless. That is how we win."

"What are you talking about?" Ravel asked, frowning at her. "Win? What might we win? If we defeat the Supreme Council, then what? Do we take over? Do we run every Sanctuary around the world? Why would we even want that? We're not in this to win. We're in it to survive. We defend ourselves. If we have to go to war, we strike at key strategic points. We weaken the Supreme Council and we chip away at their support. Then, when their rank-and-file sorcerers have had enough, we withdraw and let them sort it out among themselves."

Mist looked at him a moment longer, then sat back. "How... noble," she said, distaste curling the word.

"We don't want a war, Elder Mist," Ravel said. "If you find fault in our tactics, I invite you to offer alternatives. If you don't have any, we may as well work with what we have. Valkyrie, I see you've met Saracen. Only believe half of what he tells you. Skulduggery, you've been looking deeper into these Warlock rumours. Any progress?"

Skulduggery took a moment to answer. "Our investigation is ongoing," he said.

"Do you know something you're not telling us?"

"Yes."

"Right. Well, at least someone knows something. That's a nice bloody change."

8

SEARCHING THE AISLES

The Repository in the old Sanctuary had been much better. Its ceilings were higher, its aisles were longer, the various magical artefacts were spaced out more. But here, in the Roarhaven Sanctuary, the ceiling was low, the aisles were short and uneven, and all of these wonderful and rare objects were crammed together on the shelves, which made finding one teeny-tiny box all the more difficult.

"Can we interrogate Bernard Sult?" Valkyrie asked as they searched.

"Why would we want to?" Skulduggery murmured, his gloved fingers rifling through a large box of smaller boxes.

"Because we might get a confession out of him."

Skulduggery put the large box back on the shelf, and kept looking. "We don't need a confession. Ghastly caught him red-handed."

"But a confession might make the Supreme Council back off."

"Only if they were denying his mission, which they're not."

She frowned. "I still think we should interrogate him."

"Why?"

"To get the truth, the facts... also to gloat."

Skulduggery got to the end of the aisle, and started down the next one. "Gloating is unbecoming of you."

Valkyrie trailed after him. "You gloat all the time."

"Because when I do it it's admirable and funny. Bernard Sult is a political prisoner. The situation must be handled with great care and sensitivity – neither of which are your strong points."

"Did... you just insult me?"

He stopped, and looked back. "Not that I am aware. Let others be caring and sensitive, Valkyrie. You concentrate on being effective. It's what you're good at." He resumed his search.

"I can be effective *while* I'm being caring and sensitive," she said to the back of his head. "You've seen me with Alice. You've seen how caring I can be. I'm the most caring person in the world when I'm with her. I'm almost *too* caring."

"Let's not get carried away."

She glared. "I care. And I'm sensitive. You need to be sensitive in order to be a good big sister."

"I've clearly struck a nerve."

"No you haven't. It's not a nerve. It's just a thing. I'm a good big sister, and I'm going to keep being a good big sister while she grows up. I'm going to give her advice on school, on clothes, on boys... I'm going to make sure she's happy and safe and nothing bad ever happens to her."

Skulduggery turned. "This conversation has shifted."

"Has it?"

"It has. Who have you been speaking to?"

Valkyrie hesitated.

"Ah," said Skulduggery. "It was something you were discussing with China. I see. And what did China say that has you so confrontational?"

"I'm not confrontational."

"You think there's an argument coming so you've started arguing early. It's what you always do."

"Fine. OK. Yes, there's an argument coming. Oh, look, it's already arrived. Big deal."

"And may I ask what it is we are arguing about?"

"You don't want to know."

"Maybe not, but I think it would probably be useful nevertheless."

Valkyrie sighed, and put some irritation into it to hide her own uneasiness. "I was talking to China about the Second Lifetime Syndrome, and about maybe telling my parents the truth."

Skulduggery looked at her with his empty eye sockets.

It was very quiet in the Repository. She could hear her own breathing, and every slight rustle her clothes made as she stood there.

"Hmm," Skulduggery said.

"China's not in favour," Valkyrie said quickly. "Just in case you think she's talked me into anything."

He nodded. "Hmm," he said again.

"She gave me loads of reasons why I shouldn't, so you don't have to. I haven't even decided. I just mentioned it. It's a possibility. I don't want to lose my family. Is that so wrong?"

He didn't answer, and her eyes widened.

"I mean... I'm sorry, I didn't... That was a dumb thing to say."

"Why?" he asked, and tilted his head. Then he clicked his fingers. "Oh, yes, because my family is dead. I'd completely forgotten."

The warmth in his voice made her smile. "You're such a moron. Sorry, though."

He waved her words away. "If people had to apologise to me every time they made some random comment about dead families, I'd never get any work done. As for your dilemma, I'm not going to tell you what to do. I want you to be happy and for your parents and sister to be happy and safe. Whatever way you can achieve that is fine with me."

"Thank you."

"So long as you take into account all the possible repercussions of your actions before you do anything, I'm confident you'll make the right decision."

Her smile soured. "Cheers. Are we going to find this crystal or not?"

"Already have," Skulduggery said, and held up a small, felt-covered box. He opened it and withdrew a purple crystal the size of a peanut.

"Hmph."

He tilted his head. "Hmph?"

Valkyrie shrugged. "It's not very impressive, is it? I was expecting... I don't know what I was expecting, but I was expecting something less... meh."

"I have never admired your professionalism more than right at this moment. Anyway, this is the amethyst crystal China told you about – though, to be honest, I didn't know it could be used to affect the memory in such a selective way. It's usually wielded with such clumsiness, used to wipe a mind clear. Whoever our mystery man is, he knows what he's doing."

"If they're so powerful," Valkyrie said, "it couldn't be easy getting your hands on one."

"It's not – certainly not one as loaded with power as this is. A lot of them have been destroyed. Most of the others have been locked away in vaults and Repositories around the world."

"So our mystery man has a crystal of his very own," said Valkyrie.

Skulduggery nodded slowly. "Either that or he uses this one."

She looked at him. "Are you being serious?"

"They're really not easy to get hold of."

"So he borrows this one whenever he needs it, then puts it back when he's done? But then... I mean, if that's true, then we've probably passed him in the corridor a hundred times."

"Maybe."

"So we're pretty sure now that not only is he a Roarhaven mage, he's also a Sanctuary mage. That means he's one of us."

He looked at her. "Yes."

"Well... that's just *creepy*. Can we take fingerprints or something?"

"Crystals of this nature don't hold any oily residue," Skulduggery said, "and the box is covered in felt. We'll have someone go over the CCTV footage for this room, but I doubt we'll find anything useful. The one lead we have, though, that we didn't have before, is the description of the old man with the long grey beard. Take that description, combine it with Roarhaven, and who springs to mind?"

"The Torment."

"That being the case, what do you think our next move should be?"

Valkyrie smiled. "Scapegrace."

9

ROARHAVEN'S NUMBER ONE PUBLIC HOUSE

hen they walked into the pub, it was empty except for Thrasher behind the bar and Scapegrace sweeping up. Scapegrace brightened when he saw them. When *she* saw them. *He* saw them. God, this was confusing.

Scapegrace threw the sweeping brush away and came forward, clasped Skulduggery's hand and gave it a firm shake. "My friend," he said. "It is good to see you again."

"Uh," Skulduggery said. "Right."

"And Valkyrie," Scapegrace said, turning to her, smiling broadly. "How goes the fight?"

She had to look past the impressive figure, the pretty face, the dazzling smile, and remember the brain that lurked within that head. "What fight would that be?"

"The fight against evil," said Scapegrace. "How goes it? Does it go well?"

"Sure," Valkyrie said, a little doubtfully.

"I heard there was an explosion in the Sanctuary. Do you have any leads?"

She frowned. "Yeah."

"Any suspects?"

"The people who set the bomb were arrested at the scene."

Scapegrace nodded thoughtfully. "I see, I see. Convenient. A little too convenient, wouldn't you say? Almost as if they *wanted* to be caught."

"I don't think so..."

"Well, maybe not, I know nothing about it. But if you need our help, just give us the sign. We'll need to work out a sign. Then you can give it, and we'll come and help. Some kind of signal, or alarm, or, I don't know, maybe I could give you my phone number, or you could pop by, I suppose. We're only up the road from you, so that'd probably be handiest."

"You feeling OK?"

Scapegrace laughed, and stepped back. "Me? I'm fine. Better than Thrasher, that's for sure."

Thrasher walked up, a sheepish look on his handsome face. "Hi, Valkyrie. Hi, Skulduggery."

"You're not feeling well?" Skulduggery asked.

Before Thrasher could answer, Scapegrace did it for him. "He's constipated."

"Master!" Thrasher said, horrified.

"Oh, shut up. We're all friends here. We can talk about these things. It's just like Doctor Nye told us. We each got a blast of magic to reanimate these bodies, and that magic has been keeping us going for the past few months. But now our own biological processes are starting to reawaken and take over."

"I got hungry for the first time on Tuesday," Thrasher said, somewhat guiltily. "So I ate something."

Scapegrace grinned happily. "But while his stomach has reactivated, his bowels are still asleep."

"It's very uncomfortable," Thrasher confessed.

"As zombies, we didn't feel anything," Scapegrace said, "but now that we're human again, something like constipation is a real problem. For some of us."

Thrasher blushed and Scapegrace's grin widened. Valkyrie felt the need to step in.

"How about you?" she asked. "Have all of your biological processes reawakened yet?"

Scapegrace's grin faded immediately. "Not yet," he said. "I can feel my magic beginning to reawaken, but the biological processes are... taking their time. But it... it should be fine. I have a book about it. About what to expect. Actually, now that you're here, I was wondering... If I have any questions about, you know, certain aspects of womanhood, could I ask you?"

"No," she said.

"But just a few tips—"

"Under no circumstances. God, no. No way."

"Oh," he said. "Fair enough. I suppose... I suppose, OK, let's keep this professional."

"Professional is a good way to keep it."

"It's just... I don't have any other female friends."

She frowned. "We're friends?"

"What about Clarabelle?" Skulduggery said. "Have you asked her?"

"I have," Scapegrace said. "She tried to help, but then she started laughing, and she wouldn't stop. She was laughing so much she couldn't catch her breath, and she passed out."

"She did," said Thrasher. "I was there."

"It's all so confusing," Scapegrace said, sitting down. "I don't even know what size clothes to wear. I got a big bundle of clothes from a charity shop, but I don't even know how to wear most of it. This top, the top I'm wearing now, it took me fifteen minutes to work out how to do it up."

"It's on backwards," Valkyrie said gently. "It's got a scoop neckline. That shouldn't be on your back."

"How am I supposed to know that? That's ridiculous!"

"Also, yellow is not your colour."

"I told him that," Thrasher murmured.

Scapegrace jumped to his feet. "Now I have to figure out what my colour is? How is any of this fair?"

"It can't be all bad," Valkyrie said, trying for a reassuring smile. "You're healthy, aren't you? You're alive. That's something."

"Yeah," Scapegrace said, face in his hands. "I suppose."

"And from what I've heard, the pub is doing really well."

At this, Thrasher's face soured. "It's just a pity our clientele couldn't be a bit... classier, that's all."

Scapegrace glared. "*Our?*"

"Sorry, Master. Yours."

"There is nothing wrong with my clientele. Most of them are old friends of mine. Well, not really friends, but... but people I've known for years."

"It's nice that they're supporting you," Valkyrie said.

Scapegrace took a moment. "They treat me differently," he said. "They're nicer to me. They laugh now when I say something funny. No one ignores me any more."

"That's good."

"Yes," he said, and then shook his head. "Oh, who am I kidding? At least when they ignored me, they ignored me for the man I was, not the woman I'm not. Now I'm just an object to them. A pretty face serving them drinks."

Thrasher's eyes welled up. "They don't see you like I see you."

Scapegrace whirled round to him instantly. "Again, kind of an odd thing to say."

"Sorry, Master."

"Stop saying odd things."

"Yes, Master."

Scapegrace turned back to Valkyrie and Skulduggery. "You need something. Information? I'm your man. Sort of."

"We're looking for information about the Torment," said Skulduggery.

"Ah, the Torment. I haven't thought about him for years."

"Who is he?" Thrasher asked.

"He's before your time," Scapegrace said, somewhat wistfully. "He was a Child of the Spider, or an Old Man of the Spider, whatever. He didn't like Valkyrie because he could sense Ancient blood in her, and also he just wasn't a very nice man. He could turn into a giant spider, though, which was pretty cool. Skulduggery, remember the first time you questioned me? You wanted me to bring you to him. They were good times, weren't they? I was so different then. I wasn't a zombie. I wasn't a woman. I was me."

"You brought the Torment to Roarhaven," Valkyrie said. "You let him stay beneath this very pub."

"And did I get any thanks for that? All the work I put into converting the cellar into a place someone could live – do you know how long that took? I mean, fine, I may have stolen most of the materials, but it was still a huge undertaking."

Skulduggery tilted his head. "You stole the materials to convert the cellar?"

"Sure I did. There were enough construction supplies coming into Roarhaven to rebuild the town ten times over."

"What was it all used for?"

"Never did find out. But for ages I thought every house had another house underneath it, because there were just too many people here, you know? Too many people passing through, and I couldn't see how they'd all fit. That's how I got the idea to convert the cellar."

"There are tunnels connecting this building to the Sanctuary," Skulduggery said. "There might be more. Buildings under buildings, as you said. Streets under streets."

"Maybe," Scapegrace said, and shrugged. "I went looking one day, though. Couldn't find anything. Although that could have just been because I'm rubbish and nobody likes me for who I am."

"I like you, Master," Thrasher said.

"You don't count," said Scapegrace.

88

Skulduggery pressed onwards before the conversation derailed. "All of this was happening after the Torment arrived?"

"No, a lot of it was going on before I ever met him. I convinced him to stay here because, you know, I thought it'd make the other mages respect me if I had someone like the Torment as a friend. But he hated me. He talked to other people. Never me."

"What other people? Who did he associate with?"

"I don't know. Everyone. He had meetings. I used to call them secret meetings, but they probably weren't secret. They were just secret from me. People always wanted to talk to him, but I don't think he was interested, I think he just wanted to retire. But that didn't stop them. I remember the first time I saw Madame Mist come into town. At first I really wanted to find out what she looked like behind that veil, but then she creeped me out so much that I started to hide until she was gone."

"Ever hear him mention the Warlocks?"

"Not that I can remember. Whenever Madame Mist was around, I didn't go near the three of them."

"Three?"

"Sorry?"

"You said the three of them."

"Yes. The Torment and Madame Mist and the other guy."

"What other guy?"

"I don't know who he was."

"Do you remember what he looked like?"

"Sure. He was... well, he was regular height. Might have been taller. Or maybe below average. But anyway, his hair was... there. I think. He had a... face..."

"Do you remember anything *specific* about him?"

Scapegrace furrowed his brow. "It's like... it's on the tip of my tongue, but..."

"Don't worry," Valkyrie said. "We've been hearing a lot of that lately."

"Would you be willing to sit down with a Sensitive?" Skulduggery asked. "They can enter your mind and might be able to lift that block."

"My mind?" said Scapegrace. "No. God, no. That's the only original part of me I have left."

"We need to know who that man is."

"Ask Madame Mist. They were always together. But no psychic is going rooting around in my brainspace, you got that? I have a secret identity to protect."

Valkyrie frowned. "What secret identity?"

Scapegrace went pale. "None. No secret identity."

"What are you talking about?"

"What are *you* talking about?"

Thrasher grabbed something from behind the bar and hurried over. "Um, Valkyrie, I don't want to distract you or anything but, uh, this came for you..."

He handed Valkyrie an envelope addressed to the pub, but with her name on top. She opened it, unfolded the letter halfway and read.

"It's from Cassandra Pharos," she told Skulduggery. "She's had a new vision. She wants us to go over there tonight. There's no date, but... when did this arrive?"

"Yesterday," said Thrasher.

Valkyrie frowned. "So are we late?"

"We're dealing with a Sensitive who can see into the future," Skulduggery said. "She knew when you'd read that. She means tonight."

Valkyrie opened the letter fully. Her frown deepened. "She says say hello to the vampire for her. What does that mean?"

"Oh, yes," Skulduggery said. "I've been meaning to tell you..."

10

THE THIRTEENTH FLOOR

They didn't talk about vampires.

That was a rule Valkyrie introduced right after Caelan had tried to kill her. It wasn't possible to obey it at all times, of course – there were occasions when talking about vampires was sadly necessary – but for the most part they avoided the subject whenever possible. It wasn't that Valkyrie had developed a phobia about them, either. She wasn't *scared*. The fact of the matter was that she'd fallen into the arms of a gorgeous, brooding vampire, and he'd revealed himself to be a possessive, obsessive psycho.

The reason she didn't talk about vampires wasn't simply because of the sheer embarrassment of it all.

And now here she was, accompanying Skulduggery to Faircourt Flats, where vampires were all anybody ever talked about.

To the best of her knowledge, the situation here was unique. The ordinary tenants of the flats provided a constant supply of blood for Moloch and his pack, and in return the vampires kept the area clean from drugs and crime. Moloch's apartment was on the thirteenth floor, and it was barely furnished. Deep grooves carved the walls. Moloch himself sat in the throne that was his couch, wearing tracksuit bottoms and a silver chain around his scrawny neck. His face was pockmarked but his skin was healthy. He must have fed recently. His eyes never left Valkyrie from the moment she stepped in the door.

"You killed Caelan," he said.

"He died because of me," Valkyrie clarified. "So what? You would have killed him yourself if it wasn't for the vampire code."

"Maybe," Moloch said, "but I *didn't* kill him, did I? You did. And so you've officially joined the ranks of the Fearless Vampire Killers, up there with Blade and Buffy and other anti-vampire propaganda. You must be so proud."

"I didn't want him to die."

"I'm sure you did everything in your power to save him," said Moloch, and looked at Skulduggery. "Is that why you brought her? To send a message or something? Is this your version of a sneaky little threat?"

Skulduggery shook his head. "Sneaky little threats are not my thing. I threatened someone once, but I was too subtle about it, so when it came time to throw him off the cliff, he looked awfully surprised. These days when I threaten someone I do it loud and blatant, just to make sure my point has been taken. It could be argued that Valkyrie is responsible for the death of a vampire, but how many have I killed over the years? Vampires die, Moloch, and it's usually people like Valkyrie and me who are around to make sure it happens. May I sit?"

"The armchair's for friends."

"Do your friends ever wash? That cushion looks like someone congealed into it. I've changed my mind – I'll stand. Thanks for the offer, though."

"I didn't offer."

"But it's the thought that counts and that's the important thing. Moloch, you must know why I'm here."

Moloch chewed on something. Valkyrie didn't want to guess what it could be. "This war thing."

"This war thing, exactly. We have a lot of trouble headed our way."

"What's this *we* business, pale-face?"

"We're all in this together, I'm afraid."

Moloch laughed. "We don't have anything to do with you sorcerers. We keep to ourselves, we don't bother no one, and no one bothers us."

"And what if the Supreme Council takes over?" Skulduggery asked. "Do you think you'll be able to continue with your peaceful co-existence? You know who's one of the driving forces behind the Supreme Council? Grand Mage Wahrheit. And you know how much he loves you bloodsucking types."

Moloch scratched himself. "Looks like I'll just have to cross my fingers and hope you wand-waving types save the day at the last minute, then."

Skulduggery shrugged. "And if we fail?"

"We're all screwed."

"You could help make sure that doesn't happen."

Moloch laughed again. "This is rich, this is. You people hate us. You despise us. Most of you don't even rate us as anything above animal."

"How about we change that? I've come to you with a proposition."

"This'll be good."

"We'll help you with your serum supplies. I know how hard it is these days to find exactly what you need in large enough quantities. We can even manufacture the serum at a consistently safe level."

"That so? Serum, eh?"

"A lifetime's supply," said Skulduggery. "In exchange for your help against the Supreme Council."

"So we put ourselves in the firing line – and I assume you'd be using us as a first wave of attack kind of thing, not much more than cannon fodder – and as a reward we get all the serum we need to stay human when the sun goes down." Moloch sat forward, resting his bony elbows on his bony knees. "Do you know how

93

much I hate being human? Do you know how uncomfortable it is at night, being unable to split my skin and emerge? It's like I have ants crawling inside my flesh. And my skin, it gets so tight it gives me headaches. My gums hurt. They bleed. My teeth want to grow, but they can't. My fingernails want to lengthen, but they're held back. All I want to do is lose myself, but my thoughts jingle and jangle inside my head. And you want to give us more serum? No thanks." Moloch settled back into his couch. "We want more territory."

Skulduggery tilted his head. "I'm sorry?"

"Look at the good we've done for our local community. Crime is down. Vandalism is down. We protect the people and the people protect us. We've demonstrated what we can do and we've proved that we don't need you sorcerers looking over our shoulders when we do it. We want more territory."

"How much more?"

"Another housing estate."

"Mortal housing estates are not ours to give."

"We're not asking you to give it to us. We just want you to not interfere when we make our move."

"And how exactly would you be making your move? An army of vampires swarming—"

"Don't be ridiculous," Moloch said. "We'd do it slowly, winning over one person at a time. What, you think we haven't been asked? People see what we've done for the residents here. They might not know the full extent of who we are, but they know a good deal when they see it. They want us to spread our influence in their direction. If you agree to that, the vampires will fight on your side."

"I don't have the authority to make that kind of deal."

Moloch laughed. "Like hell you don't. You might think we're out of the loop over here, but I have my sources. You may not be an Elder, skeleton, but you run that Sanctuary as much as anyone. They'll listen to you if you tell them to agree."

"I'll inform them of your proposal."

"You do that."

Valkyrie followed Skulduggery to the door.

"Oh, girl?" said Moloch, and she turned. He gave her a shark's smile. "We remember those who have vampire blood on their hands. There's a stink about them that never quite goes away."

"Whoever said I wanted it to?" Valkyrie asked, and walked out.

11

BIG, TOUGH MAN

Dexter Vex didn't complain when he was shackled. He didn't complain as he was loaded into the van, or even when he was hauled out. He didn't complain about all the shoving and pushing and rough treatment as he was escorted into one of the American Sanctuary's support posts in rural Connecticut. He didn't complain about any of it. The same could not be said for his companion.

"I'm going to sue every last one of you," Caius Caviler raged after his head smacked into the wall for a second time. "I'm going to introduce the mortal procedure of a lawsuit into the magical community and then I'm going to sue you and take everything you own."

The man shoving him was big and broad and not in a very good mood. His name was Grim. He was an English sorcerer who'd been Quintin Strom's bodyguard the day the Grand Mage had been assassinated. He'd been fired shortly afterwards, and now here he was in America, trying to restore his honour by being as big a jerk as possible.

Vex was in America. He felt it only right to use American insults.

The sorcerer behind Vex was a much calmer fellow. Swain,

96

his name was. Vex had never met him before and, while he was blissfully unconcerned with Vex's comfort, at least he wasn't shoving him face first into walls.

"This is an illegal arrest!" Caviler went on. "You can't put shackles on someone just because of their nationality! We have rights!"

Grim shoved him into another wall. Caviler rebounded, went quiet. He sucked at his bloody lip.

They reached two rows of cells with old-fashioned iron bars in place of walls, and each bar inscribed with a binding sigil.

"In here," Swain said, nudging Vex towards the nearest one. Vex walked in and Swain locked the door. Grim pushed Caviler into the cell next to him, and Caviler stumbled to his knees beside the bunk.

"Enjoy your stay," Grim said, and went to leave.

"Big man," Caviler muttered.

Grim turned. "What was that?"

Caviler got to his feet and looked Grim dead in the eye. "You're a big man when the other guy's handcuffed, aren't you? Big, tough man. I don't think you'd be so tough if my hands were free."

"Oh, you don't, do you?"

"Caius," Vex said, shaking his head.

"Maybe I should take the cuffs off, then," said Grim.

Caviler smiled, showing bloody teeth. "By all means."

Swain took hold of Grim's arm, tried to pull him out. "Come on, we don't have time for this."

Grim shook himself free. "No, no, Mr Caviler here wants a fair go. It's only right that I should give him the chance." He took the key from his pocket and threw it at Caviler's feet. "Well? Come on now. There's the key."

"And the moment I go to pick it up you kick me in the face?" Caviler said. "I don't think so."

Grim stepped out of the cell. "There. Now you have loads of room."

Caviler chuckled. "You are smarter than you look. That's not hard, I'll grant you, but even so. Once that key is in my hand, you'll be able to shoot me for attempting to escape. Unfortunately, Mr Grim, you're going to have to do better than that."

Grim shrugged, took his pistol from his holster and held it out to Swain.

"What the hell are you doing?" Swain asked. "We have to go. Put the gun away. I'm not taking your damn—"

Grim pointed the gun at Caviler and Swain snatched it off him.

"There," Grim said to Caviler. "I'm unarmed."

Swain tried pulling Grim back, but Grim turned, shoved him, his face suddenly red with anger.

"If you don't walk away with me right this moment," said Swain, "I'll bring the Cleavers in here and they'll drag you out."

"If that's what you feel you have to do," said Grim.

Swain stared at him, then glanced at Caviler and then Vex, and walked away.

Grim stepped into the cell, closed the door, and smiled at Caviler. "Pick up the key."

"Don't," said Vex.

"Go on. Free yourself. Be a man."

"Caius, do not pick up that key."

Caviler licked his lips. His hand reached downwards slowly. Grim didn't move, not even when Caviler lifted the key off the ground and straightened up.

Grim stepped forward suddenly and Caviler flinched back, and Grim laughed like it was the funniest thing he'd ever seen. Caviler's eyes narrowed, and he worked the key until the cuffs fell.

"Put them back on," Vex ordered. "Caius, put the handcuffs back on right now. Do it."

"Caius doesn't take orders from you," said Grim. "Caius Caviler doesn't take orders from anyone. Look at him. Look how strong he is. He's going to teach me a lesson and no mistake. When the cuffs were on, I could hit because I knew he couldn't hit me back, but now... now I'm scared. Look at how scared I am." Grim's smile broadened. "What was that you were saying, Caius? Big, tough man, wasn't it? Well, your hands are free. Time to show me what a big, tough man really is."

Grim took another step towards him. Caviler backed up.

"Teach me a lesson," said Grim. "Come on." He reached out, poked Caviler's chest. "Let's go." He poked again, and again.

Caviler swung a punch that slapped uselessly off Grim's jaw.

"Good boy," whispered Grim, and replied with a punch to the ribs that lifted Caviler off his feet.

Caviler fell back, wheezing, and Grim struck him in the face so hard he cracked his skull off the iron bars. Caviler threw himself forward and Grim laughed, shot a knee into Caviler's gut and tripped him as he staggered.

"That's enough," said Vex.

"Oh, we're just getting started," said Grim, and he clapped his hands as Caviler got up. "See this? Heart of a lion, this guy! You can hit him, you can kick him, but he keeps on tickin'!"

Caviler went to swing another punch, but Grim stepped in and headbutted him.

"My turn," said Vex. "Come on, Grim. He's had enough. You want to beat up someone, beat me up. You're going to kill him."

"He should've thought of that before he provoked me," said Grim, twisting Caviler's arm behind his back. "Say uncle. Come on, tough guy. Say uncle."

"Uncle!" Caviler cried.

Grim cocked his head. "Sorry, what was that? Didn't quite hear you."

"*Uncle!*"

"Still not hearing right," said Grim, and he wrenched Caviler's arm back and Vex heard the snap of bone, and Caviler shrieked and thrashed, but Grim still wouldn't let him go. "Next time you find yourself arrested," he said, "keep your bloody mouth shut, you understand me? This here is you getting off lightly."

Grim released him and Caviler swung blindly, his elbow crunching into Grim's nose. Grim bellowed, grabbed Caviler again and wrapped his arm round his throat, hauled him back in a vicious sleeper hold.

"Let him go!" Vex shouted. "He didn't mean it, Grim! Look at him! He's beaten! Let him go!"

Caviler's face was already turning purple. His ruined arm flapped uselessly by his side, while his legs kicked and his good hand scraped at Grim's arm. Grim tightened the hold even more, walking backwards the whole time. Caviler's legs stopped kicking. The heels of his feet dragged across the floor. Both arms hung limply.

"Let him go," said Vex. "You're killing him. Grim, let him go. Release him. Grim!"

Grim's eyes widened, and he opened his arms and Caviler fell. The colour drained from Grim's face.

Footsteps approached and Swain walked back in, two Cleavers in tow. When he saw Caviler, he ran forward, yanked open the cell door and dropped to his side, checked for a pulse.

"Get a doctor," he told one of the Cleavers, and then he stared up at Grim, disbelief etched into his face. "What the hell have you done?"

12

THE DEADLINE

A photograph of Valkyrie Cain was pinned to the exact centre of the wall. Radiating outwards and linked by different coloured thread were names, locations, dates and more photographs. Along the blue thread were pictures of Valkyrie's family, including a publicity shot of the late horror writer Gordon Edgley. Red threads meant public incidents, and these threads linked newspaper reports and Internet printouts. The green thread led straight to a series of pictures of tall men in good suits, all under the banner of Skulduggery Pleasant. There were shots of a heavily scarred man, a black Bentley, and various other individuals. Some of these pictures were too blurry to make out, but most were of relatively high quality. The system for cross-referencing had started out as simple, but, as more information was collected, it had got decidedly complex.

"I don't get it," said Patrick Slattery, scratching his beard in that way he did. "You're saying that all of these guys are Skulduggery Pleasant? How does he manage that?"

Kenny Dunne collapsed into his tattered old armchair. "I don't know, but it's the only thing that makes sense."

Slattery looked sceptical. It had become his default look over these past few months. "Really? The only thing that makes sense is that all of these men we've been photographing are the same person? That makes sense to you? They look nothing alike."

"They're all tall, thin and have the same taste in well-tailored clothes. And look at their faces. The skin and hair might be different, but the bone structure's the same."

"He wears disguises, then," said Slattery. "For no reason, every day he wears a different disguise."

"I don't know. Maybe. Who knows with these people?"

Slattery shook his head, more to himself than to Kenny. "So why is he called the Skeleton Detective?"

"For the last time, I don't know, all right? Probably because he's so thin. I don't have all the answers."

"You don't have *any* of the answers."

Kenny didn't have a violent bone in his body, but there was nothing he would have liked to do more at that moment than jump up and smack Slattery right in the face. "I'm making educated guesses. It's the only thing we can do with the information we have."

Slattery hesitated, then turned from the wall and looked straight at Kenny. "We need to have a talk."

"We're talking now."

"We need to have a serious talk about what we're doing here."

Kenny's hand fluttered an invitation. "Go right ahead."

Slattery sat in the tattered old couch that had come with the tattered old armchair. "It might be time to rethink things," he said. "When you came to me with this, I thought you'd cracked. I honestly thought you'd gone mad. Magic people and possession and super-powers. I thought to myself, Kenny's gone round the bend. He's lost it. All those years chasing stories have led him into the nuthouse. I thought you'd want me and my camera down the bottom of some garden, ready to photograph fairies or something."

Kenny nodded. "Happy to know you had so much faith in me as a journalist."

"But then when you showed me what you had and, when I

saw it for myself, I thought, holy cow, we're going to change the world. Politics, religion, society – it's all going to be turned on its head. And we're the ones who are going to do it."

"Nothing's changed since then."

"Well, that's it exactly," said Slattery. "Nothing *has* changed. We had a few good months of following Valkyrie around, a few good months of collecting information and names and linking stuff up... and then it all slowed down to a crawl."

"A crawl? Have you been reading the papers? Something's going on. Unexplained destruction of property, unexplained disappearances, sightings of—"

"Kenny," Slattery said, "please. Come on. How does this help us? If we had a team, fair enough. But there's only two of us. By the time we get to the scene, it's like nothing ever happened."

"We just have to be patient."

"You need to go back to work."

"I *am* working."

"You need to work on a story that will get you paid. You're living on scraps, for God's sake. I need to get paid, too."

Kenny frowned. "That's what this is about? You want money?"

"I don't want money, I need money. I have bills to pay."

"When we release what we have, we'll be rich beyond our—"

"Release what?" Slattery said, barking a laugh. "We have photographs of people and coloured thread on a wall."

"You seem to be forgetting the recorded footage we have of Valkyrie Cain and Fletcher Renn fighting a monster."

"Could I be blamed for forgetting that? It's not like we've done anything with it. We haven't released it or sold it. We've hung on to it."

"You know why. We need more than that. We need something so concrete that no one will even try to tell us it's faked. We're dealing with sorcerers who can make you believe whatever they tell you. We can't afford to go public until we have overwhelming evidence."

"And how are we going to get it?"

Kenny sat back.

"You need the evidence to write that book you're always on about," said Slattery. "You need the evidence to make that documentary that I'm apparently going to film. Where's that evidence, Kenny? Where do we find it?"

"We stick to Valkyrie."

"Here we go again."

"We stick to Valkyrie Cain and she will take us to the evidence eventually."

"She's a teenage girl and you want us to follow her around *again*? We've spied on her enough, don't you think? We tailed her for months, and she led us to people and places that are up on that wall, and that's it. That's all we've been able to get."

"Then we have to dig deeper."

"With what resources?"

"Well, what do you suggest? That we give up on the single most important story in the history of the world? I'm not exaggerating here, and you know I'm not."

"I never said you were. I'm just saying we can't do it alone."

"We have to keep this between ourselves."

"We can trust—"

"We can't trust anyone. A careless word here and there and somehow it gets back to Geoffrey Scrutinous or Finbar Wrong or Valkyrie or Skulduggery, and they'll come for us. They'll take all this, all our work and research, and they'll wipe our minds and do a better job of it than they did with me last time."

"It's risky. I know it is. But we don't have a choice. We need support, we need money, we need help."

Kenny shook his head. "We do this alone."

"You know your problem? You don't want to share the glory."

"This isn't about who gets the by-line."

"Isn't it?"

"What are you going to do?" Kenny asked. "If I say no, if I

say we don't need anyone, what are you going to do?"

"You mean if you refuse to see sense? I don't know yet. I might just have to take what I know and go somewhere else."

"I brought you in on this. This is my story."

"See? It is about the by-line."

Kenny sighed. "Just give it a little time, OK? All this crazy stuff that's been happening, it's been leading to something, I know it has. We just have to wait. Just a little longer."

Slattery stood up. "You have till October."

"You can't expect—"

"Two months, Kenny. Then either we get some help, or I leave with what I have."

13

EYE FOR AN EYE

The news came through the normal channels, but it came quietly, buried in among everything else, like it was trying to sneak by without anyone noticing. An Irish sorcerer, arrested but not charged with any crime, killed in an American cell. Ghastly had never met the man – Caius Caviler, his name was – and to the best of his knowledge he had never had any particular involvement with the Sanctuary, past or present. As far as he could tell, Caviler's death was the tragic result of casual brutality. It was awful. It was criminal. It was the one piece of good news they'd had in weeks.

There was a knock on his door and Ravel stepped in. He looked tired. "Mind if I sit?" he asked.

Ghastly motioned to the chair, and Ravel sank into it. "I just spoke with Bisahalani," he said. "He assures me that a thorough investigation is under way to determine what exactly happened to Caviler. He said the operative responsible for the 'accident' has been suspended pending further inquiry. He apologises for the unfortunate timing."

"He apologises for the timing?" said Ghastly. "What about the death?"

"He stopped short of apologising for that. He said a formal

apology could be forthcoming once it has been determined that Caviler was not sent to America as a spy."

"Caviler has nothing to do with us," Ghastly said. "He's not an operative and never was. That's a matter of public record."

"Grand Mage Bisahalani likes to be sure."

Ghastly narrowed his eyes. "He's bluffing. Remember Prussia, right after Hopeless died? Shudder and I fell in with Bisahalani and his group of American mages. The area was completely overrun by Mevolent's forces. They were hunting us down. Relentless. They finally had us surrounded in this old farmhouse. We were exhausted, starving, injured… it wouldn't have taken much to finish us off. Bisahalani walked out, he actually *walked out* the front door, walked across the yard to where Mevolent's soldiers were crouched behind cover. No one fired at him because they were all too stunned at what was happening. He went up to whoever was in charge and he stood there and informed him that he was to take his squad of killers and madmen and scurry away before the people in that farmhouse grew irritated."

"Did it work?"

"Astonishingly, yes. He was so convincing, he was so bull-headed and strong-willed, that Mevolent's soldiers decided to cut their losses and leave. That's what he does. When he's backed into a corner, Bisahalani will talk big and talk tough and all the time he'll be crossing his fingers and hoping that you don't stand your ground. They murdered an innocent man in their custody. The core elements of the Supreme Council will stick together, but what of everyone else? We know the Scottish Sanctuary is already asking questions. The Estonians, too. Tipstaff just told me that Grand Mage Kribu is calling for all Irish prisoners to be released in the wake of what happened."

"We have the advantage," Ravel said. "We have them over a barrel for the first time since all this began."

"If we play this right," said Ghastly, "support for the Supreme

Council will crumble, and the Supreme Council itself could even dissolve."

"We have to be careful. They're going to try to shift focus away from their mistake on to one of ours."

"Then we've got to be sure we don't *make* any mistakes."

Ravel frowned. "Where's Skulduggery?"

"Skulduggery and Valkyrie have gone to talk to Moloch like we asked, and then they're off to see Cassandra Pharos. Hopefully, that'll keep them out of trouble."

"OK, good." Ravel tapped his chin. "The Supreme Council arrests our people and they treat them so badly they kill one of them. We need to show that, when we arrest their people, they're treated well. We can arrange a Global Link broadcast to every Sanctuary around the world."

Ghastly stood. "I'll get Sult ready for his close-up."

"No hitting him."

"Any assault will be to his ego, I swear."

They left Ghastly's office. Ravel went one way, escorted by his Cleaver bodyguards, and Ghastly went the other, heading for the cells.

The guard on duty was snoring in his chair. Ghastly strode forward, sending a blast of air to wake him. The young man's hair ruffled and he was almost pitched sideways to the ground, but he didn't wake. What was his name?

"Weeper," Ghastly said, remembering. "Staven Weeper. Wake the hell up."

When Weeper continued to snore, Ghastly gripped his shoulder and shook him. As he was released, Weeper slumped over and collapsed slowly to the ground. Ghastly's eyes widened.

He ran to the first cell, opened the viewing hatch, saw Adrasdos reading a book on her bunk. He went to the next cell, and the next, and the next, all of which were occupied. Then he opened the hatch on the cell that should have been occupied by Bernard Sult.

He ran back to Weeper's corner, pressed the communication sigil on the desk. "Lock the Sanctuary down," he snarled. "We have an escaped prisoner."

The conference room was humming with activity by the time Ghastly reached it. Huge screens had been set up, showing CCTV footage of the corridor leading to the cellblock. Mages chattered on phones and hurried in and out of the doors, and Ravel stood in the middle of it all with a frown etched on his brow.

He turned to Ghastly. "Anything?"

Ghastly shook his head. "I sent the Cleavers into the lower levels, but I doubt Sult would have headed down there. He'll want to get out of Roarhaven as soon as possible. If he's in the area, we'll find him. Any luck with the cameras?"

Ravel swivelled his head, like he was catching the question and passing it on to the mage at the huge screens.

"We're watching the footage now," said Susurrus. "So far, we've seen no movement at... wait a second..."

The screen flickered, flickered again, went fuzzy, and then the picture was replaced by static.

"Mr Susurrus," said Ravel, "what happened to our picture?"

"I don't know, sir," said Susurrus, furiously tapping the keyboard. "It looks like someone jammed the signal."

"Those cameras are protected, are they not?" Ravel asked, his hands curled into fists. "When we installed them, I was told they were unjammable, was I not? So will someone please tell me how this happened?"

The chatter in the conference room died for a moment while sorcerers looked away and looked at their feet and looked at each other, no one daring to posit an answer. After a moment, the silence went away, and once more the room was plunged into a chattering mess of barked orders and ringing phones.

Ravel looked over at Ghastly, gave him an exasperated shrug, and Ghastly turned as Doctor Synecdoche approached.

"Staven Weeper has just regained consciousness," she said. "He claims to have no memory of anything unusual. One moment he was doing his duty with his customary alertness, his words, and the next he's waking up with Doctor Nye staring down at him."

"You believe him?"

"We've found traces of a toxin in his blood. We should be able to identify it within minutes."

"Thank you, Doctor," Ghastly said, nodding for the next sorcerer to approach.

"We've set up a perimeter around Roarhaven," said Petrichor, a fresh-faced mage of ninety-three. "We've also been viewing any outside CCTV footage that might yield results. So far, nothing. We don't even know how he got out without being seen."

"There are dozens of secret tunnels beneath this place that we don't know about," Ghastly said.

"Um," said Susurrus.

Ghastly looked round. "What is it?"

Susurrus frowned. "The Sanctuary Global Link, sir."

Ravel came forward. "What about it, for God's sake?"

"Uh... it just activated."

Ravel glared down at him. "Do you really think we're in the mood to watch Supreme Council propaganda right now?"

"Well, that's just it, Grand Mage. They didn't activate the link. We did."

The screen pulsed, showing Bernard Sult on his knees. His mouth was gagged and his hands were cuffed behind his back.

Ravel's eyes narrowed. "What the hell is going on?"

"Elder Bespoke," Doctor Synecdoche said, hurrying back to Ghastly's side. "We've identified the toxin in Weeper's blood. It's venom, sir."

"What?"

"Spider venom."

The doors opened behind him and Madame Mist glided in, in perfect synchronicity with Syc and Portia's arrival onscreen.

110

Ravel looked at Mist. "What are they doing?"

"I have nothing to do with this," Mist said, after a moment. "Whatever their plan is, it is theirs alone."

Ravel turned to Susurrus. "Trace the signal. Find out where they are."

Syc kept one hand on Sult's shoulder, keeping him on his knees, while Portia turned to the camera. "The actions of the Supreme Council have led to this. Their repeated breaches of the accepted Rules of Law and Sanctuary Conduct have resulted in the death of an Irish sorcerer while in their custody. This cannot go unpunished."

Syc took hold of Sult's hair and pulled his head back. Sult's eyes were wide and wet with fear. In Syc's other hand, he held a knife.

"They can't," Synecdoche whispered.

Ghastly seized Mist's arm. "Tell them to stop. Make them stop!"

With a rare show of anger, Mist pulled free. "I don't know where they are, Elder Bespoke. I assure you, they do *not* have my authorisation."

"Well, do they have *phones*? Call them, damn it!"

"I have been trying, sir," Tipstaff said from another desk. "Their phones are turned off, and hidden from all scans."

"You," Mist said, looking at Susurrus, "disable the link."

"I can't," Susurrus said. "Not from here."

"So every Sanctuary around the world is watching this?"

"I—I'm sorry, but yes."

Back onscreen, Portia was talking again. "No doubt our own Sanctuary will publicly condemn us for what we are about to do, even though they will understand why it is necessary. For too long, Grand Mage Ravel has entertained the Supreme Council's excessive demands. For too long, he has indulged their whims and forgiven their sins. This latest sin cannot be forgiven. And so we offer a life for a life."

"Don't do it," said Ravel, but the words had barely left his mouth when Syc drew the knife across Bernard Sult's throat.

Ghastly stiffened and there was no sound in the room except for the sound of Sult dying onscreen.

"Let it be known," said Portia, "that if one of ours is harmed, one of yours will die."

The screen went blank.

"Turn it off," said Ravel, his voice low, his jaw clenched. "Tipstaff. Activate the shield."

"The shield is up, sir."

"Out. Everyone out." The room emptied quickly, until there were only the Elders left. "We'll go to war over this," he said. "This is everything they needed. This is the excuse they were looking for. A public execution of one of their people. Any sympathy we may have had, *any*, was washed away the moment that blade touched his skin." Ravel turned to Mist. "Those two don't do anything without your permission."

"So I had thought," said Mist. "Obviously, I was wrong. You are suspicious of me?"

"You could say that."

Mist's veil made it impossible to read her face. "That is unfortunate. Please allow me to repeat myself – I had nothing to do with this. They acted without my knowledge and certainly without my permission. I cannot, and I will not, be held responsible for their actions."

"They're Children of the Spider," said Ghastly. "Just like you."

"And that makes me culpable? Preposterous. Are you to be held responsible every time an Elemental commits a crime?"

"Children of the Spider are an especially tight-knit bunch."

"We are no closer than family," said Mist, "and yet siblings are not held accountable for each other, are they? I had no idea Portia and Syc were going to do what they did, and unless you have evidence beyond mere suspicion, we should be concentrating on bringing them to justice and dealing with the ramifications of this terrible act."

She moved for the door, but Ghastly blocked her way. "You can't just walk out of here."

"On the contrary," she said, "I can and I am about to. Administrator Tipstaff may not be able to track them, but someone has to, and by the looks of things the rest of you are too busy blaming me to do anything constructive. So if you will excuse me."

She stepped round Ghastly and walked on, and he just stood there.

14

SEEING THE FUTURE

Cassandra Pharos greeted them from her front door with a warm smile. Her grey hair was pulled back in a plait today, and she wore a loose shirt over faded jeans. She hugged Valkyrie and ignored Skulduggery's protests until he allowed her to hug him, too.

The inside of the cottage was just as Valkyrie remembered it – a bookshelf against one wall, a guitar tucked into the corner, a large rug on the wooden floor and a sofa that had seen better days. And hanging from the rafters, dozens of bundles of twigs, shaped like little men. Dream whisperers. Cassandra had given Valkyrie one as a present the first time they'd met.

"Do you still have yours?" Cassandra asked, catching Valkyrie's uneasy look.

"Yes," Valkyrie said automatically, before she even had a chance to consider telling the truth. She ignored Skulduggery's tilt of the head, and motioned to the guitar. "Do you play much?"

"Not as much as I used to," Cassandra said. "I was pretty good, once upon a time. I picked up an old one in the sixties and I was taught by one of the best guitarists of the era."

"Jimi Hendrix?"

"Angelo Bartolotti. This was the 1660s."

"Oh. Yeah. Right."

"It was a whole different instrument back then. But you didn't come here to talk about my musical past as a Baroque chick, did you?"

"You've had a vision?" Skulduggery asked.

"Yes," said Cassandra. "Or at least I will. In a few minutes."

Valkyrie frowned. "You haven't had it yet?"

"No. But I dreamed that I was going to have it, and that it involved the two of you."

"Wait. So... you had a vision that you were going to have a vision?"

"Fortune-telling is a strange business. Come down to the cellar."

She led the way downstairs to a large room with cement walls and a metal grille for a floor. Rusted pipes ran up the walls and across the ceiling like infected veins. It was cold and it was bleak. Cassandra sat in the straight-backed chair in the middle of the chamber, picked up the yellow umbrella and held it across her lap. "So how have you both been?"

"Uh, fine," Valkyrie said. "Are you having your vision now?"

"It'll come when it comes," Cassandra told her. "How's that boyfriend of yours?"

"Fletcher?"

"No, the other one."

Valkyrie felt a scowl rise. "Caelan?"

"No, the other one. Or... wait. Maybe that hasn't happened yet."

"What? You've seen a future boyfriend of mine? Who is he? What's his name? Is he hot?"

Cassandra smiled. "I'm afraid I can't say."

"Just tell me if he's hot."

"If I give you any details about him at all, it could change what happens. The future is uncertain. It's always changing. If you know who he is, he might never become your boyfriend."

"She's annoying when she has a boyfriend," Skulduggery said. "Please do me a favour and tell us who it is."

Cassandra laughed. "I've said too much already. The only reason I'm showing you this vision I'm about to have is because it relates to the one you've already seen."

"The ruined city," Valkyrie said.

"Aha," Cassandra murmured, her eyes closing. "It's starting. If you wouldn't mind?"

Skulduggery clicked his fingers and Valkyrie did the same, and they each summoned a ball of fire into their hands. They dropped the fireballs to the grille – within seconds the coals underneath were glowing orange. Heat rose, filling the chamber. Valkyrie stood with her back against the wall.

Cassandra opened the umbrella, and Skulduggery turned a little red wheel. Water gurgled through the pipes and sprayed from the sprinklers, and immediately clouds of steam began billowing. Cassandra sat in the middle of it all, the umbrella keeping her dry. When she was lost amid the swirling steam, Skulduggery cut off the water.

Valkyrie stepped forward, and Skulduggery joined her. It was quiet. The steam was as thick as fog. Even the slow dripping from the sprinklers sounded distant.

The first time she'd been down here, an image of Ghastly had run at her. But this was different. A shape moved. Staggered. There were walls around them now, in the steam, and a table, a big one. She knew this place. The conference room, in the Sanctuary. The figure stumbled into view. Erskine Ravel, dressed in his Elder robes, falling to his knees with his hands shackled behind his back, screaming in unimaginable agony.

He fell forward and the image swirled, and now they were in a city, smoke rising from the ruins. Valkyrie looked for something familiar, some way to identify what city this was – even a street sign – but the steam was lending everything a hazy quality. The city was an out-of-focus photograph, a blurred representation of reality.

Ghastly ran by, just like he had the first time, and then the street started moving around her like the whole thing, Ghastly included, was on a treadmill. It was hugely disorientating and Valkyrie had to hold Skulduggery's arm to steady herself. Ghastly turned a corner and the corner whipped by so fast that Valkyrie jerked back. He eventually slowed his run and the street slowed its movement, and when he stopped the street stopped.

Ghastly glanced behind him, getting his breath back.

"That's new," Skulduggery murmured.

Ghastly had a scar bisecting the others along the left side of his head, just over his ear. It wasn't fresh, but it wasn't old, either.

"Well now," said a voice in the steam, "don't I feel stupid?"

Steam billowed and now Valkyrie could see Tanith Low leaning against a streetlight, both hands pressing into the lower half of her torso, which was a mess of blood and ruined flesh. Ghastly rushed over to her, his eyes wide.

Steam hissed as Ghastly and Tanith talked, but their words were snatched away until Ghastly grabbed her and Tanith cried out.

"Bloody hell, that hurts!"

"I don't care," said Ghastly, and he pulled her into him and they kissed, long and hard, so long and so hard that Valkyrie began to feel vaguely uncomfortable watching them. She was saved from having to look away by fresh clouds of steam, and a new image solidified in front of her.

The first time she had seen her future self she remembered thinking how much older she looked in the steam. Her future self had been taller, with strong arms and strong legs. But now they were identical, apart from the tattoo on her future self's left arm and the metal gauntlet on her right. For the first time, Valkyrie noticed a strap that crossed her future self's chest. She had something slung across her back.

"I've seen this," the Valkyrie in the steam said, the wind playing with her hair. "I was watching from..." She looked around, narrowed her eyes. "... there. Hi."

Valkyrie frowned. This was different from last time. She hadn't said "Hi" last time.

The other Valkyrie smiled sadly. "This is where it happens, but then you know that, right? At least you think you do. You think this is where I let them die."

"Stephanie!"

Two shapes in the distance, running. Sprinting. The other Valkyrie shook her head. "I don't want to see this. Please. I don't want this to happen. Let me stop it. Please let me stop it." She held something in her hand, something the steam was obscuring as she looked at it. "Please work," she said, tears running down her face. "Please let me save them."

And then her image was swept away as Valkyrie's parents neared. Her mother turned on the spot, looking up at the sky. She was holding something.

"Oh, no," Valkyrie said weakly, watching as her baby sister clung to her mother.

"Stephanie!" her father shouted. "We're here! Steph!"

A figure in black dropped to the ground behind them, cracking the pavement with the force of her landing.

Darquesse. She smiled with Valkyrie's smile. From neck to toe she was dressed in a black so tight it was like a second skin. Desmond Edgley stepped between his wife and the monster.

"Give our daughter back to us," he said.

Darquesse continued to smile.

"Give her back!" her dad roared.

It was nothing but a moving image, it wasn't real, it hadn't happened yet, but when Darquesse burned her family with black flame Valkyrie cried out nonetheless.

Skulduggery wrapped an arm round her shoulders and she sagged against him, tears in her eyes.

The swirling steam brought a new figure, Skulduggery, dressed in a black suit, his skull bare and his gun in his hand. He slowed and stopped, reached down to pick something up off the ground. His hat. He put it on, spent a moment angling the brim. Behind him, Darquesse approached. Skulduggery turned slowly, not bothering to look up. He reloaded his gun.

The smile on the face of Darquesse widened. "My favourite little toy. You know you're going to die now, don't you?"

Skulduggery raised his head slightly, one eye socket visible under his hat. "I made a promise."

Darquesse nodded. "Until the end."

"That's right," said Skulduggery, clicking the revolver shut and thumbing back the hammer. "Until the end."

He raised the gun and fired and walked forward and fired and fired again. And then he fumbled slightly and the gun fell, and a moment later his glove followed it. His fingers spilled out across the ground.

He grunted, unimpressed, as his other hand dropped from his wrist, and now the radius and ulna bones were sliding from his sleeves and his ankles came apart and he stumbled, fell to his knees.

His hips detached and his upper body fell backwards with the sound of clacking bones. He was a ribcage and a spine and a head, trying in vain to sit up. The ribcage collapsed next.

Darquesse stepped over him, reached down, plucked his skull from his spine. She kissed his closed mouth, her lips on his teeth, then she let the skull fall and the jawbone broke and spun away.

Then Darquesse turned, looked straight into Valkyrie's eyes, and smiled.

The smile dispersed with the steam, and then there was no more Darquesse and no more ruined city, and they were back in the Steam Chamber and Cassandra was opening her eyes.

"Distressing," she said, her voice hollow.

Valkyrie didn't say anything. She went straight to the stairs and got out of there.

* * *

The tea was hot and a bit too sweet, but Valkyrie drank it anyway. Her hands had stopped shaking, thank God. Cassandra's hadn't. Having visions of that nature could not be good for your nerves.

"So you'll show me a vision of my family dying," Valkyrie said, forcing some strength into her voice, "but you won't tell me the name of my next boyfriend? How is that fair?"

Cassandra gave a shaky smile. "Because your next boyfriend might not be something you'd want to miss out on, whereas that particular future most certainly is."

"The order was different," Skulduggery said from where he stood by the window. "In the first vision, we saw Ghastly, then me, then Valkyrie, and then Valkyrie's parents. In this one, it was altered. Is that significant?"

"I don't know," said Cassandra. "Maybe. Maybe not. Your knowledge of the future changes it. Sometimes in tiny, insignificant ways. Sometimes in huge, world-changing ways."

"I spoke more this time," Valkyrie said. "Did you see that? I was actually talking to me, the me watching. And my parents... they had my little sister with them. They didn't have her in the first vision."

Cassandra nodded. "The future is in a constant state of flux."

"And Ghastly and Tanith," said Valkyrie, "and Ravel... Was he dying? It looked like he was dying." She looked up. "How do we stop it? How do we stop all of that from happening? Some things we hadn't seen before, some things were switched around, so does that mean the events we saw don't happen in chronological order?"

"Usually they do," Cassandra said. "Usually. It's a vision interpreted through my mind, remember, and so it's subject to my subconscious whims. Maybe I pulled the images of your family forward because I knew that's where your focus would be."

Skulduggery turned away from the window. "But if it was in chronological order, then Ravel in pain will be the first of those events to occur. And if we stop that from happening?"

Cassandra shrugged. "Everything else will be affected. Some of it will be changed, even avoided. Some of it won't."

"Then we do what we can," Skulduggery said. "We keep Ravel safe. He was wearing the robes of his office and he only wears those when he's in the Sanctuary, so we make sure he stays away from Roarhaven. Cassandra, thank you for alerting us. Valkyrie, we need to get going."

"Not yet," Cassandra said. "Not while those men are outside."

Valkyrie frowned at her. "What men?"

"The ones who've come to kill you. They should be arriving any moment now."

15

SPILLING BLOOD

Skulduggery whipped round. "You set us up?"

Cassandra rolled her eyes. "I'm going to pretend you didn't say that."

Valkyrie joined Skulduggery at the window as a van pulled up and armed men jumped out.

"I had another vision," Cassandra explained.

Valkyrie ducked out of sight. "And you're only telling us now?"

"I only told you at this point in the vision, too. If I'd given you any more warning, you might do something differently and you won't walk away."

"So we win this?"

"Yes," said Cassandra. "Of course, now that you know the future, you might change it. Fortune-telling – it's a tricky business."

Someone was shouting Skulduggery's name.

He grunted, took off his hat and handed it to Cassandra. "Keep this safe," he said, and walked to the door. Valkyrie followed him outside. Nine men stood waiting.

"Skulduggery," said the man in charge, an American. "It's been a while. You're looking well for a dead man."

"The same could be said for you, Gepard. Mind me asking what it is you think you're doing?"

"Obeying orders. We've been instructed to take the two of you out."

"Attacking us will start a war."

"You haven't heard? The war's already started. Your side executed Bernard Sult live on the Global Link."

"That's ridiculous," Valkyrie said.

"Afraid not. Those two Children of the Spider weirdos did it, not ten minutes ago. There's a list of people the Supreme Council needs terminated. You two are at the top of that list."

"But we're friends, aren't we?" Skulduggery asked. "Or friendly, at the very least. We shouldn't have to fight each other."

"I couldn't agree more."

"Excellent. So what are the conditions of your surrender?"

Gepard chuckled. "I'm afraid your advanced years and lack of a physical brain have led to some confusion. I have superior numbers on my side. The outcome of this day is not in any doubt – the only question is how much you want it to hurt."

"Do you know whose cottage this is? Cassandra Pharos's. She's already seen this happen. We win. You lose. Walk away."

Gepard shook his head. "You think I want to be here? You think I want to fight you? What the hell are Erskine and Ghastly thinking? The Supreme Council has a *point*, for God's sake. They're making sense. They don't want to take over, they just want to help you maintain order."

"And to show us just how eager they are to provide this help, they've sent you over to kill a few of us. No, Gepard, this isn't about maintaining order. The Supreme Council sees an opportunity to snatch up a Cradle of Magic and they're seizing it with both hands. You may not want to admit this, but you are an invading force."

Gepard sighed. "You can't win. You know that, right? So I'm giving you a chance. Walk away. The report I hand in will say you fought valiantly, but were outnumbered, so you had to retreat. You're going to lose, but that doesn't mean we have to fight."

"Actually," Skulduggery said, "your report will detail an exciting battle of legendary proportions in which we prevail despite overwhelming odds. It will be quite a stirring read, I assure you. Many will be moved to tears."

"We fought Mevolent side by side."

"And now we'll fight face to face."

Gepard looked at him for a long moment and, at his nod, the guns were raised.

Skulduggery went one way, Valkyrie went another, diving behind Cassandra's car as the air was filled with gunfire. She hated bullets. She much preferred it when they fired magical beams of energy. At least they were pretty and colourful. But bullets were too small and moved too fast to see. One of them could smack right into your head and you'd never know anything about it.

One of the men had sneaked round behind the cottage. She saw him waddling behind an old tractor, trying to keep out of sight, and she pushed herself up and ran for him. He peeked out, saw her coming and his eyes widened. He jerked his gun-hand up, but she pushed at the air and he went backwards. She crashed into him as he tumbled, both of them fighting for control of the gun. She held it away from her and he fired – a gunshot so loud it almost deafened her. She hit with her elbow, again and again, and when she hit him hard enough to knock him out she hauled herself off, and realised she was holding his gun.

Skulduggery was walking and shooting, his revolver in a two-handed grip. Bullets whipped by him and energy streams sizzled. He responded to each one in turn, firing methodically. Valkyrie saw a big guy go down, caught dead centre in the chest. A smaller guy opened up with eyeblasts. Skulduggery spun behind an old trailer, reloaded and leaned out, one-handed, squeezed off a shot that flipped the guy over backwards like some kind of acrobat. For Skulduggery, killing was easy.

Valkyrie threw her gun down, clicking her fingers and summoning fireballs into her hands. She hurled them as she sprinted, keeping a man pinned behind a van. She was very calm as she moved to his position. She could feel the blood coursing and the energy flowing – she was practically high on adrenaline – but her mind was a calm place of practical things. One step after another. No panicking. Haste makes waste. Use the fireballs to get in close.

The man stepped out and she whipped the shadows at him, sent them slicing into his arm. He dropped his gun and she clicked her fingers, threw a fireball at his legs, then seized hold of the air as he screeched and yanked him off his feet. He hit the cottage wall face first.

She turned to see Skulduggery dismantle a fat guy with bad hair. He was unconscious even before he started to topple, and Skulduggery was already darting to his next target.

Something thumped Valkyrie in the chest and she stepped back. Another bullet whizzed by her ear. A third struck her shoulder. She didn't even know who the hell was shooting her. She should have ducked, dodged, done something, but instead she glared, searching for the shooter. She saw him, crouched and firing with a startled look on his face, wondering why she wasn't going down. He shifted his aim and fired at her head, obviously figuring it out.

Move, you stupid girl, said the voice in the back of her mind.

She moved. He kept firing. Hitting someone in the head was not an easy thing to do. Hitting a moving target in the head was even harder. He emptied his gun and threw it down, fired an energy stream that missed, then ran at her. She ran at him. Dumb thing to do. He was a grown man. They collided and he flung her right over his shoulder. She crunched to the ground, tried to roll to her knees, but he grabbed her head from behind, dragged her backwards. Valkyrie wriggled and kicked, scratched at his hands, tried bending one of his fingers back. He let go and dumped her, dropped to his knee and his fist came down on her cheek. There was that moment of disorientation that comes with

125

being hit hard, and then he was pulling her hair, lifting her painfully so he could slip an arm round her throat, the opening move to a neck-break.

Let me out. I can help. Let me out.

She turned her head away, tucked her chin down, dug her fingers into his arm and brought her feet in. She got purchase then pushed, heard him grunt as they went backwards. He lost his hold and she was free. They got to their knees at the same time and she hit him, caught him in the hinge of his jaw. Lucky shot. He stopped himself from collapsing, but his face went slack. She threw herself back, giving herself room to swing her leg. She had good legs. She had good, long, strong legs. Her boot smashed into him and he went down and didn't get up.

She looked round. Skulduggery strolled towards her. Everything was suddenly quiet and still and peaceful. Valkyrie's chest and shoulder ached. The left side of her face had that dull, not unpleasant buzz of oncoming numbness. Her left eye was beginning to close as it started to swell. She could smell cordite. The smell of gunfire and carnage.

Skulduggery's revolver drifted through the air into his gloved hand, and he put it away.

"We're at war?" she asked.

"So it would seem," he said.

"They were trying to kill us. Yesterday they would have been on our side. What do we do now?"

"First, we shackle the ones who are still alive. Then I get my hat back. And then we drive to Roarhaven and hope nobody we know has been killed in the meantime."

16

THE SUPREME COUNCIL

he meeting was already under way by the time Illori Reticent stepped into the room. Palaver Graves heard the door close and glanced back, a shallow smile on his narrow face. She ignored him, focusing instead on adjusting her robes. The Elders from the other Sanctuaries couldn't see her yet, but she could see them. They were all here, Elders from the fourteen Sanctuaries who had made up the initial Supreme Council, before it had grown even bigger. The sigils that were glowing on the walls generated what were officially known as Incorporeal Visitations. These days, even though it had nothing to do with light manipulation, everyone used the mortal term *holograms*. It was just easier.

Illori stepped up beside Grand Mage Cothernus Ode, and her image appeared in twenty-three rooms just like this one around the world.

"They've already raised their shield," the German Grand Mage, Wahrheit, was saying. "From initial scans, it appears to run the entire length of the Irish coastline and forms a dome two kilometres high."

Renato Bisahalani, the American Grand Mage, nodded. They had expected this. "No matter. We have one hundred and thirty-two operatives in Ireland already, all briefed and ready for the go-ahead. Everything is going according to plan."

"It's one thing to make plans," said Kribu, the head of the Estonian Sanctuary. "Quite another to go to war. The world has changed. We are a global community, and yet we have just ordered friend to attack friend? We have fought by the side of the Irish mages since before the war with Mevolent."

"And so we know their weaknesses," said Bisahalani.

"As they know ours."

"They have one single Sanctuary," Ode said, and all eyes shifted to the source of his deep, rumbling voice. "We already have another nine Sanctuaries willing to add their might to ours. They're not going to hold out for long."

"You seem to be forgetting that Ireland is a Cradle of Magic," said Kribu.

"Not at all – but I don't view Cradles with the same superstitious awe as the rest of you. They're stronger, yes, but not by much. And twenty-two Sanctuaries against one Cradle will crush them no matter how strong they are."

"And how about twenty-two Sanctuaries against *three* Cradles?" Kribu asked, her voice calm. "If Australia and Africa get involved—"

"Why would they? This has got nothing to do with them. They're stable and they always have been." Ode shook his head. "Ireland is a mess. One catastrophe after another. They will understand that this needs to be done."

"That's not what I've heard," said Kribu. "I've heard that the Australians have told their sorcerers that an attack against one Cradle is an attack against them all."

"Grand Mage Karrik is not so naive," Bisahalani said. "He's not going to plunge headlong into a conflict if he can help it. He's going to observe the situation, make some noise and delay as much as possible. He'll be praying that we finish the job before he has to make any kind of decision."

"And Ubuntu? You realise that he and Eachan Meritorious were close friends, yes?"

"And if Meritorious were still alive, that might be a problem for us. Ubuntu is like Karrik – he'll say things to save face, but eventually, if he has to side with someone, he'll side with us. You think they don't agree with our view on this? You think they don't share our concerns? Of course they do."

"And what about the legal implications?" asked the Russian Grand Mage, a big man called Dragunov.

"Ireland cannot be allowed to hide behind a rule that was agreed upon to fulfil another purpose," said Ode. "The rule-makers didn't foresee a situation like this arising. No one did."

People started speaking over each other until Illori cut through them. "My friends," she said, "we can debate these matters for the rest of the night, but nothing will change the fact that we are at war, and we have already acted. We must press forward. If we can make the Irish Sanctuary falter before it's even taken its first steps, victory will be swift."

Wahrheit looked at her. "You're talking about the plan to take out the leaders."

"Not only the Council," said Illori, "but other sorcerers of note also. If Ravel and his Elders are dead, the Irish will look to Skulduggery Pleasant for leadership, or Dexter Vex, or any one of the Dead Men. They will look to their heroes – so it is the heroes who must fall first."

"We've already given Gepard the green light to kill Pleasant and Cain," said Zafira Kerias. "We haven't heard from him since."

"Then we had better assume he failed," said Illori. "Annoying, but not unexpected. I also propose the elimination of China Sorrows. By all accounts, her influence has been weakened of late, but she is still too unpredictable to have running loose."

"Kill China Sorrows?" Mandat said, quite visibly alarmed. "I... I'm not sure that this is the wisest course of action. Mademoiselle Sorrows could be a valuable resource to... tap.

She... I could hold her, if you want, here in France. Question her. I could—"

"Grand Mage Mandat, please stop embarrassing yourself," Bisahalani said. "As it stands, our plan is to get as many of our people through that shield as possible. We have General Mantis ready to travel to Ireland to take command of our troops on the ground. When our forces have massed, we march on Roarhaven, subdue the populace, and take control."

"You make it sound so easy," said Kribu.

"I am under no illusion. But we will seek every advantage where we can. Grand Mage Ode, I believe you have something to add to this?"

Ode looked at Illori, and she spoke up. "Grand Mages, Elders, one of the first groups we must target is the Sensitives. This will both cut the less traditional means of communication and foil any future-reading. Sensitives are not combative by nature, however, and so we may find it difficult to find sorcerers willing to deal with... *soft* targets, I believe the phrase is."

"With good reason," Kribu said. "You're talking about *murder*."

"I realise that," Illori said. "In which case, I suggest we send mercenaries."

Mandat frowned. "What mercenaries?"

"Unpleasant ones. They're Irish, though, so they stand a better chance of remaining unnoticed while they track their targets."

"And you don't think they'll switch sides and join their fellow countrymen?" Wahrheit asked.

"Vincent Foe leads a small group of nihilists who would really like to destroy the world," Illori explained. "While they're waiting for their chance, however, they accept jobs like this for money. They have no loyalty to anyone except each other, and even then their loyalty only stretches so far. At the moment Mr Foe's colleagues are languishing in prison thanks to Skulduggery Pleasant and Valkyrie Cain, but if I give the word, they will be mysteriously freed. Providing no one here has any objection to this course of action?"

Illori looked at Kribu, and watched her jaw tighten. Targeting the Sensitives was a sickening but necessary move. There'd be time enough to feel bad when all this was over.

"Very well," she said, when no one objected.

"Grand Mage Bisahalani," said Ode, "the last time we spoke in private we discussed a certain..."

"Yes," said Bisahalani, "of course."

Wahrheit did not look happy. "Private discussions are not part of the Supreme Council's agenda, gentlemen. Please – elaborate."

Bisahalani clasped his hands behind his back, the way he always did when he was about to discuss unpleasantness. "There is a single individual capable of turning the tide of this war in whichever direction he chooses. Unfortunately, despite his nationality, we have reason to doubt that he will side with us."

"Who are we talking about?" Kribu asked.

"His name is Fletcher Renn. He's the last Teleporter. Twenty years old, born and raised in London, but when his natural aptitude for magic made itself known he was, for all intents and purposes, taken in by the Irish Sanctuary. That is where he received the first part of his training. He is currently in Australia, where he continues his studies."

Mandat frowned. "And you think he'll side with the Irish if they ask?"

"That's where his friends are. Also, from what we've heard, he and Valkyrie Cain were involved."

"So he's definitely on their side," said Wahrheit.

"I'm afraid so."

"He must be targeted."

"He already is. If there is no objection, the kill order will go through." Bisahalani looked round the room. No one spoke. "Very well," he said. "The order is given."

17

MUFFINS

yra was making muffins.

The smell wafted throughout her small apartment, and Fletcher Renn put his head back on the sofa and inhaled deeply. She'd been branching out lately, experimenting with all sorts of new cakes and buns, but every few days she'd make another batch of muffins and he wondered how she could ever want to do anything else.

"I love your muffins," he mumbled.

"That's nice," Myra said, patting his cheek as she passed behind him. "Are you watching that, by the way? If you're not watching it—"

"I'm watching it," he said immediately, looking at the TV to find out what exactly he was watching. It seemed to be some sort of sporting game. "I love this," he said as she went back into the kitchen. "This is the one where they have the ball and they try to score points. My favourite is the blue team. Look, they're playing."

"You haven't a clue what you're watching, do you?"

"Yes I do. It's a cross between rugby and something that isn't rugby. Badminton, maybe."

Myra walked back in, draped herself over the sofa behind him and rested her chin on his shoulder. "It's Australian Rules football, or Aussie Rules, if you like. How do you not know this by now? You've been living here for over a year."

"I live a sheltered life."

She grinned. "I've heard it's rugby crossed with Gaelic football. That's from Ireland. Don't ask me the rules because I don't know them. And neither do you, you... you..."

He looked up at her. "Call me a flaming drongo."

She laughed. "No I will not."

"Ah, go on. Please?"

She sighed. "I don't know the rules and neither do you, yeh flamin' drongo."

He bit his lip. "I love it when you call me that."

"You're so weird."

She started to straighten up, but he took hold of her arm and pulled her down on top of him. She laughed and squirmed until she was lying across his lap, and then she said, "I love you."

Fletcher nodded. "Yup."

"Yup?"

"Hmm?"

She sat up, turned to him. "I say I love you and you say *yup*?"

"Uh," he said, "you just... took me by surprise. That's all. I wasn't expecting it. This isn't something I expected. This is kind of... y'know? A big deal, is what I'm saying. It's a big deal."

"I love you, Fletcher."

"Yes, excellent, and to you I say... wow. That's really great. I'm a lucky, lucky guy."

Myra stood. "Oh, God."

"Now, Myra..."

She shook her head. "It's fine. You don't have to... I'm not asking you to say it back to me, I'm just saying it because I'm feeling it and sometimes when you feel something you have to say it so... I'll go check on the muffins."

She hurried into the kitchen and Fletcher stood. "Myra, wait, come on."

The doorbell rang.

"Could you get that?" Myra called.

"Don't be upset with me. I'm in shock right now, that's all. I don't know what I'm—"

The doorbell again.

"Fletch, please, just answer the door."

Cursing himself for his stupidity, Fletcher went to the door and pulled it open. A pretty girl stood there, brown hair tied back, wearing jeans and a leather jacket. Behind her stood a Maori in a ripped T-shirt and with a tattoo on the left side of his grinning face.

"*Kia ora*, bro," said Tane Aiavao.

Hayley Skirmish pushed past Fletcher, into the apartment. Immediately she began snooping around. Tane came in after her, shutting the door behind him.

"Don't worry about her," he said. "She's just doing her *I have no social graces* thing. How've you been? You're looking good. Are those muffins I smell?"

There was a scream from the kitchen and Myra came running out, Hayley walking behind her, gun in hand.

In the blink of an eye Fletcher was standing between them. "Put it down, Hayley."

"She's got a gun!" Myra screeched.

Hayley almost looked bored. "I walked into the kitchen to find your girlfriend brandishing a weapon."

Fletcher turned to Myra. "Weapon?"

"A spatula!" Myra cried. "It was a spatula!"

"In the hands of a trained killer," said Hayley, "a spatula can be deadly."

"Or a really bad chef," chortled Tane, but everyone ignored him.

Myra clung to Fletcher's arm. "Who are these people? Are

these magic people? You said you weren't going to bring magic people over here."

"I didn't," Fletcher said, trying to calm her down. "I don't know what they're doing here, but I'm sure they'll tell us. Myra, the girl with the gun is Hayley. The big guy is Tane."

"Pleased to finally meet you," Tane said, smiling. "It's weird, we've been spying on you for so long it feels like we already know you."

Myra's eyes widened. "You've been *spying* on me?"

"Yeah," said Tane, then he looked worried. "But not in a creepy way. Tell her, Hayley."

"The way *he* spied on you was a little creepy," Hayley said, "but we were just doing our job. We were assigned to act as your invisible bodyguards in case all this war business got out of hand."

Fletcher frowned. "So what's happened?"

"It got out of hand."

"We've been told to bring you both to the Sanctuary," said Tane. "As the last Teleporter, Fletcher here could be a target and, if he's a target, then *you're* a target."

Myra's mouth dropped open. "Someone wants to kill *me*?"

"Maybe. Or maybe they'll try to kidnap you and use you as bait. We don't know. We only know what our Sanctuaries told us. Or rather, what Hayley's Sanctuary told *her*. The Sanctuary in New Zealand has gone all quiet."

"They might be plotting against us," Hayley said to Fletcher. "We might not be able to trust Tane. We should hit him until he loses consciousness."

Tane sighed. "Any excuse..."

"How long will we be gone?" Fletcher asked. "Myra has college and a job, and I... Myra has college."

"We'll sort all that stuff out when we get to the Sanctuary," said Hayley. "Grand Mage Karrik said we should waste no time, so... Ready to teleport?"

Myra blinked back tears. All things considered, she was handling this pretty well. "But I have to pack," she said quietly.

"No time," said Hayley.

"We'll wait," said Tane, giving Myra a smile.

Myra hurried into the bedroom, and Hayley glared at Tane. "You're just delaying to give yourself more time to strike."

"I'm not going to strike," he responded. "I'm way too scared of you."

She glowered. "Secure the door."

He frowned. "How?"

Fletcher left them to their squabbling and went into the kitchen. He turned the oven off and took the muffins out. They weren't done yet. With a heavy heart, he dumped them in the bin.

He took his phone from his pocket and stood there, leaning against the worktable, looking at it. Finally, he dialled, and held it to his ear.

"Hi," Valkyrie said when she picked up. "You've heard, then."

"Hayley and Tane have just come over," he said. "Karrik wants us taken in. Sounds like protective custody or something. Myra, too."

"Makes sense. Everyone's going nuts."

"So there is definitely a war, then?"

"Apparently so. You'd probably be better off with us, to be honest. I mean, it wouldn't be safer, in fact, it'd be a thousand times more dangerous, but you'd be of a lot more use here than there. I mean, that's if you wanted to get involved, like."

"I do," he said quickly, "and you're right. But I can't leave Myra on her own surrounded by sorcerers. She's only met you and a few others. She hasn't met the weird ones yet. I'm afraid she'd freak out if I wasn't there."

"Yeah, fair enough."

"She said she loves me."

"Sorry?"

"Myra. She said she loves me."

"What did you say?"

"I said *yup*."

"Smooth."

"We've only been going out six months. I mean, I didn't expect... you know."

"Right."

"So what do you think I should do?"

"I'm not sure," Valkyrie said. "Maybe get your priorities straight?"

He smiled. "You are a great help."

He could practically see her nodding. "Best ex-girlfriend ever. Have to go now. Things are happening."

"Aren't they always? Stay safe."

"You too." He hung up, and went out to the living room.

Tane was flicking through the TV channels. "Hayley's helping Myra pack," he said without looking up. "Or that's what she claims. She's probably in there threatening her."

"That sounds more like Hayley," Fletcher agreed. He sat on the armrest. "So what side do you come down on? Australia's a Cradle of Magic so everyone expects it to side with Ireland, but what about New Zealand?"

"You got me," Tane said with a shrug. "We're on the same page as the Aussies on a lot of things, but this is different. This is about world safety. And let's face it, the Grand Mages of New Zealand and Australia do not get along."

"So I've heard. But do you think your Sanctuary would side with the Supreme Council just because of a personal disagreement?"

"Stupider things have happened."

There was a knock on the door.

"Expecting anyone?" Tane asked, getting to his feet.

"No," said Fletcher, "but then I wasn't expecting *you*, either. Hold on."

Fletcher teleported outside and down the corridor, looking back up to the apartment door. A man stood there, waiting for the door to open.

"One man," Fletcher said as he teleported back beside the sofa, "no visible weapons. Looks normal."

"That's the best way for an assassin to look," Tane said. "I'll get Hayley, she'll know what to do. You keep your eye on the door."

Tane hurried towards Myra's bedroom. The man knocked again, then rang the doorbell. Fletcher teleported to the storage locker he rented in New Jersey, grabbed the baseball bat from the rack of weapons, and teleported back to the apartment. He held it in a two-handed grip, ready to swing. Then he turned, looking at the window behind him. A guy knocking on the door could be the distraction, allowing the second assassin to abseil down from the roof and crash through the glass, throwing ninja stars and grenades and things.

A brown envelope slid under the door.

Fletcher crouched, teleported to the door, grabbed the envelope, and teleported back. It was addressed to Myra. It looked like an electricity bill. He turned it over. Scrawled on this side was *Delivered to us by mistake!*

He crept to the door, pressed his eye to the peephole, just in time to see Myra's neighbour shuffling back to his own apartment.

"Who was it?" Myra asked, walking up beside him.

"Mr Sakamoto," he said, smiling, "who really isn't all that scary once you see how slow he moves. Ready to go?"

Myra said something and his body snapped away from the door and he fell, convulsing. Pain seized his mind. His legs kicked. His arms curled, fingers clutching at nothing, his muscles contracting with each spasm that shot through him. He tried to tell her to run, but his jaw was locked, his tendons straining against his skin. Run. Run. Why wasn't she running? She was kneeling over him, speaking, but he couldn't make out the words. Then she stood, put something on the hall table and stepped over him, heading for the kitchen.

The thing on the hall table. He could see the edge of it. It was black plastic or metal, with two little silver points. A taser.

He tried to teleport. Of course he couldn't. No one could use magic, not with that much residual electricity running through them. He gave a grunt that sounded like a gag, and heaved himself on to his stomach. He started crawling. He could hear her now. He could hear the rattle of cutlery as she searched for something.

He crawled for the bedroom.

He heard her curse. She'd found the muffins in the bin. She was not happy.

He crawled faster.

He got to the bedroom. Tane Aiavao lay face down on the carpet, a knife lodged in his skull. Hayley Skirmish sat against the far wall, her throat cut.

Fletcher nudged the door shut, swung himself round to place his feet against it, and he lay back and tried to regain control of his body.

The handle turned, and Myra pushed and Fletcher pushed back.

"This is silly," she said from the other side. "Fletcher, you're delaying the inevitable. Come on. Open up."

He would have come up with a witty retort, but it was at that moment he realised his bladder had loosened.

"I-I've w-wet myself," he said through chattering teeth.

"That's normal," Myra told him. "You're lucky that's all you did. It's nothing to be ashamed of."

"Why're you... why..."

The door shuddered violently. "Why am I doing this?" she said. "Because I've been paid to do it. It's my job."

Fletcher's teeth were chattering so hard he bit his tongue and tasted blood. "You s-said you... loved me."

"Yeah," she answered, "and you didn't say it back, you creep!"

She started kicking the door. He could hear it splintering from the other side.

"S-sorry," he called. "I... I l-love you, too."

She laughed. "Bit late, yeh flamin' drongo."

That wasn't nearly as cute as it once was.

Fletcher's fingers opened and closed. His whole body ached and buzzed, but it was slowly coming back under his control. He looked around for something, a weapon, and reached out for Tane's wrist, started pulling his body closer.

Myra was really making a racket with all that kicking. "You're annoying me now," she said. "You hear me, Fletch? Now I'm annoyed. Let me in. Let me in right now."

When Tane's body was close enough, Fletcher's hand curled round the handle of the knife. He tried pulling it free, but it was lodged deep in the skull.

"If you're hoping to have an Excalibur moment with that knife," Myra said, taking a rest from the kicking, "you can forget it. It's not going to happen. And that was my favourite blade, too."

Fletcher strained a little more before giving up, and then his eyes flickered to Hayley, all the way across the room. Somewhere on her corpse, there was a gun.

The door heaved violently and Fletcher cursed, his knees buckling against it, and Myra was lunging in, kitchen knife in her hand. He kicked out, slamming the door, catching her halfway through, jamming her against the doorframe.

"Ow!" she yelled, her free hand pressing against her forehead. Blood trickled. "Look what you did! I'm bleeding!"

Fletcher put all his strength into his legs as she did her best to push the door open further.

She slipped in a bit more and then fell towards him and he rolled, the point of the knife hitting the carpet. He sprang awkwardly to his feet and wobbled backwards on to the bed, and Myra scrambled up and jumped on top of him. He got a pillow between them, the knife slashing through to the goose feathers. He rolled again, pushing her off the side, then rolled the other way, falling to the ground beside Hayley. He found the gun tucked into her waistband and he stood, whirled, and Myra froze.

The sunlight glinted off the kitchen knife, raised as it was to stab downwards.

His hand was trembling so badly he feared he might drop the gun.

Myra smiled. "Look at you," she said. "The tough guy."

"Stay back," he warned.

She gave a laugh. "Fletch, sweetheart, have you ever fired one of those before? Do you know that there's a safety you have to flick? Do you know how to chamber the first round? It's not just a case of pulling the trigger, darling. It's a lot more complicated than that."

"Stay back or I'll—"

"Have you seen your hair, by the way? It looks *amazing*. Even more spiky than usual. Being electrocuted really suits you."

"Back off. Back off now."

Myra laughed. "I'm sorry, I'm sorry, this is mean. This is very mean. I'm playing with you, Fletch. I'm messing with you." She switched her grip on the knife, held it in front of her now, and took a step towards him. "Do you really think I left a loaded pistol in here for you to grab?"

"Stop. Don't move."

"I didn't want to use it myself because of the noise, but I wasn't just going to ignore it. There are no bullets in that gun, Fletcher."

"You're lying."

She took another step. "Pull the trigger. Go on. I dare you. Here. I'll give you an easy target."

She leaned forward, like she was going to press her head to the gun, and then her hand flashed and he felt the blade slicing through his side and sliding off a rib. He pulled the trigger and it went off, hitting nothing but floor as they crashed against the wall, struggling for the knife. It was still in him. She was trying to pull it out and he was trying to keep it where it was. Her head crunched into his face, and she pulled the knife free. He pushed her away, ran for the window, fired at it, the gun deafening and the glass breaking, and Myra came after him, but he jumped, and then he was outside, and falling, the world tilting around him and the street rushing to meet him.

18

REGIS

His phone buzzed, the screen lighting up with a one-word message. Regis slipped an old playing card into the book to keep his place and left it on the bed as he stood. He went to his bag, took out a long-bladed dagger and secured it in the sheath along his forearm. He rolled his sleeve down to cover it.

He left the room. Metric was already waiting, and fell into step behind Regis as he made for the landing. The hotel was filled with the kind of quiet that was more than just the absence of sound. It was the *deliberate* absence of sound. It was the hotel holding its breath.

Anton Shudder was an impressively intimidating man. Blessed with the uncanny ability to make everything he wore look like funeral wear, he was tall, with a face carved from flint, and short dark hair flecked with grey. Shudder's hair used to be long. In the file Regis had been given, it was long. Regis wondered if the trip to the barber had anything to do with the increasing tensions between Sanctuaries. Long hair was easier to grab hold of in a fight, after all. Was Shudder preparing for battle? Did he know what was about to happen? Did he know that for the last eleven days every room in his hotel had been occupied by sorcerers sent by the Supreme Council?

Did he have any idea that right now, right at this second, he was surrounded by enemies?

The sorcerer who moved up behind Shudder was young – somewhere around one hundred years, maybe. Too young to have fought Mevolent, too young to really understand that in war, sometimes you have to do bad things for good reasons. When he took the gun from his jacket, his hand was shaking. He raised it, and Regis saw that it was already cocked. Now all he had to do was pull the trigger, shoot Shudder through the back of the head and it'd all be over.

And then it all went wrong.

Regis could see it happening, almost in slow motion. The young sorcerer didn't mess up. Not really. Shudder's first clue that something was about to happen came when the man in front of him casually stepped to one side – out of the path of the bullet should it blast straight through Shudder and continue on. Shudder's second clue came from the young sorcerer himself, but it was a forgivable mistake. Right before his finger tightened on the trigger, the young sorcerer took a little breath and held it.

Shudder ducked and spun, one arm swinging behind him as the gun went off. He trapped the gun arm, killed the young sorcerer with a punch to the throat and spun again, the gun somehow in his hand. He fired and shot the man who had stepped out of the way. He fired again and shot the woman who reached for her own gun. Doors opened throughout the hotel and sorcerers poured out. Shudder pressed a hand to the wall and a ripple flowed through the wallpaper. Guns were aimed, triggers pulled and hammers fell, but no more shots rang out.

"He's done something to the guns," Regis said, taking his dagger from its sheath.

A stream of energy scarred the wall as Shudder dived to one side. He came up and shoved a sorcerer into another, dodged a knife and cracked the gun in his hand off the knife-wielder's temple. Someone grabbed him, lifted him off his feet, but

Shudder's heels crunched into kneecaps and there was a howl and he was dropped. A fireball narrowly missed him. He punched and punched again, dodged left and threw someone into someone else. Regis pushed his way through the sorcerers who were supposed to be working as a team and failing miserably, and his hand snapped at the air. Shudder flew backwards, hit the railing and tumbled over it.

Regis hurried over, looked down to the ground floor as sorcerers charged down the stairs. They knew they were on borrowed time. If Shudder were allowed to use his magic, it would all be over.

A German sorcerer went at him with a short sword. Shudder took it from him and used him as a shield against another energy stream. The German shrieked and collapsed. Shudder cut the fingers from the Energy-Thrower's hand. He whirled as the sorcerers tried surrounding him, taking the fight to them instead of waiting for his enemy to get into position. Regis nodded to Metric, who vaulted over the railing and landed in the middle of the crowd. They cleared a space for him and he straightened up. Shudder lunged, the sword slicing through Metric's shirt, but leaving his skin without a scratch.

Shudder took a step backwards. Metric flexed his fingers. The sorcerers around the circle calmed down. Metric would take care of it. Metric would crush him between his—

Metric stepped in and Shudder's sword plunged into his eye. Metric screamed and fell to one knee and Shudder left the sword there, already turning to the next opponent, smashing teeth with his fist.

Regis jumped, using the air to steer his course as he fell. Shudder moved at the last moment, so instead of the blade coming down diagonally into his neck, it embedded in his shoulder. Shudder went down, Regis on top, still holding the dagger. He twisted the handle and Shudder grabbed his wrist, turning into him. Regis powered forward. They crashed into the coffee table and went sprawling. Regis got a knee in the face. He tasted blood.

Shudder got to his feet and stumbled. An energy stream caught him in the side and he gasped, hit the wall and slid against it.

"Finish him," Regis ordered. "Do it now."

Energy crackled, but the wall behind Shudder opened and he fell through it. Regis ran forward, but the wall resealed, the secret escape route vanishing.

Immediately the sorcerers ran for the doors. He heard a shout from outside. They'd spotted him, and were giving chase.

He turned to find Ashione standing over Metric's dead body. "That's the problem with strength," she said. "Makes you think even your squishy parts are invulnerable."

"Were you two close?" Regis asked, wiping blood from his lip.

"Fifty years ago, he said he loved me. Could never stand the man. The most boring individual I've ever had the misfortune to know." She looked up. "So this went well."

Regis sighed. "This was not meant to be my responsibility. Glass was supposed to oversee this, or Saber. What do I know about ambushing someone?"

"You know plenty," said Ashione.

"That's on the battlefield. This is a hotel, and I know nothing about ambushing someone in a hotel."

"Apparently not," Ashione muttered.

"What was that? A note of insolence, was it?"

"Not from me, Chief. Never from me."

Regis grunted, and Ashione grinned at him.

The door opened. A mage hurried in. "Shudder, sir. He's gone."

Regis groaned. "Of course he is. OK, get everyone ready. I want this place emptied in five minutes. And keep searching, for God's sake. General Mantis is going to skin me alive when it gets here."

19

LAKEN CROSS

Music played. As Laken Cross climbed the stairs into the tattoo parlour, he worked to identify the song. He'd been to a lot of places in his lifetime, been around the world and back again, and he'd heard a lot of music. This one reminded him of nights spent in Irish pubs – the old Irish pubs, where there'd be a trad band playing every night and everyone would take their turn to sing. 'The Rocky Road to Dublin', that was it, by The Dubliners. Many a good night was had in those pubs, Laken Cross remembered. But that was years ago now. Back when his American accent made him exotic to the locals.

The tattoo parlour was empty apart from a skinny man reclining in a dentist's chair, eyes closed and listening to the music. His bare arms were inked and his lip was pierced. He had a short purple Mohawk – new – and wore a faded Sesame Street T-shirt.

"Hi there," said Laken Cross, and he watched Finbar Wrong jerk upright and almost tumble out of the chair.

"Hello!" Finbar said, doing his best to recover. "Hi, how are you? Sorry about that. Catching up on some sleep, y'know?" He turned down the music. "Something I can help you with?"

Laken Cross nodded to the photographs of tattooed limbs and torsos stuck on the wall. "I'd like a tattoo, please."

"Right you are," said Finbar. "Anything special in mind?"

"Something dramatic. Provided you have the time...?"

Finbar smiled. "I got nothing but time. Any other day, this place'd be buzzing, and my kid would be wandering around, bumping into things. But today's a slow day."

"Your kid's not around?"

"Nope," said Finbar. "Himself and Sharon, that's me wife, took off for the day. Sharon does that sometimes. She'll say she's leaving me and she'll pack her bags and call her mother and out she'll go, but that's just her way of being funny. Not being blessed with a natural wit, she has to resort to pranks. She says I'm not respecting her rights as an evolved being. I like to point out that she's been a member of three cults so far, each one stupider than the one before, and when she was in the last one she kept trying to ritually sacrifice me to her UFO supergods. I told her that doesn't sound like the work of an evolved being. I told her that sounds like the work of a loon."

"Hence the prank," Laken Cross said.

"Exactly. So, have you decided on a design or an image, maybe some words...?"

"Like I said, something dramatic. Something fantastic, you know? I like horror and science fiction and things like that."

"Right," said Finbar. "Well, I'm sure we can come up with something. Would you like some tea? I've got some lovely herbal tea."

"Sure," said Laken Cross. "I'd love some tea."

In the corner of the room there was a sink and a cupboard and a kettle, and Finbar clicked the kettle on while he searched around for some mugs.

"Do you like horror movies?" Laken Cross asked. "I love them, personally. You know what might be cool? Have you seen that movie with Michael Ironside? The one where he stares at the guy for ages and the guy's head explodes? That'd be cool."

"You want a tattoo of an exploding head?"

"Maybe just before the head explodes. God, I love that movie. I love stuff with psychics and things. You believe in psychics?"

Finbar placed two mismatched mugs on the side table, and filled them with boiling water. "Psychics?" he said. "Naw. Not really. I'm rooted firmly in reality, me. I believe in things I can see and touch. Like tax returns and... tyre treads."

"Tyre treads," said Laken Cross. "Yeah, OK, I'll admit that believing in tyre treads is a lot easier than believing in people with psychic powers. Have you ever thought about it, though? Thought about what it'd be like to be able to read minds or see into the future?"

"Can't say that I have," said Finbar, walking over and holding out the mug, his fingers gripping the rim. It was an old A-Team mug, chipped and cracked. When Laken Cross slipped his fingers through the handle and lifted it from Finbar's hand, he thought for a moment the handle would snap off. He lifted the mug to his mouth, inhaled. Finbar took his own mug and walked over to the window, sipping as he went. He stood there, looking out.

"I'd love to be a psychic," said Laken Cross.

"Wouldn't say it's all it's cracked up to be," said Finbar. "Bet there'd be a lot of thoughts a psychic would wish he'd never heard, or futures he wished he'd never seen. Just think how something like that could damage a mind."

"You might be right."

Finbar shrugged his thin shoulders. "What do I know? I just draw on people for a living. But I'd say, if psychics were real, it'd be a risky business. Hazardous to the health, y'know? What if you saw something so terrible, so awful, that your mind just kinda... switched off?"

"Like if you were forced to see it?" Laken Cross asked. "Like if something had, I don't know, taken you over?"

Finbar stiffened. "Maybe," he said. "Like I said, what do I know?" He turned. "But let's say that did happen. Some poor sap, some psychic, is temporarily taken over by an evil entity, and this evil entity forces him to look at things that'd snap his mind ordinarily... but then what happens when that evil entity leaves him?"

Laken Cross cradled his mug in his hands. "I don't know," he said. "The psychic might not be a psychic any more. Could've been short-circuited."

"Exactly," Finbar said. "Short-circuited, and no use to anybody."

Laken Cross put the mug on the nearest table, and reached for the gun tucked under his shirt.

"And then," Finbar continued, "what if ever so slowly, bit by bit, those powers returned to him?"

Laken Cross paused, and left the gun where it was. "So he was a psychic again?"

Finbar nodded. "Not as powerful as he was, maybe. Well, not at first. It'd take a few months to get back to that level. But pretty soon he'd be able to read a few thoughts, and see a few futures. Might even be able to see a future where someone comes to kill him."

"Now why would anybody want to kill him?" asked Laken Cross, speaking slowly.

"Just being careful, I suppose. He was once a powerful psychic. That's a risk in anyone's book. So they send someone to kill him. Not a soldier. Not one of their usual people. Their usual people wouldn't be prepared to do something like that. No, they'd have to... what's the word? Outsource. They'd have to hire someone. A mercenary or a hitman. A killer."

"And the psychic," said Laken Cross, "he'd have seen this?"

"Yes he would," said Finbar. "He'd have seen enough to know to cancel appointments for that day, and to send his wife and kid to her mother's. He'd have seen enough to wait around for those footsteps on the stairs and, when the killer walked in, he'd have handed him a poisoned mug of tea."

Laken Cross arched an eyebrow. "Poisoned?"

"I'm afraid so. A poison that'd take a few minutes to make itself known, but once it did? Game over, I'm afraid."

Laken Cross looked at the mug. "You poisoned that?"

"You shouldn't have come to kill me, Mr Cross."

Laken Cross laughed, and he took out his gun. "Then it's a good thing I didn't drink from it, isn't it?"

He levelled the gun at Finbar's belly and Finbar shook his head. "You didn't hear me right. I didn't say a *mug of poisoned tea*. I said a *poisoned mug of tea*. It was the handle I poisoned."

The gun fell from Laken Cross's numb fingers, and the room tilted and blurred and the floor rose up to hit him. He tried to speak, but couldn't move his mouth.

"I saw the future where you killed me," Finbar was saying. "I saw you walk up here and shoot me and kill my customer. Then Sharon ran in and what did you do? You killed her, too. Then you stood over me and you shot me twice in the head, the consummate professional that you are. In that future, you left my kid an orphan. You took away his parents. What kind of man would do that to a child? I was an orphan. I lost my parents when I was three. You think I'd be OK with you doing that to my kid? You think I'd just sit around and let that happen?"

Drool leaked from Laken Cross's parted lips. He couldn't even swallow.

"Laken Cross, you are an evil man," said Finbar. "You are an evil man for coming here to kill me and you're an evil man for forcing me to do what I've had to do. I hope you burn in whatever hell you believe in."

20

OFF TO WAR

The shield had been activated. All around the coast of Ireland, 14,271 hidden sigils had lit up, sending out an invisible field of energy that merged together and spread upwards. Skirmishes flared around the country as cells of foreign sorcerers struck and then melted away into the civilian population. Meanwhile, cells of Irish sorcerers targeted vulnerable points around the world, sowing chaos and confusion into what was already a chaotic and confusing situation.

And all of this happened over the course of one night, so that when Valkyrie woke and listened to Skulduggery's message on her phone, there was really no escaping it.

They were at war.

She got up and brushed her teeth. Outside the window, birds sang. It was a beautiful day. From the bathroom, she could look right down to the pier. The water sparkled. There was a sigil down there, glowing gently, safe from prying eyes, and although she couldn't see it, the shield crossed the bay from the pier to the tip of the far peninsula, and carried on from there. A small boat came in, passed through the shield and went to dock. If any sorcerers had been in that boat, their central nervous system would have already shut down and they'd have fallen into a coma, from which only Doctor Nye could bring them round. She watched the boat dock. It was such a nice morning, such a normal morning, for the first morning of the war.

She took a shower, dressed in shorts and a light T-shirt, and went downstairs. Her mother's voice drifted from the kitchen, accompanied by another, slightly higher-pitched voice with a certain tremulous edge to it. Valkyrie sighed, then stuck on a polite smile and walked in.

"Hi, Beryl," she said. "Morning, Mum."

"Morning, sleepyhead," her mother said, cup of coffee in her hand. Beryl sat across the table from her, her cup of tea untouched.

"Good morning, Stephanie," Beryl said. She was wearing a summer frock today. It made her look softer, somehow.

"Steph'nie!" Alice said, running over. Valkyrie scooped her up and smothered her with kisses, and Alice giggled until Valkyrie set her down again.

Beryl's smile, which had never managed to get above brittle, was replaced with a concerned frown. "Oh, dear, Stephanie. Are you lifting weights?"

Suddenly Valkyrie wished she was wearing something with longer sleeves. "Nope," she said, taking a carton of juice from the fridge. "Just exercising. Swimming. Keeping fit."

Beryl looked over at Valkyrie's mum, shaking her head. "What do you think, Melissa? It's not very ladylike to have bigger muscles than most boys your age, is it?"

"Now let's not get carried away, Beryl. She's got strong arms, but she's not a bodybuilder. And I would have loved to have arms like Stephanie's when I was her age. We're very proud of how healthy she is."

Valkyrie patted her mother's head as she passed behind her. "Thanks, Mum."

Beryl erupted into tears.

Valkyrie stared. Her mum stared. They looked at each other, then went back to staring.

"Uh," her mum said, "what are you doing...?"

"Sorry," said Beryl, pulling a wrinkled tissue from her handbag, "I'm sorry. Oh, this is dreadful. Look at me. I'm a mess." She laughed, but it wasn't very convincing, because she was still crying.

Alice waddled over to her, and patted her leg. Then she whacked it, and waddled off.

"Such a violent child," Beryl sniffed.

"Is everything OK?" Valkyrie asked, wondering when would be an appropriate time to pour the orange juice into a glass.

Beryl blew her nose. "Everything's fine, Stephanie. It's just... seeing how you two are together just..."

"We make you cry?"

Beryl smiled sadly. "Yes. I suppose you do. You're friends. You joke and laugh with each other, and Desmond's the same. I don't... I don't have that with the twins."

"Oh," said Valkyrie, and nudged her mother.

"Oh," said her mother. Then, after a moment, she said, "So how *are* the twins?"

"Oh, you know," said Beryl. "They're at that awkward age."

"They're twenty-one."

"It's an awkward twenty-one, though. They used to be so close. They'd go everywhere together, they'd finish each other's sentences... Or they'd try to. They rarely got it right. Most of the time they'd realise halfway through that they were both talking about two entirely different things. But lately... I don't know. Over the past few months we've barely *seen* Carol. She stays in her room all day. And Crystal... Crystal refuses to even speak to her. She says Carol's changed. She says there's something wrong with her."

"What does Fergus think?" Valkyrie's mum asked.

"Who knows?" said Beryl. "He doesn't talk any more, either. He spends his time reading his brother's books. I never read Gordon's work, it was all too violent and graphic for my taste, but I really can't see how that could be healthy. I'm not saying that reading, in itself, is bad although, personally, I've never trusted books, but aren't Gordon's novels just a little bit... disturbing?"

Valkyrie seized the moment to pour the juice. "Reading horror books isn't going to disturb Fergus, Beryl."

"But how do you know? Reading those books is all he does these days. I think he's even read some of them *twice*. What kind of disturbed individual would read the same book twice, I ask you?"

"It sounds to me like everyone is adjusting," Valkyrie's mum said. "You sold Gordon's boat, didn't you? Even in this market you still got enough so that Fergus and you can retire comfortably. You've got to understand that when some people retire they need time to figure out who they are now that they don't work."

Beryl hesitated, then nodded. "Yes. I suppose Fergus has always defined himself by his job."

Valkyrie frowned as she sipped her orange juice. "And what did he do?"

Beryl waved her tissue. "Sick leave, mostly. And what about the twins?"

Valkyrie's mum patted Beryl's hand. "It's like you said, they're at an awkward age. Give them time. They'll figure it out between themselves."

"Yes," said Beryl. "You're right. I'm worrying over nothing."

"Is that why you came over?" Valkyrie's mum asked. "To talk?"

Beryl nodded. "I don't have many friends, Melissa. You're probably not surprised by that, but you're too polite to say it. But it's true. I haven't been able to talk to anyone about this and it's been... it's been eating away at me."

"Well, I'm glad you feel you can talk to me."

Beryl smiled bravely. "You're my best friend, Melissa."

She blew her nose, missing the astonished looks on the faces around her. Alice wandered out of the kitchen and Valkyrie finished her orange juice and followed close behind. She picked her sister up and walked into the living room.

"Wow," she whispered. "Did you hear that? Mum and Beryl are best friends now."

Alice said something nonsensical.

"You're going to have to watch out for that, OK? Make sure Mum isn't forced to spend too much time with her. She might need a few excuses every now and then to leave the room, so you'll have to be prepared to poo yourself at regular intervals. Think you can do that?"

"Yes," Alice said immediately.

Valkyrie nodded. "Good girl. Now listen to me for a moment. I have to go away for a bit, OK? The other me will still be here, don't worry about that, but I'll be gone. I'll be in a whole heap of other countries. That's exciting, isn't it? Sort of. It might be for a week, or a few weeks... but not much more than that, I promise. Some things are happening and... Anyway, I just wanted you to know that I miss you every day I'm not home, and I'm sorry I'm not around more." Valkyrie's throat tightened. "And if... if I don't come back... please know that I love you. I love you so, so much, and all of this, everything I'm doing, is to make sure you're safe. OK?"

"Down," said Alice, and Valkyrie let her down.

"I love you," Valkyrie said, but Alice was already wandering out of the door.

Valkyrie stayed where she was for a moment, taking a deep breath. When she let it out, she let out all the sadness, too, just blew it all out between her lips. Her eyes were dry. Her throat was normal. She was not about to start crying.

She got back to her room, took off her shorts and T-shirt and let the reflection out of the mirror. Valkyrie pulled on her black clothes as the reflection dressed. When she was done, she took her backpack from under the bed and looked around the room, making sure she hadn't forgotten anything.

The reflection looked at her. "I'll talk to Carol, if you want," it said. "Make sure she's OK."

"Yeah," said Valkyrie. "Actually, yeah, that'd be cool. I don't know why she's not spending time with Crystal, but if it's got anything to do with magic, then I suppose we'd better try to sort it out."

"I'll take care of it."

"Right, thanks. I don't know how long I'll be gone, but..."

"I know."

"Yeah. Of course you do. I'll call when I can, just to see how everyone's doing, and to keep you updated."

"I'd appreciate that."

Her phone beeped. Valkyrie nodded. "He's outside."

The reflection crossed to the window, opened it and stood back. "Good luck," it said.

Valkyrie threw her bag out, used the air to lower it gently to the ground.

"I'm nervous," she said.

"You sound surprised."

"I am." Valkyrie gave a little laugh. "You know, I'm not entirely sure I want to go."

"You don't want to fight against other Sanctuaries."

"I really don't."

"But you're going to anyway."

"Yeah. I suppose I am."

The reflection hesitated. "She's getting louder, isn't she?"

Valkyrie turned away.

"She's talking to you all the time now. You listen to her too much. If you listen to her she'll get stronger. You may not want to fight against other Sanctuaries but you *need* to keep fighting against Darquesse. You've seen what she'll—"

"I don't want to talk about it."

The reflection shut up, and Valkyrie turned again, surprising herself as much as the reflection by hugging it. "If I die," she whispered, "please..."

"Don't worry," the reflection said softly. "I'll be the best daughter and the best big sister they could ever hope for."

Valkyrie stepped back, and nodded, and without another word she slipped out of the window. Before she'd even landed beside her bag, the reflection had closed the window behind her.

21

MAKING PLANS

The trucks pulled up to the Sanctuary and sat with engines idling as the Cleavers loaded themselves on. Ghastly watched as Tipstaff co-ordinated from the centre of the maelstrom, eyes constantly flicking down to the sheaves of paper he had pinned to his clipboard. Cleavers and mages and supplies and equipment, all shipping out to reinforce the outposts around the country, leaving only a skeleton crew to man the Sanctuary.

Madame Mist had spoken to her people within Roarhaven, and they claimed they would defend their town and the Sanctuary itself if outside forces converged. Ghastly had no reason to doubt them, yet he always found it difficult to trust a single word these people said. Perhaps it had something to do with the fact that three of their mages had tried to kill both Ravel and him just a few months earlier. While he had no proof that this attack had been orchestrated by Madame Mist – the three would-be assassins had so far been able to resist the psychics that Ravel had assigned to their interrogation – Mist was hiding something, of that Ghastly was certain. Quietly, and without fuss, he and Ravel had worked to reorganise the Sanctuary's structure. Madame Mist had the entirety of Roarhaven to call upon, after all – it seemed only fair that the Cleavers now answered only to Ravel, and the Sanctuary mages answered only to Ghastly.

He left Tipstaff to his co-ordinating and walked back into the busy corridors of the Sanctuary. If it hadn't been for the Accelerator, he would have happily abandoned the place altogether. It was such an obvious target for the Supreme Council, and as such it was a magnet for trouble should the shield be somehow breached. But they couldn't let the Accelerator fall into enemy hands, and neither could they let it fall into the hands of the people of Roarhaven. A dozen trusted sorcerers were to remain here, plus twenty Cleavers, whose job it was to transform the Sanctuary into an impenetrable fortress.

Swapping the grey concrete and harsh lighting of the corridors for the bright and antiseptic gleam of the science-magic department, Ghastly walked in to find two lab technicians struggling to carry away a blue-haired woman who had both hands wrapped round a narrow pillar. The technicians were red-faced, straining and sweating, while the blue-haired woman seemed quite at ease as she clung on.

"Elder Bespoke," one of the technicians gasped, "please tell her we're all evacuating. She thinks we're kidnapping her."

"Clarabelle," said Ghastly, "what's wrong?"

"This is my home," she said. "I don't want to leave. I still haven't found a sandwich I lost in here weeks ago. I can stay here when everyone else is gone. I can dust."

"The Sanctuary isn't safe any more."

"Then why is it called the Sanctuary? Sanctuaries are meant to be safe. It's where we all go when nowhere *else* is safe. I think I should stay, concentrate on finding that sandwich. I'll be fine on my own."

The door to the backroom opened and Doctor Nye squeezed through. Once clear of the doorframe, the creature straightened up, its long limbs unfolding. The surgical mask it usually wore was absent, allowing Ghastly a distressing view of its wide-gash mouth and the scab where its nose had been cut from its face. Its small eyes, yellow and blinking, fixed on Ghastly as it passed.

"Elder Bespoke," Doctor Nye said in its high-pitched, breathless voice, "you have caught us at a busy time. I've spent the last few hours instructing clumsy oafs in the gentle art of moving my equipment without breaking it. Their ineptitude has set me back weeks in some very important experiments I've been running."

"Maybe if your equipment was located in the science-magic wing," said Ghastly, "it could be moved by people who know what they're doing."

Nye waved one long hand dismissively. "Those people don't like me. They don't want me near them on account of some things I did during the war."

"You mean the crimes you committed."

"Under orders, Elder Bespoke. And am I not as eligible for the amnesty as any other follower of Mevolent? Have I not repented and paid for my sins?"

"Probably not. Sorcerers have long memories, Doctor."

"Only when it suits them. You're looking for this, I take it?" Nye passed him a triangular strip of thin metal, the size of a guitar plectrum.

Ghastly examined the symbol etched on to one side. "It does what we need it to do?"

"That and more," Nye said. "It was the simplest of tasks to construct, but it will not let you down, you have my word as a scientist. Now, if I can be of no further use to you, I have a journey ahead of me."

"And what journey would that be?"

"I intend to return to my old laboratories and wait there for this whole nasty business to blow over. I have everything I need there to continue my experiments, and if you should find yourself in need of my services—"

"You'll be within easy reach," Ghastly finished. "You're not going back to your old labs, Doctor. You're being relocated to the Keep."

Nye shook its head. "I have already had this conversation with the Administrator. The Keep's facilities are practically non-existent. How am I expected to run my experiments—"

"Doctor, I really don't care about your experiments. Everything I've heard about them strikes me as being just so incredibly *wrong*. I'm telling you what's going to happen. You're going to the Keep, and you're going to prepare. If things go according to plan, you'll have something new to keep you busy before long."

"You can't expect a creature of my talents to sit around twiddling its thumbs while—"

"There are two Cleavers outside these doors who will be accompanying you. They have strict instructions to never leave your side."

A peculiar shade of red flushed beneath Nye's natural grey pallor. "Elder Bespoke, I am *not* your prisoner and I refuse to be treated as such."

"Who said anything about being a prisoner? Those Cleavers are there for your protection. Think of them as your bodyguards."

"I have my own—" Nye said, then stopped.

Ghastly frowned. "What was that? You have your own what? Doctor, there are plenty of people out there who have lost friends and loved ones to your experiments during the war. Your safety is all that matters."

Nye looked down at him, its lipless mouth curled in distaste. "Of course," it said at last. "I will travel to the Keep and upgrade its facilities. Thank you for your... concern."

Ghastly nodded to it, and left it standing there while the technicians continued to try to pull Clarabelle from the pillar.

He got to the Medical Bay just as Doctor Synecdoche was leaving. The only patient left in here was Fletcher Renn, who sat fidgeting on one of the beds, trying to find a position to ease his discomfort. The wound he'd suffered was deep, but it was already healing, and the leaves he chewed kept the pain away. But Ghastly knew from personal experience that by now the wound and its surrounding area would be itching like crazy thanks to the ointments and the various procedures that had saved Fletcher's life.

"How are you feeling?" Ghastly asked.

"Better," Fletcher told him. "I'm just waiting for them to bring me a wheelchair. I'm not even allowed to *walk* for the next few hours, and they're saying I'm not allowed to teleport until the infection has been dealt with. That doctor with the name I can't pronounce said it could be days."

"Doctor Synecdoche."

"Days, Ghastly. I can't teleport for *days.*"

"Don't dwell on it. Just focus on getting better."

Fletcher sighed. "Ah, I'm fine. This is nothing. It's annoying, but it'll heal. To be honest, I'm more upset about my taste in women than about being injured. Valkyrie cheats on me and Myra tries to kill me. I'm not really sure I deserved either of those things, to be honest."

"Fletcher, she fooled everyone, not just you."

"Yeah," Fletcher said miserably, "but I dated her. I believed her when she said she loved me." He looked up. "Do you... do you think she really did? On some level? I mean, why would she say she loved me if she didn't have to? I know she was sent to keep an eye on me and then kill me, but... do you think she *did* fall in love with me, even just a small bit?"

Ghastly put a hand on Fletcher's shoulder. "Not really."

"Oh."

"She stuck a knife in you."

"Yeah."

"That's rarely a good sign."

"I suppose."

"But hey, you had some good times, didn't you?"

Fletcher smiled. "Yes. Yes we did."

"Before she stabbed you."

His face fell. "Yeah."

"Give me your hand," said Ghastly. Fletcher held out his hand and Ghastly pressed the metal triangle Nye had given him to the back of it. It stuck there.

"This here is a pager of sorts," Ghastly said.

"What's a pager?"

"Seriously? What's a pager? It's a... it's a device that receives messages that you carry around on your belt."

"What, like a phone?"

"This was before mobile phones. A pager was cutting-edge technology back in the... Anyway, when we need you, it'll glow, give a little beep. A different colour for different people. Providing you still want to help us, of course."

"I'm in," said Fletcher. "You didn't even have to ask."

"That's very much appreciated. Fletcher, when you're back on your feet, you'll be our troop transport. With you, we actually have an advantage over the Supreme Council. In the blink of an eye you can deliver our people to where they're needed anywhere around the world, and go in and get them if things go wrong. Because of this, you're going to be a target. Myra's already proved that."

Fletcher tapped his wound, and in his best James Bond impression said, "I got the point."

"Nice one."

"Thank you."

"Roger Moore?"

Fletcher frowned. "Sean Connery."

"Oh. Still a very good impression."

"Not if you thought it was Roger Moore."

Ghastly left him to work on his impressions, and headed deeper into the Sanctuary. He hadn't even reached the corner when a woman called his name. He turned, watched her approach. He knew her from somewhere. She was a knockout. She was gorgeous. She was...

Oh dear God, she was Scapegrace.

Ghastly's smile faded. "Yes, Mr Scapegrace, what can I do for you?"

Scapegrace came in close. Ghastly really wished he wouldn't do that. He focused on looking him in the eyes, in his beautiful green eyes, and tried to remember how annoying this man was.

"Elder Bespoke," Scapegrace said, "I won't keep you long. I couldn't fail to notice that you seem to be shipping out."

Ghastly nodded, keeping his gaze level. "Yes we are. Is that all?"

"I would never presume to ask what the Sanctuary's plan is – I have to prove myself to you, I'm aware of this. But you should know that when you are gone, this town will be safe."

"OK," said Ghastly.

"The peace will be kept."

"That's really nice."

"Justice will wear a mask."

"I'm not really sure I understand you any more, but fair enough."

Scapegrace held out his hand. "Fight the good fight, Ghastly."

Ghastly shook his hand, and then Scapegrace turned and walked off. Ghastly pulled his eyes away from that view and forced himself to carry on to Ravel's office. Skulduggery and Saracen were already here, deep in discussion with Ravel and Anton Shudder over their plans. Valkyrie sat in one of the chairs, while Bane and O'Callahan sat on the desk. Gracious was looking particularly down.

Ghastly stood in the doorway, and watched Valkyrie lean forward. "You OK?" she asked.

"No," Gracious said, somewhat grumpily. "We had plane tickets to Japan for tomorrow and now we can't go because of all this stupid war stuff. Innocent men are being targeted in Tokyo by a succubus in the form of a beautiful woman. It seduces them and drains their life force."

"And you want to kill it?"

Gracious looked at her. "*Kill* it?"

Donegan sighed. "Gracious just wants a girlfriend, that's all. He's lonely."

"It's not easy meeting single women when you hunt monsters for a living," Gracious said. Then he looked at Valkyrie like he'd just had the best idea ever. "You're friends with China Sorrows, aren't you?"

Valkyrie hesitated. "I... suppose..."

"Is she single?"

"Um..."

"Do you think she'd go out with me?"

"Uh..."

"Stop putting Valkyrie in an awkward position," Ghastly said, finally walking into the room.

"Exactly," said Donegan. "She wants to be polite and not hurt your feelings, so she's not going to laugh right now. But inside? Inside she's laughing, and so are we."

Gracious glared. "What's so funny? She may be beautiful, but China Sorrows is still just a person and, like any other person, she gets lonely, and every now and then she'll need someone to, y'know... hug."

"And you think she'll pick you for that job?"

"I have as good a chance as any. See, her problem is that she's *too* beautiful, and that kind of beauty can be intimidating for lesser men."

"Lesser men," said Ghastly, "but not you?"

Gracious shook his head. "She probably hasn't been asked out in years."

"Actually, she gets asked out all the time," said Valkyrie.

"Oh."

"She gets a lot of marriage proposals."

Gracious sagged. "Oh."

"Which isn't to say that she wouldn't go out with you," Valkyrie said quickly.

Gracious's eyes lit up. "You think she would?"

Valkyrie smiled supportively. "Probably not."

The look of dismay on Gracious's face told Ghastly it was time to change the subject. "The trucks are loaded and ready to depart," he announced. "Half of them are going now, half of them will set off in the morning when we're leaving."

"I still don't quite grasp the logic behind this," said Donegan. "If anyone should be leaving the country, it should be me and Gracious. If we get caught or killed, no big deal."

"It'd be a big deal for me," Gracious mumbled.

"But if any of you guys get captured, then we're all in trouble."

"We'll be more effective out in the field," Ravel said. "We're used to this stuff. Fighting wars is what we did."

"But you're in charge now. And who'll be left here in Roarhaven? Madame Mist?"

"That's a good point," Valkyrie said. "I mean, really, how smart is it to have two of our Elders outside the shield and fighting, while the one Elder we can't actually trust stays safe and warm inside it?"

"This is about more than it seems," Skulduggery said. "The Dead Men still carry a certain amount of weight in the magical world at large. If the sorcerers of the Supreme Council view us merely as a Cradle of Magic making trouble, they'll do their jobs and see it through to the end and it'll be business as usual. But if they see the Dead Men back together, the same Dead Men who worked so effectively against Mevolent, the same Dead Men who saved their lives and the lives of their friends all those years ago... they'll know to fear us. And the very fact that Ravel and Ghastly are part of it will tell them we are confident and powerful and no one will be able to stop us."

"Right," said Valkyrie. "So you're basically hoping that your reputations will make them run away."

Skulduggery looked at her. "Well, it just sounds silly when you say it out loud."

"And what do we do while you're gone?" Donegan asked.

Shudder looked at him. "Your first assignment will be disabling the Midnight Hotel. Aside from Fletcher Renn, the hotel is the only way to get in and out of the country without passing through the shield. The Supreme Council will want to use it to bring in their troops."

"So we stop them from doing that," said Donegan. "Gracious and I. The two of us. Against... who? General Mantis?"

"Who's General Mantis?" Valkyrie asked.

"One of the best tacticians out there," Skulduggery said. "In the war against Mevolent it was our secret weapon."

"It?"

"Mantis is a Crenga, the same species as Nye. We never lost a battle when it was in command."

"That's not making us feel any better," Gracious muttered.

"We wouldn't be sending you if we didn't think you could do it," Ravel said. "Or if there was anyone more suited. Or available. Or willing. Or—"

"Thank you," Donegan said quickly. "You can stop reassuring us now."

"Don't worry," said Ravel, smiling a little, "we'll find someone to back you up. There'll be a briefing in the morning, and then we'll move out."

"Any word on Dexter?" Saracen asked.

Ghastly shook his head. "Not yet. The most we can hope for is that he keeps his head down and stays out of trouble."

Saracen frowned. "He's Dexter Vex. When have you ever known him to stay out of trouble?"

22

STAYING OUT OF TROUBLE

The other Irish prisoners had been taken from the cells hours ago. Vex was the only one left sitting on his bunk, staring at the bars. He hadn't a clue where they'd been taken. Wherever it was, it was undoubtedly more interesting than here.

Footsteps approached. High heels. Vex sat up straighter as Zafira Kerias came round the corner. An attractive woman who always had a stern look in her eye, she seemed uncharacteristically fragile today.

"Elder Kerias," said Vex, "to what do I owe this pleasure?"

Zafira looked at him through the bars, and her whole body sagged. "What are we doing?" she mumbled.

"I'm sitting here in chains," Vex said, "and you're about to give me the key."

Zafira's smile was strained, but it was still a smile. "Not quite, Dexter. But good try, nonetheless. I meant *what are we doing* on a slightly larger scale."

"Ah," he said. "You mean this war you've started."

She ignored the jibe. "Did you ever think we'd slip into another one after Mevolent? I thought all our wars were behind us. I thought we could sit back and watch the mortals fumble around,

169

stepping in every now and then to stop them from doing something too stupid... and yet here we are."

"Humbling, isn't it?"

"You should hear Bisahalani. All these things he's been saying in private for years, now he can say them aloud and he's seizing every opportunity to do so. He's calling for the heads of your Elders. He's accusing them of treason, of betraying their own people."

"He's mean."

"You don't seem to be taking this seriously."

"I sit here in shackles, Zafira, after witnessing one of your people beat a prisoner to death. I'm taking this as seriously as I should be, believe me. I'm just wondering why you're here."

"I'm very sorry for what happened to your friend, but this... this has spiralled out of control. Your friend's death was an accident, whereas Bernard Sult was murdered."

"It's not an accident if you beat someone to death."

"Then it was manslaughter. Grim didn't mean to go that far. He made a terrible mistake, and he's been arrested and charged. But the moment your Elders decided to retaliate with Sult's execution they lost any hope they had of resolving this peacefully."

"I haven't seen the broadcast," said Dexter, "so I couldn't possibly comment on anything you've just said. But ordering an execution doesn't sound like something Erskine would do."

"Dexter, you were one of the Dead Men. You're just as respected as Ravel or Bespoke and you're liked a whole lot more than Skulduggery Pleasant. People will listen to you. If you appealed for calm, if we broadcast a short message where you asked your fellow sorcerers to lay down their arms and come to the table, talk to us, you could help put an end to this conflict before more blood is spilled."

"You want me to tell them to surrender?"

"Surrender? No, not at all. Talk. Ask them to take a moment, to think about what they're doing and the ramifications of their actions, and then come and talk to us."

"So you can arrest them?"

Zafira's eyes were sad. "Dexter, you're not seeing what I'm trying to do here. This is possibly the last chance anyone has of saving lives. You and me, here, we can do that. Renato Bisahalani won't. Cothernus Ode or Dedrich Wahrheit won't. Erskine Ravel isn't likely to back down any time soon, is he? That leaves us. We have to be the reasonable people here, Dexter. There's no one else left."

"You know what I was doing here, Zafira? Before your Cleavers hauled me in and I was accused of being a spy? Do you know what I was doing here?"

"Dexter, we don't have time for—"

"Three mortals were murdered two weeks ago. Do you watch the news? You probably heard about it. Their bodies were dumped on the front lawn of the Presbyterian church where they worshipped every Sunday. The skin had been stripped from their faces. Their hair had been torn out. Not cut. Torn. In clumps. Their eyes had been taken. Their noses and lips sliced off."

"I've seen the reports," Zafira said. "It's horrible the things mortals do to one another."

"Well, that's just it. Mortals didn't do this. I traced it back to a few members of the Church of the Faceless. Did you know those people were back in business around here? They're enjoying something of a resurgence, it would seem. All underground, of course. No sorcerer would openly admit to worshipping the Faceless Ones, not in Bisahalani's America. This was a religious hate crime, and more than that, it was a sorcerer-on-mortal hate crime. These kinds of things have a tendency to spill over if not checked carefully. If the killers aren't stopped, they'll do it again, and they'll do it bigger, and sooner or later a cop is going to catch a lucky break and suddenly we have magic splashed across the evening news. So that's what I was doing before I was put in handcuffs."

171

"Well, if you give me all the details, I'll pass it on to our own detectives and they can pick up where you left off."

"I hope they do, Zafira. Because while Bisahalani and Ode and Wahrheit and Mandat and, let's not forget, *you* are putting all of your energy into this war in a transparent attempt to finally get your hands on a Cradle of Magic and all the power that comes with it, the Church of the Faceless are killing mortals, the Warlocks are stirring all over the world, and Darquesse is still coming. But please, don't let any of that distract you from this power grab. Stumbling into a war you don't need to fight is the only thing that's worthy of your time and attention."

All the warmth had left Zafira's eyes. "I'll send someone to talk to you. You can tell them about your suspicions regarding the Church of the Faceless."

"I'll do that."

"But you won't be doing it here. You're going to be taken to a high-security prison this afternoon, where you will be held in solitary confinement until the war is over."

"Again, without charge."

"You're an enemy agent, Dexter, and you clearly have no interest in helping me avert further bloodshed."

"What you're doing is wrong and you know it."

"We're doing what needs to be done. I'm sorry you can't see that."

He sat on the bunk, watching the female Cleaver through the bars. Like the two male Cleavers beside her, she stood perfectly straight, the scythe strapped to her back and her arms by her sides. The coat was long, tight at the chest and waist, but loose down the legs, and her face was lost behind that visored helmet.

It was relatively rare to find a female Cleaver. As part of their training, Cleavers needed to undergo Behavioural Indoctrination from a young age, a lengthy process often likened to voluntary brainwashing. During the process, certain personality traits were dampened, curtailed or otherwise repressed, rewarding the Cleaver with, among other things, the ability to follow orders without hesitation. Debates had raged for hundreds of years over the moral implications of Behavioural Indoctrination. There had even been a disastrous attempt to remove it from Cleaver training and replace it with a new approach. This attempt led to a generation of failed Cleavers – the first of the so-called Rippers. Physically, they were as impressive as their grey-coated counterparts, but psychologically they were damaged. Flawed. Behavioural Indoctrination was reintroduced soon after, and it embedded itself as a necessary step in creating the perfect soldier.

There were more male Cleavers in active service simply because males responded better to the process. Females were less susceptible, and therefore harder to control. Every so often, however, came a female of the right mindset, and she'd go through the years of training and emerge on the other side, as another nameless, visored soldier. Vex never looked at male Cleavers and thought about this stuff, but whenever he saw a woman in that uniform, he found himself wondering what had driven her to choose this path. She stood there now, strong and healthy, bubbling with physical potential. But what about later? There were no old Cleavers, after all. Once they'd served their fifteen years of active duty, they had a choice – re-emerge into the world as their old selves, or continue to shun their individuality and become a Ripper. Most became a Ripper.

"Transport's here," Swain said. "Let's go."

Vex sighed and got to his feet. The door was opened and off he marched, Swain leading the way with a Cleaver directly in front of Vex and the other two behind. They climbed the stairs, walked along the corridor, and Swain pushed open the door. The sunlight on the other side was intense – Vex had to squint to watch the truck approach. He felt a sharp pressure, over in an instant, and he turned his head, frowned at the female Cleaver.

Had she just pinched his bum?

The truck stopped and Swain nodded. "OK, load him in."

The female whirled, her scythe taking the head off the Cleaver in front. The second Cleaver rushed her and she flipped backwards, her boot catching him, smacking his helmet. She landed, not giving him a moment to recover before her blade slashed through his knee and slashed again even as he was falling.

Swain stared at her in the sudden silence that followed. Then his hand started glowing.

Vex moved first, stepping between them, slamming his head into Swain's face. He dropped, unconscious, and Vex turned as the Cleaver twirled her scythe one-handed. She rammed the staff into the ground and it stayed there, swaying. Her hands went to her coat and popped it open, took it off. She wore a light cotton vest beneath. Her arms were strong. She took off her helmet, and gave him a smile.

"All right, Dexter?" said Tanith Low.

23

THE DARK AND STORMY KNIGHT

Night descended on Roarhaven like a woolly blanket of blackness with holes in it that were the stars. Scapegrace looked out over the rooftops, feminine hands on his feminine hips, a mask on his beautiful face while the breeze played with his luxurious hair, and he knew without a shadow of a doubt that somewhere out there, evil was happening. He also knew that he had no way down from this roof.

From below, there came a rattling, and a clanking, and then a voice that was rich and deep but edged with uncertainty fluttered up to him like an anxious moth. "Master? Are you there? Master?"

Scapegrace peered over the edge. Thrasher gazed up at him from the shadows, his big, strong hands gripping the ladder. He, too, wore a mask, but instead of hiding his ridiculously handsome features – his jawline, his cheekbones – it instead accentuated them, made him even better-looking than before. Scapegrace resisted the urge to drop a brick on that face and instead got down on his hands and knees and moved backwards until he hung off the edge. His foot searched below him for the ladder and he found the first rung. He started his descent, but the sound of voices made him freeze.

He waved at Thrasher to hide, then clung to the ladder and

focused on becoming one with the shadows, just like Grandmaster Ping had taught him. The voices got nearer. Three people. No, four. Three male, one female. Innocent citizens out for a late-night stroll, or something more sinister? Muggers, maybe? Or maybe they were in league with Silas Nadir. Maybe they'd been sent to kill him.

A new fear, razor-sharp and raw, gripped his heart. His magic hadn't returned yet, and he was no longer a zombie. He could be killed. If someone cut off his head now, there'd be no coming back. Death would snatch him away and never let him go, and he'd never get to do the things he'd always planned on doing, like making a list of things to do before he died.

Scapegrace leaped upwards, grabbed the edge of the roof, tried pulling himself up in one fluid motion.

Instead, he just hung there, his eyes widening in alarm, swaying slightly in the breeze. Pulling himself up in one fluid motion was not as easy as it sounded.

He glanced down. They rounded the corner. They were going to pass directly beneath him. His fingers were already burning.

"—lead by example," one of the men was saying, "and he will. He's taken us this far."

"Plans are one thing," said the woman, "deeds are another."

"You doubt him? You doubt Madame Mist?"

"All I know is that we've sacrificed so much already. It's their turn now."

Scapegrace whimpered and lost his grip and fell, and one of the men collapsed beneath his weight.

The others jumped back, shouting out in alarm, and Scapegrace scrambled to his feet and swung a punch that hit the woman. Then the air struck him like a gigantic fist and he hurtled backwards, landed awkwardly and sprawled. He looked up in time to see Thrasher charging out from hiding, his muscular arms wrapping round the Elemental who had attacked. But Thrasher was an idiot who didn't know how to fight, and wrapping his arms round his opponent was the full extent of his battle plan.

Scapegrace got up, swept his long hair away from his face, and yelled out a war cry before running away. Someone gave chase. He dodged left, squeezing between two buildings, the tangled weeds clutching at his feet. He burst out the other end like toothpaste from a tube, and someone crashed into him. He went down, cursing, scrambled up, sprinted on. Behind him, someone running. Gaining.

No. This wasn't how things were any more. He wasn't the old Scapegrace, the deluded loser, the butt of all jokes. He was the new Scapegrace, fit and healthy, student of Grandmaster Ping, warrior-in-training. And the new Scapegrace did not run from a fight.

He stopped suddenly and turned and Thrasher's eyes widened right before he ran into him. They went sprawling, finally coming to a stop on their backs, looking up at the stars.

"You idiot," Scapegrace panted.

"Sorry," said Thrasher.

They got up. They weren't being pursued, but Scapegrace couldn't take the chance that someone might follow them home. They stole into the shadows, taking the long way back to the pub. Halfway there, they removed their masks.

"Act normal," Scapegrace whispered as they stepped on to a well-lit street. Thrasher nodded, started walking like he hadn't a care in the world. "What are you doing?"

"I'm, uh, acting normal."

"No you're not. You're acting like someone pretending to be normal. Stop pretending and start acting, but don't act like you're not pretending, that'll make it worse."

A car pulled up beside them.

Thrasher froze. "What do we do?"

Scapegrace's mouth went dry. He couldn't think of anything.

A man got out, a tall man with dark hair, receding. He had a long face and a long nose. Everything about him was long.

"Evening," he said.

Thrasher stood there looking guilty.

"Hello," said Scapegrace.

The man leaned against his car with his arms folded. He carried with him the unmistakable air of authority. "And where are you off to, may I ask?"

Scapegrace tried to think of a smart answer. "Nowhere," he said instead.

The man with the long face seemed amused. "You're going nowhere, are you? Isn't that a tad pessimistic?"

Scapegrace had no idea what the man was talking about. "I'm sorry," he said, "but who are you?"

"Name's Dacanay. I'm the sheriff."

"Roarhaven doesn't have a sheriff," Thrasher pointed out.

"It does now," said Dacanay. "And I wasn't talking to you. I was talking to your girlfriend here."

Scapegrace bristled. "I am *not* his girlfriend."

"We're just friends," Thrasher muttered.

"We're not *even* friends."

"I see," Dacanay said, starting to smile. "So you're single, then."

Scapegrace frowned. "What does that have to do with anything? I'm sorry, Sheriff whatever-your-name-is..."

"Dacanay."

"Sheriff Dacanay, myself and my... associate were merely out for a late-night stroll. I didn't know that was illegal."

"Strolling's not illegal. Mugging people is."

Scapegrace tried to look surprised and offended and amused, all at once. He reckoned he just about pulled it off. "Mugging? You think we're muggers? Muggers are the *last* thing we are!"

"We're the *opposite* of muggers," Thrasher said.

Dacanay frowned up at him. "What the hell does that mean? What's the opposite of a mugger? Do you jump out at people and *give* them money and valuables? What are you talking about? How stupid are you? Tell you what, why don't you concentrate on flexing your muscles, and me and your not-quite-friend and definitely-not-a-girlfriend here will do the talking." Dacanay turned back to Scapegrace, and smiled. "And it's not that I doubt the word of someone so beautiful, but I've had a report of an attempted mugging near here."

"That's awful," Scapegrace said.

"It is, isn't it? The muggers were described as a dark-haired woman and a large muscular man."

Scapegrace swallowed thickly. "I hope you catch them."

"I think I already have."

A strained smile. "Congratulations. We'll let you get back to it, then."

Scapegrace went to move past him, but Dacanay stepped in his way. "What's your name, miss? You and your friend's?"

"Our names? Why would you want to know our names?"

"I spent the last thirty years working as a detective for the Russian Sanctuary. This is my first trip home in all that time. I need to get to know the locals again. So... your name?"

"Yes. OK. That makes sense. Our names. That's what you want. Well, my associate here... he can tell you his own name. Associate?"

Thrasher went pale. "My name is... Bond."

Dacanay peered at him. "Bond?"

"Yes. Harrison... Bond."

Dacanay grunted, and his eyes returned to Scapegrace. "And you?"

"My name," Scapegrace said, "is quite simple. It's easy to remember. You'll have no trouble remembering this."

"So?" Dacanay asked. "What is it?"

Scapegrace nodded. "Guess."

"I'm sorry?"

"Guess what my name is."

"Miss, I'm not going to do that. You either tell me what your name is or I'll—"

Scapegrace laughed. "I'll tell you, I'll tell you! My name is..." He tried to force his brain to think of a name. The last time something like this had happened he had blurted out "Adolf". Not this time. This time he needed to think of actors, not historical figures. No, not actors. Actresses. All he needed to do was think of two actresses and combine a first name with a last name. He needed to think of someone classic, like Katharine Hepburn, and combine it with someone else like... like Audrey Hepburn.

"Katharine," he said triumphantly, "Hepburn."

"Katharine Hepburn," Dacanay said, his eyes narrowing. "Like the actress?"

Scapegrace smiled, started to shake his head, and froze. Dammit.

"Katharine Hepburn Scapegrace," Thrasher said quickly. "That's her full name. It's only Katharine Hepburn to strangers."

"Well, Miss Scapegrace," Dacanay said, "I hope after tonight I will no longer be a stranger. You'd better get home now. But keep an eye out for those muggers, you hear?"

"Yes, Sheriff," Scapegrace said. "Thanks for your concern."

Dacanay got back in his car and drove off. Immediately, Scapegrace whirled to Thrasher.

"You told him my name!"

"I had to! I'm sorry, Master, but he knew something was up!"

"You told him my name!"

"I'm so sorry!"

"We have secret identities and you told him my name!"

"I thought the secret identities were only for when we had the masks on."

"That's not the point! Listen to the words! Secret! Identities! If you take away the secret, then they're just identities!"

"I'm sorry."

Scapegrace started walking. Thrasher hurried to keep up.

"Sheriff Dacanay would lock us up in an instant if he knew who we really were," Scapegrace said. "Don't you understand?

180

We're living beyond the law. We're doing the job he can't. We are vigilantes."

"Yes," said Thrasher. "Only..."

"Only what?"

"Only we haven't done anything vigilante-ish. We go out on patrol and you climb up on roofs and I go off and get a ladder and then we go home."

"Are you questioning the mission?"

"No, sir, no I am not. I love the mission. This is where I want to be. By your side. As your partner."

"Sidekick."

"Sidekick, yes, sorry. It's just... we haven't really stopped any crime or found any clues that would lead us to Silas Nadir."

"What about those people tonight? They were talking about something. Something suspicious."

"What did they say?"

Scapegrace shrugged. "I don't know, I wasn't really listening. But it's a start. We just have to find them again, follow them, and maybe they'll lead us to Nadir. Then he will taste the justice of the Dark and Stormy Knight."

"And Muscle Man."

Scapegrace glared. "What?"

"My codename," said Thrasher. "I was thinking... I was thinking maybe I'd be Muscle Man?"

"No. It can't be the Dark and Stormy Knight and Muscle Man. That sounds like we're equals. I've got the perfect codename for you. It came to me just then. You can be the Village Idiot."

Thrasher's face fell. "Sir, no, please!"

"I've decided. It's the Dark and Stormy Knight and the Village Idiot. That's who we are."

"But Master—"

"No arguments."

Thrasher sagged. "Yes, sir."

24

STAGNANT WATER

He found Madame Mist by the black lake, the morning breeze playing with the veil over her face.

"And off they go to war," she said without turning her head towards him. "I wonder how many of them will die. I wonder how many they will kill."

"Sacrifices must be made," said the man with the golden eyes.

Now she did look at him. "Yes," she said. "They must. And our turn is coming up. How can we expect our followers to make the leap if we ourselves do not?"

"I'm well aware of what I must do."

"I am glad. These are trying times for us all. Has there been any word on the Warlocks?"

"Another one of Charivari's envoys has been spotted meeting with the Maidens," the man with the golden eyes said. "I doubt they'll want to join his crusade, though. They are relatively peace-loving, for witches, and they bear the mortals no particular ill will."

"We will need Charivari's army to be strong, but not too strong," said Mist. "There is very little point in provoking him if we can't be assured victory."

"Don't concern yourself with his strength," the man with the golden eyes responded. "Charivari has yet to approach the Brides. They'll side with him, and then his army will number three hundred. An entirely manageable threat, I think. They'll attack the mortals, we'll repel them, and the mortals will welcome us as heroes."

Mist looked out across the stagnant lake. Nothing more needed to be said.

25

THE OLD GANG BACK TOGETHER

It was a nice dream. Probably. As Skulduggery shook her awake, it vanished back into the recesses of her mind. She had a feeling it had been a nice dream. She hoped it had.

"What's wrong?" she mumbled.

"It's Dexter," Skulduggery said.

She sat up in the bed, horrified. "They killed him?"

"What? No. Tanith has him."

"She killed him?"

"Stop thinking someone killed him. He's alive, as far as we know. Tanith and Sanguine broke him out of whatever gaol he was in. They're in a boat off Wexford Harbour. Ghastly's waiting in the van, so get your boots on."

It was almost 10am by the time they got to Wexford. They watched a small boat pull up to the quay. Valkyrie went to step forward, but Skulduggery put a hand out to stop her, and nodded at the low wall beside her. She peered around until she caught the faint glow of a sigil.

The boat docked, and Dexter Vex stepped out. Tall and strong, wearing a black T-shirt and jeans and scuffed boots. His hands were shackled behind his back, which made his triceps pop in his bare arms. His hair was darker than the first time she'd met him, no longer bleached by the sun on his many adventures across the globe. He hadn't lost the chiselled look, though, and she allowed herself a moment to gaze in admiration before flicking the professional switch inside her head. Climbing out of the boat after him were a well-built blonde in brown leather, and a man in a suit and sunglasses. Tanith Low and Billy-Ray Sanguine. Both had their blades drawn.

Valkyrie glanced around. No one was paying them much attention. Yet.

Tanith and Sanguine escorted Vex right up to the low wall, but stopped just on the other side of the invisible shield.

"Dexter," said Skulduggery in greeting. "Wink twice if you're being held against your will."

Despite the blades that hovered over vital areas, Dexter laughed. "Apparently they want to just hand me over to you," he said, "which is pretty nice of them if you think about it. They also want to join up."

"We can speak for ourselves, thank you," Tanith said. "Hi, Val. Hi, Skulduggery." She took a moment. "Hi, Ghastly."

"Let him go," Ghastly said.

"First we talk. Then we let him go."

"No, Tanith. This conversation will not be on your terms."

"Our terms are the only terms," Sanguine said. "We have sharp pointy blades ready to open up every artery your friend has, so you best pay attention to—"

"You," Ghastly interrupted, "are not allowed to speak."

Sanguine frowned behind his sunglasses. "What?"

Ghastly's eyes found Tanith again. "You take the shackles off Dexter, you lay down your weapons, and then we'll talk."

Tanith met his gaze. "We don't have the key."

"*You* don't need a key," Ghastly said.

Tanith smiled.

"We ain't releasing him," Sanguine said. "And you don't give us orders, scarface."

"Tanith," Ghastly said, "muzzle your pet."

Sanguine's lip curled. "Pet? That what you called me? Hey, look at me when I'm talking to you. I ain't no pet. You're just sore cos she picked me over you. That wound hasn't healed yet, has it? Still picking at it, are you? Well, here's something that'll pick at it some more."

"Billy-Ray," Tanith said in a warning tone, but Sanguine wasn't about to stop talking for anyone.

"Me and Tanith are engaged, ugly. Yeah, that's right. We're getting married."

Something inside Valkyrie curled up at the thought. She glanced at Ghastly. His demeanour hadn't changed.

"Love, honour and obey," Sanguine continued, "till death do us part, the whole nine yards. See that, Bespoke? The better man won. You can come to the ceremony if you like. You can be the ring bearer."

"Billy-Ray," Tanith said, "that's enough." She reached out, took hold of the shackles binding Dexter, and a moment later they clicked open. Sanguine's jaw clenched, but he said nothing as Dexter rubbed his wrists and shook out his arms.

Tanith sheathed her sword and, after a long moment, Sanguine reluctantly folded his straight razor and put it away.

"There," Tanith said. "We come in peace."

"Give me a reason why I shouldn't shoot you where you stand," Skulduggery said.

Tanith chewed her lip playfully. "I don't know. I'm your friend? If I hadn't been taken over by the Remnant, I'd be a good person? I'm too cute to die?"

"You *were* our friend," Skulduggery said, "and the fact is you *have* been taken over by a Remnant, which renders any hypotheticals moot."

Tanith grinned. "I notice you can't throw the cute remark back in my face."

"You also killed Grand Mage Strom," Skulduggery said, "and forced us into the path we're now on."

"That was nothing personal. That was just a job, like any other."

"Who paid you?" asked Valkyrie.

Tanith shrugged. "You know when Davina Marr couldn't quite remember who'd talked her into destroying the Dublin Sanctuary? I'm afraid I'm the same. What did you call him? Your 'mystery man'? Pretty sure it's the same guy."

"But now you want to fight by our side," Ghastly said. "Why?"

"Why not? I've been pretty busy for the last few months. My main focus has been making sure that when Darquesse arrives there will be no one who can even threaten her safety. The destruction she will wreak upon this world is going to be magnificent, and I didn't want anything to ruin that. You must understand, Ghastly, that I love Darquesse with all my heart."

Valkyrie waited for Tanith's eyes to flicker towards her, for a knowing smile to slowly grow. Instead, Tanith kept her gaze fixed on Ghastly.

"So we tracked down four God-Killer weapons," Tanith continued, "because we figured if they can hurt or kill a Faceless One they could hurt or kill Darquesse. So we retrieved them and destroyed them. I'm sure Dexter filled you in already. It was all very exciting. But now that's all over. I've done everything I can possibly do to ensure Darquesse's safety whenever she decides to turn up, and the only thing I have left to do is wait. And I hate waiting. So, when we heard about all this hullaballoo, we said to ourselves, I bet Ghastly and Skulduggery and Valkyrie could use our help. So here we are. The old gang back together."

"And me," said Sanguine.

"The old gang and him," Tanith nodded. "And we figured the best way to approach you would be while bearing gifts. Hence, Dexter Vex."

"And it was much appreciated," Dexter said.

Tanith smiled at him. "The pleasure was all mine."

Sanguine frowned, and stood between them.

Tanith looked at Valkyrie. "And the fact is, I still look at you guys as friends. Val, I know I've changed, I know I'm not the same woman you knew, but I can be. I can work at it. You're still my friend, and I still want nothing more than to look out for you and protect you."

"Excuse us for a moment," Skulduggery said. "We'll have to talk this over."

Before Tanith could even respond, Skulduggery held up his hand and the space around them shimmered. Any sound they now made would travel that far and no further.

He looked at Ghastly. "Thoughts?"

"I want to kill Sanguine," was the first thing Ghastly said. "And I want to do it slowly, in front of a lot of people. Using a hammer."

Skulduggery nodded. "Very healthy."

Ghastly sighed. "From a business point of view, we could use them. Of course we could. We know how good they are and we know what they can do. The disadvantages of using them include the fact that they're both remorseless psychopaths, and that if the Supreme Council finds out about this they can claim that Tanith has been working for us from the start, and that killing Strom was our idea. But... I don't know. Do you believe her, Valkyrie? What she said about you?"

Valkyrie hesitated. "Yes, actually. I think she'd do anything to protect me."

"I agree," Skulduggery said. "I think we should accept their offer. Use them when we need to, and keep them on a tight leash."

Ghastly made a face. "Even Sanguine?"

"I'm afraid so. We'll get them to accompany Bane and O'Callahan on their mission to disable the Midnight Hotel. If they step out of line, those two will be able to handle them."

Scowling, Ghastly nodded and Skulduggery lowered his hand.

"This is on a trial basis," Ghastly said. "You will obey our orders at all times. If you deviate, we'll kill you on sight. Agreed?"

"Agreed," Tanith said happily.

Ghastly crouched by the wall and traced a pattern back through the flow of the sigil. A section of the shield became visible, and retracted. Dexter stepped through, followed by Tanith and Sanguine. Immediately, Ghastly reactivated the section. He returned to Skulduggery's side. Silence.

"Well," Tanith said, "this is awkward."

"Allow me to break the ice," Ghastly said, and punched Sanguine.

Sanguine staggered back on shaky legs.

Tanith sighed. "That was incredibly mature."

Sanguine straightened up, rubbing his jaw and laughing without humour. He started to say something and Ghastly caught him in the ribs. He gasped, staggered, sucked in great whooping lungfuls of air, and Ghastly stood over him and watched. When he'd recovered enough, Sanguine lunged and Ghastly met him with a right cross. Sanguine hit the ground with his face and stayed there.

Tanith observed Ghastly, amusement in her eyes. "So," she said, "are we ready to go?"

They shared the most awkward van ride ever back to Roarhaven. Sanguine, when he regained consciousness, sulked while Tanith tried and failed to strike up a meaningful conversation with Valkyrie. When they arrived at the Sanctuary, the Monster Hunters were waiting.

"We're going with *them*?" Tanith asked, clearly dismayed. "But I thought we could hang around with you guys. What about everything you said about getting the old gang back together?"

"You said that," Skulduggery pointed out, "not us. We're not going to trust you, Tanith, but we'll use your talents for as long as we can. If you don't like the terms of the arrangement—"

"No, no," Tanith said quickly, "it's fine. We'll prove ourselves to you. I'm OK with that. Come on, Billy-Ray, let's go be good guys."

Gracious led them to their car, but Ghastly put a hand on Donegan's arm to keep him in place.

"If you even *think* they're going to betray you," he said, "kill them both."

Donegan nodded, and followed after them.

Ghastly looked at Valkyrie, and didn't say anything. She didn't, either.

Now that Tanith and Sanguine were not listening in, Skulduggery started telling Vex what had been happening. Valkyrie and Ghastly followed behind as they made their way to the briefing. The Sanctuary was eerily quiet – almost as quiet as the first time Valkyrie had crept down its stone corridors.

Ravel was waiting for them in the briefing room, alongside Shudder and Saracen. They didn't make a big deal about Vex's return. A few good-natured insults were tossed around, Saracen gave Vex a bag of fresh clothes, and then it was business as usual.

"OK then," said Ravel, "today is the day our war officially starts. There have been skirmishes around the world, but nothing too big. At the moment it's all very tentative. Whichever side is first to throw the big punch will take the advantage. That side will be us."

As Ravel spoke, Vex took a fresh T-shirt from his bag and took off the one he'd been wearing. Every time he moved, his muscles rolled beneath his skin. It was astonishing. He was a gleaming marvel of musculature. A smattering of scars crossed his perfect torso, evidence of a hard-lived life, each scar a signature of a different battle or enemy. Fletcher had never been like that. Caelan had never been like that. Dexter Vex was something brand-new and wonderful.

"Mmm," said Valkyrie.

Ravel looked at her. "Yes?"

Her eyes snapped towards him. "What?"

"You have something to add?"

She stared. "Nope. Just… agreeing."

Skulduggery sighed. "Dexter, please put your shirt on. Valkyrie's getting distracted."

"I'm not," she said, then smiled at Vex. "You don't have to put your shirt on."

Vex laughed, but pulled the T-shirt on over his head.

"As I was saying," Ravel continued, "our first strike is going to be a damaging one. We have traced the Engineer's energy signature but, unfortunately, they got to it first. Currently it is in a French Sanctuary facility. That means they're entering into this war with confidence. They reckon if we start to supercharge our sorcerers, they can use the Engineer to disable the Accelerator. While we have no plans to use the Accelerator at this moment in time, I think we can all agree that it is useful to have something like this as a last resort. Taking the Engineer from the Supreme Council would be a massive blow to their morale."

"What was it doing in France?" asked Vex.

"Not a whole lot," Ravel said. "When they found it, it was in a scrapyard. Whatever happened to it, it was in pieces. Grand Mage Mandat sent the remains to his top scientists to get it up and running again. The chief scientist is a man called Lamour – an odd little man, but one who claims to have a vehement opposition to the Supreme Council's actions. He got in touch through unconventional means. He won't be able to take the Engineer out himself, but he says if we can get into the facility, he can hand it over. It won't be easy, and I'm expecting heavy resistance, and I'm not willing to send a team out on what could very well be a suicide mission. So I'm going in myself."

"And so am I," said Ghastly.

Vex frowned. "Do you have any idea how unwise that is? If either of you are captured—"

"The mission is worth the risk," Ravel said. "Obviously, I can't order the rest of you to accompany us..."

"Actually, you can," said Saracen. "You're Grand Mage. You're in charge."

"Right, well, yeah, but the Dead Men have been disbanded. We're no longer a military unit."

Vex held up his hand. "All in favour of the Dead Men getting back together, raise your hands." Other hands joined his in the air. "There you go. We're now a military unit again."

Ravel hesitated. "Very well. In that case, we're going to break into the facility. We'll have to make our way there the old-fashioned way – Fletcher Renn will be out of commission until tomorrow. Because the Supreme Council will be monitoring any private planes leaving Irish airspace, we'll be travelling out of the country on a passenger jet."

Shudder looked displeased. "A passenger jet... with other passengers?"

"Yes."

"Passengers who are people? Mortal people?"

"Yes."

"I... see."

"Operational control in the field will rest with Skulduggery as always," Ravel said, then turned to Valkyrie. "I'm aware that I take my life in my hands when I say this, but I think it would be best if you stayed behind."

She shook her head. "I'm going."

"We'll be walking right into the enemy's lair."

"The best place to find the enemy."

Ravel glanced at the others. There were many things Valkyrie could have said to fill that silence, but she stayed quiet. This wasn't her decision. It was theirs. There had always been seven Dead Men – no more, no less. Originally it had been the six men standing around her and a seventh called Hopeless. When Ravel himself had been badly injured and needed time to recover, his place had been taken by Larrikin. But Hopeless and Larrikin were long dead, and the Dead Men didn't have time to hold auditions.

The last person Ravel looked to was Skulduggery. Valkyrie turned her head away, giving him the freedom to agree or disagree without judgement.

"Well, OK then," Ravel said at last, "it looks like we have a new Dead Man."

Valkyrie did her very best to stop the grin from spreading.

"Should we change our name?" Saracen asked. "The Dead People, perhaps?"

"The Dead Non-Gender-Specific Persons?" Vex suggested.

"Dead Men and a Girl? Dead Men and a Little Lady?"

"We'll keep the name as it is," Ghastly said, interrupting them before they got carried away. "Valkyrie, you'll just have to get used to being called a Dead Man. I'm sure you can handle it."

Valkyrie gave him a nod, and looked up at Skulduggery. He wasn't looking at her, though. His eyeless gaze still rested on Ravel.

"This mission," Skulduggery said. "Care to go into a bit more detail?"

Ravel straightened up. "Of course. We'll be flying into France, but we'll have to make the rest of the journey by car and foot. In all, it'll take us maybe two days. The facility is located due west of the sorcerer town of Wolfsong. It's been over a hundred and fifty years since I was there last, but they're one of the friendlier independent towns I've ever seen. It's not like Roarhaven. Since we'll be passing through on our way to the facility, we'll have a chance to speak to them and hopefully rally them to our cause."

"You think they'll turn against the French Sanctuary?" Shudder asked.

"Grand Mage Mandat is not a popular man in Wolfsong. It's a possibility. At the very least, there might be someone there who can get us close to the facility without being seen."

"And then?" Skulduggery asked.

"Then we accomplish our mission."

Skulduggery looked at Ravel and Ravel looked back at him.

Eventually Ghastly rolled his eyes. "Will you please just tell them?"

Ravel scowled. "I was working up to it."

"Working up to what?" Vex asked.

"The fact is," Ravel said, "we're not going to win this war alone. We need allies. We need the Sanctuaries of Africa and Australia to come in on our side. They're teetering on the edge right now, we know they are – but it's going to take something big to push them over and get them involved."

"Oh," said Skulduggery. "I see."

"What?" Valkyrie said. "What am I missing?"

Skulduggery looked at her. "We're going to let the Supreme Council know that we'll be going after the Engineer."

Vex laughed at the ridiculousness of the notion, but sobered when he realised Ravel had stayed silent. "You can't be serious. You actually *want* to walk into an ambush?"

"We let it leak out that we're on our way," Ravel said. "Our African and Australian friends hear about this and they know we're walking into a trap... and so they spring into action and rescue us."

"You hope," said Saracen.

"I very much hope," said Ravel.

Valkyrie frowned. "But wouldn't we be tricking them into fighting a war?"

"Tricking?" Ravel said. "I wouldn't call it tricking, no. Manipulating? It could possibly be seen as manipulating."

Ghastly looked at her. "You know what we did during the war with Mevolent. We took on the suicide missions. We did the jobs no one else wanted to do. Not all of these jobs were dangerous."

"Some of them," Skulduggery finished, "were just distasteful. We need allies. This is an incredibly risky plan that might backfire and mean the end of our fight – but there are times when a huge risk is the only risk worth taking."

"Yay," said Vex mournfully. "We're walking into another ambush. I love it so much when we do things like that. So, while all this is going on, where are we meant to find the time to recover the Engineer?"

"It won't be easy," Ravel admitted.

"I'm astonished."

"The whole thing is a set-up," said Ravel. "Even more than you think. Lamour, that lovably eccentric chief scientist, is luring us into a trap anyway. He thinks we think he's a double agent, working for them but secretly working for us. He doesn't know we know he's a triple agent, working for them but secretly working for us but really he's secretly working for them. Dexter, how's your brain?"

"Hurting."

"But in every lie there is a kernel of truth. The fact is, Lamour does have access to the Engineer, and he will be in the facility. He just won't be where he says he'll be. So while the rest of us are trying to avoid getting captured or killed, one of us will have to sneak off, track him down, get the Engineer and get back before our allies mount their magnificent rescue and whisk us all out of there."

"So who'll be the one going after Lamour?" Vex asked.

Everyone turned to look at Valkyrie.

"I have an idea," she said. "Why don't I do it?"

Vex got up and approached her. "Welcome onboard," he said, and surprised her with a hug. She wasn't surprised by how much she liked it.

Saracen was next. "You're going to make a wonderful Dead Man," he said as they hugged. "I know these things."

Ghastly came over, and when he hugged her he whispered in her ear, "Your uncle would be so proud of you."

Ghastly stepped aside and then Shudder was standing there. Valkyrie blinked up at him.

"In the past," he said, "when welcoming a new Dead Man into the fold, the tradition was to hit them across the jaw, as hard as we could."

"Uh," said Valkyrie.

"Hugging is much nicer," Shudder said, and hugged her so tight she thought her ribs might crack.

Ravel's hug was next. He smelled lovely. "You'll do us proud," he said. "And don't take our name too literally. We actually do our best *not* to die."

He released her and she turned to Skulduggery and held out her arms. "Come here, you."

He tilted his head. "My hugs are for special occasions only."

"Hug me."

"I prefer the old tradition."

"Hug."

"Would a handshake do?"

"Hug."

"A pat on the back?"

She stepped forward and wrapped her arms round him. "Hug," she said.

He sighed, and his hands settled on her shoulders. The others were warm and their embraces strong – with Skulduggery the hug was cold, and there were areas on his jacket that gave way beneath her fingers, and she could feel the emptiness within. She didn't mind.

26

THE PURSUIT BEGINS

China slipped her feet from the stirrups and swung her right leg over the saddle, letting herself drop smoothly to the grass. Sable stayed where he was as she walked to the crypt. He was a good horse. Out of all the horses she'd owned throughout the centuries, he was by far her favourite. She undid the strap under her chin, took off the riding hat and hung it on the curved tail of one of the stone scorpions that guarded the crypt door. The hinges creaked when she entered. She hadn't been to this corner of her land for over a year – hadn't been through this door in twice that.

Upon her entrance, sigils began to glow along the walls, casting a warm light on to the eight sealed stone coffins that lay before her. A ninth, in the corner of her eye, remained empty. She didn't look at it. Instead, she concentrated on the coffin in the middle. Like the others, her family crest had been carved into the lid, a scorpion atop three circles. The circles were said to represent the blank features of the Faceless Ones, while the scorpion stood for the indomitable will and immutable nature of China's bloodline.

The arrogance of it all. China's grandmother, a mere thirty years older than China's mother but two hundred years older than China, had taken it upon herself to school the children of the family in the ways of worship. The majority of those teachings were nothing if not standard – the Faceless Ones are the true rulers of the world, the mortals must be extinguished, sorcerers exist to serve these wonderfully insane gods – the same rhetoric instilled in the minds of all disciples' children.

But China's grandmother, who had in turn been taught by her grandmother, also passed down a particular addendum that was never spoken of to outsiders. The evenings China had spent with her brother Bliss, sitting by the fire while their grandmother explained the true realities of the Faceless Ones, that they *were* insane and they *were* unpredictable, and according to legend they could take over a sorcerer's body to use as they saw fit. Other sorcerers, China and her brother were told, were mere fodder for their gods – vessels waiting to be steered. But China's family believed themselves to be special. They believed they were different. They believed they were so strong and so clever that when the Faceless Ones took them over, they would retain control. *A scorpion cannot change its nature*, their grandmother always said. How right she was.

Bliss never changed his nature. He was quiet and strong and so rarely resorted to violence despite his immense strength. When he walked away, they called him traitor, blasphemer, and said he was not a true scorpion. They were so blinded by the betrayal that they couldn't see that he was the truest scorpion of them all. He had *never* been one to accept what he'd been told. He questioned. He doubted. He came to his own conclusions. And they condemned him for it.

So did she, of course. Such a hypocrite. She'd never been as strong as he was. She returned to the fold and lost herself in her worship, buried her own doubts in among the prayers and the declarations and the hatred. After he had done so much to try to save her, to try to take her away from the madness, she had responded by trying to kill him on multiple occasions. And even after she'd seen the light and walked away from it all, her own pride and stubbornness had built a wall between them. For she was China Sorrows, and she would not apologise to anyone.

The truth was she'd lost her brother long before a Faceless One had torn him apart, and it had been her own doing. Now here she was, the last of her line, standing over his coffin, one of the few possessions left to her after Eliza Scorn's vendetta. She didn't even know why she was here. Loneliness, perhaps? She smiled at that. If there was anyone who deserved a lifetime of loneliness, surely it would be her. And there she was again, feeling sorry for herself. Such a luxury. She positively bathed in it these days.

She noticed a bit of mud on one polished riding boot, and put her foot up on her grandmother's coffin to wipe it off. Such a venomous creature her grandmother had been and, like all venomous creatures, most dangerous when dying. China could still feel those fingers round her throat and see that burning hatred in those eyes. Her grandmother's death hadn't been quick and hadn't been easy, but it had been a death, and that's all that mattered.

She left the crypt, put her riding hat back on, and the sound of motorbikes reached her. Frowning, she walked to the hedge. Beyond the twisted briars and tightly-packed leaves, she saw colour. Movement. Bikers on her land. Cold anger rose inside her. She walked to a gap in the hedge, looked over. Four of them, none of them wearing a helmet. Two average-sized males – one who looked like an accountant and one, the dark-haired, unshaven one, who was clearly the leader of the pack. The third man was big, with matted hair and huge arms. The woman had short spiky hair and a cruel laugh. These were not casual trespassers. These people were here for a reason.

The accountant looked around, his eyes locking on to hers. In that simple movement alone, China knew everything about him that she needed to.

Vampire.

She spun, ran for her horse. On the other side of the hedge, engines were gunned. Foot in the stirrup, the other leg swinging, she was in the saddle and away, the ground moving with that fast, smooth rhythm.

The bikers were in the field behind her. She pointed the horse straight ahead, gave it a squeeze and cleared the ditch. One of the bikers tried to follow and ended up flying through the air while his bike tumbled into the briars. The others swung around, looking for the gate. There was a shout, and they sped to the near corner.

China galloped for the tractor trail, followed it up along the field. Behind her, wheels spun and muck flew. One of the bikes broke away from the rest, caught up with her before the others. The rider reached into his jacket, and China glimpsed the butt of a gun. Keeping one hand on the reins, she ripped her riding hat off and swung it down into his face. Blood burst from his nose and the bike reared up and flipped. She didn't bother watching him fall.

The other bikes were gaining. She galloped for the tangled hedge straight ahead, and slid both hands down the horse's side, finding the patterns she'd slowly – and painlessly – carved into the skin. The patterns became suddenly hot, and began to glow.

Two massive, beautiful, electric-blue wings sprouted from the horse's sides and the bikers cursed and one of them crashed and the horse ran and leaped and lifted away from the ground, over the hedge, his great wings beating at the air. China hugged his neck as they flew, directing him across the fields and ditches. She looked back, saw the bikers turn, speeding back to the road.

She took the horse in low, slowing as they reached the yard, and the ground came up beneath them and all at once the fast rhythm of galloping hooves replaced the beat of wings. She ran her fingers over the patterns and the wings dissolved, leaving streaks in the air. She took hold of the reins, pulled them up and slid off the saddle, calling for assistance. She kissed the horse's neck and gave it a few heavy pats, then gave the reins to the stablehand and ran for her car. The engine roared, tyres spun, and she peeled out on to the road, the bikers right behind her.

27

MANTIS

When it came down to it, the Monster Hunters were really nice guys. Sure, Tanith was pretty certain they had orders to kill her and Sanguine if they stepped out of line, but apart from that things were going swimmingly. On the drive to the Midnight Hotel they joked and laughed, and only Sanguine was left out of the fun. He was sulking again.

They parked by the side of the road, and crept through the trees. Little by little the joking stopped, until finally all four of them were creeping silently.

Donegan held up a closed fist, then motioned to the rest of them to join him. Tanith moved low, dropping to the ground beside him. Sanguine lay on her other side.

Ahead of them was a clearing in the woods. At the edge of that clearing, in a wide circle, armed men and women stood guard. About thirty of them.

"Flip," whispered Gracious. "That is just flippin' great, that is. What are we meant to do now?"

Donegan looked at his watch. "Seven seconds till noon," he said. "Four. Three. Two. One."

In the clearing ahead, wooden beams sprouted from the ground, latched on to each other while bricks and concrete bloomed and grew walls and floors. Glass stretched in window frames and colour seeped into everything. The Midnight Hotel gave one final groan of growth, and settled into place. A moment later, the front door opened.

Sorcerers filed out, each with a duffel bag over their shoulder. A dozen collected in the open space before the hotel, and they kept coming. Two dozen. Three. When the flow finally stopped, there were maybe fifty men and women standing there, talking quietly among themselves. Before the door closed over, Tanith glimpsed Cleavers within. Fifty plus the thirty standing guard, plus however many were still inside...

"I think we may be slightly outnumbered," Donegan said softly. "Unless Gracious has any new invention on his person that will even the odds...?"

"Funny you should say that," Gracious responded, "because no, I don't. Unless you count a phone as a new invention. I vote we use that to call for reinforcements."

Tanith scanned the windows. "No reinforcements. They'd take too long, our forces are stretched thin as it is, and we are not going to ask for help. We were sent to do a job and that's what we're going to do."

"Four against eighty? We don't even know how many more there are inside."

She shook her head. "We don't have to fight them. That's not our primary objective. Ghastly said we're to deactivate the teleportation system to stop more of them coming. That's what we focus on."

"I can get us past them," Sanguine said, "but I'd probably be better going alone."

Donegan frowned. "That's uncharacteristically brave of you."

"Not at all. Lugging you idiots around would slow me down and get me killed. Where's the off switch?"

"Upstairs," Donegan said. "There's a clock on the wall. Press your hand against the face and turn it very slightly to the left. There'll be a click to tell you it's done."

"Sounds easy enough," said Tanith.

"Yes it does," said Sanguine. "Kiss for good luck?"

"Maybe later," said Gracious.

"How about a handshake?" asked Donegan.

"Ignore them," said Tanith, and pulled Sanguine in for a deep, long kiss. "Now go. But don't take any stupid chances."

"Me?" Sanguine said. "Never." And then he sank into the ground.

Tanith looked at the Monster Hunters. "If he can't get to the clock, any idea how we deal with this lot?"

"With great care," Donegan suggested.

"How about we run off shouting and they follow?" said Gracious. "Then, just when they think they've caught us, they fall into our trap."

"OK," said Tanith. "And the trap would be?"

"A big hole that we'd dug earlier and covered with branches."

Tanith frowned. "I thought you were meant to be smart."

Gracious frowned back at her. "Who told you that?"

"Gracious is book-smart," said Donegan. "He leaves the real-world thinking to people like you and me and small dogs that he meets."

"The innocent are often the wisest."

The sound of smashing glass whipped Tanith's eyes back to the hotel in time to see Sanguine falling from a top-floor window. The sorcerers below scattered and he landed in the clearing between them amid a hailstorm of glass shards. Tanith stared. Sanguine lay face down, and didn't move for the longest time. Then he coughed.

Moments later, the door opened. The sorcerer called Mantis emerged from the hotel, unfolding its body as it straightened in the open air. Tanith knew a little of the general's history. The same genderless species as Doctor Nye, its arms and legs were just as long but not quite as narrow. It stood at twice the height of any of the sorcerers around it, its skin pale and puckered and clumsily wrapped in something that looked like cellophane. Only its head was hidden, encased as it was in a helmet like an oversized gas mask. It looked like a giant insect as it peered down at Sanguine.

Mantis looked up suddenly, as if it had heard something. Tanith lowered herself further, holding her breath. She risked another peek, only breathing again when she saw the ground cracking and Sanguine sinking down into it. Mantis moved impossibly fast, its long fingers closing round Sanguine's ankle. It hauled him out of the ground, throwing him behind it. Sanguine smacked into the hotel wall and fell in a crumpled heap.

At Mantis's instruction, its soldiers tied a rope round Sanguine's ankles, looped the other end round a branch, and hoisted him up off the ground. He dangled there, unconscious.

Tanith observed the scene, and Donegan asked her, "Would you be opposed to just... running away?"

She wouldn't be. They didn't even have to call it running away. They could call it a strategic retreat or a withdrawal or a regrouping. But when Valkyrie and the others heard that Tanith had abandoned Sanguine to the enemy without even trying to get him back, they'd look at her and all their suspicions would be confirmed. In their eyes, she'd be the cold, inhuman psychopath that they couldn't trust. And a part of Tanith wanted them to trust her. She didn't know what part, and she didn't know where it was located, but it was there.

"We're not leaving him," she said. "He's my fiancé, and we're going to get him back."

"Any idea how?"

"That depends," she said. "Did you bring any guns with you?"

Tanith held her hands up high and announced herself loudly, so that no one would try to take her head off in surprise. The sorcerers parted for her and she walked into the clearing, and General Mantis peered down at her.

"Hello," she said. "I just want to talk."

Mantis's small yellow eyes were magnified by the lenses of its gas mask. "Are you turning yourself in?"

"Now why would I do that?"

Its voice was strangely accented, but not as high-pitched as Nye's. "Because you are wanted for the murder of Grand Mage Quintin Strom. As is Mr Sanguine."

Tanith smiled. "Billy-Ray just got me into the room. I was the one who cut his head off. But no, I'm not here to turn myself in. I'm here to negotiate for the release of my fiancé, the aforementioned Billy-Ray."

"And what do you have to negotiate with?"

"Information. I could be a double agent. I know all the Irish Sanctuary's secrets and plans."

"Tell us how to dismantle the shield and I will let Sanguine go."

"Ah, now *that* information, unfortunately, I do not possess. But anything else. Their favourite TV shows, breakfast cereals, anything."

"Give me the current location of the Dead Men."

Tanith winced. "I would if I could, but they didn't tell me where they were going. To be honest, they don't trust me a huge amount. I can't say I blame them. I mean, here I am, offering to be a double agent. That's not exactly trustworthy behaviour, now is it?"

"Do you have any information which could be useful to us?"

"Loads," Tanith said. "For example, you haven't even asked why we're here in the first place."

"I imagine you were tasked with stopping the hotel from being used as a transportation device."

"Oh. Yeah, OK."

206

"If you have nothing more to share..."

"Now just wait a second. Just let me think here, OK? Here, how about this? I'm not alone. I'm here with the Monster Hunters."

"Bane and O'Callahan?"

"You know them?"

Mantis nodded. "I've read their books."

"Then how about an exchange? You give me Billy-Ray, I give you Bane and O'Callahan. You can imprison them, kill them, get a photograph with them, whatever you want."

"You would betray your allies?"

"My loyalties are fluid."

"That is tempting," said Mantis. "The Monster Hunters could be a fly in the ointment. Left to their own devices, they could pose a credible threat to our operations."

"So we have a deal?"

"But you and Mr Sanguine would also pose a threat – and we already *have* both of you. Exchanging you for the Monster Hunters strikes me as somewhat illogical."

"I haven't finished negotiating yet."

"Yes you have."

"I've got some cash in my pocket."

"Place Miss Low under arrest."

A Cleaver made a move.

"If you take one step closer," said Tanith, "Bane and O'Callahan will open fire."

Mantis's small eyes blinked behind its mask. "You want me to believe they are close enough to be effective?"

"They don't have to be close," Tanith said. "You know their reputations. They're both top-class snipers. Right now they're each up a tree, with you and you alone in their scopes."

Mantis sounded amused. "A moment ago, you were about to betray them."

"That was a bluff."

"How do I know this is not also a bluff?"

"I guess we'll see, won't we?"

Mantis looked at her for a few seconds, then turned its head. "Mr Habergeon, if you wouldn't mind?"

Habergeon was a bearded man with a shotgun. He walked to the edge of the clearing, put the shotgun at his feet, and rolled his shoulders. Then he held up his hands. For a moment, nothing happened. A sudden jolt passed through his body and a shield of blue energy sprang up before him, high enough and wide enough to protect the hotel and everyone standing outside.

"Habergeon's force field will protect us all from pesky bullets," Mantis said to Tanith, motioning to a pair of Cleavers. They came forward, shackles open, and Tanith drew her sword. All around her, energy crackled and rounds were chambered.

"If your next move is a foolish one, you will die," said Mantis.

Tanith hesitated, then forced a smile on to her face, and let the Cleavers take her sword.

"An excellent decision," said Mantis. It turned to a man and woman. "Regis. Ashione. Take twenty sorcerers each and track down the Monster Hunters. Take no chances."

Regis and Ashione nodded and moved out, and Mantis turned back to Tanith. "This," it said, "is probably the most ill-advised rescue attempt I have ever witnessed."

"Funny," Tanith said, "I was just thinking the same thing."

28

THE STICK

They may have been flying on a commercial passenger plane, but of course they were flying First Class.

Skulduggery sat by the window, his hat pulled low and a scarf around his jaw. His façade needed to be conserved for when he really needed it, so the plan was to sit like this for the whole flight, pretending to be asleep. He'd succeeded admirably on the flight from Dublin to Paris. But now that they were on the second leg of their journey, Valkyrie's toes were tingling, the way they did when she was restless and wanted to run around and hit something. But she behaved, because she was a good girl.

Ghastly and Ravel sat across the aisle. Ghastly wore a similar disguise to Skulduggery to cover up his scars. They needed to be as inconspicuous as possible. It wasn't easy – not with Shudder glaring at everyone who came close and Saracen chatting up the stewardesses.

Valkyrie nudged Skulduggery. "I'm bored."

"I'm meditating," he murmured in reply.

"Do they show movies on this plane?"

"It's only two hours to France. No, they don't show movies."

A thought struck her. "What happens when we pass through the shield? Am I going to fall into a coma?"

"Would that I were so lucky."

"What?"

"The shield is designed to keep people out – not to keep people in. We'll be fine."

The captain came on over the speaker. She could make out every third word he said. None of it was very interesting. She waited till he finished and nudged Skulduggery again. "Want to talk about the case?"

"Our mystery man? What is there to talk about?"

She shrugged. "I was just wondering if you'd come up with any new theories you wanted to discuss. We usually use these quiet moments to talk about cases."

"But then they cease to be quiet moments."

"So you don't want to talk about the case. OK. Want to play I Spy?"

He turned his head to her. She could see her own reflection in his sunglasses. "You're worried, aren't you?"

"I'm not worried. I'm just..."

"Anxious."

"Anxious sounds worse than worried. I'm curious, that's all. Curious to find out what's going to happen."

"I'll tell you what's going to happen," he said. "We're going to land in Annecy, sneak by security, disabling any cameras as we go. Then we're going to hire or steal a large car and we're going to drive for about two hours."

"Sounds thrilling."

"And then we're going to leave the car, and walk."

"That's the bit I'm not looking forward to."

"A nice walk will do you good."

"We'll be walking through mountains, Saracen said. That's called rock climbing."

"It's called hillwalking. You'll be fine. After a few days of that—"

She gasped. "Days?"

"—we'll get to a town called Wolfsong or, as it is otherwise known, Chant le Loup. Here, we'll try to enlist some help to get us into the research facility further on."

"Where they know we're coming."

"Yes."

"And they're planning an ambush."

"Yes."

"And the only way we're going to get out of there is if the Australians and the Africans have secretly decided to help us."

"Exactly. So, as you can see, there is nothing to be either worried, anxious, or even curious about. It's all been sorted out."

"How about, instead of all that walking, you and me just fly there?"

"I'm afraid not. We're going to have to restrict our usage of magic to the minimum until we're in areas where it won't be noticed. The Supreme Council will have Sensitives scanning the world for unusual activity."

"Seriously? But... but what's the point of having magic if we can't do awesome things?"

"My thoughts exactly. But it won't be for long."

"Then... then will you give me a piggyback?"

"Absolutely not."

They landed in Annecy and had to wait ages for the doors to open. Private jets in private airfields were so much handier, and much less annoying. Once they deplaned, Saracen took the lead and guided them away from cops and civilians and airport staff. Skulduggery fried a camera lens and they jumped a few fences to land in an outdoor car park. Vex hot-wired a minibus and they drove for a little over two hours before pulling in to the side of the road.

Valkyrie hopped out and climbed up on to a rock to take in the view. A lake on one side, mountains on the other, and the sun overhead. France certainly was a pretty place to visit.

The Dead Men were changing out of their normal clothes. She was already wearing her combat gear – the black clothes Ghastly had made her were suitable for practically every occasion.

She saw Skulduggery's bleached-white bones and looked away immediately, then laughed at her own reaction.

Shudder walked by her, eyes on the compass in his hand. She heard chatter behind her and turned as the rest of the Dead Men approached.

Skulduggery wore black leather, old and scuffed and cracked. His boots were thick and heavy, steel-toed and polished to a gleam despite their age. On his left arm he wore a dull black metal gauntlet that travelled from wrist to shoulder, with a hinge-joint at the elbow. Instead of his gun resting in a shoulder holster, it was now slung low on his right thigh. On the other side of the belt there was a sword in a scabbard.

"Whoah," said Valkyrie.

He raised his head to her. "You didn't expect me to fight a war in a suit and tie, did you? These may not be as durable as the clothes you wear, but they're close."

She looked at the others, all of whom were kitted out in a similar fashion. "Is that what you wore during the war?"

"This," Skulduggery said, "and variations of it."

"You don't even have a hat."

He reached behind him with a gloved hand, pulled a hood over his skull. "Happy?"

"Over the moon. What's the armour thing?"

He pulled the hood back down, and held up his left arm. "In the olden days, mortals charged into battle with a sword in one hand and a shield in the other. For sorcerers, this didn't leave us any hands free to use magic, so we relied on these instead. It'll stop a Cleaver's scythe – which is exactly what we need it to do."

"Cool."

"I happen to have one in your size."

"No thanks."

He tilted his head.

"I was wearing a gauntlet in Cassandra's vision," she explained.

"But that was on your right hand," Skulduggery said, "and it covered no higher than your wrist. Even if you saw yourself wearing the exact same one I have for you, it means nothing. The future in Cassandra's vision will not be decided by the gauntlet you wear. If you refuse it, that future or one like it will still happen – you'll just be a little more vulnerable to attack. The clothes Ghastly made will protect you, but something like this is an added layer."

Valkyrie sighed. "Fine. I'll wear it. Is it cool?"

"It's very cool. It's pink, though."

"I'm not wearing it."

"It's a very cool shade of pink."

"Skulduggery... you're messing with me, aren't you?"

"Slightly."

"I hate you so much."

He left her for a moment, came back with a long bag. From this he drew her gauntlet – black like his own – and held it out while she slipped her left arm through. Once in place, the fastenings tightened till it was snug but not uncomfortable. She flexed her arm, testing the hinge. It moved with her, like a second skin. "Do I get a sword?" she asked.

"No," he said, "but I did get you this."

He reached into the bag, and took out a stick.

She looked at it. "What?"

"Did you really think I'd forgotten my promise to get you a stick for Christmas?"

"It's not Christmas."

"Happy birthday."

She took it from him. It was some kind of dark wood, a little over an inch thick and hexagonal in shape, with symbols carved into it. It was oddly cold in her hand.

"It's nice, isn't it?" Skulduggery said.

"It's a stick."

"It's a special stick."

"It's a stick."

"Well, yes, but it is, as I say, a special stick. The sharpest Cleaver blade couldn't cut through this. Probably. I've trained you in stick-fighting. Tanith trained you in staff-fighting. All you have to do to turn the stick into a stun baton is press your thumb against this symbol here."

He showed her, and she pressed, and the stick remained a stick.

"Hmm," said Skulduggery.

"It's broken," Valkyrie said.

"It does appear to be not working."

"You got me a broken stick for my birthday."

"A broken stick is still a stick."

"Which brings us back to the fact that you got me a stick for my birthday. I want a sword."

"You don't want a sword. Swords are sharp. Especially these swords. You'd lose a finger on these swords. There'd be no chance of you losing a finger on that stick. It's not sharp, for one thing. It doesn't work, for another. It's perfectly safe."

"I don't want a perfectly safe weapon. I want a dangerous weapon that hurts people."

He took the stick from her, rapped it against her head. She howled and he nodded.

"See? It hurts people."

She grabbed it off him, smacked it against his skull.

"Ow," he said.

"Not so funny now, is it?"

"Of course not. It's only funny when it happens to other people. I'd have thought that was obvious."

She went to hit him again and suddenly the sigils started glowing. "Woah."

"There you go," Skulduggery said. "On its first time out, it just needed a few moments to warm up. It recharges itself just by being in contact with your skin. The shock it delivers is enough to incapacitate an average-sized person. Don't worry, the effects aren't permanent. They'll wake up with a headache, nothing more."

"Well," she said grudgingly, "I suppose that's pretty cool. So where do I keep it? Do I get a scabbard or do I have to carry it around with me?"

"Neither," he said, taking something from his pocket. It was a small disc, no bigger than a contact lens. He motioned to her to turn round, then he pressed it into her jacket near her shoulder blade. "Think of this as a kind of magnet," he said. "Go on. Put the stick away."

She moved the stick over her shoulder and let go when she felt the pull. The stick stayed there, tight against her back. She reached for it, pulled it loose, and returned it to her back. It slapped in and didn't move. "Nice," she said.

Shudder came over. "We should start now if we want to make our first camp by nightfall," he said, and without waiting for a reply he moved off.

Valkyrie looked at Skulduggery. "Last chance to give me a piggyback."

"Sorry, Valkyrie. You're one of the Dead Men now, and no one ever said it was easy."

29

TANITH'S TRUE LOVE

The sounds of people talking drifted up from the floorboards, filling the dark room with the low murmur of half-formed words. Tanith sat on the ground, cuffed to the radiator. So much for her wonderful plan.

The worst thing about the shackles wasn't that they bit into her wrists or that they robbed her of her magic. The worst thing about them was that they kept her magic just out of reach, like an itch she couldn't scratch, or a sneeze that wouldn't come. It was so close, so eye-wateringly close, and yet she had no way of getting to it.

A shudder went through her body, and Tanith closed her eyes. She'd never been good with things like this.

She heard footsteps stop outside her door. There was a moment's hesitation, long enough for a decision to be made, and then the handle turned and a small, dark-haired woman stepped inside.

"Be still my beating heart," Tanith said.

Aurora Jane shut the door quietly behind her. The last time Tanith had seen the pretty American, they'd been fighting a horde of rage-zombies in the London Sanctuary. Aurora had been there with Vex and the others, trying to steal the last God-Killer weapon to use against Darquesse when Valkyrie finally accepted the inevitable and gave in. Tanith, naturally, had been there with her gang to destroy the weapons before that could happen. Good times.

"How you doing, Tanith?" Aurora asked. "Shackled to a radiator, huh?"

"So it would appear. So did you get lonely out there or something?"

Aurora gave a little smile. "Yeah, you go on flattering yourself, see where that gets you. Sanguine's awake, by the way. Still hanging upside down with three guns pointed at him. If he even looks like he's planning on escaping, they'll shoot him."

"He's been hanging upside down for hours," Tanith said. "I bet he's so numb he can't even feel his legs any more. Does that Habergeon guy still have the force field up?"

Aurora nodded. "I'm afraid the Monster Hunters won't be shooting anyone tonight."

Tanith shrugged. "Didn't expect them to. They don't even have any rifles."

A genuine smile from Aurora. The Monster Hunters had been on her side when they went after the God-Killers. "That sounds like them, all right. Regis and Ashione have been tracking them for hours, but O'Callahan and Bane know what they're doing. They won't be found if they don't want to be."

"So what's it like," Tanith asked, "to be going up against them after fighting by their side only a few weeks ago?"

That got to Aurora, even though she did her best to hide it. "You'd be the expert on fighting your friends, wouldn't you?"

"Ah, but I have a Remnant inside me," said Tanith. "I have an excuse. I'm surprised to see you, actually. How did you even get a place in Mantis's army after what you did?"

"You make it sound so sordid. All I did was join a few friends to try and make the world a safer place."

"A few friends meaning Vex and Rue and the Monster Hunters out there. The enemy, in other words."

"They weren't the enemy a few weeks ago. At least not officially." Aurora went to the window, looked out. "But the Supreme Council might not entirely trust me, if that's what you're asking."

"Yet you signed up for the war anyway."

"Someone sensible had to."

"And now you're here, fighting against your friends."

"I am American, in case you'd forgotten, and I have more American friends than I do Irish."

"Yeah... but the Irish aren't the ones picking the fight, are they?"

Aurora turned to her. "If you didn't have a Remnant inside your head, you could take the moral high ground. As it is, you're not going to make me feel bad, so don't bother trying."

"I might not remember what guilt feels like, but I remember how it looks. And your face, Aurora my pretty, is a guilty face."

Aurora looked at her and didn't say anything for a while. Then she came over, hunkered down in front of her. If she had wanted, Tanith could have kicked her right in the face. Aurora knew that. She didn't care.

"If it was just you and Sanguine," she said, "I'd let you rot in shackles and leave him to be shot the moment he tried to run. But Gracious and Donegan are out there, and they're stupid enough to try to rescue you, and Mantis is just too good and too smart to let that happen. So, when they come for you, they'll probably die."

"So I'll ask you again. Why are you here, Aurora?"

"Wipe that smirk off your face and I'll tell you."

"Consider it wiped."

Aurora sighed. "I'm going to help you escape."

"About time you got to the point."

"I'm assuming you sent your boyfriend in to disable the hotel's transportation system, right? Do you know if he succeeded?"

"Unfortunately, he didn't get the chance to tell me."

"We have fifteen minutes until midnight. If the hotel stays where it is, Mantis will start questioning both of you to figure out how to reverse what you did. If that happens, I won't be able to get to you."

"So take these shackles off, give me my sword, and let me scram before that happens."

"And how are you going to get to Sanguine?"

"I need a diversion," Tanith said. She frowned, then brightened. "I know, I'll chop your head off and throw you from the roof. That's worked before."

"Amazingly, I'm not too keen on that idea."

"Then what do you suggest, Aurora?"

"You take my coat, pretend to be me. I'll tell Mantis I was overpowered. Meanwhile, you get to Sanguine and escape."

"I prefer my plan. In your plan I don't get to decapitate anyone, and it's a Tuesday. Tuesday is decapitation day."

"Are you going to do this or not?"

"Fine," Tanith said, holding out her hands so that Aurora could undo the shackles. "What about my sword?"

"You're pretending to be me. I don't carry a sword."

Tanith stood up, her hands free. "Maybe you could start. I'm not leaving without my sword."

"It won't be much of a disguise if—"

"I'll leave Billy-Ray before I leave my sword."

"Fine," Aurora said irritably. "You get Sanguine free, I'll see what I can do about getting you your sword."

Tanith smiled. "See? Now we have a compromise that suits everyone."

Sanguine's sunglasses and straight razor were on the ground beneath him. The three sorcerers around him were clearly bored, but didn't dare take their eyes off their captive as he hung there. Their guns didn't waver. Their fingers were held against the trigger guards, in case a twitch ended his life prematurely. Professionals.

Tanith took in all this with one glance. She had Aurora's hood pulled up to hide her face. So far, things were going well. She mingled with the enemy soldiers and kept her head down. They chatted and joked and didn't pay her any attention. Habergeon's force field was now a dome that covered the entire hotel. He sat cross-legged on the ground with his open hands resting on his knees, and he yawned. Such a useful power, but such a boring one.

Somewhere out there, in the trees, Bane and O'Callahan were being hunted. She hoped they were staying close to the rendezvous point. The only thing worse than coming back without Sanguine would be coming back without the Monster Hunters.

As she casually made her way over to her fiancé, she passed sorcerers glancing at their watches. Only seconds left. She skirted round a man softly strumming his guitar, got to within five paces of the tree from which the Texan hung, and midnight struck. When the hotel didn't disappear, all heads turned to Sanguine.

Tanith seized her opportunity. She barged past the guards and kicked Sanguine in the gut. "What did you do?" she snarled in her best American accent as he swung, gasping. "Tell us how to fix it!"

"Easy there," one of the sorcerers said, putting a hand on her shoulder.

Tanith shrugged it off, careful to keep her back to them all, and then the front door of the hotel burst open and Aurora Jane ran out, Tanith's sword in her hands, Mantis right behind her.

"Seize Miss Jane," Mantis announced, "and secure the prisoner."

Tanith grabbed the straight razor, flicking it open as she whirled. She kicked the sorcerer who'd laid his hand on her while the straight razor sliced through the rope. Sanguine crashed to the ground, Tanith dodged an energy stream, and Sanguine's hand closed round her ankle and she let herself be pulled down into the cold and the black.

"I was beginning to think you'd forgotten about me," he said once the rumbling had stopped.

"Aurora Jane," she said immediately. "She helped us. We have to help her."

She couldn't see his face, but she could imagine his expression.

"Seriously? Darlin', my legs are numb and I am quite light-headed. I need a few minutes to stay down here and get my bearings."

"Billy-Ray, she's got my sword. I am not leaving here without my sword."

"Sometimes I think you love that sword more than you love me."

Tanith said nothing.

He grabbed her, pulled her close, and the earth shifted and rumbled around them and they were moving again, and then there was a sliver of light above. She saw stars, and legs, and Sanguine's hand reaching up, and then the stars were blocked from view and they were going down again, into the cold.

"Aurora," Tanith said loudly, "don't panic. It's just us."

From the darkness right beside her, Aurora's voice. "Mantis found me," she said, speaking quickly. "I went to get your sword and Mantis found me. I said I just wanted a look at it. I guess I'm not a very good liar. I got it, though. Your sword. Got it."

"Aurora," Tanith said, "are you doing OK?"

A laugh, as sharp as it was abrupt. "A bit claustrophobic. Just a tad. A smidge. Trying not to panic, that's all. So, looks like I'll be defecting, then. Yay for me. OK. I'm going to stop talking now."

"Billy-Ray," Tanith said, "get us back to the car. Bane and O'Callahan should be waiting there for us."

They picked up speed. The rumbling got even louder. Tanith didn't mind. They'd succeeded. They'd successfully cut off the Supreme Council's only way to transport troops into the country. She grinned. Mission accomplished. This would *have* to prove to Valkyrie that Tanith was one of the good guys.

30

DEAD MEN'S TALES

Valkyrie had never noticed this before, but walking was really, incredibly boring.

She'd watched those *Lord of the Rings* films where they all went walking up and down mountains and it seemed so adventurous and purposeful, and they didn't look too tired and no one really complained and that Aragorn guy really looked sexy with his stubble and his long hair and what had she just been thinking about? Beards? *Lord of the Rings?*

Walking, that was it. Walking and boredom.

God, she was bored.

"I'm bored," she said.

"We know," said Skulduggery.

"This looked a lot more fun on *Lord of the Rings*."

"So you've said."

Dexter Vex jumped up on a rocky outcrop and looked at the mountains that surrounded them. "Check out this view. I mean, seriously. How could you ever get tired of this view?"

"I've managed it," Valkyrie said, passing him with her head down. "It's the same view we had this morning. The same view we had yesterday. I bet it's the same view we'll have this evening."

Vex jumped down, walked beside her. "You're just grumpy."

"I'm not *just* grumpy. There is no *just* here. I am grumpy on an epic scale. I'm used to driving around in Bentleys and flying through the air. This walking thing is... silly."

"I'd have to agree with that," said Saracen from up ahead, shifting his bag on his back. "I'm evidently not as young as I used to be."

"You mean you're not as *fit* as you used to be," Ravel said.

"Fitness has nothing to do with the soreness of my feet or the ache in my legs."

"You've been spoiled," said Shudder. "Too much soft living. You used to be tough."

Saracen frowned. "I did? When?"

Shudder looked at Valkyrie. "He jokes. They all do. But Saracen is one of the strongest men I have ever had the honour of knowing. We were in Siberia—"

"Not this story again," Saracen said, visibly squirming.

"Shut up," said Shudder. "We were in Siberia. Our mission was to assassinate a man so terrible his own soldiers called him the Butcher. We tried, and we failed. We were forced to run, and got separated. When we regrouped, Saracen was missing. We waited at the rendezvous point. Nothing. The Teleporter came to take us home – we didn't go. Our friend had been captured by the Butcher. We had to go back for him."

"Can we just stop the story there?" Saracen asked. "Leave it on a cliffhanger?"

"Nonsense," Shudder replied. "Valkyrie should know the calibre of the people she now serves with. The Butcher had him for three days, Valkyrie. No one endured the Butcher's interrogations for more than twenty-four hours. But, not only did Saracen endure, he found a way to escape. When we found him, he had tracked the Butcher back to his home, had subdued his wife and was waiting there for the Butcher to return. We found him, convinced him to leave with us that very night. He was almost reluctant, Valkyrie. He didn't care that the Butcher now had a dozen of his best soldiers around him at all times – he wanted to stay and see the job through to the end. That is the kind of man Saracen Rue is."

Vex was grinning. "Don't you think you should tell him?"

"Tell me what?" Shudder asked.

Saracen made a face. "Anton... the thing is, you love that story. You do. Every time you tell it, you... you just get all proud. And that's a lovely thing to see. But the story isn't the whole, entire, actual truth of what actually, truthfully, entirely... happened."

"I don't understand," Shudder said.

"The Butcher didn't capture me," said Saracen. "I never ran when the alarm was raised. I'd twisted my ankle, remember? So, while you guys took off, I hid. And, purely by coincidence, I hid in the Butcher's own cellar."

Shudder frowned. "But... but you subdued his wife..."

"Subdue is one word for it," Ravel chimed in. "Seduce is another."

Shudder stopped walking. "What?"

"She was really pretty!" Saracen said. "And she wasn't happy married to *him*. How could she be? He was ninety per cent hair."

"You spent three days with his *wife*?"

"While he was out hunting you guys, yeah. It was the safest place to be while my ankle healed. The last place he'd think to look."

Shudder turned to the other Dead Men. "And you all knew about this?"

"We didn't want to spoil the story you'd concocted," Ghastly said. "It was really good."

"Unbelievable," Shudder said, and walked on.

"Anton," said Saracen, trailing behind him. "Anton, come on."

"I used to be proud of you."

"You can still be proud of me. I've done other tough stuff. Remember going up against Vengeous in Leeds? What about Norwich? They were some tough times. Remember the psycho sisters? What were their names? Cerys and Aspen, right? They were a handful."

"Did you seduce them, too?" Shudder asked, not slowing down.

"No!" Saracen said. "Well, not at the same time..."

"I will never look at you in the same way again."

"Ah, come on."

"Anton," said Ravel, "it's really not that big a deal..."

"A man I thought I knew," said Shudder, "a man I thought of as a friend, has been letting me believe stories about him that were mere fabrications. How did you expect me to react to this, Erskine?"

Everyone stopped and looked at him.

And then he grunted. "See? I can make jokes, too."

Saracen stared. "You were joking?"

"Of course. That story may not have been true, but you are no less a worthy friend in my eyes. I have seen you in action. I have seen you rise to the occasion when lesser men would crumble. The corpse attack, for instance."

"Corpse attack?" said Valkyrie. "What was that?"

"Valkyrie doesn't need to hear this story," Skulduggery said, and they all started walking again.

"Nonsense," said Shudder. "She needs to hear every story. She's one of us now."

"The only reason you don't want this story told is because you're not in it," Vex said. Skulduggery didn't answer.

"We were in Denmark," said Saracen, "waiting for the boat to take us home. There were about thirty others with us. We'd been fighting for weeks while Quintin Strom and his lot kept Mevolent busy on the other side of the world. The last we'd heard, Vengeous was injured and we knew that Serpine was unlikely to make the trip out to face us, so were pretty confident that we'd get home without any extra hassle."

"But we hadn't heard anything about where Lord Vile happened to be," said Ghastly.

A Lord Vile story. No wonder Skulduggery hadn't wanted it told.

"So there we were," Saracen continued, "huddled round the various campfires, swapping stories, singing songs. We hadn't lost one single soldier in the last few weeks. Plenty injured, sure, but no fatalities. We were feeling pretty good about ourselves. Feeling pretty unstoppable."

"Then we found out what unstoppable really was," Ravel muttered.

"We looked around and Lord Vile was standing right there," said Saracen, "right in the middle of the camp. The sentries were dead, though we didn't know that yet. He'd killed them all without making a sound. Easy pickings, for someone like him."

"We attacked," Vex said. "Threw everything at him. He killed anyone who got too close. Larrikin was hurt pretty bad, but finally Anton here got past his defences – that Gist of his sure is persistent – and Vile disappeared. He'd had enough, he'd got bored, he didn't like it when the fight got a little fairer... whatever the reason, he left."

"He killed twelve people," Saracen said. "Those shadows of his just sliced them apart. So we gathered up their remains, by morning they were buried, and we dug in and prepared for his return. The boat was still three days away, and he was out there."

"So the sun went down," Ravel said, picking up the story. "We formed a perimeter. No one was singing any songs that night, believe me. Hours went by. The breeze rustled leaves, owls hooted, animals skittered by in the undergrowth... I remember every single sound from that night, because every single one of them stopped my heart. But nothing happened. Morning came. Some of the soldiers started to believe that Vile had run off, that maybe Anton had hurt him more than we'd realised."

"I hadn't," said Shudder. "I told them I hadn't. They wouldn't listen."

"Night came again," Saracen said. "Again, we formed a

perimeter. Again, every sound made us jump. Then we heard the voices. Voices of the people we'd buried, calling out to us, begging for help."

Ravel gave Valkyrie a half-smile. "We don't spook easily. We'd faced dark sorcerers and vampires and monsters of all descriptions. Ghosts didn't scare us. Most ghosts can't even hurt you. But those voices... They kept calling to us. All night. We had to stop people from leaving the camp to go and help.

"By morning, our nerves were in tatters. As soon as it was light, a group of us went out. The graves were empty."

"We had one more night to go," Ghastly said. "So we dug ourselves in one final time, and the sun went down. For a few hours, there was nothing. Then there was movement, all around the camp. People, just standing there in the darkness, watching us. The people we'd buried."

Valkyrie frowned. "Zombies?"

"Of a sort," said Vex. "But not the decomposing kind. Our friends had been... infected. When Vile killed them, we figured he'd left behind some little shard of Necromancer magic. Remember, some of these soldiers had been sliced to bits, but here they were, whole again, staring at us. And then they attacked."

"We were down to ten men when the sun came up," Ghastly said. "Whatever these things were, they could only live at night. At dawn, they fell apart. We gathered them, put them with the bodies of the men and women they'd killed, and we burned them all. A few hours later, our boat came and we got the hell out of there."

"If you can survive three nights like that," said Shudder, "then that is all I will ever need to know about you."

"Pick up the pace," said Skulduggery from up ahead. "We need to cover more ground before setting up camp."

Valkyrie watched him as they walked. She knew what it was like to hear people talk about you without them even realising they were doing so. Whenever anyone mentioned Darquesse, she found herself shrinking inside. She tried not to imagine their disgust, their horror, if they ever found out that Darquesse was who she'd become if she ever gave in to the voice in her head, even for a moment.

Was Skulduggery the same? Did Lord Vile whisper to him when things got quiet? Did he have to fight the call of that black shadow-armour like she had to fight against Darquesse's sheer unbridled power? Valkyrie didn't even know where Skulduggery kept the armour any more. He'd told her it was locked in a case and hidden away. He told her it was secure. It was caged. He acted so casual about it, like giving it up wasn't a big deal, like the power wasn't addictive.

Of course, maybe, for him, it wasn't. Or maybe his disgust at himself for the things he'd done, the people he'd killed, during those five years as Vile was so overwhelming that it cancelled any addiction he might have felt. That was a possibility. But Valkyrie didn't believe it.

She believed he was like her. He had a terrible secret, a secret that would cause his friends to turn on him in an instant, but it was a secret that he wanted to keep alive. She believed that the darkness, the power, the freedom, bubbling away beneath the surface, kept him going when nothing else would. Because all he had to do was give in, let it take over, and all the guilt and the shame and the pain would go away forever.

She believed he was like her because she needed to believe that. If he wasn't like her, if she was wrong, then she was alone.

And there was no one who could save her.

Valkyrie sat close to the fire, gloved hands out to catch the warmth. The rest of the Dead Men huddled in from the cold night, except for Skulduggery, who sat cross-legged on the ground without any need for heat.

She looked at each of them in turn, these men who wore their age in their eyes. Hardened men, veterans of war, warriors and killers and heroes. And villains, too, she supposed. No such thing as a true hero, not where war is concerned. Not where people are concerned. For years she had held Skulduggery himself in that high regard – he was her hero. He still was, in many respects. To have gone through everything he'd gone through, to have done the things he'd done, and to emerge on the other side as the man he was... that was pretty damn heroic. But those things he'd done when he'd given in to the darkness, when he'd surrendered to his own despair... those things could never be forgotten. Never be forgiven. She knew that better than most.

"How did this start?" she asked, breaking the silence. "The Dead Men, I mean? Who put you together?"

"No one," said Skulduggery. "We just found each other. That's what happens when people try to kill you – you form attachments. But when the war broke out, I was already friends with Ghastly and Hopeless."

"And Hopeless brought me in," said Ravel.

Ghastly nodded. "It was the four of us to begin with. We were soldiers like everyone else, fighting the good fight, trying not to get killed..."

"Some of us were more successful at that than others," Skulduggery put in. "After Serpine killed me, when I came back, I was the miracle soldier. Not even death could stop me, they said."

Vex smiled. "I heard stories about him, how he rose from the dead to lead us against Mevolent, how the war was going to be over within weeks. That didn't exactly happen. When I finally got to meet the miracle soldier, the living skeleton, I was so excited. I was expecting blazing fireballs for eyes and all this magic I'd never seen before. What I got instead was... him."

Skulduggery tilted his head. "Glad I could disappoint."

"We joined up a little while after Dexter," Saracen said, motioning to himself and Shudder. "I impressed them by attacking an entire battalion of Mevolent's troops on my own."

"You slipped," said Shudder.

"Stop saying that. I did not slip."

"I was there. You slipped and fell down the hill and rolled into their camp."

"Aggressively. I rolled *aggressively* into their camp."

"I had to save you."

"Why do you always say it like that? Like it was a chore? I was very dizzy. I probably had a concussion. However it happened, whatever the exact details were, it was a very brave thing for me to do and because of it we met up with these fine people you see before you, Valkyrie, and we became the squad of which you are now part."

"It didn't become official until Meritorious asked for volunteers to undertake a suicide mission," Skulduggery said, the orange light from the fire bouncing off his skull. "My hand was the first hand raised."

"Mine was the second," said Ghastly. "I thought he had a plan."

"I really didn't," said Skulduggery.

"I didn't know that at the time," Ghastly admitted.

"I just want it made clear that I did not volunteer for that mission," Saracen said. "I was yawning. That raised arm was me stretching. But they made me go anyway."

"By the end of it," Vex said, "Meritorious had seven volunteers. They started calling us the Dead Men when they thought we were out of earshot. No one expected us to come back."

"And we came back," said Ravel. "That's when they started calling us the Dead Men to our faces. After that, we sort of developed a reputation for undertaking impossible missions and making it out alive. There were some injuries along the way, of course. When I was recovering, Larrikin took my place. And when Skulduggery went on his little walkabout, when none of us knew if we were alive or dead, Larrikin stepped in again."

"And then when Hopeless died," Ghastly said quietly, "Larrikin became a permanent member of the squad."

"Until Serpine killed him," said Vex.

"And a few months later, Mevolent was killed," said Skulduggery. "And a few months after that, the war was over, and the Dead Men officially disbanded. We never thought we'd be needed again."

"And here we are," Saracen muttered.

"Strike from the shadows," Vex said.

"Disappear into darkness," finished Ghastly.

Silence followed, until Ravel said, "We should probably sleep. Big day tomorrow."

31

WOLFSONG

Valkyrie woke the next morning, ate a surprisingly hearty breakfast, and they set off. They stopped a few hours later for food, and almost immediately upon starting out again they came across a trail. They followed it to a larger trail which Skulduggery insisted on calling a road. They almost lost this road multiple times as long grasses threatened to swallow it. It was getting dark by this stage. A vote was taken – to set up camp or continue walking. Six to one. They kept walking.

The fog came from nowhere, blotting out the stars in the night sky. Valkyrie frowned. She no longer felt the eddying currents of air against her skin.

Ghastly snapped his fingers. Nothing happened. "Either we've stepped into a huge binding circle," he said, "or this fog has just dampened our magic."

The Dead Men turned, facing out, expecting an attack. Only Skulduggery remained calm.

"We're here," he said, as he pulled up his hood.

They were on the edge of Wolfsong and they hadn't even known it. It was an old town, stuck out here in the middle of nowhere, lit up with flickering torches. There were sigils on the outer walls, barely noticeable through the fog, and friendly faces on the people within. They didn't look like the type of people who were about to spring an attack. Skulduggery and the others immediately switched to speaking French, and Valkyrie smiled and nodded and did her best to understand what was being said. In the end she gave up and just focused on smiling and nodding.

They were directed to a tavern, and they walked in and Valkyrie's stomach started rumbling. It had been hours since she'd last eaten, and the smell of freshly cooked food was overwhelming. They took a table by the wall and ordered food and drink, and as they ate the tavern owner came over, an Englishman with a neat beard.

"Hello there," he said in English. "Not often we have tourists in our little hamlet. Name's Griff, pleased to make your acquaintance. You've been here before, have you?"

"A hundred years ago or more," said Vex. "Not much has changed."

Griff laughed. "Not much needed to. You can keep the outside world, thank you very much. We're happy where we are. And why wouldn't we be?" He looked closer at Skulduggery, peering beneath the hood. "Well, there's something you don't see every day. You must be that skeleton fellow I've heard so much about— Skulduggery someone. Welcome to Wolfsong, sir."

"Thank you," said Skulduggery. "Do you get fogs like this often?"

Griff shrugged. "It visits every day as the sun wanes, and takes our magic. The price we pay, I suppose, for living in peace. The first time it came, it brought with it wraiths."

Skulduggery tilted his head. "Is that so?"

Griff leaned in to Valkyrie, his eyes narrowing mischievously. "You ever seen a wraith, young lady? Terrible creatures to behold. Warlocks command them. I speak not one word of a lie, ask your friends. Once upon a time, they were men and women, but after the Warlocks got through with them, they shed their humanity

234

like a snake sheds its skin. Pale and terrible, they are. You hold your finger a hair's breadth from their skin and your finger is likely to freeze. But you touch their skin and it's like a heat you've never felt. They burn to the touch, and can't be killed. They get their hands on you and it's death, and a hollow kind of death, at that. They leave your ghost wrapped up in eternal torment, so the legend goes."

"Why did they attack?" asked Vex.

Griff sat back, gave another shrug. "Warlocks commanded it. Don't know why. They have a settlement, up in the mountains to the east. Or they had. Don't know if it's still there. Some of our boys disappeared one night. Their friends said they'd gone to creep up on the Warlock camp, to see if the stories of their unnatural practices were true. A week later, they still hadn't returned. There was talk of going up after them.

"Then the fog came, and the wraiths. They walked through the streets, dozens of them. Silent. They killed so many."

"How did you stop them?" Valkyrie asked.

"We didn't," said Griff. "Those who weren't killed ran until they were clear of the fog. It cleared by morning, and took the wraiths with it."

"And they never came back?"

"They haven't as of yet."

Valkyrie frowned. "But how can you feel safe here? How can you sleep? How many locks can you have on a door?"

"Locked doors mean little to wraiths," said Griff, smiling a little. "But we learned our lesson. We don't go into the mountains any more. We don't trouble them, they won't trouble us."

"So you haven't noticed anything strange?" Skulduggery asked. "The Warlocks haven't been active recently?"

"We haven't noticed anything at all," Griff said. "They might still be up there, or they might not. We don't even look in that direction any more."

"What would you say if I told you there have been reports of increased Warlock activity at all their known settlements around the world?"

"I wouldn't know about any of that. Is that why you're here, then? To see if they're stretching their legs? Because while you may be guests here, and we treat our guests well, we cannot allow you to go up there."

"We're not planning on it," Ravel said quickly. "That's not why we're here. How much contact have you had with the outside world?"

"Little," Griff admitted.

"Then you have heard nothing about the war?"

"Another one?"

"Sadly, yes, but this one is different. It's a war between Sanctuaries. Wolfsong is a small town, but it's a town with a proud history. You have defied the Paris Sanctuary's rulings and you have prospered here, alone and isolated. You seized your independence and you clung to it, fought for it, even when they tried to take this town by force."

"I remember all that," said Griff. "I was here when it happened. Now I hope you'll excuse me, because I don't speak all flowery like you Sanctuary mages, but if you want to ask a question, ask a question. Leave the flowers for the gardens."

"Well said," muttered Shudder.

"Very well," said Ravel. "Griff, we want Wolfsong to lend its strength to the Irish Sanctuary. In return, we will provide you with assistance and resources should you need them."

Griff grunted, and stroked his beard. "It seems to me that Ireland is a long way away."

"This is true. But the alternative is to add your strength to the Sanctuary in Paris, and fight against us."

"No," said Griff, "the alternative is not to add our strength to anyone. Why would we get involved in your disagreements? It's got precious little to do with us."

"War has a tendency to spread."

"Especially if invited. You all seem like nice people, but we're not nearly as strong as we were a hundred years ago. The wraiths took our strongest fighters. We wouldn't add much to your forces."

"On the contrary, you would be an invaluable asset. The more allies behind enemy lines we can secure, the greater our chances of success become. Wolfsong won't be the only one who will rally to our cause."

"How many so far?"

"I'm sorry?"

"How many towns have you rallied to your cause?"

Ravel smiled. "You'll forgive me for withholding certain details, I'm sure. Let's just say it's more than a few."

It was a barefaced lie, and Valkyrie wasn't sure that Griff was buying it.

"In that case," Griff said, "why would you need us? It sounds like you have things well in hand."

"There's always room for more."

"But not us, I'm afraid. Not with Mandat's outpost so close. They've left us alone for all this time because we have not offered them any reason to interfere. Grand Mage Mandat is not a man to cross – he's quick to anger and slow to forgive. I'm sorry, our answer must be no."

Skulduggery leaned closer. "Then we need a way into the research facility. We need to get in undetected."

Griff laughed. "And you lower your voice to tell me this? Walls have ears, is that it? You have nothing to fear in Wolfsong, my friend. Secrets do not pass beyond the boundaries of our town, you can be assured of that."

"I wish I could be as trusting as you."

"Or, if you prefer to stay suspicious, I can do the trusting for all of us." Griff laughed again. "Nobody gets close to that facility without Mandat's people being aware of it. The approach is littered with sensors and alarms. To accomplish what you need to accomplish, you would need a guide who has been there and back."

"Do you know of any such guide?"

"No I do not, and if I did I wouldn't tell you. Mandat rules his Sanctuary with a heavy fist. So unlike the days of Grand Mage Trebuchet."

"I knew Trebuchet," said Ravel. "He was a good man. Fair. Just."

"Too fair," said Griff. "Too just. Honourable men are easy targets to people like Mandat. They can never begin to comprehend the depths to which their opponents will stoop to seize power for themselves. It was a sad day for the French Sanctuary when Mandat became Grand Mage and Trebuchet was sent out into the wilds. Well, I say 'wilds'. He didn't go very far, if I'm being honest."

"He's still alive?" Ravel asked. "He might know a way into the facility. Griff, please, if you can't help us, maybe he can. Where is he?"

Griff stood, hitched his trousers a little, and nodded behind them. "He's over there," he said, and walked away.

The man he'd nodded to sat in a corner with his head down. Grey hair, cut tight. Silvery stubble. A hard face.

"He looks grumpy," Vex said. "Objectionable. You really think you can get him to help?"

"Don't worry," said Ravel, "I'll convince him."

They approached Trebuchet's table, stood there until the old man raised his eyes.

"You shouldn't have come here," Trebuchet said.

"We had to," said Ravel. "We need your help."

"My answer is no. Now leave."

"Do you remember me?"

"Of course I remember you, Mr Ravel. There is precious little I forget, no matter how much I might want to. My answer is still no."

"You don't even know what I'm going to ask."

"It doesn't matter. When I left the Sanctuary, I left it all behind. Everything and everyone I care about is in Wolfsong. The rest of the world can burn and it would not bother me in the slightest. Leave me now."

Ravel hesitated, and they all walked back to their table.

"I will never doubt you again," said Vex.

"Shut up."

Griff rented them rooms, and Valkyrie fell asleep on a soft mattress and was grateful for it. She awoke with a rumbling belly, like she hadn't eaten in days. It was still dark outside, but she dressed and went downstairs to find the rest of the Dead Men tucking into a generous breakfast – all except Skulduggery, who only joined them after she had started eating.

"We should get going," he said.

"Why do you have your hood up?" Valkyrie asked with a mouth full of sausage. "This is a sorcerer town."

"Yet as a walking skeleton I am still somewhat unique," he replied. "People tend to stare at things they are not used to. Now stop talking and eat faster. We have things to do."

They left Wolfsong and the fog started to clear, and dawn streaked across the horizon. Valkyrie looked back at the town, finding it immensely creepy the way the fog just enveloped it completely. She would have liked to stay to see it in the daytime, when the fog retreated, but Skulduggery seemed to be working to his own mysterious schedule.

Two hours later, Valkyrie's belly was rumbling again.

"I'm starving," she said.

"Me too," said Saracen.

"Same here," said Ravel. "It's like I never ate breakfast."

Skulduggery stopped, looked at them all. "What about the rest of you? Are you hungry?"

Vex and Ghastly nodded.

"Complaining is for little girls," Shudder said. "With no offence to little girls. But yes, I am hungry."

"What's the problem?" asked Ghastly.

"I didn't see any livestock," Skulduggery said. "I didn't see any crops. Where are they getting their food? Wolfsong has always been self-sufficient."

"Maybe they've started to trade," Ravel said. "Or maybe they keep their livestock and crops somewhere else. Why is it such a big deal?"

"I don't know. Something's been gnawing at me since we left."

Valkyrie sagged. "Please don't tell me we have to go back."

"I'm not saying that. OK, yes, I'm saying that, but didn't Trebuchet seem scared to you?"

"He seemed grumpy. Not as grumpy as I am right now, but grumpy." Valkyrie looked back the way they'd come. "You want us to walk up that hill? We just walked down it, and now we have to walk back up it? Why couldn't we have just stayed where we were? Why couldn't we have had this conversation while we were up there?"

Skulduggery started walking back. The others did likewise. Valkyrie glowered, and plodded after them.

They followed the trail through the trees, and by the time they emerged on to the open fields the conversation had died.

Valkyrie's feet were sore again, and she was tired and starving. No one else was complaining, though, not even Saracen, so she kept her mouth shut, but when the others stopped beside some old ruins, she gladly sat on a moss-covered slab of stone that jutted from the earth like a giant's broken tooth. She jammed her fingers into her pockets and buried her chin in her chest. A cold wind blew from the mountains in the distance and tried to sneak past her collar to send icy fingers trickling down her spine. The sky was grey and the mud was brown and the ruins were old. Timbers rotted where roofs had caved in. Stone walls crumbled and pitched at odd angles, sinking into the muck. She hadn't even noticed these ruins the first time they'd passed.

She looked round at Skulduggery, Vex and Saracen as they picked their way slowly through the remains of what had once been a town. Ravel, Ghastly and Shudder stood to one side. They spoke a few quiet words to each other, then stopped and looked solemn. Valkyrie didn't want to ask a question. Asking a question would lead to an answer, which could lead to a decision, which could lead to more walking. She was quite happy to sit on this slab and rest her feet. But, while she didn't want to ask a question, there was a question that needed to be asked.

Scowling at herself, she lifted her head. "Why have we stopped? Wolfsong can't be that far away now. What's so interesting about a bunch of old ruins?"

Surprisingly, it was Shudder who came forward. He stood beside her, the wind playing with his coat, but didn't look at her. Instead, his eyes glanced at the darkening sky, then settled on the horizon.

"Night falls early here," he said. "And the fog is coming. See it? It's rolling down from the mountains. We don't have long."

Despite Ghastly's wonderful garments, Valkyrie shivered, and reluctantly got to her feet. "Then we'd better hurry, right?"

"Hurry?" Shudder said. "To where?"

"To Wolfsong. That's where we're going, isn't it?"

Shudder looked at her, his eyes gentle. "Valkyrie," he said, "do you not think we should have come to Wolfsong by now?"

"What do you mean? It's up the road."

"No, Valkyrie. We are in Wolfsong. This is all that remains of the town the wraiths destroyed, one hundred years ago."

Valkyrie paled. "No. We were in Wolfsong this morning. Wolfsong is a proper town. It has proper houses and people in it. We talked to them. We talked to Griff. We slept in its beds. We had *breakfast*."

"We thought we had, but our bellies were fooled along with our eyes and ears. The building we were in is over there. It's nothing but a few stones and dead grasses."

"But Griff—"

"Griff is long dead, Valkyrie. They all are."

32

THE GHOST TOWN

The fog rolled in, down from the mountains, and they watched it come. When it hit the ruins, it rebuilt them, walls fading up from nothing, roofs and windows and doors becoming solid as the fog snaked through the narrow streets, and it brought with it people.

At first they were whispers and shadows, half-glimpsed out of the corner of Valkyrie's eye, and then they were solid, and passing in front of her, smiling and laughing and chatting to each other. When the cold fog covered the whole town, she felt her magic dampen, and she glanced at Skulduggery.

"They don't look like ghosts," she said softly, her breath frosting.

"No they don't," he responded. He said something in French to a passing lady, who answered him and laughed, and walked on, disappearing into the gloom.

There was a scream, from up ahead.

Valkyrie ran for the source, the Dead Men all around her. There were people running, and more screams. Panic soaked into the air and spread outwards. She could feel her own nerves starting to jangle. Something big came at her and she dodged, stumbled, and a horse galloped by, and someone ran into her, tripped over her, scrambled up and ran on. Valkyrie got to her feet, looked around. The fog quenched the sounds around her, and she couldn't see more than ten steps ahead. Her hands were freezing. She pulled her gloves from her jacket, put them on, wishing she could summon a flame to warm herself and light her way. A woman ran by, eyes wide with fear, and quickly vanished into the grey darkness.

"Skulduggery?" Valkyrie called. "Ghastly?"

Muffled cries came from somewhere to her left, and behind her in the distance there was a scream that ended as abruptly as it began. She took the stick from her back, but the sigils refused to glow. Scowling, she returned it, and pressed forward. A shape loomed in front of her, big and wide and unmoving. She put a hand to the wall and followed it round till she got to a door. It may have been a ghost door, but the wood felt just as solid as any door she'd ever seen – just as locked, too. She carried on, reached the corner. A man came running and went stumbling. He sprawled through the mud. Someone else stepped from the fog, reached down to help him up. No, not help. Those hands gripped him, either side of the face. The man screamed and the hands twisted his head all the way round. The scream died with the crack of cartilage.

Valkyrie ducked back. The thing, the wraith, so tall and grey – grey skin, grey clothes, like a person who'd had all the colour leached out of him – hadn't even turned its head in her direction. She slid away, following the wall back the way she'd come, keeping her eyes on the corner, making sure that nothing was coming after her.

The wraith walked round the corner, its eyes shining through the dark. Valkyrie's breath left her and she turned, scrambling into a run. She ran from mud to grass to mud again, almost into the waiting arms of another cold creature, but a hand gripped her shoulder, dragged her back.

"Other way," Skulduggery whispered.

They ran towards gunshots, found Vex and Ravel emptying

their pistols into an approaching wraith without slowing it down in the slightest. Shudder strode up behind it, thrust his sword into its back. The blade bounced off, but it made the wraith turn, and Shudder slammed the hilt into its face. The wraith caught his wrist, closing its fingers round his bare skin, and Shudder grunted in pain and fell to his knees. Ravel charged, shoving the wraith off balance while Vex pulled Shudder up again. Valkyrie glimpsed Shudder's wrist as he stumbled past her. His flesh was red and bubbling where the wraith had touched him.

Skulduggery jumped at the wraith, both feet hitting its chest, while Vex swung his sword into the backs of its legs. The wraith toppled, landed in the mud, and Ravel picked up a rock, brought it down on its head. It made a dull thump and muck squelched, and the wraith clutched at Ravel's ankle. Vex kicked its hand away, allowing Ravel to bring the rock down a second and third time. And a fourth. A fifth. Each time more violent than the last.

"That doesn't appear to be bothering it too much," Skulduggery noted, wiping the mud from the back of his trousers. "We should probably go before it gets up."

Ravel brought the rock down one final time, then cursed in frustration and staggered to his feet. The wraith sat up calmly. Its grey face was old and lined, devoid of expression. It started to stand.

"We're leaving," said Ravel, walking quickly. "We need to get out of this fog."

As they hurried away, Valkyrie took out her mask and pulled it on. She threaded her hair through the hole in the back and fixed the other holes over her eyes and mouth. Vex glanced at her.

"Got a spare one of those?" he asked.

"Sorry."

He shrugged. "That's what I get for not being Ghastly's favourite."

They stopped suddenly as horses galloped by. A wraith clung to one, brought it crashing down somewhere in the fog ahead.

Valkyrie heard its panicked whinnying, and then there was a wet sound and the whinnying stopped.

They adjusted their course. Valkyrie watched a man push his neighbour into the path of a wraith, only to stumble into another who'd been approaching from behind. Their fate was swallowed by the gloom and the fog, and only their screams escaped. They passed a woman sitting on the ground behind a stall. She looked at them fearfully as they passed, but didn't say a word.

A shape that moved too fast to be a wraith crashed into Valkyrie from the side. Hands grabbed her, pulled her away from the others. She cried out and saw Skulduggery lunge after her, but a moment later there was a wall of fog between them.

"Your fault," the man said into her ear. His hands were rough and he kept her moving, didn't give her a chance to regain her footing. "What did you do to bring them back? What did you do?"

Griff's eyes were wide and his face was pale.

As white as a ghost.

"We didn't do anything," Valkyrie said, tried to say, and then he flung her into the mud and stood over her, trembling with fear and rage.

"You brought them down to us. They stayed up there for a hundred years, but you brought them down to us."

"We were here," she said. "We were here the whole time."

"They're here because of you," Griff said, eyes flickering to the shapes approaching slowly from all sides. "So I'll give you to them." He turned, and ran.

A wraith stepped through and Valkyrie backed away. Scalding hot fingers closed round her head from behind, tightened their grip even as she thrashed. The wraith in front closed in and she tried kicking it back, but it just took hold of her foot. And then another took her right arm, and another her left, and a fifth wraith took her other leg, and she was lifted and stretched between them, like they were going to pull her apart. She screamed, and the scream became a wail that ended in a sob. She could feel the heat through her black clothes, trying but unable to blister her flesh. The wraiths pulled harder and she felt her joints straining to hold together. Though her head was being pulled straight back, she caught sight of another wraith drifting from the gloom. Her jacket had ridden up high, her T-shirt with it, leaving her belly exposed to the cold air. The wraith splayed its hand, brought it slowly down to rest against her.

She screamed again as it burned, a tortured scream that cut through her throat. The wraith pressed harder and then there was the sound of hooves, and two horses burst from the fog, Vex and Ghastly on their backs and a rope tied between them.

The horses passed on either side and the rope hit the wraiths at chest height. Valkyrie dropped as the wraiths were taken off their feet, some of them dragged after the horses, others sprawling in the muck. Skulduggery and Saracen came straight after. Skulduggery scooped her into his arms and Saracen used a pitchfork to shove the nearest wraith back a few steps, then they ran. Valkyrie's gloved fingertips curled into the skin around the hand-shaped burn mark on her stomach and she bit her lip to keep from crying out with every step. Skulduggery jumped over a fallen wraith and followed Saracen, barely managing to keep him in sight. They rounded a dark corner and Valkyrie heard the footsteps change from mud to a hardened surface.

Saracen stopped ahead of them, turned, looking about. "Can you hear them? Which way did they go?"

A wraith lunged from the fog and Saracen shrieked, hit the creature so hard the pitchfork handle broke in two.

"Do *not* jump out at me!" Saracen roared, driving the splintered remains of the pitchfork into the wraith's mouth. "I *hate it* when people jump out at me!"

Galloping hooves thundered closer, and before Valkyrie knew what was happening Shudder was pulling her up on to his horse. She cried out in pain, but held on as he spurred the horse forward, and they followed the road straight through the gloom. His hands gripped the reins, his right wrist badly burnt. Seconds later, the fog thinned, and then they had the night sky above them and clear air around, and Valkyrie felt magic flood her body.

The horse beneath them wasn't there any more, but Shudder held Valkyrie and landed smoothly, putting her back on her feet. She faced the fog that surrounded the town of Wolfsong like a great wall, and pulled the mask from her head. Beneath it, she was sweating. She stuffed the mask in her jacket and clicked her fingers. Thanks to Ghastly, that action still generated a spark even through the glove, and she held fire in one hand while the other curled protectively round her belly.

The other horses came through. The moment they passed beyond the fog they faded to nothing, and Ghastly and Vex dropped to the ground. Saracen sprinted out after them.

"Not fair," he panted, glaring at them.

"You need the exercise," Vex said, his hand lighting up. "Might want to get out of the way, though."

Saracen turned, saw the wraith coming up behind him. Vex let loose with a stream of energy that caught the wraith square in the chest. It moved it back a step, but didn't burn through. Ghastly hurled a fireball at another wraith that walked out next.

Saracen backed up beside them. "Damn it. I kind of thought they'd be confined to the fog."

"Me, too," Vex growled.

Shudder took off his coat and opened his shirt. "Step back," he said. "All of you."

A head pushed through his chest. It snapped and snarled as it woke, its narrow black eyes opening and blinking at the approaching wraiths. It was Shudder's face, only different, and it pushed out further till it had freed its arms. Trailing a stream of light and dark back into Shudder's chest, the Gist burst free and flew at them, screeching. Its clawed hands raked uselessly at the wraiths on its first pass and it flew upwards, fury solidifying its features. On its second pass, a wraith's arm fell to the ground, and on the third it brought a wraith high into the air, tearing into it with claws and sharp teeth, and the wraith fell in bits, back into the fog.

The other wraiths paused, then stepped back, allowing the gloom to claim them. The Gist flew overhead, unable to go after its prey, furious.

Then the fog started to retract. It rolled quickly back up the hill, taking the town and the wraiths with it, leaving only Skulduggery and Ravel standing in the ruins, swords in their hands.

The Gist shrieked as the stream went taut, and it was pulled back into Shudder's body. Ghastly moved Valkyrie away a little, to make sure it didn't try to grab her for purchase. When it was gone, Shudder's knees buckled, and Saracen and Vex grabbed him, supporting his weight.

The fog kept rolling away, and soon it was lost in the darkness.

Valkyrie walked forward on stiff legs. At her feet, the wraith's severed arm moved, its fingers clutching at nothing. "They forgot something," she mumbled.

"Bloody wraiths," said Saracen. "They'd forget their heads if they weren't so hard to chop off."

Valkyrie kicked the arm into the ruins. The wraiths could pick it up next time they visited.

Vex gave her some leaves to chew and the pain lessened considerably. He had some medical supplies in his bag and he did what he could, applying ointment and wrapping her wound in a bandage. When he was done, she could drop her T-shirt and it didn't sting. He offered the ointment to Shudder who applied a little to his wrist, but the offer of leaves to dull the pain was turned down with a grunt.

Saracen gave a low whistle. "What do you know?" he said. "The fog didn't take everyone with it."

Valkyrie and the others followed him through the ruins till they came to the few crumbling walls of what had once been the tavern. Sitting at a broken, rotten table was Trebuchet, his head down in the darkness.

Skulduggery glanced at Saracen. "Is he alive?"

Saracen nodded. "He seems alive to me."

"Of course I'm alive," Trebuchet said, not looking up. "The ghosts have it easy. They don't know they're ghosts. Every night the fog comes and rebuilds the town and the people who lived here, and they go about their business, whatever it may be. I'm the only one who knows. The only one who remembers."

"Why don't you leave?" Ravel asked.

Trebuchet looked up. "And go where? Wolfsong is my home. Its people are my people."

Skulduggery looked around for something to sit on, then chose to remain standing. "Why don't the wraiths kill you?"

At this, Trebuchet smiled. "Because then the game would be over. They come every third night, despite what Griff says. Never trust a ghost's memory, that's my advice to you. The fog rebuilds the town and everything is fine and then the wraiths come and the people all panic and scream and they all die. They die in different ways, in a different order, but they all die. The next night the town rebuilds, and the ghosts come back with no idea of what's just happened to them. It happens over and over again and there's nothing I can do to stop any of it."

"Who's doing this to you?"

"The Warlocks," said Trebuchet. "One in particular. Charivari. Their leader."

"Why?" Valkyrie asked.

Trebuchet looked at his old weather-beaten hands for a long moment. "Griff would've told you about the boys, yes? The three boys who went to take a look at the Warlock settlement and never came back? They were gone three days and me and another man went out after them under cover of night. We got to the mountains, found the boys almost immediately. Dead, they were. Hands and feet cut off, laid out on the rocks as a warning.

"Well, that didn't sit too well with us. So we went up into the mountains. Warlocks could kill three teenage boys and take no effort to do it, but two seasoned mages like us? We were going to bring the killers back with us, drag them all the way to Wolfsong.

"First Warlock we saw was a woman, cleaning her underclothes in a stream. We killed her. It wasn't easy. By the time she stopped breathing, I was the only one left on his feet, and I was losing blood and had bones broken and... Anyway. The other Warlocks, they'd heard the commotion. Tracked me all the way back to my horse. Playing with me, they were. Got to the base of the mountain and Charivari was standing there, waiting for me.

"I told him she died because of what was done to those three boys. He didn't care. I'd never seen anyone like him. His eyes... He had nightmares in his eyes. I thought it was my life next, but instead he put me on my horse, sent me back here. And sent the fog after me. It's my fault this town was murdered. It's the least I can do to suffer for it."

"You've suffered a hundred years," Valkyrie said.

"And I'll suffer a hundred more and then some. I suppose I am a lesson. Never give a Warlock good cause for revenge. I am proof of that."

"Come with us," said Ravel. "Help us. You still have supporters in the French Sanctuary, I know you do. You could convince them to rise against Mandat and the Supreme Council."

Trebuchet looked up. "Where were my supporters when Mandat ousted me? Where was their support then? I fear you overestimate my worth, Erskine. Do you know how I was ousted? Do you know how it began? I wanted to move the Sanctuary to Saint-Germain. I did not think it was healthy to isolate ourselves from the mortals. Isolation breeds suspicion, and resentment, and hatred. I felt we needed to surround ourselves with the people we were protecting. I met with Corrival Deuce many, many times to discuss these matters. You yourself were present for these conversations."

"I remember them," said Ravel. "We were compiling lists of Sanctuaries and individual sorcerers who agreed with our point of view. You were close to the top of that list."

"I didn't agree with all of Corrival's philosophies, but I agreed with most. My fellow Elders, however, did not. Mandat was particularly vehement about it. Arguments began. Petty at first. Then... not so petty. Mandat seeded doubt in the minds of those around me. They began to view me as dangerously out of touch. Two years from when I first suggested Saint-Germain, I was no longer Grand Mage. And I came here, and was welcomed, and then I got everyone killed."

"We need your help," Skulduggery said. "Mandat and the other Grand Mages have declared war on us. We need to get into their research facility."

"If you succeed in your mission, Grand Mage Mandat will be unhappy?"

"Better than that," said Skulduggery. "He will look a fool in front of his allies."

The ghost of a smile played on Trebuchet's lips. "It's a rare opportunity indeed that I get to upset the plans of Grand Mage Mandat."

"So you know something that can help us?"

"I know of an entrance. A secret tunnel that even Mandat doesn't know about. Bring me a map and I'll show you where it is."

Ravel looked at him. "You could come with us. Haven't you suffered enough?"

"For what I did?" Trebuchet shook his head. "No. For what I did, I cannot atone. I can only suffer."

33

MONSTER HUNTERS AND ME

"I don't like you."

Fletcher blinked, and looked around. "I'm sorry?"

The big guy's last name was Threatening. Fletcher didn't know his first name. When you had a last name like Threatening, first names became somewhat unimportant. And Threatening was indeed threatening. He was roughly Fletcher's age, but much bigger and stronger and much more severe, and his very voice rumbled with the promise of violence.

"I don't like you," he said again.

Fletcher nodded this time. "Ah, that's what I thought you said." He went back to reading his book. He had started carrying books around with him wherever he went. Since most of the time his job involved waiting around, it was the only thing stopping him from growing insanely bored whenever he went on a mission. It was also handy for those times when Madame Mist kept him waiting outside her office – times like right now. He was fighting fit, for God's sake. The doctor whose name he couldn't pronounce had told him he was able to teleport again. He should be out there, where the action was, not stuck in here, having to deal with morons.

Threatening reached out, thick fingers closing over the book and pushing it down. "Aren't you going to ask why?"

Fletcher looked up at him. "No."

Threatening's brow furrowed. "You're not?"

"No. Well, not unless you want me to. Do you want me to?"

"How can you stand there and have someone tell you they don't like you and not be curious as to why?"

"It's not that I'm not curious," Fletcher clarified. "It's just I assume you're jealous of my hair."

"Your what?"

"My hair, and how amazing it is. You wouldn't be the first, believe me, and you won't be the last. It is incredible hair."

"I'm not jealous of your hair."

"You are a little."

"Shut up. I don't like you because you're a coward, and even though everyone knows what you are, you're still treated as some big, important part of what we're doing here. You know what? You're not. And you can pretend to be a hero and a warrior, but we both know what you really are."

"A coward?"

"Yeah."

Fletcher gave him the thumbs up. "Righto."

"Do you not even care that I called you a coward?"

"Why would I care about that?"

Threatening shook his head, disgusted. "I don't know what she saw in you."

"What who saw in me?"

"Never mind."

"Who were you talking about?"

"No one."

"Valkyrie? You don't know what Valkyrie saw in me?"

Threatening loomed over him at full height. "You're a coward and she's saved the world a hundred times and all you've done is teleport places. So what is it? How did you get her to go out with you?"

"Do you... do you fancy Valkyrie?"

Threatening's face clouded with anger. "At least I appreciate her. At least I'd never break her heart."

"I didn't break her heart."

"Then why did she dump you?"

"That's none of your—"

"You cheated on her. You're lucky the Elders need a Teleporter because if they didn't I'd break you in half for what you did."

"Listen, what happened between Valkyrie and me is none of your business. But if you fancy her so much why don't you ask her out?"

"Maybe I will."

"Good."

"At least then she'd be with someone who really loves her."

"Hmm. Yeah. Tell me something, have you ever spoken to her?" Threatening glowered.

"So that's a no," said Fletcher. "You've never spoken to her, but you love her, yeah? Well, I can't think of a healthier way to start a relationship. You want my advice? If you're serious about how you feel and you really want to make the right impression, you know what you should do?"

"What?"

"Boss her around. Seriously. She loves that. Protect her from everything and shield her from danger, all that stuff. She likes it when people take charge and tell her what to do."

"Really?"

"God, yeah. You have to be more than a match for her."

The door to Mist's office opened, and Tipstaff walked out, nodding to him. "You can go in now, Mr Renn."

Fletcher gave Threatening a smile, and walked into the office. It was a dark room with a desk and a chair and not much else. Two men stood waiting – one tall and narrow, the other short and broad. Mist herself sat behind her desk in a chair of sweeping angles and sharp edges that reached for the high ceiling – more a throne than an office chair.

"Mr Renn," she said in quiet greeting. From the moment he'd first seen her, he'd wondered what she really looked like. Her body was slender and her hands were unlined, so she was probably relatively young under that black veil. But was she pretty? Was she ugly? Was she plain? What colour was her hair? Her eyes? Did she ever smile?

"I understand you have fully recovered."

Fletcher touched his stomach reflexively. "Raring to go."

"Good. You will begin immediately. The gentlemen beside you are Gracious O'Callahan and Donegan Bane, the Monster Hunters," she said. "You may have heard of them or read the books. By their own account, they are quite famous in certain circles."

Gracious and Donegan smiled at him.

Mist tapped a long finger once on the photograph before her. "This woman's name is Zona. She is, among other things, an expert at constructing shields from sigil magic. Likewise, her knowledge can also be used to *dismantle* our shield from the outside. We cannot afford to let this happen. It has come to our attention that she is due to be transported from the Mexican Sanctuary within the hour. By our estimation, Zona will be outside and vulnerable for no longer than ten seconds. The three of you will therefore intercept, retrieve her, and bring her back here."

"You've been to the Mexican Sanctuary before?" Donegan asked him.

Fletcher nodded. "I've been to most Sanctuaries. I can get us there. Will she have anyone with her?"

"A security detail," said Mist. "Bodyguards – Cleavers and mages."

Fletcher frowned. "And we only have ten seconds?"

"From the Sanctuary entrance to the car will take approximately ten seconds at a fast walk."

"And there's just us? Just the three of us?"

"You're not going there to engage in a battle," said Mist. "Three should be more than adequate."

Fletcher looked at the two men beside him, and Donegan smiled. "Don't worry," he said. "We've done things like this before. We'll be fine."

Gracious nodded. "Probably."

Fletcher teleported them to a rooftop in Mexico City, where they took turns with the binoculars. Gracious complained about the effects the sun would have on his delicate skin, so Fletcher teleported away for a few seconds, arriving back with a parasol that Gracious happily accepted. And then they waited.

The Mexican Sanctuary was a two-storey, flat-roofed building with an enclosed, high-walled yard. Beneath the surface, it continued downwards for many levels, but for anyone on street level it was just like all the other sun-baked buildings in the neighbourhood. No guards, no obvious security, nothing to draw the eye.

"So you're a natural, then?" Donegan asked, the binoculars fixed to his eyes.

Fletcher looked round. "Sorry?"

"A natural," Donegan said. "You didn't need any training to teleport?"

Fletcher gave a little shrug. "I needed training to control it, to be able to do it properly, but yeah, I just started one day, before I knew anything about magic or sorcerers or any of this. The first time I did it was the day my mother died. I wanted to get away, I was running out of the hospital and then, suddenly, I was at home."

"That must have been quite a shock," Gracious said.

"I didn't know what had happened. The next day I had all these theories, like I just didn't remember running home, or I'd blocked it out because of my mum. Then, a few weeks later, it happened again. The only Teleporter I'd ever heard of was Nightcrawler – you know him?"

Gracious nodded. "Kurt Wagner, from *X-Men*."

"Exactly," said Fletcher. "So I read all the comics, then watched a few science-fiction movies and TV shows for research. You know, like *Dragon Ball Z*, *Heroes*, things like that. But I stopped after I watched *The Fly*. I didn't teleport for two weeks after I saw that."

Gracious winced. "I can understand."

"And a few months later I met Valkyrie and Skulduggery and some lunatic used me to bring the Faceless Ones back. And now here I am, in Mexico City, with the Monster Hunters."

"I love stories with happy endings," said Gracious.

Donegan straightened. "We have movement," he said, and passed the binoculars to Fletcher.

Fletcher adjusted the focus slightly, saw the Sanctuary door opening, saw the Cleavers lead the security detail out. Beside him, Gracious and Donegan bent their knees and raised their fists. Fletcher took a deep breath, waited until he glimpsed a big enough gap in the group, right beside Zona, then he dropped the binoculars, grabbed the Monster Hunters—

—and then they were down there, in the middle of the security detail, and Gracious was throwing punches and Donegan was throwing energy blasts and everyone was moving and shouting and Zona looked around, her eyes wide, and Fletcher grabbed her and—

—now he was in Roarhaven, in the Sanctuary, but a Cleaver and a mage had grabbed on to Zona at the last moment, and they were turning towards Fletcher even as—

—they plummeted down the side of the tallest peak in the Alps, freezing wind biting into Fletcher's face, tumbling and rolling all together with Fletcher waiting for the mage to lose his grip and let go of Zona's arm and—

—now there was just the Cleaver to get rid of as they fell *upwards*, their momentum taking them into the air above a peaceful meadow in Yorkshire before gravity found them again and they started dipping down, the Cleaver's scythe swinging for Fletcher's throat—

—through the Auckland rain and Fletcher ducked and threw himself on Zona and they hit the hard ground and rolled—

—across the Sanctuary floor and Fletcher released his hold and he was—

—back in the Alps and falling again, the mage far below him—

—right beside him, and Fletcher grabbed him with his left hand and—

—held on as the Yorkshire countryside flipped him around and he reached out with his right and—

—grabbed the Cleaver and—

—dumped them both on the heads of the security detail as he fell between them, and Gracious whirled, pulled him to his feet and Donegan grabbed him—

—and they stood over Zona as she stopped rolling across the floor in Roarhaven.

Cleavers came forward and shackled Zona, who was too stunned to even object, and led her away. Fletcher brushed the snow from his hair as he walked out into the corridor, Donegan and Gracious on either side of him.

"We make a good team," said Donegan.

"We do," said Gracious.

"You should think about joining us, Fletcher. It's not a bad life, being a Monster Hunter."

Fletcher laughed. "I don't know anything about hunting monsters."

"Easy to learn," said Gracious, "but how are you at drawing?"

"I'm sorry?"

"We're authors, too," Donegan said, "and we've been trying to get into the picture-book market. We have this idea for a *Where's Wally* type thing, except in ours, you'd have to find the one living person hiding in among all the dismembered corpses while the chainsaw-wielding killer hunts him down. You know, for kids."

"We're going to call it *Save the Survivor*," Gracious said. "So what do you think?"

"Uh," said Fletcher, "isn't that a bit... disturbing?"

Gracious frowned. "Is it?"

"I don't think so," said Donegan.

"Yes," Fletcher said, "I think it's a little bit disturbing. I think it might give children nightmares."

"It doesn't give me nightmares," Gracious said, "and people are always saying how childish I am."

"That's true, they are," Donegan said, nodding.

They turned the corner, saw Madame Mist walking with Syc and Portia, their hands free of shackles, and Gracious pulled his gun and Donegan's hands lit up.

"What the hell is going on?" Gracious snarled.

Even through the veil, Fletcher could feel Mist's glare.

"You point your gun at me, Monster Hunter?" she said. "I am an Elder. Such an act could see you executed."

"I'm sure Gracious doesn't mean anything by it," Donegan said, energy crackling between his fingers. "I'm sure he's just wondering what the hell you think you're doing setting those murderers free."

"I do not have to explain myself to the likes of you," Mist said. Behind her, Portia was smiling while Syc looked bored. All three of them moved towards the door, but Donegan stepped into their path.

"Grand Mage Ravel ordered their incarceration," he said.

"And I am ordering their release," replied Mist. "What's done is done. They cannot bring back Bernard Sult, they cannot erase their crime, but they can make up for their mistake. They seek redemption. Who are you to deny them that?"

"You didn't clear this with Ravel," said Gracious.

Madame Mist shrugged her slender shoulders. "He is still out of reach, I am afraid. And we cannot wait. We have potential allies waiting to be brought in, but they won't wait long."

"We'll go get them," said Donegan. "Tell Fletcher where they are and we'll bring them back."

"These allies distrust Teleporters, as they distrust all sorcerers."

Gracious frowned. "What kind of allies are they?"

"Children of the Spider," said Mist. "Two of them, both old and powerful. The Terror and the Scourge. You would not be able to bring them in. They'd see you and kill you and be lost to us."

"We're Monster Hunters," said Donegan. "Hunting monsters is what we do."

Madame Mist turned her head ever so slightly. "Monsters? Do you view all Children of the Spider as monsters?"

Gracious shrugged. "Only the ones who turn into great big monster spiders."

"We're wasting time," Portia said. "You will either let us by, or attack your own Elder and be executed for treason. Which will it be?"

For a moment, it looked like Gracious and Donegan were going to go for the second option, but then Donegan lowered his hand, and Gracious holstered his gun. Madame Mist walked on like nothing had happened. Portia followed after, a smirk on her face, and Syc hissed as he passed.

Donegan waited till they were gone, then swung round to Gracious.

"He hissed at me."

"He hissed at you."

"Should I hiss back?"

"It's a bit late."

"He could still hear."

"Not unless you run after him."

"Do you think I should?"

"Probably not."

"I think I should."

"It'd be a bit weird."

"You might be right." Donegan pursed his lips, then shook his fist at the doorway.

"That showed him," said Gracious.

Donegan nodded. "He'll think twice about hissing at me again." He turned to Fletcher. "So, *Save the Survivor*. You in or out?"

"Uh," said Fletcher, "I can't draw."

"I wouldn't worry about that too much," Gracious whispered to him. "We can't write. But don't tell anyone. It's a secret."

34

RUDE AWAKENING

China woke to the sound of a door being kicked in.

She rolled over, hit the light switch and then slid off the bed. Even as the bulbs were brightening, she was pulling on her silk bathrobe and tying the sash securely at her waist. She grabbed her handbag, looped it over her head so the strap hung diagonally across her chest. It wouldn't take them long to figure out that she'd charmed the businessman down the hall into swapping rooms with her.

She ran to the spiral staircase, got to the suite's upper level just as the door burst open. An instant later, there was a bright flash and a yell of pain. If they didn't think she'd have set a few booby traps, they had no one to blame but themselves.

She knew them, of course. *Know your enemies*, her grandmother had always said. She'd identified them by the second day of their pursuit. The leader was Vincent Foe, an Energy-Thrower, nihilist and thug. Mercy Charient was his psychotic second-in-command, another Energy-Thrower, but one who preferred to emit the energy stream from her mouth instead of her hands. Less controlled, but more damaging. The big one was Obloquy, a Sensitive specialising in inflicting pain. And the vampire was called Samuel.

If she'd still had her accounts, if Eliza Scorn had not frozen her assets, China could have bid higher than whoever had paid him, solved this problem with the swipe of a credit card.

As it was, she would just have to keep running.

She emerged on to the balcony, pressed herself back against the right side, and tapped the sigils on her thighs. Immediately she felt the strength flooding her leg muscles. She bolted to the other side, jumped to the edge and sprang to the balcony across the gap. Her bare feet slapped down and she kept going, jumping to the edge and then springing again to the next one. She landed, deactivated the sigils before the magic damaged her muscles, opened the balcony doors and slipped inside.

On the level below, she could hear voices. A couple, in bed, wondering what all the noise was about. She picked her way through the darkness towards the staircase. The balcony doors swung open behind her and she turned as the vampire stepped in, still in human form. He looked straight at her.

China ran for the railing, vaulted over it, dropping to the floor below. She landed on the bed. The woman shrieked beneath her. She accidentally whacked the man in the face with her elbow as she rolled off. She glanced back, saw Samuel jumping over the railing after her. Instead of landing on the terrified couple, he kicked off from the wall, hit the ground and came up to his feet in a run. China grabbed a lamp, smashed it into his head. He staggered and she folded the fingers of her left hand, each fingertip tapping the sigil on her palm one after another. The sigil glowed red and her hand closed round Samuel's throat. He jerked upright and then pitched backwards.

She opened the door, took a peek, saw Foe and Mercy turning her way. She took the gun from her handbag, flicked off the safety and stepped out, firing. The gunshots sounded incredibly loud on this quiet Dublin night. Foe and Mercy ducked into the open doorway beside them, shoving Obloquy out of the way. China ran for the stairs. Went up.

She threw open the door at the top, ran out across the rooftop. She got to the other side and looked down. Only one balcony here. She hopped up on to the ledge. Voices behind her. She barely had time to look round before a stream of red energy burst from Mercy's big mouth, went sizzling by her arm. China spun, lost her balance and her weapon, fell, tried to land on the balcony, but her trajectory was off. She flung out a hand, grabbed an iron rail and her body snapped, almost jerking her shoulder from its socket. Grimacing against the pain, she hung, swaying, six floors above the street.

There was a man standing in the window beneath the balcony, staring straight at her. She motioned to his window with her free hand, miming opening it. He appeared unable to move.

She forced a smile on to her face even as her free hand went up to grab on to another rail. The pain from her right arm was starting to streak through her.

"Open the window," she mouthed to him.

With barely a blink, the man fumbled for the latch. When it wouldn't open, he frowned, took his eyes off China for the first time since he'd seen her, and tried again. He looked up, shaking his head in abject dismay. It wouldn't open.

"Break it," she mouthed.

He nodded, went away, and a moment later a chair smashed through the glass. Working quickly, he cleared the jagged pieces from the sill.

"Get ready to catch me," China called out.

"I love you," he called back.

"Prove it by catching me," she said, and started to swing. Back and forth she went, picking up momentum, kicking her legs up high in front and then kicking them back behind her, and when her wrists couldn't take any more she swung forward and let herself go – and the nice man caught her.

He pulled her inside and fell back, and she fell on top of him.

"I love you," he said again.

"You're sweet," she replied.

She got up, cradling her right arm, and hurried out of the room. She took the stairs down, arriving in the lobby just as the squad cars pulled up outside. She slipped into the kitchens, smiling at the chef who was preparing someone's midnight feast. He whimpered at her as she passed.

The rear door led into a narrow alley. She stepped on something disgusting, felt it squish between her toes, and kept going. She hailed a cab, could only stand four minutes of the driver's adulation before she threw him some money and got out.

Breaking into the department store was child's play. She cleaned her feet as best she could, and dressed in dark jeans and a loose T-shirt. She pulled on a pair of boots with sensible heels and a black jacket, then tied her hair back into a ponytail. Walked by the make-up section without even glancing at it, and slipped out, into the street.

Had it not been for Eliza Scorn, she would still have Skulduggery's friendship to rely on. As it was, the Sanctuary was the last place she wanted to go. She'd deal with these thugs the same way she dealt with every problem that reared its head — alone, and with an abundance of style.

35

SNEAKING IN

When Trebuchet had told them about the secret way into the research facility, it had sounded so much more impressive than it actually was.

He told them about the shaft, a tunnel that opened on the surface and took natural light and fresh water and clean air downwards into the earth. He described it as small but wide, almost as wide as the stream it was embedded in. He told them its trajectory was diagonal, and that it recycled air and water, and how it was a revolutionary idea when it was first built. Over the centuries, however, the facility grew and changed, and new ideas, technologies and magic arose to take the place of the shaft and make it redundant. These days, he said, barely anyone even knew it had even existed. They certainly didn't know it could be used as an entry point.

Valkyrie crouched down and peered into the shaft. "It's a hole," she said.

The Dead Men were dumping their backpacks on the bank of the stream. The water lapped at Valkyrie's ankles. She measured the opening. It ran from the tip of her elbow to the third knuckle of her outstretched hand.

She stood. "Are you sure we'll be able to fit?"

Skulduggery was first to come over. "I'm sure I'll be fine," he said. He had collapsed the frame under his clothes, reducing his size drastically.

Valkyrie glared. "I'm actually not worried about you. I'm worried about the rest of us. What if the shaft gets narrower in the middle or something?"

"It doesn't."

"But what if it does?"

"It doesn't."

"I'm just saying, it's... it's going to be very tight."

His head swivelled to her. "You won't get stuck."

"But—"

"You just have to close your eyes and take deep breaths. Once we climb through, the angle of the shaft will take us down fairly quickly. We're not going to be in there for longer than fifteen or twenty seconds, and the dimensions remain constant for the entire journey. To be honest, I think we'll be going too fast for you to have time to be nervous about the space. You'll be fine, Valkyrie."

The rest of the Dead Men joined them.

"Aw, hell," said Saracen when he saw what they had to fit through.

Valkyrie gave him a half-smile. "You claustrophobic, too?" she asked.

"No," Shudder answered for him, "just fat."

Vex and Ghastly laughed while Saracen glared.

"I am a healthy weight," he said. "I just... I might be a little *too* healthy to make it to the bottom."

"If he's staying, I'm staying," Valkyrie said immediately.

"Neither of you are staying," said Skulduggery. "Saracen, suck in your gut and you won't have a problem. It's Ghastly and Anton who should be worried. They're the biggest of us."

Saracen grinned. "Hear that, Anton? Maybe instead of lifting all those weights you should have joined me in eating a few pies."

"I've never lifted weights in my life," Shudder responded. "My

268

muscle mass is a natural part of my being genetically superior to you."

Saracen looked at him, then looked away. "I have no comeback to that."

Ravel was the first to sit in the stream and slide his legs into the shaft. "Oh my God," he said, immediately tensing. "The freezing water has just gone down the back of my trousers. Perhaps we should rethink this."

"Too late for thinking," said Skulduggery. "Everyone get ready."

Valkyrie pulled her trousers up as high as they'd go, then sat in the water with her legs in the shaft. So far so good. When everyone was in position, Skulduggery got to his hands and knees.

"Of course," said Vex. "You just have to go head first, don't you?"

"I like to be different," Skulduggery said.

The cold water lapped at Valkyrie's back and slipped down her trousers. She winced.

"Not nice, is it?" said Ravel.

"I really don't want to do this," Saracen whined.

Skulduggery gave a shrug. "I'm not going to force you. I'm not going to order you. Instead, I'm just going to say one little thing, and this applies to all of you."

They looked at him. He tilted his head.

"Race you."

Vex was the first to move, then Ghastly, and then Valkyrie pushed herself through and she was suddenly sliding down the wet slope, picking up speed with every metre. She hit a bump and banged her knee and scraped her chest off the concrete above, almost started turning, but then she felt the air nudge her back in place. She opened her eyes, saw Skulduggery hurtling down beside her, head first, his arms open and his hands splayed, keeping everyone in check.

She hit her knee again and straightened her legs. She grabbed her chest and pressed down and turned her head to the side, making herself as streamlined and flat as possible. She could feel her thundering heartbeat under her hand, and resisted the urge to scream. Skulduggery was right. The sheer speed she was travelling at, combined with the unmatchable exhilaration of how that felt, meant that any notion of claustrophobia had been left back up on the surface.

This was amazing.

Water splashed in her face and she blinked it away. She saw Saracen, sucking in his gut and grinning like a lunatic. On the other side of him was Ghastly. She saw him scrape against the top a few times. It looked painful. Beyond him was Vex, his T-shirt curled up around his midsection.

Valkyrie checked her own T-shirt. Yep, it was up over her midsection, too. Her fingers brushed against the hand-shaped scar that was burned into her belly, and then the shaft suddenly brightened and her eyes flickered down just as she was spat out into open space. She tumbled, then caught herself in the air and landed gently in knee-deep water.

They were in a large chamber with many angled vents and openings. Moss climbed the crackled walls. There was a single door and lots of rusted levers all in a row.

"Well, that wasn't bad at all," Saracen said, patting his stomach. "Ghastly, you enjoy that?"

Ghastly winced, and rubbed his chest. "I think I may have lost a nipple up there."

Skulduggery climbed the steps out of the water and tried the door. It wouldn't budge. "Dexter."

Vex joined him, his hand already crackling with power. They looked back at Saracen.

"It's all clear," he said. "No one around."

Dexter blasted the lock, and Skulduggery pulled the door open.

Valkyrie hurried up with the rest of them. Now that the adrenaline was wearing off, she was starting to feel things normally again, and she scowled. Nothing worse than soggy underwear.

The corridor was old and cold and barely lit. She watched the Dead Men check weapons.

"We're in the old facility right now," Skulduggery said, keeping his voice low. "They should be waiting to spring the ambush at the entry point Lamour gave us. Instead, we're going to set up our own ambush, and bring them to us. Valkyrie, at the end of this corridor, we'll be going up. According to Trebuchet, Lamour and the Engineer should be beneath us, so that's where you're going. Down."

"You still think she should go alone?" Ravel asked.

"The plan doesn't change," Skulduggery said. "Valkyrie can handle it. Besides, it's going to take all six of us to keep Mandat's forces at bay long enough for our reinforcements to swoop in and save us. Providing they're even around."

Ravel looked at Saracen. "Well? Will they be here?"

"I can't tell the future, Dexter."

"Then what use *are* you?"

"When you have the Engineer," Skulduggery said as he passed Valkyrie a small wooden ball, "bring it back to this room, then come find us."

"How will I know where you are?" she asked.

"Just follow the explosions."

Valkyrie twisted both halves of the cloaking sphere, and a bubble of invisibility blossomed out to cover her. She put the sphere in her jacket pocket and started down the stairs, her quick footsteps masked before they could start to echo round the stairwell.

From lower down, she heard voices. She slowed to a stop, and peered over the railing. Four people – three women and a man – walking up, talking French. They took up the entire width of the staircase. There was no way she could squeeze by, but the alternative was to go back up. Well, either go back up or jump over them.

She got to the next landing, turned and faced them as they

came. When their eyes were level with her feet, she ran forward and jumped, passing over their heads and then making the steep drop to the landing below. She cushioned her fall as much as she dared – if any of them were Elementals, they'd notice the shift in air pressure – and slammed into the wall and bounced to the floor. She lay there and groaned. The four people kept going up.

Still groaning, she got up, took the stairs a little slower this time. She got to level 3B and left the stairwell. She passed a group of sorcerers, talking quickly but quietly, and she really wished her reflection had paid more attention in French class. All she could decipher was that someone was waiting, and then she heard, in English, "les Hommes Mort". She smiled to herself. Her friends. She was four steps beyond them when the alarm started to wail.

She spun, certain for a moment that she had set it off, that the Cleavers were coming for her. Then, when everyone started hurrying in different directions, she relaxed – but only slightly. The alarm meant that her friends were being attacked.

Valkyrie sped up, glancing into every room she passed until she found the old man she'd seen in the photograph. Lamour was small and thin and stooped over. The man he was talking to was younger and healthier, and much more dangerous. Valkyrie stepped in. She couldn't understand a word they were saying, but it was pretty obvious that the younger man had been sent to make sure nothing happened to Lamour while all this was going on, and Lamour wasn't too pleased about it. On a hand-cart behind them was a humanoid figure covered in a sheet.

She took the stick from her back. Immediately the sigils started to glow.

"You had better work," she said to it, keeping her voice down even though she knew they couldn't hear her.

She pushed the door closed. The younger man whirled, twin fireballs flaring in his hands. Valkyrie walked up beside him and pressed the stick into his side. He jolted off his feet, and crumpled.

Lamour cried out, staggered back, and Valkyrie took out the sphere and deactivated it. His eyes widened when he saw her. "Valkyrie Cain!"

"Hello, Lamour. Pleased to finally meet you."

He blinked. "*Oui*. Yes, indeed it is. I was just... I was just on my way to meet you and your friends."

"Some others met them instead. That's what all the alarms are about."

"Ah," said Lamour. "Well... yes."

"You'd probably be doing yourself a favour by not calling for help. It'd be less painful."

He grunted, and nodded, and all the while his eyes darted about, looking for a weapon. There was a knife on the table beside him. He glanced at it, then looked back at Valkyrie. She pretended not to notice.

"Is that the Engineer?" she asked, nodding to the hand-cart.

He hesitated. "*Non*. That is a... another thing. Not the thing you want. The thing you want is... not here."

"You are a terrible liar," she said, and took hold of the sheet, pulling it off.

The Engineer was a mangled mess, but it wasn't what she was expecting. There were no wires, for a start. It seemed to have organs – solid, mechanical organs – that were dented and misshapen. Its limbs and torso were sculpted but, again, they had been bent by the accident that had led it here. Only its head wasn't trying to emulate a real human's. It had neither eyes nor a mouth, and would have been perfectly smooth were it not for the ugly gash that ran across its metal shell.

"This is what I came for," she said. "OK, Lamour, I'm going to give you a pair of handcuffs, and you're going to put one of those cuffs on your wrist, and the other on the ankle of your friend here."

"*Je suis désolé*," said Lamour, "I am afraid I cannot allow that. This mechanical marvel has been entrusted to me, and me alone.

273

I am the one who will repair it. You think I will let you give it to that monster, Nye? You think I will let this happen without a fight? Come, let us duel!"

He lunged for the desk, but Valkyrie waved her hand and the knife shot away from his grasping hand, to land clattering on the far side of the room.

Lamour straightened up, curled his hands into fists and struck an old boxing pose. "*Très bien!* We can do this the old-fashioned way! Queensberry Rules."

"Yeah," said Valkyrie. "I don't know who Queensberry is, or why she's so cool, but we're not hitting each other."

"Then you yield?"

She pushed at the air a little and Lamour went staggering back. "No, I do not yield. I just don't want to beat up little old men."

"Then a battle of wits!"

"Meaning what?"

"A game of riddles. Surely you are not afraid? I am an old man whose memory is not what it once was. I could not possibly pose a threat to someone as youthful as you... could I?"

"If your riddles are as transparent as your attempts at goading me, this should be a doddle."

Lamour grinned. "Excellent. I will start, then, yes? I run but cannot walk, I sing but cannot speak, I touch but cannot feel, and in the dark I eat. What am I?"

Valkyrie frowned. "What?"

"What am I?"

"I've to guess?"

"It is not a guess. You have to work it out from the clues I have given you."

"What was the first one?"

"I run but cannot walk."

"That's stupid."

"It is not stupid, it is—"

"How can something that runs not be able to walk? If it can run, it can walk – it just needs to run slower."

"I can say nothing more about it."

She frowned. "Wait. Is it water? It's water, isn't it?"

"I can say nothing more—"

"What was the second one?"

Lamour sighed. "I sing but cannot speak."

"A bird."

"That is not the answer to the riddle."

"A bird can't speak, but it sings."

"Yes, that is true, but it is not the answer to the riddle."

"A parrot speaks."

"What?"

"A parrot. It speaks."

"No it does not. It mimics. That is not speaking. A parrot cannot form independent—"

"What's the third one?"

"This really is not how the game of wits is played."

"Just tell me what the third one is."

"I touch but cannot feel."

"And the fourth?"

"In the dark I eat."

"Someone who likes to eat in the dark."

"That is not the answer."

"It's *an* answer. I got three out of four, so that's pretty good."

"Three out of—? No. There are not four answers. There is one answer. Each strand of the riddle adds to the answer."

"Then it's a bird that isn't a parrot who likes to swim and eat in the dark and likes to do one other thing."

"*No.*"

"Then what's the answer?"

"A Bush Stone-curlew."

"A what?"

"It's a water bird indigenous to Australia."

"And how the hell was I supposed to work that out?"

"*I run but cannot walk*. That's water. *I sing but cannot speak*. That's a bird."

"I got those two!"

"But you didn't put them together. *I touch but cannot feel*. Any physical object can touch, but in order to feel one must be organic. Inorganic objects cannot feel. A rock or stone is inorganic. *In the dark I eat*. What gathers nutrients in the dark?"

Valkyrie frowned. "Roots?"

"Exactly. The roots of a plant, or a bush. Bush, stone, water bird. The Bush Stone-curlew."

"But I've never even heard of that before."

"Is it my fault you haven't studied ornithology?"

"Fine. If that's how you want to play it, at least I got it half right."

"You really do not know how to play this—"

"Shut up. My turn to pose the riddle. Who sang 'Hit Me Baby One More Time'?"

Lamour frowned. "Pardon?"

"Who sang it?"

"That is your riddle?"

"Yep."

"But that is not a riddle, that is a..."

"You don't know, do you?"

"*Un instant, s'il vous plaît.* Just let me... What was it?"

"'Hit Me Baby One More Time.' Or just 'Baby One More Time', whichever you prefer."

"And this is a song?"

"Yes."

Lamour's forehead creased. "Is it a modern song?"

"Modernish."

"But I do not know—"

"Is it my fault you don't listen to the radio?"

"Very well, very well… It is not the American, it is not Elvis Presley, I know that, because—"

"He died on a toilet."

"He is dead?"

"A while ago now."

"He died on the toilet?"

"Mm-hmm."

"I always imagined *I* would die on the toilet."

"That's charming. Do you give up?"

Lamour sagged. "I concede. Who sang the song?"

"Britney Spears."

"You mean Brittany."

"I mean Britney."

"But she is missing an entire syllable from her name."

"Then I hope one day she'll find it. But you lose, Lamour." She threw him the handcuffs.

"I… I am not exactly sure that you won, though."

"You don't have to be sure. You just have to look at how sure I am, and assume I know what I'm talking about."

Lamour bit his lip.

"I don't want to hurt you," she said. "Just put the cuffs on and let me leave."

Lamour straightened. "If you really do not want to hurt me, you could leave now."

"I can't. I might not want to hurt you, but there's something inside me that does. And she likes it. If I let her out, even for a moment, she'll flay your skin and pull out your fingernails and take your eyes and she'll be laughing every time you scream."

"She sounds violent."

"She is violent. Please, Lamour. I can feel her in my head. She wants to get out. She wants to tear out your tongue."

"Oh, my."

"Please, Lamour…"

He hesitated, then cuffed himself to his unconscious bodyguard.

"Thank you," said Valkyrie, activating the cloaking sphere. She wheeled the Engineer out, closed the door behind her, and then carried on.

Interesting.

She got to the corner and let three sorcerers sprint by, then followed after them. The Engineer was heavy, but the cart made it manageable.

Using me as a threat now, are you? That's very interesting.

She reached an elevator, pressed the button, waited for the doors to open.

It's almost as if you want *me to take over. Is that it, Valkyrie? Is that what you want?*

The elevator pinged and the doors opened. She pushed the Engineer in, turned.

You want to feel that power again?

A woman hurried towards her, speeding up to stop the doors from closing. Valkyrie pushed gently at the air and the woman bounced off empty space, and Valkyrie just had time to see the shocked expression on her face before the doors closed.

She got back to the shaft room, took the Engineer off the hand-cart and manoeuvred it into a harness that she attached to two thick ropes. Tying the other ends of the ropes to a rusted lever she'd found on the floor, she dragged the whole lot into the water. When the Engineer was directly under the gap, she let it rest, then used the air to raise the lever upwards. Ignoring the distant sounds of alarms and explosions and gunfire, she fitted the lever into the gap and pressed upwards, watching it rattle and splash as it went, taking the ropes with it. Halfway up she began to lose control. It was getting too far away from her. She pulled it back slightly, then spent a few seconds finding the point she needed. When she had it, she focused, and then thrust both hands up. She felt the lever hurtle away from her and then it was gone from her control. All she could do was look at the ropes as they continued to unspool...

... and then stopped.

Valkyrie waited. She waited a full minute, but the lever didn't slide back down. It was up there, on the surface, in the stream. Now all they needed to do was get up there themselves, haul up the Engineer and escape.

Easy.

Making sure the sphere was still active, Valkyrie ran to the stairs and went up, following the sounds of battle. She threw open a door. The Dead Men had secured themselves in a corridor, forcing the enemy to come at them in smaller groups. Even so, they were about to be overwhelmed at any moment. Valkyrie took the stick from her back, bared her teeth—

—and then the ceiling was ripped off.

36

LOSING BLOOD

"Apologies for the interruption," Amalia said, "but you asked to be kept abreast of what was happening in France. There is news."

Illori Reticent put the report she'd been reading to one side, and beckoned the other woman into her office. It was a small office, full of books, and smelled of old paper and warm leather. After Quintin Strom's assassination, Cothernus Ode had moved into the Grand Mage's chambers and the new Elder that had been promoted to replace him had instantly laid claim to Ode's old office. Palaver Graves was a man to take untold delight in petty victories, and Illori let him have this one. Besides, at no time did Ode's office ever hold the slightest attraction for her – it was too big, too cold, and too close to the toilets for her liking.

"The Dead Men broke into the facility as we knew they would," Amalia said. "Grand Mage Mandat's forces then sprang the trap."

Illori raised an eyebrow. "By the look on your face, I can tell things stopped going to plan from that moment on."

"I don't have all the details, but it appears that the Dead Men received help from external forces."

Illori sat back in her chair. "The Australians?"

"And the Africans."

"*Both?*"

"I'm afraid so. The Dead Men escaped. Also, they have the Engineer."

Illori stared at her. "Does the Grand Mage know?"

"He is being briefed as we speak."

"This is going to be fun," Illori muttered. "Thank you, Amalia. You may return to your duties."

Once Amalia was gone, Illori pulled her cloak over her shoulders and pinned it into place with the clasp that signified her position on the Council. She fixed her hair and applied the lightest sheen of lipstick, then walked the corridors. She met Graves on the way, and with great reluctance he fell in beside her.

"I take it you've heard," he said, trying to get her to speed up.

She maintained her pace. "I did indeed, Palaver. You're not the only one who has little spies whispering in their ear."

"I would scarcely call them *spies*, Elder Reticent. Are you feeling all right, by the way? You look tired. Maybe you should rest."

She gave him a smile. "Your concern is touching. And maybe I do look tired. I tend to work a lot." They reached Ode's office, and Palaver opened the door for her. "You're looking wonderfully well-rested, though," she said as she passed through.

Palaver came in after her, glowering.

Grand Mage Cothernus Ode stood at the floor-to-ceiling window, looking out over London. While most other Sanctuaries had their premises below ground, thirty years ago, Quintin Strom decided to build upwards instead of deeper down. From the outside, the building was neither pretty enough nor ugly enough to catch the eye or hold the attention. From out there, the window Ode stood at appeared small and showed nothing but an empty room.

"Mandat has made a mess of everything," Ode said, keeping his eyes on the city. "How that's possible, I don't know. The man has a knack for plucking failure from the jaws of success."

"The Australians and the Africans—" Palaver started, but didn't get one word further.

"I know about the bloody Australians and the bloody Africans," Ode said, turning now to cast a contemptuous eye on Illori's rapidly wilting colleague, "and their involvement shouldn't even have mattered. If you manage to lure the Dead Men into a trap, you kill them instantly. You blow the entire facility. You don't try to take them *alive*. You don't try to take them *down*. You just *kill them*. The press of a button. A big explosion. Instead, he gets all of his sorcerers and all of his Cleavers to lie in wait and, when the Dead Men appear in a place no one was expecting, they all scramble over each other to claim the glory. And then, as you say... the bloody Australians and the bloody Africans."

"We should contact their Councils," Illori said.

"We're trying," Ode responded. "So far, they're not picking up the phone. It's too late. You *know* it's too late, Illori. They've shown which side they're fighting on. Their colours have been nailed."

"Then they have become our enemies," she said, "and they will be dealt with. We knew the Cradles of Magic forming an alliance was a distinct possibility."

"Doesn't make the news any easier to take," Ode said, collapsing into his chair. "Damn it, Graves, don't just stand there and sulk. Contribute to the conversation."

Palaver flushed. "Yes, Grand Mage, of course. We should also take into account the fact that the Dead Men have retrieved the Engineer."

"And that's another thing!" Ode cried. "The damn Engineer! You lure them into a trap with something they need, the very least you can do is not let them run off with the thing when they escape! Do we have *any* idea where they are?"

"I'm afraid not," said Palaver, hanging his head in shame.

"We had them," Ode muttered. "Ravel and Bespoke. Two of the three Elders. All Mandat had to do was not mess up and this war would have been over before it really began."

There was a knock on the door, and the Administrator, Merriwyn, stepped in. "Apologies, Elders. The Japanese Grand

Mage is requesting assistance. There's a strike team disabling his Sanctuary's infrastructure faster than it can be repaired."

"Please tell Grand Mage Kumo that he can deal with it himself – we're busy fighting a war."

"He knows that, sir, and he points out that we're fighting a war using his sorcerers. He barely has anyone left to defend his Sanctuary. And he's not the only one with this problem. We're getting requests for assistance from Syria, Romania, Iceland..."

"Iceland?" Ode barked. "Is there even a *Sanctuary* in Iceland?"

Merriwyn didn't bat an eyelid. "Yes there is, sir, and it's under attack."

Ode's hands curled into fists. "I don't have time for this. Ravel is sending hit-and-run teams to poorly defended Sanctuaries because he needs some easy wins. These are the actions of a desperate man. From this moment on, all reports of this nature go to Elder Graves. You can handle this, can't you, Graves?"

Palaver nodded quickly. "Yes, Grand Mage. Of course."

"Hear that, Merriwyn? Do not bother me with this again. Do you have any relevant information to share with me?"

Merriwyn turned a page. "General Mantis is on schedule, sir. There have been no reports of any delays."

"Why couldn't everyone be as efficient as Mantis? Say what you like about its unusual predilections, that creature knows how to stick to a timetable. Is that it, then? That is the one piece of good news today?"

"I'm afraid so, Grand Mage," said Merriwyn.

"Leave us."

Merriwyn bowed, and left silently.

Ode turned to Illori. "Thoughts?"

"Fletcher Renn is a problem," she said. "The Dead Men are a problem. Take Renn out of the equation and the Irish lose their ability to hit and run. Take the Dead Men out of the equation and they lose their leaders."

"Not all of them. Madame Mist is still in Roarhaven."

Illori arched an eyebrow. "You think anyone outside of Roarhaven will follow her? The Dead Men are more than just leaders and more than just soldiers. They're a symbol. They're the living embodiment of what a small group of determined individuals can accomplish against a much bigger enemy. They proved that against Mevolent. They're proving it against us."

"I didn't realise you'd joined their fan club."

"Snarkiness doesn't suit you, Grand Mage. Have you heard what our own people are saying about them? During the day, they are spoken of with trepidation and awe. But at night? At night they're spoken of with fear. The Dead Men have become the stuff of superstition and nightmares. That is why they are winning."

"Whoever said they were winning?"

"We have yet to capture or kill more than a dozen of their sorcerers, while forty-one of ours have been taken out of the fight that we know of. They are successfully targeting and attacking our support structures and we still can't get through their shield. They are chipping away at our allies and we haven't even moved against theirs. We're losing, Cothernus. With every cut, they draw more blood."

"I don't have time for this. There's a conference call with my fellow Grand Mages on the Supreme Council that I have to get to. No doubt Mandat will give us a hundred and one excuses as to how this isn't his fault. There's going to be a lot of name-calling and angry words, and nothing is going to get decided. By the end of the day, I want a new strategy from you both. Illori, I want proposals on how we handle the Australians and Africans. Graves, give me options on how to track down and eliminate the Dead Men. Get to it."

37

CHARIVARI

It had all been going so well.

Skylar and Serephia had arrived in Mozambique without detection. They'd blended into the throngs of mortals at the airport, where Skylar's English accent and Serephia's American twang wouldn't stand out. None of the African sorcerers stationed there even noticed them passing. Once they were outside, they stole a car, headed out of the city. Cothernus Ode himself had assigned them their mission – assassinate the Sensitive who was psychically co-ordinating the African forces around the world.

The Sensitive had been tracked to a large warehouse, well away from civilian eyes. Skylar had been told to expect a heavy contingent of enemy sorcerers protecting him. She didn't mind that. She had no intention of taking them on. The plan was to slip in, kill the Sensitive, and slip out before anyone knew what had happened.

So they parked and crept up to the warehouse. They found the first guard, torn apart, and that's when things started to go wrong.

"We should get out of here," Serephia said, her voice soft.

"Not until we know the target is down," Skylar replied. "And not until we know who did this."

She led the way to the wide-open warehouse door. Even for her, a seasoned assassin, the sight that greeted her was shocking. Dead bodies were strewn about like someone had carelessly tossed them aside. The carnage was fresh. Blood still dripped.

Serephia tapped her, turned her head slightly. Skylar listened. Now she could hear it. A voice. No. Two voices.

They moved into the warehouse, stepping between the bodies, darting from shadow to shadow. Serephia had her gun in her hand. Skylar realised that she'd drawn her own as well, and hadn't even noticed herself doing it.

Through the next door, there was a man on his knees. He was small, a dark-skinned man with tight silver hair. Skylar recognised him as the Sensitive. Standing over him was a ten-foot slab of muscle with pale skin and a bald head, splattered with other people's blood. Skylar's mouth went dry at the sight of him.

"I swear," the Sensitive said, "I cannot see any sign of them. Please, let me go."

The huge man laid a massive hand on the Sensitive's shoulder, and the Sensitive whimpered in pain.

"You are not looking hard enough," the huge man said. "Find me Department X or I will crush your skull."

"I need something more," the Sensitive said. "Please, I need more information. A name, or an object that one of them has touched..."

"I was told you are the most powerful psychic on this continent."

"Yes, but—"

"Find me Department X."

"I can't. Please, I'm sorry. I need more to—"

The huge man grasped the Sensitive's head between his hands and snapped his neck. Skylar's heart lurched at the sudden *crack*.

"Disappointing," the huge man murmured. Then he turned. "But perhaps I'll have better luck with you two."

Serephia was already running and Skylar was right behind her. They fired back into the room. Skylar tripped over a corpse and sprawled, lost her gun. Serephia turned, reached out to grab her, and a stream of energy melted through her like she wasn't even there.

Skylar cursed, fell back, scrambled up, and then the huge man had his hand round her throat.

"Tell me," he said, "what do you know of Department X?"

She kicked, struggled, but it was no use. She raised her hand, her magic flowing through her, but the big man took her hand and broke it. Skylar screamed and he dropped her.

"Who are you?" she shouted, clutching her arm, tears of pain in her eyes. "What do you want?"

"My name is Charivari," the huge man said. "And I am looking for the people who have been killing Warlocks. The psychic told me many things. He told me of your little war. He told me of a machine that can increase magic. But he didn't tell me what I wanted to know. He didn't tell me where I can find Department X."

"Department X isn't real," Skylar said, inching away from him on her knees. "It's a story. It's a rumour."

"Or maybe they're so well hidden that even sorcerers like you don't know they exist."

The pain was really hitting her now. "Maybe," she said. "Yes, maybe. I can... I can help you. I can—"

His lip curled. "You can do nothing. You would tell me anything I wanted to hear if you thought you could escape. So, if it is not this Department X killing my people, who is it? Who should I be hunting?"

"I... I don't know. Please, I don't have anything to do with the Warlocks. I've never even met one before."

Charivari smiled. "Well," he said, "you have now."

38

THE KEEP

Fletcher pulled his jacket tighter around himself. He didn't like being cold. That was why he'd moved to Australia. But he hadn't been back there since the war had broken out, which was, what, two months ago now. Myra had kind of ruined it for him.

The car was freezing, but he didn't ask the driver to turn up the heat. Dai Maybury was from the unfortunate Maybury clan, and he didn't take kindly to wussy complaints about the cold. From what Fletcher had heard over the past week or so, Dai was one of sextuplets, and the only decent one at that. His brother Deacon, a pretty powerful Sensitive, was a bit of a scumbag, all things considered – but at least he was still living. His other brother Davit had sealed himself in a secret room and promptly run out of air, Dafydd had fallen into a wood-chipper, Daveth had been eaten by rabid goats and Davon had died from intestinal distress.

Fletcher didn't ask him if he had any sisters.

The road became a trail, then vanished altogether in the grass. Dai stopped the jeep and they got out. The narrow meadow carried on for a kilometre or so, up a gentle incline. At the very top stood a building. They started walking.

"During the war with Mevolent, the Keep was one of our strongest positions," Dai said. "Dense woodland on either side where we would lay traps and ambushes, and behind us a sheer wall of rock, on top of which we'd lay more traps, more ambushes."

"So if you were attacked," Fletcher said, "the enemy would be forced to come up through here."

Dai nodded. "Their force would swarm in from the road and then immediately be funnelled straight towards us. Back then, our defences were second to none. There were walls, shields, gates, each one heavily manned, and that was before you even reached the Keep itself. They didn't stand a chance. Take us halfway up."

Dai laid a hand on Fletcher's shoulder and they teleported further on up the meadow and kept walking.

"We'd have our best bowmen up there," Dai said, pointing to a grassy ridge to their left. "They'd take out as many as they could, and right before their position was overrun they'd disappear into tunnels we'd built underground, emerge back at the Keep. Mevolent's army came at us again and again during the war. Sometimes it would be battalions of sorcerers, men and women filling this meadow. Other times they'd try and sneak through the trees, or come at us from the rock face. They never got close."

"So the Keep is impenetrable, then," said Fletcher.

Dai smiled. "It used to be. The war ended, the defences were dismantled, the tunnels were filled in, the walls were taken down. Now all that remains are a few small buildings."

"How long before the defences can be put back up?"

"They're not going to be."

"But the Engineer is here. If Mantis finds out—"

"We're hoping that it does."

"So we're leading them into a trap?"

"More or less."

The closer they got to the Keep, the more figures Fletcher could see moving about behind the low, broken walls. He smiled. "Let me guess. Hidden up there is our army, right? Mantis comes up, expects an easy victory and then *bam*. We strike."

Dai put his hand on Fletcher's shoulder again. "See for yourself."

They teleported beyond the wall, into the Keep itself, and immediately Fletcher jerked away from a Hollow Man as it shuffled by.

"Relax," said Dai, laughing, "they're ours."

They were everywhere. Paper-skinned, shoulders slumped as their heavy fists swung, their faces had indentations where the eyes and mouth should be. At a distance, they could pass for human, but up close they were a hulking mockery. Fletcher watched one of them snag itself on a rusty nail, tearing its skin. It kept walking as green gas billowed from the tear, deflating itself with every step. It collapsed, emptied, and then the breeze took hold of its skin and tossed it across the ground, where it tangled in the feet of another Hollow Man and was dragged from sight.

Bane and O'Callahan walked up. Gracious was not looking happy.

"This is ridiculous," he said. "You see what we have to work with? You see the quality of these things?"

"They do seem to be on the cheap side," Dai conceded.

"Worst quality skin I've ever seen on a Hollow Man," said Gracious. "Where did Ravel get them? No, I don't want to know. I don't want to taint myself with knowing the name of the person who made these skins."

"We just inflated the last of them," said Donegan. His eyes were rimmed with red and his nose was running. "Foul stuff, that green gas. I got a blast of it, right in the face."

"He threw up," Gracious said.

"I did," Donegan admitted. "And I'm still seeing blurry outlines of everything."

"Um," Fletcher said, "can I ask a stupid question?"

"There are no stupid questions," Gracious said, "just stupid people. Ask away."

"Well, from what I can see, there are only Hollow Men here, is that right? No sorcerers or Cleavers apart from you guys?"

"That is correct," said Donegan.

"And if Mantis does find out that the Engineer is here, and if it does come with its army, you don't really have any defences to... defend yourself with."

Gracious nodded. "An accurate summation. What part was the stupid question?"

"That's coming up," Fletcher said. "If Mantis attacks, you've got that rock cliff behind you so there's nowhere to run, either."

"Waiting for the stupid question..."

"Well... I mean... If they come, you can't fight and you can't run. You'll be trapped."

Gracious looked at him. "That wasn't even a question."

"You're quite right," Dai said. "When Mantis attacks, we'll be overwhelmed. The Keep will be surrounded, and they'll breach our pathetic wall with laughable ease. At which point they'll realise that all these people they've seen moving around are, in actual fact, really cheap Hollow Men."

"By which time," said Donegan, "Gracious, Dai and I will have run back to Nye and Clarabelle and the Engineer, and we'll call for you. Then you come, and you teleport us to safety."

"But what's the point?" Fletcher asked. "Why lure them here in the first place if... oh."

Gracious smiled. "Look. He's getting it."

"So they'll be here," Fletcher said, "in this terrible position with no defences and no escape, and they'll turn round..."

"And realise that the Dead Men have moved into the valley behind them," said Donegan, "and they have an army with them."

Fletcher grinned. "That's pretty smart."

"That's why they're called tactics," said Gracious, "and not..."

The others looked at him. Gracious just shrugged. "Fletcher, you want to go talk to a robot?"

Fletcher grinned. "Sure."

Gracious led him into the Keep, the inside of which was not quite as disappointing as the outside. The walls held up the ceiling. The floors held up the walls. It was a good system.

The only room that had anything in it looked like a mad scientist's garden shed. It was small, cramped, and full of beeping machines and wires running everywhere. Doctor Nye had to almost bend double to move. Clarabelle waved as Fletcher walked in. She stood beside a six-foot robot.

Its metal surface was battered, and deep scratches ran over the magical symbols soldered on to its sculpted torso. It was also not exactly *here*. There were small gaps in its body, like a jigsaw missing some of its pieces that somehow managed to stay together. Within those gaps there was a blue glow, which turned white the more Fletcher stared. Its head was smooth, and had a smiley face scrawled over it.

"That is so cool," said Fletcher.

Gracious was practically giggling with excitement.

Nye looked round, looked back at the Engineer, and sighed. "Clarabelle," it said, "did you draw a smiley face on the robot?"

Clarabelle furrowed her brow, like she was searching for the perfect lie. Then she brightened, and said, "No."

"You didn't?"

"No, Doctor."

"Do you know who did?"

"I think it was one of the Hollow Men."

"I think you're lying."

She sagged. "It just looked sad, standing there without a face. Now it looks happy."

"It looks ridiculous."

She brightened. "Ridiculously happy?"

"No," said Nye, "just ridiculous. Mr Renn, aren't you going to say hello to our mechanical guest?"

Fletcher peered closer. "Is it working?"

Gracious nudged him. "Ask *it* that."

Fletcher cleared his throat, and stepped towards the robot. "Excuse me," he said, "are you operational?"

The Engineer turned its head towards him. "I am," it said, its voice undoubtedly robotic but surprisingly warm. "I was reactivated forty-three minutes ago. My available systems are back online."

Fletcher looked round to Gracious. "Do Skulduggery and the others know about this?"

Gracious nodded. "They've asked me to get all the information we need. Engineer, are you ready to answer a few questions?"

"Yes I am, Mr O'Callahan."

"The Accelerator," Gracious said, "can it be shut down?"

"Yes. In doing so, a locking mechanism will seal it from use. Once deactivated, only I can activate it again."

"Would you have any objection to shutting it down?"

"Not at all. That is my purpose. In the event of the Accelerator's activation, I am to facilitate its deactivation before it is too late."

"Well, OK then," said Gracious, smiling broadly. Then he frowned. "Wait, before it's too late to do what?"

"The Accelerator's power is on a constant loop," said the Engineer. "With every loop, the power builds, and the stronger the link to the source of all magic becomes. Eventually the Accelerator will overload, delivering a boost to every magical being around the world."

"A boost," said Gracious cautiously. "Like the boost it gave to Kitana Kellaway and her friends?"

"I'm afraid not. Their power was merely tripled, and while my creator could not calculate this accurately, he estimated that an uncontrolled overload would result in a boost to between ten and twenty times a sorcerer's current level."

Nye looked around, its small eyes widening. "But a boost that big would drive all sorcerers *insane*."

"My creator believed this was a possibility, yes."

"So the Accelerator is a... a time bomb," said Gracious. "A doomsday device."

"Not intentionally," said the Engineer. "A nuclear reactor has carbon rods that can shut down the fission reaction at any moment, preventing a catastrophic meltdown. You may think of me like those carbon rods. I am what prevents the Accelerator from being a bomb."

"Except you didn't," said Gracious. "Because you weren't around."

"I got bored."

"You're a machine."

"Machines can become bored, too."

Gracious looked suddenly concerned. "My toaster is bored?"

"Perhaps," said the Engineer. "I do not know many toasters. My cognitive functions are perhaps a little too sophisticated for my own good. But I can still switch off the Accelerator before it reaches catastrophic levels, if you take me to it."

Gracious let out a sigh of relief. "See that? There's a threat, and now it's averted. That, I think, qualifies as a victory for the good guys." He turned to Fletcher, held up his hand. "High five!"

Fletcher looked at him. "Really?"

"Don't leave me hanging, man."

Fletcher gave him a high five. It really hurt.

"Mr Engineer," Gracious said, "would you be so kind as to accompany us back to the Sanctuary and deactivate the Accelerator?"

"Of course," said the Engineer. There was a pause. "Hmm," it said.

"That didn't sound good," Fletcher said warily.

"Apologies," said the Engineer. "A part of me seems to be malfunctioning."

Nye swivelled its head on its long neck. "What did you say?"

"My memory-processing unit is malfunctioning," said the Engineer. "I am afraid that I cannot access the relevant protocols."

"Let me see it," said Nye. "I'll fix it."

The Engineer shook its smiley-faced head. "I am afraid it will not be that simple, Doctor. A self-diagnostic reveals the unit to be irreparably damaged."

Fletcher stepped forward. "Wait a second, so now you *can't* shut down the Accelerator?"

"Not without my memory-processing unit being replaced."

"There *is* no replacement," Nye said angrily. "This is a one-of-a-kind piece of technology. Give me six months and I might be able to reverse-engineer it, but—"

"I am afraid you do not have six months," said the Engineer. "In a matter of weeks – without my processing unit, I cannot be any more specific than that – the Accelerator will overload."

Gracious looked at Fletcher. "So now we're back to the end of the world? I take back my high five. This is not a high-five situation."

"May I offer a possible solution?" said the Engineer.

"Please," said Gracious. "A possible solution would be awesome right about now."

"My creator, Doctor Rote, had many scientists working on different aspects of the Accelerator, and therefore me, at the same time. They did not know how their projects interacted, or what they would combine to form, but the woman who designed my brain made a prototype before she started work on the finished version."

Fletcher frowned. "You have another brain somewhere?"

"In essence," said the Engineer, "yes. It is not as advanced as the one I have been using, but the memory-processing unit could be salvaged from the prototype and used in place of my own."

Gracious clapped his hands, delighted. "See that? Problem averted. We are good. I don't mind telling you. We are *good*. So, Engineer, where is this prototype brain of yours?"

The Engineer looked at him. "It currently resides in the Sanctuary in London, England."

"Oh," said Gracious, and looked like he might cry. "Oh, good."

39

ENEMY COMBATANTS

Autumn brought with it shorter days and darker evenings. It swept the warmth of summer to one side, replaced it with grey skies and chill winds like some great switch had been flicked. Grey skies to match grey moods, Valkyrie reckoned, in everyone around her except the Dead Men. There had been moments over the past few weeks – during the ambush in France, at the raid in Moscow, after the battle in Arizona – where she genuinely thought that these men had probably never been happier than right now. They had a clear purpose once again. They were fighting for something. They were warriors, and they were back doing what warriors did.

Making war.

She didn't say any of this out loud. It wasn't because she didn't want to make them feel bad – it was merely because she didn't want them to start questioning *her*. The fact was, despite the fighting and the killing and the sheer discomfort of being at war, she was enjoying herself. She hadn't yet been forced to seriously injure anyone, she hadn't been seriously injured herself, and they hadn't failed even one of their missions so far. Sure, things hadn't always gone according to plan, and they may have missed one or two opportunities along the way, but they were striking fast and getting out of there before the enemy could counter. They were winning. Sort of.

Sometimes it was hard to tell which side was in the lead. The Supreme Council forces were massive and overwhelming, but slow to move. The Irish sorcerers stayed in small groups and darted in and out – sometimes with Fletcher's help, sometimes on their own. They'd suffered some losses, some crushing defeats, but they kept going. Like Shudder said, you stab a giant enough times with a tiny knife, sooner or later he's going to topple over.

Not that the Irish were the only side using this tactic, of course. General Mantis and his few hundred soldiers may have been denied the reinforcements they'd been expecting, but so far they were successfully evading capture in Ireland – and they hadn't yet taken the bait and attacked the Keep. Skulduggery suspected that they were hiding among the mortals, and every so often they'd regroup, hit a target and dissipate back into the cities and towns. Except for Mantis himself, of course. A creature like that would have to stay hidden.

For the last few days, their base camp had been an old hotel on the outskirts of Frankfurt. There were twenty Irish sorcerers staying here, plus three Americans and four Germans who had decided to follow their conscience. Valkyrie crossed the dark courtyard, saw Tanith through a window and stopped, peered closer. Tanith was leaning back against the wall while Ghastly worked at her boots. Ghastly said something and she laughed, and at her reply he smiled. He put the first boot on the ground and she slipped her foot in, balancing herself by resting a hand on his shoulder. He knew, of course, that her balance was perfect. He didn't object to the hand, though.

Sanguine walked in, stopped suddenly when he saw them. Tanith took her hand from Ghastly's shoulder, used it to pick up her second boot. She pulled it on while standing on one leg, chatting away. Sanguine glared at Ghastly. Ghastly gazed back, and stood, and when he moved he brushed by Tanith gently. Sanguine went for him.

Valkyrie stopped herself from rushing in. Even Tanith didn't try to break up the fight. Sanguine hit Ghastly and Ghastly hit Sanguine. They crashed over furniture and rolled on the floor, and Ghastly was first up and he clipped Sanguine as he rose. Three more punches followed and Sanguine staggered, then his hand went to his pocket and his straight razor flashed.

Tanith grabbed his wrist, held it in place. Stern words, softly spoken.

Sanguine shook his hand free, but didn't resume his attack, and a moment later he stormed out of there. Tanith looked at Ghastly, but he turned away, and Tanith shook her head, and followed Sanguine out of the door.

"Spying is rude," Skulduggery said from Valkyrie's shoulder.

"We have loads of spies," she said, annoyed that once again she hadn't even heard him approach.

He nodded. "And they are very rude people. Who were you watching?"

"Ghastly and Tanith and Sanguine. Ghastly and Sanguine had a fight."

"Did Ghastly leave him alive?"

"Yeah. Tanith stepped in before it could get any worse. She's changed, don't you think? She's getting more like her old self. I think the real Tanith is re-emerging."

"From what I know of Remnants, I'm afraid that's not possible. If it seems like she's back to her old self, then she's pretending. Which, by itself, isn't necessarily a sinister development."

"You think she's doing it to try to be our friend again?"

"She doesn't want to be our friend," Skulduggery said, "she wants to be *your* friend. She knows you're Darquesse. In her eyes, you're her messiah. Her idol. Who wouldn't want to be closer to their idol?"

"Well, if that's what she's trying to do, at least we can trust her to a certain degree."

"To a certain *limited* degree."

"You're worried that I might start to think of her like I thought of the old Tanith, aren't you? Well, I won't. No matter how much I might want to."

"I wasn't worried."

"So you didn't come out here to check on me?"

"No, I came out here because we're about to decide what to do about the Accelerator problem."

She looked at him. "If we shut down the Accelerator, you won't be able to power the Cube, and the Cube is the only thing that's going to be able to hold Darquesse."

"I'm afraid, for the moment, we don't have a choice."

"For the moment?"

"I'll think of something, Valkyrie. I always do. Now, enough dawdling. Fetch Fletcher and drag him to the briefing in ten minutes?"

"The briefing," Valkyrie said, giving a salute. "Yes, sir."

"Dear God. That was the worst salute I've ever seen."

"Oh, you're exaggerating."

"It was like someone slapping a dead fish across their forehead. Please don't salute again. It doesn't suit you. Just give that cute little impish grin of yours from now on, OK?"

She grinned. "What, this one?"

"No," he said, "the cute one."

She glared and he walked off, chuckling to himself. She walked the other way, climbed the stairs to Fletcher's room. She walked in to find him freshly emerged from the shower, wearing a towel around his waist and looking at himself in the mirror.

Valkyrie sighed. "You're never going to change, are you?"

Fletcher turned, and her smile faded. The scar cut across the left side of his midsection, and stood out red and raw against his wet skin.

"Doctor Synecdoche says it'll fade in a few weeks," he said.

She nodded. "Keep applying that stuff they give you. Does it hurt?"

"No. Itches, though."

"I remember. That burn the wraith gave me is already fading. It doesn't even sting any more."

He nodded, didn't say anything. It was odd, seeing him with his hair flattened by his shower. Made him seem vulnerable, somehow.

"You OK?" she asked. "We haven't had a chance to chat since this all started. You know, about Myra and everything."

He shrugged, started laying his clothes on the bed. "What's there to chat about? We dated, she was an enemy agent, she tried to kill me. It's funny. While I was recovering, that's all I could think about. I wasn't able to teleport anywhere or do anything, so the same things kept running through my head. *Why did she do this? What's wrong with me? Poor little Fletcher. Boohoo.* But then, when I was through feeling sorry for myself, I got angry. She murdered Hayley and Tane. Murdered them, like they were nothing."

Valkyrie leaned back against the wall. "I know," she said, suddenly feeling drained.

"I still can't understand it. I don't understand how it's possible. Hayley and Tane. They were my friends. They were your friends. They were cool and funny and so much fun to be around. But because they were the ones to tell us that the war had started, because they happened to be there when we found out, she killed them. As easy as that." He snapped his fingers. "How is that possible? How is it fair? What kind of person do you have to be to kill two people who have never done anything to harm you?"

"We'll find her," Valkyrie said.

"How? She's not even a sorcerer, as far as I can tell. She's just an assassin. A mortal assassin. How are we going to find one of those?"

"She was used once, maybe she'll be used again. When she does, we'll hear about it. Then she'll pay."

He grunted. "She made good muffins, though."

"I'm sure you'll find another muffin-maker just as good as she was. And maybe this one won't try to kill you."

"Well, that'll just be weird."

Valkyrie couldn't help it, she laughed. Fletcher did, too. She felt lighter now, better, and she stood up straighter.

Fletcher held his arms out wide. "Dry me."

She raised an eyebrow. "Pardon?"

"Use your water power thingy."

"I'm not a hairdryer, Fletch."

"I don't want you to *touch* my hair. It'll go frizzy. Just dry the rest of me."

She sighed and raised her hands, and he closed his eyes and waited. Grinning, she took hold of the air and sent it blasting into him, knocking him back a few steps, thoroughly disrupting his hair and sending his towel spinning into the bathroom. Then she spun on her heel and walked out. "Briefing in five minutes," she called.

"I hate you so much," he called after her.

"I know."

Tanith turned up for the briefing without Sanguine. Valkyrie said nothing, but watched Ghastly pretending not to notice that she was standing right beside him. Fletcher arrived with his hair perfectly ridiculous as usual. Valkyrie grinned at him from across the large table and he did his best to ignore her, but she could see the smile edging on to his lips.

"OK then," Ravel said, his voice bringing an end to the low murmuring in the room, "good news first. Squads of African sorcerers have obliterated seven of the Supreme Council's facilities around the Middle East, and our Australian friends have gone straight to New York. I've heard unofficial reports that Grand Mage Bisahalani himself had to be evacuated before he was captured. These actions have taken so much pressure off us. Without them, I'd say we'd be well on our way to losing the war. So... that's the good news. The bad news, you've all heard. If the Accelerator overloads, a power boost that big wouldn't just affect sorcerers. The Engineer said *every* magical being. So we're talking Warlocks and witches and creatures and—"

"And mortals," Skulduggery said. "Mortals with magic in them. Ordinary people, who would have lived out their lives without a hint of what they actually are. That's more than catastrophic. That's an extinction-level event. The human race would be wiped out."

"And what about Darquesse?" Ghastly said. "The Accelerator was supposed to help contain her, not make her more powerful. Someone like her, boosted to that degree..."

"She'd be a god," Skulduggery murmured.

"Oooh, this is fun," Tanith said, grinning and looking straight at Valkyrie.

"Suddenly we have a new priority," said Ravel, missing the glare that Valkyrie shot back. "We need to be able to shut down the Accelerator the moment this war is over, or within a matter of weeks – whichever comes first. To do that, the Engineer needs one missing piece of its brain, which sits in the London Sanctuary."

"I might be able to just teleport in," Fletcher said, a little uneasily.

Saracen shook his head. "Every Supreme Council Sanctuary will have anti-Teleporter sigils set up. We'll have to go in the old-fashioned way."

"I know a secret entrance," said Tanith. "No problem."

"Getting in isn't our main problem," Ravel said. "We've been keeping an eye on them, just as we've been keeping an eye on as many of the major Sanctuaries around the world as we can. On the table before you are surveillance photographs. Take a look at the sentries. We can only assume the sentries *inside* are the same as the sentries *outside*."

Vex frowned at the images. "Half of these are teenagers. They're rookies. What the hell is Ode playing at? Is he running out of full-powered sorcerers?"

"The success of this mission depends on us retrieving the prototype without setting off a single alarm," Skulduggery said.

After a moment, Vex's face changed. "Oh."

Valkyrie frowned. "What? I'm obviously missing something."

Ghastly looked at her. "The only way to guarantee that nobody raises the alarm is to kill each sentry we come across. Ruthlessness is the quickest and quietest way."

"But we can't kill kids," Saracen muttered.

"Taking the time to subdue them is going to increase the risk of discovery," Shudder said. "They are enemy combatants. They should be treated as such."

"They're too young," Vex said. "No. We can't go in."

"That is exactly why Ode assigned them," said Ravel. "Anton's right – we should view them as any other enemy. We don't want to do it, but we have to. You want to blame someone, Dexter? Blame Cothernus Ode for deliberately placing them in harm's way."

"In *our* way," said Saracen.

"This is war," Ravel said. "Bad things happen. We're the Dead Men. We're used to making unpalatable choices."

"Not like this," said Vex. "We never did anything like this, Erskine, and you know it. This is what Guild's lot did. His Exigency Mages wouldn't think twice about killing a bunch of raw recruits. But not us."

"The Exigency Mages aren't around any more – we're the only option *left*. And the moment we start putting the safety of the enemy above our own is the—"

"It's Skulduggery's decision," Ghastly interrupted. "He's got full operational control of this mission."

"Agreed," Ravel said. "Skulduggery? What do you say?"

Skulduggery looked up. "The mission is still a go, but we use non-lethal means to subdue these sentries."

Saracen was the one to break the silence that followed. "Astonishing," he said. "You've managed to find a solution that pleases absolutely nobody."

"Tanith," Skulduggery said, "where is this secret entrance?"

"In the alley to the east," Tanith said. "That'll take us into a storeroom. From there—"

"You're not coming with us."

"What?"

"We'll be able to restrain ourselves from killing," Skulduggery said. "You won't. Fletcher will teleport us all into the alley. You will open the entrance, and Fletcher will teleport you both back. *We* will go in, the seven of us. We'll split into teams, retrieve the prototype, then clear a room so that Fletcher can teleport in."

"It sounds so easy," said Ravel.

Skulduggery looked at him. "It won't be. We can expect heavy resistance. We can expect them to do whatever it takes to stop us from achieving our goal."

"So how do we get round that little obstacle?" Saracen asked.

Skulduggery tilted his head. "We disguise our goal with another one."

40

WOLVES AT THE DOOR

China pulled up, away from the streetlamps, and checked her rear view. Satisfied that there were no motorbike headlights approaching, she pushed open the door, grimacing as she got out. The car was a Mini Cooper, a nifty little thing. But it wasn't hers. It was the second car she'd borrowed since losing her own. And even this one had bullet holes in it.

Holding her side, she crossed the street, walking quickly. She followed the narrow alleyway, weeds spilling from cracks in the concrete, to a house that had once been small and unassuming and which now stood proudly, refurbished, remodelled, rebuilt. Eliza Scorn had been busy.

Even the door was new. It was heavy, built into an arch. Everything about this place screamed 'church', though there was no religious symbology that any mortal would recognise. China pushed open the door, stepped in and closed it behind her. Inside was quiet. Still.

There was a knock on the door behind her and China spun, her heart lurching. But no. Vincent Foe kicked doors down – he didn't knock on them.

She answered it, and the expression that greeted her was most unusual. It managed to be awestruck, captivated and lustful, while at the same time shocked, shamed and terrified. Octa Gregorian Boona stared at her, his mouth opening and closing, but no sound emerging. Then he spun round, started walking away.

"Octa," China said in a soft voice.

Octa stopped walking immediately, but didn't turn round. His shoulders were shaking. He was crying.

"Come back here."

He shook his head, but turned despite himself and walked back, dragging his feet. His head was down. He sniffled as he stopped in front of her.

"You probably didn't expect to see me when you knocked on the door," China said, careful to keep any hint of accusation from her tone. "I'm sorry if I startled you."

"It's OK," he sobbed.

"I haven't seen you in a while. Not since my library was destroyed. Have you missed me?"

He nodded quickly.

"Is this where you're bringing your little snippets of information now? To Eliza?"

Octa fell to his knees. "I'm sorry, I'm so, so sorry. I didn't want to betray you. I love you. You know I love you. But Eliza pays for the things I know. She pays me. With money. Not... not promises or..."

"Octa," said China, "when did I ever promise you anything?"

He looked up, tears in his eyes, his face splotchy and red. "You didn't promise with your words. It was the... It was my own hope."

"I can hardly be held responsible for that, now can I?"

"No."

"And I didn't think I *had* to pay you. I never viewed you as an informant, Octa. To me, you were a friend. If you wanted me to pay you, you should have told me. Then I'd have known things were strictly business between us."

"No," said Octa, "they weren't. There's something between us, China. I don't care about money. I care about you. I love you."

"You are so sweet. So what did you come to tell Eliza about?"

"Just something I heard about the Warlocks. One of them was seen in Mozambique this morning. He killed eighteen sorcerers."

"One Warlock killed eighteen sorcerers?"

"That's what they're saying, yes."

In the distance, the sound of motorbikes.

"I love you," said Octa. "Miss Scorn might think I'm her informant, but in my heart, I will always be *yours*."

"I knew you'd stay loyal," China said. "Thank you, Octa. I'll make sure she gets your message."

China stepped back and closed the door, and turned to see a weasel-faced man in a three-piece suit staring at her. "Hello, Jajo," she smiled.

He backed off, practically ran away. China sighed, walked deeper into the church. The pews were hand-carved. On the wall, two circles, one big, one small, barely intersecting, both made of solid gold.

Eliza Scorn walked from a backroom, Jajo Prave following along in her wake. She looked well, China had to admit. Her clothes were wonderful. Her hair, luxuriant. Her lips, curled in a cruel smile. "I'd heard you were being hunted," she said.

"I still am," China replied.

"How delightful! Are you still scurrying from place to place like a scared little fox, while the pack of wild dogs is closing in?"

"That's how you picture it, is it?"

"I picture lots of shivering in dark and lonely places. I did wonder, of course, why you didn't just go running to the Skeleton Detective or those nice Sanctuary people, but then I remembered. That pride of yours. I bet you shudder at the very thought of running to your friends for help."

"They're not my friends, Eliza. You made sure of that."

Scorn smiled.

China answered her smile with one of her own. "I look around at the power and the wealth you've accumulated and, I must admit, I envy you. Not long ago, I had all of this."

"And then you let it slip away."

China shrugged. "I was arrogant. Foolish. I placed too much value in the games I played. When you arrived back, I was caught unprepared. I deserved what happened to me."

"I am so glad you see it that way. But if you think the Church of the Faceless will allow you back in after everything you've done..."

"Oh, no, Eliza. I'm not here to seek help. I still view the Faceless Ones as insane beings of enormous power and their worshippers as the most deluded people I have ever had the misfortune to know – yourself included, of course."

"Then why are you here, China? To waste my time? To try my patience?"

"To spread the pain. I had my status, my reputation, my possessions, my library... I thought they made me strong, but they merely made me an easy target. Now I have nothing. *Now* I am strong. And you? You have everything. And that makes you weak."

"Is that what this is? You came here for a last physical confrontation before the wild dogs catch up to you? How disappointingly pedestrian of you. And so ill-advised. I beat you easily the last time we fought. I'll beat you easily again."

"I'm not here to fight you, Eliza."

"Then what? Why are you here?"

China smiled. "It's not dogs who chase me. It's wolves. And I've led them to your door."

Eliza lost her smile. "Out. Out, get out."

"Too late, I'm afraid. They're already here."

"Then I'll throw you to them," said Scorn, grabbing China's arm.

China whipped her arm free, smacked Scorn across the face

and stomped on the back of her leg. Scorn fell to one knee and China's fingertips dug into either side of her trachea.

"You beat me last time because I had grown complacent," she said softly. "I had lost my edge. But I've had a year to get that edge back. Feel how sharp I am, Eliza?"

Scorn made a sound, deep in her throat.

Prave came clattering down the steps. "There are people outside," he said. "They have the church surrounded."

China released her grip, and Scorn stepped away, hand at her throat. "They'll burn this place to the ground and they'll burn you with it, Eliza."

"We'll tell them we're not protecting you," Prave said.

"They won't listen," Scorn said, her eyes glinting with anger. "Activate the defences."

China left them to it, found a small room and took the thick piece of chalk from her pocket. She drew the sigil on the floor quickly. She could hear crashes and breaking glass. She lay down on top of the sigil, took a deep breath, and tapped the edge.

The sigil glowed, and China gritted her teeth as a pulse of light shot upwards, hit the ceiling, lighting up the whole room. Her cracked ribs burned as they healed. Pain ran the entire length of her body, but there had been no time for subtlety. She'd needed a safe place to do this ever since that vampire had thrown her into that wall.

She tapped the sigil and the light cut off and she gasped. She turned over, tried to stand. Her body trembled. She was sore, bruised and battered, but at least her ribs were no longer broken. From elsewhere in the church, she heard the door being kicked down.

So much for Eliza's defences.

She forced herself up, stepped from the room in time to see Scorn running and Prave scrambling after her.

"She's that way!" Prave screeched, pointing in China's direction.

Foe and Mercy came into view, stumbling. Whatever defences

Scorn set up had obviously had *some* effect, but they looked more annoyed than hurt. Still, it was something, and China would take whatever she was given. She ran for a narrow set of wooden stairs, found herself climbing into a loft space with a large, stained-glass window at one end. No other way down.

A voice crept up inside her mind, Obloquy's voice, bringing with it distant promises of pain. Her psychic defences were higher than most – secrets had been her livelihood, after all – but this kind of attack could not be blocked by conventional means.

Pain, said Obloquy and China cried out, her knees buckling beneath her. She fell, turned to watch Obloquy climb the stairs after her, his eyes narrowed. *More pain. More pain than you've ever felt*. China tried to scream, but her body was seizing up, her muscles contracting. Obloquy was in the loft now, coming closer, closer, and when he was within range China clutched her head with both hands, her fingers digging through her hair to press against the tattoo on her scalp.

Her thoughts turned jagged. Grew thorns. Spikes. Obloquy grunted. Tried pulling away. His thoughts caught on her thoughts. Caught on the spikes. Spikes ripped him. Tore him. China jabbed. Slashed. Obloquy flailed. Panicked. China's thorns spread, piercing, then retracted, pulling.

China blinked and sat up. Obloquy stood over her, swaying slightly, his face slack. She got to her feet, wincing as a headache began to pound behind her eyes. She tried to hurry away, but her legs were like lead. She'd only had to use that sigil once before. The after-effects had been similar. A few minutes. That's all she needed. Just a few minutes and her strength would return.

The window smashed ahead of her and Samuel climbed through. Typical.

She tapped her forearms. Whether she had enough strength to use magic at all proved irrelevant – Samuel darted at her so fast she didn't have time to find out. His palm found her chest and she flew backwards, hit the ground and sprawled. Even before she could open her eyes she felt his cold hands on her, lifting her. He threw her into the wall. She turned her head at the last instant, saved herself a fractured skull, but her shoulder crunched and pain blossomed.

She'd come here to heal her broken ribs, and now had a broken collarbone.

She got to one knee as Samuel came for her. She held out a hand to stop him, to keep him away, and he grabbed her wrist, stepped back and yanked. China spun through the air, but he still had hold of her, and he turned and swung her back into the wall.

She dropped, gasping, unable to breathe. Collarbone broken. Those ribs again. Shoulder dislocated.

His fingers closed round her ankle, and Samuel started pulling her after him as he walked. They passed Obloquy, still standing there with his eyes half-closed. China managed to wrap an arm round his leg, but Samuel barely noticed. He tugged her and she slipped by, almost missing the knife in Obloquy's boot. She reached out, snatched it, and then she was being pulled along the floor again.

She sucked in a sliver of breath. Then another. Then she sat up and plunged the knife through Samuel's arm.

His grip opened and he stumbled, gave a roar that was more outrage than agony. China scrambled up, ran at him, jumped and crunched her forehead into his face. He collapsed backwards and she fell on him and rolled off, crying out in pain. Darkness swarmed, but she fought against it. Samuel might have been unconscious, but it wouldn't be long before Obloquy's brain came back online. If she passed out now, he'd kill her. If she took even one moment to rest, she'd never make it out of here alive.

Groaning, China sat up, got to her knees, got to her feet. Forced herself to walk to the broken window. She climbed out on to the roof of the extension. Below her, the motorbikes were parked.

China sat on the edge of the roof, dangled her legs over. Taking a deep breath, she let herself fall.

Her feet hit the ground and gave out and she collapsed in a

screaming heap. She turned the scream into a string of curses and used her anger to make herself stand.

She straddled the biggest bike there, clicked her fingers and the engine growled to life. She flicked back the kickstand, put it in gear and spun it in place. With one arm held tight against her side, she released the brake and took off.

41

GUNNING FOR ODE

An eyeblink, and they were in London.

The Dead Men turned in all directions, silenced weapons already locked and loaded while Tanith moved to the alley wall. Valkyrie stood beside Fletcher, realised she was holding her breath and started breathing again.

Tanith ran her hands over the bricks. "Just give me a second," she murmured.

Without taking his eyes off the rooftops, Ghastly frowned. "You said you knew how to get us through."

"I know how to get us through from the other side," she said. "I just have to find out how to do it from this one."

The more seconds that dragged by, the more Valkyrie expected the alley to fill with Cleavers. Ghastly and Ravel were keeping their mouths shut, but she could tell they were furious.

"Saracen," Skulduggery said, "I don't suppose you could help her out, could you?"

Saracen shook his head. "I have no idea how to get us through, I'm afraid. Although I can tell you that if we do get through, there isn't an army lying in wait for us."

"Well, that's something."

"Found it," Tanith said. "See? Told you I could do it.

Everyone face the wall now. When you start to tingle, walk on through."

They formed up, and Skulduggery looked at Fletcher. "The moment we're inside, teleport out. When we're in position, we'll signal you."

Fletcher nodded, gave a good luck wink to Valkyrie, and then a light hit them and Valkyrie felt her whole body start to buzz. Skulduggery was in front of her and the light was making him glow so much he was almost transparent. Suddenly they were all moving, walking forward, through the wall, and Valkyrie couldn't help it, she closed her eyes as she passed through the bricks. When she opened them, they were standing in a dimly-lit storeroom, and none of them were glowing any more.

No words were spoken. Saracen moved to the door, nodded to the others, and they swarmed out into the corridor, weapons ready to fire. Valkyrie stayed in the middle. She'd been through the door enough times with Skulduggery to know what to do in situations like this, but it was very different going through with a team. At any given moment there were guns pointed in five or six different directions. When it was just the two of them, Skulduggery would scan all corners, check all doorways and clear all rooms. As a squad, though, they all seemed to rely on Saracen's hand signals for which rooms were empty and which rooms were occupied. Obeying without question, they avoided every possible confrontation. *Saracen Rue knows things*, they'd said. They hadn't been exaggerating.

Their passage through the building was done in silence. Even the way they moved was silent – their quick footsteps strangely muted on the polished floor. Security cameras were disabled as they went.

Almost one minute after they had arrived, they split up without a word. Valkyrie and Skulduggery took the stairs towards the Repository, avoiding all sorcerers who passed. They reached a corner, and peered round.

At the doors to the Repository, a boy of around fifteen was standing beside a Cleaver. While the Cleaver stood straight and unmoving, the boy was obviously having a hard time keeping still. Valkyrie felt Skulduggery's arm encircle her waist, pull her tight to his side. They waited there for the boy to get so bored that he started to look around. And then he did it. The boy glanced at the Cleaver beside him, taking his eyes off the corridor, and Skulduggery lunged, taking Valkyrie with him. They flew towards the Repository. The Cleaver snapped his head round, but it was too late. Valkyrie slammed into the boy and Skulduggery collided with the Cleaver. Such was the force of the collision that the Repository doors burst open and all four of them fell through.

Valkyrie rolled with the boy, glimpsing his wide eyes, the shock on his face. She got to her feet, hauled him up. He tried to hit her, but she caught his arm, pinned it between them. He struggled, but she was stronger than he was. She didn't want to hurt him. He was still in training. He was just doing what he was told. But then he opened his mouth to shout and she didn't have a choice. Her gauntlet-clad elbow cracked into his jaw, and he was suddenly a dead weight in her arms. She laid him on the floor and turned to Skulduggery just as he managed to get the Cleaver in a sleeper hold. When the Cleaver's struggles ceased, Skulduggery dumped him on the ground and straightened his tie.

The Repository was bigger than the one in Ireland, but as Valkyrie walked the aisles she decided that the artefacts on display were simply not as impressive, and there were a lot of gaps on those shelves. She reached the end of the first row, saw an empty glass case up a few steps. The plaque on the side informed her that it was meant to hold the God-Killer sword, and she wondered why they hadn't bothered removing it yet. Tanith had stolen the sword and Sanguine had melted it down. No matter how much they hoped and prayed, that case was going to remain empty.

She started down the second row, scanning the shelves. She got to the end, to where Skulduggery had shackled the Cleaver and the boy, and then Skulduggery walked out of the aisle to her right.

"Found one," he said, tossing her the cloaking sphere. They moved to the doors and she twisted the hemispheres away from each other. A bubble of invisibility enveloped them as they stepped out.

Staying close, they jogged the length of the corridor, took the stairs up. They passed a half-dozen mages, each one as oblivious to their presence as the last. When they got to the top floor, their progress slowed, as Skulduggery had to deactivate each security measure they came across. Finally, they made it to a set of white marble steps that led up to another corridor, this one decorated with paintings on the walls. A dark-haired girl dressed in black, around Valkyrie's age, stood at the base of the steps with her eyes fixed on the floor as an older mage scolded her.

"You have an assignment," he was saying. "Do you know what that is? We brought you in here with the others because we thought you were up to the task. You want to work in the Sanctuary once your training is complete, don't you?"

The girl muttered something.

"What was that? I didn't hear you, Ivy."

"Yes," the girl said sullenly.

"And is this how you intend to achieve that goal? By slacking off?"

Ivy shrugged. "It's boring."

The mage stiffened. "What?"

She looked at him. "It's boring. Standing in the same place for hours. I got bored."

"So you went for a walk?"

"I just want to be near the action."

"There is no action, Ivy. Everyone on guard duty is as bored as you are, but they don't let it affect them. They do their duty. You should feel honoured. You're the last sentry before the Grand Mage's office. I expect more from you, do you understand?"

"Yeah," Ivy said, then added a "sir" for good measure.

The mage sighed. "Return to your post. I'll be back shortly."

The mage walked off, passing within arm's reach of Valkyrie, and Ivy rolled her eyes at his back, then plodded up the steps.

"I'll take him out," Skulduggery said. "You take the girl."

Skulduggery stepped out of the bubble and hurried after the mage. Valkyrie reduced the size of the bubble so that it was just big enough to conceal her, then put the sphere in her jacket pocket. She climbed the steps and stood right in front of Ivy for a moment. Such an odd feeling, to be this close to someone without them knowing. She moved around behind, loosened her arms in her sleeves, and stepped up for a sleeper hold.

Then the sphere fell from her pocket and bounced on the floor, and she looked down at it as it rolled away. The instant she was out of the bubble the sphere vanished from sight.

She looked up again. Ivy was staring at her.

A moment.

Valkyrie moved, but Ivy was faster. Her hand shot out, the heel of her palm smacking into Valkyrie's cheek. Valkyrie stumbled, absorbed two knee shots to the belly without much trouble, but was too slow to avoid the elbow that slammed into her ear. She reeled, cursing with the pain, and Ivy jumped on her back, legs wrapped round her while she went for a sleeper hold of her own. Immediately Valkyrie tucked her chin to her chest, but Ivy's arm tightened across her face instead. Valkyrie staggered. The pressure increased. Her jaw felt like it was about to dislocate.

Valkyrie bent over, tried to throw Ivy off, but her hooks were in good and tight. The pain from the face crank was making her eyes water. Her mouth was open. She couldn't close it.

She tilted again, almost losing her balance, almost falling. She couldn't fall. If she fell, it was game over. At least standing she had a chance of shaking Ivy off.

Ivy's weight shifted slightly. She was trying desperately to stay in place, but gravity was dragging her forward. Valkyrie shook herself harder. She stopped trying to pull the arms away from her face, and instead she went to Ivy's feet, dragging them slowly apart. She gave another jerk and Ivy slid off her back and the pressure was gone. She straightened, gasping, but Ivy pushed at the air and Valkyrie crunched into the wall. She rebounded, stumbled towards Ivy as she stood, and went for the stick on her back. Her hand grasped at empty space and Ivy hit her, right on the chin.

The world spun and Valkyrie's knees gave out and she fell. The stick was lying on the ground next to her head.

"I just want to tell you," Ivy said, standing over her, "that I am a huge fan."

She kicked and Valkyrie tumbled down the steps and sprawled out across the floor.

"We're the same age, actually," Ivy continued, walking down after her. "You're a few months older, but we're basically the same age. We kind of look alike too, don't we? You're a bit taller, but we could be sisters, if people didn't know us. They'd probably think we're sisters."

Valkyrie got to her hands and knees and Ivy slammed a kick into her ribs.

"I used to hear all the stories about you and Skulduggery. I mean, you were my age, you hadn't even had your Surge, but you were out there, saving the world and fighting the Faceless Ones and Remnants and... OK, this is going to sound really lame, but it's because of you that I decided to be an Elemental."

Ivy waved her hand, and Valkyrie shot off the ground, flipping head over heels into a wall. She crashed to the ground.

"I had wanted to be an Energy-Thrower," Ivy continued, "because my friend was going to be an Energy-Thrower so I thought I'd do it, too. But then you came along and I mean, yeah, OK, you do a little Necromancy, but really you're an Elemental, right? Like, that's what you're going to choose when all this is over, isn't it? Have you ever tried Energy-Throwing? It is *so* cool."

Valkyrie pulled herself up and a stream of energy burst from Ivy's hand and struck her shoulder, spinning her on the spot.

"But if you become an Elemental after the Surge, then I want to as well. It'd be another thing we have in common. Wouldn't it be great? Maybe we could team up sometime. That would be *amazing*."

Valkyrie backed away.

"I know I probably sound like the biggest nerd in the world," Ivy laughed, "but you've just... you've inspired me the way no one has before. I heard you were doing all this fight training so *I* started to do fight training."

Ivy lunged with a jab straight to Valkyrie's nose, followed it with an elbow to the side of the face and then she grabbed her, hip-threw her to the floor.

"We're even dressed alike," she continued, as Valkyrie struggled to get up. "But your clothes are those special kind, aren't they? They protect you? Yeah, they're really hard to get, so..." She blushed. "And I can't believe I'm about to ask this, but do you think maybe you could talk to your tailor for me? Get him to make me some clothes? Do you think he would?"

Valkyrie got to one knee, wiped her eyes to clear them and felt her nose. It was tender to the touch. A trickle of blood ran down to her lip. "Make you clothes?" she muttered. "What size are you?"

Ivy's eyes widened in delight, and her hands went to her mouth. "You'll ask him? You'd do that for me? You have no idea how much that—"

The moment Ivy took her hands away from her face Valkyrie's fist found her jaw. Ivy pinwheeled back, hit the wall and slid along it, doing her best to stay upright.

"You have issues," Valkyrie told her. "Seriously. You do."

Ivy lurched towards her, then her eyes rolled back in her head and she dropped, unconscious.

Resisting the urge to kick her, Valkyrie wiped the blood from her nose and went back to pick up her stick. Then she walked from wall to wall in a tight pattern, eyes on the floor, until she stepped through the invisibility bubble and the cloaking sphere appeared in front of her. She deactivated it, put it in her pocket, made sure it wouldn't fall out this time.

"You look a little worse for wear," Skulduggery said as he strolled back.

Valkyrie scowled at Ivy's unconscious form. "She cheated. She was better than me."

Skulduggery shrugged. "And yet you're standing and she isn't. You even managed to stop her from sounding the alarm."

"She didn't even try to," Valkyrie said. "She was too busy yapping. Apparently I'm her hero."

"There really is no accounting for taste," he responded, starting down the corridor.

She walked beside him. "Shut up. I'm a great role model. I have many admirable features."

"Tight trousers don't count."

"What, now there are criteria?"

They quietened down as they approached the door to Ode's office. Skulduggery took off his hat, laid it on the ground and then pulled his gun from its holster. Valkyrie's hand went to the door handle. At Skulduggery's nod she twisted and pushed it open and Skulduggery stormed in.

Ode lurched to his feet behind his desk as Skulduggery pushed at the air, and managed to brace his open palm against the rippling onslaught, deflecting it around him. Valkyrie darted to one side, whipping shadows at Ode's arm, but the air moved sharply and cut through the tendril. Even as it dissipated, a column of air slammed into her chest and drove her back. She tumbled, glimpsing Skulduggery jumping over the desk and colliding with Ode. Shadows coiling round her hand, she crossed to the desk in three strides, only relaxing when she saw Skulduggery's gun jammed beneath the Grand Mage's chin.

"Hello, Cothernus," Skulduggery said.

42

MISDIRECTION

His free hand taking hold of Ode's robe, Skulduggery pulled him to his feet. Valkyrie hurried around, shackling the old man's hands behind his back. Only then did Skulduggery step away. But he kept his gun levelled.

"You're not going to win," Ode said, his face tight.

"War isn't about winning or losing," Skulduggery replied. "It's about playing the... oh, no, wait, it *is* about winning or losing. And we're winning. We have you, don't we?"

"I am not the Supreme Council," said Ode.

"No, but you're a pretty big piece."

"So what are you going to do? Parade me around in chains? Execute me? It doesn't matter. The others will not stop until you are defeated."

"Nonsense. The others will stop when this becomes a war they cannot afford to fight. They'll stop when they run out of leaders. They'll stop when they run out of supporters. There are many reasons they'll stop, Cothernus. You just have to use your imagination."

"Glib answers won't win this war, but that's all you have, isn't it? How do you expect to get me out of here? Do you even have a plan? Someone like you—"

Valkyrie took a hood from her pocket, and pulled it over Ode's head. The moment it was in place his words were muted. He could be screaming at the top of his voice and no one would hear it.

"Thank you," Skulduggery said to her. "I fear he was about to start insulting me."

"I couldn't let that happen," she said. "Your ego is a fragile and delicate thing."

"You see? You understand me."

A bubble of invisibility enveloped them again, and they hurried through the Sanctuary. No alarms raised yet, which was a good sign. When they got to the Great Chamber, Saracen was already here, a bag slung over his shoulder. He had found a sigil carved into the wall and was in the process of making his own adjustments, which would render it inert. Ghastly and Ravel led Illori Reticent into the Great Chamber, her head covered like Ode's. Vex and Shudder came next, Palaver Graves unconscious and carried over Shudder's shoulder.

"He put up a fight?" Vex asked.

"He wouldn't stop screaming," Shudder answered. "Have all of the sigils been found?"

"There should be another one over there somewhere," Saracen said, nodding to the wall on his left, but not looking up from what he was doing.

Ravel hurried over, started running his hand over the wall's surface.

"Encounter any resistance?" Skulduggery asked.

"Some," said Ghastly. "We probably don't have an awful lot of time." An alarm started wailing. "Though I could be wrong."

Skulduggery drew his gun and Valkyrie joined him at the doorway. Cleavers and sorcerers ran by. Skulduggery closed the door and splayed his hand, the air pressure keeping it tightly shut. "How are the sigils coming along, gentlemen?"

"Disabled," said Saracen, running over to help Ravel just as he found the last one.

The door handle turned. Someone knocked, and a man's voice called, "Uh, hello?"

Valkyrie looked at Skulduggery, looked back at the others, looked at Skulduggery again.

"Hello," Skulduggery said, speaking loudly to be heard over the alarm.

"Hi," said the man. "The door's locked."

"Is it?"

"Yes."

"That's funny," said Skulduggery. "Hold on a moment." He reached out, jiggled the handle a few times, then stepped back. "Yes, it's locked. You wouldn't happen to have the key, would you?"

There was a delay in response from the other side. "I'm sorry," the man called, "who am I speaking with?"

Skulduggery tilted his head. "Who am *I* speaking with?"

"This is Oscar Nightfall."

"Are you sure?"

"What?"

"Are you sure you are who you say you are? This is the Great Chamber, after all. It's a very important place for very important people. It is not beyond the realms of possibility that someone, and I'm not saying that this applies to you in particular, but someone could conceivably lie about who they are in order to gain access to this room. I have to be vigilant, especially now. There's a war on, you know."

Oscar Nightfall sounded puzzled. "Who are you?"

"Me? I'm nobody. I'm a cleaner. I'm one of the cleaners. I was cleaning the thrones and the door shut behind me. Now I can't get out. Could you try and find a key?"

"What's your name? Give me your name."

"No. It's mine."

"Tell me your name!"

"My name is Oscar Nightfall."

"What? No it isn't. That's my name."

"It is? Since when?"

"Since I took it!"

"You didn't ask me if you could take it. I was using it first."

"Open this door immediately."

"I don't have the key."

"I'll fetch the Cleavers."

"I found the key. It was in the keyhole. It's always the last place you look, isn't it? I'm unlocking the door now. Here we go."

Skulduggery relaxed the air pressure, opened the door, and pulled Oscar Nightfall inside. Valkyrie stuck out her foot and Oscar stumbled over it and Vex shoved him to Ghastly and Ghastly punched him. Oscar fell down and didn't get up again. Skulduggery closed the door once more.

"Sigil?" he asked.

Ravel and Saracen walked over.

"Disabled," Ravel said, pressing a flat piece of black metal he'd taken from his pocket. A moment later, Fletcher appeared, wincing at the volume of the alarm.

"That is loud," he said. "Everyone ready?"

"Down!" Skulduggery barked, swinging his gun round. Fletcher vanished and Valkyrie saw the Cleaver behind him, climbing from the hidden compartment in the floor. Skulduggery thought better of firing his gun and he pushed at the air. The Cleaver wove through the rippling space and Skulduggery sprang at him, even as two more Cleavers emerged from the compartments on either side.

One of them dodged Vex's energy stream and the other slashed at Ghastly as he ran up. Valkyrie hurried to the Elders, making sure they didn't run off. Fletcher was beside her. Three more Cleavers climbed through.

Behind them the doors burst open. Sorcerers spilled into the Chamber.

Valkyrie grabbed the Grand Mage and spun him round, kicked

at the back of his leg to bring him to his knees. Her fingers curled, sharpened shadows pressing into his throat beneath the hood. "Nobody move!" she shouted.

The fighting froze. All eyes turned to her.

"Anyone tries anything," she said, "and I'll take his head off and Fletcher will teleport us out of here before you can blink. Skulduggery. Gentlemen."

Skulduggery picked himself up, his fallen gun drifting into its holster. The other Dead Men backed away from their opponents, taking the Elders with them. A sorcerer Valkyrie had met once stepped forward slowly. His name was Scarecrow something. Severn, she remembered.

"We can't allow you to take them," said Scarecrow Severn. "The Elders would rather die than be used against their own people. And I don't believe you'd kill the Grand Mage, Valkyrie. We all know you. We all know you're a decent and honourable person."

"Desperate times," said Fletcher. "We can all go a little crazy."

Skulduggery moved closer to Valkyrie and all around the room weapons were raised.

"Not one more step," said Scarecrow, "any of you. One more step means we attack."

"Then we seem to be at an impasse," said Ravel. "If you move, violence erupts. If we move, violence erupts also. That's a lot of erupting violence."

"You can leave," said Scarecrow. "The Elders remain with us, but you can teleport out of here. That way, nobody gets hurt."

"Oscar's a little hurt," said Vex.

"But nobody likes him."

Beneath his hood, Palaver Graves was shaking his head quickly. He was ignored.

"How about a compromise?" Skulduggery said. "We'll leave you with Elder Graves and we'll just take the other two."

Scarecrow gave a little smile. "Sorry, Skulduggery. No compromises."

Ravel sighed. "But we've gone to all this trouble. We got in here, split up, sneaked around, got all three of your bosses... If we leave empty-handed, what's the point? It's a tad anticlimactic, is all I'm saying."

"You won't be leaving here empty-handed. You'll be leaving here with your lives. And you won't even have to kill any of us along the way. We're friends, Erskine. You don't want to kill me, do you?"

"I'm not sure," said Ravel. "You are pretty smug right now."

Palaver Graves tried standing, but Shudder put one hand to his shoulder and kept him down.

Scarecrow lowered his weapon. Everyone else kept theirs raised. "I don't like what the Supreme Council is doing," he said, "but I agree with what they say. Ireland is too unstable. It needs help. I'm not going to get into an argument with you because I know I won't win. I don't like this war, as necessary as it may be. I don't like fighting my friends. I'll fight and I'll kill if I have to, but, if I'm given a fair chance to avoid it, I'll take it."

Someone was making their way through the crowd. Valkyrie tensed. A slender woman appeared by Scarecrow's side.

"Pardon the intrusion," she said.

Scarecrow glanced at her, frowning. "Uh, this is our Administrator, Merriwyn Hyphenate-Bash. Merriwyn, can this wait? We're kind of in the middle of a stand-off."

"I understand that, Mr Severn," said Merriwyn, "but I have just heard some news that may facilitate the departure of the Dead Men at their earliest convenience. If I may?"

Scarecrow hesitated, then, "Sure... go ahead."

Merriwyn's eyes moved over the Dead Men. "You will, of course, doubt what I am about to tell you, but I assure you it is the truth. Your allies, the Councils of both the Australian and African Sanctuaries, have been killed. It was the result of no

328

military action undertaken by us or our colleagues on the Supreme Council, although my knowledge of their plans is admittedly limited."

Ghastly stared at her. "What?"

"Grand Mage Karrik and his Elders were caught in a bomb blast as they met with their military advisors. Grand Mage Ubuntu and his Elders were slaughtered in their beds. Nobody has been arrested or detained for the assassinations."

"When?" Skulduggery asked.

"Less than five minutes ago," Merriwyn said. "Both sets of assassinations occurred within moments of each other."

Ravel's frown deepened. "Something this sneaky, this brutal, has Renato Bisahalani's fingerprints all over it. And if Bisahalani was involved, then Ode was involved."

"You don't know that," Scarecrow said.

"If the Supreme Council didn't do this, then who the hell did?"

"There are plenty of suspects," said Scarecrow. "What about the Warlocks? They've been making trouble, right? It could have been them."

"If the Warlocks were behind this," Skulduggery said, "it wouldn't be just the Elders who were killed. Their entire Sanctuaries would be devoid of life and dripping with blood."

Ode shook his head. Valkyrie hesitated, then pulled off the hood.

"We didn't do this," Ode said immediately. "I give you my word, I had no knowledge of any planned action against Karrik or Ubuntu and I am willing to bet my life that Bisahalani didn't, either."

"You're on your knees in the hands of your enemies," Shudder murmured. "Your word means little."

Ode shifted round to look at Skulduggery and Ravel. "Damn it, we didn't do this. We didn't want them dead. We just wanted them to stay out of the fighting. How does this help us? Their sorcerers are going to be calling for our blood now. Their deaths mean we now have three Cradles of Magic fully invested in this war and that is *not* what we wanted."

"We'll have our Sensitives pick through your mind," said Ghastly. "They'll get to the truth."

Scarecrow took another step forward. "I told you," he said, "you're not taking them. Release them and we will let you leave – on that you have *my* word. Anton Shudder, is my word good enough for you?"

Shudder observed Scarecrow for the longest time, and nodded. "Aye," he said.

Valkyrie stayed where she was, and only stepped away from Ode when Skulduggery nodded to her. The Elders were left where they were, and the Dead Men surrounded Fletcher. Palaver scrambled to his feet, shaking his head violently, until someone pulled the hood off.

"They're not after us!" he screeched. "They took something from the Science Archive! Stop them!"

And then they teleported.

43

UNDERCOVER

Keeping the town safe, Scapegrace embarked on his nightly patrol with narrowed eyes and a keen sense of smell. Evil had an aroma, a stench, and if there were anything that would lead him to Silas Nadir, it would be his nose. Maybe.

He quite liked having a nose. But he had spent so long without one, as a head in a jar, that there was perhaps a slim chance that he was putting too much faith in his new one. Could noses smell evil? He didn't know.

"We should probably hold hands," said Thrasher.

Scapegrace scowled at him. "What?"

"We're undercover, sir. We're a loving couple, out for a midnight stroll. That's what loving couples do."

"We're not holding hands."

"It might look suspicious if we don't, sir."

Against his better judgement, Scapegrace allowed Thrasher to take his hand, and they walked on.

"Beautiful night, isn't it?" said Thrasher.

"Shut up."

"Oh, but we should talk, sir. It might look suspicious if we don't talk."

Scapegrace glowered. "Fine. Yes, it's a nice night. The moon is nice. The stars are nice. The town is nice. Everything is nice."

"Do you see yourself settling down here, Master?"

"What?"

A car approached. "We should kiss, sir."

"We are not kissing."

"It might look suspicious if we don't kiss."

The car was getting closer, and Thrasher turned to him and leaned in, lips pursed, and Scapegrace leaned back, lips in a tight line. Thrasher's eyes were closed, his eyebrows raised. Scapegrace put a hand to the idiot's face and pushed back. The car passed and, in the swoop of the headlights, Scapegrace saw something.

A figure stole through the shadows ahead of them. Slim, dressed in black. A woman. Scapegrace shoved Thrasher away and crept after his quarry. An acolyte of Silas Nadir, perhaps? Scapegrace had heard stories about the kind of lunatics who were drawn to serial killers. Maybe this woman wasn't the only one. Maybe there were dozens. Hundreds. Could this entire town be one big cult, obeying Silas Nadir's every poisonous word?

Scapegrace forced himself to keep going. Fear had no place in the heart of Roarhaven's protector.

With Thrasher stumbling around behind him, Scapegrace followed the woman to a clearing behind a short row of houses. He squatted down as the woman stopped walking.

Thrasher hunkered down beside him and stared at the woman. "Is that... is that Madame Mist?" he whispered.

Even as he asked the question, Scapegrace saw the black veil, and he sagged. Madame Mist was an Elder. She was scary and made his insides go cold, but she wouldn't have anything to do with someone like Nadir. Disappointed, he was about to turn round and head back when a man appeared before Mist, his image flickering.

"That's shunting!" Thrasher whispered excitedly. "That's what it looks like! That must be him, sir! That's Silas Nadir!"

The man stopped flickering. He was small, slim, wearing a long coat and carrying an umbrella that was dripping wet, as if he'd just been in a rainstorm. Scapegrace gazed into the face of his arch-nemesis. He couldn't really see a whole lot because of the distance and the fact that it was dark, but that in no way detracted from the drama of the moment.

Some words were said, and the man handed the umbrella to Mist, who held it over her head despite the clear night sky. Then the man took hold of her other hand and she flickered, and vanished, leaving him alone in the clearing.

Scapegrace pulled on his mask, and Thrasher did the same.

As the man started walking, they crept after him, keeping low and sticking to the shadows.

They moved parallel to him for the most part, then Scapegrace gave a series of sharp hand signals.

"Is there something wrong with your hand, Master?" Thrasher whispered.

Scapegrace scowled. "Let's rush him."

"Oh," said Thrasher, suddenly sounding even more nervous than usual. "OK. If you think that's wise."

Scapegrace didn't bother answering him. They crept closer, and closer, and then Scapegrace led the charge, slamming into the man from behind. Thrasher came with him, roaring in fear, and they all went down. Scapegrace rolled clear of the scuffle, then shoved Thrasher on top of the struggling man.

"Get off me!" the man cried.

Scapegrace sneered down at him. "You'd like that, wouldn't you?"

"Yes!" the man gasped.

"Village Idiot, stay where you are."

Thrasher whimpered something about Muscle Man, but did what he was told. Scapegrace put a foot on Thrasher's back, pressed down, and the man gasped again.

"What do you people want?"

"Justice," said Scapegrace. "A world where the innocent are free to enjoy their lives, safe in the knowledge that they won't be horribly killed by a crazed, dimension-hopping serial killer."

"You... you think I'm Silas Nadir?"

"I *know* you're Silas Nadir."

"I'm not Silas Nadir."

"That's something only Silas Nadir would say."

"No it isn't! That's something that anyone who *isn't* Silas Nadir would say!"

Scapegrace frowned. That made sense. Then he shook his head. "Nice try, Nadir, but you won't defeat me with logic. I am the Dark and Stormy Knight, I am Roarhaven's protector, and logic holds no sway over me."

"I'm not Nadir, you idiot."

"Then who are you? And where did you send Madame Mist?"

The man glared. "You saw that?"

Scapegrace sneered again. "I see all."

"Then you're a dead woman."

The sneer dropped. "I'm sorry?"

"I don't know who you are, but if you've been spying on Madame Mist, then you don't have long to live. Once she hears about this, she will hunt you down. There is nowhere you can run that she won't be able to find you."

"Now just hold on a second..."

"You think they're going to let two morons in masks ruin their plans? Do you have any idea what they've done to get this far? Do you have any idea what they're willing to do?"

"What *who* are willing to do?"

"Master," Thrasher said, "I think I should get up. He's scaring me."

"They've been planning this for a hundred years," the man continued, breathing easier now that Thrasher had moved off him. "Their reach stretches around the globe. They have people *everywhere*." The man stood, still glaring. "You have no idea, you could not even begin to *fathom*, the depths to which they have sunk. You don't know what they're prepared to risk."

"What *are* they prepared to—?"

"Annihilation," the man said. "Extinction. You're looking for Nadir, is that it? He's not here. But what you've found instead is your own destruction."

"We haven't found that," Scapegrace insisted. "And we haven't been following Madame Mist. We just saw her once. That's all. There's really no need to tell her, or anyone, about this. It was a mistake. We thought you were Silas Nadir. Obviously, you're not. Huge, gigantic apologies. Still, no harm done. We'll part ways here, go about our lives, and never speak of this again."

"Please don't kill us," Thrasher said.

"It's too late for that," said the man.

Then Scapegrace had an idea. "Run!" he said to Thrasher, and sprinted away.

As they raced through the back alleys of Roarhaven, he tore the mask from his face and hurled it into the darkness.

Let them try and find him now.

44

THE CALL TO ACTION

As with everything lately, there was good news and there was bad news.

The good news was that Doctor Nye was already at work in the Keep, installing the new memory-processing unit in the Engineer. Once it was in, the Engineer could shut down the Accelerator before it drove insane everyone who had even the slightest spark of magic in them. This was good. This was something to be celebrated.

The bad news was that Merriwyn Hyphenate-Bash had not been lying about the African and Australian Councils being hit. Suddenly Ireland's only allies were reeling against the ropes, and there was nothing they could do about it. Valkyrie didn't like feeling helpless. She much preferred having something to hit.

"Ow," said Myosotis Terra.

"Sorry," Valkyrie said, breathing hard and grinning as they circled each other.

Myosotis came in low then switched high with a kick that turned out to be a feint. When Valkyrie swerved to avoid it, Myosotis spun, her foot crashing into Valkyrie's legs. She hit the ground and Myosotis dropped on to her. They rolled. Myosotis found her back and Valkyrie tried to turn into her, but the choke was on and Valkyrie had no choice but to tap.

They sat up. Valkyrie wiped the sweat away.

"Are you all right?" Myosotis asked. Valkyrie had known her for years, but only remembered her when she was in sight. A handy trick for a thief and a spy. Not so handy for maintaining friendships. "You don't seem like your usual self."

"I'm fine," Valkyrie said. "Well, maybe I'm still a little annoyed that that Ivy girl beat the hell out of me."

"Ah." Myosotis smiled. "Wounded pride."

"No, it's not that, it's... Well, OK, maybe it is that. But I'm supposed to be the cool one. I'm the youngest, the strongest, the most special..."

"And then this little upstart," said Myosotis, "this little *neureiche*, comes in and shows you up by being younger and stronger and cooler than you."

"Well," Valkyrie said, frowning, "I don't know about cooler..."

"Face it, Val," Myosotis said, lying back on the training mat. "You're getting old."

"Shut up. I'm only eighteen."

"And she's seventeen. You're over the hill. Yesterday's news."

"I swear to God, the only reason I'm not pounding your face into smush right now is because I'd hate to embarrass you in your home country."

Myosotis laughed. They got up, used the hotel showers, and Valkyrie went to look for Skulduggery. He was heading to Ravel's makeshift office when she found him.

"You look freshly scrubbed," he said as she fell into step.

"Yeah," she said. "Just had a workout."

"Did Myosotis kick you around the place again?"

She frowned. "Who?"

Ravel looked up when they walked in. Skulduggery took a seat. "You look dreadful."

Valkyrie glared. "Skulduggery. Be positive."

"Sorry," said Skulduggery. "You look positively dreadful."

Ravel gave the briefest of smiles. "You know, I'm starting to think I may be in over my head here."

"Really? You?"

"Do you think I am?"

"I'm going to be polite and encouraging, and say it doesn't matter what I think."

"Skulduggery," Valkyrie said.

"No," Ravel said, "he's right. I was never meant to be Grand Mage. Corrival Deuce was. He would have been a great Grand Mage. This wouldn't have happened if he were in charge."

"If only he hadn't been bludgeoned to death by a Remnant," said Skulduggery.

Ravel winced. "Don't say bludgeoned. He was struck *once* on the head."

"And it killed him," said Skulduggery. "And that counts as a bludgeoning."

"But bludgeoning makes it sound a lot more violent than it actually was. When I think about it, I like to think that he was taken by surprise. That he never even knew what hit him." Ravel sighed. "He was a good man. I learned so much during the years I spent at his side. The people he met with... sorcerers who hated mortals, who wanted to rule over them, who wanted to enslave them... Corrival would meet and talk and listen and by the end he'd almost have them convinced that the only way forward was to step even further back into the shadows. I used to just stand there and watch in amazement. If he had lived, I'd say we'd already be in the middle of discussions on how to effectively curb the use of magic in our day-to-day lives."

Valkyrie made a face. "I don't much like the sound of that."

Ravel smiled. "Corrival would have convinced you. Magic, he used to say, should only be used to protect the mortals. And look at us now. Will any of us even *think* about the mortals until this war is over?"

"Now that you've broached the subject," said Skulduggery, and let his words hang.

"Our friends in Australia and Africa don't know what to do. They're... panicking, I suppose. Angry. Scared. They don't want to hold elections – they want to hit something. They've asked me to appoint interim Elders from within their Sanctuaries until all this is over."

"The files?"

Ravel lifted a folder from the pile and let it fall again. "All likely candidates. We know most of them. Some are astonishingly ill-suited to the task, but others are... possibilities. Ghastly's helping me go through them, but it's..."

"It's not what you signed up for," Skulduggery finished.

"We're finding it hard enough to run our *own* Sanctuary. And now they want us to help run theirs? The new Elders, whoever they end up being, won't have half the experience of Ubuntu or Karrik. They'll be looking to us for leadership and we'll be... flailing around, trying to look like we know what we're doing."

"You've managed to be pretty convincing so far."

"I've led us into a war."

"But you've done it convincingly. The best thing to do now is probably let the dust settle for a few days, see how everything lies—"

"No," Ravel said.

Skulduggery tilted his head. "No what?"

"No, I can't let you go. That's what you're going to say, right? You want a few days off so you can look deeper into this Warlock activity? The killings in Africa? I can't spare you. Either of you. Not at this stage. Things are too... unstable."

"If the Warlocks attack," Valkyrie said, "things are going to get a lot worse."

"We don't know that they will attack. We don't know that they even *want* to attack. The last time Charivari was even seen was a hundred years ago."

Skulduggery nodded. "When he killed an entire town for the death of one Warlock."

Ravel frowned. "You sound like you have something to say."

"Someone has been killing Warlocks, Erskine. Dozens of them, over the last five years. If Charivari killed a town for one, what will he do for dozens?"

"Who's killing them?"

"All the evidence points to Department X."

"Department X doesn't exist."

"I didn't say they did. I just said all the evidence points to them."

"So… Someone's setting up a non-existent organisation?"

"A non-existent *mortal* organisation."

Ravel closed his eyes. "Oh, this just gets better. Dare I ask who is setting up the mortals?"

"The Torment."

Ravel cracked one eye open. "He's still dead, right?"

"Yes, but his associates aren't. We're looking for a mystery man who associates with Mist and other unsavoury characters."

"And why the hell am I only hearing about this now?"

Skulduggery shrugged. "You've had a war to blunder through. We didn't want to burden you unnecessarily."

"But now you've decided to burden me anyway? Thanks. So where did you want to go?"

"I got a message from China," Valkyrie said. "A Warlock's been spotted in Africa."

"Africa's a big place."

"Mozambique."

"Mozambique is a big place."

"This Warlock, we think it might have been Charivari himself. He killed eighteen sorcerers."

Ravel blinked. "Eighteen?"

"Sixteen African, plus two foreign. We think they were Supreme Council operatives."

"Do you have any idea where you'd even start looking?"

"We're detectives," Skulduggery said. "We follow the trail."

"And how long would that take? I can't let you go. You know I can't let you go. If you didn't already know it, you'd be convincing me right now to let you go. But you're not, so..."

"The Warlocks are a threat, Erskine. And someone from Roarhaven is luring them towards the mortals, using Department X as bait. It's tied up in this war somehow, we just haven't figured out how yet."

"Please don't tell me we have to go to war with Roarhaven."

"Not yet. Look, if you can't send us, send someone else. Either way, we need to—"

The door opened and Ghastly walked in, lips set in a straight line. "They've taken the bait," he said. "Mantis is attacking the Keep."

45

UNDER ATTACK

letcher arrived in the lab as Nye and Clarabelle were manoeuvring the Engineer up to a standing position. Alarms wailed.

"Where are the others?" Fletcher asked, making Nye jerk round, its small yellow eyes opening wide.

"Do not do that!" it said. "I have a delicate heart!"

"That it keeps in a jar on its desk," Clarabelle whispered loudly.

Nye glared at her, then looked back at Fletcher. "The Monster Hunters and Mr Maybury have not reached us yet. Perhaps we should teleport without them. They may very well be dead."

"Or we could wait a minute," Clarabelle suggested.

"What about the Engineer?" Fletcher asked. "Is it working?"

"I am, Mr Fletcher," the Engineer said. "Fully functioning and mobile. How are you?"

"I'm good," Fletcher muttered, hurrying to the door and peeking out. "Everyone stay here," he said. "I'll be right back."

He took off running, hearing now the sounds of explosions over the alarm. There were Hollow Men up ahead, shuffling quickly for the exit, eager in their own way to join the fight. Fletcher got to a cracked window. Through the clouds of green gas he saw stumbling figures and flashes of coloured energy, and then a dark shape ran straight at him.

He ducked back as Gracious came smashing through the glass, landing in a spectacularly bad roll/sprawl combo. Donegan jumped through next, followed by Maybury. All three of them were coughing, with tears streaming from their eyes.

"They've taken the bait," Donegan wheezed. "We should probably go."

They linked arms and Fletcher teleported them back to the lab, where he collected Clarabelle and Nye and the Engineer and then they were outside in the fresh air, down the other end of the valley, right where Fletcher had teleported the Dead Men and their army a mere two minutes earlier.

Skulduggery looked round. "You took your time."

"Our fault," Gracious coughed. "We wanted to see how many of the enemy we could take down before we had to retreat."

Valkyrie walked over. "How many did you manage?"

"I didn't get any," Gracious said. "Donegan, you almost took down that tall guy, didn't you?"

Donegan was too busy coughing to answer.

"But then the tall guy started hitting you, so you stopped and ran away. Maybury?"

Maybury pressed his fingertips against his closed eyelids. "I was going right for Mantis, but then that bloody gas got in my eyes and, I don't know, some massive bloke reared up in front of me. I hit him but I swear, it was like hitting a wall."

Gracious nodded. "You hit a wall."

Maybury blinked at him. "I what?"

"I saw it. You ran into a cloud of gas and stumbled around for a second until you reached a wall, and then you shrieked and punched it. It was very heroic."

Fletcher moved away from them, looked up the valley towards the Keep. Hundreds of sorcerers, just realising they'd been had.

Valkyrie stood beside him. "Scary sight, isn't it?"

"They've got an army up there."

She shrugged. "We've got an army down here. Skulduggery expects them to hunker down in the Keep for the time being until they come up with some kind of plan."

"And what's *our* plan?"

"You teleport Nye and Clarabelle and the Engineer back to Roarhaven, and we wait right where we are. They'll have to come to us eventually."

"So... it worked. The plan worked."

Valkyrie grinned. "Don't you love it when that happens?"

Fletcher took Dr Nye, Clarabelle and the Engineer back to the Sanctuary, where the Engineer immediately began the deactivation process for the Accelerator. He returned to the valley minutes later, and Gracious saw him, walked over, and clamped a hand on his shoulder. "The Fellowship is together once again."

"Sorry?"

"We quest, young Fletcher. We travel far, to strange lands, seeking strange people, eating strange food, saying strange things. We are a Fellowship of Three. Comrades-in-arms. Friends. Brothers."

"Uh..."

"We've been assigned to investigate some Warlock activity in Mozambique," said Donegan. "We were told it could be incredibly dangerous, so we're taking you along with us to get us out of there if things go wrong."

"It will be a great adventure," said Gracious. "They will sing songs of this!"

"Seriously," Donegan said, "stop talking like that."

"But we go questing!"

"We're going hunting. Just like we always do. Don't let him worry you, Fletcher. We've done this a thousand times and we'll do it a thousand more. We're professionals."

"I'm going to wear my shorts," Gracious announced.

Donegan glared. "You'll get sunburnt."

"I can handle it."

"No you can't."

"We're going to Mozambique! I have to wear my shorts and my *Lion King* T-shirt and sing 'Hakuna Matata'. It's the only words of Swahili I know."

"And what happens when you get sunburnt? Who has to hear you complain about it, eh? I do. Fletcher, have you been to Africa before?"

"Yes," Fletcher said. "I've been to all three Sanctuaries and, like, a few other places. I went over to see lions and stuff."

"Did you see any?"

"Yes. Lots. It was cool."

"Excellent," said Donegan. "Well, we probably won't be seeing any lions on this trip, I'm afraid. We'll be going to Maputo, asking a few questions, and staying away from dangerous things."

"Danger is my middle name," said Gracious.

"No it isn't," said Donegan. "We'll be leaving as soon as I find fresh ammunition for my gun."

Fletcher frowned. "I thought you said we'd be staying away from dangerous things."

"I did. But there's no guarantee they'll stay away from *us*."

46

THE NEW CAPTAIN

hree days they'd been trapped in the Keep, and Regis almost wanted someone to fire the first shot just to relieve the boredom.

He raised the binoculars to his eyes and watched the Irish. Good people, good soldiers, experienced in battle and unforgiving to enemies. He never thought he'd have to go up against them, but life is what life is, as his mother used to say, and life's damn unfair when you think about it.

"How many now?" asked Ashione, appearing so quietly beside him he almost jumped out of his skin.

Scowling, Regis said, "Four hundred, maybe five. Those woods down there are probably teeming with Cleavers, though. I can see movement."

"Five hundred at the very least," Ashione said. "Well, that's not so bad. That's practically two to one. And here I thought Mantis had led us into trouble."

Regis glanced round to make sure no one had overheard. There wasn't a soul on the planet that he trusted more than Ashione, but the woman had a smart mouth that was going to get her killed one of these days. Not today, though.

She squinted up at the sun. "What do you reckon the chances

are of the bosses having a big friendly conversation and the war being called off before we have to hit anybody? It's a nice day. Too nice to be killing people we used to call friends."

Regis grunted. "If they didn't call it off during those weeks we were skulking about and hiding in bushes, I doubt they're going to call it off now. You're just worried you'll find yourself face to face with Saracen Rue. And then you'll fall into his arms like last time."

Ashione punched his shoulder. It hurt. "I didn't fall into his arms. If anything, he fell into mine. No man can resist my smile."

"I've managed to these long years."

"Well, you're an especially grumpy man."

"That I am. To be honest, though, I'm rather hoping I don't see Saracen Rue on the battlefield. For a start, I have no interest in falling into his arms. And for another, if he's here, the rest of the Dead Men probably are, too."

Ashione laughed. "You don't believe the stories, do you? They're good, don't get me wrong, but they're not some unstoppable force. They *can* be beaten."

"Have you ever seen Anton Shudder on a battlefield? What about Skulduggery Pleasant? What kind of man can bring himself back from the dead with the pure power of his hatred alone? I don't want to go up against *any* of the Dead Men – but those two in particular."

Ashione wrapped an arm round his shoulders. "Don't you worry, Regis. You just situate yourself behind me and I'll bat my eyelashes at them. No man can resist my eyes. Or you could go after Cain – she'd be an easier target."

"Mm. Don't know about that. She's still a girl. Feels wrong to fight someone who hasn't even had their Surge yet."

"Well, what do you know? Regis has a streak of nobility left in him, after all."

"That's me, all right. Regis the Noble."

"Regis the Dim-witted, more like," said Rad Crockett, coming up behind them. A punk of a mage who'd taken his name in the 1980s and had failed utterly to live it down ever since, Rad had a thing for Ashione, and for everyone else he had nothing but a sneer and a smirk. Except for Mantis, of course. When Mantis was around, that sneer was nowhere to be seen.

"The General wants to see you," Rad said, delivering his message and immediately turning his attention to Ashione. "Hey, baby. You're looking well today."

Ashione looked at him coldly. "As opposed to yesterday, when I was ugly?"

"What?" said Rad. "No, I meant—"

"You calling me ugly, is that what you're doing?"

"No, I'm – what? I'm saying the opposite. You misunderstood."

Ashione rounded on him. "Oh, so now I'm stupid as well as ugly?"

She came forward and Rad stepped back, and Regis shook his head. "Ashione, will you give the poor lad a break? He doesn't get your sense of humour."

Rad spun round. "I don't need your help, Grandpa. Why don't you shuffle off and let me and Ashione talk?"

Regis sighed. "Ashione, have at it," he said, and walked away to the sound of Ashione berating the little punk to within an inch of his miserable little life.

The camp at the Keep was small and neatly ordered. The jeeps and trucks were parked bumper to bumper round the perimeter, like in the old days when they used to circle the wagons. Bolstering the defences were a whole heap of sigils and contraptions and things Regis didn't understand. He only knew that they kept him safe, and that was good enough for him. He passed sorcerers cleaning guns and sharpening swords, talking and laughing among themselves. There was a nervous energy in the air, like maybe this was the day they'd meet the enemy. There were plenty who said they wanted to fight, but most who said that they were either stupid or lying or both. There were, of course, those who wanted to fight and were neither stupid nor lying, and they were the dangerous ones.

For most of his adult years, Regis had done his best to avoid fighting if it were at all possible. Sometimes it was, sometimes it wasn't. Life is life, after all.

The General's tent was uncoloured canvas held together with patches and clumsy stitching. It was charmless to say the least, and despite the warmth of the day the inside was cool to the point of coldness. Regis nodded to the Cleavers at the entrance and passed between them. The activity within was centred round a large table with a large map spread over it. Standing with his hands flat on the table was Captain Glass, whom Regis could find few nice words to say about. To Glass's left was Captain Tortura, a woman who never looked at Regis with anything more than mild distaste. And beside her was Captain Saber, who seemed to have developed a deep-seated loathing of Regis since the last time they'd met.

The exact centre of the tent was the highest point, and the only spot General Mantis could stand without having to stoop. Mantis was a Crenga, a species that had hovered on the edge of extinction since long before Regis was born. But somehow those long-limbed, genderless creatures had never quite slipped into the crumbling pages of history. When Regis was a boy, there had been stories of whole colonies of Crenga living in the hills of some far-off mystical island. But, when Regis had been a boy, there were stories of practically everything.

"Mr Regis," said Mantis, its tortured voice filtered through the bizarrely oversized gas mask it wore, "we are in need of a fresh pair of eyes. Perhaps you would look upon this map and tell us what you see?"

Regis came forward. It was a map of the surrounding area, its hills gathered in clustered lines and a river snaking through it. No towns, no settlements, no mortals. On the largest hill on the map there was a tin figure of a man waving a little blue flag.

Saber's toys, he knew. Further on down the shallow valley there were three other tin men close together, and a fourth in the middle of the woods. All of these carried red flags.

"Well," said Regis, taking his time to make sure he hadn't missed anything, "it seems to me that we're about to be overrun by four tiny little men who, to be honest, shouldn't cause us too much trouble."

"Will you please take this seriously?" Saber growled.

"I'll do my best," said Regis, resisting the urge to pick up the tin men and start doing silly voices.

Mantis traced its long, cellophane-wrapped finger round the edge of the hill. "Our defences are solid to the north, south and west. To the east, our enemy lies."

Regis frowned. "Wouldn't it be prudent to reinforce our defences on that side, sir? It would seem to be the logical move."

Mantis nodded its head. "That it would, Mr Regis, were we planning on staying here even longer than we already have. However, due to our dwindling supplies we cannot put this off any longer. Our plan is to pour forth, to charge our enemy and take the fight to them. It will be *glorious*."

It will be suicide. "Um," said Regis, "but wouldn't we be running straight into, you know... superior numbers? And we'd also be giving up the high ground, which is something we maybe shouldn't give up."

"What's the matter, Regis?" said Captain Tortura, a mocking smile on her lips. "Afraid of a little fighting?"

"Yes," Regis answered. "I'm terrified of the stuff. It's bad for your health and should be avoided at all costs. Begging your pardon, General, but why? We've been sneaking around for weeks. We've been playing the long game. Why suddenly change our tactics?"

Mantis looked at him, its small yellow eyes magnified by the helmet until the General resembled some kind of great blinking owl. "You don't approve?"

Regis hesitated. "It's not that I don't approve, sir. It's just that up till now we have demonstrated great patience and cunning. I'm simply wondering why we have chosen this point in time to start charging and screaming and fighting and dying. Sir."

"You're a coward," said Saber.

"You show me a brave man and I'll show you a dead one," said Regis.

"We may well be giving up the high ground," Mantis said, "but we are not doing it without good reason."

"I see, sir," Regis said, but he didn't really see in the slightest. "Beg pardon, General, but why am I here?"

"Because, when we decide to go, we will need a company to lead the charge."

"Are you looking for volunteers, sir? Under whose command would this company be?"

It wouldn't be Glass, Regis knew that much. Might get his boots dirty. It might be Saber, but the danger would be he'd want all the glory for himself, and get everyone else killed. Tortura, then? She'd be more than capable, but whether or not Mantis was willing to risk losing his best captain in the field was another matter entirely. Regis looked up, realised that everyone was looking at him, and the bottom dropped out of his stomach.

"Congratulations, Captain Regis," Mantis said. "You've just been promoted."

47

AJUOGA

Maputo was a city reeling.

Not on the outside, of course. Its streets were full of the noise and bustle that Fletcher had come to associate with the place on his half a dozen trips to Mozambique. As far as the mortals were concerned, nothing had changed. Life continued plodding onwards. But for the sorcerers, their whole world was in upheaval.

Grand Mage Ubuntu and his Elders had been powerful and wise. Many criticised them for taking too long to come to important decisions, but they acted when it counted and that, as far as Fletcher was concerned, was all that mattered. And now they were dead, all three of them murdered as they slept. Their replacements were doing their best to keep it together, both to make sure the African Sanctuaries didn't fragment during all this chaos and suspicion and also to ensure that the Supreme Council didn't take advantage of the turmoil to launch an attack. So far, they were doing a good job. Since the Warlock attack that killed eighteen sorcerers, they'd recalled most of their operatives to bolster their strength and, as far as Fletcher could tell, the Supreme Council's forces were staying well away. No one wanted to provoke the beast Africa while its fangs were bared.

But it did mean that there was no way to get any kind of official help from the Mozambique Sanctuary in their hunt for this Warlock. Donegan Bane didn't seem to mind, though. He had friends all over the world, many of whom were of significant ill repute. Just the kind of people to help them, then.

An air-conditioned limousine pulled up outside the bar Donegan had brought them to, and they got in, sitting beside each other on the long seat. Seated opposite was a beautiful woman swathed in white linen.

"I am Ajuoga," she said as the limo started down the street. "I believe you have been enquiring as to the Warlock."

"Yes we have," said Donegan. "This is Fletcher Renn, Gracious O'Callahan, and I am Donegan Bane. Thank you for agreeing to meet with us."

Ajuoga smiled brilliantly. "The pleasure is mine, Mr Bane. I am such a fan of the books you write with Mr O'Callahan. And Fletcher Renn, the last Teleporter. I am honoured to be in your presence."

"Thank you for smiling at me," Fletcher said, and Ajuoga laughed.

"Such a delight, you are! I had heard tales of your hair, but not your charm. Rest assured, the tales I tell of you shall not skimp on the details. But look at me, taking up so much of your time with my fawning. You have come here on business. You have questions."

"We do," said Donegan. "A Warlock killed eighteen sorcerers a few days ago on the outskirts of the city – including your Sanctuary's top Sensitive. The assassination of your Elder Council has obviously overshadowed this, but we would appreciate any information you might have. My associate said you are well connected."

"People talk to me," Ajuoga said, smiling gently. "From what I know, however, killing those sorcerers, or that Sensitive, was not the Warlock's primary business in Mozambique."

353

"Do you know what his primary business was?" Gracious asked.

"Recruitment," said Ajuoga. "A Warlock had already been to Ireland to talk to the Crones of the Cold Embrace, but they are frail, and would not join Charivari's army. Next, a Warlock went to Sweden to talk to the Maidens of the New Dawn, but the Maidens are meek, and would not join Charivari's army. Then Charivari himself came here to talk to the Brides of Blood Tears, and the Brides are strong, and he found them receptive."

Donegan raised an eyebrow. "It was *Charivari* who killed those sorcerers? He came here *himself*? And the Brides, they... they said yes?"

"Indeed they did," said Ajuoga. "From what I have been told, Charivari is looking for war. He wants the Warlocks and witches to stand together against those who would dare hurt them. Once his business with the Brides was concluded, he found the Sensitive, in order to extract information about this Department X. Tell me, what do you know of it?"

"We know it doesn't exist," said Gracious.

"Oh, I know that," Ajuoga responded, "but there have been stories about it since the Second World War. Rumours have to start somewhere."

"It's an urban legend, nothing more," Donegan said.

"I see. Yes, of course. But where are its headquarters? Dublin or London? I have heard Dublin."

"It doesn't have any headquarters," said Fletcher, frowning. "It doesn't exist."

Ajuoga laughed. "Of course it doesn't, of course it doesn't." She leaned forward, and patted his leg. "It is so good to meet you."

She kept patting his leg. Fletcher was pretty sure she was coming on to him. Awesome. It was pretty blatant, though. Right in front of Bane and O'Callahan, who were not looking happy. In fact, they were looking at Ajuoga with something approaching suspicion. And now that he thought about it, Fletcher could see their point. She was still patting his leg. She was even leaning forward in her seat. He couldn't blame her, of course. He was gorgeous, and his hair was spectacular. But even so, this behaviour could possibly be labelled as *odd* if his sheer animal magnetism were ignored and you just focused on—

She suddenly had a knife in her other hand and she was slashing towards his neck, and Bane and O'Callahan were lunging for her and Fletcher teleported—

—but took all three of them with him and they tumbled to the ground back in the valley in Ireland, surrounded by sorcerers.

Ajuoga snatched him away from Gracious and Donegan and Fletcher tried to get free. He glimpsed Valkyrie running forward, shadows curling round her fist, but then Ajuoga's blade came for him again and he teleported without thinking, then teleported again, and again, trying to shake Ajuoga off, trying to dislodge her, and then he felt the knife pressing into his throat and she said, very softly and right into his ear, "Stop."

He stopped. They were in a field in Texas. It was morning here.

Ajuoga kept the knife where it was. "When I tell you to," she said, "you will teleport us back to that bar I picked you up from. Don't worry, it has been emptied of patrons."

Fletcher didn't feel brave. He had a knife to his throat and of all the feelings rushing through him, bravery wasn't one of them. Even so, he found himself saying, "If you're going to kill me, get it over with."

Ajuoga gave him another one of her brilliant smiles. "I do not wish to kill you, Fletcher. You are the last Teleporter – why would I wish to kill you? No, no. I assure you, I only wish to kidnap you."

48

ASSASSINS

Things were not working out the way Ghastly had hoped.

Losing Fletcher was a major setback. They had done their best to keep him out of the fighting and as far away from danger as they possibly could. He was the one advantage they'd had over the Supreme Council and, for all they knew, he was already dead. The Monster Hunters were pleading to go back to Mozambique and Valkyrie was trying to convince Skulduggery to help her track down this Ajuoga person, but Ravel wouldn't let any of them go and Ghastly agreed with him. Once Mantis was defeated, once its army was in shackles, they could find Fletcher and bring him back. If he were still alive.

At least this part was going according to plan – so far. Mantis and his army were still hunkered down in the Keep for the fourth day in a row, and Ghastly was down here with everyone else at the bottom of the valley. Another night had fallen and – Fletcher notwithstanding – no one was hurt and no one was dead. Ghastly was experiencing a rare moment of relief. And then his phone rang.

"Doctor," he said, "what can I do for you?"

"Elder Bespoke, I'm so sorry for bothering you." Doctor Synecdoche sounded worried. She talked fast, and he could practically hear her frown over the phone. "If there were anyone else I could call, I wouldn't be wasting your time with—"

"Doctor, please, it's no trouble. Tell me what's wrong."

"Well... this sounds ridiculous, but I can't get into Roarhaven."

He answered her frown with one of his own. "I'm sorry?"

"When Doctor Nye arrived back in the Sanctuary, I decided to take a few days off. Nye was busy with the Engineer and I had some leave owed me, so I drove into Dublin to see some friends. But I've just driven back and... they won't let me in."

"Who won't let you in?"

"The Roarhaven mages. They have the road blocked off. I can see more of them on the hill. They know who I am. They know I work for the Sanctuary. But they said they're not letting anyone through."

"Doctor, I don't know what's going on, but if I give you Administrator Tipstaff's number, you can call him and he'll—"

"He's not answering," said Synecdoche. "I called Elder Mist, too, and I got talking to a man I've never spoken to before and he told me Elder Mist is unavailable. He wouldn't give me his name. Sir, I really don't mean to pester you, I know how preoccupied you must be right now, but... something's not right."

"Doctor, thank you for bringing this to my attention. Go back to Dublin. Keep your phone on. When this is resolved, I'll have someone call you, or I'll call you myself, and hopefully I'll have a satisfactory explanation for you. Thank you, Doctor."

He hung up, his frown deepening. He found Ravel strolling through the camp, talking with Saracen.

"We may have a problem," he said. "There are roadblocks up around Roarhaven. Our people aren't being allowed in. No one inside is answering their phone."

"The Supreme Council could have sneaked some people into Roarhaven," said Saracen, "using Mantis as a distraction."

Ghastly shook his head. "Synecdoche said it was Roarhaven

357

mages who stopped her. Whatever's going on, the Supreme Council isn't behind it."

Ravel sighed. "It's probably just some new piece of bureaucracy that Mist has introduced to 'improve security' since we've been gone. What do you want to do? You want to check it out? You could even take the nice doctor with you, and demonstrate how full of authority you are."

Saracen nodded. "That's sure to impress her. It'd impress me."

"See that? If it'd impress Saracen Rue, it's *sure* to impress a lady."

"Would the both of you just shut up about that?" Ghastly said. "With all this badgering about meeting a nice girl, you're worse than my mother ever was."

"Chicks dig scars," said Saracen. "That's all I'm going to say about it."

"You're a veritable font of wisdom, you know that?"

Laughing, Saracen wrapped his arms round Ghastly and Ravel and slowed their walk as he pulled them in. "Two men with knives ahead of us," he muttered. "A third coming up on our left, a fourth on our right."

Ravel grinned, but spoke softly. "This is technically an army camp. Everyone has knives."

"They're waiting for us."

"Maybe they're fans," Ravel whispered, but veered to the left as Saracen went right, leaving Ghastly to keep walking straight ahead. Typical.

A man and woman walked out from behind cover with their heads down. They each had a hand hidden from view. They parted to allow Ghastly to walk between them. Instead, he stopped, and raised an eyebrow.

"You don't really think you're going to catch me unawares, do you?"

They moved and he snapped his palm against the air and the woman went flying back. The man brought the blade

358

swinging low and Ghastly grabbed his wrist with both hands and yanked him into a headbutt. The knife-man collapsed and Ghastly clicked his fingers, threw a fireball into the chest of the woman as she ran at him. She shrieked and beat at the flames and Ghastly waved his hand. The flames went away and she looked up and Ghastly hit her so hard he heard her jaw break.

Behind him, Ravel was practically posing for photos with one foot on the head of his unconscious opponent. Saracen dragged his own would-be assassin across the ground and dumped him in the clearing between them. Saracen's hand was bleeding from a deep cut across the back of it. He looked annoyed.

"What's your name?" asked Ghastly.

The failed assassin snarled.

"I know him," said Ravel. "His name's... something nervous. Like Worrying or Fretting or—"

"Anguish," the assassin said. "But that's all you're getting out of me."

Ravel looked at Ghastly. "Roarhaven mage."

Ghastly rubbed his head where he had butted the knife-man. It was starting to swell. "This isn't the first time Roarhaven mages have tried to kill us. You'd think they'd have got the message by now. Mr Anguish, we're not going to be killed by the likes of you, so do yourself a favour and tell us who's behind this."

Anguish's sneer was becoming unsightly. "You're dead. All of you are dead. Everyone who stands between us and our destiny is dead."

"And what destiny would that be?" Saracen asked.

"Ruling over the mortals like we were born to do," Anguish told him. "And don't try to read my mind. We all have Level 4 barriers."

"I'm not psychic," said Saracen. "Why does everyone think I'm psychic? I just know things."

"Do you know who sent them?" Ravel asked.

Saracen gave a sigh. "I said I know *things*. Most of these are random things. Not especially useful things."

By the time Saracen rejoined them with his hand wrapped in a bandage, the assassins had been hauled away and the rest of the Dead Men were gathered in Ravel's tent. Ghastly kept his eyes on Valkyrie. Since Fletcher had been taken, she'd barely spoken to anyone except to argue her case in going after him.

"Madame Mist appears to be making her grab for power," said Skulduggery. "Although it would seem to be an especially clumsy one for someone as meticulous as she is."

"Maybe she just saw her chance," said Vex. "Erskine and Ghastly are in the field, along with most of the sorcerers loyal to them. She's not going to get an opportunity like this again."

Valkyrie rubbed her forehead like she was trying to get rid of a headache. "But what's the point?" she asked, her voice irritable. "Mist sets up roadblocks and takes over the Sanctuary... and then what? She's seized a building. So what? That doesn't mean she's in charge, not while the other two Elders are still alive."

"I'll be sure to ask her when I get there," Ravel said.

Ghastly saw a flicker of apprehension in Valkyrie's eyes. Something about what Ravel said made her uneasy.

"That's not a good idea," said Skulduggery.

"Staying in this camp is not a good idea," Ravel countered. "If Mist had four assassins hidden here, she could very well have more. You know me, Skulduggery – I have no patience for this kind of thing. If someone wants to kill me, I'll meet them halfway."

"You were in one of Cassandra Pharos's visions," Valkyrie blurted. "We didn't tell you because of the whole, you know, affecting-the-future thing. But we saw you in the Sanctuary. You were in pain. A *lot* of pain."

"I see," Ravel said, raising an eyebrow. "Did she see anything else?"

"Nothing more to do with you," Skulduggery said.

Ravel nodded, then shrugged. "The future can be changed just by knowing what's going to happen. I'll be fine."

"It's really not a good idea."

"If Mist takes over, all this will be for nothing. I'm going back to Roarhaven, Skulduggery. It's my decision."

"I'll go, too," said Ghastly. "Cassandra didn't see me in that vision, did she? So I'll stick with Erskine, and make sure that future doesn't happen."

"Fair enough," said Skulduggery. "Anton, you're going, too, you're on bodyguard duty. Valkyrie, Dexter, Saracen and I will stay here."

Saracen frowned. "We're splitting up," he said. "When we fought against Mevolent, we had a rule. We don't split up until the job is done."

"It won't be for long," said Ravel. "A few days at the very most. If we get to Roarhaven and it's too much for us to handle, we'll hang back, wait until Mantis and his army are taken down. Then we'll all march in together."

"Unless *you've* had a premonition of something bad happening," Vex said to Saracen.

Saracen glowered. "I'm not a psychic."

"Then what are you?"

"Wary."

"The awesome power of wariness," Vex grumbled. "One of these days you *are* going to tell me what your magic discipline is."

"How many times do I have to say this? I know things."

"I hate you."

"See? I knew that."

"We've got two Australian mages with us," Skulduggery said, still on topic, "Nixion and Zathract. Take them with you, they're good in a fight. And the Cleavers have been given strict instructions to obey the Grand Mage above all else – you'll need them, too."

"Makes sense," Ravel said. "How many?"

Skulduggery looked at the map. "All of them," he said.

"But that'd cut our numbers here by a third," said Ghastly. "If Mantis attacks, you'll be crushed."

Skulduggery tapped their position on the map. "We know Mantis has eyes in these woods," he said. "If you leave now, they'll need a few hours to verify that you've really gone. Maybe they're behind what's happening at Roarhaven or maybe not, but I bet they know something's up. When you leave, taking the Cleavers with you, they'll report back. Mantis won't be able to let an opportunity like this pass, and it *will* attack."

Valkyrie frowned. "Yay. It'll attack and kill us, falling right into our trap."

"Val's right," said Saracen. "I fail to see how any of this is to our advantage."

"Mantis won't know how long our forces will be depleted," Skulduggery said. "I doubt it'd even wait until morning to attack. Under cover of night, it'll come for us. They're so fond of their shields over there. We'll construct our own, all the way across this line. And up here, on this ridge, we already have Moloch and fifty vampires."

The men around the table were too seasoned to show it, but the sudden silence that followed those words was proof enough of their shock.

"They're up there?" Vex asked.

Skulduggery nodded. "I called Moloch this afternoon. They mobilise quickly, I have to say. They arrived before nightfall and set up a cage. If there's one thing vampires know how to build well, it's a cage." He trailed his finger from Mantis's position on the map to their own. "Mantis will charge straight at us. When its forces reach this point, the vampires will charge at them from the ridge, catching them in the open. The Cleavers will stand and fight, but all the sorcerers in the rear will know better. They'll retreat. The sorcerers at the front will be caught between the vampires and our shields. We'll be accepting their surrender and taking prisoners – Mantis among them."

"Uh, OK," said Vex. "And then there'll be fifty vampires roaming around in this area here."

"Moloch says he can control them. He's already taken the serum, so he'll stay human and herd them back to where they can do no harm."

"He's sure he can do that?"

"He seems confident. All we can do is take him at his word."

"So your entire plan hinges on the word of a vampire?" Ghastly pressed. "Skulduggery, you hate vampires. I mean, out of all of us, you trust them the least. And we don't trust them at all."

"I trust that Moloch can't afford to let us fail," Skulduggery said.

"But what if he can't control them like he thinks he can?" asked Saracen.

"Then we take them out," Skulduggery said, "and solve Dublin's vampire problem along the way."

49

INTIMIDATION TECHNIQUES

As Scapegrace swept the floor, he wondered if this was it. Was this his life? Was this the full extent of what he would achieve? Ex-zombie, now woman, owner of a modestly successful pub? What had happened to his dreams? Was he sweeping them up along with the dust? Was he abandoning them?

He'd dreamed of being the greatest killer the world had ever seen. He'd dreamed of having a horde of zombies at his command. He'd dreamed of being Roarhaven's masked protector. But now, as he swept, a great sadness came over him, for he realised he was a failure. He'd lost his pride, his honour… even his magic was reluctant to return to him. He had nothing left.

Well, apart from the pub. A smile broke through his sadness. That was the one thing he hadn't messed up yet. So what if he wouldn't be a notorious villain or an adored hero? He could still be a good person. He could still live a good life, now that he'd thrown the mask away.

The door opened behind him and three men walked in, looking around like they owned the place.

"Hello, gentlemen," Scapegrace said. "What can I get you on this fine evening?"

"Hello, Vaurien," said the man in front.

"Do I know you?"

"What matters is that I know *you*, Vaurien Scapegrace. I have to say, you're looking good these days. If I hadn't heard so many reports on what you looked like in your old body, well... you and me might have had a shot."

"I'm sorry??"

"Unfortunately," the man continued, "I *did* hear all those stories. I know what you were like both as a disgusting zombie and as a pathetic human. You talked big. You boasted. You never did anything. You're a coward, Mr Scapegrace, and you're just not very bright."

Scapegrace stood his ground. "Who the hell are you?"

"My name is Mud," the man said, "and these are my friends, Shun and Bagatelle. We've been sent to give you a warning."

"Oh, really?"

"Really," said Mud, and at his nod the bigger of the other two men, the one called Bagatelle, picked up a chair and threw it over the bar. The mirror cracked, bottles smashed, and the shelf collapsed.

"Hey!" Scapegrace cried out, but Shun grabbed him, pulled him back, while Bagatelle threw another chair that demolished the freshly cleaned glasses.

"Master!" Thrasher shouted, charging out from the backroom. A stream of energy erupted from Mud's hand, caught Thrasher full in the chest and launched him across the room.

Scapegrace tore himself free and stumbled, looking up to find himself surrounded.

"You've been going out at night and getting yourselves in trouble," Mud said.

Scapegrace hesitated. "I... I don't know what you're talking about."

"You wear silly little masks."

"Then how do you know it's us?"

Mud raised a fist and Scapegrace recoiled sharply. "OK, OK! It's us!"

Mud lowered his fist into his other hand, started rubbing his knuckles in a threatening manner. "We're here to tell you that you're going to want to stop doing all that stupid stuff."

"We've stopped! We've already stopped! When you walked in, I was thinking about that, how we've stopped. Because we have! We're not even looking for him any more."

"Looking for who?"

"Silas Nadir."

"Silas Nadir isn't even in the country, you moron. No one knows *exactly* where he is, but he's not in Ireland and he's definitely not in Roarhaven. You're also going to want to forget you ever saw Creyfon Signate."

"Who?"

Mud smiled. "Good man."

"No," said Scapegrace, "who's Creyfon Signate? Is he the other Shunter? Did he bring the dog-creature here? A dog-creature attacked Thrasher. Did he bring it here on purpose, or did it sneak through on one of the shunts? Why is he shunting? What's he doing here anyway? Where is everyone disappearing to?"

"You're asking questions you shouldn't be asking."

"Am I?"

"I was told to make sure you stayed out of everyone's business. I asked around, mentioned your name, and they all said you were a coward and a moron. They said some stern words and a little destruction of property and you'd fall right in line. But something tells me they've all misjudged you. I was instructed to kill you only as a last resort."

"Wait," said Scapegrace. "Kill me?"

"You picked the wrong time to have a change of heart."

Scapegrace narrowed his eyes. "And you picked the wrong time to threaten me."

With the speed of a cobra, Scapegrace lashed out at Bagatelle,

366

catching him on the ear with a vicious chop. He ducked as Shun reached for him, and spun with a kick that came dangerously close to landing. Mud fired off a punch that Scapegrace blocked with his chin, and Scapegrace countered with a flailing hand to the air as he fell. He landed on the floor and the three thugs glared down at him.

Then the door opened, and everyone looked round.

"Forgive me," Grandmaster Ping said, "but today I have business with Miss Scapegrace."

"Get out of here, old man," said Mud.

Ping shuffled forward. "I am so sorry, but my ears are not what they used to be. Could you repeat that, please?"

Bagatelle stepped in front of him. "He said leave."

Ping peered up at Bagatelle, his curious eyes blinking. "My, my. You are a tall one. Still, as my honourable father used to say, the taller the tree, the further the fall."

Bagatelle took hold of Ping's bathrobe, and Ping's liver-spotted hand closed gently round Bagatelle's. He twisted and leaned in and Bagatelle cried out and fell to his knees. Before Mud or Shun could react, Ping struck Bagatelle with a lazy slap and Bagatelle lurched sideways and crumpled.

Shun ran at him and Ping avoided the kick and swept the supporting leg from under him. As Shun fell, Mud fired, and Ping stepped sideways and shoved the falling man into the path of the energy stream.

Mud cursed, tried backing away, but Ping was already too close to avoid. Mud tried punching, but that didn't work. He tried kicking and that, too, failed. Then he tried being flipped through the air and landing on his head. That seemed to do the trick.

Scapegrace got to his feet as Ping turned. "That was amazing," he said.

"That," Ping said, "was kung fu. You are all right?"

"I am," said Scapegrace.

"I'm OK, too," moaned Thrasher.

"Nobody cares," said Scapegrace. "They came here to kill me because we're getting too close to the truth. We'll... we'll have to go into hiding."

"Not to worry," said Ping. "I will protect you."

"Uh, I don't think I can keep paying you."

Ping chuckled, reached up, and pressed his long, bony finger to Scapegrace's lips. "I do not help Miss Scapegrace for money. I help Miss Scapegrace for love."

Scapegrace stared down at him. "*Whu?*"

50

THE BATTLE
AT THE KEEP

Ghastly and Ravel had left with the Cleavers hours earlier. It was just gone four in the morning. The sky would be brightening soon, turning from black to blue, preparing for dawn.

The first strike came without warning. The enemy must have had a few cloaking spheres, because suddenly there were bullets and rockets and energy streams lighting up the shields. Someone behind Valkyrie launched a flare that illuminated the valley, casting the hundreds of charging sorcerers in a hellish red glow.

"Return fire!" Skulduggery roared, and the shout went up the line and things got louder. A writhing ball of energy slipped through the shield and exploded next to a truck, spinning it over on to its side.

An enemy Elemental used the air to propel himself high overhead. He landed on the curve of the shield, every touch lighting it up. He rolled until he found a gap and dropped off the edge, using the air to slow his descent. But the moment he hit the ground sorcerers jumped on him and he was lost to Valkyrie's sight.

Skulduggery stuck his gun through a gap and fired. He pulled it back, reloaded. "Where the hell is Moloch?"

Valkyrie jumped back to let a trio of mages run by. Everyone had a job to do but her. She looked up to the ridge. Where the hell *was* Moloch?

Keeping low, she ran back and to the east, looping around out of the camp and towards the trees. She brought the shadows in to hide her as she sprinted across the open ground. She sank into the treeline, keeping her head turned away from the brilliant flashes of light from the battle. If Mantis had people creeping through here, she needed to be able to see them first.

She moved as quickly as she could, using the sounds of fighting to mask her footsteps. Every time she thought she saw someone in the dark, it turned out to be nothing. Which was odd. If she'd been in charge in place of Mantis, she would have sent a squad of her best fighters down here in an attempt to outflank the enemy. She knew that's what Skulduggery was expecting. So where were they?

The ground turned steep and she slowed, creeping up the side of the hill towards the ridge. Up ahead she could hear snarling. Lots and lots of snarling. That low, guttural, savage snarling that could only tear itself from the throats of vampires.

She fought the irrational urge to rush forward, but it was her slow steps that prevented her from tripping over something lying in the undergrowth. She nudged it with her foot. It moved, then moved back, settling into its original position. She knelt, reached out. Felt a leg.

She cursed under her breath and fell on to her backside. Whoever it was didn't move. She could see the outline of a shoulder. He was sitting up, resting against a tree.

Her mouth dry, Valkyrie got to her knees. When he still didn't move, her hand went back to his foot. Soft rubber and laces. Running shoes. Her hand moved up. A tracksuit. Beneath it, a cold, cold leg.

Shielding one hand with the other, she clicked her fingers, summoned a small flame. Moloch's tracksuit. She shuffled closer.

Moloch's blood. She raised her hand. Moloch's dead body, sitting here in the woods, missing its head.

She let the fire go out before she saw too much, but had to fight to keep from throwing up. She stood, backed away, praying she didn't kick anything head-shaped in the dark.

The white-skinned vampires were packed into a massive cage, climbing over each other for their chance to snarl and snap at the man in black pacing back and forward just out of their reach. Dusk. It took her a moment to realise he was snarling back at them.

He stopped suddenly, his head snapping towards her. Valkyrie turned to run, but he was on her in an instant. She felt a hand on her jacket and then she was flying through the air. She hit the ground and rolled and before she'd even come to a stop he was beside her, a hand closing round her throat. He lifted her off her feet and held her there. She kicked out, tried to breathe, his fingertips pressing into her arteries, stopping the blood supply to her brain, her head pounding, lights dancing before her eyes.

And then he let her go, and she fell to the ground.

The vampires were going crazy now. She was an arm's length from the cage, the only thing stopping them from ripping her to pieces. She looked up at Dusk.

It was quite beautiful, the way the bursting light from the battle hit the angles of his face. The side with the scar was hidden in shadow. The scar she'd given him.

"Why?" Valkyrie asked.

He looked down at her. She knew the rule as well as anyone. There was only one cardinal sin when it came to vampires – the killing of one of their own. Caelan had broken that rule and was shunned. In order for Dusk to do the same, he would have needed a very good reason – and, in order to do it in front of all these other vampires, Moloch must have wronged him in some unforgivable way. But what did a vampire deem unforgivable?

"He stole my life," Dusk said quietly. "Cursed me with undeath. I've been waiting for him to leave his squalid fortress ever since I found out. I suppose I owe you for drawing him into the open."

"But we need him," said Valkyrie. "We need the vampires. We'll lose without them. Please. Help us."

"If I open this cage, these vampires will kill me."

"You said you owe me."

"I do. And at some later date I will tell you a secret about yourself that even you do not know. But not tonight."

He turned, started walking away.

"No, Dusk, please... Please!"

When the darkness had swallowed him, Valkyrie stood. The vampires howled in frustration. Some of them started to fight among themselves. She walked quickly away from the cage and looked down into the valley. Mantis's forces were battering at the shields. It would only be a matter of minutes before they got through. Even if she could find the key to open the cage, there was no Moloch around to herd the vampires away once they'd done their job. Besides, once the cage opened, she'd be the first one to fall to their hunger.

But down there... down there Skulduggery and the others would fight. They'd fight and kill and die. She had to do *something*. She couldn't just stand up here and watch as...

Her eyes widened, and her heart surged. Lit up by the uncertain staccato of the fighting, of explosions and flashing energy streams, there were people moving in from the other end of the valley. Ghastly. Ravel. Cleavers and sorcerers. They'd turned back.

Reinforcements.

She laughed. She couldn't stop herself. Despite having fifty vampires a mere stone's throw away from her, she jumped up and thrust her arms in the air. She even did a little dance, up there on that ridge, the vampires snarling themselves into a frenzy.

When she was done, she looked down at the valley again. There must have been hundreds of people on that road. She frowned. Hundreds. Too many to be Ghastly and Ravel and the Cleavers. Too many to be reinforcements.

She cried out as the newcomers crashed into Skulduggery's army from the rear. They swarmed the camp, adding to the terrible symphony of machine-gun fire and shrieking energy streams. She watched as it played out, as her fellow sorcerers realised they'd been outmanoeuvred. Half of them turned to fight while the other half struggled to keep the line. And then the shield broke. Under pressure from too many points it just dissolved, and Mantis's army swept in on a wave of destruction.

Valkyrie screamed and brought the wind in to boost herself high into the air and far from the ridge. She lost control at the peak of her jump and didn't bother correcting herself. She fell towards the valley floor, only bringing the air in at the last second. She hit the ground at a run. She came up on one of Mantis's sorcerers, lagging far behind the others. She slammed her stick into the back of his head and kept running.

There was a huge explosion from the camp. She could hear screams above the roars and the shouts. Another straggler ahead. A woman. Valkyrie hit her so hard the woman flipped over as she fell.

Then she plunged into the battle.

Gunfire and screams assaulted her ears. Men and women fought and cursed and stabbed and shot each other. Enemy Cleavers cleared spaces with whirling scythes. Someone crashed into her just as an energy stream passed where she'd been standing. She glimpsed his face. What was his name? Threatening? That was it, Threatening. Threatening got up, gun in hand, shooting a man who ran at him. The bullets hit armour, didn't slow him down, and Threatening dropped the gun and went for his sword and the man stuck a blade in Threatening's throat and left him to die.

Valkyrie sent a wave of shadows crashing into the man who'd killed him. Her stick flashed as she struck another enemy mage and he crumpled.

She saw Dai Maybury scrambling backwards, trying to get away from a big man with a black beard and a huge axe. She sprinted towards them, pushed at the air. The big man staggered and she lashed him with shadows that drew blood across his face. Snarling, the big man swung his axe for Valkyrie's head and she stumbled, lost her momentum, managed to dodge a second swing, but he caught her with his free hand. She whirled and sat down with a bump, the left side of her face stinging. Dai rejoined the fight and the big man lost interest in her, so she sat there, dazed, while people died all around.

Let me out.

Figuring she'd probably do better on her feet, she stood and looked around. So many people fighting. How did they even know which opponent to pick? Was there a system for that kind of thing? Did people with swords go for people with swords? Did people go for opponents their own size? How did they even know who was an enemy, in the dark and the chaos? The whole thing seemed astonishingly unfair.

You're panicking. You tend to fixate on irrelevant details when you panic. Have you noticed this?

A sword came for her, flashing in the moonlight. She brought her left arm up to meet it, felt the jolt through the gauntlet. She'd barely deflected that strike. This wasn't like in training. Her blocks needed to be a lot stronger.

The man with the sword swung again. Valkyrie slipped on something and fell, rolled, came up, blocked. She lunged into him, headbutted his chest. He grunted and stepped back and she flicked her stick at his head. There was a bright blue spark and he howled, wheeled, the sword falling from his grip. She hit him on the arm and he collapsed to the ground, jerking like he'd been electrocuted.

A sun exploded in front of her and she flew backwards, hit someone and they both went down. She blinked but couldn't see, felt hands on her, didn't know whose they were so she found the face and hit it. She got an elbow in the mouth for her trouble and her lip burst. She snarled, found an eye and jabbed at it with her thumb. She heard a scream and pushed him off, stumbled away, her vision returning. Something hit her shoulder and spun her, then hit her back and she landed face down in the dirt. Someone ran by, tripped over her, kicking her in the head on the way down. She blinked again. The world was blurry but getting clearer. Among all the shouts and yells and running footsteps, she picked out the footsteps that were coming for her and she rolled on to her back.

A sorcerer let loose with a dazzling energy stream that would have burrowed through her belly were it not for her jacket. She swept her arm towards him, her shadows slicing through the backs of his legs. He screamed and fell and she dived on him. They went rolling, cursing and biting and snarling. They came to a stop with Valkyrie on the bottom, his weight on her, spittle spraying from his mouth and his hand crackling with energy.

He's going to kill you. Let me out.

Valkyrie clutched at the air and her stick slid into her hand. She jammed it into his ribs and he convulsed so violently he practically leaped sideways. She rolled the other way, clicking her fingers and hurling a fireball into the helmet of a Cleaver fighting a mage she knew. She went low, her stick cracking into his knee. He jerked back but didn't fall. His uniform protected him.

His scythe scraped against her gauntlet and he whirled, kicked her, sent her stumbling over the body of a woman. He jumped at her and she pushed at the air, but he passed through it and she pushed at the air again and sent herself sliding along the grass. He sprinted after her as she got to her feet, wobbling slightly. She swept her hands in and up and a gust of wind lifted her. She hurtled diagonally away, not caring where she landed until she hit the ground and lost her stick and rolled to a stop, gasping for breath. Her hair was in her face and the blood was sticking it to her lips. She raised her head, gazed at what she could see of the battle, saw a big man with a black beard and a huge axe striding towards her.

Strong legs in brown leather stepped between them. A sword caught the flashing lights prettily.

The big man swung that axe and Tanith moved under it, cut his hands off. The hands fell, still clutching the axe, and the big man's eyes widened and he started hollering. Someone picked Valkyrie off the ground, put the stick back in her hand. It took her a moment to realise that Sanguine was beside her.

A bullet hit her shoulder and she winced, turned to watch three mages run at her. The woman in front reloaded as she ran, Sanguine moving to intercept. He dived on her and the ground swallowed them. The second mage faltered, then a hand burst from the ground, grabbed his ankle and yanked him down beneath the surface. The third mage had fireballs in his hands and he was hopping from one place to the other, screaming at Sanguine to bring his friends back. Sanguine rose up behind him, grabbed him and snapped his neck.

Tanith was suddenly beside Valkyrie, looking into her eyes. "You OK? Val? You hurt?"

"No," Valkyrie managed to say.

"Can you fight?"

No, she wanted to say. No I can't fight. Take me away from this. Please God, take me away. Instead, she said, "Yes."

Tanith gave her a wicked grin, and leaped at the nearest Cleaver.

Valkyrie brushed the hair from her eyes and turned in a circle. Everywhere around her people were fighting. She watched a woman fighting a sorcerer she knew. The woman gripped the collar of his coat and yanked it down, and steel flashed in her hand as she plunged a small blade into his throat. The sorcerer toppled, the woman staying close all the way down. When he went limp, she picked up her sword, looked around, saw Valkyrie. She ran at her.

Valkyrie pushed at the air, but the woman dodged to one side, came up and ducked the shadows that came after. Cursing, Valkyrie fell back, using her stick and gauntlet to defend against that swinging sword. The woman's face was covered in blood, but her eyes were clear and bright and terrible. The woman brought the sword down heavily, but Valkyrie held the stick in both hands, planted her feet wide and blocked upwards, just as strong. And then the woman kicked her between the legs.

Blinding pain shot through Valkyrie's body and she curled up, dropped to the ground and fell sideways.

The woman crouched over her, the tip of her sword pressing into Valkyrie's neck. "Hurts, doesn't it?" she said, panting for breath. "People think it's just guys that works on. If only, right?"

Valkyrie's eyes were filled with tears, and every muscle was seized in pain. She couldn't even whimper.

"Ashione," a man barked. He stood over them, keeping an eye out. He was old but solid, and carried a short sword that dripped with blood. "Do the job and stop talking about it."

The woman, Ashione, nodded to him, then looked down at Valkyrie. "War's no place for a girl," she said, and hit her with the hilt of the sword and the world went black.

51

THE MAN WITH
THE GOLDEN EYES

Ghastly hunkered down in the darkness, eyes on the two shapes moving towards him. He could hear their footsteps from here – every scuff and stumble and kicked pebble. Their whispers drifted by on the breeze – harsh words and abject apologies. When they were close enough, Ghastly stood.

"Over here," he said quietly.

Scapegrace jumped in shock and Thrasher gave a muffled cry of horror. For some reason they were both wearing masks. There was someone else with them, too, someone Ghastly hadn't noticed before. An old Chinese man in a bathrobe. He, too, wore a mask.

Scapegrace hurried over. He wasn't wearing anything too revealing. For this, Ghastly was thankful, yet also strangely disappointed.

"Elder Bespoke," Scapegrace whispered. "We came as fast as we could, but we doubled back a few times to make sure we weren't being followed, so that may have delayed us. I hope you weren't waiting long, but you can never put too high a price on security, that's what I always say."

"Why are you wearing masks?"

"In case we're recognised. We're wanted men in this town.

Our never-ending war against darkness recently ended, but we have made some serious enemies."

Thrasher stepped up. "Excuse me? Elder Bespoke? Where's the force field?"

"Right in front of you," said Ghastly.

Thrasher started to raise his hand.

"I wouldn't do that if I were you," Ghastly warned.

Thrasher's arm lowered, but Scapegrace gave him a push and Thrasher hit the force field with a sharp crack of energy that launched him backwards.

"Wow," said Scapegrace, as Thrasher sprawled to a groaning stop.

"The force field covers the whole town and a lot more besides," said Ghastly. "It's a particularly nasty one, as you can see, which is why we need you to deactivate it on your side."

"Of course," said Scapegrace.

"First thing to do is find the sigil. It'll be carved on to something solid, and it'll be glowing."

Scapegrace went hunting through the undergrowth, and Ravel and Shudder walked up behind Ghastly.

"Any luck?" Ravel asked.

"We've just started," said Ghastly.

The old Chinese man stood on the other side of the force field, smiling at them.

"I don't believe we've met," said Ravel.

"My name is Ping," the old man said. "I am romantically involved with Miss Scapegrace."

Ghastly raised an eyebrow. "Is that so?"

"It is not," Thrasher said, struggling to sit up.

Ping nodded. "We are very, very happy together. Waiting for the big, stupid man to move out."

"That's never going to happen," Thrasher said, trying to stand on trembling legs.

"Found it!" Scapegrace said, jumping up excitedly. "It's carved into the back of this rock!"

Ghastly and Ravel watched him jiggle for a moment. "Good," said Ghastly. "This next part is trickier. You're going to have to follow my instructions exactly, understand?"

"Yes, sir," said Scapegrace.

"OK. Press your fingertip to the centre of the sigil, just where it starts to loop. Got that? Now slowly move your finger down at a forty-five-degree angle..."

It took twenty minutes and dozens of attempts, but finally that small section of the force field retracted. Ravel gave a sharp gesture and suddenly Cleavers detached themselves from the shadows around them and marched through the gap, three abreast, 114 in all. The two Australian mages followed, and when Shudder and Ravel were through, Ghastly reactivated the force field and turned to see Scapegrace standing right there.

"I've been keeping an eye out," he said. "I saw Madame Mist. She vanished."

"What do you mean?"

"Vanished. Disappeared. Shunted."

Ghastly frowned. "You saw this?"

"Yes, sir. I thought it was odd so here I am, reporting it."

"Well, that's... That's good to know. Thank you."

"Sir, yes, sir. Also there was a dog-creature, but I took care of that. Orders, sir?"

"Uh, well, to be honest, I think your work is done for tonight. You should go home and recuperate."

Scapegrace looked dismayed. "But we're here to help."

"You have helped. But things could get messy in a few minutes, and I need to know we have back-up waiting should we need it."

"I'm your back-up?"

"Yes. Yes you are."

"Because I've been training in the fighting arts. Master Ping has been training me."

"That's good to know."

"I think he loves me a little bit, though."

"I may have noticed that, yes. Go home, Scapegrace. If we need you, we'll call."

Scapegrace bowed, then twirled round and darted into the night. Thrasher ran after him, and Ping shuffled after them both. What an odd group.

They moved slowly through Roarhaven, careful not to be seen. The closer they got to the Sanctuary, the more uneasy Ghastly became. The town was quiet, like it was holding its breath.

Two mages guarded the entrance. Ravel sent a pair of Cleavers to incapacitate them. Ghastly drew his gun, and led the way inside. It was unnaturally still. Zathract and Nixion took off down one corridor, taking half the Cleavers with them. The rest of the Cleavers stayed with Ghastly and Ravel and Shudder, as they made their way through to the heart of the Sanctuary. Any mages they encountered along the way were taken down by non-lethal means. Until they got to the bottom of whatever was going on, the Roarhaven mages were being treated as *potential* hostiles. There'd be no killing them. Not yet.

A figure lurched from the shadows and Ghastly spun, but it was China Sorrows who fell into his arms.

"Just the man I wanted to see," she mumbled. "You don't have your sewing kit on you, by any chance...?"

Her clothes were dirty and torn and stained with blood. She was hurt, and exhausted and even paler than usual.

"What happened?" asked Ghastly.

She rested her head against his chest and closed her eyes, but she smiled with cracked lips. "What didn't? I've been... hunted from one side of this country to the other. Thought I could make it alone, but no... no woman is an island."

"How did you get through the force field?"

She smiled a pale smile. "No sigil can stop me."

Ghastly lifted her, passed her into a Cleaver's arms. "Take her to the Medical Bay. Find someone to treat her. Force them." The

Cleaver nodded and moved away, carrying China as if she were as light as a feather.

They continued on. Ravel posted guards at every doorway they passed. By the time they reached the Round Room, there were twenty Cleavers left.

Ghastly rested his hand on the door, and looked at Ravel. "Ready?" he whispered.

Ravel glanced at Shudder, then looked at Ghastly. He took a deep breath, and nodded. Ghastly pushed the doors open and strode in, Ravel and Shudder on either side of him and the Cleavers spilling in behind.

Ahead of them, Madame Mist stood with Portia and Syc and two other Children of the Spider, people Ghastly recognised as the Scourge and the Terror. None of them looked remotely surprised to see them.

"The warriors return," said Syc, giving a little laugh.

"Cleavers," Ghastly said, "arrest Elder Mist and her friends."

"On what grounds?" Mist asked, her voice unhurried. The Cleavers didn't move. Any action taken against an Elder would have to be ordered by the Grand Mage himself. "We have done nothing but keep the home fires burning."

"And the force field?" Shudder asked.

"I thought it prudent, with General Mantis still out there. Was I wrong? Should I not have worried?"

"You sent your people to kill us," said Ghastly. "For a second time, I might add."

"My people? My people are here with me. Were you attacked by any one of them? Were you attacked by a Child of the Spider?"

Her tone was low, mocking, and completely confident. Ghastly didn't like it. She was completely outnumbered, but acting like she was the one with the upper hand. He pressed a finger to his headset.

"Nixion," he said. "Status?"

His earpiece crackled into life. "A half-dozen people, all in shackles," said Nixion. "This area's secure. Want us to check the lower levels?"

Ghastly's eyes stayed on Mist. "Not yet," he said. "Hold for further instructions."

"Can we finish this now?" Portia asked. "I'm bored."

Mist shook her head. "This is a moment to be savoured, my sweetling. Not rushed over. Not fumbled. But look. You've spoiled it now. You've robbed it of its fun."

"Wasn't fun for us," said Syc.

"Of course not," Madame Mist said. "Because you're young, and impetuous, and have yet to learn such subtleties as patience. When you have learned this subtle art, then you will never want moments like this to end. Elder Bespoke, we never got along, you and I. You distrusted me from the start – wisely, as it turned out. Do you have anything else to charge me with?"

"You were behind the Warlock killings," Ghastly said. "You were framing the mortals."

"Of course. But I assure you, the Warlocks are merely a means to an end. Once they attack Dublin City, Sanctuaries around the world will unite, and we will save the mortals from these evil, evil beings and be hailed as heroes. We'll take over, and the mortals won't even get to set off one of those bombs they love so much. An elegant plan. Not my own, I have to admit. But an elegant plan nonetheless, don't you think?"

She was building up to something. Ghastly had found it wise over the years to never let his enemies build up to something.

He took another step forward, raising his gun. "Hands on your head, all of you. You're under arrest for conspiracy to commit murder."

"One moment, please," said Mist.

"Hands on your head *now*," said Ghastly.

"Indulge me, if you will, as one Elder to another. My final request before I am led away in disgrace. Your associates, elsewhere in this building. Call them."

"What?"

Mist said nothing more.

Frowning, Ghastly pressed his headset again. "Nixion. Any change? Nixion? Zathract?"

There was movement behind Mist, and something came flying through the air to land wetly in the space before Ghastly. Nixion's head rolled to a stop, joined a moment later by Zathract's.

"Oh, dear," said Madame Mist. "Oh, I have been unforgivably rude. I seem to have forgotten to introduce you to our new bodyguard that Doctor Nye has generously donated to our cause."

A figure stepped into the light. Dressed all in black, carrying a scythe, his face hidden behind a visored helmet.

"He's darkened his colour since the first time you met," said Mist, "but the Black Cleaver is still the same man who almost killed you six years ago. I think it only fitting that he be here to witness your death."

Something cold and sharp thudded into Ghastly's back and he took a step forward, his gun dropping from his suddenly numb fingers. He looked round, saw the Cleavers falling upon Shudder, their scythes piercing the unarmoured sections of his clothes as easily as they did the flesh beneath. They knew exactly where to strike. The Gist burst from Shudder's chest, screaming in pain and fury, but a scythe took Shudder's head and the Gist dissipated like smoke in a breeze.

Ghastly fell to one knee. He reached behind his back, clumsy fingers searching for the scythe blade. Instead, he found a knife. It was pulled free before he could grip it, and he toppled, turning over to land on his back.

"I am sorry, my friend," Erskine Ravel said, bending over him. Ghastly closed his hand around Ravel's wrist, tried to keep the blade away – "No," he whispered, "no, don't" – but his strength was gone and Ravel easily disentangled himself and pushed the knife into his throat.

In that moment, Ghastly became aware of a great many things.

He became aware of how cold he suddenly was, and how hot his blood felt, splashing on to his skin. He became aware of Anton Shudder's head lying on the floor, turned away from him. He became aware of how many regrets he'd stored up over the years, and despite them all and despite his age, he still wasn't ready to die. And he became aware of Ravel's eyes, brimming with tears, those eyes of his that had many a lady swooning over him down through the centuries. Those golden eyes.

52

A REASONABLE REACTION

Finding Tanith was the only thing that Sanguine cared about, but after an hour of searching he had to return to the small primary school with nothing to show for his efforts. The school was in the middle of nowhere, with doors that were easily forced and windows that gave them a good view in all four directions. A good temporary base – providing they didn't have to defend it.

Rue and Vex were already back, and Gracious O'Callahan was working away at the little school computer, tapping the keys by the dim light of the screen. A few minutes later, Pleasant dropped from the midday sky and strode into the classroom.

"Any sign?" Vex asked.

"Nothing," Pleasant said. "We'll have to expand our search."

"No," said Rue. "Skulduggery, I know you're worried, but Valkyrie's a prisoner of war now. She'll be treated well and she'll be kept out of danger. If we keep looking for her, we're going to run into the people who are looking for *us*. They're closing in and you know it. We have to leave the area."

"We're not going anywhere without Tanith," Sanguine said quietly. "Valkyrie will be released when the war is over, but Tanith is a wanted fugitive. She's gonna be thrown in prison for the rest of her life if we don't get her back *now*."

Vex shook his head. "It's too risky. I'm sorry."

"So that's how it is, is it? You'll let her fight for you, but the moment she needs help you cut her loose? I thought you were meant to be the good guys, all noble and honourable. I don't see much nobility in leaving your people behind."

"We're not leaving," said Pleasant. "Once Mantis figures out who he has, he'll set his Sensitives on them. They're probably already at work. We have to get to Valkyrie before they push too deep."

Rue frowned. "Why? They don't know where we are. They don't know of our plans because we don't have any plans."

"That's not what I'm worried about."

"Then what, for God's sake?"

By the way he stood, it looked like Pleasant was about to say something he really didn't want to say, but he was saved the trouble by O'Callahan.

"There's something you should see," he said.

Sanguine stepped forward. "You've found them?"

O'Callahan shook his head. "This computer isn't powerful enough to crack Mantis's communication codes. Instead, I've been trying to find out why we can't get in touch with Ghastly. Whatever else she's done, Madame Mist hasn't changed the codes for the security feed yet, so I've accessed the cameras in the Roarhaven Sanctuary."

"Let's take a look," Pleasant said, and Sanguine rushed forward before all the good places around the computer were taken. The monitor showed the empty Round Room.

"At the moment nothing's happening," said O'Callahan, sitting at the keyboard. "So I... I went a few hours back. And I... I found this."

He clicked a file and they saw Madame Mist and a few other

creepy-looking individuals facing off against Bespoke and Ravel and Shudder, plus a whole army of Cleavers at their backs. Words were being spoken.

"Where's the audio?" Vex asked.

O'Callahan frowned, started opening and closing windows while the stand-off continued onscreen.

"I know the pretty ones," said Sanguine, "I know Syc and Portia, but who are the ugly people?"

"The Terror and the Scourge," said Rue. "Contemporaries of the Torment. They can turn into giant spiders, just like he could. If anything, though, they're even less friendly and... wait, who the hell is this?"

A man in black stepped into view. He looked like a Cleaver.

"Got it," said O'Callahan, and there was a slight hiss and then Madame Mist's voice drifted from the speakers.

"—but the Black Cleaver is still the same man who almost killed you six years ago," she was saying. "I think it only fitting that he be here to witness your death."

Ravel was the first one to move. But instead of moving against the Children of the Spider, he slipped a knife from his sleeve and plunged it into Ghastly Bespoke's back.

Pleasant stiffened and Vex cursed and Rue jerked away from the monitor, and Sanguine's eyes would surely have widened if he'd had any.

Rue found his voice and shouted as Bespoke fell and Anton Shudder was sliced from shoulder to sternum. The Cleavers hacked at Shudder with detached ferocity, not affording him a moment's mercy, not even when they took his head. Bespoke was on his back by now, with Ravel crouched over him.

"I am sorry, my friend," Ravel said, and plunged the knife into his throat.

Vex turned from the monitor and Rue staggered against the wall. Only Pleasant stayed where he was, watching his scarred friend choke on his own blood and die. It was as if the skeleton were frozen in place. Sanguine felt the ridiculous urge to reach out and poke him, just to see if he'd react, but he'd seen that kind of anger before. It was the quiet kind. The dangerous kind.

On the monitor, there was sudden silence. The Cleavers stepped away from Shudder, their scythes dripping. Ravel stood slowly, looked at the knife in his hand.

Syc walked forward, peered down at Bespoke's dead body and laughed.

Ravel moved so fast it was almost scary. In an instant, Syc was on his knees with the blade that had killed Bespoke pressed into his throat. Portia cried out and the Terror and the Scourge moved, started to grow, their arms and legs lengthening.

"Stand down!" Ravel roared. "Stand down or I'll kill him and then I'll kill every last one of you!"

Sanguine leaned in, eager for more bloodshed, but the Terror and the Scourge stopped growing, and after a moment they returned to their original forms.

"You let him go," Portia said, her voice shaking with fury.

Ravel ignored her. He hauled Syc to his feet, and leaned in. "You do not laugh at this man. You understand me? Compared to him, you're nothing. You're less than nothing. He was one of my friends, but you? You're not worthy to even be killed by the same knife that's marked with his blood."

Ravel shoved Syc away from him, and Syc glared but retreated to Portia's side.

Only Madame Mist seemed to have kept her composure. "We've had reports from the battle at the Keep. Our forces have been decimated by Mantis and his army. Some are dead. Most are captured."

Ravel looked at her, something unreadable in his face. "Good," he said at last. "Skulduggery and the others?"

"Escaped," said Mist. "Although Mantis has Valkyrie Cain."

"OK. That should keep Skulduggery occupied for a while, at least. I want Vaurien Scapegrace rounded up. He helped us get in, so he'll help others. Get Dacanay on it."

"Of course, Grand Mage."

"And get someone in to... clean up in here. I want these men given proper burials."

"Of course."

Ravel looked down at Bespoke and Shudder, and walked out. The Black Cleaver was the first to follow, and then the others, until only Syc and Portia remained behind.

"Why do we take orders from him?" Syc asked when they were alone, anger bubbling beneath his words. "I should kill him for what he did. No one lays a finger on me. *No one.*"

Portia took hold of his arm. "It's just for a little while longer," she said. "Then we won't need him any more. We won't need any of them. Come on. Come." She took his hand, and led him out of the room. They had to step over Bespoke's body to do so.

O'Callahan hesitated, then pressed a key and the image froze.

Sanguine stepped back, so he could watch all three Dead Men. He saw the horror in Rue's eyes, the disbelief in Vex's. It almost made him laugh, to see them in such distress. He'd never liked Ghastly Bespoke. His only regret was that he hadn't been the one with the blade to his throat.

There was a mirror on one wall with magnetic numbers stuck on to the surface. Pleasant walked over, cleared the numbers to one side and examined his reflection. He straightened his tie. Vex, Rue and O'Callahan watched him. It occurred to Sanguine that everything Pleasant was wearing had probably been made by Bespoke.

"What do we do?" Rue asked.

Pleasant took off his hat, adjusted the brim. "Replay the footage. We need to hear everything that was said. Then we release it over the Global Link. Our people need to know that Roarhaven is no longer a refuge."

"About Erskine," said Rue. "What do we do about Erskine and Mist?"

"Oh, that," Pleasant said, putting his hat back on. "We kill them. We kill them all."

53

IN HER HEAD

alkyrie was in her uncle's house when the phone rang. She looked at it and listened to the ring until it filled her head, and then she picked it up.

"Hello?" she said.

"Who is this?" a man asked.

"My name is Valkyrie Cain," said Valkyrie. "I'm twelve years old and my uncle has just died."

"I know Edgley's dead," said the man. He sounded angry. "What are you doing in that house? Why are you in his house?"

Valkyrie frowned. The ringing had made her head hurt. "Um... wait..."

Someone pounded on the front door. "Open up!" the man shouted. "Open the damn door!"

Valkyrie jumped up off the couch, ran to the fireplace and grabbed the poker. The pounding on the door stopped, and she turned to the window beside her. The curtains were open. Outside was pitch-black. She could see her own reflection in the glass. She didn't look twelve years old. She was too tall, too broad, and her clothes were too small, too tight. They stretched across her.

A hand knocked on the window. "Are you alone in there?" the

man asked, but before she could answer, the window exploded and the man leaped in.

She went to swing at him with the poker, but realised she wasn't holding it any more. Instead, she wore a black ring that left a trail of shadows in its wake, so she used those shadows and sent them snapping into him. The man tumbled backwards, into the corner. She looked down at herself. She was wearing black now. Everything fitted. The man charged at her and she pushed at the air and he went hurtling into a bookcase.

The door opened behind her and a skeleton in a nice suit walked in.

"Hello, Skulduggery," she said.

He tipped his hat to her, and they watched the man get to his feet, and start to sweat, and then the man melted and disappeared between the floorboards.

"Why are you here?" she asked Skulduggery. "Did you know I was going to be attacked? Were you using me as bait?"

He turned his head to her. "The less you know about all this, the better. You're a perfectly normal young lady, and after tonight, you're going to return to your perfectly normal life. It wouldn't do for you to get involved in this."

She frowned. "We've had this conversation before, about how involved I get."

"But we can limit that involvement."

"I don't understand. Why am I twelve? I'm not twelve. I'm eighteen. That man didn't dissolve here, he dissolved in the canal. You threw fire at him and shot him. I don't... I don't think this is real..."

"But it's what's best for you."

She winced. "I've got a headache. I don't understand this. It's like *déjà vu*, but... but it's staying with me. I don't feel well."

"But it might—"

"I'm going to be sick. I'm going to throw up. Why does my head hurt so much? This isn't real. Something's wrong. Don't you feel it? What's the last thing you remember? The last thing I remember is... fighting. I remember lots of people fighting and... We were at war. My God. How could I have forgotten? Skulduggery, we were at war and all the other Sanctuaries were trying to take over and somebody hit me and—"

"Don't you want to get back to that world?"

"What world? What are you talking about?"

"It's safer there."

"You're not making any sense."

He cocked his head. "Funny. When I first met your uncle, that's what he said, too."

She stepped back. "You're not Skulduggery. Who are you? This isn't right. This isn't how it happened. What's going on? Who are you? I don't know you."

She turned and ran into a vast library where bookshelves grew like great oaks, stretching towards the ice-blue sky. In the clearing of the forest of books stood China Sorrows.

"He has anger in him like you have never seen," said China. "He has hatred in him that you would never dream about. You should have been there during the war, you know. You should have seen him then."

Skulduggery emerged from the shadows beside China, his eyeless gaze fixed on Valkyrie. "You asked me what is my nature? It is a dark and twisted thing."

Valkyrie tried to focus, but it was hard with the pain in her head and the constant buzzing.

"Has he corrupted you yet?" Solomon Wreath asked from behind her. She turned, squinting at him through the gloom. "He corrupts everyone he meets. Have you noticed that? Have you noticed how much you're changing, simply by being around him?"

The pain jabbed at her and her knees went weak and she fell back into a chair in Bespoke Tailor's. She looked up and watched Ghastly working at the sewing machine.

"Did Skulduggery ever tell you about my mother?" he asked

without looking up. "She was a Sensitive, did he tell you that? She told me that Skulduggery would take a partner some time in the future, a girl with dark hair and dark eyes. She said there was an enemy you had to fight. A creature of darkness. She said Skulduggery fought by your side for some of it, but... She *sensed* things more than she saw them, you know? She felt terror, and death, and futility. She felt the world on the edge of destruction, and she sensed evil. Unimaginable evil."

"I don't want to hurt anyone," Valkyrie said quietly, and sat back. The seatbelt was tight across her chest. Skulduggery always insisted on the seatbelt whenever they were in the Bentley. She looked at him now, sitting beside her, and she took a deep breath. "Are you ready?"

"I am," Skulduggery said.

"You're sure?"

"Quite sure."

"OK. So I'll tell you. Here I go. Skulduggery..."

"Yes, Valkyrie?"

"I'm... I don't know how to say this. I..." She swallowed. "I'm—"

She wanted to say "I'm Darquesse", but the car was suddenly filled with light and noise and now she was sitting somewhere else, in a hard chair, and her ankles and wrists were held in place, and she opened her eyes and saw the woman sitting in front of her.

The woman grunted, frowning in surprise. "She's awake."

They were in a barn. It was big. Sunlight streamed in. Old farm machinery was stacked against one side. Valkyrie's mouth was dry. Her left eye was swollen. She turned her head. Tanith was in a chair beside her, dried blood on her face, and beside Tanith, Donegan Bane. Their hands and feet were shackled, and their eyes were closed. There were people sitting in front of them, too. Sensitives.

General Mantis walked into Valkyrie's field of vision. It peered down at her. "I thought she was the only one of them *without* psychic defences," it said.

The woman nodded. "She is. This should be easy. But there's something... it feels like there's something in there, in her mind, keeping me out."

"Try again," Mantis said. "She must know where Skulduggery Pleasant has retreated to, and we don't have time to waste. Go deeper."

Valkyrie tried to speak, but she was too tired, and the woman leaned forward and pressed her fingers to Valkyrie's forehead.

"It will really be easier on you if you stop resisting," the woman said quietly. "The more you fight, the more it hurts."

"Please," Valkyrie managed to whisper, "stop. Don't wake her up."

"Don't wake who up?"

Tears rolled down Valkyrie's cheeks. "Please. She'll kill you all..."

"It'll be all right," said the woman. "Just relax. I'm going to poke around in your head a little more and then it'll all be over."

"No..."

"Shh," said the woman. "Everything is going to be all right. I promise."

"No," Valkyrie said, "you don't understand... you don't understand..."

The headache started again and she closed her eyes, wincing, the pain in her head coming in rapid beats, like a knife on a chopping board. She looked up, realised she was in her kitchen back in Haggard. Clarabelle was hunched over something on the table. No, not something. Someone. Valkyrie moved round. Clarabelle's lips were black, and she had a scalpel in her hand that she was using to chop up Kenspeckle Grouse's fingers like they were carrots. There was no blood, though, and Kenspeckle didn't seem to mind.

"Valkyrie," he said, smiling at her, "I haven't seen you in weeks. Staying out of trouble?"

"Not really," she said, frowning.

"Nor did I expect you to."

"What are you doing in my house? What if my parents come home? Professor... I think I'm in trouble. There's something wrong, but I can't remember what it is. It's important, though. It's... Professor, doesn't that hurt?"

Kenspeckle gave a little laugh. "Don't you worry about *me*, Valkyrie. I'm tougher than I look." With the last of Kenspeckle's fingers cut into thin slices, Clarabelle reached for a bigger scalpel, and started slicing his hand. Kenspeckle watched her work, smiling in appreciation of a job well done, then looked back at Valkyrie. "So what has he dragged you into this time?"

"Skulduggery doesn't drag me anywhere," Valkyrie said, immediately defensive. Then she felt bad. She shouldn't be cross with Kenspeckle. He was dead, after all. "We're at war," she explained. "The other Sanctuaries, they want to take over. There was a... a battle. They won. I think I was... I might have been captured. But Skulduggery got away."

Kenspeckle's eyes flickered to someone standing beside Valkyrie. She realised Skulduggery had been there all along.

"Do you not feel one iota of responsibility?" Kenspeckle asked him. "She could have been killed. Yet again, while out with you, she could have been killed. Would you have felt anything then? Do you remember ever actually *having* a heart, or were you *born* dead?"

Skulduggery's façade flowed over his skull, but instead of imitation flesh it was blackest shadow. "The world is a dangerous place," he said. "In order for people like you to live in relative safety, there need to be people like me."

"Killers, you mean."

An arm draped itself round Valkyrie's shoulders while she looked at Skulduggery standing there. "Don't worry, sweetie,"

Davina Marr whispered in her ear. "I know what it is. All those hormones raging, you have all these conflicting emotions... You had a crush on him before he was pulled into hell, didn't you? You can tell me. It's sad and pathetic and highly amusing, but I promise I won't laugh."

Valkyrie went to shove Marr away from her, but it was Fletcher she pushed.

"You look at Skulduggery and that's who you model yourself on," he said. "He's brave, you're brave. He's cold, you're cold. He's ruthless, you're ruthless. Well done, Val, you share the emotional range of a dead man."

She turned back to Skulduggery. The others were gone now. All that remained of Kenspeckle were chopped-up bits of dried flesh. Skulduggery looked at her with his black skull.

"You're a bad influence on me," she said.

"I never claimed otherwise."

They'd spoken those words before. This conversation was a rerun. It wasn't real. None of it was real. She wasn't in her house. She was in a... a barn... She'd been captured and there was someone in her head.

Valkyrie walked out into the hall. It was suddenly dark outside. "Hello?" she said loudly. "I know you're here. I can feel your frustration."

She opened the front door and stepped out into the middle of the battle she'd been taken from. It was quiet, and everyone moved slowly, like time was crawling. She walked through them until she found the woman who had been sitting opposite her in the barn.

"You're in my head," said Valkyrie.

The woman frowned. "You're not supposed to be able to see me."

A bullet moved lazily through the air. Valkyrie checked its trajectory. It wasn't going to hit anyone. She examined a fist striking a face, watched the spittle erupt from the distorted mouth with agonising slowness.

"You want to know where Skulduggery is," she said. "I don't know where he is. I can't help you. You'd better leave me alone."

The woman nodded. "And I will. I just have to make sure you're telling the truth."

"And this is how you go about it?" Valkyrie asked. "Stringing together a bunch of memories to get me to open up?"

"It works."

"Not on me."

"Why is that?"

"You don't want to know." Valkyrie ducked her head under a sword and moved past a falling man with all the time in the world. She got closer to the Sensitive. "You'd better leave. She's coming."

"Who is?"

"My bad mood."

The Sensitive smiled. "I'm going to have to push a bit deeper now, OK? I apologise in advance for anything embarrassing I might uncover."

"Is that part of it?" Valkyrie asked. "Do you use a person's embarrassment and shame against them? That doesn't really seem fair."

The woman shrugged. "Exposing uncomfortable truths breaks down the biggest walls. You should save yourself the trauma. Just let me in."

"It's not up to me."

"Then who is it up to?"

"Me," said Darquesse.

Valkyrie opened her eyes. The Sensitive opposite her sat ramrod straight, her eyelids fluttering, her mouth open. Her nose was bleeding.

It was dark outside. The barn was empty apart from Valkyrie, Tanith and Donegan and the three psychics who were trying to break into their minds.

"Release me," Valkyrie said.

The Sensitive moaned, then shifted forward and fell to her knees. She took a key from her pocket, undid the ankle restraints first, then the wrist shackles. Magic flooded Valkyrie's body and she stood up. The Sensitive whimpered. Valkyrie could see into her mind. It was such a fragile thing. Easily broken.

"Release my friends," she said, and the Sensitive scampered over to Tanith to do just that.

Valkyrie went to Tanith's psychic, wrapped an arm round his throat and tightened. By the time he withdrew from Tanith's mind, he was already sliding into unconsciousness. Valkyrie let him fall and did the same thing to the psychic opposite Donegan, even as Tanith was standing on shaky legs.

"What the hell just happened?" she murmured.

Valkyrie didn't answer. She waited until Donegan was free, and then ordered the Sensitive to stand. Blood was now running from the woman's ears. It would have been so easy to reach a little further into her mind and wrench everything sideways.

Do it.

Instead, Valkyrie moved behind her, strangled her until she went limp.

Donegan blinked. "Is this real? Are we really out of our shackles?"

"It's real," said Valkyrie, struggling to get her thoughts in order, struggling to push her bad mood down. "We have to get out of here. Either of you have your phone?"

Donegan searched his pockets, scowled and shook his head. Tanith went searching through the barn, found her coat and sword on a bench nearby, but no phones. Valkyrie took the Sensitive's phone as Donegan limped to the door and took a peek outside. "We're not getting out this way," he said.

Tanith walked up the wall, the wood groaning slightly under her weight. She disappeared into the gloom beyond the rafters.

"I think we can get out here," she said after a moment. "I'll need something to prise a few boards loose, though."

Valkyrie went to the workbench, found a crowbar and used the air to send it drifting upwards. Tanith's hand emerged from the shadows, took the crowbar and vanished with it. There was a scraping from up above, and a creak and a snap, and a broken board bounced off the rafters and fell. Donegan caught it before it hit the ground, and laid it carefully to one side.

Tanith dropped, crouching, to the thickest rafter. "Come on up," she said.

Donegan looked at Valkyrie. "Do you mind?"

"Not at all," she said, and the air rushed in and Donegan shot upwards like he'd been fired from a cannon. Tanith caught his arm before he started to drop back down again, and pulled him up the rest of the way. Moving carefully, he stood on the rafter, hands out to steady himself. Tanith clasped her hands and boosted him up into the gloom. Valkyrie heard him climbing, and then Tanith nodded to her. One more rush of air and then she, too, was being pulled up on to the rafter.

Now that she was up here, she could see the narrow gap that Tanith had made in the roof. Donegan was reaching down to her. Valkyrie stepped on Tanith's clasped hands and straightened, and Donegan pulled her through. Outside, the stars glittered coldly.

Moving slowly, she crawled to the edge and looked down. Mantis had taken over an old farmhouse. The enemy were everywhere, sitting round campfires, chatting and laughing and slapping each other's backs. They weren't bad people. She knew they weren't. Their laughter wasn't cruel. They were just soldiers who needed to let off a little steam after a battle. The more Valkyrie listened, the more their joviality sounded forced, like they were trying to drown out their own doubts over what had just happened.

She crawled back, joining Tanith and Donegan on the other side of the roof, where things were quiet and dark. A sentry patrolled below them. Before Valkyrie could stop her, Tanith dropped on to him. She didn't know if he were dead or just unconscious, but he didn't make a sound. Linking arms with Donegan, she used the air to lower them from the roof. They landed silently, and followed Tanith through the trees.

When they were far enough away, Valkyrie took the stolen phone from her jacket.

"No," Donegan said quickly. "We can't use that. They'll be able to pinpoint where the call is picked up. We'd lead them right to Skulduggery and the others."

Valkyrie muttered a curse, went to drop the phone, but she stopped. A message was flashing. "There's something on the Global Link," she said. "The subject is 'Roarhaven Compromised'."

Donegan frowned, took the phone off her, tapped it a few times. Valkyrie and Tanith stood beside him. An image filled the screen – Ghastly and Ravel and Shudder facing off against Mist and the Children of the Spider. Donegan tapped the screen again, and the footage began to play.

54

STEPHANIE EDGLEY

Stephanie's parents had understood.

She'd had a speech rehearsed. It had been impassioned yet sensible, sincere yet witty, and it had made some very valid points on the importance of taking a year out to decide what she wanted to do with her life. The colleges and universities weren't going anywhere, after all, so why rush into anything?

It had been a great speech, and she hadn't needed one word of it.

So here she was, on a Wednesday afternoon in the middle of October, alone in the house and wondering what to do with the rest of her day. Wondering what to do with the rest of her *year*, come to that.

She climbed the stairs, humming a Rhianna song. She walked into her bedroom and went suddenly cold, like a hand of ice had seized her heart. There was a cloaking sphere on her desk. Then she noticed Valkyrie, sitting on the bed with her head down.

Stephanie stared at her for a moment. Here she was again, here to take back everything Stephanie loved.

"Ghastly's dead," Valkyrie said in a broken voice.

Stephanie frowned. "What?"

"Ravel killed him. Shudder, too. Ravel betrayed them, he..."

"What do you mean dead? Like, *really* dead?"

Valkyrie nodded.

Stephanie felt something. What was that? Sadness? She'd liked Ghastly, or at least she'd liked Valkyrie's memories of him. She wondered if she'd miss him.

"You look terrible," she said.

Valkyrie did look bad. She looked exhausted, like she could do with a sleep and a long shower. "It's all going wrong," she muttered. "They fell into our trap. We had them. We were going to beat them. Then... I don't know. There were more of them. We were all split up. I was with Tanith and Donegan."

"You're not with Skulduggery?" Stephanie asked.

Valkyrie shook her head. "We were captured. They had a psychic digging around in my brain. I've been hearing..." She faltered, but Stephanie knew.

"Darquesse," she said.

Valkyrie nodded. "She's talking to me. Right now, she's talking to me. I'm doing my best to ignore her, but..."

Valkyrie grimaced, and Stephanie knew that Darquesse had just said something.

"Where are Donegan and Tanith now?" she asked.

Valkyrie gave a quick shrug. "Donegan said we should split up. We're going to meet tomorrow. I'm so tired. I need to sleep." She looked up. "Where is everyone?"

"Dad had to go into work," said Stephanie. "Mum and Alice are over in Beryl's. Beryl and Fergus are worried about Carol. They say she's become very withdrawn lately. She won't even spend time with Crystal."

"Right," said Valkyrie, barely even listening to details about her own life, details she should be caring about. Instead, she just stood up and took off her jacket. If ever Stephanie had harboured doubts over what she had to do, they vanished then and there.

"I should probably get back in the mirror," she said.

Valkyrie murmured something.

Stephanie opened the wardrobe. She looked at her own reflection in the full-length mirror. A reflection's reflection. She peered into her own eyes, saw the life in them, then she stepped through, into the two-dimensional mirror image of a slice of the bedroom. It used to seem so right to her, once upon a time. These days it was so jarring it made her queasy, especially with the flipping. She didn't know what the technical term for it would be, but for some time now she'd been able to flip her image whenever she emerged. When all this started, a watch worn on Valkyrie's left wrist would appear on Stephanie's right. But not with the flipping. Just another little thing, another improvement, another piece of evolution that Valkyrie had thoroughly missed.

She turned and faced Valkyrie through the glass, watched her touch her fingertips to the mirror on the other side. She saw the slight frown when Stephanie's image didn't alter to match her own.

Valkyrie's memories flooded into her, and she allowed her own memories to flood Valkyrie's. She even added a few of the secret ones, the ones she'd been hiding. She let Valkyrie have the memory of the day Carol died, and she let her experience the memory of being tortured in Mevolent's dungeon, of having her fingers cut off.

Valkyrie staggered back, hands to her head, eyes wide. Stephanie stepped out of the mirror, back into the three-dimensional living world, and rooted through the bottom of the wardrobe.

"What did you do?" said Valkyrie, knocking over the bedside table. "What did you do?"

Stephanie straightened up, the Sceptre of the Ancients in her hand.

Valkyrie jerked away, stumbled back towards the door. "What are you...?"

"My name is Stephanie. I'm a person. I'm real. The Sceptre only bonds to people who are real, right? It's bonded to me."

There were tears in Valkyrie's eyes. "You killed Carol."

"She won't be missed. Not really."

"Why? I don't understand why you—"

"Too lazy to sort through the memories?" Stephanie asked. "Just like you're too lazy to go to school and too lazy to study and do homework? I'm taking over, Valkyrie. I'm taking Mum and Dad and Alice and I'm making them mine."

Valkyrie walked backwards, out on to the landing, her jacket still clutched in her hand. Stephanie followed at a respectable distance.

"You're broken," said Valkyrie. "You're malfunctioning. Get back into the mirror and we'll fix you."

The Sceptre flashed and black lightning turned the wardrobe to dust. She turned back to Valkyrie. "No more mirror," she said. "I'm out here for good."

Valkyrie backed off the top step of the staircase. For a moment, Stephanie thought she might tumble down, but no, she kept her balance. Pity. "You're going to kill me?"

"Of course," Stephanie said. "I kill you, and you won't kill my parents."

"I don't kill them. That's Darquesse."

"Darquesse *is* you," said Stephanie, following her down the stairs. "That little voice in your head? That's not another person. That's your nasty side. Your dark and twisted side. Even when your magic is bound, you could still hear that voice. And you're so close to giving in to it, aren't you? Especially now, after Ghastly. So, so close. I can't allow that."

"Skulduggery will know. He'll—"

"He'll think you were recaptured. And if he figures it out, I'll kill him, too. He won't suspect a thing. None of them will."

"I won't let you take my place."

"Bit late."

Valkyrie reached the bottom of the stairs. Her eyes blazed with anger. "You say you love them? Look at yourself. You're

406

damaged. You understand? You're not safe to be around. You're not a person, you're a malfunctioning *thing*. Five years ago, Skulduggery shot you to fake my death. Ever since then you've been getting worse."

Stephanie gave a smile as she followed Valkyrie into the living room. "Actually, it was a few moments before that. It was when he pulled me from the puddle – that's when things started to change. See, I know everything you know, but you don't know everything I know. Here are the rules when it comes to reflections. Rule one: a reflection shouldn't be left out for too long. Oops. Rule two: reflections can't do magic. Rule three: each person has only one reflection. Once that reflection's physical body is destroyed, it can't return, and no new reflection can be conjured. Why do you think this war isn't being fought by thousands of reflection foot soldiers? Because they've all been destroyed by now. And rule four – once conjured, a reflection must emerge only from its original surface. In my case, the mirror I just destroyed. Skulduggery knew it was risky conjuring me from a second surface. He knew something could go wrong. But he did it anyway. So really, when you think about it, all this is his fault."

"Listen to me. You don't have to do this. We can—"

"Say my name."

Valkyrie frowned. "What?"

"My name. Say it. I want to hear you say my name."

"Why?"

"Because you abandoned it and I picked it up, and I want to hear you acknowledge that."

Valkyrie looked at her, but didn't say anything.

Stephanie raised the Sceptre. "Say it."

"No."

Now it was Valkyrie's turn to see anger flash in Stephanie's eyes. "Say my name."

"No."

407

Stephanie stepped forward and cracked the Sceptre off Valkyrie's head. Valkyrie stumbled against the back of the sofa.

"Say my name or I'll turn you to dust."

Valkyrie held her hand to her forehead as blood started to trickle. She looked at the black crystal, and then—

"You're not going to win, Stephanie."

That name. That simple name, spoken by the girl who had abandoned it, brought a glow of pure joy to Stephanie's being the likes of which she'd never felt before. And that joy brought tears. The first tears that weren't part of simulated emotion for the benefit of others. The first real tears. And in that moment, in that wonderful moment, Stephanie became truly whole.

Valkyrie whipped her jacket at the Sceptre and stepped in with a punch that sent Stephanie reeling. Stephanie's arm went wide to stop her fall, and she swept half the mantelpiece clear. Valkyrie had the Sceptre now, and was pointing it straight at her.

"This is for Carol," she snarled.

And nothing happened.

Stephanie crashed into her, taking them both over the sofa. They sprawled out the other side, and Stephanie got up, grabbed Valkyrie by the hair and kneed her in the head. She tried it again, but Valkyrie grabbed her legs and sprang. Stephanie's back hit the coffee table and the wind rushed out of her. She slid on to the floor and Valkyrie got on top, started hitting her. Stephanie covered up as best she could, trying to breathe. She tasted blood.

Her hand went searching for a weapon and instead found the leg of the coffee table. She pulled the table over her head, struggled to keep it there while Valkyrie tried pushing it back. A few moments to blink and clear her head and then Valkyrie lifted the table off her completely. Stephanie shot her hips off the ground and twisted and they turned over and over again, knocking over the lamp that Stephanie's grandmother had left them.

There was a mad scramble and then Stephanie was flat on the floor and Valkyrie had grabbed her wrist, tried to break her arm.

Stephanie saw the move coming and countered, flipping Valkyrie on to her belly. She dived on her, her arm snaking round Valkyrie's throat, but Valkyrie bit down hard and Stephanie cried out and moved her head just in time to catch Valkyrie's elbow right in the eye socket.

Stephanie rolled off, howling in pain. A moment later, Valkyrie's boot slammed into her side. Through bleary eyes, she watched Valkyrie stride into the kitchen and take a knife from the rack.

Stephanie forced herself up, looking for the Sceptre. She lunged to the fireplace as Valkyrie came back, grabbing the poker.

"You're going to stab me?" she said, panting. "You're really going to stab me to death?"

"You're not alive," Valkyrie said, closing in.

Stephanie swung the poker and Valkyrie swayed back, came in with a straight stab, but Stephanie flicked the poker into her wrist. The knife dropped and the poker flicked again, whacked into her head. Valkyrie stumbled and Stephanie kicked, sending her into the patio door, cracking the glass. Valkyrie ducked the next swing, caught Stephanie with an elbow and Stephanie lashed out blindly, hitting nothing. Valkyrie grabbed her and lifted and then the floor smacked into her head and Stephanie lay there in darkness. Over her own breathing, she heard Valkyrie groan as she got up. And then she heard a car.

She opened her eyes. Valkyrie stood over her, frozen. The car's engine shut off. A door opened and closed.

"Mum's back," Stephanie mumbled. "You really want her to find two of us here?"

Valkyrie looked down at her, her eyes wide with alarm.

"You'd better run," said Stephanie. "I'll give her your love."

The front door opened.

"Steph?" her mum called. "We're home."

"Mum!" Stephanie shouted. "Help!"

Valkyrie whirled, grabbed her jacket off the ground and held it in front of her as she sprinted for the patio door. Stephanie's mum rushed into the room, Alice in her arms, as Valkyrie leaped. She hit the glass and crashed through it and Stephanie's mum cried out. Valkyrie stumbled but kept going, running to the back of the garden and vaulting over the wall.

Alice was crying and Stephanie's mum was on her knees beside Stephanie and Stephanie tried her very best not to smile.

55

REFUGE

Valkyrie cut across the fields, staying away from the roads as she left Haggard behind her. The cops would be out looking for a girl in black, and she didn't think it'd be a good idea for them to pick her up and have her folks arrive at the line-up. She got to the next town over, walked the beach as the sun set, and chose a spot in among the sand dunes to lie down. She covered herself with her jacket and curled up. She didn't think she'd be able to sleep. It wasn't that she wasn't tired – she was, she was exhausted – it was just that her mind was too active. Her thoughts jostled against each other and she couldn't calm them. She had no phone, no money to get a taxi, and her car was at her house, the keys with the reflection.

Stephanie.

Yes, Stephanie, as she now called herself. Stephanie, the murderous lunatic with the Sceptre and Valkyrie's family in her possession. It was all Valkyrie's fault, of course. She'd known something was wrong with the damn reflection. She'd known it for years. She'd even talked to Skulduggery about it, but she'd never pressed the issue. She'd never demanded a solution. She was too afraid that the solution might be to get rid of the thing altogether, and then Valkyrie would have had to resume her old life. And that would never do. Not when there was adventure and excitement to be had around every corner with Skulduggery. She could never give that up.

Just like with Darquesse. The moment she'd realised the truth, the moment she'd realised that she herself was the one all the Sensitives were having nightmares about, she should have quit. She should have walked away. She should never have done magic again, never spoken to Skulduggery again, never given the voice within her any more power. But of course she hadn't quit.

You were having too much fun.

How many sorcerers had thanked her for saving the world? How many had called her a hero? The truth was she was too selfish to be a hero. She was too... what was that word?

Narcissistic.

That was it. She was too narcissistic. She'd lied to herself: she'd told herself she was doing good, she was saving lives. She'd told herself when the time came, when Darquesse tried to take over, she'd be strong enough to fight back, to retain control. Even after all these slip-ups, she was delusional enough to think she could emerge victorious when it really mattered.

Bless.

Valkyrie turned over, tucking the jacket under her chin. She made herself think about Ghastly, and felt that part of herself start to ache again. She thought about Shudder, felt guilty that she'd barely considered his death, but then her thoughts went back to Ghastly, and she cried.

She didn't think she'd fall asleep, but she did, and she dreamed of her fingers being cut off and her eye being plucked out, and she dreamed of killing Carol. When she woke it was morning. She stood, shivering, and brushed the sand from her clothes. She pulled on the jacket and zipped it up, then left the beach, her arms wrapped round herself. Her belly rumbled. She got to a bus stop and stood beside people waiting to go to work and to school. She kept watch for cop cars. The bus trundled up and she let her fellow commuters get on ahead of her. She let her hair out of its ponytail, then climbed on and smiled at the driver.

"I don't have any money," she said.

"Do you have a ticket?" he asked.

"No. But I really need to get into the city."

"I'm afraid I can't help you." He kept the doors open, waiting for her to disembark.

kill him kill him kill him kill him kill him kill him

He looked at her. "You don't appear to be getting off."

"I know," she said, "and I'm sorry. I've never done this before, but I just don't have any money, I don't have my phone, I need to get into town and..."

The driver sighed. "One free ride. Don't try this again."

"Thank you. Really. Thank you."

She found an empty seat and slid into it. Thank God for cool bus drivers.

She got into town, gave the driver a peck on the cheek for his kindness, and hopped off. She crossed the Liffey, hurried down the Quays, and fought her way through the crowds of tourists in Temple Bar. Finbar Wrong's tattoo parlour was tattooed itself, a mural-covered building that stood out beside its slightly more conservative neighbours. The ground floor was empty, as usual, but as she turned for the stairs a voice behind her said, "About time you got here."

She spun as Skulduggery emerged from the backroom, and she ran to him, hugging him so tight she thought she might break his bones. Her tears soaked into his jacket. Dark blue today. It was good to see him out of his combat gear and back in a suit.

"Everyone else is upstairs," he said. "Apart from Saracen and Fletcher. Saracen's out getting lunch. Tanith and Donegan told us what you've been through. It's going to be OK."

She looked up at him. "Ghastly..."

"I know," he said, his voice soft.

"But Cassandra's vision... We saw him with Tanith, we saw them kiss..."

"We also saw Ravel on his knees, which is why we sent Ghastly and Anton with him in the first place. We changed the future, Valkyrie. But we'll make Ravel pay for everything he's done. You have my word. Come on. We have plans to make." He started for the stairs.

"Wait. Skulduggery, my... The reflection. She tried to kill me."

His head tilted. "What?"

"She's calling herself Stephanie. She's not... she's different. She wants my family. My life. She has the Sceptre."

"How?"

"I brought it with me, or Darquesse did, she brought it back with her, but I thought it had stayed in the alternate reality. But she has it. Stephanie has it. We have to go back."

Skulduggery paused for a moment. "If you want to go, we'll go. But I don't think we should. Right now your family has a protector with your knowledge, your skills and your intelligence. The reflection mightn't have your magic, but it has the Sceptre. Valkyrie... I know it sounds warped, but they couldn't be safer right now."

"But she's malfunctioning."

Skulduggery nodded. "Say the word and we'll go."

She stared at him, then sagged. "Yeah," she muttered. "OK. She can wait."

"We'll get your family back, Valkyrie. I promise," he said, and led the way upstairs.

Saracen arrived back with lunch, and Valkyrie ate ravenously and washed it down with scalding hot coffee. Tanith was sitting upside down and cross-legged on the ceiling. Below her, the Monster Hunters drank soft drinks while Saracen and Vex stood by the windows, keeping an eye on the street outside. Sanguine sat apart from everyone else, and Finbar waited patiently for the conversation to begin.

Skulduggery took his hat off, adjusted the brim, and put it back on again. His house was being watched, so he couldn't get at the rest of his suits.

"The hat looks fine," said Vex.

Skulduggery shook his head. "It's out of shape. It's ruined. May as well just throw it away. There's nothing that can be done for it now."

"Ghastly wasn't the only tailor in town, you know."

"But he was the best," said Skulduggery. "How can I go back to an ordinary tailor now? I have standards."

"You also have a room devoted entirely to hats that he made you. I think you'll do OK."

"I'm not so sure," Skulduggery said, and everyone went quiet until he snapped his head up. "All right then, for the benefit of those who haven't been around in the last few days, here's what's been happening. The shield is down. We don't know how or why it came down, but it's down. The Supreme Council has taken over Ireland. The only place not under their control is Roarhaven, which is protected by another shield that is, thankfully, still up. General Mantis has the place surrounded, of course, and it's only a matter of time before they find a way in.

"Meanwhile, Sanctuaries within the Supreme Council have been turning against each other with delightful regularity. I'd like to think they were arguing among themselves because the injustice of the war had finally got to them, but I suspect there is something bigger going on."

"What about Ravel?" asked Valkyrie.

Skulduggery looked at her. "He's still in Roarhaven."

"I mean, why did he do it? What does he want? He is our mystery man, right? He's the one we've been hunting? He's been with Mist from the start. All this time we thought it was him and Ghastly standing together and Mist isolated, when actually it was Ghastly who was standing alone. But for God's sake... why?"

"You saw the footage," Skulduggery responded. "You heard

what Mist said. They want the Warlocks to attack Dublin, and all the sorcerers to team up to fight them. Once we've been made public, once we've been called heroes, we take over. The mortals will love us. Until they realise they're no longer in control. By which time it'll be too late to do anything to stop us."

"Ravel's a lot more cunning than I ever gave him credit for," said Vex. "He went around with Corrival Deuce for all those years, talking to people like the Roarhaven mages, convincing them that our duty is to protect the mortals, not rule them. And at the end of it all? He had a list of sorcerers around the world who agreed with his point of view. Who knows what else he's been up to?"

"Let's make a list," said Skulduggery. "Conspiring with the Torment and Madame Mist, Ravel was behind the destruction of the Sanctuary here in Dublin, in which dozens of lives were lost. The move to Roarhaven was his idea. I think we can safely assume that he murdered Corrival Deuce in order to replace him as Grand Mage, using the Remnant attacks to cover it up, and then orchestrated assassination attempts on himself in order to gain full control over the Cleavers. He released Sean Mackin, maybe hoping that Kitana and her friends would attack the mortals in full view of the world. When that didn't happen, he returned to his Warlock plan, which had been set in motion five years ago, but which had probably been on his mind for the last century."

"It'd almost make me admire him," said Saracen, "if I didn't hate him so much."

"But the fact remains," Skulduggery said, "that while we may have our issues with Erskine Ravel, we need Roarhaven to stay strong against the Supreme Council and others. Finbar?"

Finbar nodded and stood, cleared his throat. "Yeah, thanks, Skul-man. Well, as most of you know, the last two years haven't exactly been easy for me. Someone, or something, who shall remain nameless but may very well be sitting upside down on my ceiling right now, got into my head during all that Remnant drama and forced me to push myself further than I'd have liked, psychically."

"You say that like it wasn't fun," Tanith said.

Finbar looked at Skulduggery. "I'm not talking to her. Please tell her not to interrupt. I can't handle talking to her."

"Finbar," said Tanith, sounding hurt, "why can't we be friends? I used to *be* you. I know everything there is about you. All your secret thoughts, all your little desires..."

"Tanith, shut up," said Skulduggery. "Finbar, please continue."

Finbar cleared his throat again. "Right, yeah, OK. So anyway, I have to be careful about what I open myself up to these days. But this morning I had a vision. And it was a vision of, of me. I don't... Sensitives don't normally get visions of themselves, but there I was, here, in this very room, and I look out this window and... and there are these people, walking through the streets, some of them hovering in the air, and they're shooting these beams of light and buildings are exploding and people are going bananas and vaporising when they're hit and there are cops, there are loads of cops, shooting at them, having no effect. Then this place gets hit, and there's all this noise and rubble, and I'm trapped and I look up and one of them, one of these people, passes by me, and then my vision goes deeper, because I kind of... I go into his head, y'know? And I see what he's seen.

"And suddenly I know who he is, and that he's a Warlock, and I see him in the Sanctuary, in this big machine, and from the sounds of it it's this Accelerator you keep talking about, and there's this guy and, I don't know, maybe thirty or forty others. All getting jacked up on Accelerator juice. And leading the pack is this huge big bald fella, with more muscles than I've had hot dinners. And I've had a lot of hot dinners. Sharon makes a wicked curry."

Valkyrie looked at Skulduggery. "What would the Warlocks be doing in the Sanctuary? They think Department X is real. Shouldn't they be attacking mortal targets?"

"What the hell does it matter?" Sanguine asked. "The Roarhaven shield ain't letting anybody through, Warlock or not."

"That's not what I saw," Finbar said. "When I saw into this bloke's head, I saw them kill all the sorcerers who went against them. They get in, they use the Accelerator, and after that there's no one to stop them. Dublin... Dublin's destroyed. And it's probably only the start of what they'll do."

A city in ruins. Valkyrie had seen that before.

"It wasn't just us who evaded capture in the valley," said Skulduggery. "A few other groups got out, too. I've been in contact with some of them. They've heard that six experts in science-magic are scheduled to enter the country today in a small convoy. It's safe to assume that Mantis will be using them to try to bring down the Roarhaven shield."

"So we intercept?" asked Saracen.

"You do," said Skulduggery. "If possible, subdue and detain. But it won't be easy. Security will be very tight."

"And what about you?" Sanguine said. "While we're going up against overwhelming odds, what are you gonna be doing?"

"We change the future. In order to stop the Warlocks, and the Supreme Council for that matter, from getting to the Accelerator, we'll need a way to get through the shield ourselves. So Valkyrie and I will be going after Fletcher."

Donegan sat up a little straighter. "The woman my contact put us in touch with, Ajuoga – it turns out she might very well be a Bride of Blood Tears."

Skulduggery looked at him. "This contact of yours, can he help us find her?"

"I'm afraid not. He was found dead two days ago. The Brides don't leave loose ends."

"Efficient but annoying. Very well – we have other ways of tracking them down."

"I can come, if you want," said Saracen.

"You'll be needed to take down the convoy."

"Ah, I'm sure Dexter has that covered."

"No I don't," Vex said. "Sorry. If I don't go hunting for Brides of Blood Tears, then you don't go hunting for Brides of Blood Tears."

Valkyrie frowned. "What's so special about the Brides of Blood Tears?"

Saracen looked at her. "You'll see," he said. "If ever I had to be captured and shackled by anyone, I'd want to be captured and shackled by *them*. Oh, and take sunscreen."

"Sunscreen?" Valkyrie echoed. "Why? Where are we going?"

Skulduggery looked at her. "Africa," he said.

56

THE DOCUMENTARY

China's shadows never left her. Everywhere she went in Roarhaven, they were behind her. She didn't know their names. Two mages, that's all they were, but they were impossible to lose. Not that she tried. She was focusing on getting her strength back, not on ditching the people who'd been assigned to keep an eye on her. She'd been from one side of this dreary little town to the other. She'd walked round the stagnant lake and approached the shield. On the other side, she could see Mantis's army, preparing for attack. They'd been preparing for days.

When she got back to the Sanctuary, Ravel was waiting for her. It was the first time she'd seen him since he'd murdered Ghastly Bespoke. Behind him stood the Black Cleaver, as silent and still as a corpse.

"You're back early," Ravel said. "You don't usually return from your walk for another hour."

She gave him a smile. "My shadows looked weary."

"Ah, yes, they're not very subtle, are they? I hope you'll forgive me, China, but you have a proud history of treachery. I doubt it'd take much to get you to add us to your list."

"Betray the only people keeping me safe?" she said. "You know me well enough to know that I am entirely self-serving. Vincent

Foe and his group of miscreants are on the other side of your rather glorious shield. Believe me, I have no intention of doing anything to jeopardise my place *within* said glorious shield."

"Madame Mist tells me you've had a lot of phone calls lately. Don't worry, we haven't been listening in. With the number of firewalls you have in your phone, I'm surprised even you can hear what's being said. But one of her little spidery acolytes had been making a note every time someone calls you."

"I'm a popular girl."

"Well, that's just it. You're not, are you? You once were, before Eliza burned your library to cinders."

"A temporary lapse, I assure you. Informants are notoriously fickle people, and they're scared of uncertainty and loud noises. But now that I'm part of the Sanctuary, now that I have been seen to ally myself with Erskine Ravel himself, some old lines of communication are opening back up. I'm hearing whispers again."

"Anything interesting? Maybe something useful enough to allow you to remain under our protection for a while longer?"

"I may have something for you."

"Skulduggery?"

"The Warlocks."

"They don't worry me. They may be powerful, but there are only a handful of them. And I don't think we'll be their target anyway. I have reason to believe they'll be striking Dublin."

"Maybe you should start to worry. Do you remember what Wretchlings are?"

Ravel frowned. "Yes. I think. They're before my time, before yours too, but in the simplest terms, they were organic Hollow Men. Artificial, man-made people."

China nodded. "But instead of being made from foul gases and paper skin, they were made from meat and blood and entrails. Because of this, they were in a constant state of rot. No one has constructed any for a thousand years because of their sheer savagery. It would appear that thousand years is now up."

"Charivari has Wretchlings?"

"Indeed he does. As to how many, I couldn't say. It all depends how long he's been planning this."

Ravel nodded slowly. She could tell he hadn't expected this. It felt good to watch him frown after what he'd done.

He snapped out of it. "That is interesting," he said, "but I'm sure it's nothing we can't handle. I have a favour to ask, actually."

"Oh?"

He gestured, and two men came hurrying forward. The sloppy one with the beard held a camera. The clean-shaven one held a notepad.

Ravel smiled, all charm. "China Sorrows, allow me to introduce Kenny Dunne and Patrick Slattery."

They stared at her, and the one called Kenny started to blush. Slattery stepped forward. "I don't make much money, but I will give you all of it. Whatever you want. I know we've just met, but I feel a connection between us, a real connection, and that's not something that happens every day, it's not something you can ignore. So here I am, a boy, standing in front of a girl, telling her he loves her."

Kenny barged forward. "He stole that from a movie."

"I did not," said Slattery quickly.

"He did. He stole it from *Notting Hill*."

"Only the last bit."

"I'd never steal a line from a movie for you," Kenny said, gazing deep into China's eyes. "You deserve more than that. You deserve poetry and originality and you deserve everything, everything in the whole world. I don't deserve *you*, but... but if you give me a chance, then maybe I can become a man that you could some day love."

"He stole that from a movie," Slattery said.

"No I didn't," said Kenny. "It just sounds like I did because it's from the heart."

"Mine was from the heart."

"Yours was from a DVD collection."

"I don't own *Notting Hill*," Slattery said, derision in his voice. "The only Richard Curtis film I own is *Love, Actually* because it's actually a really lovely film."

"I haven't seen it," China said.

"You could have a loan of mine if you like," said Kenny.

"Gentlemen," Ravel said, "I asked China to talk to you in an effort to convince you to get our message across. China, some of my people stumbled across these two in Dublin, asking all sorts of odd questions. They brought them to me and I saw a way to help the Arts and our cause. Gentlemen; you're making a documentary about us, after all. Wouldn't it be better to let us help you make it?"

Kenny spoke to Ravel, but couldn't take his eyes off China. "We're journalists," he said. "We have journalistic... integrity. What you... what you were talking about sounded like you'd be telling us what we could and could not... you know... film..."

"That's not what I meant at all," Ravel said. "All I meant was that if, God forbid, some people attack the mortal population of this country, you would have documented proof that we leaped to the mortals' defence the first chance we got. Something like this, broadcast around the world, would show people that we weren't a threat to them – that there was really no need to fear us. That in fact they might benefit from our... guidance."

"Sounds like propaganda," Slattery said, smiling at China. "We're journalists... our duty is to the... the... the whatchamacallit... the truth..."

China looked at them both, and smiled. "Please?"

Slattery whimpered and Kenny nodded so fast he could have given himself whiplash. "OK, no problem, I love you."

"Aw," China said, "thank you."

57

SUNBURN

The jeep slowed, and Skulduggery turned off the engine and they got out. The first thing that struck Valkyrie was how cold it was. There were no clouds, and more stars in that vast sky than she had ever seen. Her sense of wonderment was ruined by the yawn that overtook her. It had been a long flight and then a long drive and she was sore and tired. She didn't know the name of this village, but it perched quietly on the edge of the Sahara Desert like an obedient puppy waiting to be petted.

A man emerged from the shadows, walked over to them with a smile on his face. "Detectives," he said, shaking their hands. "My name is Tau. The Council of Elders asked me to meet you here, and offer you any and all assistance. I believe you wish to visit the dwelling of the Brides of Blood Tears, is that right?"

"They're holding an associate of ours," Skulduggery said. "We're just here to ask for him back."

"The Brides are not known for giving up those things they have taken."

"We plan on being persuasive," said Valkyrie.

Tau smiled. "Indeed. The Brides live in a vast pyramid to the west of here. Come with me. I will take you to your transport."

Tau led the way round the outskirts of the sleeping village. A dog crossed their path, looked at them without interest and continued on.

"Hey," said Tau, "did you hear? Renato Bisahalani is dead."

There was surprise in Skulduggery's voice. "By whose hand?"

"He was struck down by assassins, so I've been told," said Tau. "They're dropping like flies, aren't they? I am glad I have never been respectable enough to become an Elder." He chuckled.

A truck was parked behind a crumbling white wall. Valkyrie's Necromancer ring turned cold.

She reached out, a hand on Skulduggery's arm, and they slowed. A dark mass lay crumpled by the truck's rear wheel. Tau noticed it and jerked to a stop. Skulduggery tapped her, nodded to a pile of broken pots beside them. Behind it, another dead body.

Tau turned, the shadows falling over his face. Then his hand started crackling with energy and he raised his arm and a large figure rushed him, a sword cutting through the arm at the wrist.

Tau screamed, staggered backwards, and the sword swung again and took his head.

Skulduggery remained absolutely still, so Valkyrie fought the urge to leap forward. She couldn't see in the dark like he could.

"Apologies for the drama," Frightening Jones said, wiping his sword clean as he neared. "Their associates ambushed me this morning. One of them stayed alive long enough to tell me what they planned. Skulduggery, you're looking well. Valkyrie, a pleasure as always."

Whenever she met Frightening, Valkyrie had to consciously stop herself from bowing. There was just something so inherently regal about this calm African – the way he carried himself was almost king-like.

"Who were they?" Skulduggery asked.

"Pirates," said Frightening. "There is really no other word for it. They steal and loot and if their prize is worth enough, they sell it on. That's what they were planning to do with you. The

Supreme Council would pay handsomely for either of you in shackles."

"But you guys are on our side," Valkyrie murmured, her eyes irresistibly drawn to Tau's head, lying in the sand.

"There are three Sanctuaries in Africa," Frightening pointed out. "At the best of times, there are opposing factions. But now that our Elders are dead, more sorcerers are breaking away and looking out only for themselves."

"How are the replacement Elders?" Skulduggery asked.

"Doing their job. Doing their best. Ravel made some good choices when he appointed them." He lowered his eyes. "I... was sorry to hear about Ghastly. He was a friend, and a good man. I couldn't believe that it was Ravel who did it."

"We'll make him pay," Skulduggery said.

"Is it true?" Valkyrie asked. "About Bisahalani?"

"It is," said Frightening. "Zafira Kerias has assumed his place as Grand Mage of America. These are turbulent times we live in. But for now, your chariot awaits." He led them round the truck. "It'll take you most of the way, but from its endpoint on, you'll need to walk. The Brides live in a pyramid that's only visible from a certain angle, and they value their privacy. I've never been there myself, but I've been told if you stay on a south-south-westerly trajectory, you will eventually reach it."

"Eventually?" Valkyrie said, frowning. "How long is 'eventually'?"

"No more than seven hours."

"Wow. It's a good thing Skulduggery can fly, then."

"Ah, no flying, I'm afraid."

"What?"

"The Brides will detect any extraordinary usage of magic. Throwing a fireball will be fine. Flying, I am afraid, will not."

Valkyrie sagged. "So we have to walk? For seven hours? On sand?"

"I have some water for you."

"How about a piggyback instead?"

Frightening smiled. "If I were accompanying you, I would be honoured. Unfortunately, I have business in Egypt."

She immediately looked at Skulduggery, who immediately shook his head.

"I'm not giving you a piggyback."

"But I got tired walking from there to here," she whined. "Think how bad I'll be after seven *hours*."

They stopped beside a double seat that someone had torn from a bus, and when they didn't walk past it, Valkyrie's frown deepened.

"Please don't tell me this is our chariot," she said. When no one answered, she continued. "It's a seat. There's no car around it. There's no engine. There aren't any wheels. Chariots are meant to be pulled by horses. Where are the horses?" Her eyes widened, and she looked around them. "Are they invisible horses?"

"Even the Brides of Blood Tears need to occasionally shop for supplies," said Frightening. "This is the transport they have arranged for themselves. It travels at over two hundred kilometres per hour and cannot deviate from its course. I am told the journey to its endpoint will take nine hours."

Valkyrie stared. "So we sit on that thing for nine hours, travelling at a ridiculous speed, and then we have to walk for another seven hours? How is that practical?"

"The Brides do not shop often."

"Apparently not."

Frightening handed her a canteen. "Here is your water. Granted, you probably don't need this. You're an Elemental, after all, you can conjure water from the moisture in the air."

Valkyrie made a face. "How much moisture is there in desert air?"

Skulduggery brushed the seat clean of sand, and sat. "How many Brides should we expect to encounter?"

"If you're lucky?" Frightening said. "None. Hopefully, you'll sneak in, find Fletcher, and you can all teleport back to Ireland before they notice you're there. I don't like dealing with witches.

427

I don't understand their magic and they, you know... they creep me out. But to answer your question... I was told there could be as many as three hundred Brides in that pyramid. And for every Bride there are at least two Devoted trailing after them."

Valkyrie sat beside Skulduggery. "Devoted?"

"Mortal men who toil in servitude," Frightening told her. "Some call them willing slaves. They obey without question and without complaint – mostly because their tongues were cut out once puberty set in."

"They can't talk? I honestly cannot think of anything more terrible."

"I could see some advantages," Skulduggery murmured.

Frightening laughed. "Good luck, my friends, and enjoy the ride. Apparently it's just like a rollercoaster."

He slapped the back of the seat and the whole thing lifted into the air, high enough so that both Skulduggery's and Valkyrie's feet cleared the ground.

"And you might want to hold on to something," Frightening said as he walked away, and in that instant they sprang forward, accelerating so suddenly that Valkyrie was pressed back into the seat.

They moved straight out, away from the village, soundlessly skimming over the sand, picking up even more speed. The air filled Valkyrie's cheeks, ballooning them out while her hair went nuts. Giggling, she glanced at Skulduggery, who sat there with a hand held in front of him. Not even a breeze ruffled his shirt.

"Don't be boring!" she roared at him over the wind. He moved his head a fraction. "Come on! It's fun!"

His head moved in that way that was his equivalent of rolling his eyes, but he took off his hat and held it to his chest, and then he dropped his hand. Immediately the wind whipped his tie across his jaw.

The seat skimmed over a high dune and plunged down the other side, and Valkyrie screamed and laughed and gripped

Skulduggery's arm. Tears streamed from her eyes, but she could barely lift a hand to wipe them away. Beside her, the wind was making a deep whooshing noise as it passed through Skulduggery's eye sockets.

"Façade!" she shouted. "Put your façade on!"

He hesitated only a moment, then tapped his collarbones. The false face crept quickly across his head, but the features struggled to stay where they were supposed to. His cheeks were like Valkyrie's, ballooning outwards, but even his eyes were being dragged round his head. The wind went up his nostrils and flipped his nose inside out and Valkyrie laughed until their speed made it hard to draw breath. For the first time she noticed how cold she was, and she tightened her grip on Skulduggery's arm and he held up his hand, deflecting the air around them.

Valkyrie gasped in the sudden quiet. Skulduggery's face settled into position, and he looked at her with a raised eyebrow.

"Enough fun for you?"

"My skin stings," she said.

"You've just had sand blasted at you at two hundred kilometres per hour. I'm not surprised your skin stings. You should have worn your mask."

"You could have told me that at the start."

"Then how will you learn?"

They hurtled down another dune. Below them, around them, the sand was dark. Above them, a vast sky with countless stars.

"It's beautiful," she said softly.

"It has its moments."

Valkyrie awoke with her head resting on Skulduggery's shoulder and, even before she'd opened her eyes, the world was bright and hot and harsh.

She sat up a little straighter, cracked her eyelids. The dark dunes beneath had become golden, and the countless stars were now hidden behind a sky of perfect blue. The seat slowed as it came to the top of a dune and the moment Skulduggery stopped deflecting the air the heat closed in on Valkyrie like a fist.

"Woah," she croaked.

The seat stopped, and lowered to the sand. Skulduggery stood, put his hat back on. Valkyrie held out her hand and he pulled her to her feet. Her back was stiff, her legs were numb, and she was hot. She was so incredibly hot.

She tied her hair back, then fumbled in her pocket for her sunglasses and put them on. She took a long swig of warm water, and wiped her mouth before speaking. "We have to walk for seven hours? In this heat? I can't do it. I literally cannot do that."

"You'll be fine," Skulduggery said, nodding to their left. "We go that way."

He started walking. Valkyrie followed.

"It's too hot. I'm being serious. My clothes are meant to cool me down in hot weather, but they're doing nothing."

"They'd cool you down on a hot summer's day in Ireland," Skulduggery said. "The Sahara is quite another matter, I'm afraid."

It was hard to walk in the sand. It sucked at her boots, her lovely boots, her lovely boots in which boiled her lovely feet. She was already sweating. She took off her jacket, tied the arms round her waist. The gauntlet made it awkward, but she managed.

Skulduggery glanced back. "You can't wear that," he said.

She looked down at herself. Her pink T-shirt, the one Stephanie had bought. She resisted the urge to rip it off and burn it. "Why not?"

"It's pink."

"So? We're not in camouflage."

"I mean it's pink and it's not armoured. You should put your jacket back on. We're going up against some very dangerous and unpredictable people."

"Who are seven hours away from our current position."

"You're going to get sunburnt."

She took a tube of suncream from her pocket. "Extra strength," she said.

He shook his head and carried on. She followed, spreading the suncream over her arms and shoulders, her face and neck and chest. "Do my back," she called.

"Do your own back."

"I can't. Please?"

"Do you know how hard it is to get suncream off these gloves?"

"No," she admitted truthfully. "Do you?"

He stopped and sagged. She passed him the cream and turned, and he spread it brusquely over the back of her neck and down to her shoulder blades.

She grinned as he handed the tube back to her. "Thank you."

He grunted, then put his hat on Valkyrie's head and moved off.

"Want to sing songs while we walk?" she asked.

"God, no," he said.

They'd been walking for hours and the canteen had long since been emptied. Valkyrie licked her dry lips. She'd come with sunglasses and suncream, but no water of her own.

Pretty dumb for a smart girl.

She applied more suncream to her sizzling skin, having gone through most of the tube already. The fedora was hot on her head, but it did its part to keep her face in the shade, and for that she was grateful. Anything she could do to cool down was welcome beyond measure. If Skulduggery hadn't been here, she would have had no problem in abandoning her clothes altogether.

What a sight that would make.

She laughed.

Skulduggery looked back. "Everything OK?"

"Not really. I think I may be delirious."

He stopped, and watched her as she walked up to him. "You're burnt."

431

She looked at her arms. "No I'm not."

"Take off the sunglasses."

She dipped them lower on her nose, and could suddenly see how red her skin was. "Oh, bloody hell! Look at me! I'm a lobster!"

"I told you to leave your jacket on."

She glared. "You think that now is the time to say things like that? Really? There is *no* time to say things like that, but *especially* now. This is going to hurt so *much* tonight, and all I get from you is 'I told you so'? Water. Give me water."

"I've taught you how to draw the moisture from the—"

"I'm tired and I'm cross and I'm hot and I'm sunburnt and you have just committed an *unforgivable* sin so you'd better give me water right this *second*."

"Well," he said, "since you put it like that..."

He raised his hand and the air started to shimmer, and a small mist formed above her. She could feel the air currents against her skin, feel what he was doing, how he was manipulating the moisture around them. She tilted her head back and the mist became droplets of water that fell into her open mouth.

"Oh, that's good," she said, her eyes closed. "More."

"You want any more," he said, walking away, "you do it yourself."

She stared after him in dismay. "Oh, come on, just—"

"You're never going to learn if I always do these things for you. I'm not going to be around forever, you know."

"You planning on leaving me?"

"Not if I can help it. But things happen."

Valkyrie sighed, and trudged after him.

She did her best to draw water from the air, she really did. At best she could form a little pocket of drizzle, though, and the more she walked, the less she was able to concentrate. Finally, she couldn't stand it any more.

"Water," she said. Her mouth was so dry it hurt to speak.

Skulduggery didn't look back. "You need to do these things—"

"Water, or I'll die. I will die. To spite you."

He stopped, turned to her, and sighed. "Fine."

"And more," she said. "This time, more. Lots."

He plucked his hat from her head, and raised both hands. Valkyrie took off her sunglasses and once again she tilted her head back while a mist formed above her. It was a big mist this time. A serious mist. She felt the air currents twisting and turning with every gesture Skulduggery made, as he dragged the moisture into droplets of water. A lot of droplets. And not droplets any more. Drops now. Proper-sized drops, hanging there, bumping into each other forming bigger drops, forming a puddle that rippled in mid-air, a big puddle, a serious puddle, a—

The puddle collapsed and drenched her and she squealed, she actually squealed, and jumped to one side way too late to avoid it. She swallowed whatever water had landed in her mouth, almost choked on it with the outraged laughter that bubbled up from somewhere within, and she stared at Skulduggery through strands of wet hair and he just stood there, and she discovered just how smug a skull could look.

"I can't believe you did that," she said.

"You wanted more."

"You are so immature."

"And you're smiling for the first time in hours."

She laughed again, put a hand to her face and rubbed the water into her cheeks and forehead. It felt so good. Having wet hair felt so good. And yet even as she stood there she could feel herself starting to dry.

"Could you do that again?" she asked.

"My pleasure," he said.

Once she'd had her fill of water, and once she'd topped up her canteen, they started walking again. Another hour and her stomach started to rumble. An hour after that, her energy left her. Skulduggery picked her up and carried her, and she drifted off in his arms. She didn't know how far he carried her, but she opened her eyes when that voice in her head said, *Wakey-wakey.*

Before them, the desert shimmered in a heat haze like she had never seen. The shimmering air rose as tall as a skyscraper, but it was localised to the area directly in front of them. Skulduggery let her down, and Valkyrie stood on shaky legs. She untied the jacket from around her waist and put it on, hissing in pain as it slid over her skin.

For her benefit, Skulduggery moved slowly down the dune, and she managed to follow without collapsing. They approached the heat haze, which didn't retract before them. Instead, it stayed in place, like a wall. Skulduggery tilted his head and made an amused sound. Then he took Valkyrie's hand, turned her slightly, and the heat haze parted, and behind it she saw the pyramid.

58

THE BRIDES OF
BLOOD TEARS

It took close to half an hour to climb the smooth stone steps to the first opening. Valkyrie lasted less than two minutes before her legs cramped, and she happily settled into Skulduggery's arms for the rest of the journey. When he finally set her down, she straightened, and it was like unspooling from a hot, humid swamp. Every part of her was sticky and covered in sweat.

"I feel gross," she said softly, holding her arms out from her sides. "Oh my God, I need a shower."

Skulduggery read the air. "First we rescue Fletcher, then you can have your shower. How are you feeling aside from hot and burnt?"

She wanted to tell him she felt fine, that there was no need to worry about her. But lying about something like that would be dangerous to them both. "I feel a little weak," she said.

"Then you stay behind me. If I tell you to run or hide, you do what I say. Going up against a witch is not like going up against a sorcerer. These people are much more dangerous."

They moved in through the opening, and the sudden shade would have made Valkyrie smile were it not for the sunburn that kept her face as blank as possible. She pocketed her sunglasses.

There were rooms to either side of them, no doors, containing shelves of clay pots of varying sizes.

"If we get separated," Skulduggery whispered, "we meet up back here."

She gave the slightest of murmurs, and followed him to the heavy curtains at the end of the corridor. He pulled the curtains back and a warm light chased the shade away.

The centre of the pyramid was a vast, hollowed-out cavern in which numerous plateaus had sprung, stretching from one side to the other. These plateaus were connected by a spider's web of rope bridges and ladders, stairs and slopes. Some plateaus were narrow, some were wide, some were solid and some looked flimsy as paper. There were buildings on some of them, solid buildings of stone, but mostly the dwellings seemed to be tents and marquees of varying sizes.

Valkyrie hunkered down beside Skulduggery, neither one speaking for the moment, and they watched the Brides. Now she understood why Saracen had said there were worse people to be held captive by. Their hair was tied in a series of golden bands, and the lower half of their face was covered by a red veil. They wore skirts of silk, slit high to the waist, and a choli blouse, all in red, with their bellies exposed. The cape was red, too, although Valkyrie was pretty sure that it wouldn't be called a cape. Whatever it was, it was some kind of mix between silk and chiffon, and it was attached to the shoulders by small golden rings and to each wrist by a golden bracelet. The cape rippled with every movement, no matter how slight. Another bracelet curled round the right upper arm, and their sandals had interlacing straps that looked way too complicated and annoying to be practical. Each Bride had a curved dagger in a jewelled sheath on her hip.

Wherever each Bride went, a man followed. Wearing nothing but a plain white sarong around their waist, their heads were shaven and their bodies were muscled. The Devoted kept their eyes down as they walked, each one exactly six steps behind the Bride they followed. Not a bad system.

"Do the Devoted have to do *whatever* the Brides tell them?" Valkyrie whispered.

Skulduggery looked at her. "Stop drooling."

"I wasn't—"

"Stop it."

She sighed. "Fine. So where do you think they're keeping Fletcher?"

"I don't know," Skulduggery said. "From what I've read of the Brides, their evenings and nights are for themselves. Everything gets shut down. Doors are locked and off they go to do whatever it is they do in their spare time. That's our best shot at moving around."

"How? I don't have the cloaking sphere any more."

"We'll just have to do it the old-fashioned way," Skulduggery said. "We'll have to sneak."

"That sounds hard."

"Nonsense. Sneaking is easy. You just have to be careful about where you—"

He stepped out from hiding and accidentally kicked a pebble that skittered along the ground and bounced off a pot with a nice loud *ping*.

"Me and my big articulate mouth," he muttered, as a Bride looked up and saw him.

The alarm went out, the Brides shouting warnings to each other. Valkyrie started to stand.

"Stay down," he ordered.

She stared at him. "What are you going to do?"

"Something inadvisable," he said, and ran forward.

Valkyrie stayed where she was, tucked behind cover, listening to the shouts and the sounds of crackling energy and exploding rock. He was leading them away from her.

He's leaving you alone.

Keeping low, she moved back through the curtain, squinting at the rectangle of unforgiving light that would usher her outside. Where would she go? Where would she hide? She was weak, sunburnt, and probably had heatstroke or something. She wouldn't get far out there. She wouldn't get far in here, either. The thought of throwing a punch made her want to cry.

Footsteps on the other side of the curtain made her dart into the room on her right. She pressed herself back against the wall, careful not to disturb the clay pots. Two voices – no, three – talking quickly. Only one of them spoke English. She didn't recognise either of the other two languages.

One of the Brides babbled urgently.

"Let me," said the Bride who spoke English.

More babbling, then—

"We will."

Valkyrie would have scowled if the pain hadn't stopped her.

Just our luck that the only one we can understand is a lackey and not a boss.

She peeked out. Two Brides hurried into the sunshine and disappeared down the steps. Made sense. Their secret pyramid had been breached, after all – they needed to know if there was anyone else out there.

The third Bride, the one Valkyrie couldn't see, walked back towards the curtain, and Valkyrie coughed softly. The footsteps stopped. Valkyrie picked up one of the pots. She couldn't hear anything now, but it was highly unlikely that the Bride was still standing in place. No, if the Bride was anything like Valkyrie, she would already be sneaking to the doorway, ready to lunge in and catch the intruder unawares—

The Bride lunged into the room and Valkyrie smashed the pot over her head, giving a muffled scream as her sunburn sent claws of stinging pain ripping through her. The Bride stumbled to her knees and Valkyrie stepped back and kicked her in the head.

Oooh, that felt good.

Valkyrie looked down at the unconscious Bride while she waited for the pain to fade. An idea came to her, and grew into a plan. It wasn't a very good plan, but it was a plan, and that's more than she had a moment ago.

Valkyrie took off her clothes, folded them neatly and put them on a shelf behind a pot, and dressed herself in the Bride's outfit.

Not right, is it? Leaving these wonderful clothes here with all manner of dangers ahead.

No, it wasn't right, especially given what she was now wearing. Red silk and a stupid veil and sandals she couldn't even do up right.

You look great. You look like a homicidal belly dancer.

She slipped the Necromancer ring into a small pouch she found beside the knife, then shackled the Bride's wrists, tied her feet, and used one of Valkyrie's own socks as a gag. She apologised about that one. Of course the Bride didn't hear it, but that was hardly the point.

The only way this was going to work was if no one got too close to her. Then they wouldn't see the mess she'd made of the sandals or how her hair wasn't bound right or how, instead of a healthy tan like the others, her skin was glowing painfully red. Also, the Brides walked with a sway that she didn't have, and they walked lightly, like they were each on individual clouds. Valkyrie was well aware of how she walked. She walked functionally. She was used to wearing trousers and boots.

Trousers and boots that Ghastly Bespoke made. Doesn't seem right to abandon them like this.

Taking a deep breath, Valkyrie left the room and walked through the curtains. The heat made her start to sweat again, and made her sunburn sting like crazy. She walked for the nearest rope bridge. It was surprisingly steady.

One of the Devoted was ahead. She faltered, then straightened up and walked swiftly by him. He didn't shout out. Didn't raise the alarm. This was good. This was going to work. She glanced back. He was right behind her.

She whirled and he stopped. She waited for him to make a move. He didn't. He just stood there with his eyes down. She frowned, backed away, turned and walked on. He followed.

She stopped again and so did he.

"What do you want?" she asked. If he recognised the difference in accents, he didn't react to it. But neither did he answer.

She was about to stride off and leave him there when she saw a Bride and another Devoted walking closer. Cursing under her breath, she retraced her steps back to the rope bridge. The Devoted came after her.

"Would you stop?" she hissed. "Just stop, all right? Stay!"

He stopped walking and she hurried, passed the rope bridge and kept walking until she came to a junction. She hid as another Bride passed, a Devoted walking behind her with his head down. Everywhere a Bride walked, there was at least one Devoted trailing in her wake.

A Bride walking around without a Devoted will probably arouse suspicion.

Valkyrie headed back to the rope bridge. He was still there.

"Hello," she said. "Would you... I need to get to our prison cells, but I have forgotten, uh, how to get there. Take me to them."

The Devoted bowed slightly, but didn't move.

"Well?" she pressed. "Let's go."

He took a step backwards, bowing as he did so, and she understood. She walked by him and he followed. When she got to the top of the slope, she hesitated, looked back, saw the angle of his shoulders and moved right. It wasn't the fastest or most effective way to get where she needed to go, but it worked. In one narrow corridor they were forced to pass within arm's length of another Bride. The Bride nodded to her and she nodded back, and they each continued on. Valkyrie breathed out and relaxed.

440

They walked until they came to a giant door. She looked at the Devoted. "This is it?"

He bowed a little deeper.

It was locked. Of course it was locked, the day was over. Everything shut down when the day was over. There was no way she was getting through this tonight, not without bringing every Bride down on top of her.

"I need to sleep," she said.

He bowed, stood to one side, and she walked by him. Again, he directed her with the turn of his shoulders until they came to a wide plateau of tents and marquees. Doing her best to keep away from other Brides, Valkyrie chose a tent on the outer edges.

"Get me food," she said to the Devoted. "And water. Please. If you wouldn't mind."

The Devoted bowed and walked away, and Valkyrie stepped inside, letting the flap close behind her. The floor was covered in cushions, and she stepped over to the biggest one and sat. She wished she had her phone. She didn't even know what time it was. She tried to fix her hair back into the golden bands, but abandoned the task before she grew too annoyed.

A few minutes later, there was movement outside her tent. Resisting the urge to come up in a crouch and prepare for trouble, Valkyrie lay back and feigned sleep. That wasn't easy with her sunburn. She listened to someone come in and cracked open an eye. A Devoted laid a tray of food down on the small table. The lamplight flickered over his muscles and his bald head – but they *all* had muscles and bald heads. She waited until she saw his face, until she was sure he was *her* Devoted, before she sat up.

"Thank you," she said.

He said nothing. He went to the entrance and stood there, hands by his sides, head down, like a statue.

Valkyrie crawled over to the table, filled a goblet with water and lifted the veil to drink it down in one go. There were meats and grapes and fruit piled on to the tray and she ate what she could and left the rest of it.

She crawled back to the big cushion, piled a few on top of each other and lay against them, propped up. The curved dagger was digging into her thigh. The arm bracelet was digging into her bicep. Her hair was too loose and her damn sandals had slipped down again. She was anxious. She was anxious and bored. She was anxious and bored and tired, but there was no way she could sleep, not with the enemy all around, not with Skulduggery held captive and—

She woke. She couldn't have been sleeping for that long. She was still propped up on the cushions. She hadn't moved.

The Devoted had, though. He had laid out small jars of sweet-smelling oils on the ground before her, and beside them was a large pail of water. He stood behind the pail, a cloth in his hands.

"Uh," said Valkyrie. "What's going on?"

He didn't say anything. Of course he didn't. She sat up, almost cried out with the pain and he quickly scooped up one of the jars and knelt by her. He dipped a finger in, then touched it lightly to her arm. That spot, the spot he'd touched, immediately cooled. It didn't even look as red any more.

"Well," she said to the Devoted, "aren't you full of surprises?"

59

THE RISE

Morning came and she led the Devoted out of the tent. Her sunburn had become a tan overnight and she could move without pain once again. At her instruction, the Devoted had even fixed her hair into the golden bands and done up the sandals properly. She looked like a Bride of Blood Tears now, and tried to give her hips that extra bit of sway to complete the transformation. She needn't have bothered. None of the other Brides gave her anything more than a cursory glance as she walked back to the giant doors.

They stood open. One of the Devoted waited to one side, his head down. A sentry?

Kill him. Snap his neck. Cut his throat.

Valkyrie passed him warily. His eyes stayed downcast. Her own Devoted stopped beside him. Obviously, they weren't allowed any further. That suited Valkyrie just fine. She gave one last admiring glance to the bald man with the big muscles and hurried on, following the tunnel round to another set of large doors. They stood slightly open, warm firelight seeping through the crack. She slowed, and approached in silence. She heard voices, and took a peek.

A stone cavern, lit by a single torch on the wall. A Bride with

443

skin the colour of chocolate walked slowly round a circle of linked asymmetrical shapes carved into the ground. Within the borders of those shapes, sigils had been etched. It looked to be an exact match to the necklace the Bride wore. Valkyrie had seen that kind of thing before, and she knew that to break the necklace was to break the circle. Within the circle stood Skulduggery and Fletcher. Fletcher appeared unharmed, though Skulduggery seemed to have lost his hat.

He loved that hat.

Valkyrie slipped her Necromancer ring on to her finger. She called in the shadows to mask her, and crept through the doors, blending immediately into the gloom around the edges of the room. The Bride was saying something about not getting comfortable.

"I honestly don't see us staying here for much longer," Skulduggery responded. "Could I ask a question, though, before you continue on what I'm sure will be a delightful monologue? Charivari, the scamp, is making all sorts of threatening movements and whatnot. Does he still believe that Department X is responsible for the deaths of his people?"

"You think I would know?" the Bride asked.

"You've been in contact with him, Ajuoga. We know you have."

"Maybe," Ajuoga said, and laughed. She had a pretty laugh. "Very well. Yes, we have been *in contact* with him, as you say. A most impressive man. When he left, he spoke with many people, enquiring about this mysterious mortal agency that had been killing his Warlocks. As did we. But now it is plain, Department X is nothing but a rumour. How embarrassing for us all."

"And what are Charivari's plans now?"

"I'm sorry, I do not understand. His plans are what they have always been. Find the ones responsible and make them pay."

"How will he do that?"

"The Warlocks are powerful, and Charivari is no simple-minded barbarian. Our true enemy tried to provoke us into attacking the mortals. Only sorcerers who hate mortals would do such a thing. And they are easy to find."

"And if he finds them?"

"If? Oh, dear, no. You misunderstand. He has *already* found them. All this trouble emanated from your Sanctuary, Mr Pleasant. That is where the Children of the Spider have congregated, is it not? That is where the Torment lived. We know of his involvement."

"The Torment is dead," Fletcher said.

"But his brethren live, and they plot against us and our kind. Your Sanctuary will fall, make no mistake. I have to say, however, we like what we hear about this Accelerator. Is it truly as powerful as they say? That will be quite something. I am looking forward to that."

"You've joined with the Warlocks, then," Skulduggery said.

"Of course. We are witches. They are Warlocks. We practise the true magic. Your kind despises us."

"I'm a living skeleton," said Skulduggery. "I have no *kind*."

Ajuoga sounded amused. Beneath her veil, she was surely smiling. "A living skeleton, indeed. We have all heard so many stories about you, Mr Pleasant. Your legend permeates even here, where we care little for your Sanctuaries or your petty squabbles. And yet I must admit to feeling slightly underwhelmed. Subduing you was tragically simple."

"Have you ever heard of being lulled into a false sense of security?" Skulduggery asked.

Ajuoga opened her arms. "Then where is the surprise attack? Where are your reinforcements?"

"I'm not sure," Skulduggery admitted. "They're probably lulling you into a false sense of security, too. I'm not sure it works if everyone is lulling, to be honest – then there's no one left to do anything. We may have to work on our strategy for the future."

"The future?" Ajuoga echoed. "Maybe you would have a future if you had been captured by the Maidens of the New Dawn or the Crones of the Cold Embrace – although I doubt it. But you are among the Brides of Blood Tears, the most fearsome of all witches, and you, Detective, don't have much of a future to worry about."

Valkyrie crouched slightly. Ajuoga was nearing.

"I see," said Skulduggery. "And what do you want with young Mr Renn here, may I ask?"

"He's a Teleporter," said Ajuoga. "He's a natural. We want his blood."

"I don't think so," snarled Fletcher.

"We want his genes."

"That one's a bit more vague..."

"We want him to breed with us."

"I reckon I'll be OK here on my own," Fletcher said to Skulduggery.

Skulduggery ignored him. "And when you're done breeding with him, what will you do then? Kill him?"

"We'll never be done breeding with him."

"I'll hold them off," Fletcher said. "You save yourself."

"I'm not leaving you here, Fletcher."

"Ah, go on."

Valkyrie burst from the shadows, but Ajuoga spun and her hand flashed and Valkyrie ducked and stumbled as the wall behind her exploded in shards of rock. She threw a fistful of shadows as a distraction and then went low, her shoulder slamming into Ajuoga's stomach while she grabbed the back of her legs. She tried to lift, but the woman was already shooting her legs back, adjusting her balance.

This one could be trouble.

An elbow dropped sharply between Valkyrie's shoulder blades and she barely turned her head fast enough to avoid taking the knee square in the face. Stars burst behind her eyes. Ajuoga moved round her, an arm encircling her throat, hauling her up straight.

This one knows what she's doing. This one has experience.

Before the choke could come on, Valkyrie turned and slammed an elbow into her nose. Ajuoga released her, the red veil already darkening as blood soaked the material. Valkyrie snapped her palm straight and the air rippled, and Ajuoga went tumbling head over heels.

"Finish her," Skulduggery said from inside the circle. "Don't give her time to—"

But Ajuoga had already recovered. Her hand flashed white and Valkyrie threw herself sideways. The energy stream sizzled past her bare skin. Shadows crashed into Ajuoga's back, making the second shot go wide, but now the curved dagger was in the woman's hand and slashing across Valkyrie's arm. Blood flew. Fletcher yelled out frantic warnings as the dagger slashed again and Valkyrie jerked back and Ajuoga came forward, slashing and drawing more blood.

"Don't retreat," Skulduggery instructed calmly, as if they were in practice, as if she wasn't fighting for her life. "Every step backwards you take gives her more room to work. Meet her. Get in close. Guard, Valkyrie. Where's your guard?"

Valkyrie held her arms in front, turned her palms facing in. Ajuoga circled her. Valkyrie dropped her guard slightly, giving her a gap, and Ajuoga saw it and slashed, and Valkyrie sprang into her.

"Good girl," Skulduggery said.

Valkyrie blocked and grabbed the knife arm in one movement, held it tight to her side while she threw palm shots into Ajuoga's face. The veil tore away. Beneath it, Ajuoga was bloody but beautiful. Valkyrie stepped into her, hip to hip, and flipped her in an old-fashioned judo throw. Ajuoga spun in a whirl of cape and dress and crunched to the ground, the dagger dropping. Valkyrie lost her balance, stumbled over her, Ajuoga pulling her down. They clawed and raked and punched and snarled and hissed and bit. Valkyrie got on top, but Ajuoga's legs flashed up, trapping Valkyrie's head and one arm between her thighs.

Triangle choke.

Valkyrie could put it on, but she had no idea how to get out of it. She clicked her fingers, tried summoning a flame, but Ajuoga arched her back, lifted her hips off the ground, tightening the squeeze. Valkyrie's own arm pressed against her throat, cutting off the blood supply to the brain. Her eyes bulged.

Let me out and I'll help.

Fletcher was shouting curses and Skulduggery was issuing instructions, but she couldn't hear either of them. Her head was fuzzy. Tears blurred her vision. Her face was red. She knew her face was red. She probably looked ridiculous. She hated it when her face got red.

Fletcher, still shouting curses. Skulduggery, still issuing instructions.

She was making that noise, the noise people make when the triangle choke is put on. Like a gurgle. Spittle dripped from her lips. Not very attractive. She was going to pass out. She couldn't get out of this and she couldn't use magic.

Let me help. Let me take over.

Skulduggery. What was he saying? What was that he was saying?

Beyond the roar in her head, she heard, "Valkyrie, you still have your own dagger."

Oh, yeah.

She reached down with her free hand, rapidly numbing fingers pulling the dagger from its sheath, and with all that remained of her strength, she drove it up. Into Ajuoga's right buttock.

Ajuoga shrieked and Valkyrie was kicked sideways and she rolled, gasping, while Ajuoga contorted on the floor beside her. With slowly clearing vision, she watched Ajuoga yank the dagger from her cheek and hurl it away, then she turned to Valkyrie with murder in her eyes.

Uh-oh.

Ajuoga threw herself at Valkyrie, bloodied hands curling round her throat, cursing at her in some exotic language.

Kill her.

Valkyrie hammered at those hands, but they wouldn't budge. She hooked her fingers, dug her nails deep into Ajuoga's face and ripped downwards, leaving bloody furrows in her wake. Ajuoga recoiled and Valkyrie threw her off, tried to get up, but Ajuoga jumped on her back.

Kill her.

Valkyrie stood, bent forward, tried to shake her loose. She closed her eyes to avoid losing one of them. Ajuoga pulled her hair and bit her ear and Valkyrie screamed. She twisted and Ajuoga hit the ground and scrambled up, blood running from her mouth. Valkyrie backed up, horrified, one hand pressed to the side of her head.

KILL HER.

Ajuoga ran at her and all Valkyrie wanted to do was keep her off, that's all she wanted to do, just stop her, just stop her and end the fight, just push at the air hard enough so that she flies back and knocks herself out on the wall, just push at the air—

Ajuoga jumped and Valkyrie sent a spear of shadows slicing through her.

She hung there, Ajuoga, held off the ground by the shadow. Hands at her side, legs not kicking, head down. Peaceful and dead.

Valkyrie looked up at her. She looked at the shadow, saw how it had gone all the way through. Saw how sharp it was. Her eyes flickered, following it as it gently turned and twisted through the gloom, following it all the way back down to the black ring on her finger.

Wait. No. That wasn't right. She'd pushed at the air. Ajuoga had run at her and jumped and Valkyrie had pushed at the air.

No you didn't.

She'd pushed at the air because that's what she did. She'd needed to keep Ajuoga away from her so that's what she did. She'd used Elemental magic because that's what Skulduggery had taught her.

You killed her.

"Valkyrie," Skulduggery said, speaking quietly.

"Mm?"

"Valkyrie, look at me."

She looked at him.

"Put her down, Valkyrie."

She nodded, and the shadow laid Ajuoga on the ground next to the circle and then it sank back into the darkness of the room, like it was never there.

Murderer.

Fletcher's eyes were wide. He said nothing. Skulduggery was looking at her. He stood perfectly still. His head was perfectly straight.

"Valkyrie," he said. He liked using her name. "I need you to break her necklace now. Can you do that? Break her necklace and we can get out of here. Come on now. We don't have much time. Someone will have heard. They'll be coming."

Killer.

She walked over to the woman

that you killed

and looked down at her. Despite the blood, she was beautiful.

"Valkyrie, I can hear them," said Skulduggery. "They're coming. Break the necklace. Valkyrie. *Valkyrie.*"

"*Look out!*" Fletcher cried.

She turned and a Bride came through the door with her hand already lighting up.

60

ONE LITTLE WORD

think we should talk.

It's OK, you keep doing what you're doing. I'll say what needs to be said. Don't let me distract you. Hit her again, though. You need to hit her again. OK, good. I think you broke her jaw. Nice one.

Skulduggery. I have to help Skulduggery and Fletcher.

They're fine. Skulduggery's managed to snag Ajuoga's cape. Look at him. He's pulling her into the circle. He'll break the necklace and they'll be free. We don't have to worry about them. We have to get you out of here. Let's run. Go on. Run.

Good girl.

I know things haven't worked out the way you wanted when all this began. You wanted fun and adventure and all these exciting things. Of course you did. That's nothing to be—

Duck.

Now throw a shadow at her. Throw a – oooh, nice. Now where was I?

Nothing to be ashamed about.

Yes, thank you. Wanting a life less ordinary is a perfectly natural wish to make. Everyone makes it. The only difference is, for you it came true. You're one of the lucky ones.

I should have stayed where I was.

What do you mean? Back in the room with Skulduggery or—?

I should have stayed normal. I'm sorry now I pestered him to take me along.

No you're not. You can fool most people, but you can't fool me. I know you've missed your parents and I know you regret not seeing your sister's first steps with your own eyes, but sacrifices had to be made. You made them, in exchange for the extraordinary. And you're not sorry you did it. Not one bit. Take this left.

The way's blocked.

They're only Devoted. They won't be able to stop you.

I can't hurt them.

Of course you can.

I don't want to.

What am I going to do with you? Just push them aside. Use the air. See how easy that was? Keep running now.

The Brides have seen me.

Of course they have. And they're gaining. They are quite fast for belly dancers, aren't they? They probably hate being called that. Shout it back to them, see what they say.

No.

I swear, Valkyrie, you are no fun any more. Better duck. Woah. That was a close one. You realise, of course, that if one of those energy streams hits you in the head, we're both toast, right? I'm not going to have time to swoop in and save the day. Maybe you should throw a fireball or two, just to distract them. That's it. Just click aaaaand... throw!

Huh. I never noticed before. You have terrible aim.

I wasn't trying to hit them.

In that case, you've succeeded admirably.

Just wanted to slow them down.

Suuuure. Hey, did you know that you're missing the top of your ear?

She bit it off.

That cow. That horrible, horrible cow. I wish you'd done worse to her now. I wish you'd made her suffer. There's someone up ahead. Did you hear me? There's someone up—

Oh, this is brilliant. Oh, this is just great. Rolling around on a cave floor

452

with another psychotic belly dancer is exactly what you want to be doing right now. We should have sold tickets for this. If you want, I could help. Just step aside and I'll—

No.

Your choice, of course.

These skirts don't exactly allow you to keep much of your dignity, do they? Better hurry up. The others are almost here. You have her arm. Break it. All you have to do is break it and you can get up and keep running. Stop trying to look for another way to finish this and just break her damn—

Yowch. She's a screamer, isn't she? You never can tell, I suppose. OK, back on your feet.

The thing is, Valkyrie, you didn't ask for this. I know you didn't. Wanting a life of adventure is one thing – wanting a life where the fate of the world rests on your shoulders is something else entirely.

Run in here. Hide.

Hold your breath. Hold it or they'll hear you. Hold it...

Are they gone? Take a peek. Are they gone? They're gone. See that ledge up there? Use the air.

Wheeeeeee.

OK. I'm pretty sure I know the way out from here. Proceed with caution, though. I'll fill this awkward silence with words of great wisdom and passable wit. You never asked for the burdens you've been given. At the start you were a victim of your own bloodline, and by the time that passed you were already in too deep. You'd developed a taste for the life these sorcerers led, and you were proving yourself, again and again. Much was asked of you, and you stepped up, Valkyrie. You understood that with great power comes great responsibility.

That's from *Spider-Man*.

What?

It's what Uncle Ben said to Peter Parker.

No it's not. I made that up right there. We just have to go down this little tunnel here and we should see daylight.

We should have waited for Skulduggery.

He'll be fine. He's probably already waiting for us at the car. Then we can all drive away and – you're slowing down. Why are you slowing down? Are you crying?

I can't do this any more.

You don't have to. Valkyrie, you've been through so much. Too much. The reflection has taken over your life. You've been tortured. You've lost your uncle and your cousin. You lost Kenspeckle Grouse. You lost Tanith to that Remnant. And now you've lost Ghastly. One by one they're snatched away from you. You can't be expected to keep going through all that. You've risked everything to save the world, again and again, only to wake up one night and realise that you're the one who's going to end it.

You're going to end it. Not me. You.

I am you.

No. You're twisted and evil and wrong.

That's hardly a healthy attitude to take to your own psyche. I'm part of you. When you let me take over, you don't go away, do you? You're still there. Every thing I've done and every life I've taken, you were there. You remember it all. You tell yourself that I'm the wicked one and you don't have any choice in the matter. That's how you sleep at night. But it gets to you. Of course it does. You have so much blood on your hands.

Walking quickly won't change that. Wherever you go, you take me with you, remember?

You kill people. Not me.

You've forgotten Caelan already, have you?

I didn't kill Caelan. The saltwater did.

And who pushed him in? Who held him under?

He was going to kill Fletcher. He was going to kill me. I had to do it.

I agree. But let's not pretend. His death is on your hands. But, of course, he was a vampire, wasn't he? He was a thing, a monster. It's easier to justify killing a monster. Easier to ignore, too. But Ajuoga wasn't a vampire.

She wanted to kill me.

So you killed her first.

It was an accident. I didn't mean to.

Valkyrie, please. I'm inside your head. You wanted the fight to end. Your

454

conscious mind, the civilised part of you, wanted to use Elemental magic to keep her away. But what did you actually do? You used Necromancy, a discipline Skulduggery has warned you against so many times in the past. Why has he warned you?

Because it's easy.

Exactly. Because it's easy. Because it obeys your more primal nature. Necromancy isn't civilised. It's power. It's easy power. And you embraced it, because you like easy power. Power that doesn't take years to master.

I still didn't mean to kill her.

It wasn't about killing her. You just wanted the fight to end, so you ended it. You chose the simplest, most direct option. The easy option. As usual.

What are you doing?

Ajuoga. A beautiful name, isn't it? She's the first Ajuoga you've ever met, the only Ajuoga you've ever known, and you killed her.

What are you trying to do?

Keep going. We're almost there.

Are you trying to make me let you take over?

Of course.

I won't do it. I can't.

You can and you will. You're about to. You're ready to give up. You want all this to be over, don't you? So choose the easy option. You know you want to.

You'll kill too many people. You'll kill my family.

Our family. And I have no intention of killing our family. You've already seen how Cassandra's visions can change. You saw Ghastly kiss Tanith – that's not going to happen any more, is it? Because the future was changed. And it can change again. I might not destroy the world. I might have a change of heart.

No. Leave me alone. Leave me—

Oh, dear.

Ooooh, now I remember. Yes, we should have taken a right where we took a left. If we had taken the right, that would have brought us to the surface. Instead...

They're everywhere.

They look mad.

I have to get out of here. I have to—

And they're blocking the way back. Between you and me, these are some angry-looking belly dancers. I don't think I've ever seen belly dancers look as angry as this.

You led me here. You led me into a trap.

That's a terrible thing to say. It's quite true, but terrible. Watch out, I see a hand lighting up. If I were you, I'd—

Too late.

That... OK, that is gross. That was one of my favourite legs. Could you stop screaming, please? Could you pay attention? They're closing in. Another hand is lighting up. Valkyrie? Stop screaming and look—

Wow. That was a good shot. I know, I know, we no longer have a left arm below the elbow, but did you see that shot? Textbook.

Help.

Sorry? What was that? I couldn't hear you over the sound of your own screaming.

Help me.

Sure. Let me take over.

Heal me.

I will, absolutely. I'll reattach that leg and regrow that arm and I'll even regrow the chunk of ear that cow bit off. Just step aside and let me at the controls.

For a moment. Just a moment.

No, no. I'm sorry, Valkyrie, you can't just use me when you want to and then push me aside. Not any more. My time has come. Our time has come.

And there goes the other arm. These belly dancers are a sadistic lot, aren't they?

The pain...

Is pretty bad, I have to agree. Let me shut it off. I can do it. You know I can. You like it when I do that. You love being me. Admit it.

Please.

Just say the word. Let me come in and take over. For good, this time. No more sharing. Not any more. We're way past that now. This is what you want,

456

Valkyrie, deep down in your twisted little heart. Just say the word and I can make all your pain and doubt go away. I can erase your confusion and regret. You'll never have to be afraid again. Just say the word. One little word...

Yes.

Good girl. Good girl.

Now watch these witches burn.

61

THE REAL GIRL

Stephanie was working her way through a book – *The Stand*, by Stephen King – when Fletcher teleported into her room. She shrieked and bounced off her bed and stumbled against her desk, the book falling to the ground with a thud.

Eyes wide, she stared at him. He had an armful of black clothes, with a pair of boots, a gauntlet and a stick on top. Valkyrie's stick.

"She's gone," he said in a hollow voice.

Stephanie frowned. "Valkyrie?"

"She's..." Fletcher gave a little laugh. "What am I doing, tiptoeing around it? You know she's Darquesse. Of course you do. Well, now she's Darquesse full-time."

Stephanie straightened up. "What happened?"

"A lot of stuff. She was captured, did you know that? She had a psychic poking around in her head. And then she and Skulduggery came looking for me and it all went wrong. She was surrounded, she was going to be killed. We went after her, but... you should have seen it. There must have been a hundred of them and she – she killed them all. The amount of blood..."

"But she might recover," Stephanie said.

Fletcher shook his head. "Skulduggery said that Darquesse

had slipped out a few times before, but it was never for more than a few minutes. But she's been Darquesse now for two days. No one knows where she is, no one knows what she's going to do..."

"How did the others take it?"

"What, you mean the news that Valkyrie's the one they should have been fighting all along? They don't know yet. He hasn't told them. He's going to tell them today."

"Does he know you're here?"

"Skulduggery? No. Why should he? I just thought you needed to know. If you see her, you call me, OK?"

"OK. You brought back her clothes."

"Yeah."

"That was nice of you."

She took them from him and he sat on the bed. "I didn't know what else to do. Skulduggery's just gone really quiet and... I don't have anyone else to talk to. I mean, I just found out yesterday that Ghastly was dead."

"Oh, God. Fletch, I'm sorry."

"I'm not sure that he ever liked me, but he talked to me, you know? He always had time to talk."

"And I'm sorry about Myra as well."

"Ah, yes, Myra. The girlfriend who tried to kill me. I suppose I should be flattered, actually, that she went to the trouble of starting a fire in her dorm *hoping* that I'd teleport in and save the day. That shows dedication, right? That shows commitment. Not to me, or the relationship, but to her career as a hired killer. You've got to admire that. But what a track record, eh? You cheat on me, the next girlfriend tries to kill me..."

"*I* didn't cheat on you."

He blinked at her. "Hmm? I know that. Did I say that? Oh, God, I did. Sorry."

"How about you call me Stephanie?" she said gently. "It might make a difference if you know I have a name."

459

"Yeah, sure. Sorry, Stephanie, I didn't mean you."

"That's quite all right, Fletcher. So what's the plan now? What's the next move?"

"The plan is to teleport into Roarhaven and shut off the Accelerator, then take down Ravel and find some way to beat Mantis's army and then the Warlocks, who are on their way. Easy, right? It's just that Skulduggery's going to tell the others that Valkyrie is Darquesse. I don't know how they're going to take that, or the fact that he kept it from them for all this time. Gordon will be there, too. How's he going to react?"

"He already knows. You're meeting at his house?"

"We were over at Finbar's place, but we have to switch. Y'know, for security reasons. Stephanie, what will Darquesse do? I mean, what does she want?"

"I don't know."

"All the psychics say she'll destroy the world and kill everyone. But Valkyrie wouldn't do that."

She sat beside him, and held his hand. "When she's Darquesse, she's different, Fletch. To her, it's not about who she hurts or who she kills, it's about the feeling she gets when she does it. It makes her... happy."

"Happy?"

"In a way. It's kind of freeing, not to be held back by laws or rules or conscience."

"But she loves her family. She'd never do anything to hurt her family."

"Fletcher, I can't think like Darquesse. I can only think like Valkyrie. And you're right, Valkyrie would never hurt her family, just like I never would. But Darquesse is different."

"She'll find a way to beat it. Valkyrie will. She's strong. She won't let herself hurt anyone she loves."

Stephanie turned to him fully. "Valkyrie's confused. She's always been confused. She has all these conflicting thoughts and feelings. I'm afraid she mightn't know what she's doing."

Fletcher raised his eyes to hers. "Did she ever love me?"

Stephanie hesitated. She wanted to lie. She wanted to make him feel better. But she couldn't. "No," she said. "But she cared about you. She still does."

"But she didn't love me."

"I'm sorry."

His eyes grew colder. "What about the vampire? Did she love him?"

"No. She barely liked him."

"Then why was she with him?"

"Because she's confused. She thought she wanted someone dangerous."

"What did they—?"

"Oh, Fletcher... what are you trying to do? Are you trying to torture yourself? You're an amazing guy. You should be with someone who sees that. You should be with someone who appreciates you and... and your cool hair."

That raised a smile, and she gave him a smile of her own, and then she leaned in and kissed him. For a moment he froze, and then he kissed her back. His left hand went to her face, his thumb stroking her cheek.

Gently, he broke off the kiss. "You're... not real."

"Of course I'm real," she said. She kissed him quickly. "You felt that, didn't you?" She kissed him again. "And you felt that, right? Valkyrie may not have loved you," she whispered. "But I can."

When Fletcher was gone, Stephanie went downstairs and changed Alice's nappy, then picked up her little sister and smothered her with kisses. Alice laughed so hard she made Stephanie laugh, and just when the laughter was subsiding Stephanie blew a giant raspberry on Alice's neck that set her off again.

Their mum walked in, smiling.

"Mammy!" Alice said, delighted. "It's mammy!"

Stephanie passed her over. "You'd swear she hadn't seen you in days."

"Oh, she's a drama queen," her mum said as Alice wrapped her little arms round her neck. "Were you on the phone just now? I could have sworn I heard two voices coming from upstairs."

"Radio," said Stephanie. "Oh, listen, I was thinking I might head over to Gordon's for a few days."

The smile faded on her mother's face. "When?"

Stephanie shrugged. "Now, actually."

"Do you think that's wise? The last time you were alone in a house, we were burgled and you were attacked by a crazy girl. And that's the second time you've been attacked in this house."

"But I've never been attacked in *Gordon's* house," she said, and technically that was true.

"Steph, I don't know if I like the idea of you being alone."

Stephanie smiled. "So what should I do? Develop a phobia about it? Mum, I'll be fine. I just want to spend a few days by myself, reading books and, you know... thinking about what I'm going to do with my life and stuff."

"And 'stuff', eh? Have you had any more thoughts on that?"

"Some thoughts," said Stephanie. "No decisions. Not yet. I just need to clear my head."

Her mum took a moment. "OK, but you call every hour to let me know if you're OK."

"Maybe not *every* hour."

"But close enough."

"I'll do my best. I'm just going to change and grab my bag and then I'll be gone. Love you."

"Love you back," said her mum, and they hugged and Stephanie kissed Alice and then she climbed the stairs to her room.

All she'd ever cared about was her family. All she'd ever wanted was to live the life of a normal girl. And now that Valkyrie was gone, all of Stephanie's dreams were coming true. It should have been perfect. She could now spend time with her parents and her sister while Skulduggery and the others fought their magical wars and dealt with Darquesse.

Only she couldn't let other people fight for her. That's not who she was. She had to do something. She had to help. Darquesse was as much her problem as anyone's. And what if Skulduggery faltered? What if he couldn't bring himself to deliver the killing blow if the opportunity presented itself? Then Darquesse would more than likely kill him, and who'd be next? Everyone?

Stephanie got changed into Valkyrie's black clothes and took the Sceptre from its hiding place, placing it and Valkyrie's stick into a bag already half filled with fresh underwear and T-shirts. She took her phone, transferred some money into her pockets, and grabbed her bag. Then she got in the Oompa-Loompa, and drove to Gordon's.

She used the back road, the hidden road, approaching the house from the rear, and stopped the car before anyone had a chance to hear the engine. Slinging her bag over her shoulder, she jogged up to the utility door, used her key to open it and slipped inside. Immediately she heard raised voices.

"What the hell were you thinking?" Vex was saying, almost shouting. "The biggest threat the world has ever seen and you had a chance to do something about it and you *didn't*!"

Skulduggery's response was too low-key to travel, but Vex's came through clear as day.

"Bull! You didn't do what needed to be done because you're too close to her! You couldn't bring yourself to do it and now look, look what's happened. Valkyrie's gone. Darquesse is free. She's out there. And that's *your* fault."

Stephanie crept out of the utility room, went to the library and took down a set of encyclopaedias. She slid open the hidden hatch and peered into the living room. Skulduggery was standing in the middle of the room. He wasn't wearing a hat. Vex and Saracen and the Monster Hunters were on their feet, facing him.

Fletcher was against the far wall and Sanguine was standing next to Tanith, who was the only one seated.

Gordon came into view, his head down, his face creased with worry. "What do we do?" he asked. "How do we get her back? This is her worst nightmare. This is the one thing she was terrified of."

Vex glared at him. "You knew about this?"

"Of course I knew," Gordon snapped, "I'm her uncle. I don't care if I'm not the *real* Gordon, I'm real enough to love my niece."

Vex shook his head. "Anyone else know about this little secret?"

Tanith raised her hand. "Me."

Sanguine stared at her in surprise. "You knew? Why didn't you tell me? It seems to me that this is information that could be shared with someone you're gonna marry."

"Please don't remind us of that," said Saracen. "It really creeps us out."

Vex looked back at Skulduggery. "We went looking for the God-Killers to *stop* Darquesse. We risked our *lives*."

"And if you had told me what you had planned," said Skulduggery, "I would have talked you out of it."

Vex went to the nearest chair and sat in it heavily. He sighed. "There was a time when you wouldn't have hesitated to kill her."

"Yeah," said Saracen, "you really picked a great time to soften up on us."

"She can still be saved," Skulduggery said.

"How?" Donegan asked.

"I just need to talk to her. If I talk to her, I can calm her down. I can bring Valkyrie back, you don't have to worry. I've done it before."

"How do you know she won't just kill you before you have a chance?"

"Because Darquesse likes to play games. That's what you have to understand about her. In her own way, she's an innocent. Every time she emerges, she discovers something new about herself, something more she can do. She'll pull your arms and legs off, but there won't be anything malicious behind it. She just wants to find out how easy it is."

"Yeah," said Gracious. "That really sounds like we shouldn't worry."

"I trusted Valkyrie before," Skulduggery said. "I trust her now."

Vex looked at him. "You really think you can reach her?"

"I just need to get close enough to talk."

"I hope you know what you're doing."

Skulduggery tilted his head. "Me too."

"See?" Tanith said to Sanguine. "Now you take everything they said and you pretend we said it and you won't be so mad at me any more."

Sanguine looked unimpressed. "That ain't how this works."

"Excuse me for a moment," Saracen said, walking out of the room.

"So is that it?" Donegan asked. "Are we finished arguing about this now? Because we still have to figure out what we're going to do about Roarhaven. We intercepted the convoy, we've locked those shield experts away where no one can find them, so now the way is clear, right? Now that we have Fletcher back, we can just teleport in. Anything else we should take into consideration?"

"Things have been happening quickly over the last two days," Skulduggery said. "Mantis still takes its orders from what remains of the original Supreme Council, but at the rate those original members are falling, those orders could stop coming at any moment."

"Maybe Mantis will give up and go home and the war will be over," said Fletcher.

"Maybe," said Skulduggery, "but Mantis isn't our primary concern. The Warlocks are. Once Charivari is dealt with and the Engineer has shut down the Accelerator, we can start looking for other people to hit – Erskine Ravel being number one on our list."

There was a click behind Stephanie and she froze, and a soft voice said, "Turn around." She turned, slowly.

Saracen stood there, finger on the trigger of the gun pointed at her. "Apparently you can heal gunshot wounds to the head. If you make any sudden moves, I'm going to let you prove it."

She swallowed. "I'm not Darquesse."

"If you're Valkyrie, why are you spying on us?"

"I'm not Valkyrie, either. I'm Stephanie. I'm her reflection."

"You're not a reflection."

"I am, I swear."

Saracen frowned, and the gun dipped. "Good God. You're not like any reflection I've ever seen. You're practically... human."

"I am human," she said. "I'm Stephanie."

He looked at her for another moment, then motioned to her. Taking a deep breath, she closed the hatch and followed him. He walked into the living room first, but she faltered just outside the doorway.

"We have a guest," she heard him say. "And before any of you overreact, you need to know that even though it looks like the real thing, even to us, this is actually Valkyrie's reflection. It calls itself Stephanie."

Stephanie walked in. Fletcher looked surprised to see her, but Vex and the Monster Hunters looked astonished. They came over immediately, peering at her, stopping just short of prodding her. Behind them, Tanith and Sanguine stood watching, and Gordon frowned in puzzlement.

"Step away from it," Skulduggery said.

Vex and Saracen went one way, Gracious and Donegan the other. Stephanie looked at Skulduggery and she felt afraid.

"I'm not an it," she managed to say.

"You're wearing her clothes," said Skulduggery. "Just more things for you to steal. You got what you wanted, though. You made her run from her mother. You took her life and her family. So why are you here?"

"What was that?" asked Fletcher. "Val ran from her mum?"

"It tried to kill her," Skulduggery said, and now Fletcher was looking at her like she was some kind of thing, some kind of inhuman creature. There was something else in his eyes, too. A kind of hurt.

"I can explain," she said, but they were already starting to ignore her words.

"How did it get like this?" Vex asked. "Leaving aside the homicidal tendencies for a moment, how did it get so real?"

"This is fascinating," said Gracious. "Did you alter the conjuring sigil? I always thought the sigil could be improved, but who has the time to focus on reflections? But this one. It's magnificent."

"I'm not an it!" Stephanie said sharply. "I'm a her! I'm a person! My name is Stephanie Edgley. My parents are Melissa and Desmond Edgley and my sister is Alice. I live in Haggard in County Dublin."

"And you murdered Valkyrie Cain's cousin," Skulduggery said.

Stephanie went quiet. Fletcher collapsed into a chair.

"I did what I had to do," Stephanie said, her voice brittle. "The only things I care about in this world are my parents and my sister. I care about them because my whole purpose was to pretend to be Valkyrie and pretend to care about her family. Only it stopped being an act. I stopped pretending and I started caring. I love them. I'd do anything to protect them. That's why I'm here. You're going to need all the help you can get to stop Darquesse."

Skulduggery tilted his head. "You think you're coming with us? You think you can take Valkyrie's place?"

"We're the same person."

"You're a thing who murdered Valkyrie's cousin."

"And she's a thing who will murder the world," Stephanie said, anger biting into her voice. "Skulduggery, you don't want to hear it, I know you don't, but I *am* her. I don't have her magic, but I have everything else she had. And I have the Sceptre."

"The Sceptre of the Ancients?" Tanith asked.

"That was destroyed," said Donegan. "Wasn't that destroyed? Didn't I read that somewhere?"

"This is the Sceptre from the alternate reality," Stephanie said, "the one Mevolent rules. It's bonded to me. And correct me if I'm wrong, but we're kind of lacking a few God-Killer weapons right about now, aren't we? When Darquesse turns up, I'll be the only one able to stop her."

"Or we could kill you here and now," said Skulduggery, "and take the Sceptre off your hands."

"You won't kill me."

"You're so sure?"

"You won't kill—"

Skulduggery took his gun from its holster and Stephanie's mouth went dry. He thumbed back the hammer and aimed right between her eyes.

"Skulduggery," said Vex, "just hold on a second..."

"It's not Valkyrie," Skulduggery said. "It's not a real person."

Saracen took a small step forward. "You just can't shoot her."

"It's not a her."

"I think we should all calm down for a moment," said Gordon.

"Please don't kill me," Stephanie said quietly.

Fletcher appeared between them. "Stop."

Skulduggery's voice was cold. "Get out of my way."

But Fletcher held his ground. "What if Val doesn't come back? You're going to let her folks think she just ran away, or something horrible happened to her? The whole point of having the reflection in the first place was to step in when Valkyrie wasn't around. Killing Stephanie wouldn't be about justice or making the world a better place, it'd be about you and your anger. That's all. Valkyrie would want us to think of her parents and Alice at a time like this, you know she would."

Tanith brushed by Skulduggery and gestured at Fletcher to step aside. "Move it, hairdo. I'll sort this out." She looked Stephanie up and down. "Look at you. You're a marvel, is what you are. You're something to behold. And I'm not like these guys, I know what you mean when you say you are Stephanie. Of course you are. I happen to be very discerning when it comes to friends, and you? You are someone I could see myself being friends with. But the real question here, Stephanie, is not are you a person, or can you be trusted. No. The real question is—"

Tanith's sword flashed from its scabbard and Stephanie barely had time to flinch before Skulduggery came crashing into them both. Stephanie hit the ground, tangled beneath all those arms and legs. The sword came to a rest on the carpet beside her. Saracen went to snatch it up when Sanguine hit him, sent him spinning.

Hands grabbed her, dragged her out from the scuffle. Fletcher, pulling her to her feet, and then in a heartbeat they were in a quiet apartment and it was dark outside.

"Thanks," said Stephanie.

Fletcher said nothing. Without turning on any lights, he moved to the other rooms, checking them. He came back and she felt an irrational need to fill the silence between them.

"I shouldn't be surprised, I suppose," she said. "Tanith was only part of the group to make sure Valkyrie stayed safe until Darquesse could emerge. Now that Darquesse is out, Tanith can go back to being the enemy. And, since I have the Sceptre, I'm the biggest threat to Darquesse. Stands to reason she'd try to kill me."

Fletcher murmured something.

She looked around. "Are we in Australia? Is this your place?"

"Yeah," he said. "Well, it was. Don't know why I chose to come here."

"Maybe you still think of it as home."

"That'd be pretty messed up of me, then, wouldn't it? So which one did you kill? Carol or Crystal?"

Stephanie looked away. "Carol."

"Does Crystal know what happened?"

"They don't know anything's different. Carol's reflection took over from her. I made sure."

"Well, aren't you nice?"

"I... I wish I could say that I didn't want to have to kill her, but honestly... at the time I didn't see it as being wrong. I mean, I knew it was a terrible thing to do, but I didn't feel one way or the other about it."

"And now you do?"

"Yes."

"Why? Because you're suddenly so close to being human? Isn't that convenient? Just when we find out about it, you start to feel guilt. You poor thing."

"Fletch..."

"You know what? I believe you when you say you're not an *it*. I believe you when you say you're a person."

"Thank you."

"No problem. And, as a person, I really don't like you."

"Yeah," she said.

He vanished. She stayed where she was and a moment later he returned, took hold of her arm, and then they were back in Gordon's living room. A small section of floor was cracked, and Gracious was in the process of pulling a rug over it.

Skulduggery looked at her. "Tanith and Sanguine have decided to spend some time away from us. You're not going to be safe at home, so you're coming to Roarhaven with us. You have the Sceptre with you?"

"It's in her bag," said Saracen.

"Then we can leave immediately," Skulduggery said. "Fletcher, what is the remotest part of the Sanctuary you've been to that's near the Accelerator Room?"

"Probably one of the bathrooms," Fletcher said. "There's one on the third level down that's full of leaky pipes? It's pretty horrible and it's always cold."

"Sounds perfect," said Skulduggery, and his gun floated into his hand.

62

ROARHAVEN REVEALED

They teleported into the bathroom. It was dark and smelled bad. Skulduggery held up his left hand, reading the air, then he moved to the door and peeked out. Stephanie sneaked out after him with the others. They got to the corner and Skulduggery went on ahead. Stephanie heard a strangled cry, and then silence. Moments later, she was stepping over the unconscious form of a Roarhaven mage, into the Accelerator Room. Skulduggery was already talking to the Engineer.

"Who are you loyal to?" he asked.

"I am loyal to myself," said the Engineer. "And to the Accelerator."

"Not to Erskine Ravel?"

"It is not possible for me to have loyalty to people, organisations, doctrines or beliefs."

"Has the Accelerator been used recently?" Vex asked.

"It has not been used in six months, one week and two days."

"That's when it was used to boost Kitana's power," Stephanie said.

Skulduggery turned his head to her and she did her best to ignore him and keep her eyes on the Engineer.

"So there are no super-sorcerers running around," said Saracen.

"OK, that's a good start. Engineer, we'd like you to deactivate the Accelerator now, please, before anyone can use it."

"Very well," said the Engineer. "It will take me fourteen days to initialise proceedings."

"Fourteen *days*?" Fletcher said, staring. "We need it shut down *now*."

"I am afraid that will not be possible."

"But the Warlocks are on their way."

"If you do not want them to use the Accelerator before it is deactivated," the Engineer said, "you will have to hold them off for the next three hundred and forty-three hours and eight minutes."

"Great," Vex muttered. "Well, that's that. Nothing we can do here. Let's refocus on Ravel and get this done."

Saracen led the way to the stairs, then up. It took three times longer than usual to make it up to the surface level. Certain rooms were being emptied, while certain other rooms were being crammed full of furniture and materials. Stephanie got the impression that they were preparing for some major refurbishment.

They got to the surface level and Skulduggery took over, leading them through the smaller corridors, the ones that weren't lit right, the ones that rarely saw activity. They heard footsteps ahead. Half of them darted into one room, half of them into the room opposite. High heels – and, behind them, more footsteps.

Stephanie waited beside Vex. He looked calm. In control. His eyes only widened when they heard Skulduggery say, "Hello, China."

Vex lunged out and Stephanie and the others followed. They filled the narrow corridor, facing off against China and two Roarhaven mages. The mages were frozen on the spot.

"Skulduggery," China said, "wait..."

Skulduggery's voice was cold. "I knew you'd be the first to turn traitor."

"No, you don't understand."

"You just can't stop betraying people, can you?"

China stepped forward, wringing her hands. "What was I supposed to do? I didn't know what Ravel was planning, I swear!" Stephanie glimpsed a glowing sigil on China's palm. "They forced me to stay! I didn't want to! You have to believe—"

And China whirled, planting her hand on the face of the nearest Roarhaven mage, sending a bolt of power through him. At the same moment, Skulduggery used the air to pull the second mage into an elbow that sent him crumpling to the floor beside his partner.

China smoothed her dress. "I was beginning to think you'd abandoned me."

"At least you've been safe," Skulduggery said. "Where is he?"

Stephanie joined the others in looking puzzled.

"I don't know," said China. "But wherever Ravel is, the Black Cleaver is with him. You need to leave. Every sorcerer in this building has orders to kill you all on sight." China looked at Stephanie, and her eyes narrowed. "And who do we have here?"

"I'm Stephanie. Valkyrie's reflection."

China gazed at her. "Curious."

"You two planned this from the start," Stephanie said.

"We improvised," Skulduggery said, "not planned."

"Why didn't you tell me? Valkyrie, I mean. Why didn't you tell Valkyrie?"

China smiled a little. "Because he didn't want her to assume we had patched things up. He hasn't forgiven me for the things I did and I don't expect him to. But one must be pragmatic in times like these."

Skulduggery grunted. "What have you found out?"

"Precious little, I'm afraid. Mist has me followed every time I step outside. You're right, though. There are too many people for this town. You could walk the streets at the same time every day of the week and you'd see the same number of faces, but never the same faces. There is more to Roarhaven than I have been allowed to see."

"It has to be below the streets. But how big? And how many people? And, more importantly, why? Why has Ravel gone to all this trouble?"

"This is the least of the trouble he's gone to. I've just heard that the German Elders have been killed by their own mages. They're not even bothering to blame it on assassins any more."

"And Ravel's involved?"

"From what I can gather, he is more than merely *involved*. The sorcerers he appointed as interim Elders in Australia and Africa? His supporters. Zafira Kerias in America, Palaver Graves in England? His supporters. He has had Elders turning on Elders, mages turning on Councils, and Sanctuaries turning on Sanctuaries – and, in every single case, the people who have taken over are people who support Ravel's views on a world run by sorcerers."

"So that's it?" Fletcher said. "He's won? I mean... if the Supreme Council are all dead, then everyone is taking orders from Ravel now."

"Not quite," said China. "Ordinary mages would never support a move to turn the mortals into slaves, so he's going to need something big to unite the sorcerers around the world."

"The Warlocks," Skulduggery said.

"I believe so."

"China, we need to get Ravel alone."

"That's not going to happen. The Elders are under constant protection. Ravel never goes anywhere without the Black Cleaver, and Mist never goes anywhere without Syc and Portia. Your best bet is to draw him out into the open, which is easier said than done. It's just a pity you didn't get here sooner."

"What do you mean?"

"He's scheduled to deliver a speech to the good people of

Roarhaven in under an hour, right outside the Sanctuary. It would have been perfect for you if you'd had time to prepare."

"It might still be perfect."

She frowned. "Don't let his betrayal lure you into doing something stupid."

"When was the last time *I* did anything stupid?" Skulduggery asked, and handed her a phone before she could answer. "Take this. If you need to contact us, send a message. It's untraceable, but only good for thirty words before the protective sigils burn it out. I've got its twin."

China nodded, looked down at the unconscious mages at her feet. "I suppose I'll have to dispatch these two charming individuals myself. Joy of joys."

Skulduggery started moving, and China looked up. "I'm sorry, by the way. About Ghastly. I liked him."

Skulduggery paused, and nodded, and continued on. They followed him down a little-used corridor until they could go no further without looping back on themselves.

He started tapping the bare wall. "There's a tunnel that runs from here to the cellar beneath Scapegrace's pub, where the Torment lived. From what I understand, he never told his fellow Children of the Spider about either the tunnel or the cellar."

"Thank heaven for private people," Gracious murmured.

The wall rumbled and yawned open, revealing a gullet of darkness. Skulduggery clicked his fingers, summoning flame.

"We're going to have to run," he said.

Stephanie took off after them down the slanting slope, cutting straight through this labyrinth. If they took one wrong turn, she knew, they'd find themselves at a dead end with no time to make it back before the walls squashed them all to a red and pink paste. She stumbled, almost fell, but Fletcher grabbed her hand, pulled her onwards.

The walls started rumbling again. The tunnel was closing back in.

His hand still clutching hers, Fletcher jumped so he could see over the heads of the people in front, and when his feet touched down again they were both in the lead, emerging from the tunnel into a dimly-lit bedroom. Stephanie went sprawling across the bed, landing on her feet on the other side. A few moments later, Skulduggery and the others joined them, and the tunnel resealed itself.

"Cheat," Saracen managed to gasp to Fletcher, who shrugged.

For the first time, Stephanie became aware of music playing. 'Shake a Tail Feather' by Ray Charles. Gun drawn, Skulduggery led the way out of the bedroom, Stephanie right behind him. They got to the living room, with its tatty armchairs and battered couch, awful 1970s wallpaper, a painting of a ship on a stormy sea, an old, cracked TV, a record player... and, in the middle of the room, Scapegrace and Thrasher and some old Chinese man, dancing to the music.

The others crowded in around Stephanie. She could feel their frowns.

Scapegrace was doing the mashed potato. Thrasher was doing the twist. The old Chinese man was doing the bird. They all had their eyes closed, faces screwed up as the music ran through them. Skulduggery used the air to lift the needle from the record, and the music cut off and the dancing stopped, and the dancers looked round in confusion until Scapegrace saw Stephanie and the others standing there.

"My friends!" he cried, delight widening his eyes. He rushed over, shaking Skulduggery's hand, gripping Stephanie by the shoulders, and then beaming at the rest. "I'm so glad you're here. We've been hiding out for days. We haven't even been able to go out on our nightly patrols. Have you heard? About Elder Bespoke?"

"We heard," Skulduggery said.

"Sheriff Dacanay is hunting for us. At least twice a day he sends people in to search the pub. They haven't found us yet.

We're too clever. Although we didn't bring any food down with us."

"I can fix that," Fletcher said, and vanished.

Scapegrace gestured to the furniture. "Please, everyone, sit. Welcome to the Knight-cave. Most of you will know my sidekick Thrasher, and this is Grandmaster Ping, my instructor in the martial arts."

Ping bowed deeply. "Very honoured to meet you," he said in halting English. "Miss Scapegrace and I are in love."

"We're not in love," Scapegrace said quickly, smiling to cover up his awkwardness.

"Very much in love," said Ping.

"For the last time," said Scapegrace, "I am a *man*."

Ping looked at him, and shrugged. "Ah well, nobody is perfect."

"I'm sure this is all very interesting," Skulduggery said, only putting his gun away now, "but we need to use this cellar—"

"Knight-cave," said Scapegrace.

"—as a base. We're going to be striking at Ravel, taking him down and everyone who stands with him. Are you in?"

Scapegrace beamed, then took something from his pocket and turned away from them. He pulled it, whatever it was, over his head, spent a few moments fixing it in place, and then he whirled. He was wearing a mask. It wasn't a very good one. "The Dark and Stormy Knight will fight for justice," he announced.

Skulduggery hesitated. "The Dark and Stormy Knight... is that you?"

"Oh, yes, sorry. It is."

"Right."

"And I'm the Village Idiot," Thrasher said happily. Whatever reaction he had expected to this confession, Stephanie reckoned it wasn't a pained, embarrassed silence. Thrasher flushed red and shut up.

Fletcher appeared by Stephanie's side, laden down with groceries. "I risked a peek," he said. "There's a crowd already gathering outside the Sanctuary. Whatever he's going to talk about, Ravel's going to have an audience."

"Good," said Skulduggery. "I'd hate if we were the only ones there."

There was no plan. Stephanie stood with her head down, beside Skulduggery and the others, slightly apart from the huge crowd that was buzzing with anticipation. The only thing Skulduggery had said was that if an opportunity presented itself, they were to take it. Stephanie couldn't see how an opportunity would present itself. There were Cleavers and Roarhaven mages everywhere, posted at strategic points and mingling with the spectators. If the Dead Men, or what was left of them, were to make one move, they'd be cut down instantly.

There was a podium set up outside the entrance to the Sanctuary, and behind it a giant screen. At the moment the screen showed the crowd. Some people ignored the camera in their faces, others openly scowled at it, but most grinned and laughed and waved. Their moment of glory. Stephanie only had time to wonder who was operating the camera before Erskine Ravel stepped on to the podium, the Black Cleaver right behind him. He waited until the cheers and applause died down before speaking.

"Sorcerers of all disciplines," he said, his voice coming across loud and clear, "friends... brothers and sisters... I stand before you in the peaceful town of Roarhaven whose borders are even now being threatened by those many of you view as your enemies. But I also speak to them, for I know they can hear me. I speak to General Mantis and the men and women of the army it leads, and I speak to mages around the world, viewing this on the Global Link.

"We have been through some troubling times. Not since the

days of Mevolent have we experienced such divisions in our society. But, as destructive as it was, that was a good war to fight. We stood side by side and we fought for survival against a cunning and ruthless foe. When we fought, many of us didn't even believe that the Faceless Ones were anything more than the superstitions of an old religion. We weren't fighting against insane gods – we were fighting against their insane worshippers, dark sorcerers who were planning a genocide against the people we were sworn to protect. We fought for each other. We fought for the mortals. And we won.

"But this war is different. There are no villains in this conflict. There are simply opposing sides. Through circumstances beyond our control we have been forced to take up arms against each other. At first it was the Irish Sanctuary against the members of the Supreme Council. Then it was the Cradles of Magic against the Supreme Council. And then fractures began to appear as the moral implications of our own actions took their toll. You saw the footage yourself. My own best friend, Ghastly Bespoke, conspired against me. Not for any selfish reason, but because he thought he knew best. In defending myself I took his life, as many of you are aware. Not a day goes by that I do not shed a tear for my friend. But I also thank him. Because in doing what he thought was right, he reinvigorated my own strength and resolve to do the same.

"My friends, many of the Grand Mages who sit on the Supreme Council are different Grand Mages from the ones who formed it in the first place. In the last hour, I have been informed that Cothernus Ode and Illori Reticent have been found murdered in their own Sanctuary. Palaver Graves is now Grand Mage of England, but he is no less passionate and no less fierce than Ode ever was. I have reached out to Grand Mage Graves and the others and they have reached out to me, for we have seen what divisions like these can lead to if not healed in time. Isolation. Suspicion. Hatred. We have spoken of our grievances and agreed upon a truce. As I speak, word should be reaching General Mantis, confirming what I have just said."

Ravel took a moment, looking out upon the sea of faces. "We have also spoken of our duty, above all else, to protect the mortals. This is, after all, how the conflict started. In too many instances over the past few years, the Irish Sanctuary has teetered on the brink of disaster. It is only thanks to people like Ghastly Bespoke and Skulduggery Pleasant that none of Mevolent's Three Generals were able to succeed in their plans. Even more recently, Dreylan Scarab's plot to kill eighty thousand mortals was foiled, the Remnants were recaptured, the Necromancers stymied and the sorcerer known as Argeddion defeated. In all of these cases, however, the threat of being discovered by the mortals was dangerously high. The camera capturing this message is being wielded by a mortal, a journalist who has uncovered the truth, who has found us. He is but the first. We could wipe his mind, but there would still be others after he's gone. Would we wipe their minds, too? How many wiped minds are too many?

"The world has changed, my friends. Technology has changed it. Secrets are harder to keep. Do you know how many dark corners of the Internet there are dedicated to amateur, blurry footage of sorcerers in action? We are urban legend now. It is only a matter of time before we become front-page news. And just like that, overnight, we will be the enemy. We will be hunted, imprisoned, experimented on, until we are forced to fight back. But we cannot fight back. How could we? It is our duty to protect the mortals.

"It is time to match the world, to change with it. I have spoken with the Supreme Council about protecting the mortals in a more overt fashion, not to run from the spotlight but to step from the shadows. We have broached the subject of revealing our existence. I know, I know, this goes against everything we've ever believed in, but our choices are few and we have little time to decide.

There is a threat on the horizon. The Warlocks are massing. They have joined with the Brides of Blood Tears, and they are on the march. We have even heard rumours that they have an army of Wretchlings with them. With that level of sheer power and savagery, they could decimate a small country within days. Millions of mortals would die and the world would wake up to the harsh reality that magic is real, but not everyone who wields it is good and honourable.

"If such a tragedy were to take place, we would need to act swiftly and decisively. We would need to push back the Warlock threat in full view of the mortals so that they would rightfully view us as their protectors. And once the Warlocks are defeated we slip into their society. We let their gratitude enhance us and we use our magic and our science to enhance them, to improve their lives, to protect them to the fullest of our abilities. We co-exist. We thrive.

"Of course, no decision about any of this has been made, and no decision could be made without the full support of every Sanctuary around the world. This is a paradigm shift of epic proportions. We all need to be in agreement.

"At my command, our shield will be lowered. Under the terms of the truce, General Mantis and its army can enter Roarhaven. They will not be harmed. They will be welcomed. They are our brothers and sisters, and Roarhaven is nothing if not hospitable. There is also more to this town than at first appears. Decades ago, its citizens discussed how best to grow their town. They were proud of their magical heritage, and they wanted Roarhaven to be a shining light for magical communities the world over. So they worked. And they built. And people came. Whispers spread from like-minded individual to like-minded individual. There is a place, they said. A place for people like us. But such a rapid and extravagant expansion needed to be kept from mortal eyes, and so they enlisted the help of Creyfon Signate. Creyfon comes from a long and distinguished line of Dimensional Shunters, explorers into realities few of us would even dream about. Creyfon heard the citizens' plans and he agreed to help, and he is with us today for the grand unveiling."

A man came forward, small and slim with close-cropped hair, and joined Ravel on the podium.

"I know him," Scapegrace whispered. "We beat him up. We thought he was Silas Nadir."

Creyfon Signate raised his arms and lowered his head. Stephanie frowned.

The town began to flicker with new buildings superimposing over the old.

"The citizens of Roarhaven had a dream," said Ravel, "to rise beyond the limitations set on them. They dreamed of a town strong enough to withstand any assault and big enough to house any number. They dreamed until their town was a town no longer. Sorcerers, friends, brothers and sisters, I present to you Roarhaven City!"

Signate gave a cry of effort and the flickering buildings became solid. Towers and steeples raced each other skywards, overshooting the residential blocks, apartments and houses and homes. The roads were broad and intricately layered, and the old Main Street was now little more than an alleyway. The old buildings were still there, but above and around them there were all manner of improvements and modifications.

When his speech had begun, Ravel had been standing in front of a squat, unimpressive Sanctuary building. It was now nothing less than a palace, and it stood shimmering in the sun. Smaller than Mevolent's palace had been, perhaps, but just as luxurious, and it seemed to be occupying the exact centre of this new city like a vibrant, beating heart. Even the stagnant lake was different. Swirling bridges criss-crossed its sparkling surface, and on those bridges people cheered. People cheered in the streets, too. Thousands of them. Men and women and children, who hadn't been there moments earlier.

And around the outskirts, a wall, complete with watchtowers and buttresses.

"This isn't a city," said Vex softly. "It's a fortress."

At Skulduggery's command they moved backwards cautiously, keeping their faces hidden from the thousands who now surrounded them on all sides.

63

THE TRAP

The relief was a tangible thing, heavy in the air, like a low-lying heat that wouldn't go away. Those who had fought under Mantis's command, sorcerers from all over the world who had never wanted to go to war in the first place, laughed and sang with the people of Roarhaven and the mages they had been trying to kill just days earlier.

Grievances were forgotten. Grudges were dismissed. No one, it appeared, bore any animosity towards anyone else.

No one except China.

In one of the vast and empty rooms of this strange new Sanctuary, she sat and watched Vincent Foe walk in, followed by his gang of mercenaries. They had been drinking and carousing with the best of them, but now their fun was over.

"You sent for us," said Foe.

"I did," said China.

They stood in front of her, and Foe tried a smile. "Listen, Miss Sorrows, we were hired to do a job. You can't take this stuff personally."

"I happen to take being hunted down very personally."

"We're the bullet. We're not the finger that pulled the trigger. The Supreme Council—"

"I know who pulled the trigger, Mr Foe. And it's not even who you think. There were systems in place behind this war. Strings being pulled. I know exactly who ordered my death."

"Then that's who you should be angry with."

She raised an eyebrow. "How could I be angry? It's what I would have done in their place. You see, to the finger that pulled the trigger, ordering my death was a purely business decision. But you and your friends took to it with relish. Too much relish, if I'm being honest."

"We were hired—"

"Step forward, please."

Foe frowned. "I'm sorry?"

"There are five circles drawn on the floor in front of you. Each of you pick a circle and step into it."

"We're not going to—"

"Mr Foe, I'm sure I don't have to remind you that I am a personal guest of Grand Mage Ravel's, and that he has instructed you to do whatever I ask."

Foe's merry band of mercenaries glanced at each other uneasily. Except for Samuel. Samuel just kept his eyes on China. Even as they all stepped into the circles, his eyes never left her.

"Thank you," China said, as she stood up and tapped the sigil on her elbow.

The circles lit up and their bodies went rigid, eyes bulging, fingers curled as pain seized control.

"I could kill you all with another tap of my finger," China said, walking between them. "You dare to hunt *me*? You dare to make an attempt on *my* life? Do you even know who I am? Do you know the things I have done? I'm sure I cannot even begin to comprehend the audacity with which you thought that my life would be quashed by the likes of you. In all your years on this planet not one of you has done anything to deserve the *right* to kill me. Not you, Mr Foe, and not one of your pathetic, mewling little band of killers."

Her finger hovered by her elbow. One twitch would be all it took, and the pain would rise so suddenly their hearts would burst. Instead, she flattened her hand and brushed it over her elbow, and the circles stopped glowing and the mercenaries dropped, gasping, to their knees.

"I'm not in the habit of being merciful," she said to them, "but you have your uses, as clumsy and thick-fingered as they may be. Mr Foe, please look at me when I'm talking to you."

Foe raised his head. Sweat poured down his face. Immediately China felt the need to shower.

"For the indignity I have suffered at your hands, you owe me. When I come to collect my favour, you will obey without question. Do I make myself clear?"

"Y-yes," Foe said.

"You work for me now. Remember that. Leave me now, I have another appointment to keep."

They dragged themselves away, and China allowed herself a moment of pleasure before shaking it off. She headed for the busier sections of the Sanctuary, where mages walked and talked quickly. A pair of Cleavers let her through to the Round Room. Ravel and Mist sat in their chairs, the Black Cleaver standing behind Ravel while the Children of the Spider stood around them. Ghastly's chair was, of course, empty.

"China," said Ravel, "thank you for joining us. I apologise for taking you from your work, but I think there's something you can help us with. You may have heard talk of some missing mages?"

She inclined her head in a nod. "I've heard the gossip. Four mages have failed to turn up for their Sanctuary duties. Their houses are empty. Their friends don't know where they are."

"We know where they are," said Ravel. "We've been keeping it quiet so as not to spread panic. They're dead. And it's been more than four. Eight dead, in the last week. All of them killed in the line of duty. Another eleven gone missing. Taken. Two of them were the mages sent to keep an eye on you."

"That's terrible."

"Isn't it? I suspect that while the war between Sanctuaries is over, there is another war being fought within these city walls."

China could feel Mist's gaze on her, despite the veil that covered her face. The Terror and the Scourge were looking at her calmly. Only Syc and Portia had open hostility in their eyes. She didn't know how much they knew, but she knew how much they suspected. A lie here could land her in shackles, or worse.

China gave them all a smile. "The Dead Men," she said.

"Or what's left of them," said Ravel. "This was more our style than leading an army across a battlefield, after all. Drop behind enemy lines, take the opposition out one by one, whittle down their numbers."

"Strike from the shadows," China said. "Disappear into darkness."

"That's our motto, and that's our system. And now it's being used against me. I never realised how annoying it could be. Of course, the system is a lot more effective when you have a Teleporter on your team. I'm assuming they have Fletcher back?"

"You're assuming I know?"

"Of course you know," Portia said. "You're Skulduggery Pleasant's *friend*. You have a history."

China locked eyes with her. "The same could be said for Erskine, and look how that turned out."

"Ladies," Ravel said, "we're not here to throw accusations around. We're not playing the blame game. You're standing in a circle of trust, China. We're all on the same side. Isn't that true?"

China thought about her answer before voicing it. "Somewhat."

Ravel laughed. "That's why I like you, China. You're so hard to trap in a lie. When was the last time you spoke with Skulduggery?"

Erskine Ravel and the Children of the Spider in front of her. The Black Cleaver behind. The truth, then.

"Six days ago," China said. "The day you unveiled your city, actually."

"Execute her!" Syc growled, stepping forward. A slight turn of the head from Madame Mist, though, and he glowered and stepped back.

"Were they here for the speech?" Ravel asked. "I hope they liked it. Not nearly enough people have come up and congratulated me on that speech. It took me ages to get it right. Skulduggery, now, Skulduggery would have appreciated it."

"I wouldn't know what he thought," said China. "I haven't spoken to him, or any of them, since."

"Oh. That's a shame. Well, since we're on the subject, what did you speak to them about?"

"They asked about your plans. I answered honestly. I don't know anything about your plans. They asked when you would likely be alone. I said you're never alone, you always have bodyguards around you."

"Such is the world we live in," Ravel said, shaking his head sadly. "Were you of any use to them at all?"

"I don't see how I could have been."

"Mm. Well, apart from not *reporting* it to me immediately. I mean, you aided them in *that* sense."

"I suppose you could look at it like that."

Mist spoke. "And now, Miss Sorrows, where do your loyalties lie?"

China looked at her. "Where they have always lain, Madame Mist. With me."

A spider scurried out of Mist's voluminous sleeve and across her pale, slender hand, before disappearing from sight.

"I'm going to be frank here," said Ravel. "It's not looking good for you, China. You come to the Sanctuary for, well, sanctuary, and we take you in. You have work you need to do? We give you the tools. Your little spies aren't speaking to you any more? We put you in a position so that they do. We've done so much and

489

asked so little. And the first chance you get, you fail us by aiding the enemy."

"If I hadn't, they might have killed me. It wouldn't take much to convince Skulduggery that I had betrayed him yet again."

"I suppose you're right," said Ravel. "You did get his wife and child murdered, after all. Something I've always wondered about, actually. Why did you do it? I mean, I know it was to lure Skulduggery into the trap so that Serpine could kill him, but you could have sent anyone to snatch them up. You could have sent the Diablerie. Instead, you went. Alone. You went up against his wife. Alone. For someone who never exposes herself to any unnecessary danger, that's quite a risk you took."

"I was young. Impetuous."

"In love?"

"What an odd notion."

"Is it? We had plenty of theories throughout the years, but we always returned to that one. Back when he was alive, before the war started, you were in love with Skulduggery. And he was in love with you."

"Ridiculous. I barely knew him back then."

"That's what Dexter said, but then we remembered that your brother had tried to take you with him when he stopped worshipping the Faceless Ones. You spent months with people who weren't lunatics – and one of these people was Skulduggery."

"It doesn't say much for our supposed love if I returned to my old ways soon after, does it?"

Ravel gave a smile. "You returned to your old ways after Skulduggery met his future wife. Ghastly's opinion was that you were spurned."

"Ghastly Bespoke's opinions were not always right. It was his opinion, for example, that he could stand with his back to you and you wouldn't stick a knife in it. How wrong he was."

Ravel's smile slipped. "I'm not going to try to justify my actions. I killed Ghastly. There's a special hell for traitors, and that's where

I'm going. But he had to die. As did Anton. I had to send a message to my supporters. They needed to see that I was as committed to this revolution as they were. Just as they had to spill the blood of their Elders and fellow mages, I had to spill the blood of my brothers. Now we're all damned together."

"And if you manage to capture Skulduggery and the others?" China asked. "Will they also have to die?"

Ravel shook his head. "It'll be shackles and a cell for them. You know me well enough to know that killing is, and always will be, a last resort. I may have done this terrible thing, but I haven't changed who I am. I'm not some moustache-twirling vaudeville villain. I'm still me."

"And who are you? You say I know you well enough? I don't know you at all. You used to be such a proud exponent of Corrival Deuce's teachings. Where did it all go so wrong?"

Ravel shook his head sadly. "My eyes were opened long before I started regurgitating Corrival's words. During the war with Mevolent, I was captured. Tortured. After a few days, I told them everything I knew, but they didn't stop torturing me. They finally had one of the Dead Men in their grasp, and they were enjoying every single scream. Then one day I heard screams that weren't my own, and I thought *they're here. My friends are here.* But when the door burst open, it wasn't Skulduggery or Ghastly standing there. It was the Torment. Larrikin took my place in the Dead Men while I recovered, and I spent almost a year with the Children of the Spider. Do you know of the conditions in which they were forced to live? Squalor. And not because of the war, but because of the mortals. A Child of the Spider can't walk among us for very long without revealing how... different they are. And these days it's even harder to hide."

"So that's what all this is about?" China asked. "Equal rights for Children of the Spider?"

"Equal rights imply that they're equal to mortals. They're not. They're superior. We all are. My eyes were opened, China. Why should we live in squalor? Why should we hide who we are? Because that's the way it's always been? That's not a valid reason."

"So you orchestrated a war."

"I orchestrated a revolution under the guise of a war. Corrival Deuce was wrong. We shouldn't just be the guardians of the mortals. We should be their leaders. The only reason you're still alive is because I know you share my views."

"You're so sure?"

"One hundred per cent positive."

"That doesn't mean I agree with your revolution."

"Of course you don't agree with it," said Ravel. "You hate change. You want the world to remain steady and predictable. So does Skulduggery. I've just done away with that possibility. The Warlocks are hunting for Department X. They're going after the mortals. When we are forced to step in, when we defeat them, every sorcerer will be united under my rule. Then we take over. It's a New World Order, China, and I'm giving you the chance to get in on the ground floor."

"So you need something from me."

"I need the Dead Men. I need Skulduggery and the others."

"I don't know where they are."

"But you can get a message to them. You can tell them I'm going to be alone and vulnerable at a particular time."

China hesitated. "You want me to lead them into a trap."

"The Warlocks are close to attacking the mortals. To the best of our reckoning, we expect them to attack Dublin in a matter of days. We need to be ready to take them down. You said they had the Wretchlings with them, and that's something we didn't anticipate. If anything goes wrong before they attack, if Skulduggery disrupts our plans, the Warlocks might actually win. And then where would we be?"

"Dead," said China.

"Dead," Ravel echoed. "So, yes, I want you to lead Skulduggery and the others into a trap. We'll put them in shackles, put them

492

in cells, and we'll deal with the Warlocks. Once we've established our dominance over the mortals, the cell doors will be opened, and I'll turn myself in."

China frowned. "You're not going to lead?"

"Me?" Ravel said, and laughed. "What would I know about running a world? Every country's Sanctuary will absorb that country's government and it'll all continue as before, just with people like us in charge. I'll confess to my crimes, be put away or go into exile, and my friends can live in peace."

"That's almost noble."

"Were it not for the manipulations and murders," Ravel nodded.

"Be under no illusion," Madame Mist said quietly, "if the Dead Men fail to turn up, or if they are somehow ready for us, you will be killed instantly."

"I'd expect nothing less," China said.

64

THE TRAP IS SPRUNG

Ravel made a big show of shaking the hand of General Mantis right on the steps of the shiny new Sanctuary. Mantis's army dissolved, soldiers becoming sorcerers once again – independent and curious – and they explored Roarhaven while the city's people grinned proudly – both at what they had made, and for the secret they had kept for all this time. The various Elders of the Supreme Council, itself undergoing a slow dissolution, sent their warmest congratulations and made promises to visit soon.

But there was tension in the air. Stephanie could feel it whenever she left Scapegrace's Knight-cave. The Irish sorcerers who had fought under Erskine Ravel had seen the footage, they had seen Ghastly Bespoke and Anton Shudder being murdered by their own Grand Mage, and they weren't buying his lies. They met in small groups, talked quietly among themselves, their conversations dying whenever a Roarhaven mage walked too near.

And they weren't the only ones. Sorcerers from other Sanctuaries, men and women who had never wanted to fight a war in the first place, were asking questions about their own Sanctuaries' involvement. Upon closer inspection, facts and motivations didn't add up. The assassins who had caused so many

Elders to be replaced had either disappeared or had yet to be even identified.

And then there was the Big Question, the question that everyone was asking.

Where was Skulduggery Pleasant?

They were saying the reason the shield around Roarhaven had been put back up when Mantis came through was because Grand Mage Ravel was afraid of what the Skeleton Detective would do once he got to him. They said that Ravel went everywhere with the Children of the Spider to protect him, and had the Black Cleaver as his own personal bodyguard. They said he couldn't sleep at night.

How Stephanie hoped that was true.

No one expected her to have feelings. She could see it in their faces. Vex and Saracen and the Monster Hunters were at least civil to her, and friendly enough, but Skulduggery and Fletcher ignored her. She tried not to show how much that hurt. She deserved it, of course she did. She'd murdered Carol. She'd tried to kill Valkyrie. In their eyes, she was probably still a reflection, still a thing, still an *it*.

When Valkyrie had first told her about Ghastly, Stephanie wasn't sure how she felt. She knew she felt something. There was something inside her, something that felt like Valkyrie's memories of heartache and loss. But Stephanie had shoved it aside, because she was able to do that. Shove it aside, deal with it later. But when she'd dealt with it later, she realised that what she was feeling was real. It was actual heartache. It was actual loss. And it was hers, it wasn't Valkyrie's.

But nobody wanted to know about how much Stephanie grieved.

Seven days after the war ended, she woke to discover that China had sent a message. She walked into the Knight-cave living room to find everyone here, deep in discussion. They hadn't even bothered to wake her.

"This is our chance," said Gracious.

Skulduggery kept looking at the message on his phone. "So it would seem."

Gracious frowned. "You think it's a trap?"

"I don't know. It's perfect. It's not too easy, but it's nothing we can't manage. It's ideally suited to us."

"So it *is* a trap."

"It may not be."

"So it's *not* a trap."

Skulduggery turned to him. "Gracious, I sincerely don't know. But if it is a trap..."

"Then China's betrayed us," Vex said.

"She wouldn't do that willingly," said Skulduggery. "But if they've put a gun to her head and we don't walk into the trap, they'll assume she tipped us off somehow. Ravel might very well throw her in a cell, but Madame Mist is not so forgiving."

Saracen rubbed his hand over his mouth. He hadn't shaved in two days. "You think they'll kill her?"

"It's a distinct possibility."

"So what do we do?"

Skulduggery held up three fingers, and one at a time he ticked them off. "We kill Ravel. We rescue China. We don't get caught. It's going to be tricky. Gracious, is there any way you can access the camera feed again?"

Gracious shook his head. "They changed the access codes the moment they realised we'd infiltrated their system. But if Ravel's going down to the Accelerator Room, I think I can patch into the signals received by the Engineer's audio-visual processors. I don't think even Nye thought about installing safeguards for that. We'll be able to see what the Engineer sees, and hear what it hears."

"Excellent," Skulduggery said. "We'll need every advantage we can get. I'm not going to lie to you, this is going to be dangerous. I can't make any of you come with me on this one. Questions?"

Everyone put their hands up.

"Sorry," Skulduggery said, "I meant 'volunteers'. Thank you. Gracious, get to work. The rest of you, prepare. In two hours, we're going after Ravel."

He didn't say anything about Stephanie staying behind, so she prepared alongside everyone else. Well, almost everyone.

Scapegrace cornered her on her way back from the toilet. "Let us help," he said. "I've been training in the martial arts. Thrasher has big muscles. Grandmaster Ping is really good at kung fu. Please don't leave us behind. I want to be one of the good guys."

"You *are* one of the good guys," Stephanie said, "but this isn't up to me. Skulduggery and the others... they need to see you in action before they'll let you come along, and we don't have time for that right now."

"But this is *it*," said Scapegrace. "This is the big one. I... I need to do this. The Black Cleaver is my fault. I got Thrasher to pick up all the little bits of him after Lord Vile made him explode. I gave the bits to Nye as payment for putting our heads in new bodies. If it wasn't for me, Ravel wouldn't have the scariest bodyguard in the world and—"

"Scapegrace," Stephanie said, "it's OK. No one's blaming you."

"If ever there was a moment to prove myself, to show people that I'm not a joke any more, that it's time to take me seriously, it's now. This fight you're going into is important to you. We want to be there. I want to be there. I want to fight alongside the good guys and whatever happens, victory or defeat, life or death, I'm ready for it."

"It isn't up to me."

"But they'll listen to you."

"No," Stephanie said. "They won't."

She left him there, and got back to the living room as a picture flickered into life on Gracious's laptop. The Accelerator Room. Empty, apart from the Engineer itself. Everyone crowded around.

"Keep an eye on the walls," Skulduggery said. "They need a large sigil on each one if they want to debilitate Fletcher upon arrival."

"Can't see any," said Vex.

"You'd better be sure," Fletcher said. "I got hit with one of those things before and it is not fun. I couldn't teleport for hours afterwards."

Skulduggery leaned away from the screen. "The walls look clear."

"So maybe this isn't a trap, after all."

"Maybe. Here they come."

The Engineer swivelled its head and the monitor showed two mages walking in, followed by Ravel with the Black Cleaver behind his right shoulder. The Engineer looked away for a moment, as Clarabelle wandered by, and when it returned its attention to Ravel, the Grand Mage was peering directly into its face. Nye stood by his side, stooping over. The Black Cleaver, Syc and two Roarhaven mages formed a loose circle round them both. Ravel reached out, tried wiping the smiley face from the Engineer's head. As he did so, he turned the camera slightly, and they glimpsed Portia, standing guard by the door.

"Saracen, Dexter and Gracious, take Syc and his two friends," Skulduggery said. "Donegan, Portia is yours. The most dangerous person in that room is the Black Cleaver. Stephanie, the Sceptre is the only thing guaranteed to put him down fast. If he moves, turn him to dust. Ravel is mine. Fletcher, you stay away from any fighting. If this is a trap, you grab whoever is closest and get the hell out of there. Everyone clear on what they have to do? OK then, get in position."

Stephanie didn't even get to blink and they were standing inside the circle of bodyguards with Ravel and Nye. The Black Cleaver was the first to spin, but Stephanie was already holding the Sceptre out, ready to fire. She was aware of the scuffles all around her, of the shouts and curses and threats, but she didn't take her eye off the Cleaver as he stood there, his hands frozen halfway to his scythe.

Fletcher was beside her, gently moving her as Vex dragged Syc past them, Syc turning purple in a sleeper hold. The Sceptre didn't waver. The Cleaver didn't move.

When Syc slumped into unconsciousness, Vex said, "Clear."

Behind her, Gracious said, "Clear."

"Clear," from Saracen.

"Clear," from Donegan.

"Put down the scythe," Stephanie told the Black Cleaver. "Back up against the wall."

For a moment, the Cleaver didn't move.

"Do as she says," said Ravel from somewhere to her right. The Cleaver laid the scythe on the floor and backed up. Stephanie's mouth was dry.

"I've been held here against my will," Nye said, its voice wavering with fear.

"Shut up," said Skulduggery. Stephanie glanced at him. He had Ravel on his knees, gun pressed to his head.

"What's it going to be?" Ravel asked. "Assassination, arrest, or kidnap?"

"Keep talking," Skulduggery said. "I haven't made up my mind."

"Well, if these are my final few moments, I'd like you all to know how sorry I am about Ghastly and Anton."

"Assassination it is," Skulduggery muttered, taking a step back to avoid the blood splatter.

"Hold on," Ravel said quickly. "Just hold on a second, OK? I didn't want to do it but I had to. I'm changing the world. In fifty years you'll look back on all this and, I don't know, maybe you'll see that I was right."

"I doubt that very much," Saracen said.

"Yeah," said Ravel, "I thought it may have been a tad far-fetched myself, but what else am I going to say with a gun pointed to my head? Apart from if you surrender now, none of you will be harmed."

"Is this the part where you spring the trap?" Skulduggery asked.

Ravel smiled. "So you knew?"

"Of course."

"But you came anyway?"

"Of course."

"See? That's why we're friends. I'm going to stand up now. You can shoot me if you want, but I'm standing up." Ravel got to his feet slowly. The gun stayed pressed to his temple. "You're not going anywhere, by the way. You're certainly not teleporting out of here."

"Is that so?" Fletcher said. "And what's going to stop us?"

Ravel looked at him. "Your hair is really cool."

The pager on Fletcher's hand crackled and he jerked back. Vex caught him as he fell.

"Don't worry," said Ravel, "he's still alive. But he won't regain consciousness for a while. Just a little something extra I had added to the pager. Voice-activated. I had to pick a phrase that no one else would say to him, ever."

"They're coming for us," Saracen said. "Mages and Cleavers. Dozens of them."

"Gracious, pick up Fletcher," Skulduggery said. "We're shooting our way out of here."

"No you're not," Ravel said, almost angrily. "You're going to get yourself killed. Just surrender, OK? You've lost. Accept it. You'll be in a cell for a few months and when you emerge we'll be ruling the world, the way we were always meant to."

The doors burst open. Skulduggery swung Ravel round and stood behind him.

"If any of us takes one single step," Ravel told the mages and Cleavers who were flooding the room, "kill us all."

Skulduggery thumbed back the hammer of his gun. "You're so eager to die?"

"I won't let you ruin everything," Ravel said. "I won't let Anton's and Ghastly's deaths be in vain. This will be seen through to the bitter end – with or without you and me."

"I should just kill you right now."

"You could. But then all of you would die. Even Valkyrie there. You want her to die, Skulduggery? I don't. I don't want any of you to die."

Stephanie waited for Skulduggery to correct him, to tell him that she wasn't the real Valkyrie, but he stayed quiet.

There was a voice from behind the crowd of Cleavers. "Let me through. Let me through, damn it." A moment later, a narrow man pushed his way to the front.

"Flint," said Ravel, and for the first time Stephanie detected a hint of surprise in his voice. "Everyone, allow me to introduce Flint, our new Administrator."

"What happened to Tipstaff?" Stephanie asked.

"Tipstaff is... enjoying some time off," said Ravel. "He's spending most of it in a cell, but he's always been the solitary type. Not everyone understood why I did the things I did."

"Grand Mage," Flint said, "we've spotted the Warlocks."

Ravel brightened. "Perfect timing! Where are they? Dublin?"

"No, sir," Flint said. "They're here. They're outside the city gates."

Ravel stared at him. "But why... why the hell have they come here? They're meant to be attacking the *mortals*."

"Looks like they're not as gullible as you thought," Skulduggery murmured, and released his hold. "Everyone, stand down." He held out his gun.

Ravel hesitated, then took it. "Cleavers," he said, "cuff them."

The Cleavers moved in. Stephanie allowed them to take the Sceptre away from her, and cold shackles closed round her wrists.

Ravel turned to Nye. "Doctor, keep Fletcher nourished and hydrated while he sleeps."

"Of course."

"And no experimenting, you understand me?"

Nye hesitated, then bowed. "Of course."

Ravel looked at Skulduggery, then spoke to the Black Cleaver. "Bring them up to the wall. They've come this far, they may as well see the damn Warlocks."

65

THE WARLOCKS

he Cleavers herded them into a tight group and they followed Ravel through the Sanctuary. The old familiar corridors, concrete and grey and utilitarian, now opened up into grand walkways of marble and stone. The ceilings, so low, so oppressive, blossomed into arches and domes. They passed a group of men knocking down walls between the old and the new, the drab and the splendid, and it was like peeking into another world. Which, in a way, was exactly what they were doing.

They gathered on a platform. At Ravel's command, it sank smoothly into the floor, the gap sealing itself above their heads. They came to a stop at the mouth of a wide, well-lit tunnel, and started moving again, forward this time.

"Bloody Warlocks," he muttered.

Skulduggery sounded oddly pleased. "After you'd gone to all that trouble to frame Department X..."

"Exactly," said Ravel, exasperated. "I mean, how many breadcrumbs do I have to drop to lead them to attack mortals? Everything worked out according to plan. Everything. Yet still they turn up here. What use is that? We need them to attack *Dublin*, for God's sake. We need mortals to see them, to fear them, we need the world to panic. Only then can we swoop in and save the day."

"And then take over," Vex added.

"Taking over is our right," said Ravel. "This is the most painless way we can do it, for both us and the mortals. What, you'd prefer if our plans consisted of mass destruction on a global scale? I'm trying to do this with a minimum of hardship. You're all looking at me like I've enjoyed this, like I've enjoyed getting innocent blood on my hands or betraying my friends."

"If you really feel bad about it," said Stephanie, "take off our shackles."

"Well," Ravel said, "I don't feel *that* bad about it." He smiled, but nobody else did, so he sighed and held up the Sceptre. "And where did you get this, may I ask? Have you been visiting alternate dimensions again?" He examined it closer. "There are other God-Killer weapons. The sword, the dagger, the spear, the bow. There are more, too, if you believe the legends. But this... this is the one. This is the weapon that drove back the Faceless Ones. An army that carries the Sceptre before it... is invincible."

Stephanie looked him straight in the eye. "So are you going to kill me? The only way you can use that is to kill me and claim ownership of it for yourself."

"You really think I'd kill you, Valkyrie?"

"You killed Ghastly. And Shudder. And Corrival Deuce. And who knows how many others."

Ravel looked away. "Yeah. Well. I'm not going to kill *you*."

Gracious was standing with his head tilted back, looking at the lights as they flashed by. "We're underneath the streets?" he asked.

"Yes we are," Ravel said. "The Sanctuary is connected to all major points in the city by these tunnels. You should see some of the materials we've discovered in the dimension where all this was built. Rocks, minerals, metals – we have nothing like them in this reality. No humans over there, but plenty of weird animals and fascinating vegetation. We've had experts examining everything and they've discovered some kind of basic intelligence in the plant life. Can you imagine that? Intellectual carrots. The mind boggles."

"What are you trying to do?" Vex asked quietly. "Are you trying to make friends with us? Are we chatting now? You murdered Anton and Ghastly, you son of a bitch. There's no coming back from that."

Ravel looked away, and nobody said anything as the platform slowed to a stop.

The ceiling opened above them and they rose into it and kept going upwards, picking up speed. Stephanie had to open her mouth wide and make herself yawn so that her ears would pop. Just when she thought the ride would go on forever, they stopped and the door in front of them opened and the wind rushed in.

They stepped out on to a wall so thick you could park two cars side by side and still have enough room to squeeze by. There were battlements on one side and a metal railing on the other, the side that looked out across the city. It was an impressive sight. Stephanie peered over the railing, straight down to the streets below, and a dizzying wave of vertigo washed over her. A Cleaver nudged her onwards, and she caught up with the others as they walked. Skulduggery had once told Valkyrie the names of the various sections of the battlements. He'd told her to think of the wall as the gums of an old man—the gums themselves were called crenels, and the jutting teeth were merlons. Valkyrie had forgotten the lesson within minutes. Stephanie remembered everything.

The wind up here was strong and cold, and it snatched Skulduggery's hat from his head. Ravel raised his hand and the hat swung around and settled into his grip. He put it into Skulduggery's shackled hands, but Skulduggery said nothing.

General Mantis didn't have to peer between the merlons to look out over the surrounding land. It just stood there, ridiculously tall, wrapped in that cellophane. Now that she was close enough,

Stephanie could see its pale, hairless flesh beneath. It looked down at them as they approached, its face hidden behind that mask.

"Grand Mage Ravel," it said. "Congratulations on capturing your enemies. If you wish to fling them from the wall, I know the perfect spot."

Ravel frowned. "I'm not altogether sure you're joking."

"The General is like that," another man said as he walked up, a woman by his side. "Its sense of humour takes a little getting used to. Hey, Saracen."

"Regis," Saracen said, nodding to him. "Hi, Ashione."

Ashione, the woman, made a point of ignoring him.

"You're probably wondering why I didn't call," Saracen said to her. "I was going to, I really was. But then I lost your number. And war broke out. And then my phone stopped working. I have to get a new one. Any recommendations? I was thinking about a—"

Ashione glared at him and he shut up.

"Grand Mage," Regis said, "we're setting up a vantage point for you. If you'll follow me?"

They left Mantis standing there and walked over to a young woman.

"This is NJ," Regis said. "She's chosen the language of magic for her discipline, and we have her studying under China Sorrows."

"Miss Sorrows is a wonderful teacher," NJ said, eyes wide. "She really is so good at this. I'll never be half as good as she is. That's what she keeps telling me. She's magnificent."

Regis sighed. "NJ is a little enamoured of Miss Sorrows at the moment."

Ravel smiled as NJ blushed. "Hey, don't worry about it. We've all been there, believe me. Most of us are still there, if we're being honest. But how about you put all your doubts out of your head for the moment, and show us what you can do?"

NJ nodded. "Yes. Yes, sir."

She took an ornate pen from a silver case, and pressed it to one of the merlons. The tip of the pen began to glow, and it carved through the stone like it was made of butter. NJ may have been nervous, but her hand was sure, and she completed the sigil without a single hesitation. Once it was finished, she repeated the process on the next merlon.

She checked her work, blew on the pen then put it back in its silver case. She pressed the first sigil and it glowed, and when she took her finger away there was some kind of transparent film attached to it. She drew the film all the way across the crenel, and touched it against the second sigil, where it held. The film shimmered in the strong wind, but through it the surrounding countryside was magnified.

In the distance, they saw people.

"That's them?" Ravel asked. "How many are there?"

"Thirty, sir."

"That's all? Where's Charivari?"

"We haven't been able to see him."

Ravel shook his head. "So they've come to make war on us with thirty people?" He looked at Skulduggery. "Thoughts?"

Skulduggery took his time before answering. "Right now I'm thinking, wouldn't it be great if they all came in here and ripped you apart?"

"Well," Ravel said, "that's helpful. Regis, ask the General what it thinks."

"Something's happening," Stephanie said.

The Warlocks were clearing a space for an old man. He straightened both arms over his head and started making circular motions with his hands. White energy glittered around his fingertips.

"Is that Charivari?" Gracious asked.

"No," said Vex. "Charivari's younger. More physically impressive. What's this guy doing?"

"Ashione," said Regis. "Stop him from doing what he's doing."

"Yes, sir," said Ashione, and took her rifle from its covering.

"Some Warlocks can't be killed by bullets," Donegan said.

"These bullets are special," Ashione murmured, putting her eye to the scope. The man brought his hands apart slightly, teasing out a small circle of energy. Ashione pulled the trigger, and the man's head snapped back in a mist of blood. The circle stayed where it was, though, hovering in the air.

A woman came forward, held her hands to both sides of the circle, started stretching it. Ashione adjusted her aim, fired again. The woman's body toppled over the man's.

Another man came forward, stretched the circle even further. You could ride a bike through it now. Before Ashione could fire, another man calmly stepped in front of him, blocking her shot. And another man stepped in front of him. And another.

"This is ridiculous," she said, picking up the rifle and jogging to another vantage point. She fired again, and again, but the others protected the man as he spread his arms wide and stepped back, and the circle pulsed with light and with every pulse it grew. You could drive a car through it now. A van. A truck. A bus. And still it pulsed, and still it grew, until it was wide enough to fit ten buses through.

And then it stopped, and it hung there like a giant smoke ring.

"I don't get it," said Saracen.

It dipped a little, dipped more, dropping closer to the ground. Upon contact its curved edge started to flatten, until it looked less like a smoke ring and more like a punctured tyre. And then it settled, and stopped deflating.

Ravel scowled. "Does anyone know what the hell that is?"

"It's a portal," said Skulduggery.

Figures emerged. Stephanie heard Regis mutter something under his breath, something that sounded like "Wretchlings". She didn't know what a Wretchlings was but she didn't think she could count them as human. Some had hair. Most hadn't. Some were big, some scrawny. All of them had boils or sores of some sort. They wore leather and fur, but their clothes were stitched into their rotting skin, and their rotting skin was stitched through their clothes. They bulged, like they'd been overstuffed, like their insides had yet to settle into place. Some of them, their faces twitched like every muscle was in spasm, while others had faces so slack it was like they had no muscles at all. One thing they all had in common though, was a weapon. They carried their swords or their axes or their war hammers in their meaty fists or their skeletal hands and they walked with a single, hostile purpose.

And they kept coming.

A hundred. Two hundred. Five. A thousand. Two thousand. They kept coming, spreading out across the fields. Three thousand. Five thousand.

When they were all out, the portal closed behind them.

"I make it around twelve thousand," said Dexter.

Ravel grabbed Regis's arm. "Get Mantis over here. I need him to take control of the city's defence." When Regis hesitated, Ravel's eyes narrowed. "*What?*"

"We'll fight," Regis said, "but *your* people won't."

"What are you talking about?"

"The Irish sorcerers," said Regis. "I've spoken to them. They don't trust you, not after what you did to Ghastly and Shudder, and they won't fight for you."

"They won't just stand by and let Roarhaven be destroyed."

"I wouldn't be too sure about that."

"Well, what the hell do you expect me to do about that now? Explanations can wait. If I tell them to fight..." He faltered. "Damn it." He turned to Skulduggery. "They'll fight for you."

Saracen barked a laugh. "You have some nerve..."

Ravel ignored him. "Take over, Skulduggery. Take command. Mantis's people and ours will fight if you're the one giving the orders. Forget about me, about what I've done. There is a city here, with sorcerers who aren't fighters, thousands of them. Men, women and children. The Warlocks will slaughter them, you know they will."

509

Skulduggery tilted his head. "And after?"

"What happens, happens."

Skulduggery looked over at the twelve thousand Wretchlings, and held out his hands. "Then you'd better take these shackles off, hadn't you?"

66

THE SIEGE AT ROARHAVEN

The Roarhaven sorcerers didn't bother with magic at that range. A long barrel and a bullet, that's all they needed to slow the advance. From up high on the wall, Stephanie couldn't see the blood. She just saw the Wretchlings jerk, topple and fall. One after another.

There were others in among them, men and women whose hands were lighting up. Hot beams of energy burst forth, but while bullets passed through the shield without slowing, magic sizzled against the invisible barrier and went no further. A one-sided battle if ever Stephanie had seen one. Suddenly the Warlocks' great numbers didn't mean so much any more. If they couldn't get through the shield, where was the threat?

She watched a skinny man down below, shouting up at them. His words were lost long before they reached the top of the wall, but that didn't seem to bother him. He screamed and shouted and shook his fists and stamped his feet. Skulduggery joined her looking down at him.

"That's a little odd," he murmured.

"Looks like he's doing the haka," Stephanie said.

Skulduggery motioned to Regis. "Captain, if I could focus your attention on the gentleman having the tantrum."

Regis peered over the side. "What about him?"

"The Warlocks aren't known for being normal, but even so, this does strike me as unusual behaviour."

Regis grunted. "Ashione, see the guy kicking up a fuss? Take him out before he does something weirder."

"You got it, chief," Ashione said, taking careful aim.

A piece of wall exploded beside her and she jerked back. "What the hell...?"

Energy beams hit the shield, sizzled, and broke through.

"He's taking down the shield," Skulduggery said, snatching Ashione's gun from her and lifting it to his shoulder.

He fired, but a Wretchling jumped in front of the shouting man, caught the bullet in the neck. Skulduggery fired again, and again a Wretchling sacrificed himself. The shouting man spread his arms wide and stomped his feet and his words drifted above the gunfire. Stephanie heard a few garbled words of old magic and then someone on the wall was shouting, "It's down! The shield is down!"

The Warlocks' energy beams carved great scars into the wall. Smaller darts of energy flew like angry insects, pocking against the battlements. A sniper who had leaned too far screamed, dropped his rifle and staggered back, clutching his face. He fell to one knee, then toppled on to his side, and went limp. When his hands fell, half of his melted face went with them.

The sense of calm evaporated. They still had the high ground and they still had their defences, but soldiers were now ducking as they moved, scurrying from one vantage point to the next. Those beams of white energy tore chunks from solid stone.

Ashione had her rifle back and she was popping up, taking a shot and then immediately ducking down again. Every time she popped up, it would be in a slightly different place. The Warlocks had already identified her as a major threat – her section of the wall was under constant bombardment.

Stephanie glanced down in time to see the Wretchling clear a space around a big man, maybe seven feet tall. His torso was glowing like he was being lit from within. He suddenly threw his shoulders back and a whirling ball of white energy shot out of his chest. It rose quickly, growing as it came. A few snipers tried taking shots at it. Elementals sent waves of air to shoo it off course. Neither of these had any effect. Vex let loose an energy stream of his own, but it hit the ball and passed through. And still the whirling mass of white rose towards the top of the wall, and it slowed, and hung there.

"Back!" Skulduggery roared. "Everyone back!"

The ball exploded with a deafening crack. The blast lifted Stephanie off her feet and flung her over the railing. Screaming, she started to fall to the city streets far below, but a hand snagged her ankle and she swung to the wall and slammed into it. She hung there, upside down, unable to even blink. The grip on her ankle was tight. Blood rushed to her head.

She was pulled up, and a hand clutched her leg and kept pulling, and now the hands were on her hips, and she was pulled under the railing and back on to the wall. She turned over, shaking, expecting Skulduggery or Dexter, instead finding a Cleaver, just another anonymous Cleaver.

"Thank you," she gasped.

The Cleaver picked up his scythe and went to help an injured sorcerer, and within moments she couldn't tell him apart from all the other Cleavers. Rubble littered the walkway. A chunk of the wall was missing, and great clouds of dust rose like smoke. She saw Skulduggery, looking for something. She waved to him, watched him visibly relax and then turn away, getting back to work.

Stephanie got up, went back to the wall. Something hit the merlon beside her, spraying her with chips of rock. A metal dart, buried in the stone, trailing a rope of white energy.

She peered over the edge. More of these darts shot into the wall, fired from the hands of Warlocks in a burst of white. Once

513

attached, the Warlocks secured the other end to the ground, and the rope went taut. Stephanie ducked as a dart skimmed her cheek. She glanced again a moment later, saw dozens of these energy ropes in place. What were they hoping to do – pull the wall down?

Instead, the Warlocks stepped away, and the Wretchlings ran forward. They jumped on to the ropes with their bare feet and they kept running, like overeager tightrope walkers, sprinting up the steep incline like this was a Sunday morning jog.

The shout went out. Bursts of gunfire sent Wretchlings falling, but there seemed to be a limitless supply, and by now the Warlocks were keeping the snipers busy with their energy beams.

Stephanie reached over her shoulder, took hold of the stick. It buzzed lightly in her hand. She took another look at the Wretchlings. They were getting close. A few sorcerers were trying to cut the energy ropes with no success. Others still hit the ropes with their swords, trying to dislodge the dozens of Wretchlings running up each of them. It was no use. And then the Wretchlings were upon them.

One of them scrambled over the wall in front of Stephanie. The first thing to hit her was the stench – rotting meat and putrefaction. The second was his fist – a blistered thing of mismatched knuckles. She used the stick to hit him back in a burst of blue light, then turned to the battlement as another Wretchling crawled up. She jabbed him in the throat and then pushed, forcing him backwards. He screamed and vanished and she turned again, ducked a curved sword that whistled for her head. The Wretchling came forward, slashing wildly, his face contorted with hatred. She blocked clumsily, giving ground, then lunged. But he sidestepped, the hilt of the sword crunching against her head.

She fell, biting her tongue, the world spinning around her,

but her mind staying alert enough to curse herself. She rolled, the sword slicing across her side, but unable to get through her jacket. The Wretchling jabbed at her and stabbed at her and finally it occurred to him that maybe he should try going for the part of her that wasn't swathed in black. Stephanie blocked a slash at her head and swung for his body, but the curved blade parried the stick and took it from her hand. She dived on him, fingers clawing at his face. His flesh was clammy and soft, like ripe fruit. They staggered against the railing and she bit his neck, gagged on the foulness, and jammed her thumb in his eye. He screeched and pulled away and she shoved at the same time and he flipped backwards over the railing, falling to the streets below.

The Wretchlings were everywhere now, their swords clashing with the scythes of the Cleavers. Sorcerers took them on hand to hand when they had to, but ranged magic was preferred. Stephanie wiped her mouth and returned her stick to its place between her shoulder blades, then took the Sceptre from her bag. Black lightning flashed and a Wretchling who was just scrambling over the wall turned to dust, and the wind snatched that dust away in a swirling mass. The Sceptre fired again and again, Wretchlings exploding like 2,000-year-old clay pots being dropped from a great height. Three more Wretchlings, bursting dryly apart, and then from the clouds of dust came a fourth, running straight at her.

He took her off her feet and she lost the Sceptre before she even hit the ground. He kicked her and she rolled, then scrambled, grabbed him, got her legs under her even as he was trying to get free and she stood, heaving him on to her shoulders with a roar, and ran for the battlements. She hit them and he toppled off her and over the top, his scream quickly fading.

Strong fingers grabbed her, turned her towards the hot breath of a Wretchling, who punched at her quickly but ineffectively.

She looked down, realised he had a small triangular knife in his fist that was searching for weak points. She grabbed his wrist, held on, feeling the skin shift beneath her grip, but his other hand was on her face, fingers digging into her eyes. She turned away and the fingers came after her. One of them strayed too close to her mouth and she bit down, heard the crunch of bone and felt the spurt of hot blood, and then the Wretchling was wrenched away from her. A sorcerer had him round the throat, was hauling him to the railing. The Wretchling twisted into him, plunged the knife into his gut half a dozen times in less than a second, and the sorcerer stumbled back and the Wretchling pushed him, and he fell screaming to the city below.

Stephanie grabbed her stick, ran at him. The Wretchling blocked her swing and snarled. She spat a mouthful of his own blood back into his face and kicked his knee, and then she slammed her stick into his head. The sigils weren't glowing any more. It was out of charge. She hit him again and again, knocking him out the old-fashioned way. He collapsed and she fought the urge to throw up.

She pushed aside a dead Cleaver and pulled the Sceptre from beneath his body, then returned to the battlements. There weren't as many ropes as before. As she watched, one of them went from white to grey, and then it faded altogether. The handful of Wretchlings who were halfway up fell, howling, to the ground. The other ropes started to fade. There were no more Wretchlings climbing them.

When the last rope had faded, the Warlocks retreated, and a cheer went up along the wall. Victory.

Stephanie took a look at the dead and the dying. She looked at lifeless sorcerers and lifeless Wretchlings and still Cleavers, and the damage done by all that white energy. Her hip bled from where that knife had nicked her. Her right shoulder was on fire – torn muscles from when she'd lifted that Wretchling. She tasted blood. Some of it was her own. Some of it wasn't.

The Warlocks' first attack and they'd repelled it. Victory indeed.

She was assigned a room with a bed and a shower. She washed, groaning with aches and pains, and when she was done she went down for something to eat. Skulduggery came to see her as she sat alone. Stephanie looked up, but didn't say anything, waited for him to start.

"I heard you saved a few lives," he said.

"That's what we do, isn't it?"

"It's what myself and Valkyrie do. You kill defenceless girls."

She nodded. "I'm not arguing with you any more."

"I'm sorry?"

She took another bite, chewed and swallowed. "I get that you hate me. Of course you hate me. I've done horrible things. Not as many horrible things as Valkyrie, but still... But that's not why you hate me. You hate me because I'm not her. And it's fine, if you want to continue like that. Then whenever you hear that I've done something good or nice, you can pretend to be surprised, because everyone knows you think I'm nothing but the evil version of Valkyrie.

"But I'm not the evil version of Valkyrie. *Valkyrie* is the evil version of Valkyrie. And now that I'm real, now that I'm a real person, I'm not going to hurt any more innocent people. Can she say the same?"

"I'm going to get her back."

"How? You have no idea, do you? You're terrified that the next time you see her you'll have to kill her, because you'll have no other choice. So you can say all the mean things you want. It doesn't bother me. You're just scared."

Skulduggery's head tilted, and he looked at her for the longest time before turning, and walking away.

She woke to shouts and sat up in the dark, her hand finding the Sceptre and holding it out in front of her. The shouts continued

517

and she threw back the covers, jammed her feet into her boots. She searched around for her jacket, pulled it on, made sure the stick was in place. As she walked to the door, she pulled the bag over one shoulder. She stepped out, saw four figures walking up the street towards her, and she went cold.

Wraiths.

67

WRAITHS

Horrible freaky things came through the darkness and the Dark and Stormy Knight pulled on his mask and prepared for battle. There were screams in the distance, and flashes of light and gunfire. Then more screams.

The Dark and Stormy Knight would not scream. The Dark and Stormy Knight was this city's protector. Was it the one it needed? No. But it was the one it deserved.

He crept out from hiding, approaching one of these sinister figures from behind, and then he leaped, wrapping an arm round the figure's throat.

Even as he applied the stranglehold, he could feel the terrible heat from the figure's skin seeping through the thin fabric of his skintight top. But he ignored the pain and tightened his hold. Pain meant nothing. Pain was transitory. Pain would fade. Only justice was forever. Justice and a little bit of this pain. Oh, this pain. Oh, this hot, hot pain, pushing everything else from his mind. But only a few more seconds. He just needed to hang on for a few more seconds.

The Dark and Stormy Knight released the stranglehold and staggered away, yelping as he shook his arm to cool it down. The figure turned to him slowly, as if it had just noticed him.

"Back-up!" he screeched. "Where is my back-up?"

The Village Idiot thundered into view, head down and arms out, yelling a war cry. He crunched into the figure from behind and folded like a cheap accordion. Useless. Then Grandmaster Ping arrived.

"Ping!" said the Dark and Stormy Knight. "You go low, I go high!"

"I have a new strategy," Ping called out. "Run away."

And that's just what Grandmaster Ping did.

The Dark and Stormy Knight stared at him as he vanished into the shadows, then the figure obstructed his view and he stepped back, cornered. His mouth was suddenly dry. All his dreams, all his stupid ideas about being a hero, about being one of the good guys, none of it meant anything. He'd failed. He was a joke. They were right to laugh. He pulled the mask away. If he was going to die, he was going to die as Vaurien Scapegrace, a proud man in a proud woman's body, not as some pathetic joke.

The figure reached for him and a golden stream of energy hit it, sent it staggering. Sheriff Dacanay and another man strode towards them. The other man fired again, hitting the figure in the chest, driving it back, and then Dacanay raised his hand and a stream of purple energy burrowed a hole through the figure's head. It keeled over and didn't get up.

Scapegrace let out the breath he'd been holding, his legs almost collapsing beneath him.

"Interesting," Dacanay said, standing over the figure's body. "You can hurt it, but I can kill it."

His companion nodded. "Must be something to do with the power level of your energy. I'll spread the word."

He took off, and Dacanay looked at Scapegrace. "You again. It might be best if you stayed indoors tonight. We got a wraith infestation to deal with and we can't afford to have civilians running around. It's a sure-fire way to get yourself killed."

Scapegrace nodded quickly. "OK."

"You might want to pick up your boyfriend while you're at it."

"He's not my boyfriend."

"Well, whatever he is, he can't just lie around on the street like that. It's a public safety issue."

Scapegrace hurried over to Thrasher, kicked him in the side. Thrasher groaned, opened his eyes.

"Master?"

"Get up," Scapegrace commanded. "And take off that ridiculous mask."

Thrasher did as he was told as Dacanay's radio crackled into life, and the voice of the man who had just run off came through loud and clear. "Multiple wraith attacks just north of your position," he said. "I'm dealing with one of them, but there are three kids being chased along Amrita Street, and a woman with blue hair is cornered by the fountain. Over."

Dacanay held the radio to his mouth. "I'm taking Amrita Street," he said. "Out."

"Wait," Scapegrace said. "The woman with blue hair. That's Clarabelle. She's our friend. You have to help her."

But Dacanay was already running. "Sorry," he said. "Kids come first."

Scapegrace watched him go, and turned to see Thrasher looking at him.

"Master?"

Scapegrace didn't know what to do. Thrasher was looking at him with that big, stupid face, and Scapegrace didn't know what to do. He swallowed. "We help Clarabelle."

They sprinted to the top of the street and turned right, towards the fountain in the square. The moment it came into view Scapegrace wanted to run the other way, but then he saw Clarabelle. She had climbed into the fountain itself. Around her, three wraiths were closing in.

"Scapey!" she yelled. "Gerald! Help!"

"We're coming!" Thrasher yelled back.

Scapegrace looked around, scanning their environment for a weapon, or an idea, or some kind of plan. He couldn't find anything.

"Master?"

A shout bubbled up from somewhere within him. "Hey!" he screamed. "Hey, wraiths! Hey! Come get us!"

Thrasher joined in, jumping up and down and waving his ridiculously muscled arms. One of the wraiths noticed them, started walking over.

"Now what do we do?" Thrasher whispered.

"We lead it away," Scapegrace said. "Look how slow it moves. It's walking. We can run. It'll never be able to—"

A breeze rustled through the square and the wraith came apart like smoke, solidifying again right in front of Scapegrace.

Scapegrace screamed as the wraith reached for him, and Thrasher lunged, his big fist clunking off the wraith's pale, angular cheekbone. The wraith barely noticed yet Thrasher staggered away, clutching his hand, his knuckles burning. Scapegrace kicked at the wraith's knee, but missed, and his supporting foot slid out from under him and he fell. The wraith looked down at him... then raised its head. Scapegrace craned his neck, the world upside down, and saw someone walking towards them. He rolled over.

The Black Cleaver approached.

Thrasher grabbed Scapegrace's arm and dragged him out from under the wraith, hauled him to his feet as the Black Cleaver pulled out his scythe. The wraith observed the Cleaver like he was a species it had never encountered before. Behind it, the other two wraiths abandoned their pursuit of Clarabelle and started walking over.

The Cleaver moved, his scythe flashing, and the first wraith's hand fell to the ground. There was no blood, no pain, and the wraith looked at its stump without emotion. The Cleaver whirled, taking the wraith's right leg off at the knee. The wraith fell, tried to get up and the Black Cleaver took its head.

But even that didn't stop it.

While the Black Cleaver turned to face the other two, Scapegrace stepped forward, kicking the disembodied head away from the wraith's grasping hand. It wasn't that long ago that he himself had been a head, but he didn't feel bad about what he'd just done. Let the wraith put itself back together on its own time.

The remaining wraiths became smoke that blew apart, coming together again on either side of the Black Cleaver as he spun, ducking under their attempts to grab him. The scythe caught the crescent moon and sliced through the throat of one of them. It lurched, its head lolling back, held in place by a flap of pale skin. The last wraith caught the Cleaver's arm. Scapegrace heard the snap of bone, but the Cleaver didn't even flinch. He rammed the top of his helmet into the wraith's face, broke its leg with a single stomp that drove it to its knees, and wrenched his arm loose. Then he gave a little jump back as he brought his scythe up and over, and the blade embedded itself in the wraith's head with a solid *thunk*.

Scapegrace and Thrasher watched in awe as the Black Cleaver pulled his scythe free and the wraith crumpled sideways.

There was a scream, somewhere off to their left, and without a word the Black Cleaver was gone.

Clarabelle hurried over. The water from the fountain had drenched her, but she didn't seem to notice. "You rescued me," she said, her big eyes bright.

"Well," said Scapegrace, "it wasn't really us…"

"You rescued me," she insisted. "You really *are* my friends."

"Of course we are," said Thrasher.

The wraiths were slowly turning to smoke, and that smoke was linking up with its missing body parts. Scapegrace didn't want to be around when they solidified. "We should go," he said.

Clarabelle clamped a hand over her mouth as they hurried away. "I've never had friends before," she said. "Not really. I had one. We grew up together. Everyone thought we hated each other, but I just assumed that she was imaginary, and she assumed *I* was imaginary, so we never spoke to each other when there were other people around."

Thrasher hesitated. "Sounds reasonable."

"But she died, thirty years ago," said Clarabelle. "So I've had thirty years without a friend. And now... now I have two of the best friends in the whole world. I'm the luckiest girl *ever*."

Roarhaven was full of empty buildings just waiting to be filled by an influx of sorcerers who wanted to be part of the first capital city of sorcerers. Scapegrace led them into one of these buildings, closed the door behind them and barricaded it.

"We'll wait here," he whispered. "Maybe by morning they'll be gone. Clarabelle, what were you even doing out here alone? There's a war on – we were told to stay indoors."

"I was looking at houses," Clarabelle said. "I was told I could choose one to live in, because I work for the Sanctuary and everything. I don't like any of them, though. None of them feel like home. I don't think this place will ever feel like home."

"Why don't you just live with us?" Thrasher asked.

Clarabelle's eyes widened. "Could I? Scapey, could I live with you?"

Scapegrace peered out through the window, making sure the wraiths hadn't followed them. "Sure," he said. "Why not?"

Clarabelle hopped up and down, but Thrasher managed to get his hand over her mouth before she started squealing. When she was done, she whirled, grabbed Thrasher in a hug. "Oh, thank you, thank you, thank you! My two best friends ever! Gerald, my dear, sweet Gerald. You risked everything to save me. You have the heart of a lion."

Thrasher beamed. "You think so?"

"I do." She whirled again. "And Scapey, my dear Scapey. When I looked up and saw you running towards me, I just knew everything was going to be all right. I knew you'd save me. You're my hero."

Scapegrace blinked at her. He was her hero?

He stood a little straighter. His chest didn't need any puffing out, but he puffed it out anyway. He was her *hero*.

"Oh, Master!" Thrasher said, his eyes wide.

"Shut up," said Scapegrace.

"Do you know what this means?"

"Be quiet."

"It means you didn't have to learn kung fu. You didn't have to put on a mask. You didn't have to be the Dark and Stormy Knight. Master... you were a hero all along."

"Yes," Scapegrace snapped. "I got that. I realised that myself. But now you've taken a moment of personal triumph and validation and you've ruined it by making it obvious."

Thrasher's face fell. "Oh."

"Stand over there and don't speak for the rest of the night."

Thrasher turned, and slouched towards the corner.

Idiot.

68

BLACK SMOKE, WHITE FLAME

The wraiths were gone by morning, but the dawn brought with it a fresh bombardment. Those floating balls of energy drifted to the wall and did their damage there or beyond. Watchtowers fell, mages and Cleavers were killed by the blasts or, more likely, falling masonry. A few explosions rocked the city itself, damaging houses and other dwellings, though casualties here were not as high as they could have been. After the night of horror they'd just witnessed, most citizens of Roarhaven were moving towards the Sanctuary and away from the wall. An exact death toll had yet to be calculated. The wraiths had retreated before the sun came up, but there had been reports all morning of people missing as well as dead.

Stephanie remembered a time when she didn't need sleep. As a reflection, all she'd had to do to regain her strength was to step into the mirror and she'd emerge like a freshly charged battery. But now that she was a person, eating and drinking and sleeping took up so much of her time she felt sure she was doing it wrong.

She ate breakfast and checked the Sceptre. The black crystal was still glowing as fiercely as ever, and she wondered if it ever needed to be recharged. Her stick did. It hung between her shoulder blades, solid and heavy and reassuring, but utterly devoid of magic. It had saved her life, though, and she wasn't about to throw it away simply because it didn't keep its stun effect for long.

Bane and O'Callahan were comparing bruises when she found them, and together they went to the top of the wall. Skulduggery was already up there with Vex and Saracen and General Mantis. Everyone moved hunched over. The Warlocks' aim was improving.

"They've been at this for hours," Vex said as another explosion rocked the wall. "How long before they get bored, do you reckon? Before or after the wall topples over?"

"We need to take the offensive," said Saracen. "We need to get our people down there."

"General," Skulduggery said, "tell the others your suggestion."

Mantis swivelled its gas mask towards them. "Thank you. Some of you may have noticed that our enemy leaves itself vulnerable when it attacks. Its number is split into three. The Wretchlings are closest to the wall, twelve thousand of them. Behind them, Warlock Energy-Throwers, twenty in all. And behind them, Charivari has been glimpsed, sitting on the hill with approximately fifty Wretchlings and a further twenty Warlocks. That is our opportunity."

"You want to go after him?" Gracious asked.

"Three cloaking spheres ought to conceal my troops," Mantis said, nodding. "I am sure Grand Mage Ravel has one or two secret exits from which we could leave the city. We would then move around behind them, attack from the rear, and either kill or capture Charivari."

Vex frowned. "And if you're noticed, the attacking force will return and you'll be wiped out."

"If the attacking force notices, that will be your signal to open the gates and charge at the Wretchlings. Without Charivari to issue commands, they will find themselves fighting a battle on both sides."

Stephanie didn't know if her words would be welcomed here,

but someone had to say it. "There are more of them than there are of us."

"Surprise is a sharp weapon to wield," Mantis replied. "But you need not engage them fully. You would just have to sow enough confusion to allow us to slip backwards, still under cover of the cloaking spheres. Then you would return to the safety of the wall and leave our enemy confused and standing in the middle of a field, not knowing which way to turn."

"In order to be ready at the gates, we'd need to drastically reduce our numbers on the wall," said Vex. "The Wretchlings could swarm us."

"I did not claim this plan to be without risk."

"If it goes wrong," Saracen said, "you'll be out there alone. We won't be able to get to you. And Warlocks aren't known for taking prisoners."

"Death comes for us all. But I do not believe we will fail."

A few days ago, Mantis was the enemy – alien and unknowable. Today it was a friend, and Stephanie didn't want to see it risking its life on something so dangerous.

"What does His Highness say about this?" Vex asked.

"Ravel doesn't *get* a say," Skulduggery responded. "On this wall, I'm in command. Mantis has a plan, and it's a good one, and I'm inclined to agree to it. Unless anyone here has a reason why I shouldn't."

Stephanie could see it in their eyes. They wanted to object, but they didn't have a choice.

"OK then," Skulduggery said. "General, prepare your people."

Mantis gave a sharp salute, and left them where they crouched.

"It's suicide," said Donegan.

"Maybe," said Skulduggery. "But if it works, this battle is over."

"And if it doesn't, we're down half our number."

Skulduggery looked out over the battlements. "Fortune favours the bold. He who dares wins. The only easy day was yesterday. *Signa Inferemus*. Take whichever slogan you like the most and lean on it. That's how you get through decisions like this. Stephanie, stick."

She frowned, took the stick from her back and handed it to him. He gripped it, and the sigils started glowing again. He handed it back, fully charged, without saying anything.

The morning passed without any more deaths. The bombardment slowed, as if the Warlocks were getting tired. When the Warlock had attacked Valkyrie and Skulduggery in that alleyway eighteen months before, he'd used up so much power that he tried to eat Valkyrie's soul in order to get his strength back. Stephanie didn't like to think about what the Warlocks outside the gate would have to do to get their energy up again, and she certainly didn't want to see it. She found a spot against the wall where she could sit and no one was going to trip over her, and she closed her eyes and tried to doze.

She woke to find a camera being shoved in her face. She recoiled, slapping it away. The cameraman adjusted focus as he hunkered down, and before she could rip the camera from his hands, another man joined him. She recognised him – the journalist, Kenny Dunne – and suddenly it all slipped into place. His annoying little investigation, Ravel's documentary crew... Of course they would find each other. Of course they would.

"Hi, Valkyrie," Kenny said. She couldn't be bothered to correct him. "You remember me? You questioned me about Paul Lynch's murder, a year and a half ago. Skulduggery pretended he was a cop, Detective Inspector Me. Remember that? I'm Kenny Dunne, and this is Patrick Slattery. I was wondering if you wouldn't mind talking to us."

"Talking to you about what?" Stephanie asked, holding her hand in front of the lens and turning her face away. "Seriously, stop filming me."

"Valkyrie, this is your chance to set the record straight. This is your chance to tell your side of it."

"Side of what?"

"Of everything," said Kenny. "Of everything that's going on. We've been here for days, in among these people, and we don't understand them. We can't. They're all hundreds of years old, and yet they look better than we do. They can do magic and shoot laser beams from their hands and throw fireballs and... and we can't wrap our heads round any of that. But you... you're one of them, but you're also one of us."

"You don't know anything about me," she said, and stood up. They stood with her.

"I know plenty," Kenny said. "These people call you Valkyrie, but I know you as Stephanie Edgley, eighteen years old, from Haggard, in north County Dublin. Recently left school and is considering college. According to your old teachers, you're a bright girl who holds herself back for some reason. Your classmates liked you, even though they viewed you as a little weird."

The anger rose in her throat. "You talked to my friends?"

"A few of them," said Kenny. "Don't worry, I didn't make it obvious. I'm a journalist. Getting information out of people is what I do."

She grabbed her bag, went to walk off. "Go pick on someone else, would you?"

"I'm not picking on you, Stephanie. I'm trying to tell your story."

She turned to him. "What's this for?"

"A documentary. The Grand Mage believes that the normal world will find out about sorcerers soon enough, and we want to use this documentary to answer questions and allay fears."

"That's what Ravel wants?"

"Yes."

"He's lying. He's a murderer and a traitor and he wants to take over. Everyone in Roarhaven does. They want to rule the mortals because they think the mortals are inferior. But I've seen what that's like. I've been to a world where sorcerers rule the planet and the mortals, the normal people like you, are slaves. That's all they are. So this little documentary of yours, Kenny, will be used to calm them down while Ravel gets things organised. You're going to help him take over the world."

"The Grand Mage explained all this to us," Kenny said, shaking his head. "There's been a huge misunderstanding. He doesn't want to take over, he wants to co-exist. He says once the Warlocks are defeated he'll talk to you and make you see that—"

"See them?" she said, pointing over the wall at the Warlocks. "They were meant to attack Dublin. Ravel's been planning this for years. He set the mortals up. But it's all gone wrong, and instead of attacking the poor defenceless mortals, the Warlocks are here, attacking us."

"Stephanie, you don't have all the information. I sat down with the Grand Mage and talked about—"

"He lied to you, Kenny. Hasn't anyone ever lied to you before?"

"Then why are you fighting alongside him, if he's so bad?"

"Because the Warlocks have to be stopped."

"That's what the Grand Mage said. That's all he wants."

"No it isn't. But none of this will make it into the documentary, will it? You'll either edit it out, or Ravel will. So what's the point of talking to you?"

"Because this might be your last chance to tell your family you love them," Kenny said gently. "If you have a message for them, I can make sure they get it if something happens to you."

Stephanie leaned forward. "My family know I love them. If I needed a documentary to tell them that, then I don't deserve the opportunity."

Resisting the urge to take the camera and hurl it over the side, she walked over to where Skulduggery was standing as NJ conjured up another magnifying window between the battlements. When NJ saw Stephanie, she smiled.

"Hi."

Stephanie grunted.

"I was in the Sanctuary earlier," NJ said, apparently unaware that a grunt was meant to indicate an unsociable attitude. "Fletcher's awake. The doctors say he'll be able to teleport in a day or so."

Stephanie frowned. "You know Fletcher?"

"Oh, yes," said NJ, and then her smile faltered. "I mean, not well. We're not close, or anything. We're just friends. Not even good friends. Just ordinary ones. Ordinary friends. I have a boyfriend. Well, I don't, but if I did, I mean, it's not that—"

"NJ," Skulduggery said, "could you please stop talking and finish what you're doing?"

"Yes," NJ said, blushing. "Sorry."

A moment later, she was done.

"There," she said. "Sorry, again, about the babbling. Sometimes I babble. I don't mean to. But I babble. I do. I'm trying to stop. Or at least cut down. It's not easy. Once, I babbled so much—"

"NJ," Stephanie said sharply. "Thank you for your help. You can go now. Go check on Fletcher, there's a good girl."

NJ nodded, smiled, and ran off.

Skulduggery peered through the magnifying window. "I see you were talking to Kenny," he said.

Stephanie didn't look at him as she answered. "They're making a documentary. That's what they think they're doing anyway. It's just propaganda that Ravel's going to use."

"What did you say?"

"Nothing much."

"He probably thinks you're her."

"Yeah, I got that. But don't worry. So long as you're around to constantly remind me that I'm not good enough, it shouldn't go to my head. Has Mantis reached them yet?"

"See for yourself," Skulduggery said, stepping to one side. Stephanie peered through the window. She could see nothing different. Charivari and his Warlocks were still on that hill with those Wretchlings, still focusing on the wall. She moved slightly, just in time to watch a sentry being yanked backwards and vanishing.

"They're there," Stephanie said. Whispered, actually.

Skulduggery nodded, looking through the window with her. Mantis's invisible army had sneaked right up on the hill without being noticed. Another sentry was lost to sight.

Any moment now the army would charge. Any moment...

Warlocks and Wretchlings vanished as a wave of invisibility swept over them, leaving only empty tents. From where Stephanie stood, there was no hill that seemed more peaceful. But down there, she knew, within those bubbles of invisibility, a battle was raging and people were dying. Blood was being spilled. Limbs were being shattered. Lives were being ended.

A fireball burst outside of the bubble. A stream of white energy emerged from mid-air, high above the hill, fading to nothing the further it travelled. A stream of purple energy carved a furrow in the grass.

So far, the Warlocks attacking the wall hadn't noticed that their commander and his company had disappeared.

"How long will it take?" Stephanie asked.

Skulduggery turned his head fractionally. "To subdue fifty Wretchlings and twenty Warlocks? I don't know. The Warlocks would be Charivari's personal guard."

"So the best and the toughest, then."

He didn't say anything.

They stayed there, watching the hill while the slow bombardment of the wall continued. Stephanie lost track of time. She started looking around, shifting her position to look through the magnification window at the Wretchlings. She found them fascinating. Artificial creatures. Just like she had once been.

"Something's happening," Skulduggery said, his voice low. She looked back at the hill as, one by one, the cloaking spheres collapsed, revealing the dead and the injured and the captured.

"Oh, no," said Stephanie, and her insides went cold. From

where she stood she had a wonderful view of the hill, and could clearly make out General Mantis and its soldiers, on their knees and surrounded by Warlocks.

That evening, Stephanie watched the Wretchlings drive stakes into the ground, all in a line that stretched from one side of the field to the other. The prisoners were brought forward, and each one was chained in place. Mantis itself was chained to the stake directly before the gates. Stephanie saw Regis down there as well, and Ashione. She was hurt. She could barely stay upright.

The Warlocks stood behind the line, watching the wall silently. Charivari stepped between them, until he was the only one out in the open. He was pale, and bald, and tall. Taller than Mevolent had been, certainly. Maybe ten feet tall, with scars that criss-crossed his muscles. He looked at the wall, maybe counting the cracks and the gaps, maybe calculating how much longer it'd stay up. He didn't say anything. He didn't shout up threats or insults. He didn't wave any flags or make any gestures.

When he was satisfied, he walked back through the line, the Warlocks parting for him. Moments later, white energy started to glow in the hands of his soldiers.

"Get ready," Skulduggery called. "Snipers, take careful aim. Try not to hit any of our own."

But the barrage didn't come. Instead, the glowing energy started to flicker, became white flames. Stephanie felt the alarm that rippled along the wall, but she didn't understand it. She didn't understand it until the prisoners began burning.

There were horrified cries beside her as the screams reached them. The prisoners strained against their bonds, but there was no escape. Mantis writhed on its stake like an insect in a frying pan.

"Rifle," Skulduggery said. Then, "Rifle!"

He snatched a gun from someone, put the stock to his shoulder and fired. Mantis jerked back and sagged against its chains.

Skulduggery shot the next man over. Then the next. Then he shot Regis, caught him in the chest, stopped his screaming. Ashione was rolling on the ground, trying to stamp out the flames. It took two shots to end her agony.

By now the other snipers along the wall had taken up the responsibility. Each shot took the life of a fellow soldier, and gradually the screaming grew less, and then stopped altogether.

The bodies continued to burn, black smoke rising from white flames.

69

QUIET MOMENTS

Night fell. The Energy-Throwers roamed the streets, waiting for the wraiths to come back. Stephanie stayed up on the wall. She couldn't sleep, not after what she'd seen. Her insides were knots sliding in acid. Her mouth was always dry, no matter how much water she drank. Fear, she supposed. This was true fear. She didn't like it much.

Losing Mantis and its army like that... that was a blow. That was a serious blow, and not just to their numbers. There were no smiles up on the wall. No jokes, no matter how bleak. Losing Mantis had robbed them of their humour. This was probably what hopelessness felt like.

She looked north, out over the dark countryside. Dublin was north. And north of Dublin, Haggard. Her family. Lying in bed, asleep, no idea that their fate was being decided out here under the sickle-bladed moon. She wanted nothing more than to be in her own bed in her own room, and not for the first time she wondered how Valkyrie could have done this for all those years. There was nothing brave about it. Nothing noble. Valkyrie had chosen magic and danger over her family, and that was something Stephanie could not understand. She wouldn't be here if she had any other option.

"You're really not her," said Fletcher.

She turned. He stood there, pale in the moonlight.

"I'd never have been able to sneak up on Valkyrie," he said. "I'd have had to teleport right behind her. But she'd have known. Whether she'd hear something, or feel it in the air, or just sensed that someone was behind her, you know that way sometimes you just know you're being watched? Or maybe you don't. Maybe it's a human thing."

"I'm human," Stephanie said. "If you cut me, do I not bleed? If you poison me, do I not die? And if you wrong me, shall I not have revenge?"

Fletcher looked at her. "Did you just make that up?"

She smiled softly. "It's Shakespeare. Kind of. I changed it a little. Paraphrased."

"Oh, that's right," said Fletcher, "you've got full access to all your memories, don't you?"

She nodded. "Everything I ever read. Or Valkyrie ever read. Or heard or saw or did. It's why I'm so good at exams. Are you feeling better?"

He shrugged. "Still shaky, but I'm OK. Woke up a few hours ago and no one would tell me what was going on. Have to admit, I didn't think Ravel would still be in charge."

"Well, apparently it's complicated," said Stephanie. "It's all about seizing the right time. If it were me, I'd just go right up to him and turn him to dust."

"Yeah, you're good at that, aren't you?"

His voice was tired and lacked venom, but his eyes were still full of hurt and anger.

"I did what I did so that I could live," she said. "It was self-defence."

"It was murder and it was attempted murder. You tried to kill Valkyrie."

"She never loved you, Fletcher."

"That's got nothing to do with—"

"Stop treating her like she's perfect."

He laughed. "Oh, I know she's not perfect. I know she's—"

"You know she's selfish," Stephanie cut in, "and vain, and egotistical, and you know she's uncaring. But look at you. You'd go back to her in an instant if she asked. Even if you knew that she was just with you for something to do, you'd fall in love with her all over again. You've forgiven her for cheating on you. You've forgiven her for treating you like an annoying, lovesick puppy."

"I really don't need to be insulted by you," Fletcher said, and started walking away.

"I would never cheat on you," she said before she could stop herself.

Fletcher stood still. She looked at his back. Her face was burning. She was blushing. She tried to fight it, tried to regain control and push down this horrible feeling of embarrassment, but every push made the feeling spill over even more. Fletcher turned.

"I don't understand you," he said. "You're not..."

"Don't say I'm not real. Don't say I'm not human."

"But you're not," he said, almost angrily. "You came out of a mirror. You're a stand-in. You're a, a weak imitation of the real thing."

"Good," said Stephanie. "I'm glad I'm a weak imitation. I wouldn't want to be a good one, because then I wouldn't care what you thought. I've grown, Fletcher. I'm more than I was."

"You're a killer," he said, and Stephanie darted forward, grabbed his arm before he could leave.

"And I regret it," she said. "I'm sorry I did it. I'm sorry I had to do it."

"Feeling bad doesn't make it OK."

"But feeling bad is new to me. Feeling anything is new to me. I still don't know how to deal with it. It's scary and ugly and makes me feel sick most of the time but, Fletcher, please, don't treat me like a thing."

"Then how should I treat you? After everything you've done, how should I treat you?"

She looked at him, into his eyes. "Like a girl," she said, and kissed him.

He shook his head. "You're not... you're not her."

"No." She kissed him again. "I'm me."

The breeze picked up, and the smell of rotting meat wafted to them.

"Wretchlings!" someone bellowed. "They're coming!"

Her heart lurching in her chest, Stephanie ran to the parapet. The darts were being fired, trailing white ropes. And now the Wretchlings came, emerging from the gloom, running up those ropes like demented acrobats, knives and swords and war hammers in their hands, swarming like ants over dropped food.

She whipped her head round to Fletcher. "The Energy-Throwers are in the streets. We need them up here. Get as many as you can."

Fletcher nodded and vanished.

Stephanie pulled the Sceptre from her bag, took aim, and black lightning cleared four Wretchlings from the nearest rope. But there were more behind. There were always more. She leaned out to get a better shot, only noticing the floating ball of energy at the last moment. She turned away, squeezed her eyes shut, heard the explosion as the blast picked her up and tossed her away like just another piece of rubble. She crunched to the ground, rolled three times and came to a groaning stop.

Skulduggery stood on the battlements, sending great gusts of wind to knock the Wretchlings from their ropes. Every few seconds he'd have to dodge to one side to avoid an energy stream from down below, but then he'd get right back to it. The handful of other Elementals on the wall followed his example. Some of them weren't so effective. Others weren't so good at dodging. Despite their efforts, the first Wretchling came over the wall and others followed.

Stephanie blasted one of them to dust and got to her feet. Three came at her. She got the first two, but the third grabbed the Sceptre, pushed it back while his other hand closed round Stephanie's throat. He had boils all over his face and a dagger in his belt. She pulled the dagger out and stuck it into his side. He made a sound like an angry cat and pushed her back further. She clawed at his face, bursting the boils, then slipped her finger into his mouth, her nail scraping by his clenched teeth. Curling her finger, she raked it out, felt his cheek split open in a spray of blood and pus. He howled, recoiled, and she jammed the Sceptre against his jaw and it flashed and he exploded into dust.

A flurry of movement and she ducked, spun, ran, Wretchlings right behind her, their hands snatching at her hair, at her jacket, pulling the stick from her back, too many to fight, their blades too close.

"Skulduggery!" she roared, running for the ledge, unable to stop, and they grabbed her and she jumped and they all went over.

Stephanie plummeted.

Below was darkness sprinkled with streetlights. The wind whipped away the screams of the Wretchlings before they reached her. She turned over as she fell, watching them fall with her, their eyes wide and mouths open, terror etched on their faces, their eyes fixed on the ground below.

And then someone else was falling between them, the skull betraying no emotion as gloved hands found her, and she slid into his arms and Skulduggery looped up, leaving the Wretchlings to continue their descent while Stephanie held on for dear, sweet life. He set her down on a rooftop across the street from the wall.

Her legs were shaky and every nerve was jangling and all she wanted to do was collapse, but she narrowed her eyes as he hovered over her. "Am I missing something?"

"You've done enough," he said. "Go back to Haggard."

"I can *help*."

"We're going to lose."

"No. We can use the Accelerator, start boosting magic."

"And when that happens there's going to be a lot of unstable people looking to do violent things. Whether we win or lose, Roarhaven isn't safe."

"But I have the Sceptre."

"And someone's going to kill you for it. Stephanie, go home. You can't help us any more. If we fail, you'll need to protect your family."

"No, I can—"

"I don't have time to argue. Valkyrie, please, for once in your life, do what I say."

She looked up at him. "I'm not Valkyrie."

His head dipped, the brim of his hat cutting across his brow like a frown, and then he rose higher. "Good luck," he said, and flew back to the wall.

70

SUPERCHARGED

They kept coming, a never-ending stream of Wretchlings. By morning the dead were three-deep up on that wall, and then their focus shifted, and they stopped trying to get over the wall and just came through it. The gates opened with a great splintering crack, and Wretchlings and Warlocks swarmed in and the Sanctuary mages met them. Magic was tossed to and fro and men and women went down screaming, but up close it was battle the old-fashioned way. Blood and blade and grunts and spittle. Vex hated the old-fashioned way.

A Wretchling with a face like a battered shovel came at him with a sword in his fist. Vex knocked the sword to one side, tried to swing his own, but there were too many people around, too much jostling for space. He almost apologised for the delay. *Hold on there like a good fellow and I'll kill you the moment I'm able. Nice weather for it, eh?*

Suddenly his arm had space and he jabbed out, puncturing the Wretchling's chest and shoulder and throat with the tip of his blade. Someone shoved him and he knocked the Wretchling to the ground. Vex stood on him, kicked him, stabbed him a little more until a Warlock barrelled through, roaring curses in some language Vex neither knew nor was interested to learn. Still too tight to really swing, Vex could only bash the opposing sword with his, making sure it didn't get too close. The crowd around them surged in all directions at once, and Vex found himself pressed up against the Warlock with his hands trapped below him. The Warlock had one arm pinned to his side, the other crushed against his own chest. They headbutted each other while they waited for a space to open up. The Warlock had a great big beard. Vex bit the beard and pulled back and the Warlock roared in displeasure. The beard tasted horrible.

Vex slipped on something and went under, cursing, suddenly lost in a forest of legs and boots that threatened to trample him into the ground. He tried to rise, got a knee in the face that knocked him sideways, finally reached up and grabbed hold of someone and dragged himself towards the light. He broke the surface, pressed the point of his sword under the bearded man's chin and thrust skywards. The sword jarred a little when it hit the underside of the man's skull, and he pulled it out again.

The fighting was spreading out a bit, now that the sudden, illogical eagerness for death and dying had abated. Energy crackled in Vex's hand and he blasted a Warlock who was about to do the same to him. A Wretchling leaped over Dai Maybury, who was rolling around in the dirt with a Warlock, and came at him with a swing that would have taken his head off if he hadn't blocked. Their swords clashed again and scraped off each other, screeching like fingernails on a chalkboard. Vex pushed him back, hacked at his arm, cleaving through muscle and bone. The Wretchling's sword fell, still gripped by his hand, and Vex slashed downwards into his throat. The Wretchling died standing, then toppled backwards, ripping Vex's weapon from his hands.

A sword caught him across the back, would have cut through to his spine were it not for Ghastly's clothes. He turned, grabbing on to the Warlock who powered into him. They went down in a tangle of arms and legs. God, this one was heavy. Vex tried

543

pushing him off and it was like pushing a wall of muscle. He poured his magic into his hand and unleashed it into the man's ribs, and the Warlock grunted and rolled sideways. His clothes were armoured, too, though, and he got to his feet a fraction of a second behind Vex. And he still had that sword.

He stepped in and swung, knocking Vex back. Vex pushed a Wretchling into the Warlock's next swing and grabbed his dagger as he died. He slashed at the Warlock's throat, missed, and the Warlock went low and took his leg out from under him. Vex rolled to avoid the sword that clanged off the ground next to his ear, wondered if the Warlock's boots were armoured. He plunged the dagger into his foot, got a screech in return. Obviously not.

Vex threw himself between the man's legs, ignoring the sword strikes his clothes absorbed. The Warlock started to hop about, trying to get at him, but Vex stayed on his knees, scurrying about underneath, keeping his head tucked below the Warlock's groin. Not the most dignified of ways to fight a battle, perhaps, but since when had dignity ever kept a man alive?

Someone dropped a war hammer and he dived at it, swung without looking. The hammer crunched into the side of the Warlock's knee. The knee caved in sideways and the Warlock screamed, toppled, landed on his elbows, still screaming. Vex stood, the Warlock screamed up at him, and the war hammer met his face and brooked no argument.

He turned to another Warlock, who backed away, his eyes focused on something behind him. Vex risked a glance, found himself staring along with everyone else. Six sorcerers hovered in the air, smiling. Vex recognised two of them. They had not been able to fly the last time they'd met.

The Accelerator-boosted mages sent columns of air rippling towards the enemy, so fiercely that they snapped bones and ruptured skin. They threw fire like napalm and Vex had to scramble to avoid being caught in the inferno. Flesh melted and dripped to the ground as the screams rose to the skies. The six sorcerers landed and strode towards the enemy, each one of them keeping the smile on their face. Wretchling and Warlock fell before them, and suddenly the unceasing tide through the gates slowed to a trickle.

A Wretchling jumped on one of the sorcerers, but increased strength seemed to be among the gifts the Accelerator bestowed. The sorcerer laughed as he held the Wretchling by the throat, legs kicking uselessly. He didn't even seem to care about the dagger in the Wretchling's hand, at least not until it was buried up to its hilt in his neck. The Wretchling was dropped and the sorcerer fell to his knees, gurgling blood, a look of surprise on his face.

Smiles faded on the faces of the other five sorcerers. A Warlock caught one of them full on with a beam of energy. It took her head off. The remaining four roared in anger and swept forward in a bloody swathe of destruction, but the enemy had their measure now. They could be killed, and so they were.

But, as the last of the six sorcerers fell, another ten appeared in the sky above them. And none of these were smiling.

Someone grabbed Vex from behind and he whirled, but when his elbow crunched into flesh he was standing on top of the wall.

"Fletcher! Sorry!" he said as the kid went stumbling. Saracen caught him, made sure he didn't fall.

"It's OK," Fletcher said, both hands to his face. "I really should have expected that."

Once he was sure he hadn't busted Fletcher's cheekbone, Vex joined Skulduggery and the Monster Hunters at the parapet, looking down. Each supercharged Roarhaven mage was dying, but they were taking down dozens of Wretchlings before they went. "Can't believe Erskine used the Accelerator," he said. "He knows it'll turn them nuts."

"As long as they're directed at the Warlocks and not us, I'm not complaining," Gracious muttered. Then he frowned. "Of course, it's only a matter of time before he *does* direct them at us, isn't it?"

"Ravel will send them after us the moment the tide turns in Roarhaven's favour," Skulduggery said. "By the looks of things, that could be anytime in the next few hours. So we need to strike now. Or rather, *I* do."

Saracen looked at him. "What?"

"I need you all to stay here. One of us won't be missed, but any more than one and the alarm will be raised and I'll never be able to get near him."

"So you're going up against Ravel alone?" Donegan asked. "Him and Mist and all their cronies?"

"I won't be alone," Skulduggery said, "and it's our best chance to catch him unprepared."

Saracen shook his head. "Splitting up again. How many times do I have to tell you what a bad idea that is? The Dead Men work best when we stay together."

"There is no Dead Men," Skulduggery said, sounding almost surprised that no one else had realised it. "Ghastly and Anton have been murdered. Ravel's betrayed us. Valkyrie is... gone. The Dead Men have had their last stand and we've fallen, Saracen. The three of us are all that remain."

The sounds of war faded for a moment as that quiet, simple fact settled into Vex's mind. They'd lost members before, but never so many, and they'd never lost one to betrayal. He looked at Saracen and Skulduggery, his friends, his brothers, and although they had history that would hold them together forever, he could feel the bonds between them start to loosen, and fall away. Suddenly Saracen Rue looked old and tired, and Skulduggery Pleasant came into focus as what he really was – a genius, a killer, a tortured soul, and the only true dead man among them.

71

IN THE SANCTUARY

China stepped over the sorcerer's unconscious body and sat at the desk, the monitors before her arranged like a shrine to voyeurism. Rooms, corridors, entrances and exits, all of them displayed in glorious, pixel-perfect definition. She found a card, wrote down the unconscious sorcerer's name – Susurrus – and the password she'd got out of him – mydogrex1 – and left.

In here, deep in the Sanctuary, she couldn't hear the explosions at the wall. She couldn't hear the fighting or the screams or the battle cries. She could see the tension on the faces of the people she passed, though. Everyone walked quickly, everyone spoke urgently. These were Roarhaven mages, people who had been part of Ravel's plan from the very beginning. It amused her to see them panicking. It made her smile.

She checked her watch. It was a delicate thing, thoroughly unsuited to what was to come, but she had to make do with what she had available to her. Gone were the days when she could afford the luxury of choosing a specific watch for a specific purpose. Ever since Eliza Scorn had destroyed her apartment – and most of her belongings – China had been forced to adopt a more practical approach to life. She acquitted herself well, as one would expect, but that didn't mean she liked it.

As the appointed minute clicked into being, Skulduggery Pleasant walked round the corner, holding a carved wooden stick. The face he wore was grave and humourless, the kind of face a person wouldn't want to examine too closely. Without even acknowledging his existence, China turned and started walking. He fell into step beside her, and they made their way to the cells. When Ghastly and Anton Shudder had been murdered, these cells were quickly filled by the sorcerers who tried to fight back. Once the Warlocks attacked, however, most of these sorcerers were released so that they could fight under Skulduggery's command. Most, but not all.

Skulduggery let his façade melt away, and opened the first two cells they came to. "Tipstaff," he said, "Mr Weeper, would you care to lend a hand in exacting a little justice?"

Staven Weeper emerged first. Young and a little too earnest for China's liking, he had nonetheless tried to attack Ravel on three separate occasions for what the Grand Mage had done. That earned him a few points in China's book, and so she did her best to ignore the way he mewled like a kitten when he saw her. Tipstaff, the ex-Administrator, stepped out and nodded to both her and Skulduggery. Ever the professional, he got straight to the point.

"By justice," he said, "I assume you mean bringing Erskine Ravel to task for the crimes he has committed."

"You assume correctly," Skulduggery said. "But we'll need your help to do it."

Weeper looked suddenly worried. "Um, my magic isn't really combat-based..."

"We know," China told him. "We won't need you to fight."

"Then I'm your man," Weeper said immediately. "Or I'd like to be. If you'd have me. Because I love you. I love you so much. If I were married, I'd leave her for you. I'm not married. But I'd still leave her. Just say the word."

"Focus, Staven."

"Yes. Sorry. I love you. Sorry. You must get that all the time. Sorry."

"Hush, boy," Tipstaff said. "Detective Pleasant, Miss Sorrows, what do you need us to do?"

"The Terror and the Scourge are being kept busy overseeing the boosting process in the Accelerator Room," said China, "which leaves Ravel and Mist protected by Syc and Portia and the Black Cleaver. We need you to find them, then call me with their location." She handed Tipstaff a card. "That name and password will get you into the security room."

Tipstaff gave a curt nod.

"We won't let you down!" Weeper said. "I vow to you, upon my very life, that I will succeed, or die trying."

"There's really no need for—"

"If I die, think of me fondly," Weeper said, his lower lip trembling.

Tipstaff sighed, and walked off towards the security room. Weeper dragged himself after him.

"That must get annoying," said Skulduggery.

"You have no idea," said China.

They walked the opposite way, deeper into the Sanctuary, avoiding large groups of mages if they could help it. No one stopped them. No one asked what their business was. Everyone was too concerned about the battle outside.

"I was on the wall earlier," China said. "Not for long. I just wanted to see what all the fuss was about. I did see a little bit of fighting, however."

"I'm sure you're coming to a point," Skulduggery said.

"Naturally. The reflection that prefers to be called Stephanie. Such a curious thing. It reminded me of a black-clad Pinocchio, battling side by side with the boys, just like the real Valkyrie would be doing, were she not an evil world-breaker."

"Annoyed, are you?" Skulduggery asked. "That this little slice of information got by you?"

"Somewhat," China admitted. "All it would have taken was one Sensitive who knew Valkyrie's face to have had a vision... I don't like being the last to know. In fact, I despise it."

"You can't know every little secret, China."

"But I want to. Do you know where she is?"

"Valkyrie? If I knew, I'd be there right now."

"Instead, you have her doppelgänger to occupy your time."

"Not any more. I sent her home to be with Valkyrie's family."

"Her?"

"Sorry?"

"The reflection. Stephanie. It's a her?"

Skulduggery didn't respond.

"There's nothing wrong with it being a her," China said. "Especially now. And maybe Valkyrie would even be proud to know that some part of her is still capable of fighting the good fight, even if she herself has fallen to the darker side of her nature."

Her phone buzzed, and she answered.

"The Grand Mage and Elder Mist have just entered what would appear to be the new Hall of Remembrance," said Tipstaff. "Syc and Portia have remained outside."

"And the Black Cleaver?" China asked.

"We can't see him," said Tipstaff. "We can see *you*, however."

There was a brief scuffle, and then Weeper came on with "Hi, China," before Tipstaff regained control.

"Apologies," he said. "As I was saying, we can see you. Continue down this corridor, take the second right, and then a left. The entrance to the Hall will be around the next corner."

China hung up. "We're close," she said, leading the way. They followed Tipstaff's directions, slowing as they approached the final corner. China pulled her hair back into a ponytail, and Skulduggery took off his hat, laid it carefully on the ground beside the carved stick.

They rounded the corner. At the far end of this corridor was a heavy door. Halfway between the door and the corner, Syc and Portia stood.

"What are you doing here?" Syc asked, a sneer on his lips. "The fighting is outside."

Skulduggery didn't answer, and neither did China. They just kept walking.

Portia's eyes narrowed. "Syc, I think we are being betrayed. I think they mean to betray us."

"Finally," said Syc, his face lighting up. "I've been wanting to pull them apart for ages."

Portia and Syc stood side by side. China walked right up to Portia and Skulduggery walked right up to Syc. Portia smiled, knees bending, getting ready to fight. At the last moment, Skulduggery darted across, smacked her in the jaw and took her off her feet. Syc appeared frozen for a moment, and the sigils on China's knuckles flashed into his line of sight right before she broke his nose.

He went stumbling, howling in pain. China kept close. She couldn't afford to let him regain his senses. Her fist crunched into his side, smashing ribs. Letting him regain his senses would mean letting him turn into a giant spider. Another punch, this one to the belly, forcing the air from his lungs. And letting him turn into a giant spider was not on the agenda. He tried to grab her and she batted his arm away and drove an elbow into his temple. Not today.

Syc went sideways, his face a bloody mess, his equilibrium shot to hell. She glanced back at Skulduggery, but he was already following Portia round the corner. Portia was not looking like her usual composed self. She looked positively dishevelled.

That's what China liked about these kinds of people, and she'd seen plenty of them in her time. Young, strong, vibrant and cocky. Syc came at her and she smashed his face into the wall. It was so satisfying, making them hurt. She tapped the sigil on her palm and planted her hand over his face. She felt the power snap through him and his whole body jerked wildly and he collapsed.

She looked down. So, so satisfying. She allowed herself a moment to imagine how satisfying it was going to be, doing the same to Eliza Scorn.

She closed her eyes, relaxing. When she opened them, she walked to the corner and stopped.

Portia was on the ground, motionless, her eyes closed. Unconscious or dead, China didn't know. Didn't care. But walking up the corridor was the Black Cleaver, scythe ready. Skulduggery walked towards him, the carved stick lighting up in his hand.

The Cleaver moved in, straight for the kill. Skulduggery deflected the blade and the Cleaver whirled with a kick that Skulduggery avoided. The scythe flashed, sweeping in again and again, and Skulduggery blocked and moved and parried. The stick flashed whenever it struck the Cleaver's reinforced uniform, its effects muted but noticeable. The more Skulduggery hit him, the warier the Cleaver became, until he focused his efforts on taking the stick out of the equation. The scythe's handle smacked against Skulduggery's hand and the stick dropped, went skittering across the floor. Immediately Skulduggery grabbed him and slammed him against the wall, and the Cleaver had to drop the scythe to free up his hands.

They pushed away from the wall and the tempo of the fight increased, both fighters getting the measure of the other. The Cleaver, much like Tanith Low, was agile enough to jump and spin and throw extravagant, unexpected kicks, whereas Skulduggery was the down-to-earth fighter he'd always been. Elbows and headbutts and grabs. He left the fancy stuff to other people. Always had.

The Black Cleaver caught a punch and drove his forearm into the back of Skulduggery's elbow. There was a sound, somewhere between a crack and a pop, and Skulduggery stumbled, his sleeve flapping. The Black Cleaver looked, almost in surprise, at the half-an-arm it now held in its grip. Skulduggery fell to his knees, groaning in pain. The Cleaver dropped the arm and picked up his scythe, and China stepped round the corner, her sigils glowing.

But, as the scythe swung down, a wave of darkness burst from Skulduggery, hurling the Black Cleaver into the far wall with enough force to shatter every bone in his body.

China stepped back out of sight, but kept watch. The shadows hovered over Skulduggery's hunched form, surrounding him like a shell, pulsing softly. A tendril wrapped round the broken piece of his arm and pulled it slowly across the floor, dropping it at his knee the way an eager dog might drop the day's newspaper. Without looking up, Skulduggery threaded the arm through his sleeve and it reattached. His gloved fingers flexed, and he got to his feet, moving like a weary man. Even though he had no lungs, and no need for breath, he inhaled deeply, and as he did so the shadows were pulled into him, disappearing into his chest.

China ducked back, trying to process what she had just seen.

The sudden silence tugged her from her thoughts. She dragged Syc to the corner, and flung him as far as she could. His head smacked off the ground and she followed him, making a show of smoothing down her hair.

Skulduggery looked over and she gave him an easy smile. He nodded back, and picked up his hat.

"You're not finished here," said a voice behind her.

She turned. The Terror and the Scourge stood there, thick black liquid running from their eyes, nostrils and mouths, seeping over their skin, their clothes, through their hair. Their limbs jerked, lengthening, hands becoming talons. They reared back – giant spider-legs bursting from their torsos – and then dropped forward to land on all fours. Or all *eights*, really.

They chattered as they grew, a third eye opening on each of

their heads, becoming giant black spiders with rapidly hardening armoured shells.

Skulduggery walked up to them, handing China the Black Cleaver's scythe as he passed. He held Valkyrie's stick in his hand.

Smiling, China accompanied him.

72

RESCUE

Watching Fletcher Renn fight was an incredible experience.

The boy had no skills as such, he couldn't throw a punch to save his life, but he had talent, and talent went a long way. Vex did his best to keep track of him, and it wasn't easy. Appearing and disappearing in and around crowds of Wretchlings, turning up with all manner of weapons – baseball bats, sledgehammers, iron bars and tasers. Vex even saw a few axes in there. He got knocked around a fair bit, a few times he even got jumped on, but he would always vanish and then arrive back without his assailant. Moments later, those same assailants would drop from the clouds, screaming all the way down.

Fletcher teleported to the top of the wall to get his breath back, and Vex frowned. Up close, the boy looked remarkably pale.

"How are you feeling?" Vex asked.

Fletcher gave him the thumbs up as he panted, but Vex shook his head.

"You're exhausted. You need to rest."

"I'm fine," he said. "Just gimme a... second..."

"Fletcher, look at me. You need to rest. Using magic is the

same as any other physical activity. It drains you. If you go back down there in this condition, you'll make a mistake and you'll wind up dead."

Fletcher looked like he was about to argue, but he was too weak to start.

"There," Saracen said, pointing through the magnifying window. "Charivari."

Vex hurried over to him, scanning the ground outside the city walls. He saw him then, Charivari, in among all the Wretchlings and the Warlocks, but looming over them, a bald-headed mass of muscle and ferocity.

"Right," said Vex. "Wow. OK. In the flesh he's a bit bigger than I'd... expected. Gracious. You're the strongest of us. Care to have a go?"

Gracious took a moment to peer through the window, then shook his head. "God, no, no way, see the size of him? He'd step on me."

"But you're really strong."

"To be honest, he looks like he's more Donegan's type of opponent anyway. I'd hate to keep him all for myself."

"I don't mind," said Donegan.

"No, no, I insist."

"I really don't mind, though."

"Or we could tell one of our super-sorcerers to do it," said Saracen.

Vex looked at Fletcher. "Sorry to do this to you, but do you think you can take us down there?"

"No problem," Fletcher said, wiping the sweat from his forehead. "Everyone hold on to each other."

They linked up and Fletcher teleported them into the streets, and suddenly they were surrounded by chaos and shouts, screams and roars.

"Hey!" Saracen called, running up behind three Roarhaven mages who were practically glowing with newly-boosted power.

"Charivari's out there! He's the big one! Take him out and these guys won't have a leader!"

The three mages turned, and Vex muttered a curse. Only two of them were from Roarhaven. The third was English, and the last time Vex had seen him, he was strangling Caius Caviler to death.

Grim's eyes found him, and he smiled.

He barrelled past Saracen, shoved Fletcher out of the way and grabbed Vex, lifting him off his feet. "I was hoping no one would kill you," he said. "Wanted the pleasure of that all to myself."

Gracious jumped on Grim from behind, wrapped an arm round his throat, and there was a surge from the gate and then the Wretchlings were everywhere. Vex fell, saw Gracious and Grim go down, had to scramble up to avoid being trampled himself. He fired an energy stream into a Warlock's face and smashed an elbow into a Wretchling's jaw, and all the while he was being carried back on a wave of snarling movement.

And then, from that wave, a monstrous shark. Vex tried to twist away, but Grim had him. Up this close, he could see the madness in those eyes. Vex poured magic into his hand, but Grim took hold of his wrist, crushed it. Vex's scream evolved into a string of curses as he staggered free, two Wretchlings now hacking into Grim with their blades. Vex didn't expect them to last long, but Grim tore through them faster than even he'd anticipated.

Vex tried to run, but one of Grim's friends caught him, turned him as Grim strode forward. He sneered and pulled back his fist for the killing blow, and then for his next trick he turned to dust.

Vex blinked. He what?

Black lightning hit the sorcerer behind him and Vex fell to his knees, eyes widening as Stephanie Edgley emerged from the fighting, Sceptre in hand.

She fired again. Two Wretchlings exploded into dust and the third super-sorcerer took to the skies, but lightning found him and fried him and reduced him to a grey swirling cloud that the breeze took deeper into the streets of Roarhaven.

Stephanie grabbed Vex's arm, helped him stand. He held his injured wrist close to his chest, and managed a smile.

"I thought you'd gone home."

"No one would lend me their car. Where's Skulduggery?"

"Gone after Ravel."

"Alone?"

"Apparently not," Vex said, and looked around them. Fighting everywhere. "No way out," he muttered.

Stephanie hefted the Sceptre in her grip. "Good," she said.

73

WAR DESPONDENT

War is hell.

That's what was going through Kenny's mind as he followed Slattery through the chaos. War is hell and it's scary and how on earth is anyone supposed to know what side they're on? He saw magic people fighting other magic people and some of them threw fire and others had light coming out of them, and there were these things that looked like badly-stuffed monster-men running about snarling at everyone. Everywhere there were explosions and gunshots and screaming, and energy beams and swords and those people in grey with the scythes. It was a blur of confusion and panic and fear and exhilaration, but mostly fear.

Kenny saw someone he recognised, a girl in black.

"Valkyrie!" he shouted, and grabbed Slattery's arm, pointed. Slattery nodded, his camera moving with him. Kenny was sweating and his eyes were wide and he knew he had a terrified expression on his face, whereas Slattery had never looked so calm. He envied him.

They moved along the outskirts of the fighting, keeping Valkyrie Cain in sight. The closer they got, the more faces Kenny recognised. Ravel had given him their names. Dexter Vex, Saracen

Rue, Donegan Bane, Gracious O'Callahan. They looked bloody and battered, but they fought off those misshapen monster-men like it was just another day at the office.

Kenny found a place to crouch, out of the way of the chaos, and he pulled Slattery in beside him. They watched Valkyrie Cain fire black lightning from a golden stick, and a monster-man turned to dust as it ran for her. He heard Slattery say "Whoah" under his breath, and despite himself he started grinning. This was amazing stuff. This was *beyond* amazing. This was going to change the world.

Someone was fighting his way towards them, surging through the battle, tossing monster-men and sorcerers alike out of his way. He burst through and Kenny stared. He must have been ten-foot tall, bare-chested and bare-armed, veins standing out like cords against his skin, and all the more terrifying for it. He was a mountain of a man with a bald head and hands made for crushing.

"Charivari," said Dexter Vex, and whatever he said next was lost amid the racket and the screams.

The big man, Charivari, walked into the middle of the group, seemingly unconcerned that he was surrounding himself with the enemy. More words were spoken, more words lost. Kenny only hoped the camera was picking them up. They'd do their best to isolate them in post-production later. He had a feeling whatever was being said was important.

Gracious O'Callahan suddenly jumped forward, the small man going up against the mountain, but when his fist connected, it shook Charivari, drove him back a few steps. Dexter Vex raised his left hand and a beam of energy crackled into Charivari's shoulder, sending him spinning. Valkyrie missed with the black lightning, but Donegan Bane caught him in the back with another energy blast. And then O'Callahan again, jumping high, slamming a fist into the bigger man's jaw, and Charivari fell.

Kenny realised he'd been holding his breath. He let it out. Was that it? That was it. The big man was beaten. Good guys win again.

Charivari reached out and grabbed O'Callahan's ankle and flung him into Valkyrie. They went down and she lost the golden stick. Bane fired off another blast, but Charivari rolled out of the way, came up on one knee. The veins that covered his body suddenly pulsed, and a ball of energy shot from his hand into Bane's chest, taking him off his feet. Rue jumped in, swinging a sword that Charivari dodged, and Vex joined him, his right hand cradled across his chest, his left hand crackling. Kenny saw Slattery moving up behind them and his eyes widened. How the hell had he got all the way over there?

Vex fired and the energy stream hit Charivari, rocked him but didn't drop him. Rue's sword opened a gash on Charivari's leg.

Kenny waved frantically at Slattery. He was too close. He was going to get spotted. Slattery saw him but ignored him, moving around for a better angle.

Cameramen. They believed the lens was a shield, protecting them from harm. He was going to get himself killed.

Muttering curses, Kenny moved forward. He stayed low, keeping his eyes on the clearest route to Slattery, ignoring the fight going on right beside him. O'Callahan was back in the action and Bane was running in, but Kenny kept his eyes fixed straight ahead. He could marvel at it all in the editing room when it was all over. First he had to get there.

He went to grab Slattery's arm and a stray beam of energy sizzled through the cameraman's chest, killing him instantly. He fell backwards, dead with his eyes open, a look of surprise on his face.

Kenny stared down at him.

This was confusing. This was... He looked up, feeling the need to call a halt to everything, to point to Patrick Slattery, to tell them that something had gone terribly, terribly wrong. But all around, people fought and died, and none of them felt the need to call a time out.

He didn't quite know what to do. What was the protocol at a

time like this? He was vaguely aware of the possibility that he was in shock.

Kenny picked up the camera, turned it and filled the lens with Slattery's body. Then he stood up straight, turned the camera towards Charivari. As he watched the fight, something was building in his chest. It wasn't fear any more. Not really. It was just... an urge. An urge to get away. To just run.

He looked into the viewfinder. He saw O'Callahan hit Charivari and Charivari blast Rue. Charivari's veins pulsed again and another ball of energy barely missed Vex, exploding against the wall behind him. And there was Valkyrie, searching for the golden stick, and Charivari saw her and fired another ball of energy and it exploded and Valkyrie Cain was... gone.

Kenny took his eye away from the viewfinder. She was gone. Vaporised. Dead. Valkyrie Cain. His subject. The girl who risked her life to save the world. The girl who gave her life.

Kenny turned, and he ran, and he kept on running.

74

THE THICK OF IT

tephanie fell to the ground and Fletcher released her, went tumbling, vanishing and reappearing as the residual energy crackled through him. She looked up to see a forest of legs. Someone crashed into her, a sorcerer fighting a Wretchling. They were all around. She was outside the wall and they were all around. Fletcher called her name and she reached for him, but he teleported, and didn't come back.

Right then. Out here all alone.

A Wretchling ran at her and she jumped up. Instead of retreating against the swinging axe, she charged into him, twisting her hip and flipping him, and they both went down and went rolling. Stephanie's fingers curled around an open wound on his face and she tore downwards, splitting the skin and he screamed, and she tore the axe from his grip and buried it in his head. She saw the blood and jerked away. Killing with the Sceptre was easy – it was all black lightning and dust. It was clean. But this... this was messy and horrible and she didn't like it. Too much could go wrong. She needed the Sceptre.

She looked up. She could see the gate from where she was, but between the gate and where she stood there was a war being fought.

She took the mask from her pocket, pulled it on, threaded her ponytail through the back. She pulled on the gloves and zipped the jacket up to her chin. Then she tugged the axe free, and ran for the gate.

She swung the axe into a Wretchling's leg as she passed, took an arm off another. One of them burst through the fighting. She blocked his sword with her gauntlet and her axe bit into his neck, almost took his head off. He fell awkwardly, tearing the axe from her hands. She picked up his sword, used that to chop and stab her way through. There was a ring of Cleavers, their scythes a blur, their grey uniforms spattered with blood. Wretchlings ran at them and died. Then suddenly a stream of yellow energy cut through two of them like they weren't even there. A Warlock strode forward, building up to another blast.

Stephanie altered course, squeezing past two fighting women, and as the Warlock raised his glowing hand, she brought the sword down on his wrist. The hand fell and light spilled from the wound, and Stephanie slashed at his midsection and more light spilled. The Warlock fell to his knees and Stephanie turned as a screech rose up behind her, almost avoided the blade that crunched into her head.

The world spun and she went sprawling. The screeching Wretchling kicked her, kicked her again, then brought his sword down into her chest. It hurt. Not as much as the blow to the head, and definitely not as much as it would have done were she not wearing these clothes, but it hurt nonetheless.

She'd lost her own sword when she fell, so she scrambled up empty-handed as the Wretchling swung at her. She caught the blade under her arm and stepped in, grabbed him and kicked at his knee. He screeched again, in pain this time, and she kicked that knee twice more before she felt it splinter. He fell back and she ripped his sword from his hands.

Through a gap in the fighting, she saw the Warlock. The cut to his midsection had healed, and the injury to his wrist had closed over, leaving him with a stump. His mouth was widening, his teeth long and dark, and his eyes were on her.

Stephanie turned, started hurrying for the gate.

A Wretchling stumbled into her, realised she was the enemy, and swung. She blocked, the impact juddering up her arms, but when she blocked the return swing, she lost her sword. She immediately lunged into him, biting at his neck as they staggered into someone else. She found a dagger in his belt and pulled it out, jammed it up into his armpit. His strength began to fade and she tripped him, fell on top, withdrew the dagger and used his face to push herself to her feet. He grabbed her ankle and she kicked him and he let her go.

Before her, a sorcerer and a Wretchling held each other in headlocks and lurched about like an exhausted, four-legged spider. The point of a spear whistled by Stephanie's face – she felt the shifting air flow through the eyehole of her mask – and a Wretchling pulled it back, tried stabbing her again. She ducked behind the four-legged spider and the Wretchling followed, cursing her, jabbing with the spear. The fighters around them closed in and the Wretchling was swallowed by the surge, and Stephanie left him to it. She slashed at an arm to move it out of her way, almost tripped over a screaming man, and looked back to see the Warlock barrelling towards her.

His left hand closed round her jacket and he picked her up and slammed her to the ground. He knelt on top of her, mouth widening as it opened, those teeth longer and darker than they had been a moment before. She'd cut off his hand, weakened him. He needed her soul to grow strong again.

The Warlock lowered his head to bite, and stopped. He pulled back, looked at her weirdly, and she took the opportunity to plunge the dagger between his ribs. Warm light spilled from the wound and he jerked away, and she stabbed again and again and pushed him off. She rolled on top of him, went to stab his chest. His good hand grabbed her wrist. She snatched the dagger into her other hand and sank the blade into his throat. He gagged. She got up. He rolled on to his side, light shining from every wound. Then the light faded, and turned to blood, and the blood leaked out of him as he died.

She got to the gate, squeezed through, but tripped, went stumbling, and hands reached for her, pulled her up, right into the snarling face of a female Warlock.

Stephanie cried out as the Warlock lifted her, then slammed her to the ground. Punches came next, rocking Stephanie's head from one side to the other. When the Warlock realised her punches were having little effect, her finger scrabbled at Stephanie's neck and she pulled the mask from her head. She threw it into the crowd of fighters and Stephanie tried to heave her to one side. That was her mask. Ghastly made that for her. She started to rise, but the woman punched her and this time there was nothing to disperse the impact. The fist crunched against her cheek and her teeth rattled. She fell back, her thoughts disconnected from the world around her.

The Warlock opened her mouth wide, wider, wider, those teeth small and sharp, that mouth getting big, bigger and bigger, and Stephanie sat up, thrust her fist into the Warlock's mouth, punching the back of her throat.

The Warlock gagged, recoiled, her eyes bulging, but Stephanie went with her, kept her fist in there, driving her back, snarling as they rolled. Now she was on top, and she put her weight behind it and curled her hand and jammed it down the Warlock's gullet. She grabbed something, she didn't know what, her fingers tightening round it, and she yanked, twisted it sideways, and the woman's eyes rolled in her head and she stopped struggling.

Stephanie yanked her arm out, taking a few teeth with it, and she hauled herself up and ran back to where her friends were battling Charivari. She broke through a wall of bodies.

Charivari had them beaten. Saracen lay on his side, unconscious or dead, Stephanie didn't know which. Donegan was against one wall, trying to stand. By the way he held his ribs, she could tell they were broken. Dexter was staggering away from Charivari and Gracious stood, covering his retreat. He was battered and bloody, but his fists were raised.

"That all you got?" he called out.

Charivari struck him and he flew backwards, hit the wall and dropped. He took a moment in the dirt to feel sorry for himself, then pushed himself up into a sprinter's start. Stephanie watched him take a couple of deep breaths and then he bolted, ran straight at Charivari, who hit him again, and again he flew backwards.

Suddenly Fletcher was at Stephanie's elbow. "You're all right," he said, panting for breath. "I thought you were – I thought you'd been—"

"Fletcher, the Sceptre. Where is it? Help me look for it."

He shook his head. He looked weak. "I'll handle this," he said. "I'll tap him, drop him from the sky."

"Fletcher, no."

She grabbed him, but he took her hand, removed it from his arm. "Stephanie, I'll be back in a second."

He teleported to the spot right behind Charivari, but he swayed, like he was dizzy, and the back of Charivari's hand smashed into him.

"Where are your heroes?" Charivari asked, walking up behind Vex. "Where is Ghastly Bespoke, or Anton Shudder, or Skulduggery Pleasant? Where are the men you send to take down men like me?" His fist came down on Vex's shoulder and Vex cried out, dropped to his knees.

Stephanie looked away, her eyes searching for the Sceptre.

"And where is Erskine Ravel," Charivari asked loudly, "your great and glorious leader?"

"Ravel's no leader of ours," Vex answered.

"No? Then why do you protect him? Send him out to me. I know his secrets. I know what he was trying to do. Let me look upon the face of the man who started all this. I want to see him. I want to look into his eyes as I crush everything he has built."

"Stay right here," Vex said, trying to stand. "I'll go get him..."

Vex's legs gave out and he collapsed.

"Ravel!" Charivari shouted. "Show yourself!" He picked up a fallen sword and crouched, letting the blade rest on the back of Vex's neck. "Show yourself or I start taking the heads of your friends!"

He looked around, waiting for a reply, then shrugged and looked down at Vex. "You need better friends."

"He's not my friend."

"Obviously."

Charivari raised the sword.

"Stop!" Stephanie shouted, running forward.

Charivari looked at her. "I was wondering what had happened to you."

"If you kill him," Stephanie said, "you'll never find Ravel. We'll hide him away. You'll never get to him."

"Where is he?"

"Don't hurt anyone else and I'll take you to him."

"You have three minutes to bring him to me."

"No, you'll have to come with—"

"Three minutes."

Her argument died on her lips when she glimpsed the Sceptre, half hidden by a dead Wretchling, a mere arm's reach away from where Charivari was crouched.

"OK," she said, walking forward, trying to keep her eyes locked on to Charivari's, trying to get him to focus on her. "I can call him from up here. Or Dexter can."

"And who is Dexter?"

"The man whose head you want to take."

"Oh," said Charivari, "*Dexter*. Is that true, Dexter? Can you call Ravel from up here?"

Vex didn't respond. In annoyance, Charivari raised the sword a little higher.

"No!" Stephanie cried, darting closer. "Stop! I can do it! Just let me do it!"

"No tricks, girl. Or I take your head, too."

"No tricks, I promise," Stephanie said. "In his jacket there's a black box. If you give that to me, I can use it to signal Ravel."

Charivari's free hand patted Vex's jacket, and Stephanie waited for him to glance down, just glance away from her, that's all she needed him to—

Charivari looked down at Vex and Stephanie dived. She rolled and Charivari's sword cut the dead Wretchling in half and Stephanie fumbled with the Sceptre as she kept rolling, and she fired and missed as she got to her feet and fell back as Charivari flung the blade. It missed her by a hair's breadth, and she tripped and reeled and he came for her, smacked into her, lifting her off her feet as easily as she'd swat a fly. She hit the ground and rolled and came up and backpedalled, and Charivari grabbed another sword and threw it and it hit her shoulder and spiralled away and she toppled. But as she toppled she fired, and Charivari dived out of the way of the black lightning. She fired again, but he grabbed a corpse, used it as a shield. It turned to dust and he grabbed another, threw it and Stephanie had to scramble to avoid it. A shadow fell over her and she turned, and his huge hand closed round her throat and pinned her against the wall and she jammed the Sceptre under his chin.

They froze.

Charivari's eyes flickered down to the black crystal, then back up to meet hers.

"All I have to do is squeeze," he said.

"All I have to do is think," she replied.

"I am not the monster here, girl. Ravel had my people killed. He is responsible for all of this."

"I know."

"Then let me kill him."

"I would, but how do I know you'll stop there? You've moved against the Sanctuaries. You'd probably expect them to retaliate. Best thing for you to do, from your perspective, would be to wipe them out while you have the chance. Then what happens to the mortals?"

"I have no interest in mortals."

"But I do. I want them to live normal lives. You jeopardise that."

"Then it appears we are at an impasse. If I kill you, you kill me. If you kill me—"

Black lightning flashed and Charivari turned to dust and Stephanie rubbed her throat. "I kill you."

Stephanie looked around, chose Fletcher to run to first. He groaned as she made him sit up. The left side of his face was badly swollen, his eye was closed and blood ran from his burst lips. If he was lucky, the only thing that was broken was his jaw.

"Look," said Vex.

Stephanie looked around, then followed his gaze upwards, and her insides went cold.

Vex pulled Fletcher to his feet. "Fletcher, listen to me. I know it hurts. It's going to hurt a lot more in a few minutes. I know you're tired. But you have to teleport one more time, OK? You have to teleport us back up to the wall. Can you do that?"

Fletcher nodded, his eyes glassy. Stephanie and Vex held on, and Fletcher took a moment. He swayed again, then furrowed his brow. Just when Stephanie thought he wasn't going to be able to do it, they were on the wall.

Vex put Fletcher sitting down, then joined Stephanie at the parapet, looking up.

Valkyrie stood in the sky, below the clouds, looking down at them all.

No, not Valkyrie. Darquesse. Valkyrie was gone now. Only Darquesse remained.

75

UNEVEN ODDS

thousand questions rattled inside Stephanie's head. She chose the simplest one. "What is she wearing?"

"She's dressed like a Bride of Blood Tears," Vex said.

The wind whipped at her clothes. It must have been freezing. Darquesse didn't seem to notice.

"How long has she been up there?" Stephanie asked.

"I don't know," Vex said. "She just drifted down out of the clouds, like she wanted a better look. God knows how long she's been watching."

Below Darquesse, the fighting continued. The Roarhaven mages killed dozens of Warlocks and Wretchlings, and the Warlocks and Wretchlings eventually took each one of them down. The mages who flew only looked downwards – never up. The Warlocks who fought only looked at their enemies – never beyond them.

"What's the range on the Sceptre?" Vex asked.

"I... I don't know."

"You might not get a better shot. She's not moving."

Stephanie looked at him. "You don't want to try and talk to her?"

"She's too dangerous. We take the shot when we have the shot."

"Maybe we should let Skulduggery know."

"You know as well as I do that he's not going to make the right decision. I don't want to kill Valkyrie. I want to save her. But we don't have a choice. Kill the girl, save the world. It's a simple equation. I take full responsibility for this, do you hear me? Do it. That's an order."

Stephanie raised the Sceptre, and hesitated. "She's very far away, and this thing doesn't come with a targeting system. If I miss, she'll come down here and kill us."

"That's probably what she's going to do anyway," said Vex. "May as well give her a reason."

Lightning travels at 3,700 miles per second. By the time Stephanie registered the black crystal flash, the lightning would have already struck its target. She took a deep breath, and aimed.

And just as she was about to fire, Darquesse turned her head and looked right at her.

"Oh, hell," Stephanie breathed.

But instead of attacking, Darquesse waved. And then, like she was diving from an invisible board, she arced up and swooped down, and sped towards the earth.

She hit the ground with such force that Stephanie could *see* the shockwave that threw back Warlocks and Wretchlings and mages alike. Darquesse stood slowly in the clearing, the battlefield suddenly quiet as both sides appraised this new player in the game.

A Wretchling stepped forward. Darquesse allowed him to approach. His sword glinted in the sunlight. He sprang at her and she killed him. Stephanie didn't see exactly what she'd done, but it involved a lot of blood and it was over in a flash.

A Warlock tried next. He raised his arm and she raised hers. His hand lit up and a beam of white energy hit Darquesse's open palm. He stepped forward, curling his body, putting everything he had into it. Darquesse just stood there. When the beam failed and the Warlock sagged, Darquesse flicked her hand and his body came apart.

One of the flying Roarhaven mages thought this was hilarious. Stephanie could hear his laughter, the laughter of a fool who saw victory because he was too dumb to recognise defeat. The Warlock's head came to a rolling stop near Darquesse. She picked it up, threw it. It went straight through the laughing mage's chest like a cannonball.

A floating sphere of white energy drifted to Darquesse as she stood there. She observed it, reached out to touch it. Stephanie was pretty sure she saw her smile, and then it exploded so brightly that she had to look away. When she looked back, Darquesse was still standing there.

Stunned silence. Every moment that passed, Stephanie expected to hear a battle cry, as either the Warlocks or the mages took the fight to Darquesse. But no. No battle cry. In the end it was Darquesse herself who instigated the slaughter.

Stephanie stepped to the magnifying window just in time to see Darquesse gently sweep her arm to one side, her fingers curling. She suddenly snapped her arm back and a line of Warlocks split apart, limbs twisting in the air. Warlocks and Wretchlings ran at her, then, and she danced through them, ignoring their swords and their magic, her wounds healing even as the blows landed. Her hands were her swords, her fingers her daggers. She moved impossibly fast, spinning and whirling. Bodies and body parts went flying over the heads of the Warlocks and mages who swarmed her. And swarm her they did. Stephanie watched as they piled on top of her, a mountain of men and women. For a moment she thought they might even succeed, but then she heard the screaming, and a moment later the mountain blew apart.

A Roarhaven mage staggered to his feet in the stillness that followed. He sent a torrent of flames straight into Darquesse's face. The flames swirled around her, but they were darkening, and when she sent a handful back to him they were black, and they enveloped him and he burned where he stood.

Stephanie had seen black flames like that before. It wasn't her memory, it was Valkyrie's, but she owned it nonetheless, and she knew it as well as if she had been standing in Cassandra's steam chamber herself. In the vision, it was those black flames that had killed Stephanie's family.

Warlocks and mages and Wretchlings alike tried to run, but the unnatural fire leaped from Darquesse's hands and spread through them like they were dry trees in a forest. She rose up off the ground, her arms outstretched, orchestrating the flames with her fingers. The fire swirled, and surged, and roared, and Wretchlings burst apart before the fire even reached them, their rotten bodies unable to cope with the heat. Warlocks and Roarhaven mages died screaming, and still the black flames spread.

Stephanie watched, fascinated. "She's going to kill them all," she said.

Vex didn't say anything, and Stephanie felt something else stirring within her. Behind the fascination, beneath the admiration, there was something else, a feeling, growing more powerful the more she saw.

It was fear, she realised. It was horror. She was looking at the end of the world, and it was wearing her face.

76

CHINA'S FINAL ACT

Every Sanctuary had a Hall of Remembrance. Some were simple affairs, with photographs and portraits of deceased Sanctuary operatives lining the walls. Some were more imaginative, with floating head projections appearing when a certain floor panel was stepped on. The Hall of Remembrance in Roarhaven was as lavish as China was expecting. A large room with a massive wooden pillar in its centre, reaching from floor to ceiling and shaped like a volcano. Upon that pillar were carved hundreds of names.

Erskine Ravel and Madame Mist were carving even more when China and Skulduggery walked in.

"Do you mind coming back later?" Ravel asked without turning. He was wearing his Elder robes. "There are quite a few names we have to add to the list of fallen sorcerers. Once we're done here, we can talk."

"There won't be any talking," said Skulduggery.

"Ah, I see," he said, "I wondered which one of us would be the first to move against the other." He put down the carving tool, scanned the pillar, and pressed a name. A full-body image of Anton Shudder appeared to his left. He pressed another name, and Ghastly Bespoke appeared. Their images were so solid that China half expected them to start moving and talking.

"Pretty good, aren't they?" said Ravel. "Very lifelike. Some of them aren't so good, some of the conversions from old photos and paintings haven't worked out so well, but all in all I'm happy with what we've done to honour their memories." He paused. "The moment the first mage stepped out of the Accelerator, I should have sent him to kill you."

"But you didn't," said Skulduggery.

"No I didn't. Too distracted. You must think we're going to win, then, right? If you expected me to move against you at any moment, the battle must be tipping in our favour. Is it?"

"With these boosted sorcerers of yours," Skulduggery said, "maybe."

"Good," said Ravel. "Good. Bloody Warlocks, eh? Why couldn't they have just attacked Dublin like I'd planned?"

Skulduggery's voice was cold. "You killed Ghastly and Anton for nothing."

Ravel gazed back at him, and didn't say anything for a bit. When he did finally speak, he sounded so incredibly sad. "You don't understand any of this. That's the worst thing. You, all of you, you think I'm another Serpine or Scarab. You don't see that what I've done is necessary. You don't believe me? Turn on the damn TV. Look what the mortals are doing to themselves. Look at what they've done to the world. They're bleeding the planet dry. They're poisoning the air, the land and the sea, and they know exactly what they're doing, but their politicians are so corrupt and compromised that nothing is being done to stop it. They focus, again and again, on the little things that divide them and not the big things that unite them. They need to be governed. We need to step out of the shadows and take control. In the long run, they'll be happier."

"They'll be slaves."

"You keep on using that word," Ravel said, getting angry. "*You* keep on using it. I've never used that word. None of us have, because that's not what we're after. We don't *want* to *rule*. We *need* to *govern*."

"That's not our job."

"It should be. Think of what could have been avoided if someone like me had done this a long time ago. There would be no extremism. No fundamentalism. No terrorism. No hate crimes. People could be whatever they wanted to be, and as long as they didn't hurt anyone else, they could live in peace and happiness. But we had to stay out of sight, didn't we? Let them decide their own fates. We policed our own people and we trusted the mortals to do the same. We succeeded. We beat Mevolent. We beat his Generals. But the mortals? They failed. So they've had their chance. Now we take over."

"No, Erskine," said Skulduggery. "We don't. When the Warlocks are beaten, we'll return to how things were before."

Ravel shook his head. "It's too late for that. Who's running the Sanctuaries now? My people. Shoot me. Kill me. It makes no difference. It's bigger than me now. It's bigger than you, bigger than all of us. The revolution cannot be stopped."

"There may be people like you running the Sanctuaries, but the Sanctuaries themselves are made up of people like me. The only way your plan would have worked is if the Warlocks attacked the mortals. Then the sorcerers would have united and taken them down in full view of the world's media. But the Warlocks are about to fall – thanks to your own sorcerers."

Ravel smiled. "You're so smart. So, so smart. And yet even you can overlook the obvious. The Warlocks were just one option. Kitana and Sean and Doran? They were another. You see, all we need is a threat. All we need is someone big enough and powerful enough to burn mortal cities to the ground. And now we have that, with Valkyrie."

Skulduggery remained very, very still.

"Darquesse is in all the visions now," Ravel continued. "All the Sensitives are seeing her, clear as day. I was told about it last night. The girl with the Sceptre, that must be Valkyrie's reflection, am I right? You'd said it had evolved. I had no idea quite how much. Impressive."

"Valkyrie won't be used by you to—"

"Skulduggery, come on, don't be ridiculous. Valkyrie's gone. You don't get to tell me what she will or will not do. And you can forget about any self-righteous anger on your part. You protected her. You knew what she was, what she would become, and you hid her from us. You allowed her to blossom, and because of that, now she's the one we'll need to kill."

"You won't be killing her," said Skulduggery, taking off his hat. "You won't be doing anything."

Ravel undid the clasp, and let his robe fall. Underneath he was wearing a suit that Ghastly Bespoke had probably made for him. "So what's it going to be?" he asked. "Bullet to the head, or are you going to beat me to death?"

"I don't know," said Skulduggery, walking towards him. "I'm just going to see what happens."

Skulduggery lunged and Ravel slipped by him, kicking his leg out and grabbing him when he stumbled. He threw Skulduggery against the pillar, and every carved name that Skulduggery brushed against brought a still figure into the Hall.

China lost sight of Madame Mist in the sudden crowd. As Skulduggery and Ravel fought, more and more dead sorcerers were appearing. China moved around them, searching for the woman in black. Her elbow passed through the arm of a mage she had once known, without any sensation at all. These images may have looked solid, but they had no more substance than a hologram. And then Madame Mist burst through, hands curled into claws.

China staggered back, trying to fend her off, but Mist's strength was astonishing. She caught China with a backhand that took her off her feet and sent her sliding along the floor, through the legs of a half-dozen dead mages. As she slid, she glimpsed Skulduggery and Ravel, hanging on to each other and trading elbows and hammerfists.

She got up, tapped the sigils on her arms and flung them wide, catching Mist with a wave of energy that sent her stumbling. The sigil on her palm lighting up, China rushed in, but Mist knocked her hand away and so China slammed into her. They hit the floor, separated, and once again China lost sight of her. Then the images started to fade, and one by one they began to disappear. China saw Mist, out of the corner of her eye, coming for her.

She knocked her fists together, lighting up the sigils on her knuckles. Strength flooded her body and, when Mist reached for her, China grabbed her wrist and twisted, locking Mist's arm straight and forcing her to her knees. The sleeve of Mist's dress bunched up near her shoulder, exposing the pale skin of her arm, and with her free hand, China struck the back of the elbow. Mist shrieked and the elbow shattered and shards of bone ruptured the skin. But instead of a spray of blood there was a swarm of spiders. They were already on China's hand, moving quickly up her arm. China pulled away, snagging Mist's veil and taking it with her. The woman's face was pale, her lips dry and cracked. Tiny spiders moved beneath her skin.

Mist turned her head and black spiders started crawling from her nostrils and her ears and squeezing out from behind her staring eyes. She opened her mouth, vomited out more of them, the torrent hitting China in the chest. China slipped and fell and covered her face with her hands, but the spiders were already there, trying to get past her tightly-pressed lips, scuttling over her screwed-shut eyes. They were in her hair, in her clothes, crawling all over her, and still they came, the weight pressing down.

She couldn't see and couldn't breathe. She tore handfuls of

spiders away from her face, but it was like clawing at a landslide. She tried to get up, squashing them beneath her, but slipped on the mess and fell again, grunting on impact, her lips parting slightly.

And then the spiders were in her mouth.

She kept her teeth locked together, but they were there, filling her cheeks, surging down her throat, and she was choking now, and going to die.

The least she could do was take Mist with her.

Her hand went to her chest, her middle finger pressing through her clothes to the point of her sternum. She traced it down, following the tattoo that she could feel glowing to life, as all of her other tattoos started glowing also. The tattoo swerved left and her finger followed, then swirled, and cut across, and she felt the heat rise from within her. And, as she finished tracing the symbol she had cut into her own skin so long ago, the heat burst from her.

It incinerated her clothes, her shoes, the scant make-up on her face and the light polish on her nails. And it incinerated the spiders, too – burned them all, outside and in, turned them to ash and turned the ash to vapour. She opened her eyes and her mouth and sucked in air that turned superheated and scorched her throat and lungs. She stood, the ground melting beneath her bare feet. She looked at her arms, looked down at herself. She glowed. Her body was a furnace. She could feel her eyes starting to boil.

Madame Mist was struggling to stand. Dismayed at the loss of so many of her spiders. Clutching her ruined arm. So pale and so frightened. China reached out with both hands, clamping her fingers round Mist's shoulders. Mist tried to scream, but she was dead before she could make a sound. China let her go and she crumbled, a smoking, charred, blackened thing, not even recognisable as a corpse.

China allowed herself a single moment of satisfaction, of

something approaching smugness, and turned and saw Skulduggery looking at her.

"What have you done?" he asked.

She could barely hear him over the roar in her ears. Ravel was on his knees, his hands shackled behind his back.

"I'm sorry," she said. "I'm sorry for what I did to you. I'm sorry for what I did to your family."

He shook his head. "Turn it off. Whatever you're doing, deactivate it."

She gave him a smile. She wondered how it looked through the heat haze. "There is no off switch, I'm afraid. And don't come any closer. Nothing can withstand its power. I added this tattoo once I learned that you had returned from the dead. It was Mevolent's idea, actually. A last resort. He helped me craft it. If ever you had found out what I had done, and you'd got your hands on me, I was to use this to kill both of us."

"That's insane."

"Not really. Burning myself alive from the inside was a far less scary thought than what you'd do to me."

"China—"

"Shut up, Skulduggery. You talk too much, has anyone ever told you that? Shut up and listen. I'm sorry for the part I played in the murder of your child and the woman you loved. I neither deserve nor expect your forgiveness. I don't even want it." Her mouth was dry. It was getting harder to speak. "I deserve this. I deserve the pain that's going to arrive, any second now."

"I'll get you to a doctor."

"It won't do any good."

"Then we'll bind you."

"With what? I'll melt any shackles that get close."

"For God's sake, there has to be something I can do. I can't just watch you die in front of me."

"Turn away and you won't have to."

"*No!*" he roared, then stepped back, standing straight. "No," he said again, calmer this time. "You did terrible things hundreds of years ago. So did I. I'm no hypocrite. I can't hate you any more than I can hate myself."

She laughed despite the pain that was building. "Skulduggery, darling, you *do* hate yourself."

"Nonsense," he said. "I love myself. I think I'm hilarious. And you're not going to die."

"Do you know why I like you, you dear, sweet man? Because, while you may not have ever loved me, you have never bored me, either. That's a rare quality, and one which I have always found most... attractive."

"I need you, China."

"How I have longed to hear those words..."

"I need you to help me get Valkyrie back."

"... followed by those. I wish I had more time to think of something suitably pithy to leave you with but, unfortunately, the pain is becoming quite distracting. Goodbye, Skulduggery."

Of course, even on the brink of death, things still refused to go her way. Darquesse walked into the Hall, successfully stealing China's big moment away from her. China almost laughed.

"Valkyrie—" Skulduggery started, and was lifted off his feet by an invisible hand and slammed back against the far wall.

China's eyesight was failing, so she couldn't be sure, but for some reason Darquesse seemed to be dressed like a Bride of Blood Tears as she walked up to Ravel.

"You killed my friend," Darquesse said with Valkyrie's voice.

"Yes I did," said Ravel, standing. "I didn't want to have to do it, but a change had to be made and I—"

"He was your friend, too," Darquesse interrupted. "But you killed him."

"Look at you," he said. "Look at your power. Look at the things you've done. Why should you have to live in a world run by mortals? Why should any of us? We're stronger than them. We're better than them. Join us, Darquesse. You're one of us."

China's insides were cooking themselves. Her strength was almost used up. It was all she could do to stay standing. And her eyes, her pale blue eyes, her beautiful pale blue eyes, were already sizzling in their sockets. But even so, she could see the look on the face of Darquesse.

"I'm one of you?" Darquesse repeated. "Is that what you think? You look at me like we're equals? The gap between you and a mortal is far less than the gap between you and me, Erskine. To someone like me, a mortal could be viewed as an insect. But a sorcerer? A sorcerer is only a slightly bigger insect."

Ravel looked at her, his face unreadable. "Do what you came here to do, Darquesse. I'm not going to beg for my life. I don't deserve your mercy."

"What mercy? But no, death is too good for someone like you. You know what isn't too good for you, though? You know what's just right? Pain. Lots and lots of pain."

Darquesse smiled, and a small ball of light started to glow between her eyes. It moved slowly down, glowing through her skin, moving down her throat. It did a little twirl when it reached her clavicle and she giggled, and then it moved under her clothes and off to one bare shoulder, and down her arm to her hand, to her fingertip, where it stayed, pulsing gently.

Darquesse tapped Ravel's forehead, and the little ball of light transferred to him. He jerked away, panicking, as it pulsed and pulsed again, and faded.

Ravel frowned. Darquesse smiled.

Ravel's shriek caught China by surprise as his body snapped back. He fell sideways to the floor, convulsing.

"Agony," said Darquesse. "Constant agony for twenty-three hours a day. No painkillers or sedatives will do anything to alleviate what you're feeling. If and when your body compensates, if you find that you're starting to get used to it, the pain will increase. One hour a day, it'll stop. You can eat, drink – sleep, if you can. But mostly you'll just dread the agony returning." Darquesse looked up, forgetting all about Ravel as he kicked and thrashed on the ground. She looked at China.

"What have you done to yourself?" she asked softly.

China took a step forward. And another. If she had to die, the least she could do was take Darquesse with her. She held her hand out. Darquesse came to meet her. The closer she got, the clearer she got. It was Valkyrie's face. Those were Valkyrie's eyes.

China took her hand back an instant before Darquesse could clasp it.

Darquesse smiled. "You are an interesting woman, China Sorrows. In your last moments you might have a chance to stop me and save the world – and you hesitate."

China tried saying Valkyrie's name, but her tongue was frying in her mouth.

"Who am I to you?" Darquesse asked. "Who was I? The daughter you never had? The sister you always wanted? Was I a friend? A plaything? A chance at redemption?"

China's vision failed. She could feel her eyes about to burst.

Darquesse's voice in front of her. "You know who you were to me? A mystery. An enigma. A rare and beautiful creature, to be admired and... Oh, China. You are magnificent."

Two words. China wanted to say two words. She only wanted to say *I'm sorry*, as she reached out through the darkness, found Darquesse's arm and closed her hand round it.

"Oh, dear," she heard Darquesse say. "Did you really think that would work?"

China tightened her grip, but she had no more strength and her knees were about to buckle and she stepped back and then there was something cool pressing against her chest.

"It's going to be OK," she heard Darquesse whisper.

The darkness shifted to gloom and then brightness and she had eyes again, and she could see Darquesse standing there, her left hand sucking the heat from China's body. It filled Darquesse now, making her glow, incinerating her clothes, burning through the gold bands in her hair, turning the arm bracelet to ash. The Necromancer ring burst open as it disintegrated, the shadows curling and twisting madly.

China stepped back, repelled by the heat, but in an instant it was gone, absorbed, and Darquesse stopped glowing. The twisting shadows latched on to her, flowed across her strong arms and broad shoulders like oil, down her chest and her belly and her long legs, covering her body like a second skin. China remembered the young girl who had walked into her library six years earlier, and compared her to the young woman who stood before her now. That dimple. Those eyes. That smile. So similar. So incredibly different.

Skulduggery approached slowly. "Valkyrie," he said.

Darquesse turned to him. "She's gone. She's not even a quiet little voice in the back of my mind any more. I won't tell you how easy it was to take over. You don't want to hear things like that."

"Let me talk to her."

"There is no *her* any more. There's only me. There are no tricks you can pull to change that. You've used them all up."

Skulduggery tilted his head. "Then what do you want? I've seen the visions. I've seen you kill and destroy. I've seen what you do to Valkyrie's family."

"*My* family," Darquesse corrected. "And I've seen that too, remember. But I don't want to hurt them. I don't want to hurt anyone. I just want to live."

"If you're really not a threat, come with me. Let us run some tests."

"So you can figure out how to stop me? Imprison me? No thanks. I'm out, and I have no intention of going back in. But

I'm not your enemy, Skulduggery. I'm still the same girl I always was. Just, you know... don't stand in my way."

"What happens if I do?"

She smiled as the ceiling melted above her. "I don't know," she said. "But won't it be fun finding out?"

She rose up through the ceiling, and was gone.

77

THE SACRIFICE

For a city that had just come into being, Roarhaven had had its fair share of ups and downs. Its glorious unveiling, its citizens so excited, the gates ready to open to tens of thousands of new sorcerers, flooding in from around the world... and now look at it. Quiet, subdued, anxious. Its outer wall, originally so imposing, so strong, was now a smoking, cratered, fragile shell. Its people no longer strolled with confidence through its broad streets. Now they hurried, their eyes furtive and darting, wary of the Cleavers who were no longer under Erskine Ravel's control.

Every single one of these people knew of Ravel's plan. Even the children knew. Their parents told them stories of what was to come as they tucked them in at night. They were all complicit in Ravel's crimes. They all shared his guilt.

"What the hell do we do now?" Vex muttered.

He stood with Saracen on the steps of the Sanctuary. The bodies had been cleared from the streets and the blood had been washed away, but the memories left stains everywhere he looked. And the people, the few to pass within sight, kept their heads down, like they didn't want to be noticed.

"How about we build up another shield," said Saracen, "but

this time it's to keep people in, not out? We charge everyone here as accessories to the murders of Ghastly Bespoke and Anton Shudder, and we turn Roarhaven into a prison. See how they like it then."

Vex didn't say anything. He didn't say how much he agreed with that idea.

The Bentley pulled up and Skulduggery got out, joined them at the top of the steps and they all walked into the Sanctuary without uttering another word. Vex didn't like when Skulduggery went quiet. Bad things tended to happen.

It took them longer than necessary to get to the Accelerator Room – the corridors were different in this new palace, the rooms were switched around, and everything was so much bigger than before. They passed the Medical Wing, where Doctor Synecdoche was now in charge, and picked up the Monster Hunters along the way, who already had their bags packed for Tokyo. Fletcher Renn had offered to teleport them straight there, and possibly help out if he could. He didn't want to go back to Australia. Not yet.

They eventually got to the Accelerator Room, and the Engineer swivelled its head to them as they entered.

"Good afternoon," it said. "Is there something I can help you with?"

When Skulduggery didn't respond, Vex spoke up, grateful for the opportunity to tackle problems that could be solved. "One or two things, actually. These mages whose magic has been boosted – some are dead, some are in shackles, but some are on the run. How long will they stay at this power level?"

"By Doctor Rote's calculations, no more than five weeks."

Donegan made a face. "Five weeks? These people are bordering on *insane* as it is. Is there any way to, I don't know, de-boost them?"

"Not that I am aware," the Engineer said. "Their power levels will begin to fluctuate after the first two weeks, however. If you can catch them while their power has dipped, they would be easier to apprehend."

"Wonderful," Saracen muttered.

"So there's nothing you can do, or the Accelerator can do, to help us?" Vex asked.

"Regretfully, nothing."

Vex sighed. "OK then. In that case, the fourteen days are up, so we'd like you to shut the Accelerator down now, please."

"Of course," said the Engineer. "Which one of you shall be contributing?"

Skulduggery looked round. "I'm sorry?"

"Oh, yes," the Engineer said, "I lacked a piece of information when last we spoke of this. Very well, I shall explain. It is quite simple. The Accelerator can be powered down without incident for up to four weeks from its initial activation. We have obviously missed that deadline. After that, the deactivation requires a substantial sacrifice."

"What kind of sacrifice?"

"A soul," the Engineer said, "willingly given."

Saracen frowned. "What?"

"The chosen person steps inside the Accelerator thusly." The Engineer stepped on to the dais and turned to face them. "Death is instantaneous and, one would imagine, painless. Upon their death, their soul is released," the Engineer mimed something flying from its chest, "and is then used to close the rift between this reality and the source of all magic, thus deactivating the Accelerator."

Gracious crossed his arms. He did not look impressed. "Someone has to sacrifice themself? That's a tad drastic, isn't it? As far as off switches go?"

"Is there any way to bypass it?" Vex asked. "Isn't there a plug we could pull?"

The Engineer stepped out of the Accelerator. "There is no bypass. There is no plug. It must be a soul, willingly given."

"How would the Accelerator know if it's willingly given or not?"

"I would know," said the Engineer. "It is only with my permission that the soul can be used, and my creator was quite specific in his requirements. He said this machine must only be activated as a last resort. He reasoned that only a noble person of pure intent would go through with it once he was warned of the price that must be paid."

"But you weren't here to warn us," said Saracen. "So that's your fault."

"Indeed it is. But that does not change the fact that it must be a soul, willingly given."

"Well?" Donegan asked. "Anyone here willing to sacrifice their life to shut this down?"

Gracious took one step backwards. "I have, uh, a lot of online subscriptions that depend on me..."

"How long do we have to decide?" Skulduggery asked. "When is the Accelerator going to rupture?"

"Twenty-three days, eight hours, three minutes and twelve seconds," said the Engineer.

Vex stared. "So not only do we have Darquesse on the loose," he said, "and not only do we have nineteen supercharged sorcerers running around, and virtually every Sanctuary on the planet in a state of chaos, but now we have twenty-three days to decide who's going to kill themselves to save the world? How the hell are we meant to manage *any* of that?"

"We'll manage it the same way we manage everything," China Sorrows said from behind them, and they turned to her as she stood in the doorway, as beautiful as always. "With extraordinary amounts of style and good grace."

"We don't even have a Council of Elders any more," said Saracen. "How will we co-ordinate? Who's in charge?"

"From now on we won't be needing a Council," China said. "I think we've gone as far as we can with that approach, wouldn't you agree? And as for who's in charge, I'd have thought that would be obvious."

Vex frowned. "You?"

"Unless you can think of someone better suited to the task. Maybe you yourself? Or Saracen? Or Skulduggery, perhaps? If any of you would like to take on the overwhelming responsibilities of the post and forgo a life of freedom and adventure, please, be my guest."

Vex didn't say anything. Neither did Saracen or Skulduggery.

China smiled. "That's what I thought. Any other objections? No? You're quite sure? Very well then. I hereby accept, with great reluctance and humility, the post of Grand Mage, and I swear to only use my newfound powers to protect the magical and mortal communities of Ireland, and possibly to extract small bits of personal vengeance against those who have wronged me in the past." She clapped her hands. "There. It's settled. All right gentlemen, first order of business is tracking down the supercharged sorcerers. Mr Vex, Mr Rue, they are your responsibility. I'm sure the Monster Hunters will lend their assistance when and if you require it."

China looked at Skulduggery, and her voice softened. "Detective Pleasant, you have one task and one task only. Find Darquesse. Stop her if you can... kill her if you must."

78

AFTER THE WAR

tephanie's parents had been relieved to have her home.

It wasn't that they didn't think she was a good driver, they said. It was just that whenever she got behind the wheel, they started to worry. It was silly, they knew it was – she had her full licence, she was as good as anyone else, and they knew she was a sensible girl. But hey, worrying was a parent's job.

Stephanie couldn't understand how Valkyrie had come to the conclusion that her folks were ready to hear the truth. They worried enough about the most ordinary, mundane things in everyday life. If they knew about the magic and the fighting and the danger and the death, they'd never sleep again.

But she was home, and that was the only thing that mattered. She'd survived. She'd done her bit to stop the Warlocks, to stop Ravel, and her family were free, and happy, and safe – at least for the moment.

While her mum made them lunch, Stephanie played with Alice in the living room. She sat on the floor, adjusted the bag strap on her shoulder, and dumped out a tray of building blocks. Alice went at them with glee, flinging them over her head. They hit the wall, the mirror, banged against the new patio door that had been put in to replace the one Valkyrie had smashed through.

"Careful now," Stephanie said. "You don't want to break anything, do you?"

Alice cackled, threw the last block, and Stephanie grinned, grabbed her and started tickling. Alice howled with laughter and Stephanie rolled on to her back, blowing raspberries into her sister's neck. She eventually let go, and Alice clambered off, then sat on the ground beside her. Stephanie stayed where she was, looking up at the ceiling, and when she found her mind drifting back to the events of the last few days she caught herself. Valkyrie was gone and Stephanie had inherited her family. She had what she'd always wanted, and she wasn't going to waste a moment of her new life by thinking about death and destruction when she didn't need to.

Alice was unusually quiet. Stephanie turned her head and her heart lurched. Her bag had fallen open, revealing the Sceptre, and Alice's little fingers tapped against the black crystal. Stephanie moved with thinking, snatching the bag away as she whirled to her knees. Alice burst out crying and Stephanie stared, eyes wide.

Despite her racing pulse and the surging adrenaline that made every nerve ending jangle, Stephanie picked up her sister and held her close as she stood. "Oh, I'm sorry," she said, talking softly. "I'm sorry, sweetie. I didn't mean to scare you."

She hadn't even needed to. Alice was descended from the Last of the Ancients, the same as Valkyrie, which meant she could touch the black crystal without dying. Stephanie herself hadn't dared to touch it herself. She didn't know if that rule applied to reflections, no matter how evolved they had become.

"Here," she said, lifting the bag a little higher so that Alice could reach into it. "This is the Sceptre of the Ancients. See the crystal? You can touch it if you want. There you go. The crystal was made by the Faceless Ones, these horrible old gods, and anyone who touches it turns to dust. Apart from the Ancients. Apart from you. You're a very special girl, Alice, but I promise to do everything I can to make sure that you have a normal life. I won't let you turn out like Valkyrie did. I swear. Kiss?"

Alice looked up at her with her big eyes, and tilted her head forward so that Stephanie could kiss it. When Alice moved her head back again, Stephanie glanced behind her, saw Skulduggery Pleasant standing in the back garden.

She put Alice down, let her run around collecting the building blocks, and she climbed the stairs and went into her bedroom. She closed the door behind her and opened the window, then stepped back. Skulduggery sat on the sill.

"There's a problem with the Accelerator," he said. The way his head was turned, the way his hat fell, all she could see was his jaw. "Shutting it down won't be quite as straight-forward as we'd hoped. It'll require a sacrifice."

She nodded. "I'm sure you'll be able to handle it."

"I'll think of something. Ravel was transported to prison this morning. They tried to sedate him, but nothing works."

"Right."

"The Children of the Spider went with him, and seven others. The investigation into who else knew about his plan is ongoing."

"OK."

"We decided not to go after his people in the other Sanctuaries. We know they were a part of it, and we'll be using that against them to ensure we're never attacked again. They're our people now."

"Well," said Stephanie, "that works out well for everyone."

Skulduggery nodded. "The Warlocks have gone into hiding again, and we have teams of Cleavers rounding up any remaining Wretchlings. They won't have got far. We have perimeters set up from—"

"Skulduggery," Stephanie cut in, "what do you want?"

He raised his head, looked at her. "We don't know where Darquesse is," he said. "We don't know where she vanished to after Africa, and we don't know where she's gone now."

Stephanie patted her bag. "That's why I'm carrying the Sceptre around with me everywhere I go."

"Do you think she'll go after her family?"

Stephanie hesitated. "No," she said. "But she might come after me."

"That's what I thought. Stephanie, I need your help. We have to find her, we have to bring Valkyrie back."

"Valkyrie's gone."

"I don't believe that."

Stephanie went to her desk, turned on the radio to mask their voices. "It doesn't matter what you believe, because you don't know what it was like living with Darquesse in your head. Valkyrie knew that one more slip would be all it took. She doesn't have the strength to survive. A big part of her doesn't even want to."

"You're lying."

"No, I'm not. She loves that power. She loves becoming Darquesse. It's so incredibly freeing for her."

"Then help me stop her."

"But you don't want to *stop* her, do you? If we find her, if I have the chance to kill her, will you let me?"

Skulduggery turned his head slightly, away from her. "If I can't get through to Valkyrie, then yes."

"Not good enough," Stephanie said. "You tried talking to her. It didn't work. If you try to talk it again, Darquesse will kill us both. We won't have time for your way and then my way. We'll only have time for one way. So, if I help you, and we find her, and I have a chance to kill her, will you let me do it?"

Skulduggery didn't answer for the longest time. Then he said, "Yes."

Stephanie nodded. "OK then. You've got yourself a partner."

79

THE PACKAGE

Kenny was done.

He'd already cleared the research out of his apartment. The walls were now bare, the floors were uncluttered, and there was suddenly space on the table to put a coffee cup. He'd cleaned out his hard drive, wiped his browsing history, deleted every related file that existed online. And then he took Patrick Slattery's footage and photographs and he destroyed every last bit.

Almost every last bit.

He did a little editing. It took him a few hours. It wasn't pretty, and the seams were obvious and amateurish, but he got it done with what little skills he possessed, and then he destroyed everything that remained.

He lit a small bonfire at the back of his building, and every few minutes he'd add something else to the flames as he stood there. It occurred to him that he was watching his career go up in smoke. He was OK with that. He had reached a point that so few journalists reach, and he'd found himself with a choice to make – reveal the truth and watch the world change, or hide it forever, and let the world continue to spin.

Before the battle at Roarhaven, he'd wanted to change the

world. The people deserved to know, he reckoned. The story needed to be told.

But should a story be told simply because it's there? Should a truth be revealed simply because it's uncovered? He'd taken it upon himself to expose this hidden culture of magic and he hadn't looked any further than that. But now he knew. If these sorcerers were forced to go public, people would get hurt. People would die. Normal people would rise up with their guns and tanks and bombs, and sorcerers would fight back with their energy beams and fireballs, and more people like Patrick Slattery would die.

Slattery had had a wife. Kenny didn't even know her name. He'd never spoken to Slattery about anything other than the story. Slattery's wife would never know what happened to her husband, and that burned through Kenny's soul. There was nothing he could do about that.

But there *was* something he *could* do about Valkyrie Cain. Over the last year, he'd got to know her, in a way. She'd been a normal girl, plucked from her ordinary life, thrust into a world of magic and death and terror. She had fought the forces of darkness and she hadn't asked for rewards, or recognition, or parades in her honour. She had fought because she was a good person, a decent person, a hero, and she had died a hero's death in a blinding flash of light.

That was all Kenny had needed to see. That was all he could stand. He'd found a car and he'd fled, leaving the fighting in the rear-view mirror. If the world was going to be overrun by terrifying, powerful beings like that Charivari, Kenny wanted to be with his own people when it all went down.

He got home. Watched the news. Waited. Slept. Waited again.

And then he figured that Charivari had been stopped, that the world had been saved, that Valkyrie Cain's sacrifice had not been in vain.

He knew, then, that his career was over, and he only had one more thing to do before he quit being a journalist forever. Valkyrie Cain was a hero, and those closest to her deserved to know that.

When the last bit of evidence was burned, he got in his car and he drove out of Dublin City. He got where he needed to go and he sat there for two hours. Finally, he lifted the package from the passenger seat and got out. Stomach churning, he crossed the quiet road, walked up to the front door and knocked. He waited. He resisted the urge to turn and run and forget about this, and he waited. Finally, the door opened.

"Hi," Desmond Edgley said. "Can I help you?"

SKULDUGGERY PLEASANT
THE DYING OF THE LIGHT

He's dead.
She's still in high school.
But together they're going to save the world.

Read the ninth book in the bestselling
SKULDUGGERY PLEASANT series…

Following the loss of Valkyrie Cain, Skulduggery Pleasant

must track down Darquesse before she turns the world

into a charred, lifeless cinder – and so he draws together

a team of soldiers, monster hunters, criminals…

and Valkyrie's own murderous reflection.

Not everyone gets out of this alive.

Read on for a taste of *Resurrection*, the tenth book in the bestselling Skulduggery Pleasant series.

1

A new beginning.

That's what this was. A fresh start. He was going to deliver this one piece of information and then leave. He could go home, back to New York, or maybe Chicago, or Philly. Ireland didn't suit him any more. He was done with it – and it, apparently, was done with him. He was OK with that. He'd had some good times here. He'd had some fun. He'd made some friends. But a new day was about to dawn. All Temper Fray had to do was survive the night.

The wall up ahead cracked. By the light of the streetlamps, the cracks spider-webbed. Any last vestige of hope that he'd just be able to walk out of here vanished with those cracks. Temper had seen this trick before. A redneck psycho called Billy-Ray Sanguine used to jump out at people as they passed, kill them before they blinked. Temper had met Sanguine once. For a hillbilly hitman, he'd been all right. Whoever this guy was, he was no Billy-Ray.

The wall spat out a skinny little runt who came at him with a big knife and a bigger snarl. Temper ignored the snarl for the moment, focused on the knife, batting it away and slamming an elbow into the runt's mouth, dealing with the snarl almost by default. The runt went down, all flailing limbs and broken teeth, and Temper hurried on.

Yep. Things were going badly. But of course they were. Nothing ever went well for Temper Fray.

A motorbike came round the corner ahead of him, its single headlight sweeping the storefronts, and slowed almost immediately. Temper kept walking, keeping his head down, his hands swinging loosely by his sides. The guy on the motorbike wasn't wearing a helmet, and he wasn't looking at Temper. He was focused on the road, keeping his head straight. Just a guy on his bike, that's all, going about his business. As he drew parallel, his right hand drifted into his jacket.

Temper lunged, shoving him as he passed, and the bike toppled and the driver cried out as he fell. Temper kicked the consciousness right out of him and the guy flattened out. Bending over him, Temper reached into his jacket, found the gun and pulled it free. He checked it was loaded, then flicked off the safety. His own gun was on the kitchen table in the house he'd been staying in, alongside his phone. He'd have traded all the guns in the world for his phone right now. What he wouldn't give for a chance to call in reinforcements.

What he wouldn't give to call in Skulduggery Pleasant.

Resurrection is available now.

Contemporary American monologues
for men

RARY
RICAN
GUES
R MEN

6/98

CLERKS: Please checkout
only 1 monologue book per
patron!!!

CONTEMPORARY
AMERICAN
MONOLOGUES
FOR MEN

EDITED BY TODD LONDON

THEATRE COMMUNICATIONS GROUP

This publication is made possible in part with public funds from the New York State Council on the Arts, a State Agency.

Library of Congress Cataloging-in-Publication Data

Contemporary American monologues for men / Todd London, editor.
—1st ed.
p.   cm.
Includes bibliographical references.
ISBN 1–55936–134–4 (alk. paper)
1. Acting—Auditions. 2. Monologues. 3. American drama—20th century.
4. Men—drama. I. London, Todd.
PN2080.C645 1997
812'.04508'081–dc21
                                                                97–5738
                                                                CIP

Cover design by Paula Scher
Book design and composition by Lisa Govan

Distributed to the trade by Consortium Book Sales and Distribution, 1045 Westgate Drive, St. Paul, MN 55114–1065

First Edition, April 1998

ACKNOWLEDGMENTS

The playwrights whose words appear in this volume are, of course, its authors. They have been consistently encouraging, generous and remarkably tolerant of the piecework I've made of their art. I'm grateful to them all.

Special thanks to Nancy C. Jones, Kerry Lowe and Timothy Mennel, who did much of the hard labor on this book. Thanks, too, to Gino Dilorio, Daniel Swee, the writers and staff of New Dramatists and, especially, Terry Nemeth.

My deepest appreciation goes, always, to Juanita and Guthrie.

Editor's note: Many of the monologues that follow have been cobbled together to make sense out of context. Where lines of dialogue or stage directions have been cut, three open boxes—□□□—mark the deletion.

CONTENTS

INTRODUCTION

This collection has a simple aim: to make matches. You're an actor searching for the right monologue—for auditions or acting class—and here are cuttings from dozens of the most exciting American plays of the past two decades. The material might be said to be searching, too. It's on the lookout for actors who will connect deeply, who have the emotional availability and the craft to deliver these monologues into the world with their complexity intact. It seeks actors who think on their feet, who understand in their bodies the impression contemporary life makes on a character. Like any match-maker, though, this book offers only an introduction. The work is left to you.

Some of the excerpts collected here will read like nothing else you've found. Some are more difficult than others, some more strange, but they all offer a freshness of voice, an originality that can be fully felt/heard/appreciated only in context. So, I encourage you, once you've discovered a monologue you like (or two or ten), to read the complete play. (In the interview that follows, Daniel Swee, one of New York theatre's most respected and experienced casting directors, says that "without reading the play, you're exploring a town without a map.") They're all published and easy to lay hands on.

This volume gathers solos from well-made plays, autobiographical performances, experimental playwriting and unabashedly political theatre. Often, these scripts mix dramatic or tragic tones with comic and farcical ones—even in the same monologue. Thematically, too, while many of these writers tackle matters of life and death, love and loss—themes with great traditions in the theatre—they also go where plays haven't gone in quite the same way before. Racial and sexual identity, cannibalism, cross-dressing, corporate brutality, pedophilia, cockfighting, AIDS, spiritual revelation—it's all here, dished up with fierce intelligence and terrific wit. You can't make rich sense of any of it from a single speech.

This book assumes not only that you love to act but also that you love to read plays. That's one of the reasons it's divided into named chapters instead of into more standard categories, such as by age range or, tragic and comic. Also, more than a few of these monologues can be played in a variety of ways by a variety of "types" of actors. As mentioned above, the sensibilities of contemporary playwriting make it harder, too, to classify works as "comic" or "dramatic." Is it merely funny to watch a clown suffer a heart attack at a birthday party while desperately singing "A hundred bottles of milk on the wall"? What about a guy in a Santa suit who punctuates his plans to assassinate the president with songs from *West Side Story* or a Nazi leader who cracks jokes before his trial for crimes against humanity?

These monologues are grouped (and the groups titled) with the hope of sparking an immediate connection. They're organized by subject (men and work, early loves, dealing with a father or being one), by emotional impulse ("I'm dying, that's what's wrong") and by action ("I thought of killing people"). Some headings are designed to suggest a common thread of character or predicament—"I choose not to be inconsolable," for example.

You might want to thumb through the book the way you would an anthology of short stories or poems, until one piece grabs you and inspires you to try it out. Or, if you need information about age and character type right off the bat, go straight to the introductory paragraphs, and they'll tell you what you need to know. There's a range of men's experience represented here, for actors of every age, temperament and ethnic background, actors of every stamp.

This book has another aim, too, shared by its publisher, Theatre Communications Group, from whose play list these brave new works are culled. That goal is to get new American plays out into the world. For this mission, too, the interests of actors and playwrights overlap. Actors need words, and writers need real voices for their interior ones; you need compelling roles, and they need disciplined, resilient actors to breathe stage life into their characters. Both want to make thrilling, important theatre. Neither can do so without the other. It's a natural match.

—**T. L.**

AN ACTOR CHOOSES

AN INTERVIEW WITH DANIEL SWEE

Daniel Swee has been casting director for New York's Lincoln Center Theater for the past six seasons. Prior to that, he was casting director for the Hudson Guild Theatre, Theatre Communications Group and Playwrights Horizons. His recent work includes Tina Howe's Pride's Crossing *with Cherry Jones, Anton Chekhov's* Ivanov, *starring Kevin Kline at Lincoln Center,* Art *on Broadway and the film,* The Object of My Affection.

What do you do as a casting director?

My job is to know as many actors and their work as well as possible. Then I come up with ideas, make suggestions, offer advice and opinions to the directors, producers and writers I work with in order to cast their plays the way they would like them cast.

So it's an advisory position?

Right. I advise and assess.

Assess?

I have to assess the levels of people's talent, their abilities and their particular qualities.

Under what circumstances do you listen to actors perform monologues?

Usually at LORT [League of Resident Theatre] Lottery auditions and Equity Performer Auditions [EPA], which are auditions required by the actors' union. The specifics vary depending on the contract your theatre works under, but they often require you to see a high volume of actors over the course of one, two or three days. Generally, the actors have only two or three minutes in which to do their monologues.

How many monologues do they do and what kind?

The typical thing is two contrasting monologues. Usually, "contrasting" means classical and contemporary or comedy and drama. It's a nebulous term. Too often, I find that contrasting monologues aren't contrasting; they don't really show different qualities.

So actors should pick works that show different qualities?

Most important, they should pick things that show them off well. The fact is, 95 percent of the time an actor is being asked to do a monologue on the same day as many other people. He's going to be one of fifty, a hundred, a hundred and fifty people that day. And these auditions are usually not something he'll be cast from. No one's going to say, "Oh look, he was great in that monologue; let's give him the role." It's only one step in a process. You want to interest someone enough to bring you in again to read for a specific project or to remember you down the road. So, you need to pick something that sits comfortably with you.

And it should be something you can do clearly and well. These auditions—when you're seen with hundreds of other actors—aren't the times to stretch yourself. A twenty-five-year-old should not come in and audition as Amanda Wingfield [the mother in *Glass Menagerie*], even if she did it well in college. If you're someone who conveys great vulnerability all the time and don't have much access to anger or power, you shouldn't come in and do Stanley Kowalski. Even if it's a good exercise, we're going to get a blurry picture of who you are and what you can do well. It's helpful to cast yourself well when you pick a monologue. It's the equivalent of giving someone a clear snapshot of you, because it's often their first time meeting you. Maybe later on they will see the whole range of what you can do.

What about contrast?

People feel very differently about this. The thing I care about most is that actors are good. Essentially, I don't care if their monologues have similarities, as long as they're good. If the work is interesting, it makes me want to see them in something else. On the other hand, you should try not to repeat yourself by choosing two emotionally identical pieces.

I've been surprised, collecting monologues for this book, at how rare it is for these contemporary writers to write in either a strictly comic voice or a purely serious or tragic one. I couldn't have divided them into those categories if I'd tried. These playwrights seem, for the most part, to mix things up, to cross genres, comic-serious, tragic-farcical, and so on.

Yes. There's really no difference, no way of saying, "This is comedic. This is dramatic." Though there are certain things that can never be done comedically, there is humor in, for example, Tennessee Williams. Still, you wouldn't say, "Oh, Williams writes for the comic actor." Similarly, Jon Robin Baitz writes serious plays, but his work is deeply, deeply funny. So are his characters. A lot depends on what you pick and how you go about presenting it.

Okay. Let's say we're at a general audition or EPA. You're not casting for a particular show but getting an overall sense about a lot of actors new to you. And let's say an actor feels comfortable in a range of roles. How does he decide what to show?

First, he should know who he's auditioning for, who his audience is. One of an actor's jobs is to educate himself as much as possible about the field and to know as much as possible about the auditions he's going into. Then, pick monologues that work well. For example, if you're auditioning on a day when you think there are going to be a lot of other people, you'll go a lot farther with something funny, if you do it well. If you're a good actor and you've found a funny monologue, people will enjoy it more.

Is it harder to fulfill a serious piece—a weighty emotional moment—in a couple of minutes than a funny one?

No, I think it's harder to enter with something extremely funny. Too many people feel they've got just two minutes to show the entire range of human emotion. It's just insane, and it's impossible. You see people trying to emote and thinking that if they don't get to the point of crying, it's not successful. That's not the point. People aren't going to cast you because you cry. They'll cast you if you're good and you're honest.

Also, monologues that work as audition pieces have movement in them. All good writing does, but often this movement takes place over different stretches of time. You're looking for something that moves in a shorter period of time. You have to be shrewd about that. That doesn't mean you should impose anything artificial and suddenly go into hysterics for no apparent reason. But there's got to be some way to chart the change of emotions within the context of a monologue. It can be a twenty-second monologue, a forty-second monologue or a sixty-second monologue. I've seen forty-second pieces that work beautifully because they're concise, truthful and honest and, in them, someone starts one place and ends up in a very different place. They tell a story.

Doesn't "honest" mean different things? There's honest within the circumstances of a play, but some actors aren't sure how to direct their energies, so they want to display a range of honest emotions . . .

That to me is dishonest. If you think you've got to show the entire range of emotions you're capable of—that doesn't happen in real life. How can you honestly convey those feelings in so short a time without imposing something? Specific, honest choices that work for that character within the scene—that's all anyone can ask for, all anyone wants.

What about choosing material that's close to yourself? You gave extreme examples of wrongheaded choices—Amanda Wingfield, Stanley Kowalski. Can you say more about that?

AN ACTOR CHOOSES

It's a hard call. I don't want to tell people that they can or can't do certain things. Some actors have greater range than others; some have a good sense of themselves and others don't. It's analogous to a résumé picture. A picture should look like the actor. It should show an expression that's actually one of his expressions, not one he'd *like* to have or that he's practicing having in front of a mirror. It should convey a thought—someone specific thinking of something. And it should convey a quality that he, as a person and as an actor, actually possesses.

Other than choosing suitable material, are there other general guidelines for selecting a monologue?

There are certain things not to do, certain generalities and all of them have exceptions. For instance, it's often not a good idea to do a monologue from a play you've performed. Once you take it out of context, it might not stand well on its own. People watching do not have the benefit of the last half hour of your performance. Having rehearsed and performed the play helps to inform the character and emotionally form what you're doing, but at a certain point, you have to take it out of context and make it work within its own thirty-, sixty- or ninety-second life.

If they're taking the monologue out of context, why do they need to know the whole play?

Again, it's not a hard-and-fast rule. There are good actors who can create a very specific world and stay emotionally honest without playing the character as written. Some people watching get offended by that, but I actually think it's fine. In general, though, without reading the play, you're exploring a town without a map. You can discover it, but you might end up making assumptions. You assume you're on Main Street when, if you looked at the map, you'd know it's Maple Drive.

How about guidelines for performing the pieces you choose?

The first ten seconds—the first moments—are the most important.

Why?

Because if you're not specific, if you're slightly off your game (which happens with actors when they're nervous, slightly spacey or on autopilot for a few seconds), people's minds wander. It's hard to win them back. I don't mean you've got to *sell* it, but the first moment has to have an immediacy to it. You need to engage. From the first moment, you have to be speaking in response to something. Because of that, some monologues are difficult to do, others have an easier entrance.

It's never easy to overcome the fact that you're an actor in a room auditioning. Performing monologues is an artificial situation. It takes a lot of talent, skill and canniness to overcome that. You have to be so specific about all your choices and actions that those of us watching come to believe you're living within the world of the character rather than being an actor in a room auditioning.

Does this contemporary material make unusual demands of actors? Does it require something that isn't demanded in other kinds of theatre writing?

It's a hard generalization to make. Jon Robin Baitz, for example, demands actors with a facility for language-oriented material, who have the verbal dexterity to handle fairly complex language. Eric Bogosian's work requires that actors convey a sense of verisimilitude. They have to seem real and avoid coming off actor-y. On the other hand, his writing is less naturalistic than it seems, so you need people who have the skills to keep the emotions pitched high enough, the energy high enough, real but not too small. His work is both theatrical and real.

Writers like Harry Kondoleon and Nicky Silver need naturally comedic actors. You can't go at their material thinking, "I'm going to be funny." But their stuff has a natural wackiness. It needs to be real and truthful, and the characters' eccentricity has to come organically rather than be pasted on. As with almost all comedies, the humor comes from the emotional stakes running high. Often in auditions, the stakes aren't high enough. The actors aren't committing enough to what they're doing. They hope to be truthful and are simply casual instead. Raising the emotional stakes doesn't mean raising your voice or sobbing. It means filling each moment, making specific choices and committing to them.

Do you have dos and don'ts for auditioners?

Everyone you talk to will have different rules. For me, addressing an imaginary person in an empty chair is usually a bad choice. I end up thinking to myself, "He's talking to an empty chair." If you simply make clear choices about who you're speaking to, your relationship to them and where they are, you do a lot better. And you should be shrewd about the placement of that person. Whether you place them onstage or in the direction of the audience, do it at a smart angle, downstage of you, unless there's some reason not to. Doing the entire scene in profile doesn't work either. And look for a way to do it naturally, so that you can be seen. Be flexible, too, since you don't know what the setup of the room will be until you're there.

My feeling—and other people feel differently—is that you shouldn't lock onto someone who is watching you audition. Do not use them as the person your character is speaking to. It makes a lot of people uncomfortable. It's also harder for the actor to concentrate if that person suddenly looks down to write or stops paying attention.

There are other dos and don'ts: Don't throw chairs or other items. Keep props to a bare minimum if you use anything at all. With props and costumes—you shouldn't carry or wear anything that you'd be embarrassed to carry or wear on the subway. You'll look nuts. Costume yourself in something that works for the character without actually costuming yourself as the character. If you're playing a nineteenth-century gentleman, don't wear jeans. On the other hand, don't wear some sort of foppish hat that's going to get you arrested. Don't wear hose just because you're playing Shakespeare.

Another one: I hate monologues where people play actors. You know, those monologues with the character of an actor who is frustrated because he just had an audition. It gets on my nerves and seems insular, lacking in imagination.

What about dos? The rules are always don'ts.

Dos are simply good acting. Come in and act well. If you've chosen a good monologue, come in and do it truthfully, cleanly, with focus. Then walk out of the room knowing you've done your best work. What happens next is up to everyone else. You have no control over that.

"I WAS JUST THINKING ABOUT MY FATHER . . ."

THE FILM SOCIETY

BY JON ROBIN BAITZ

Durban, South Africa, circa 1970. Jonathan Balton has just assumed the post of headmaster of the Blenheim School for Boys, a conservative academy for the preparation of British South Africa's ruling class. His administrative ascent has had a considerable cost, including many of his ideals and beliefs. He is about to fire his closest colleague and refuse to rehire his oldest friend. He speaks to them after returning from the funeral of the school's most hard-line, rightwing teacher, whose burial has set off Balton's memories of his own father's death.

BALTON: I was thinking of the farm. Every Saturday night, Father'd give one of the cows to the natives. A treat. Few farms did that. But actually, it was no sacrifice, just a small feeble animal. And yet, cane-cutters, herd boys, all of them . . . would look forward to Saturday night. The compound would come alive. That mad Zulu pop music on the Bantu radio. I'd sit in nanny's lap, watching. It was all very festive. *(Beat)* I was mostly interested in the killing of the cow. Used to be, they used a knife and that was vivid, very much a thing of the bush. To see the creature's dull eyes flashing, hooves scraping at the dirt as the knife was led across the throat—and the blood running into a gourd on the ground. But the part that fascinated me the most was when it was dead. Its evisceration. The skin drawn slowly back and the veins exposed, black blood clotting into the reddish dust of the compound which would be dead quiet, somber. Little ivory-colored and purple-hued sacks filled with bile and acid and urine. Balloons of undigested grass, bones cracked and muscles pulsing gently as a fire was readied, and the tongue, the great curled muscle, unravelled, cut out, and the teeth and jaw laid bare. *(Pause)* But it is one Saturday in particular that I remember. It was my birthday and I was given the honor of killing the cow. I was eleven. The knife was dispensed with and my father gave me a pistol with tiny silver-tipped bullets. I was to blow out the brains from a little spot between the eyes and this death had none of the ritual of the knife. It was an assassination and I believe the natives knew this. Unbearable to have this cow led to me, docile and uncomplaining. She was tied to a post with a little strand of rope and I tried to do the thing very quickly. But you see, I did not do a proper job of it. And the bullet ricocheted off her skull and down into the jaw—this shattered pulp of bone and blood through which she screamed, you see, as I recall it. And tore loose from her feebly tied rope. And there she was with saliva and plasma all about, bolting into the cane fields, everyone stunned. She was gone. And I stood there. Frozen. *(Pause)* And I looked up and saw my father standing on the verandah of the main house with my mother—and he whispered something to her and went inside and nanny came to me. And of course, by this time, I was crying. The natives staring at their feet—mortified. No laughter—which might have been preferable. *(Pause)* And then my father came out of the house with his shotgun, got on his horse and rode into the field, and there was a single muffled blast and nanny put me to bed. A quiet supper that night, no singing or dancing, and of course, not long after, we moved into the city—my mother's idea. So I was just thinking about my father and all.

ROOSTERS

BY MILCHA SANCHEZ-SCOTT

The American Southwest. When Hector's father, a great breeder and trainer of roosters for cockfights, goes to prison for killing a competitor, the young man is forced into the field work he loathes and which his father has always claimed is beneath him. His charismatic father returns today from prison, a kind of conquering hero to everyone but Hector, who despises him for, among other things, neglecting his family in pursuit of the perfect fighting bird. Gallo tries to provoke in his son feelings for their heritage by asking Hector if he remembers his first cockfight, to which his grandfather, Abuelo, took him. Hector pretends not to remember, but moments later, alone on a porch, with a stylized cockfight swirling around him, he recalls.

HECTOR: It was in Jacinto Park . . . the crowd was a monster, made up of individual human beings stuck together by sweat and spittle. Their gaping mouths let out screams, curses, and foul gases, masticating, smacking, eager for the kill. You stood up. The monster roared. Quasimoto, your bird, in one hand. You lifted him high, "Pit!" went the call. "Pit!" roared the monster. And you threw him into the ring . . . soaring with the blades on his heels flashing. I heard the mighty rage of wings and my heart soared with him. He was a whirlwind flashing and slashing like a dark avenging angel then like some distant rainbow star exploding he was hit. The monster crowd inhaled, sucking back their hopes . . . in that vacuum he was pulled down. My heart went down the same dark shaft, my brains slammed against the earth's hard crust . . . my eyes clouded . . . my arteries gushed . . . my lungs collapsed. "Get up," said Abuelo, "up here with me, and you will see a miracle." You, Father, picked up Quasimoto, a lifeless pile of bloody feathers, holding his head oh so gently, you closed your eyes, and like a great wave receding, you drew a breath that came from deep within your ocean floor. I heard the stones rumble, the mountains shift, the topsoil move, and as your breath slammed on the beaches, Quasimoto sputtered back to life. Oh, Papi, breathe on me.

THE LOMAN FAMILY PICNIC

BY DONALD MARGULIES

Life in eleven-year-old Mitchell's Coney Island high-rise apartment reminds him a lot of Death of a Salesman, *except that it's 1965 and his beleaguered dad, instead of traveling, sells lighting fixtures out of a showroom in Brooklyn. Alone with his father at the kitchen table, they run out of things to say, so he talks to the audience.*

MITCHELL: For school, Miss Schoenberg made us read this play that Arthur Miller wrote a long time ago, before I was born, about this salesman with two sons who lives in Brooklyn? Sound familiar? I know; I read it like three times 'cause I couldn't believe it either. There are all these similarities. Except Willy Loman, the guy in the play?, the salesman?, doesn't sell lighting fixtures. *(A beat)* Anyway, in the play he goes insane and kills himself by smashing up his car so his family can collect his insurance money, even though I thought you can't collect if you commit suicide, which is what I said in class but Miss Schoenberg said not necessarily. *(A beat)* Arthur Miller himself grew up in this very same spot practically. Many years ago. He walked the same streets I walk every day. He played in our schoolyard probably. I heard that his family's house was one of the houses they wrecked so they could build our middle-income luxury building here in Coney Island. At least that's what Miss Schoenberg said. *(A beat)* Anyway, we have to get up in front of the class and do like oral book reports?, but instead of doing the usual if-you-want-to-know-how-he-kills-himself-you-have-to-read-the-play kind of thing, I decided I'm gonna do something else, something different. *(A beat)* So, I'm writing this musical-comedy version of *Death of a Salesman* called *Willy!* With an exclamation point. You know, like *Fiorello!? Oklahoma!? Oliver!?* So far I've come up with a couple of songs. Like, when Biff and Happy are up in their room and they hear Willy downstairs talking to himself?, they sing this song called "Dad's a Little Weird" which goes: *(Sings)* "Dad's a little weird, he's in a daze. Could it be he's going nuts, or is it just a phase?" *(A beat)* Well, it's a start. What do you think?

THE HOUSE OF RAMON IGLESIA

BY JOSÉ RIVERA

Javier Iglesia is Ramon's oldest son, the only one of three to go to college. Although born while the family still lived in Puerto Rico, he's the only brother to achieve stability and develop prospects for material success in the United States. In Javier's view, his father is a failure, an embarrassment and a drag on his life. Ramon has worked at numerous menial jobs—including janitor at Javier's high school. He has seen his own attempt to start a business go down the tubes. He's also a diabetic and, despite its particular dangers for him, a sometime drunk. Because of difficulties documenting ownership, the father's plan to sell his Long Island house and move the family back to Puerto Rico has, like much else, fallen apart. The two men fight, and Ramon leaves the house. Javier then goes in search of his father, missing a job interview to do so. He finds him drunken and disoriented, limping through the snow.

JAVIER: I can just leave you here. You know that? I'll just leave you here and you can die in the cold. I'll leave you here if I want! □□□
   Half of me wants to do that. Lie right down there, Dad! Cover yourself up! Go to sleep! Let them find you tomorrow morning! You'll be doing me a favor! I won't have to point to you, saying, "That's my father, that janitor there!" See the bent old man with the mop? The old slave dragging his feet? That's my proud old man! *(Ramon falls in the snow)* GET UP FOR CHRISSAKES! *Don't you have any pride at all?* Are you going to let this snow kill you while I stand here watching you? If you don't get up, I'll walk, I'll leave, I swear! *(Bending down over his father) Why can't you help yourself? Why? (Low)* Why can't you help . . . yourself? You should never have bent down so I could wipe my feet on your back. I never asked you to do that for me. Why did you do that for me? Why were you that way for me? Why did you suffer so fucking *quietly?*

SIGHT UNSEEN

BY DONALD MARGULIES

When The New York Times *ran a magazine cover story called "Jonathan Waxman: The Art Scene's Bad Boy or Visionary?" Jonathan thought it would make his father proud. It didn't. The elder Waxman was confused and alienated. "All these words," he said, "are about you? What is there to say about you?" Less than a week after his father's death, Jonathan heads to England for his European debut, a retrospective of the enfant terrible's paintings. He visits an old girlfriend, Patricia, whom he'd thrown over fifteen years before.*

JONATHAN: I went to pack up his house the other day? My parents' house? All his clothes, my old room, my mother's sewing machine, all those rooms of furniture. Strange being in a place where no one lives anymore. □□□

(A beat) Anyway, what I found was, he'd taken all the family pictures, everything that was in albums, shoved in drawers—hundreds of them—and covered an entire wall with them, floor to ceiling, side to side. I first saw it years ago, when he'd started. It was his Sistine Chapel; it took him years. He took my hand (I'll never forget this) he took my hand—he was beaming: "*You're* an artist," he said to me, "*you'll* appreciate this." He was so proud of himself I thought I was gonna cry. Proud and also in a strange way competitive? □□□

So, there was this wall. The Waxman family through the ages. Black-and-white, sepia, Kodachrome. My great-grandparents in the shtetl, my brother's baby pictures on top of my parents' courtship, me at my bar mitzvah. Well, it was kind of breathtaking. I mean, the sweep of it, it really was kind of beautiful. I came closer to examine it—I wanted to see how he'd gotten them all up there—and then I saw the staples. □□□

Staples! Tearing through the faces and the bodies. "Look what you've done," I wanted to say, "How could you be so thoughtless? You've ruined everything!" But of course I didn't say that. How could I? He was like a little boy. Beaming. Instead I said, "Dad! What a wonderful job!" (A beat) So, there I was alone in his house, pulling staples out of our family photos. These documents that showed where I came from. Did they *mean* anything to him at all? I mean as artifacts, as proof of a former civilization, when my mother was vibrant and he was young and strong and we were a family? (A beat) That's all gone now, Patty. It's all gone.

LOSING FATHER'S BODY

BY CONSTANCE CONGDON

Combine the facts laid out in this monologue with the title of Congdon's play and you've caught the premise and style of this satirical romp. In his forties, George Boyle has been the Anderson family's loyal, put-upon, company lawyer for more than fifteen years. Now, Mr. Anderson has died on a Canadian fishing trip with his brother and business partner, Cecil, and George has to explain certain complications to the children, Scott and Kimberly, a pair of thirty-something workaholics whose idea of mourning is a set of doubles tennis and cocktails at the club with chums. As long as Mom stays sedated and their serves go in, they should sail smoothly through funeral time. George's news, though, presents the first snag. Before he speaks, he breaches family order by lighting up a cigarette while sitting on the living-room couch. (Kim and Scott smoke outside over an ashtray they wash after each use.)

GEORGE: Well. Scott. Kimberly. Fact is, we've hit kind of a snag. It's no big thing, really big thing, anyway. I mean, everything is legally going forward. It's a personal, more of a personal— *(Blows out some breath, starts over)* Basically, it's this: your Uncle Cecil feels very strongly that the chartered plane costs too much and has decided to drive your father back in the station wagon. Himself. From Canada. He's stored him—your father—under the canoe, on the roof, carefully wrapped, and has been advised by some Mountie up there— some guy who knows what he's talking about—that game is transported at this time of year with no problems in—ah—you know, preservation. So. Now, I know this may seem a little bit—I mean— ah—a little, ah, a bit uncomfortable. But Canadian law on the transport of, you know, remains is incredible. Incredible. I mean, the red tape— *(More than George can express)* Now, I know what you may be—what's running through—what you may be thinking—I mean, it's, it's NOT, by any stretch of the imagination, ideal. I realize that, and so does your Uncle Cecil. But he is—you know how he is. He and your father built this company from a very modest—well, you know the story, of course. All of this from these principles of frugality and practicality, which I admire so much—have always admired in them both, and in you, and in Pauline. And determination. It's incredible, really, Cecil's determination is incredible, really. I wish you could hear him on this subject. I mean, the immediate subject at hand . . . that we're discussing here. So, what do you think? Before you say anything, though, here are some things to consider. It's not a long drive, and he is driving straight through, so our basic timetable would be the same. The other thing is, well, this is really the thing, he's on the road, you see, already.

"A MAN WHO LOVES HIS WORK"

IMPERCEPTIBLE MUTABILITIES IN THE THIRD KINGDOM

BY SUZAN-LORI PARKS

This pair of monologues, the first two appearances of Mr. Sergeant Smith, tell us almost everything we know about him. He is in the armed forces, stationed on an island that isn't much more than a rock, at some time in history. His current job—from which he hopes to be "distinctioned" and promoted to a desk of his own—is to clean the rock. The context tells us, though the author never does, that he's African American. The "Third Kingdom" of the title includes the two worlds of the African American—preslavery Africa and America from slavery on—as well as all the sea in-between. The first speech appears to be delivered to a photographer, imagined or real, who's meant to take pictures of Smith to send to his family. The second is probably a letter to that family, which expands by one child each time he receives a furlough visit from Mrs. Smith.

MR. SERGEANT SMITH: I'll have four. Four shots. Four at thuh desk. Go ahead—put in thuh colored film. Mmsplurgin. Splurging. Uh huh. Wants em tuh see my shoes as black. Shirt as khaki. Stripes as green. No mop n broom bucket today! I'll sit first. No. Stand. I kin feel it. In here. Mmm getttin my Distinction today. Thuh events of my destiny ssgonna fall intuh place. What events? That I dont know. But they gonna fall intuh place all right. They been all along marchin in that direction. Soon they gonna fall. Ssonly natural. Ssonly fair. They gonna fall intuh place. I kin feel it. In here. This time tomorrow mm gonna have me my Distinction. Gonna be shakin hands with thuh Commander. Gonna be salutin friendly back n forth. Gonna be rewarded uh desk cause when uh mans distinguished he's got his-self uh desk. Standin at thuh desk. My desk. Sssgonna be mines, anyhow. Fnot this un then one just like it. Hands in pockets. No— out. Ready for work. Here is Sergeant Smith at his desk. Ready. Ready for work. Next, second shot: right hand on the desk. Like on the Bible.

God and Country. Here is a man who loves his work. The name of this man is the name of Smith. You get the stripes in? They gonna be bars by evenin! Ha! Bars by evenin! Having a desk is distinguished. All of us have them. Because when there is danger from above, we stop. We look. We listen. Then we—dive underneath our desk (being careful that we do not catch our heads on the desk lip). Dive! Dive under our desks where it is safe. Like turtles. In our shells we wait for the danger to pass. —I don't wanna do uh shot uh that— don't want em tuh worry. Next, third shot: Here—oh. I will sit. Hands folded. Here I am—no. Arms folded. Next, shot number four. Ready? Hands on books and books open. A full desk and a smiling man. Sergeant Smith has got stacks of papers, but, not to worry, he is a good worker and will do well. Wait. Uh smile. Okay. Go ahead. Take it. Smiling at work. They like smiles.

IMPERCEPTIBLE MUTABILITIES IN THE THIRD KINGDOM

BY SUZAN-LORI PARKS

MR. SERGEANT SMITH: Here I am on a rock. As you can see, the rock is near water! We of the 20-53rd are closer to water than you can guess. We are in the water! But we are not on boat! But, we are not on a submarine! We of the 20-53rd are on an ISLAND!! A big rock in the middle of the ocean. Next time your mother takes you to visit the ocean, Buffeena, look very far out over the water and give me a wave. I will waaaave back! You may have to put on your glasses to see me, and I expect that to you I'll look like just a little speck. But if you look very far, you'll see me and if you wave very hard, I will waaaaaaave back! Next time your mother takes you to visit the ocean, Buffeena, throw me a kiss and I will throooooow one back! Now, Buffy, to reach me at the 20-53rd you are going to have to throw me a BIG kiss. Ask your Mother to help you. She will help you just as we here at the 20-53rd help each other, working together, to get the good job done. Here at the 20-53rd different men have different jobs. Some read maps. Some fly airplanes. Some watch guard over our island home. It is my job to watch over this rock. The rock I'm standing on right now. Our Commander, the man in charge, likes a clean rock. See my broom? See my mop? It is my job to keep this rock clean! My rock is very clean. My rock is the cleanest of all the rocks on our island home. I make the Commander very happy because I do a good job. I help him and in turn he will help me. My Commander, when the time is right, will reward me for a good job well done. My Commander will award me soon and put me in charge of bigger and more important—more important aspects of our island home. And your daddy will then have his Distinction. And your daddy will then come home. He will come home with bars instead of stripes and you and your Mommie will be just as proud! Well, it is time for work! Your daddy loves you, Buffy, and sends a big kiss and a big smile.

THREE HOTELS

BY JON ROBIN BAITZ

Kenneth Hoyle is a rising vice president for a multinational business that aggressively markets Iris and Rose baby formula to Africa and the rest of the Third World. Since coming to work for the company after a stint in the Peace Corps, he has hardened into the role of corporate hatchet man, increasingly alienating his wife, Barbara, and winning the encouragement of his superiors, Kroener and Mulcahey. He appears alone, in a hotel suite in Tangiers, Morocco, wearing "a rather exquisite summer suit." He speaks to the audience.

HOYLE: Anyhow. This Brit kid who works for us. We're at a party for the London office. Me. My wife, Barbara. Bunch of the guys. And the kid says to me, "Mr. Hoyle, sir," (and you know they're gonna fuck ya when they call you sir) "I must tell you I think that what we are doing in Africa is morally indefensible."

Well. I mean. There you are. His wife stands there grinning at me like a mad little Staffordshire terrier and there is my *own* wife, grinning, thrilling. And Kroener and Mulcahey taking it in too. "Morally indefensible," I say. "How so?" And he sputters like a boiling tuber. "You've got saleswomen dressed up as nuns and *nurses* for God's sake running around *hospitals* in Lagos and Nairobi. You're treating baby formula in the Third World as if it's tonic water, which it is not, though by the time the mothers dilute it and the babies drink it, it may as well be. You've got billboards with *doctors* on them, for Christ's sake, proclaiming "Iris and Rose is better than breast milk." And the only reason you're getting away with any of this, Mr. Hoyle, is because you are doing it in a place where white people do not go on holiday. Come on," he says. "Defend *that*." □□□

At World Headquarters you learn a kind of manufactured thuggishness. It is a sort of currency, if you will. The coin of our realm. It means nothing. Less than nothing. It's totally made up.

I look at the boy. "For years," I begin, "this company was run by uncomplicated men who had a clear goal: make a buck. And with the opening of so many world markets, it's taken these men a while to learn that you can't do business in Togo the same way you do in Elbow Lake, Minnesota." I stop for a moment. "'Cause in *Togo*, pal, things are different." What I'm doing is, I'm doing my gentleman farmer number. (Someone said poor Georgie Bush might have seen me on PBS, that documentary on corporate accountability, and stolen my style.)

Anyhow, back to the party. I say, "Listen. You and I both know that *you* know that. I can see from your tie that you did your hard time at the London School of Economics, so kiddo, clearly you're bright. Therefore, I'm not gonna stand here and play sandbox ethics with ya, so let me offer you this. *Quit*."

I take a breath. The room, it is glistening; it is limpid. He is beginning to look queasy but I'm not about to let this cocksucker off the hook. □□□ "If it's so very morally indefensible sitting here overlooking Green Park with your glass of stout and sausage on a toothpick, well then, this must be your resignation, and happy am I to accept it right here and now. *Sir*."

Exactly eighteen days later I was made Vice-President in charge of Marketing and Third World Affairs.

DRINKING IN AMERICA

BY ERIC BOGOSIAN

Junkie, wino, conventioneer drunk on champagne, tough guy wreaking exaggerated havoc while on whiskey, 'ludes and triple-strength acid, Bible-thumping terrorist—these are a few of the self-absorbed and hyperkinetic blowhards who strut their stuff in Bogosian's 1986 solo show. This wheeler-dealer's got Arnie on hold on one phone line while doing business with Sid on another. It's nine o'clock in L.A. In place of coffee with cream, he snorts lines of coke chased with a triple shot of bourbon. "He wakes up, talking very fast."

Yeah? . . . SID, SID, SID, SID, SID, SID! Listen to me: YES! Do you hear me saying yes? I said yes. Yes. You have Richard Chamberlain. . . . Richard Chamberlain, *The Bhopal Story*, it's gonna happen. . . . Yes, *The Bhopal Story: The Tragic Story of a Misunderstood Multinational* starring Richard Chamberlain, name over the title, one hundred percent of the title, filmed on location in India with a cast of a thousand beggars. You're gonna make a million bucks on this thing, Sid. . . . Yes, you have the blind beggars . . . yes, you got the crippled beggars. . . . Will you get off my case, it's gonna be the greatest miniseries in the history of miniseries.

Huh? What do you mean you have some more people you want me to look at? Who? . . . Who's he? . . . The greatest actor in India? I never heard of him. . . . I never heard of him, Sid, I don't care if he's Mahatma Gandhi's grandson, if I never heard of him he's not coming in on this picture. . . . Because he's an unknown, that's why. . . . Why is he unknown? Because he doesn't have a name. . . . Sid, we're talkin' Richard Chamberlain here, OK? One of the greatest, if not the greatest, American actors of our time! I cannot have this great actor acting opposite some two-bit, unknown Hindu! I don't care if everyone in India has his face tattooed on their chests, he's an unknown in the States. . . . Wait a minute, wait a minute. . . . Sid, Sid, Sid, Sid, Sid . . . can I . . . can I . . . can I get a word in edgewise here for a second?

This guy, is he in the union? Is he in SAG? All right, listen, bring him down to the set, we'll give him some water to carry around, he can do a little Gunga Din routine for us there. . . . It's the best I can do, Sid. . . . Sid, I'm getting off the phone. . . . Have a nice time in India, watch out for the prime rib. . . . OK, yeah, ha ha. . . . *(punches the hold button again)*

Yeah, Arnie, I'm still here. . . .

ROOSTERS

BY MILCHA SANCHEZ-SCOTT

Gallo lives for the breeding and training of fighting roosters. A knife fight with a Filipino breeder got him sent to prison for manslaughter, but now he's back, dreaming of the cockfight and a champion bird. He's "a very, very handsome man in his forties," a Mexican-American charmer and sweet-talker, willing to sacrifice everything and everyone to his calling.

GALLO: Lord Eagle, Lord Hawk, sainted ones, spirits and winds, Santa María Aurora of the Dawn. . . . I want no resentment, I want no rancor. . . . I had an old red Cuban hen. She was squirrel-tailed and sort of slab-sided and you wouldn't have given her a second look. But she was a queen. She could be thrown with any cock and you would get a hard-kicking stag every time.

I had a vision, of a hard-kicking flyer, the ultimate bird, The Filipinos were the ones with the pedigree Bolinas, the high flyers, but they had no real kick. To see those birds fighting in the air like dark avenging angels . . . well like my father use to say, "Son nobles . . . finos. . . ." I figured to mate that old red Cuban. This particular Filipino had the best. A dark burgundy flyer named MacArthur. He wouldn't sell. I began borrowing MacArthur at night, bringing him back before dawn, no one the wiser, but one morning the Filipino's son caught me. He pulled out his blade. I pulled out mine. I was faster. I went up on manslaughter. . . . They never caught on . . . thought I was in the henhouse trying to steal their stags. . . . It took time—refining, inbreeding, cross-breeding, brother to sister, mother to son, adding power, rapid attack . . . but I think we got him.

NO MERCY

BY CONSTANCE CONGDON

On the eve of the first atomic-bomb detonation, Young Roy, a twenty-year-old army corporal brought in to staff the Trinity test site, comes face-to-face with the bomb's mastermind, Robert Oppenheimer. Young Roy stands in awe of the brilliant scientist; he's thrilled to be "a kind of forward observer" of the world-changing event, even as Oppenheimer appears tired, haunted and confused.

YOUNG ROY: I'm not afraid of tarantulas. I'm really not afraid of anything out here. Two months ago, if I thought I'd be here in New Mexico, well, I would've laughed. I got my orders home in Berlin, and they told us we'd get a month off then go back to, you know, clean up. But when I reported for duty, they put us on this train and the next thing I know, we're heading west. A whole train of soldiers heading west for no reason. Seemed like then. And we stopped in Nebraska—*Nebraska*—for three days and played baseball to kill time. And still we have no idea where we were going or why. And then, and then, back on the train and further west, and the ground starts to change. My buddy wakes me up and presses my face to the window. Lord! There's a herd of antelope galloping alongside the train and I look up and got my breath took away again! Mountains! Blue-green, almost black the pine is so thick. They are so still and big, they look painted on. Well, that's when I knew I was going somewhere important. Something about the speed of that train—I swear once we got close to here, we went faster and faster—I think those guys could've lost control like *that. (Snaps fingers)* I mean, that prairie blurred into the desert and the day went *by.* And then, bang, we were stopped. 'Cause we were here. Stopped. Dead. And it was so quiet. The sky was full of stars. And I could feel that train moving inside me for the whole next day. ☐☐☐

This is just about the most excitng thing that has ever happened, sir. I mean, I missed the invention of the motor car, I missed Christopher Columbus, I missed the time when Lord Jesus was walking around on earth, I missed the invention, no, *discovery* of electricity. I was beginning to think that absolutely nothing was ever gonna happen to me. You know?

When I think that the smartest men, why, in the whole world are here. And all the knowledge that's went into this, from way back there. When the first guy got an idea, like a little light bulb going on over his head, and, wham, he invents that light bulb. And then another guy makes it better. And another guy says, "We got a light bulb, we need a socket." And then, wham, we got a socket. And then a lamp. And then, the next thing you know, the whole world is lit up. Lamps everywhere! No more darkness.

RAISED IN CAPTIVITY

BY NICKY SILVER

After four-and-a-half years of psychoanalysis, Sebastian feels that he's made "not an iota of progress. He returns from his mother's funeral—she was killed when her shower massage flew off—determined to terminate therapy. Here, he attempts to describe to his doctor the family dementia around birthdays and to pinpoint the exact moment his twin sister Bernadette "slipped, irredeemably, 'round the bend."

SEBASTIAN: It was hot, August, and the temperature must've reached a hundred and ten in that front yard. There were about two dozen children there, none of whom I particularly liked, and none of whom was having a particularly good time. We just sat there, sad, withered children on a patch of brown, burned-up grass. My mother had, as always, planned every moment of the day with military precision. Two o'clock: three-legged races. Two fifteen: passing oranges under our chins. At three o'clock, the entertainment arrived. A clown: Mr. Giggles. Mr. Giggles was *extremely* old. It's true that all adults seem old to small children, but Mr. Giggles would have seemed *very old* to very old people! He was old. His skin was the texture and non-color of white raisins.

In any event, Mr. Giggles made flowers spring from umbrellas and foam balls appear from behind our ears. He was maniacally cheerful, despite the fact that none of us joined in or laughed or moved. Mr. Giggles thought some singing might rouse us from our collective coma. He sang "A Hundred Bottles of Beer on the Wall." Only we were ten, so he sang "A Hundred Bottles of *Milk* on the Wall." Not very imaginative was Mr. Giggles. He sang loudly and with what should have been infectious joy: "A hundred bottles of milk on the wall, a hundred bottles of milk!" And we tried! We did. At first. All of us, I think, joined in. Mr. Giggles ran around in a desperate frenzy, wild for us to perform—but it was so hot! We made it through ninety bottles of milk on the wall and eighty bottles of milk. And then . . . I could take it no more. I just stopped. I lay down, put my head on the earth and shut my eyes. Well, Mr. Giggles ran over and knelt down and sang *right* at me, loud, shouting more than singing really. Screaming right at me: "EIGHTY-TWO BOTTLES OF MILK ON THE WALL! EIGHTY-TWO BOTTLES OF MILK!" I refused to stir. I just opened my eyes and stared at this *fascist* clown. Then another little boy stopped. Tommy Leonardo, I think. He let his head fall forward and fell silent. Giggles leapt upon him and shrieked with rage, "EIGHTY-ONE BOTTLES OF MILK ON THE WALL! EIGHTY-ONE BOTTLES OF MILK!" Then very quickly, other children followed suit. Like spontaneous suicides, their voices fell silent. By now Mr. Giggles was in the throes of a demented fit! Running crazily from child to child, screaming, spit flying out of him, sweat spraying off of him.—But he would not give up! By now, no one was singing, except for my sister, who would participate in this deranged duet at any cost! I watched as Giggles flapped his arms like spastic birds and lost the count completely: "FORTY-TWO BOTTLES OF MILK ON THE WALL! FORTY-EIGHT BOTTLES OF MILK!" And then he fell over in a sad, wet, broken-pencil heap. *(Pause)*

The silence was palpable. My sister, abandoned, looked at me. "He's dead," I whispered. Bernadette shrieked and ran in horror from the yard and into the street, where a bread truck swerved to avoid her and ran headlong into a mammoth oak tree, shaking from its perch our cat, which fell to an ugly, bloody death, impaled by the truck's antenna and splattered on the windshield.

COASTAL DISTURBANCES

BY TINA HOWE

Andre Sor, forty-nine, is the European-born owner of the most impor-
tant photography gallery in New York. He comes to a beach on the
North Shore of Massachusetts to see his twenty-four-year-old girl-
friend, Holly, a photographer. She describes him: "power and promises
. . . beautiful women falling all over him . . . the whole charismatic
thing . . . sweeping into rooms and making everyone's heart stop. . . .
Lowering his voice and swearing allegiance to only you." The exquis-
ite story he tells Holly below is, in fact, an explanation or excuse—
the reasons he must leave her for several weeks (as, clearly, he's
done often before) to see new work in Paris and Brussels. They're
on the beach together in the drizzling, overcast August afternoon;
Andre's wearing "knockout" Italian shoes and "a chic raincoat. He
carries an umbrella."

ANDRE: As I said, my father was a diamond cutter. His gems were
prized by the most beautiful women of Europe. He was a master. It
was his *eye!* He could see the jewel where none existed. As a handy-
man in this country, he acquired boxes of castoff junk—clock springs,
sewing-machine parts, glass doorknobs, old eyeglasses. After a day
of haggling in the streets, he'd haul out his boxes of treasures and
lose himself in the minutiae of small gold springs and moving parts
. . . ☐☐☐

Well, three or four times a year as we were finishing our meager
Friday evening Shabbas dinner, he would suddenly announce, "I have
something to show you, my children." You see, my father was also
an amateur watchmaker. He built fantasy clocks that played tunes
instead of telling time—mechanical toys that flew around the
room—ticking bifocals . . . ☐☐☐

As our circumstances worsened, his creations became even more
fanciful. They reached their height the winter my sister Sophie almost
died of pneumonia. Just as she was fluttering back into consciousness, my father whispered, "Ich hab epes eich zu veissen, mein
kinder." . . . He reached under the bed and pulled out this crystal
sphere about the size of a football. Inside it was a miniature render-
ing of our cherished view—the Woolworth Building, the Bank of

Manhattan, Farmer's Trust . . . □□□ But what was most astonishing of all was . . . he'd fashioned it as a clock with tiny numbers around the circumference. *(Rotating and miming the movement)* Every hour on the hour, something within the sphere moved. At eight o'clock, the Woolworth Building bent at the middle and doffed its roof. At nine o'clock, one of the little barges suddenly sent off a blast of steam. At ten o'clock, a flock of seagulls wheeled up over the courthouse. . . . As you can imagine, there was no sleeping that night. My father's fancy had not only animated our secret world, it also made it tangible—something we could hold in our hands. For Sophie, it was like being given back her life again. For me, it was a testament to the transforming eye of the artist. I don't have those gifts. *(Pause)* I can only admire. Innocence eludes me. But you—you and my father— you walk with the angels. Think of it—living a life promoting a talent you'll never have, a beauty you'll never be able to create.

"I'M DYING, THAT'S WHAT'S WRONG"

SWIMMING TO CAMBODIA

BY SPALDING GRAY

Spalding Gray, author, performer and subject of the evening-length monologue from which this is excerpted, comes to Thailand to play a small part in The Killing Fields, *a movie about the Cambodian genocide. As his work on the film comes to an end, though, he finds himself hard-pressed to return home, at least until he has a "Perfect Moment." His girlfriend Renée, visiting for a couple of weeks, has just wrenched from him a commitment to meet her in New York, whether or not he has had such a moment by July 8. After they resolve their feud, it is "time for pleasure." So Gray joins his devilish companion Ivan, a South African cameraman, in a few tokes of Thai stick on the beautiful starlit beach, even though "marijuana tends to unlock my Kundalini in the worst way."*

When I opened my eyes Ivan was there but Renée was gone. She must have wandered off down the beach. I had no real sense of where I was. It all looked and felt like a demented Wallace Stevens poem with food poisoning, and in the distance I saw what looked like a group of Thai girl scouts dancing around a campfire. I thought that if I could get in that circle and hold hands with them I would be whole again. I would be cured and back in real time. I got up and tried to walk toward the fire and found that I was falling down like a Bowery bum, like a drunken teenager or the fraternity brother I'd never been. And all of a sudden I realized I was going to be very sick and I crawled off like a Thai dog to a far corner of the beach.

Up it came, and each time the vomit hit the ground I covered it over with sand, and the sand I covered it with turned into a black gauze death mask that flew up and covered my face. And so it went; vomit-cover-mask, vomit-cover-mask, until I looked down to see that I had built an entire corpse in the sand and it was my corpse. It was my own decomposing corpse staring back at me, and I could see the teeth pushing through the rotting lips and the ribs coming through

the decomposing flesh of my side. I looked up to see Renée standing over me saying, "What's wrong, Hon?"

"I'm dying, that's what's wrong."

"Oh. I thought you were having a good time building sand castles."

She had been looking on at a distance.

Two men, I don't know who, carried me out of there, one arm over
one shoulder and one arm over another, like a drunken, crucified
sailor. And I was very upset because the following day I was scheduled to do my big scene in the movie.

AS IS

BY WILLIAM M. HOFFMAN

*Saul and his ex-lover, Rich, both in their thirties, are dividing up their
belongings after a long separation, the result of Rich leaving for
another man. Saul's jealousy his risen up throughout the scene, but
just now he is grappling for control of it, working to keep the man he
still loves in the room with him. The monologue, from this early, important AIDS play, reflects a moment in the history of the disease circa
1990, when the 1985 play was revised.*

SAUL: I visited Teddy today at St. Vincent's. It's very depressing. . . .
He's lying there in bed, out of it. He's been out of it since the time
we saw him. He's not in any pain, snorting his imaginary cocaine,
doing his poppers. Sometimes he's washing his mother's floor, and
he's speaking to her in Spanish. Sometimes he's having sex. You can
see him having sex right in front of you. He doesn't even know you're
there. □□□

Jimmy died, as you must have heard. I went out to San Francisco
to be with him the last few weeks. You must have heard that, too. He
was in a coma for a month. Everybody wanted to pull the plug, but
they were afraid of legal complications. I held his hand. He couldn't
talk, but I could see his eyelids flutter. I swear he knew I was with
him. *(Pause)*

Harry has KS, and Matt has trouble breathing. He went for tests today. . . . I haven't slept for weeks. Every morning I examine my body for swellings, marks. I'm terrified of every pimple, every rash, even though I've tested negative. If I cough I think of Teddy. I wish he would die. He is dead. He might as well be. Why can't he die? I feel the disease closing in on me. All my activities are life and death. Keep up my Blue Cross. Up my reps. Eat my vegetables.

Sometimes I'm so scared I go back on my resolutions: I drink too much, and I smoke a joint, and I find myself at the bars and clubs, where I stand around and watch. They remind me of accounts of Europe during the Black Plague: groping in the dark, dancing till you drop. The New Wave is the corpse look. I'm very frightened and I miss you. Say something, damn it.

THE LOMAN FAMILY PICNIC

BY DONALD MARGULIES

Herbie, manager of a lighting showroom and father of two boys, lives in a high-rise apartment in Coney Island, Brooklyn, circa 1965, surrounded by identical buildings. He's rarely home, though, indentured as he is to his job. He recently worked through his eighteenth anniversary and worried through his son's bar mitzvah that missing a Saturday of work would put his job at risk. When he is at home, he's stymied, can find next to nothing to say to his sons or his wife, Doris. In the first monologue, Herbie, staring across the Formica table at Doris, comes suddenly to life, as he, in fantasy, tells her the story of the day she died. In the second, he stares out, stuck in the midst of dressing for work, and speaks to the audience.

HERBIE: It was around eleven one night. ☐☐☐

We were in bed, watching the news. You got up to go to the john; I dozed off; you came back. The toilet was still running. And then you shook, like. ☐☐☐

The kind of shake you do when you're in a dream, falling? ☐☐☐

Well, your shake woke me up and I looked at you and you looked funny to me. ☐☐☐

Very white; and I touched you and you felt funny. □□□

I shook you: Doris, Doris. It was like you passed out, only worse. □□□

9-1-1 I called. I held your cold foot and told you, we're gonna get you some oxygen, Doris, everything's gonna be okay. And the sirens came soon, red lights flashed 'round the windows, and the buzzer buzzed and I buzzed 'em in. They're on their way up, Doris, don't worry, any minute. . . . The bell. I let 'em in, I was still in my shorts and didn't even care, didn't even think to put on my pants. And they came in, noisy with oxygen, stretcher; they *zetzed* some furniture on the way in. □□□

Easy, I said, and led 'em to the bedroom, and I sat up in bed watching them work on you. Boy, they hit you hard. □□□

Don't hurt her, you got to do that so hard? They pumped on you, your pajama top was open, and I wasn't even embarrassed 'cause these guys are professionals, I thought, they do this all the time. Remember the time the car died on that bad part of Ocean Avenue and the Triple-A guys started her right up? □□□

That's what I thought: Come on, guys, start her up. □□□

Let's go. One more press, two more, come on Doris, three more, come on, okay this time, this time, come on baby. You were gonna snap out of it like when you think in the movies somebody drowned but they cough up water and they're fine. Cough, Doris. Come on, cough. And then you were gonna sit up and turn pink again and say what the hell happened, Herbie? □□□

I waited. *(A beat)* What the hell happened you were supposed to say.

THE LOMAN FAMILY PICNIC

BY DONALD MARGULIES

HERBIE: Maybe I don't have dreams anymore. I mean I must, but I don't remember. I don't remember a thing. My childhood? The war? Show me a picture of me taken someplace and I couldn't tell you where. I won't remember the name of the buddy I had my arm around. Ask me what year my kids were born, I couldn't tell you. Either of them. I know I was married eighteen years ago 'cause that's what Doris told me; the other night was our anniversary. I know how old I am; I'm forty years old. I was born in '25, but the exact date they're not sure, and the midwife who signed the birth certificate put my sex down as female. So I don't know; I don't know. I remember Dame May Whitty was in *The Lady Vanishes* . . . but I don't remember my father even shaking my hand. □□□

Did my father throw me a bar mitzvah? I don't even remember being bar mitzvahed. If I was you can be sure nobody thought twice about it. They say we were very poor when I was young. *(Shrugs)* I don't remember. Supposedly we were on relief. Six kids in three rooms. No doors. No privacy. Hand-me-downs from my brothers. . . . Nothing ever started with me, it ended with me. I didn't have much; that much I remember. You stop wanting, so what you don't have doesn't matter. This is the Depression I'm talking about. I got through those years with my eyes shut tight and holding my breath like when you're underwater. Got the hell outta there, straight to the Army. War was an improvement. Then I met Doris, then I married her, got this job, kids. . . . And I go through every day with my eyes shut tight and holding my breath, till the day is over and I can come home. To what? What kind of home is left to come home to by the time I come home?

IV
"DESCRIPTION OF THE SO-CALLED VENUS"

VENUS

BY SUZAN-LORI PARKS

Parks's play follows a woman transported from her South African home to be displayed as a human wonder—"The Hottentot Venus"—because of the extraordinary size of her "bottom." "The year was 1810," we're told, "three years after the Bill for the Abolition of the Slave-Trade had been passed in Parliament, and among protests and denials, horror and fascination her show went on. She died in Paris 5 years later." Below are two descriptions of the Venus Hottentot. The first is a postautopsy presentation made by The Baron Docteur during the play's intermission. The Docteur, an anatomist fascinated by the woman, first sees her in a filthy freak-show cage. He buys her from the head of the show, keeps her as both subject and mistress, falls in love with her and then, as his own family life and career are threatened, allows her to be thrown into jail, where she, infected with "the clap," inevitably dies. He then autopsies her, building a career off his research. His monologue might be a good exercise in subtext: his fascination, attraction, love and guilt bubble under the scientific presentation of fact. The second speech includes quoted material from the Docteur's journal. It's read out by a former grave digger, who now watches the jail where Venus is caged and left to die. He functions as a narrator and chorus through the play. Parks's frequent use of (Rest) means, "Take a little time, a pause, a breather; make a transition."

THE BARON DOCTEUR:
The height, measured after death,
was 4 feet 11 and 1/2 inches.
The total weight of the body was 98 pounds *avoirdupois*.
In the following notes my attention is chiefly directed
to the more perishable soft structures of the body.
The skeleton will form the subject of future examination.
(Rest)

External Characteristics:
The great amounts of subcutaneous fat were
quite surprising. On the front of the thigh for instance
fat measured 1 inch in thickness.
On the thighs reverse the measure of fat was
4 inches deep.
On the buttocks proper, rested the fatty cushion, a.k.a.
Steatopygia the details of which I'll relate in due course.
(Rest)
The Skin:
Prevailing color: Orange-brown tolerably uniform in tint
on all parts of the body save on abdomen and thighs:
2 shades darker.
(Rest)
The palms of the hands
and soles of the feet
were almost white.
(Rest) □□□
The hair on the scalp was black.
Arranged in numerous separate tufts
each tuft composed of a bunch of spirally
curled hairs. Much interwoven.
The length of the tufts atop the head were from 1 inch to 1.5
becoming shorter and smaller at the scalps edge.
Several of the individual hairs when pulled out straight
were found to measure a full 7 inches.
On the scalp were several spots completely bald:
The subject when alive wore wigs which
could have produced the bare patches.
(A warning, Gentlemen, to us all.)
Eyebrows were very scanty.
Eyelashes short: .2 inch hairs.
On the *pubes* and *labia majora*
a few small scattered tufts
of crisply curled black hairs were present.
When pulled out straight these stretched out
over 3 inches long.
(Rest)
(Rest) □□□
The *mammae*, situated exactly

over the fourth and fifth ribs,
were a full 6 inches apart at the inner edge of their bases.
They were soft
soft, flaccid and subpendulous:
4 inches in diameter at the base
and about the same from base to apex.
Nipple very prominent of blackish-brownish hue
and 1 inch in diameter. An areola
darker than the neighbor skin
extended around for 1 and a 1/2 inches
from the nipple's center.
(Rest) □□□
Her shoulders back and chest had grace.
Her charming hands . . . *uh hehm*.
Where was I?

VENUS

BY SUZAN-LORI PARKS

THE NEGRO RESURRECTIONIST:
Footnote #7
Historical Extract. Category: Medical.
(Rest)
A DETAILED PHYSICAL DESCRIPTION OF THE SO-CALLED VENUS
HOTTENTOT:
(Rest)
"Her hair was black and wooly, much like that of the common Negro,
the slits of the eyes horizontal as in Mongols, not oblique; the brows
straight, wide apart and very much flattened close to the top of the
nose, but jutting out at the temple above the cheekbones; her eyes
were dark and lively; her lips blackish, terribly thick; her complexion
very dark."
(Rest)
"Her ears were much like those found in monkeys: Small, weakly
formed at the *tragus*, and vanishing behind almost completely."

(Rest)

"Her breasts she usually lifted and tightened beneath the middle part of her dress, but, left free, they hung bulkily and terminated oblique-ly in blackish areola about 1 and 1/2 inches in diameter pitted with radiating wrinkles, near the center of what was a nipple so flattened and obliterated as to be barely visible: The color of her skin was on the whole a yellowish brown, almost as dark as her face."

(Rest)

"Her movements had rapidity and came unexpected calling to mind well, with all respect to her, the movements of a monkey. Above all, she had a way of pushing out her lips just like the monkeys do. Her personality was sprightly, her memory good. She spoke low Dutch, tolerably good English—the men at the Academy and I tried to teach her French. She danced after the fashion of her own country and played with a fairly good ear upon a little instrument she called a Jew's Harp."

(Rest)

"She had no body hair apart from a few short flecks of wool like that on her head, scattered about her pubic parts."

(Rest)

"The wonders of her lower regions, will be fleshed out in greater detail at a later date."

(Rest)

"This information was gleaned, as has been said, upon the first and subsequent examinations which were performed in the office of her personal physician. As stated for the record, she submitted to these examinations as willingly as a patient submits to his doctors eyes and hands."

COASTAL DISTURBANCES

BY TINA HOWE

Leo Hart "used to be a lot of things—a car mechanic, a double-A ball player, a contractor." Currently, at twenty-eight, he's a slightly-too-old-to-be-doing-this lifeguard on a private beach on Massachusetts's

North Shore. He's also handsome, strongly built and noticeably "well-endowed in the uh . . . hoo-hah department." Not long ago, he and his girlfriend of three years, whom he'd hoped to marry, broke up. More recently, while working at the beach, he met another woman, Holly Dancer, and (for the moment) their romance seems sexy, exciting and fun. They've just spent their first night together, making love on the beach. It's early morning. They're alone, sharing stories. When he's finished this one, Leo will ask her to run away with him and sail up the coast of Maine.

LEO: Juanita Wijojac—Christ, I haven't thought about her in years. □□□

I was thirteen and she was eleven. Juanita Wijojac was the most exotic girl I'd ever seen. It wasn't just her beauty, which was phenomenal—her mother was Portuguese and her father was Hungarian or something, so she had all this hair—chalk white skin and clouds of black hair □□□

All the guys in school were in love with her. We used to fantasize: if she has extra fingers, what *else* does she have tucked out of view . . . ? □□□ We couldn't figure out what she was doing in Essex. She must have been studying with some famous organist in the area. She didn't stay long. Only a year, but what a year . . . ! I used to climb the elm tree next to the First Congregational Church where she practiced in the evening and watch her. I lived in that fucking tree! On a clear night, there were as many as forty guys up there with binoculars. But no one was as loyal as me. . . . It's funny, I don't remember the music at all, and she was really good. I mean, when she cut loose with those preludes and fugues, she practically shook the stained glass right off the walls—those lambs and apostles jitterbugged like nothing you ever saw. . . . No, it was all her—the way she hunched over the keys, how her hair fell across her face, and of course all those flying fingers. Sometimes I counted as many as eight on a hand . . . □□□ Yeah, after a couple of hours up in that tree, the old imagination went nuts. I saw extra eyes, extra mouths. . . . Finally, I couldn't take it anymore, I had to do something. I'll never forget it. . . . One night I was up in my tree as usual, when all of a sudden I found myself marching right up into the organ loft and bam—there I was, face to face with her. She was so flushed and beautiful, I could hardly keep my balance. . . . I reached out to steady myself and set off this blizzard of sheet music. She lets out this piercing scream as if she's just met up with Jack the Ripper, I mean we are talking disaster city here . . . and then I notice some of her fingers kind of . . . disappearing down into her palm . . . □□□ and she's wriggling around on the bench as if she's trying to hide something. □□□

It was awful. I immediately regretted having come, but seeing her so flustered trying to reel everything in, just heightened my desire . . . □□□ I threw myself at her feet. □□□

I didn't know what else to do. I began telling her that I loved her, that I'd always love her, that I wanted to marry her and be with her forever. But she didn't seem to understand so I grabbed her. □□□

I couldn't help it, she suddenly seemed so fragile. I wanted to protect her. By this time, she was screaming in every foreign language you've ever heard. The louder she screamed, the tighter I held on to her. It was a nightmare, Her heart suddenly started going crazy. It raced from her chest, to her side, down her legs, back up to her neck. I tried to steady it with my hands, but it was all over the place! □□□

Finally, some rector or deacon showed up and pulled us apart. It was shortly after that, that her family moved away. I thought I'd never recover. I mooned around for almost two years. I'll tell you one thing— she could have given one hell of a backrub.

CASANOVA

BY CONSTANCE CONGDON

Congdon's play spans the life of the world's most notorious womanizer (1725–1798) and takes place in cities throughout Europe. More than a dramatization of Casanova's famous memoirs, though, this theatrical epic provides a woman's-eye view of the seducer's life. The ghost of a woman who loved him narrates and witnesses his conquests, and, as the syphilitic, decrepit old rake makes his way toward a final appearance at the reemergent French court less than a decade after the Revolution, his abandoned daughter Sophie, now forty, anticipates his return. Sophie's companion is a sixty-year-old transvestite named Bobo, who appears throughout in full woman's makeup and gowns. Bobo loves the old royal French world, in which he was a chevalier, before Casanova humiliated him in public. In the decades since his fall from social grace, he has made a living as a tutor and seamstress and harbored two powerful memories (which follow in separate monologues) of the man who disgraced him. One is an image of social cruelty; the other of the transforming power of erotic love. "All these years I thought you hated him," Sophie says of Casanova near the end. "No," Bobo replies, with the resonance of a secret stored for forty years.

BOBO: He humiliated me in court, the Venetian brute. He'd just escaped from prison and didn't we hear THAT story until we were all ready to scream. I was dressed as a man that day and was a person to be taken seriously. There was talk that I was going to be ambassador to England! He came up to me in front of the entire court at the Palace and proceeded to smell me from head to . . . my nether regions. Well, I was stunned, to say the least. I just stood there amazed! And then he said in the worst French I have ever heard: *(In an Italian accent)* "This is not a man. This man is a woman!" *(Back to his own voice)* And everyone froze—believe me, when every second of one's life is controlled by rules of decorum, an incident like this is cataclysmic—and then, Louie, King Louie—thank God he didn't live to see the horrible things, unspeakable things that happened to his grandson at the hands of barbarians, *beasts*. The world is a dreadful, horrible place, my sweet. And, if I could take us both to the moon tomorrow, I would! *(Pause. He's remembering the French Revolution)* Paris—you are despicable.

You have been made despicable.

It's a shame his makeup's become politically incorrect—yea, even dangerous. But I'm going to wear it until the day I die.

CASANOVA

BY CONSTANCE CONGDON

BOBO: In a garden, at dusk, I watched him once.

It was a large function, and everyone had gone to hear the concert by the ornamental waters, but I had stayed behind to relieve myself. I was in a gown with some intricate underpinning and the process of relieving myself promised to be somewhat complicated and potentially alarming to anyone who might observe it. So I approached a section of hedge that contained an enclave and a very tall topiary. And that's when I heard his voice—it was unmistakable, and his French had gotten much better. The demands of my bladder disappeared entirely from my consciousness as I positioned myself to observe, my mouth dry, quite certain that I was to see the most erotic vision.

There he was, your father, with a woman—a rather ordinary-looking woman, I thought. They were sitting on a stone bench, very close, but not touching. She was speaking now, telling of some incident, growing more and more animated in her speech, enjoying herself, and he was simply there, listening, his face mirroring her emotions, laughing, then intent, then serious. So strange—he did nothing and yet his simple attention seemed to have the most erotic effect on her—suddenly she took his face in her hands and kissed him, passionately, on the mouth. When she released him, his head fell back, and I could see the ecstatic expression of his face. He closed his eyes and reached for her breast, like a drowning man reaches for the shore. He must have been gentle in his grasp because she gave—all. I watched him swim through the satin that encased her, unbuttoning himself as he went. Not my taste, but, oh God, it was lovely.

They lasted through the rest of the Vivaldi and were into several measures of the Boccherini when she heard something—not me. I was transfixed. I was silent, still. I was topiary. Topiary of an exquisitely dressed, very tall woman with a rampant hard-on. She left him, she bolted, suddenly alarmed. And he collapsed, face down, like he'd been shot. I couldn't bear it. I crept, limped away.

A few heartbeats, I swear, a few steps, breaths, and he was right behind me. "Madam," he said, "Madam," in a voice clouded with lust. I stopped and he pressed himself up against my back. "Mademoiselle." And then he ran his tongue up the back of my neck.

I'd always thought my neck was ugly.

CLOUD TECTONICS

BY JOSÉ RIVERA

Aníbal de la Luna picks up a strange and beautiful woman in the middle of a rainstorm flooding Los Angeles. She is pregnant—has been, it seems, for two years—and in search of her lover, the father of the unborn child. Aníbal shelters her for the night in his modest home. After Celestina tells her story, the conversation centers more and more on sex and love. Aníbal describes his girlfriend Debbie and how, as they made love the night before, memories of his first experience of love—when he was still a boy—were unleashed.

ANÍBAL: One night I was on the second floor of my cousins' house. I remember walking past a dark bedroom: the door was open. I thought I heard a voice inside calling my name. I went in. My cousin Eva was there. She was older than Ernie or Cheo. Much older than me. I remember her standing by the window. I could see her face lit up by a streetlight—or was it the moon? I remember there was a heavy smell in the room. And I don't know how I eventually got there . . . but I ended up lying in bed with Eva. I was on my back, looking at the ceiling. Eva was kneeling next to me. Then Eva lifted her dress and she was straddling me and pressing her pelvis into me. I think she had her underwear on. I had my pants on and I didn't know why she was doing this to me, though I knew I had to do this because she was my older cousin, therefore she had authority. I remember her legs being smooth. I remember her face. She was looking out the window. I don't remember how long this lasted. I don't remember if anyone came in. I don't remember if anyone ever knew about this, though, later on it seemed that everybody knew. I liked Eva on top of me. I remember her weight. I liked her weight. I don't remember if I got hard or not: I was only a little boy! I liked watching Eva's face, the way she looked out the window. How the light struck half her face. I wish I could remember her mouth! I think it was open. But I don't remember. Was there a smile? Did she bite her lower lip? Was she talking to me? Did she say something in Spanish? I remember her eyes. (*Beat*)

So I fell in love with Eva. She was all I thought about. And I think my mother suspected something and she was worried about us, though first cousins had married several times in my family. One night my mother and I were washing dishes together, side by side. And we had the only conversation about sex we were ever to have. Without looking at me, she said: "Aníbal, remember: there is some fruit you are not allowed to eat." And that's all she said. And I knew *exactly* what she meant. And it was all she had to say to me. (*Beat*)

I've never forgotten Eva. Even in Debbie's arms after five years of missing her and wanting her, I thought easily of Eva. It's like . . . the space around my body was permanently curved—or dented—by Eva's heaviness. I wonder if love sometimes does that to you. It alters the physics around you in some way: changing the speed of light and the shape of space and how you experience time.

V

"MY SHIT'S INTENSE"

POUNDING NAILS IN THE FLOOR WITH MY FOREHEAD

BY ERIC BOGOSIAN

Bogosian's solo show barrages the audience with men. These characters, originally played by the author, wear their personal shit on their sleeves: aggression, rage, paranoia, need. They are the voices he's trying to pound out of his head in order "to think a clear thought"; they are "the boogeyman of my inner thoughts." Here is a "fan" accosting a performance artist who is, or might as well be, Bogosian himself. The time is 1994; the place, America.

"The Fan"

Hey man, man, excuse me, man, I just want to tell you, man, uh, I just saw the show and it was . . . it was really intense. And I wondered if I could ask you a question? I've been taking this course on performance from Willem Dafoe, well actually from this woman who used to work with Willem Dafoe and uh, she's been teaching us about breathing and honesty in breathing and I was watching you tonight, man, and uh, you breathe so honestly, man.

And I was wondering uh, could I buy you a cup of coffee, man, we could just hang out and rap for an hour or two?

Oh, yeah of course, cool, cool. I understand. No, you're busy, that's cool.

I just want to tell you, man, that I think your shit's great. And uh, I think like you and Gary Oldman and Steven Seagal are doing like the only interesting shit out there right now. I mean it, I think you're a genius.

Me? I make performances like you. I mean, not like *you*. But uh, like you. It's funny, like some of the shit you do out there, man, it's like you've been to one of my shows and you're like stealing my shit. I mean I know you're not . . .

But I wish you could come see what I do, man. I like perform and I have this friend who does this music while I'm performing because you know you have to have music with your shit for like marketing purposes and stuff, you know? They won't put you on MTV if you don't have music. I mean, you don't have to worry about that shit, you're old and everything . . .

But I wish you could see it. I know you'd dig it.

I do this one thing, where I take this human skull and I cover it all with cheese food until it looks like a real head and I stick it on this stick and stick the stick on like this spring on my back and like when I'm jumping around the head is like bouncing around and I'm like: "Whoa! A *head*!" And I grab it and I bite it and all the skin's like falling off and the audience gets totally grossed out . . . and . . .

Oh! And last week, man, you would have loved this. . . . We went down to the meat market and we got all these pigs' guts and blood and shit and we filled up these ziploc bags with 'em, stuck 'em under our clothes. The audience didn't even know they were there.

And we're like jumping around and doing our show and like all of a sudden we pull out these straight razors and sliced our stomachs right open and all the guts and blood are like falling out and chicks are screaming and I'm slipping on the blood. Fell down, took three stitches over my eye, man. See?

Like art imitating life.

Yeah. Yeah. That's what everybody says. My shit's intense.

FREE WILL & WANTON LUST

BY NICKY SILVER

Philip is the only person in his mangled, manic family unable to over-come his loneliness with sex. His mother Claire, a chatty, narcissistic and somewhat grotesque sophisticate possesses the skill in spades: by keeping herself in perpetual heat over a continuous supply of much younger lovers whom she pretends to love, she can fill up every void. Philip, a twenty-year-old music-school dropout with no such charm or talent, appears, according to Silver, like a Bertolt Brecht character in his mother's Noël Coward play. This speech, taken from a much longer monologue to the audience, exemplifies Philip's direct, aggressive style, at war with Claire's witty, glamorous one. Just prior to this, Philip has stumbled in on his apparently sexless girlfriend loudly enjoying raucous intercourse with Claire's lover. This is only one of Philip's recent crises.

PHILIP: I don't find my sex organs particularly attractive. I don't mean that. I mean, I don't find my sex organs particularly attractive. That's the same thing, isn't it? Let me clarify—oh hell! I don't think mine are any less attractive than anybody else's. I don't think my penis is any uglier than yours, say, or yours. But then, I'm assuming a lot, because I haven't seen your penis. But then you haven't seen mine. And let me tell you right now, you're not going to! And not because I think it's any uglier than anybody else's, but just because *I don't want to!* So, my point is: sex parts are ugly. Which, of course raises the invariable question, what is ugly and what is beautiful? We are all trained to see certain things as beautiful and other things as ugly, or less so. I haven't decided whether this is entirely environmental or whether genetics has a hand in it. But the pictures in *National Geographic* of women with long, pendulous breasts and disks, like garbage can lids, implanted into their lips, leads me to the conclusion that it is largely environmental conditioning. (I don't know if conditioning was the right way to end that sentence, but it was long and I lost the thread—DON'T JUDGE ME!)

Anyway, we are all trained that certain lines are attractive, angles, pleasing to the eye, cleanness of line and so forth. Anyone who's studied design or the Munsell color wheel knows what I'm talking about. And let's face it. *The scrotum* really falls through the cracks of what is generally considered attractive. Is it me, or does the scrotum look like you've been in the bathtub a long time before you even get in? Wrinkled and soggy. I know it's not me, so don't try to make me feel bad, I feel bad enough already. I have a terrible stomachache from fish or pork or something.

And I don't think women have it any better! What? Is the vagina such an oil painting? Apologies to Georgia O'Keeffe, but it's no Mona Lisa, which I realize is a mixed metaphor, I think. But they're not pretty. Although my penis has, from time to time, been my friend. It has, more often, not. It has been my enemy. Oh hell! That may be too strong. . . . I used to love to sit on the edge of my bed, naked, holding the head of my penis between my thumb and index finger, squeezing the hole on the end so it opened and closed, while I threw

my voice and carried on a conversation. . . . YOU HAVE NO BUSI-
NESS JUDGING ME! Everyone has done that! Haven't they? . . . Well,
everyone with an imagination.

SYMPHONY OF RATS

BY RICHARD FOREMAN

*In avant-garde director/writer Richard Foreman's second collabora-
tion with the Wooster Group, he created an extravagant, multimedia
nightmare for his main character, a U.S. president "bounced back and
forth by forces outside his control." In Foreman's words: "The
President is receiving messages telepathically, and he doesn't know
whether to trust them or not. . . . In our culture, especially for white
males in power, there's a compulsion to suppress any ambiguity that
arises in our emotional or intellectual life. . . . Suppose we had a
President who allowed his imagination to function full time, would he
be able to make the straight-ahead decisions he's expected to . . . ?"
In Foreman's stage directions leading up to this speech, the President
crosses to his presidential desk, enclosed in a glass booth, and
climbs onto it as a reporter snaps photos and an actor in a rat's head
creeps around the outside of the booth. The President looks around,
disoriented.*

PRESIDENT: Where . . . am I now? Remind me? □□□ I am deeply into
the seventh realm. Archangels are visible. Taking the shape of self-
evident pulsation factors. □□□ Hard for other people to understand
what that means probably, so doubly, I don't have to explain myself.
□□□ Can I offer anybody besides myself a refreshing glass of water?
□□□ No. That water can't enter into someone else's world. Remember, everything I'm saying is coded. Therefore, my real purposes are
not understandable. □□□

Be careful. I'm going to teach you about life now, more than you
care to know. It turns out you all live on a planet upon which you daily
perceive . . . only one of seven possible levels of reality. Animals, however—elephants, zebras, rats—perceive two such levels, neither of

them the level that we, as humans, perceive. Lucky? No. It's not a matter of more desirable or less desirable levelwise. It's time, however, for you to have a so-called ultimate adventure. Remember, I'm speaking in code. Plus I am not going to be kind. Remember, my friends: God does not like strangers who stay strangers. So . . . □□□ let's be friends. □□□ You can't reach into this world! Don't even try! But there has to be another solution. Join me! You figure out how . . . !

FAT MEN IN SKIRTS

BY NICKY SILVER

Bishop Hogan and his mother are the only survivors of a plane crash on a deserted island. A pigeon-toed, hunched-up, eleven-year-old with a stutter and a Katharine Hepburn obsession, Bishop comes into his own on the island. He's transformed from a scared, deformed mess into a cannibal and, ultimately, a murderous maniac. This speech to the audience begins his transformation; in it, he loses his stutter and straightens up.

BISHOP: Katharine Hepburn made *Suddenly Last Summer* in n-n-nineteen-fifty-nine. It was based on a one-act play by Tennessee Williams. B-b-both she and Elizabeth Taylor were n-n-nominated for Oscars for the film. It is the story of Violet Venable, Katharine Hepburn's efforts to have her n-n-niece, Elizabeth Taylor, loboto-mized by Doctor Montgomery Clift. She wants to stop Liz from telling the world about her son, Sebastian—named for St. Sebastian, who was pecked to death by crows, like Tippi Hedren in the movie, *The Birds*. *(His stutter is gone)* It seems, Sebastian was this homo who used to use Katharine to lure young men on tropical islands, until she got too old and he had to use Liz. (And Katharine had the hots for junior herself, sorta) But last summer he was eaten to death by homo-cannibals, which according to the movie had something to do with sea turtles and Elizabeth Taylor's bathing suit becoming trans-parent when it got wet. *(His voice drops to a deeper register. He looks at his feet, which straighten themselves from their pigeon-toed stance)* According to legend, and her biography, by Charles Higham, Katharine Hepburn had to have homosexuality explained to her by Joseph Mankiewicz. Now, I don't think it's possible to have worked in Hollywood for twenty-five years and not to have figured it out. I think anyone who claims not to know that kind of thing is hiding something because they're nervous. I think this probably relates to why Katharine Hepburn only lived with her husband, Ludlow Ogden Smith for a few months, but had the same secretary, Laura Harding, for over twenty years. *(He takes a moment and stands up perfectly straight, for the first time)* Anyway, in the end of the movie, Monty saves Liz and Katharine loses her marbles. It was in black and white. *(He now speaks strongly, coldly)* I do not mind it on the island. The sky is almost always blue. I can do what I want. I can be by myself. It was not like that at home.

VI

"I THOUGHT OF KILLING PEOPLE"

STILL LIFE

BY EMILY MANN

Mark, an ex-Marine, still carries the violence he experienced and committed in Vietnam. It erupts in his marriage to Cheryl, whom, despite his love, he sometimes beats. His active violence also plays out in his artwork—the remnants of bones and battle memorabilia he seals in jar sculptures and the horrific photographs he shows to the audience in this direct-address, testimonial-style play.

MARK:
I thought of killing people when I got back.
I went to a party with a lady, Cheryl, you know,
later we got married—
She was into seeing people who were into LSD.
And I had tried a little acid this night,
but I wasn't too fucked-up.
And we went to this party. □□□
And there was this big guy.
I was with a friend of mine who tried to rip him off,
or something like that.
He said, the big guy said:
Get the fuck out of here
or I'll take this fucking baseball bat
and split your head wide open. □□□
I started to size up what my options were. □□□
In a split second, I knew I could have him.
He had a baseball bat,
but there was one of these long glass Coke bottles.
I knew . . . Okay, I grabbed that.
I moved toward him, to stick it in his face.
I mean, I killed him.
I mean in my mind.
I cut his throat and everything. □□□

My wife saw this and grabbed me.
I couldn't talk to anybody the rest of the night.
I sat and retained the tension and said:
"I want to kill him."
They had to drive me home.
It was only the third time I'd been out with my wife. ☐☐☐
It wasn't till the next day that I really got shook by it.
My wife said,
"Hey, cool your jets."
She'd say, "Hey, don't do things like that.
You're not over there anymore.
Settle down, it's all right." ☐☐☐
I think my wife's scared of me.

STILL LIFE

BY EMILY MANN

*Mark's confession reveals something of the anger, guilt and terror
that propel him so violently through civilian life. Nadine, mentioned
here, is an older woman artist, his mistress.*

MARK:
I . . . killed three children, a mother and father in cold blood. ☐☐☐
I killed three children, a mother and father. ☐☐☐
I killed them with a pistol in front of a lot of people.

I demanded something from the parents and then
systematically destroyed them.
And that's . . .
that's the heaviest part of what I'm carrying around.
You know about it now, a few other people know about it,
My wife knows about it, Nadine knows about it,
and nobody else knows about it.
For the rest of my life . . .
I have a son . . .

He's going to die for what I've done.
This is what I'm carrying around;
that's what this logic is about with my children.

A friend hit a booby trap.
And these people knew about it.
I knew they knew.
I knew that they were working with the VC infrastructure.
I demanded that they tell me.
They wouldn't say anything.
I just wanted them to confess before I killed them.
And they wouldn't.
So I killed their children
and then I killed them.

I was angry.
I was angry with all the power I had.
I couldn't beat them.
They beat me. □□□

I lost friends in my unit . . .
I did wrong.
People in the unit watched me kill them.
Some of them tried to stop me.
I don't know.
I can't. . . . Oh, God . . .

A certain amount of stink
went all the way back to the rear.
I almost got into a certain amount of trouble.
It was all rationalized,
that there was a logic behind it.
But they knew.
And everybody who knew had a part in it.
There was enough evidence,
but it wasn't a very good image to put out
in terms of . . .
the marines overseas, so nothing happened.

I have a child . . .
a child who passed through the age

that the little child was.
My son . . . my son
wouldn't know the difference between a VC and a marine.

ASSASSINS

BY STEPHEN SONDHEIM AND JOHN WEIDMAN

One of a gallery of fourteen Americans who have tried, successfully or un-, to assassinate a president, Sam Byck hijacked a 747, which he hoped to crash into the White House when President Nixon was home. He outlines his complaints and ideas onto tapes that he sends to famous cultural figures. Here, he speaks to Leonard Bernstein. Throughout this musical, Byck appears in a Santa Claus suit, carrying a picket sign.

SAM BYCK: Hey, I know what you're thinking. Who the hell is Sam Byck with his fat ass and his tongue on rye to give a shit hot guy such as yourself advice? Well, Lenny, it's a fact that my unwillingness to compromise my principles and kiss ass like some people I could mention has cost me the so-called good life which others have enjoyed. So be it, Len. Fuck me, fuck you. But Lenny, listen. Listen to one small piece of advice from a true fan . . . Forget the long-hair shit and write what you write best. *Love songs*. They're what we need! They're what the world needs! "Lonely Town!" "Maria!" Tender melodies to cherish for a lifetime! Timeless strains which linger in the memory and the heart! Love, Lenny! What the world needs now is love sweet love! Love makes the world go round! *(He takes a slurp of Yoo-Hoo)* Well, not exactly. Bullshit makes the world go round. You know that all too well, a worldly guy such as yourself. You know the world's a vicious, stinking pit of emptiness and pain. But not for long. I'm gonna change things, Lenny. I'm gonna drop a 747 on the White House and incinerate Dick Nixon. It's gonna make the news. You're gonna hear about it and I know what you're gonna ask yourself: What kind of world is this where a decent, stand-up guy like Sam Byck has to crash a plane into the President to make a point? You're gonna wonder if you want to go on living in a world like that. Well, lemme tell you, Len. You do. And you know why? So you can keep on writing love songs! Yes! There's a gorgeous world out there, a world of unicorns and waterfalls and puppy dogs! And you can save it! Through the medium of your God-given talent! *Do it*, Lenny! Save the world! Is that too much to ask?! . . . Oh, Lenny. One more thing. When you hear about my death you're gonna wonder if there's something more you could have done. Lenny, you did everything you could . . . *(He clicks off the tape recorder. A beat. Then he clicks it on again)* Well, maybe not *everything*. Maybe not absolutely everything, you know. Maybe one day you could've picked a phone up. Just picked up a phone and said, "Hey, Sammy, how's it going? Hang in there, Sam. This Bud's for you." How long would that have taken you? A minute? Half a minute? That was too much, wasn't it? You probably had your limo double parked. You and your shit hot buddies had a plane to catch to Paris, France for dinner and a blow job. Hey, I understand. I understand too well, my friend. You're just like all the rest of them— *(He flips through the tapes, reading names)* Jonas Salk, Jack Anderson, Hank Aaron . . . You knew where I was. You *all* did. And you know what you did? You left me there! You jerks! You shits! You pricks! You had your chance and now it's too damn late! Fuck me?! Fuck you! I'm outta here! I'm history, Lenny! Understand?! I'm *history*! *(He takes a big bite out of his sandwich, chews. Lights fade, as he starts to sing . . .)*

I like to be in America,
O.K. by me in America,
Knobs on the doors in America,
Wall-to-wall floors in America!

THE WASH

BY PHILIP KAN GOTANDA

Nobu carries a shotgun into the apartment where Masi, his wife of several decades, moved after separating from him. After a lifetime of quiet submission to this sixty-eight-year-old Japanese-American man—Masi still picks up and washes his dirty laundry—she has asked for a divorce in order to marry another man, a widower she's recently begun dating. Unbeknownst to Nobu, the other man lies napping in the next room. Although Nobu has been portrayed as an emotionally contained and often mean man who has verbally degraded his wife for years, nothing has prepared us for overt violence. His action, driven as much by confusion and shame as anger, has surprised him as well.

NOBU: It's not loaded. *(Pause)* At first I said,"No, no, no, I can't believe it. I can't believe it." I got so pissed off. I got my gun and drove over here. I drove around the block twenty or thirty times thinking "I'm gonna shoot this son-of-a-bitch, I'm gonna shoot him." I drove right up, rang the doorbell. No one answered. I kept ringing, ringing. . . . I went back to the car and waited. You cheated on me. How could you do that to me? I'm a good husband! I'm a good husband, Masi. . . . I kept seeing you two. The two of you together. I kept seeing that. It made me sick. I kept thinking, "I'm gonna shoot that son-of-a-bitch. I'm gonna shoot him. I waited in the car. It was three o'clock in the morning when I woke up. It was so cold in the car. You weren't back. I got worried I might catch a cold, and my back—you know how my back gets. I drove home, took a hot bath, and went to sleep. I've been sick in bed all week. I just wanted to show you. Both of you. That's why I brought it. Don't worry. It's not loaded. *(He cracks the shotgun and shows her that it is not loaded)* I just wanted to show both of you how it was, how I was feeling. But it's all right. You two. It's all right now.

THE FOOD CHAIN

BY NICKY SILVER

This monologue, taken from an alternate ending Silver wrote for the play, comes at the end of a running tirade by Otto, a "hugely over-weight," insecure, rage-filled, Jewish, out-of-control "verbal tornado." When he's not talking, he's cramming fistfuls of groceries—donuts, bagels, pretzel rods, Yodels—into his mouth. Who's he talking to? There's Serge, the man he dated briefly four years ago and whom he's been hounding with his unwanted affections ever since; Ford, the only man Serge has ever loved; Amanda—Ford's wife—is there, too; as is Otto's bane, his mother. Otto's got a gun.

OTTO: No one ever liked me. Mother, you carry pictures in your wallet of people you never met, instead of pictures of me! . . . When I was a child, I was in the sixth grade, I think, we had a dance at my school on the first day of May, a Sadie Hawkins dance. It was silly, it was nothing—is it hot in here as Buchenwald, or what?—Anyway, the girls were supposed to ask the boys to dance. And I was not an unattractive child! Tell them, Mother. I wasn't fat then. I didn't have clubbed feet or dandruff or anything. I was quite normal looking, and maybe even a little better than normal looking. But NO ONE asked me to dance . . . no one. The entire dance went by and not one little girl ever came over and asked me to dance. I went to the cloak room and cried and cried. The teacher, Miss MacFarland, I'll never forget her, Miss MacFarland heard me. She came to the cloak room, drawn there by my hideous, shrieking sobs. And she knelt down, next to me, down to where I'd curled myself into the fetal position, on the floor, buried under a mountain of coats. She uncovered me and said . . . "Otto? Otto, why are you crying?" I could barely talk. But I spoke in that spastic, convulsive way children do when they're sobbing. I said, "No one will dance with me." She nodded very sagely, the chain that held her glasses around her neck bobbed up and down. And then she said, "Oh." I wasn't satisfied. That wasn't the comfort I needed. I asked her, "Why?" She thought for a very long time. And then she answered me . . . "No one likes you, Otto. No one likes you and no one ever will. . . ."

POUNDING NAILS IN THE FLOOR WITH MY FOREHEAD

BY ERIC BOGOSIAN

Rage and paranoia are just two of the emotional states driving the boogeymen who parade through Bogosian's solo show. In "Rash," a wealthy man stands at his $3,000 Hammacher-Schlemmer barbe-

cue on his fifteen-acre estate, which is surrounded entirely by barbed-wire-topped fencing, talking to a friend while the children from his most recent marriage run around the pool. He hates to leave his house these days and fantasizes about napalming the Bowery. The title of the sketch refers to the rash he got when a beggar shook his hand in thanks for a twenty-dollar bill and infected him with "some kind of bum disease." It is America, 1994.

"Rash"

I ever tell you about my friend, George, down on Wall Street? Now, here's a guy, about three years ago, makes a killing. Shorts some stock, makes fifteen million dollars on one deal. Says to himself: "That's it, I win." Gets off the street. Goes down to the South Pacific, buys an island. They're not that expensive, about two million bucks. Moves his whole family down the island.

I'm talking to him on the phone yesterday, says it's great down there. Beautiful weather every day. Inexpensive. He's got a satellite dish, gets a hundred and fifty stations. Gets it all: *Seinfeld*, the Knicks. No problems with parking, car hijacking, drugs . . . it's his own island, he's the king of the island. And I know how he feels . . .

I mean, look, I'm the world's biggest liberal. But you know I'm watching that CNN, I'm watching those riots in L.A. and I'm thinking to myself: "What if they start doing that around here? What if they start running around like that around here?"

I mean, look at this house, Charlie. You can't see this house from the road. We're vulnerable up here. What happens, we're up here one Sunday, we're hanging out: reading the paper, eating bagels, grinding coffee beans. I pick up the phone to call my mother: "Oh, the phone is dead!"

I look up, a couple of black guys are at the back door. Breaking down the back door. They don't even have to be black guys, could be anybody. Then what do I do? What do I do then? "Oh, come on in, would you like a cup of coffee? Maybe you'd like to rape my wife, kill my kids, burn my house down?"

What do I do then, Charlie? What do I do then?

That's why I have the gun. □□□

I would; I would shoot them, for the kids I would shoot. If they were from the phone company, I would still shoot them.

Anyways, these are ready. □□□

Jeremy, honey, come out of the bushes, Daddy's not angry anymore. Come on out, we'll discuss it later. We're gonna have din-din now. No, no hot dogs, we've got fifteen-dollar-a-pound prime sirloin from Dean & DeLuca, now come out of the bush. COME ON! COME IN THE HOUSE!

THE CONDUCT OF LIFE

BY MARIA IRENE FORNES

Orlando, an army lieutenant in an unnamed Latin American country, rises to the rank of lieutenant commander through his talents as a torturer. His sadism infects his home, too; amid quieter horrors in his relations with his wife, he imprisons a young woman in his cellar, where he regularly beats and rapes her. Ultimately, his cruelty begins to rebound against him. After a man in his custody, whom authorities want alive, dies accidentally, Orlando is called in for questioning. He fears the interrogation is a trap, his undoing. He's speaking to Alejo, another officer and his family's closest friend.

ORLANDO: That's funny. That's very funny. They want to question me. They want to punch my eyes out? I knew something was wrong because they were getting nervous. Antonio was getting nervous. I went to him and I asked him if something was wrong. He said, no, nothing was wrong. But I could tell something was wrong. He looked at Vélez and Vélez looked back at him. They are stupid. They want to conceal something from me and they look at each other right in front of me, as if I'm blind, as if I can't tell that they are worried about something. As if there's something happening right in front of my nose but I'm blind and I can't see it. □□□ You understand? □□□

What kind of way is this to treat me?—After what I've done for them?—Is this a way to treat me?—I'll come up . . . as soon as I can— I haven't been well.—Okay. I'll come up. I get depressed because things are bad and they are not going to improve. There's something malignant in the world. Destructiveness, aggressiveness.—Greed. People take what is not theirs. There is greed. I am depressed, disillusioned . . . with life . . . with work . . . family. I don't see hope. *(He sits. He speaks more to himself than to Alejo)* Some people get a cut in a finger and die. Because their veins are right next to their skin. There are people who, if you punch them in the stomach, the skin around the stomach bursts and the bowels fall out. Other people, you cut them open and you don't see any veins. You can't find their intestines. There are people who don't even bleed. There are people who bleed like pigs. There are people who have the nerves right on the skin. You touch them and they scream. They have their vital organs close to the surface. You hit them and they burst an organ. I didn't even touch this one and he died. He died of fear.

A BRIGHT ROOM CALLED DAY

BY TONY KUSHNER

Weimar Germany in the early days of Adolf Hitler's rise to power. Gregor Bazwald (Baz), in his thirties, is a homosexual who worked at the Berlin Institute for Human Sexuality until it was closed by the Nazis three days ago. He was brought in for questioning, slapped around a bit, then let go. He tends to explain history in terms of sexual frustration and release and, as the early horrors of his historical moment grind on around him, he responds with good-humored hopelessness and pleasant resignation.

BAZ: I went to Munich. □□□
    To kill myself.
    Really. I'm very much afraid of them, I have been for years, all police, but these are much more frightening. Being alone with them in a room with a locked door is paralyzing. I looked at the carpet the whole time. I thought, good, they have a carpet, they won't do anything that would get blood on the carpet. When the main one grabbed my face and slapped it I started crying. *(Pause)* I have always been terrified of pain. He said to me, "In the woods outside of Munich, do you know what we are building?" I said no, and he said "A camp. For people like you." I have a criminal record, I can't get out

easily. I expected them to arrest me immediately after letting me go—something to do. So I decided to kill myself. ☐☐☐

I wanted to go to another city so that none of you would be asked to identify me afterwards. I took the night train. When I got there I bought a revolver and four bullets. Extras. I can't imagine why I thought I'd need extras. Anyway. I wanted to be found by people who aren't particularly frightened or upset by death. Nuns who care for the terminally ill. Better that than in some cafe, ruining some waiter's whole day . . . ☐☐☐

But I felt that killing myself in the midst of a bunch of nuns was probably a much more serious sin than doing it discreetly in a secular location. So I went to the park. ☐☐☐

Agnes, I met a remarkably attractive young Silesian there. I was exhausted. Fatigue makes me easy to arouse . . . ☐☐☐

I realized after my Silesian friend left that it had been nearly a week since my last orgasm. Too much pent-up energy. The result: depression. Add to it the nightmare of the last few days—suicide. One brisk interlude with a pliable friend and my desire to live returned to me in all its hot, tainted glory. ☐☐☐

There's more. The best part. ☐☐☐

Well, here I am in Munich with a little money, a loaded gun, and a whole day to kill before the night train to Berlin. What to do? ☐☐☐

I went to the cinema. And you are absolutely not going to believe what happened. ☐☐☐

It was a Dietrich film. And there was hardly anyone there, it being early in the day, just me and some old people and some war vets. When all of a sudden into the theatre marches a squadron of brownshirts and guess who else? ☐☐☐

It was him. In a slouch hat and a trench coat. ☐☐☐

Hitler. And he sat down three rows in front of me. The S.A. sat in back of him but I had a clear view of the back of his head. I could see the oil in his hair. ☐☐☐

The film got going and I was thinking to myself, "Life plays funny tricks. Here we are, watching a Dietrich film: ten pensioners, six war-cripples, Adolf Hitler and me, a homosexual Sunday anarchist with a loaded gun in his pocket."

(He shapes the gun with his fingers, aims carefully, and makes a soft "bang")

So I left.

VII

"GOD'S LIGHTNING OPENS UP THE GROUND"

THE GOSPEL AT COLONUS

BY LEE BREUER

At the end of his bitter life, blind Oedipus seeks a resting place. His fate—killing his father, marrying his mother, fathering his sisters and brothers—allows no respite, though; it pursues him to the end. Breuer's version is a radical retelling, an African-American gospel "oratorio set in a black Pentecostal service, in which Greek myth replaces Bible story. It is sung, acted and preached by the characters of the 'play'." Here, Oedipus is a visiting preacher who narrates his role and, below, speaking as Oedipus, "delivers a meditation from the pulpit."

PREACHER OEDIPUS:
Though he has watched a decent age pass by,
A man will sometimes still desire the world.
I swear I see no wisdom in that man.
The endless hours pile up a drift of pain
More unrelived each day; and as for pleasure,
When he is sunken in excessive age,
You will not see his pleasure anywhere.
The last attendant is the same for all—
Old men and young alike, there being then
No music and no dance. Death is the finish.
Not to be born surpasses all philosophy.
The second best is to have seen the light
And then to go back quickly from whence we came.
The feathery follies of his youth once over,
What trouble is beyond the range of man?
What heavy burden will he not endure?
Jealousy, faction, quarreling, battle—
The bloodiness of war, the grief of war.
And in the end he comes to strengthless age:
Abhorred by all men, unfriended,

Without company in that uttermost twilight
Where he must live with every bitter thing.

That is the truth, my friend,
Not for me only, a blind and ruined man.

I think of some shore in the north
Concussive waves make stream
This way and that in the gales of winter.
It is like that with me sometimes—
(Chanting)
The wild wrack breaking over me
From head to foot, and coming on forever.
Now from the plunging down of the sun.
Now from the sunrise quarter.
Now from where the noonday gleams.
Now from the night and the north. □□□
Hear it cascading down the air!
The God-thrown, the gigantic, holy sound!
Terror crawls to the tips of my hair!
My heart shakes! My soul is salvation bound.
And where my body shall repair,
God's lightning opens up the ground. □□□

Bless his name!

TRAVELER IN THE DARK

BY MARSHA NORMAN

*Three generations come together around the death of a devoted
family friend, Mavis. Everett, the grandfather, is a country preacher,
"a one-time fire-breathing evangelist" with "a direct personal relationship to God." His son Sam, a world-famous surgeon, has, after a
childhood of devotion patterned on Everett's, built a life of fierce,
rational nonbelief. Now Sam verbally wrestles with his father for the*

soul of Stephen, Sam's own twelve-year-old son. The playwright sums Sam up: "a brilliant loner. . . . He can seem preoccupied, impatient and condescending. But he can also be counted on to handle any situation. His sense of humor is what makes you put up with his infuriating personal security."

SAM: He's lying to you, Stephen. He lied to me and now he's lying to you and I won't have it! God had nothing to do with Mavis dying. It just happened. It was a goddamn rotten thing to happen, but God didn't do it. No. God is not in control and hasn't been in control for some time. *(He pauses and shifts into the master storyteller he can be)* He lost it . . . over Job. God made a bet with the Devil and lost it all. □□□ The Devil said, "Sure Job loves you. Why shouldn't he? He's the richest man on earth. But you take all that away, and he won't pray to you then, no sir."

Well, God just had to find out. So in one afternoon, He killed all his sheep, all his camels, all his oxes and his asses and his daughters and his sons. And Job still prayed. So the next afternoon, God set a fire that burned up his house and everything in it, turned all his friends against him, sat Job down in the ashes and gave him leprosy.

And even then, Job prayed. Job suffered more than any man had ever suffered. As much, in fact, as God had ever suffered. And when God realized that Job could suffer just as well as He could, everything changed. For God saw that He had sinned, but Job loved Him still. And in that moment, God found God, and it was man.

And ever since that time, God has been up there believing in us with all His heart, believing we can do whatever we want, and wondering why, exactly, we do what we do. We must have our reasons, but He can't, for the life of Him, figure out what they are.

So He watches, but He can't help us. So He weeps. All God can do now is cry. The oceans, Stephen, are the tears God has cried since Job. □□□

God is not in control. We are. There is no heaven, there is no hell. There is this life, created, in your case, by your mother and me. Life on earth, which we can make better through careful thought and hard work. But *we* make the progress, and *we* make the mistakes. Not God. God has nothing to do with this, so there is no point in believing in Him. He's just another fairy-tale king, as far as I'm concerned. If you want to believe, believe in yourself. In your power, in your mind, in your life. This life. Because that's all there is.

WHITE WATER

BY JOHN JESURUN

A thirteen-year-old boy named Mack has a vision: a formless woman in a glowing ball of light repeatedly visits him and turns a muddy well into a healing spring. Seven hundred and twenty-five people, with ailments from cancer to AIDS to broken limbs, get cured by the water. Medical reports describe Mack as having "a delicate constitution, with a lymphatic and nervous temperament. Thirteen years old though he seems not more than eleven. His face is pleasant, his eyes have a lively expression." Throughout the play, a mix of live and televised interview, he confidently withstands interrogation by a talk-show staff, imagined by the playwright as lawyers. When asked about one cure, presumably the first, Mack responds . . .

MACK: I didn't have nothing to do with it I was just standing there and I told them I had nothing to with anything and I couldn't do anything and so not to come near me and they could go to the spring if they wanted to but they couldn't come near me. So I went home but they dragged me to the house and I could taste the poor mother's salt tears, they were all over my arms. Then he fell to the floor and cried a big long cry. Then someone picked him up and his feet stuck out like they were dead. Shall I go to the hospital with you. No, I can go alone, they said. I should go with you. No, I can go alone. I just want to get him right in there. I'll go with Pepito. I'll call Pepito. But I knew all about it. It was happening while I knew it was happening. I was scared, so I walked around the door and he was in there sleeping so I walked outside by the fence and someone was wailing. There was only one star out. Then, I walked by the door and they were in there and he was sleeping sick. I hear crying but I didn't believe it so I looked over by the bed and the mother cried and fell on me and I moved because I didn't want her tears to touch me. I don't want your hot sweaty salty tears to touch me. Then he picked his body up and the legs were stiff so I looked and cried and fell on the floor. My arm was out and my face was wet. Then I stood up and someone else was gone and they tried to push my hand on him and I said, This is unchangeable, he's erased. Then the body fell down and his back was to the floor forever. They pushed my hand on him but I didn't want to touch it. They wanted me to pray. I said, Get up, get up. And he got up. I screamed and ran away. Stop staring at me. What are you looking at?

VIII

"WE ARE THE MASTER RACE"

GREENSBORO

BY EMILY MANN

On November 3, 1979, five protesters at a "Death to the Klan" rally in Greensboro, North Carolina, were shot and killed by a group of Nazis and Ku Klux Klan members. Greensboro *explores the event and its repercussions through documentary testimony from many people—on both sides—involved with or affected by the killings. Part of the White Aryan Resistance, this skinhead is a thin young man, "almost waiflike . . . hunched over, vulnerable."*

YOUNG MAN: It starts early. They start to drain your white pride in school.

We are the master race—intellectually, creativity—we are the master race.—How did we come enslaved by the Jews? I think the answer is easy—it's in our culture, it's in our heritage, it's in our blood from day one to be honest, honorable, hard-working people. It's in their blood from day one to learn how to deceit the Gentiles.

You know a Jew is not a white man. Y'ever heard the expression "blood in the face"? Well, lemme ask you, can a Jew blush? Listen, he's just a nigger in disguise.

And now what do we have? A whole bunch of reverse discrimination. We have the anti-hate law which might as well be called the anti-white law cuz I never heard it used against any of those mud races.

There are a lot of angry white people out here now. We have to prepare for war, and we know that. The time has come—it's going to be too late. That means food storage, target practice, ammunition. . . . There's going to be a lot of bloodshed. Personally, I can't think of a better way to go than to die for my people. *(He raises his arm in a Heil Hitler salute)* White Power!

GREENSBORO

BY EMILY MANN

*The Klansman speaks at a White Aryan Resistance (W.A.R.)
Conference. He's described as "a middle-aged man in a white shirt
and a white cap with a black insignia," positioned in front of a
Confederate flag, a National Socialist flag, and a silver Viking
broadsword. He's mid-speech and quite agitated.*

KLANSMAN: We can't use the same techniques we've been using for
the last forty years. Look at Louis Farrakhan—black leader, sepa-
ratist—Nation of Islam. He should be a model to the Klan. And when
Louis Farrakhan speaks, he doesn't speak in a small church like this.
He gets a sports amphitheater that seats 50,000 people. A half million black men went to Washington. That just shows you what white
people are up against. We're going to have to get started here.

We are the White Knights of the Ku Klux Klan. We are not
supremacists. Okay . . . We are separatists. We're not supreme anymore. We've been degenerated. The last thirty years the white race
has gone downhill so fast it's unbelievable.

We of the White Knights of the Ku Klux Klan are not going to sug-
arcoat our ideology. We are pro-white. We like the "r" word. We are
revolutionaries. Look—the masses respect power. Look at the IRS.
They grumble and groan but come April what is it? April 14, they
come right out with their 1040 forms. The masses respect who's in
power. And I don't think it shows power when you have half a dozen
Klansmen walkin' down the street in sheets with a hundred cops
around in fronta five hundred jeerin', screaming white protesters.
When Joe Six-Pack sees that, he's got nothin' but contempt for the
Klan. But we can win over Joe Six-Pack with our ideology. Why?
Because Joe Six-Pack agrees with us.

Let's talk about tactics. Let's talk about invisibility. It's time for the
Klan to go Invisible. Put on a coat and tie like

David Duke can get forty percent of the vote in Louisiana. David
Duke hasn't changed his ideology one bit but he's changed his tactics. We have to get started here. Now let's talk about courage and
let's talk about fear. Most of the Knights have lost their jobs. We live
near the ghetto. We live near these blacks. You have to deal with fear

every day. But when you get fulla anger and rage, you'll overcome that fear. We'll ally with you—National Socialist, Identity Christian, Aryan Nation, militia—what have you. We'll work with you. We make the best fighters. Why? The White Knights have been hurt by the system, knocked down by the system, kicked by the system. We make the best fighters because we got nothing more to lose.

PACIFIC OVERTURES

BY STEPHEN SONDHEIM, JOHN WEIDMAN AND HUGH WHEELER

Pacific Overtures *is a musical in the style (freely adapted) of Japanese Kabuki theatre. The action begins in 1853, when American ships approach the island empire of Nippon (later called Japan), which has lived in total isolation from the world for 250 years. This monologue is performed as a story by the Reciter, the evening's narrator who steps into several roles, including that of Storyteller. The tale acts as a parable for the events onstage. The Courageous King stands for the Emperor, who has for years been ruler in name only, dominated as he is by the warlord Shogun (retold as the Lord High Protector). The Kingdom of the Giants is, of course, the West. As in the story, the apparently slumbering Emperor will enact some revenge on both usurpers.*

STORYTELLER: The Tale of the Courageous King. Long ago and far away, behind the highest mountain peak, there lay a magic land of peace and harmony, ruled by a young king, little more than a child. One day, a royal hunting party set out from the young king's palace in search of tigers near the river bank. While his hunters beat the bush, the King retired to a sunny glade, and sipped green tea ▢▢▢ prepared by his companion, his Lord High Protector. Around his head buzzed sleepy bees ▢▢▢ and past him darted brilliant butterflies. ▢▢▢ Then suddenly the butterflies were gone—for like the young King they heard the beaters drawing closer through the bush. ▢▢▢ Deep in the forest, the underbrush began to dip and wave ▢▢▢ and snapping twigs ▢▢▢ and tearing leaves all heralded the beast's approach! The Lord Protector drew his sword to meet the tiger's rush □□□ the bamboo trees were thrust aside and there appeared—no tiger, but a man! Then two men, three, then more than one could count. Bearded ogres with gray skin and matted hair, waving swords and spears. "We are emissaries from the Kingdom of the Giants, come to open up your backward land!" When he heard that, the Lord Protector cast aside his sword and fled. The King was left alone. Oh, what will become of him, abandoned by his treacherous protector? Surely the savages from across the sea will cut him down! But look . . . how superbly he stands his ground! Look how his sword leaps from its scabbard! One invader—gored in the stomach! Another! See how the head flies from the body! Another! And another! Now hear the shouts, hear the roars of defiance as the King's faithful beaters rush to his side. All join in the fray as the screams of the dying savages echo and re-echo down the forest ravine. Oh yes, here was a great victory—for in an hour not a single barbarian was left alive, as once again the butterflies returned to float and shimmer over the wild flowers, dyed crimson by the blood of foreigners. And then, just as the young King sheathed his sword, into the glade strode a magnificent tiger. "Your Majesty," the tiger said, "I am the king of all the jungle beasts. But from the forest I have watched you fight these Western dogs, and surely you, and you alone, deserve to wear the royal crown." So saying, he kow-towed and led the hunters in a shout: "All Hail the King! All Hail our Courageous King!"

BY ROMULUS LINNEY

Herman Goering, Germany's reichsmarschall and Adolf Hitler's number-two man, is brought to trial after World War II. Charged with "Crimes Against Peace, War Crimes and Crimes Against Humanity," he faces a tribunal of judges from France, Russia, Great Britain and the United States. Despite the predetermined outcome of his hearing—he will be sentenced to die by hanging—he demonstrates his drive to dominate others, including his jailers. Even his humor works to humiliate or seduce, to divide and conquer those around him. Compared throughout to Richard III, Goering entered prison "a great white pig," addicted to morphine pills. Three months later, he's dropped one hundred pounds, been weaned off drugs and restored to fighting trim. This scene occurs as he readies for the first day of trial. An American captain hands him the "red-on-white polka-dotted aviator's scarf" he requests for adornment; he washes his face and hands the towel to a black sergeant. As always, he finds time for a joke.

GOERING: Ah, Great American Hunter! ☐☐☐ I thank you for this small decoration, as I go to battle. Wonderful. There. ☐☐☐ Wash my face! Look my best! ☐☐☐ Staring at me, aren't you. Well, guards look through a hole in my cell door every minute of the day and night. The only time they can't see me is when I take a shit. Which is the only time I wish they *could* see me! ☐☐☐ Very well! The great Inter-Galaxy Armies of Venus and Mars are packed into gigantic Space Ships. The Universe itself is to be invaded and conquered by these invincible forces, and the first planet to be conquered is Earth. The Supreme Leader of this overwhelming Air Force has studied the situation thoroughly. He sends his Ambassador, a great Martian soldier, to issue an Ultimatum, to the first man on Earth he sees. The Ambassador lands—at a filling station in Cleveland, Ohio, by a large gas pump. "Well," says the Supreme Leader, when he returns, "did you find an Earthman?" "I did," says the Ambassador. "Did you issue our Ultimatum?" "I did," says the Ambassador. "What did he say?" says the Supreme Leader. "Nothing," says the Ambassador. "He just stood there, with his dick in his ear." ☐☐☐

Oh, come on, gentlemen. Laugh! Why not? Scarf! Uniform! Boots! I'm ready! Once Hermann Goering was known and loved all over Germany! And by God, years from now, he will be again! All right, not loved maybe, but known, and admired! ☐☐☐ Thank you, nigger. ☐☐☐ I beg your pardon! That *is* what they call you? You'll end up in a camp, too! Just watch!

IX

WOMBmanWARs

WOMBmanWARs

BY JUDITH ALEXA JACKSON

Conceived and staged as a solo performance, WOMBmanWARs begun as a response to what the writer saw as the "'high-tech lynching' of Anita Hill" at the Clarence Thomas hearings. From this impulse, Jackson used story, movement, political satire and mixed media to characterize the war between the sexes, often in a racial context. Jackson, an African American, originally played the Reverend at a microphone in this stand-alone sermon.

REVEREND: I'm not saying we should cast aspersions on the hussy. Mike Tyson's accuser deserves the same consideration as David Duke in the eyes of the Lord.

All I'm saying is every time a black man tries to get ahead he is brought down by a black woman. Black man takes two steps forward . . . who pulls him three steps back? Black woman. Black man reaches for a star. Who snatches his hand down? Black woman. Black man have a dream. Who wakes him up? Black woman! You know it's true. I got proof.

Adam Clayton Powell. Congressman from Harlem, USA until who brought him down? Black woman. Marion Barry. Mayor of Washington, D.C. until who told on him? Black woman. Clarence Thomas a United States Supreme Court Justice by the skin of his teeth. All brought down by who? A BLACK WOMAN.

And now look who she's after. Our young brother Mike Tyson. World-champion boxer. Warrior in the ring. Hard as a rock butt-kicker and millionaire to boot. (*He wipes his brow*)

Black women have got to stop stomping on the black man's dreams. Stop holding the black man down. Stop putting the black man on the back burner. What a black man needs is somebody to help him stand up. Somebody who will help him shake that monkey off his back. Get off me monkey. Offa my back. There's a war going on out there . . . and black men have got the heaviest casualties.

We not saying, the black man is perfect. You got problems? Don't run to the enemy. Don't call 911. Keep it in the family. Come to the church . . . that's what you do. That's where we can begin to sort things out. Pray for him black woman but don't bring the black man down. Raise him up. Raise him up.

SIGHT UNSEEN

BY DONALD MARGULIES

Nick is an archaeologist from rural, working-class England. He lives and works beside his wife, Patricia, far from the city, in near poverty, knowing, on some level, that she married him, years ago, in order to stay in the country. When her old boyfriend, now a rising star on the world art scene, pays them an unexpected visit, buried memories and feelings surface. Nick surprises Jonathan, the former lover, as he's about to sneak back to London in the middle of his first night in their home.

NICK: Not that I was ever her type. There was a certain challenge to be found in that. I thought she would never, not with me. She was so . . . *attractive*, you know, so confident, so American. The first time she slept with me I thought it must have been because I was her supervisor. I'm sure that was why. When it happened a second time, well, I didn't know *what* to think; I chose to think there was hope. Yes, I opted for hope. In a moment of uncharacteristic brazenness, I asked her to marry me. She accepted. I don't know why. I have my suspicions. *(A beat)* From time to time, I'll fortify myself with stout and kiss her neck, feel her tit, lay with my head there. □□□

Sometimes she'll let me. She'll even stroke my hair. Once she kissed my head. I wanted to reach up and kiss her mouth, but why get greedy and piss her off? □□□

Some nights she'd respond—oh, she'd respond, or initiate even—and I would rush into it foolishly, trying not to feel I was somehow being rewarded. I take what I can get; I'm English. *(A beat)* She succumbed to my charms tonight, though. Tonight she acquiesced. Did you hear us?

(Jonathan shakes his head; he's lying.)

Oh. What a shame. It was brilliant.

HOT 'N' THROBBING

BY PAULA VOGEL

The author encourages actors playing the Man "to go gangbusters on this role. The bigger the asshole you are, the more we'll love you." This prototype, the compelling animal asshole, is part of what Vogel skewers here, in a play that shows domestic violence in all its complexity and horror. The specifics: the Man has disregarded a restraining order keeping him from his wife, who, having suffered ten years of drunken violence at his hands, is, with their two children, building a life without him. Drunk and disheveled, he breaks into the house. She shoots him in the ass and then tends to him. He continues to draw her in, alternately seducing her, revealing and threatening. He has lost his job, he explains; nothing turns him on anymore. The following confession, for all its self-deprecation and pathos, shows one side of him. Moments later, he beats and strangles her to death. He's over thirty-four, Vogel tells us. "Holes in dungarees. Almost a beer belly."

MAN: Okay, this is hard for me, all right? It's . . . it's a fuckin' Friday night. Right?

And so what do we do, Friday night? Go out, drink some beer, and . . . ya know . . . cruise the strip. I mean, if you're a guy who's alone, that's what there is to do in this town on a Friday. ☐☐☐

Right. So . . . I take a shower, you know, spruce up a little bit. And I count out the change I have left. And it's not much. And that gets me a little depressed, but I think, okay, shit, I'll economize, I'll buy a six-pack for the truck, and I won't drink out, you know? So I go downtown, and hit the streets . . . and I go in a few . . . places . . . but mostly there are minimums. So I think, fuck, I can't even watch the live action. ☐☐☐

So . . . so . . . so I go into a corner bookstore, and it's packed. And I change a five into quarters, and slip into the booth . . . □□□

And all it does is get me even more agitated. I'm thinking, this is not what I want, on a Friday Night, the feeling of my own fist in a booth—I'm like numb to that by now—and so I get back into my own truck, and I drink a few beers, to get my nerve up—and I empty out my pockets . . . I check the dash and under the seats, and I count—and I come up with a lousy eighteen dollars and thirty-seven cents. □□□

Well, I think, you know, times are hard, maybe some working girl will consider it—you know? Maybe I'll get lucky, or I'll hit someone green on the street—so I crank up the engine, and start to drive it slow, down the side streets. And I see them, it's warm out tonight, and they're there, in groups—laughing, wearing next to nothing, and they're so close, they're laughing at me, calling out to me— □□□

They were all together. I couldn't get one off by herself; I thought they'd laugh—I couldn't just call out, you know, "How about $18.37?!" I just . . . I just lost my nerve, I was so . . . down by then . . . then . . . and then I just kept driving and the truck kind of drove here by itself.

"THUH CHILDREN"

THE DEATH OF THE LAST BLACK MAN IN THE WHOLE ENTIRE WORLD

BY SUZAN-LORI PARKS

"Because so much of African-American history has been unrecorded, dismembered, washed out, one of my tasks as playwright is to . . . locate the ancestral burial ground, dig for bones, find bones, hear the bones sing, write it down," Suzan-Lori Parks writes in an essay that could serve as introduction to Ham's tour-de-force list of begats below. This monologue will give you a sense of the play as a whole: language that moves musically and rhythmically—like a theme with variations, alternately telling a story and thwarting it, rephrasing the familiar (in this case Bible text) in stereotypical African-American vernacular and then refracting that language through Parks's own wild, experimental idioms. The time is the present, but the Last Black Man whose death the play concerns seems to have died in the past, present and future—"before Columbus" and tomorrow—all at the same time, falling from a spaceship, fried in the electric chair and hanged from a tree. Ham, who appears late in the play in order to recall the history of the line that dies with this man, is the one who knows history, who "re-members." The author doesn't tell us more about Ham, not even that Ham's a man (there's a reference to "Ham-bone girl" that might be addressed to Ham or to the "Black Woman with Fried Drumstick."). In other words, the actor can find some freedom here.

HAM: Ham's Begotten Tree (catchin up to um *in medias res* that is we takin off from where we stopped up last time.) Huh. NOW: She goned begotten One who in turn begotten Ours. Ours laughed one day uhloud in from thuh sound hittin thuh air smakity sprung up I, you, n He, She, It. They turned in engaged in simple multiplication thus tuh spawn of theirselves one We one You and one called They (They in certain conversation known as "Them" and in other certain conversation a.k.a. "Us"). Now very simply: Wassername she finally gave intuh It and tugether they broughted forth uh wildish one called simply Yo. Yo gone be wentin much too long without hisself uh comb in from thuh frizzly that resulted comed one called You (polite form). You (polite) birthed herself Mister, Miss, Maam, and Sir who in his later years with That brought forth Yuh Fathuh. Thuh fact that That was uh mother tuh Yuh Fathuh didnt stop them 2 relations from havin relations. Those strange relations between That thuh mother and Yuh Fathuh thuh son brought forth uh odd lot: called: Yes Massuh, Yes Missy, Yes Maam n Yes Suh Mistuh Suh which goes tuh show that relations with your relations produces complications. Thuh children of That and Yuh Fathuh aside from being plain peculiar was all crosseyed. This defect enhanced their multiplicative possibilities, for example. Yes Suh Mistuh Suh breeded with hisself n gived us Wassername (thuh 2nd), and Wassernickname (2 twins in birth joinded at thuh lip). Thuh 2 twins lived next door tuh one called Uhnother bringing forth Themuhns, She (thuh 2nd), Auntie, Cousin, and Bro who makeshifted continuous compensations for his loud and oderiferous bodily emissions by all thuh time saying excuse me n through his graciousness brought forth They (polite) who had mixed feelins with She (thuh 2nd) thus bringin forth Ussin who then went on tuh have MeMines. □□□

MeMines gived out 2 off spring one she called Mines after herself thuh uther she called Themuhns named after all them who comed before. Themuhns married outside thuh tribe joinin herself with uh man they called WhoDat. Themuhns in WhoDat brought forth only one child called WhoDatDere. Mines joined up with Wasshisname and from that union come AllYall. □□□

Yo suddenly if by majic again became productive in after uh lapse of some great time came back intuh circulation to wiggled uhbout with Yes Missy (one of thuh crosseyed daughters of That and Yuh Fathuh). Yo in Yes Missy begottin ThissunRightHere, Us, ThatOne, She (thuh 3rd) and one called Uncle (who from birth was gifted with great singin and dancin capabilities which helped him make his way in life but tended tuh bring shame on his family)

BUCK

BY RONALD RIBMAN

Buck Halloran's ex-wife keeps changing the rules on his visitations with his son, Kenny, making it difficult for Buck to be part of the boy's life. Buck's having a hard time being part of his own life, too. He produces murder reenactments for a sleazy cable station—"one step up" from cheap porno reels. His clubfooted boss, who appears ominously from an infernal elevator, terrorizes him. Worse, he's haunted by one of the murders he's re-creating, which spurs him to seek the truth of what happened instead of just hacking out sexual violence for thrills. His writer, Charlie, to whom he confides here, urges him to toe the line or risk losing his job and, as a result, access to his son. Marion is his ex-wife; Douglas, her current husband.

BUCK: They got me in the playground again, Charlie. The same cruddy playground across the street from the apartment I spent five years of my life in with Kenny . . . first rocking him in the carriage, then watching him walk, holding onto my fingers, then one day just going off by himself. And I can see the two of them standing on the terrace, staring down at me through those rotting ficus bushes he planted. And when the reconnaissance is finished with, they move inside for the discussion: "Should we send the kid out, or risk another battle over visitation privileges?" You know how many times I've been to court with them in the last year-and-a-half since the divorce? Four times. Four times! And I always win because we always get the same judge—a sixty-year-old lesbian who knows injustice when she sees it. She issues order after order demanding that I be allowed to see my son. The only problem is it never does any good. My wife has a special dispensation from God which allows her to throw my court orders into the garbage can while I have to obey hers down to the letter of the law or suffer immediate death. "If you don't have him back in four hours, I'll get a court order!" And, by God, she will. She's got an East German refugee with stainless-steel eyeglasses who represents her as a special favor to Douglas's accounting firm. He specializes in court orders. You could call him when he's just starting to boil a soft-boiled egg, and by the time the egg is ready to eat he's got the court order and fifteen documents proving he spent all of

World War II as a medic on the Russian front. He keeps dumping me back in the park again with the rest of the divorced leftovers. I sit there watching them waiting for their kids to come out with little gift boxes on their laps, and I'm scared, Charlie. I'm so scared. Scared that they're not going to bring him out to me, scared that if I can't keep up my support payments they'll keep him away from me for good, scared that no matter what I do I'm gonna lose him anyway. □□□

Now all I want is just for it to be ordinary again between me and Kenny. But it's never gonna be ordinary again. Ever. The first few months I tried, pretending Saturday or Sunday or whatever the hell day it was they let me see him was just another day of the week . . . but after a while it sinks in. It's gone. The whole damn cord of life that used to hold the two of us together is pulling apart like a piece of wool from an old sweater. And even if I wanted to live with the pretense, I can't, because sure as hell he comes into the park one day and I can see in his eyes he's pretending, too. And he tells me this jerk, this accountant, this Mr. Perfect Mate Lovey-Dovey with three college degrees and a Jaguar, wants him to call him Dad. "Just call me Dad." Well, I told Kenny, "You just call him Douglas. You tell him your dad told you to call him Douglas."

WOMBmanWARs

BY JUDITH ALEXA JACKSON

The conflicts Danny describes, preferring the male over the female, are at the heart of Jackson's play, originally performed as a one-woman show. WOMBmanWARs *combines stylized and satirical sketches with the more naturalistic story of an African-American family—Danny, his wife Sapphire and their daughter Danisha.*

DANNY: When Danisha was born □□□ I was the happiest man on earth. She curled up around my thumb and I knew right then nothing would ever be the same again. I became a man that day. Before that, I thought being a man meant getting some. □□□ But one look at my baby girl changed all that. I could cup her whole seven pounds in my hands like that. It was my job to protect her.

Man, I'd stand there, holding her, thinking about my first car. A Ford Mustang. I kept that baby pretty. Bought her everything she needed. Didn't let nobody touch her. Didn't have a scratch on her for six whole months. Then somebody banged her up and I just about had a nervous breakdown. My first car, man.

I wasn't gonna let nobody hurt Danisha like that. Nobody's gonna mess with her paint job.

Don't laugh man. I know I ain't no poet. Sometimes I wish I was so I could say what I'm trying to say. *(He sits on stool and leans toward audience member)* Mind if I tell you something kinda personal? And don't let me catch you telling nobody what I'm about to say. *(Pause)* Sometimes I see you out there playing catch with Jerome and I get jealous man. *(Pause)* Jealous. *(Pause)* Seems like a man's not fully round 'til he's had a son.

I'm going to tell you something I'd never admit to Sapphire. I wanted a boy. Still do sometimes. *(Pause)*

Danisha tries hard though, bless her little tomboy heart. You know she's named after me. Danisha. Little Danny. Climbing trees. Playing ball. Jumping fences. But she'll grow out of all that. Be a lady. I'll see to it.

SWIMMING TO CAMBODIA

BY SPALDING GRAY

Although Spalding Gray's full-length monologue tells the story of his time as a bit player in The Killing Fields, *a movie about the Cambodian genocide, it contains many digressions. Here, he departs from the tale of his Southeast Asian misadventures, while staying with many of its themes: horror versus pleasure, the guilt of being a shallow, fortunate American and the way even history's most sweeping human atrocities can give way to thoughts of money and the easy life.*

When I was in therapy about two years ago, one day I noticed that I hadn't had any children. And I like children at a distance. I wondered if I'd like them up close. I wondered why I didn't have any. I wondered if it was a mistake, or if I'd done it on purpose, or what. And I noticed that my therapist didn't have any children either. He had pictures of cats on the wall. Framed.

He may have changed since then, but my therapist was the kind who, if you asked him a personal question, would take the entire session to answer. You had to take the responsibility to stop him. You had to learn to be selfish. So I always said that he was like a drinking partner, except we never went drinking and I paid for the drinks.

I asked him, "Why didn't you ever have any children?"

And he said, "Well, I was in Auschwitz when I was nineteen and the death marches were moving out as the Russians moved in. And I said to my friend, who was also nineteen, 'I think now we have a beneficent Gestapo. Now we must run for it.' And my friend said, 'No, I am too tired. I must first rest.' So I am watching him sleeping and I see blood from the corner of his mouth and I realize he is dead from exhaustion. So I run and escape and I make it to the border of Poland and Germany, and another death march of twenty thousand goes by, not so beneficent this time. They are shooting from horseback, and I surrender.

"They take us to the edge of this great pit and machine gun the whole lot of us. Everyone falls dead except maybe some twelve or fifteen who fall into the snow and live. I am one. I am shot in and around the genitals so it's a kind of automatic vasectomy. Two days later the Russians find me in the snow."

I said, "Two days in the snow and you didn't freeze to death?"

"What . . . ," he answered, "it was just *snow*." (And *I* was the one in therapy?)

"Listen, this is going to sound weird, but I really envy you."

"What, are you one of those who think suffering ennobles?"

"No, it's not that. We're all born by chance, no one asked to get born, but to be reborn by chance, to live like that, it must have made your life—you know—much more conscious and vital. Things must have changed enormously for you. Also, you don't have to make a decision about whether or not to have kids. It must have changed your life in a very dynamic . . ."

"No. Uh-uh. Nothing changes, no. We thought that, you see. In the first reunions of the camps everyone was swinging, like a big sex club with the swinging and the drinking and the carrying on as though you die tomorrow. Everyone did what he wanted. The next time, not so much, not so much. The couples stayed together. The next time, we were talking about whether or not we could afford a summer home that year. Now when we meet, years later, people talk about whether or not radioactive smoke-detectors are dangerous in suburban homes. Nothing changes."

HOW I LEARNED TO DRIVE

BY PAULA VOGEL

"Sometimes to tell a secret, you first have to teach a lesson," *explains Li'l Bit as she embarks on a story that spans thirty years of* *her life. The secret she reveals: her sexual relationship, from ages* *eleven to eighteen, with her Uncle Peck, a man in his forties. Lessons* *form the narrative structure of Paula Vogel's play—scenes are built* *around the dos and don'ts of driving, for instance, and "Greek* *Chorus" monologues include such instructions as "Recipe for a* *Southern Boy," which describes Peck: "A drawl of molasses . . .* *Bedroom eyes—A dash of Southern Baptist Fire and Brimstone—a* *curl of Elvis on his forehead . . . The steel of army in his walk." Here,* *the lesson concerns pompano fishing, taught to an unseen boy. The* *context tells us that this is an intricate, patient, loving seduction, of* *the sort Peck plays out with his niece over the course of years.* *Context also suggests that he'll attempt some consummation of this* *seduction in the "secret place" he describes at the end. Peck, we dis-* *cover, first molests Li'l Bit when she's eleven. It's a good bet that* *"Bobby" is that age, too.*

PECK: I get back once or twice a year—supposedly to visit Mama and the family, but the real truth is to fish. I miss this the most of all. There's a smell in the Low Country—where the swamp and fresh inlet join the saltwater—a scent of sand and cypress, that I haven't found anywhere yet.

   I don't say this very often up North because it will just play into the stereotype everyone has, but I will tell you: I didn't wear shoes in the summertime until I was sixteen. It's unnatural down here to pen up your feet in leather. Go ahead—take 'em off. Let yourself breathe—it really will make you feel better.

We're going to aim for some pompano today—and I have to tell you, they're a very shy, mercurial fish. Takes patience, and psychology. You have to believe it doesn't matter if you catch one or not.

Sky's pretty spectacular—there's some beer in the cooler next to the crab salad I packed, so help yourself if you get hungry. Are you hungry? Thirsty? Holler if you are.

Okay. You don't want to lean over the bridge like that—pompano feed in shallow water, and you don't want to get too close—they're frisky and shy little things—wait, check your line. Yep, something's been munching while we were talking.

Okay, look: We take the sand flea and you take the hook like this— right through his little sand flea rump. Sand fleas should always keep their backs to the wall. Okay. Cast it in, like I showed you. That's great! I can taste that pompano now, sautéed with some pecans and butter, a little bourbon—now—let it lie on the bottom—now, reel, jerk, reel, jerk—

Look—look at your line. There's something calling, all right. Okay, tip the rod up—not too sharp—hook it—all right, now easy, reel and then rest—let it play. And reel—play it out, that's right—really good! I can't believe it! It's a pompano. —Good work! Way to go! You are an official fisherman now. Pompano are hard to catch. We are going to have a delicious little—

What? Well, I don't know how much pain a fish feels—you can't think of that. Oh, no, don't cry, come on now, it's just a fish—the other guys are going to see you. —No, no, you're just real sensitive, and I think that's wonderful at your age—look, do you want me to cut it free? You do?

Okay, hand me those pliers—look—I'm cutting the hook—okay? And we're just going to drop it in—no I'm not mad. It's just for fun, okay? There—it's going to swim back to its lady friend and tell her what a terrible day it had and she's going to stroke him with her fins until he feels better, and then they'll do something alone together that will make them both feel good and get sleepy. . . .

(Peck bends down, very earnest) I don't want you to feel ashamed about crying. I'm not going to tell anyone, okay? I can keep secrets. You know, men cry all the time. They just don't tell anybody,

and they don't let anybody catch them. There's nothing you could do that would make me feel ashamed of you. Do you know that? Okay. *(Peck straightens up, smiles)*

Do you want to pack up and call it a day? I tell you what—I think I can still remember—there's a really neat tree house where I used to stay for days. I think it's still here—it was the last time I looked. But it's a secret place—you can't tell anybody we've gone there—least of all your mom or your sisters. —This is something special just between you and me? Sound good? We'll climb up there and have a beer and some crab salad—okay, B.B.? Bobby? Robert . . .

XI

"NOTHING LEFT BUT TO RUN"

DRINKS BEFORE DINNER

BY E. L. DOCTOROW

Michael is a guest at a posh dinner party in a "modern, well-appointed" New York City apartment. In the middle of the evening's conversation, another guest draws a gun and, while railing at the meaninglessness of life and society, almost offhandedly terrorizes the men, women and children present. Michael is forced to consider out loud a world that seems to be coming to an end.

MICHAEL: Years ago I saw a man running on a beach. A middle-aged man running alone at low tide. He was the first one I noticed. The runners those days ran alone. They ran on the beaches, or they ran on the tracks behind the universities. You'd see one. You'd see two. Today there are so many runners, they go in packs. And they are dressed to run. They're dressed in shoes that have been manufactured for them and sweatsuits and shorts and headbands manufactured for them. They run in the city along the river and they run in the streets of the suburbs. They run along the edges of highways past the gas stations and fast-food places. They run along the highways to enlarge their lungs and breathing capacities, to make their hearts strong and muscles firm, but I don't know why, because the cars get the air first, they can't run past the cars, and what is making their lungs large and hearts strong is pure carbon monoxide. Still, they run and there are more of them than ever. Not only white middle-aged men, but boys and girls and older people and black people and most of all women. A lot of the runners are women. They do not appear as women, they appear as runners. Even when they're attractive, they're attractive as runners rather than as women. But as I say, they are all running. And I wonder, What is it their bodies have decided that their minds have yet to announce? Perhaps it is their secret acceptance of the need to train for what is going to happen. Perhaps the runners training along the roads of the country, training on the trails of our national parks and down the main streets of small towns and in parks in our cities and in traffic packs on the highways are the unconscious training of the nation for the terrible thing to come. When this terrible thing comes, our runners hope to outrun it. I see no other reason to run along the highways and breathe car exhaust. They are learning not only to have strong hearts and limbs and large lungs, they are learning the directions in which to run, they are learning the routes, it is very interesting. But of course, if you talk to runners, they all tell you how much better they feel since they began to run. They'll not admit to be training for the time that will come when it is time to get away from whatever it is that is coming. They will not admit it, perhaps because their minds do not yet know it. And each day their number increases because more and more people want to be ready for the time when there is nothing left but to run, when nothing else will avail but to run, and they do not want to be among those who cannot run or who falter and stumble and collapse from the attempt to run. They do not want that. They intend to be able to run. Their bodies are in training but their minds haven't made the announcement. When will they make the announcement? I have no idea why they haven't already made the announcement.

SHIMMER

BY JOHN O'KEEFE

"It was the end of a long bad time," John O'Keefe writes at the beginning of this extended autobiographical monologue about his escape from the Tama County Juvenile Home, where he was taken, through no fault of his own, after the breakup of his brutal, alcoholic family. He recalls the fall of 1956, between Tama and Toledo, Iowa, "just off Highway 30." The excerpt below captures the moment of flight, with his only friend, Gary. They are pursued by Mr. White, a vicious and violent man and patron of Hoover Hall, the hellish residence of their detention.

We came to the edge of the highway and were just about to cross it when we saw it, Whitey's truck sitting on the shoulder of the road pointing at us like a big ugly nightmare.

"What are we gonna do?"

"Let's cross the highway."

"Right in the traffic?"

"Yeah, right through the traffic. He'll have to do a U-ee."

"We'll get killed."

"What's the difference?"

We shot across the highway. White revved his truck and started coming at us. We ran in front of him into the oncoming traffic. Car horns blared at us. I saw Gary silhouetted in the truck lights. A big rig's horn blasted. It sounded like the five-o'clock whistle. I saw Gary dive out of the lights and then they were coming at me and I dove. A pair of eyeballs flashed at me as I hit the wall of the ditch. I think I was what you call "knocked out."

I hear all these horns and people shouting. I push myself off the ground and look over the edge of the ditch. I see Gary grinning at me. He's pointing his finger. I follow it. I see White standing in the middle of the highway, trying to stop the cars. All around him cars are skidding and screeching and blaring their horns.

Then it's over. The oncoming traffic is gone and the cars behind him are gone. There was only us and the Chevy.

We're running in the middle of the highway. We're running and holding our thumbs out like we're hitchhiking. It's beginning to dawn on me how crazy this all is when out of the night a pair of car lights appear.

Gary's on the side of the road. He's picking up something and he's running to me. He's giving me something. It's a big rock. He's got one too. The car approaching us is slowing down. We can hear Buddy Holly coming out of it. It's a Chevy Bel Air convertible and it's pulling to a stop.

"Where are you going?"

A guy in Levi's and a motorcycle jacket, ducktail and all is looking at us. I'm gripping my rock.

"Marshalltown," I croak.

"Hop in."

He's saying "hop in." We're not hopping in, we're diving.

The guy is burning rubber and we're shooting off into space. Whitey is pulling his truck in front of us, unbelievable! The guy is swerving around him.

"Hey, you stupid mother, you crazy?"

Gary and I looked at each other, our faces flushed, our eyes bugged as we slid down into the plastic turquoise backseat.

"Fag?"

The guy held up a pack of Camels. I took one. A Zippo was bundled in the pack. Gary snapped open the lid and spoked the flint. We put our heads together over the oily flame and sucked. God, the taste of those Camels. We looked into the night, the glowing beauteous Bel Air beneath us, and it was no dream. Gary leaned over, carefully avoiding the rearview mirror, gripping his rock.

"I'll kill him if I have to, Spacy."

But we didn't have to. The guy brought us out of captivity like some kind of rock-and-roll Moses. He did in twenty minutes what would have taken us hours. The wind blew through my hair and as the lights of Marshalltown appeared I felt new life. Looking over at Gary I could tell he was feeling it too.

XII

"WILL THE PAST RELEASE US?"

ANGELS IN AMERICA, PART TWO: PERESTROIKA

BY TONY KUSHNER

The lights come up on "The World's Oldest Living Bolshevik," an "unimaginably old and totally blind" man (originally played by a woman). He speaks this once and is never heard from again.

ALEKSII ANTEDILLUVIANOVICH PRELAPSARIANOV: The Great Question before us is: Are we doomed? The Great Question before us is: Will the Past release us? The Great Question before us is: Can we Change? In Time? And we all desire that Change will come.

(Little pause)

(With sudden, violent passion) And *Theory?* How are we to proceed without *Theory?* What System of Thought have these Reformers to present to this mad swirling planetary disorganization, to the Inevident Welter of fact, event, phenomenon, calamity? Do they have, as we did, a beautiful Theory, as bold, as Grand, as comprehensive a construct . . . ? You can't imagine, when we first read the Classic Texts, when in the dark vexed night of our ignorance and terror the seed-words sprouted and shoved incomprehension aside, when the incredible bloody vegetable struggle up and through into Red Blooming gave us Praxis, True Praxis, True Theory married to Actual Life. . . . You who live in this Sour Little Age cannot imagine the grandeur of the prospect we gazed upon: like standing atop the highest peak in the mighty Caucasus, and viewing in one all-knowing glance the mountainous, granite order of creation. You cannot imagine it. I weep for you.

And what have you to offer now, children of this Theory? What have you to offer in its place? Market Incentives? American Cheeseburgers? Watered-down Bukharinite stopgap makeshift Capitalism! NEPmen! Pygmy children of a gigantic race!

Change? Yes, we must must change, only show me the Theory, and I will be at the barricades, show me the book of the next Beautiful

Theory, and I promise you these blind eyes will see again, just to read it, to devour that text. Show me the words that will reorder the world, or else keep silent.

If the snake sheds his skin before a new skin is ready, naked he will be in the world, prey to the forces of chaos. Without his skin he will be dismantled, lose coherence and die. Have you, my little serpents, a new skin?

Then we dare not, we *cannot*, we MUST NOT move ahead!

CHILDE BYRON

BY ROMULUS LINNEY

1852. The long-dead Lord Byron appears to his dying daughter as part of a hallucination. She has business to finish with him, business begun when he abandoned her, a baby, to the care of her mother. Byron's wife forced the separation by threatening to have the club-footed poet committed to the madhouse on the basis of behavior considered reprehensible and disgusting, and therefore crazy: homosexuality, incest with his sister, and coerced sodomy in the marriage bed. He defends himself to a chorus of others, including his wife, whom he calls Bell and, after Shakespeare's famous shrew, Kate. Below, Byron defends himself again, explaining to his daughter his abandonment of another child by another woman, during his exile in Italy.

BYRON: So. I have committed some sin against you all, so elemental none of us knows what it is. Come now. Why do you hate me so? Because of my boy feelings, which I will not kill within me, and the sweet dreams they bring? For the foolish love of my foolish sister, and in her face and body, the sad family I inherit from God, and will not disown? For my physical bestiality, which, given the incredible phallus your gossip has bestowed upon me, not only would damage my wife's pride, but split her rectum up to her palate? How do I threaten you? With verse? My stanzas will overthrow the Church?

My rhymes will bring down Parliament? I am only another guilt-ridden writer, returning every night like a dog to brandy, verse, and the vomit of memory, to make my music from it: what has that to do with you? Because I am rich? I owe my creditors thirty thousand pounds! Because I am a dandy? Any one of you can enter a British drawing room gracefully. I must bobble in, like a cork. Because I am a Peer of the Realm? I was born to squalor, and you know it. To your great noble family you must admit me, you have no choice, but around the accident of my title, you hold your noses. Because I am both obvious and overpraised, and you can forgive anything but that? Or, finally, is the cause too simple ever to be discovered? *(Pause)*

Why, whatever the reason, you monumental gentlemen who tell lies about me and beat your own wives, you regal bitches who invite me one day into your bodies and into a social slaughterhouse the next, you are shameless frauds—*I* blush for *you*—you are priests without religion, you are saints without morals—you defy burlesque!

(Passionately) You are the canker and the worm! You are the death of the heart! And you will never, ever admit that you are also, at the bottom of your souls, man and woman, every last one of you, the same poor *animal* I am: the slave of your unfound love, as I am the slave of mine! *(Pause)*

Bell! Still do I cling to the wreck of my hopes, before it sinks forever. Were you never happy with me? You were. Did no affection pass between us? It did. We can have our place in life together. We should. We will. Leave these people. Say but one word, and I will come to you this moment, and buckle you, Kate, against a million!

CHILDE BYRON

BY ROMULUS LINNEY

BYRON: No. I saw something. A shape, a form. ☐☐☐ I lived with my countess and her husband, for a while. That is the custom in Italy. You become a cavaliere servente. Rhymes with plenty. A flatterer of tenors, a fan-carrier of dowagers, an expert in the arrangement of shawls and lace. It was life as it really is: the opera. Five notes of plea-sure, one scene of hysteria, and four acts of boredom. The count left his countess. I remained, steadfast. Shelley came, with his hopeless poems, his radical self-righteousness, and his talented wife he con-stantly dreamed about choking. Visions of dead babies in the foam of the sea, huge breasts turning into eyes, staring at him. Shelley's wife brought along her younger sister, who climbed in bed with me—and, I suspect, with Shelley—until finally she could say, like her sister, she'd also had a baby by a poet. Which poet? I couldn't tell. The baby was beautiful, like me, crazy like Shelley, and nobody knew. I took her in, at their request. A little girl, like you. I fed her cake. □□□

Shelley was a good critic. We read our poems to each other, talked the candles down, rode with our women through the forests, by the lakes. I began—with great pleasure—*Don Juan*— □□□ Which every-one insisted I stop writing because it was obscene. It was only funny. □□□

Our little natural baby died in the convent school where I put her, to grow up as she should, with other children, and her mother accused me of murder, Shelley had fits. She died of a fever, asking a nun for a piece of cake. □□□

I wasn't Childe Harold anymore. I got fat again. My skin turned sal-low. My teeth came loose. My curls went limp. On hotel registers, where it said Age [I wrote one hundred]. □□□

The form, the shape began to emerge. My life—I saw it plainly—what a mess. A man's soul, *parboiled* by his youth. □□□

Like poor Shelley's brains in the cauldron of his skull, seething, bubbling, boiling there, when we dug him out of the sand of an Italian beach, and cremated him in a tin oven, making a ceremony out of a suicide, which is what he was. And what I would be, too. *(Pause)*

The shape of his life, and mine. Complete. But how to do it? I had always been the great swimmer, so it would really be too embar-rassing to drown, like Shelley. Or put a bullet in my head, since I had pointed so many pistols so many times elsewhere. But there it was, like a ship in the fog, waiting to take me—where?

JACK

BY DAVID GREENSPAN

Character 8, the "Jack" of the play's title, remembers an early scene from a life now over. Jack is dead. Suffering from brain tumors and more than one hundred lesions (AIDS is implied though not named), he committed suicide. Until this scene his life has been recounted by three female speakers, illuminated to appear like "floating busts," in overlapping, partial and mostly unpunctuated sentences. They've described Jack's mother, a beauty who, gone fat and mean after contracting lupus, beat and persecuted her son. Aunt Rosie and the father, presumably long gone by the time Jack dies, are detailed here for the first time.

CHARACTER 8:

So. Okay. So now . . . now I'm lost on the beach. And this is like—this is the time when Aunt Rosie is out from Chicago. And . . . oh—and Aunt Rosie, you know, Aunt Rosie, I mean was like four feet tall, and she had this orange hair—like from the beauty parlor, and she looked like . . . well, that's kind of what she looked like. And I'm lost because . . . well, I went along the . . . shore looking for shells; I used to collect shells—from the beach, and I've . . . gone, you know, too far I'm . . . lost; I'm . . . well, I'd just gone too far. So . . . now I'm look-ing for the umbrella—for our umbrella. But it's hard, because . . . well, there are thousands of umbrellas. I mean everybody has an umbrel-la, you know—you can rent an umbrella—they have stands where—even if you don't have one you can rent one, and . . . anyway, that's just to say that there are thousands of umbrellas; and I can't locate—you see, every time I think I've located our umbrella, I run up to it and there are people I don't recognize. I mean, I don't know, you know, like when you think you've located your family and you run up to their their umbrella and it's not your family; it's people you don't know. So . . . and I was frightened that my parents are going to leave without me, and (I don't know why I thought that) but I was scared because . . . well, there are people on the beach, adults, you know, who obvi-ously know that I'm lost and want to help me, But every time some-one—I mean I was just scared that—I don't know that they'll arrest me or something, or that I'll get in trouble or something. You know,

I'm just frightened. So if someone asked me if I was lost I'd just say no and try to look like, you know, I wasn't lost. I mean . . .

Anyway. So . . . anyway, suddenly I see my father. Well, actually it's my Aunt Rosie I see first because, you know, she had this orange hair that's very distinct. Distinctive. But I see my father next to her, and my father is walking towards me, and he has a big smile on his face, and I'm really happy—I must have been so relieved to see him; and maybe I start to cry or something like that. And he's calling out to me; he's calling my name. "Jack. Hey Jackie. Jack." My father. So I drop my shells; I had a plastic cup full of . . . ummm shells, and I run to him and I'm crying I'm pretty sure I'm crying at this point, and I throw my arms around his waist and I bury my face in his swimming trunks—which are wet and sandy—and wet. And my father is laugh- ing. My father is . . . I don't know, embarrassed(?) because I'm cry- ing—and he's laughing. I mean this is what it was always like; my mother would be screaming and yelling and throwing things around the apartment and

(Hold. Turning sharply to the upstage right offstage) What? *(Back to his audience)* Wait; wait a minute. *(Back to the offstage, very angry)* What?! No! No; we're not finished yet! We're not finished! All right, but we're not finished yet! *(Turns back to his audience, upset at being interrupted. Slight aggravated "Pheww")* Don't put that on the tape. Don't leave that on the tape. You're not going to leave that on the tape (?). Yeah, don't leave that on the tape. All right, so where was . . . oh, right; she'd be screaming and yelling, right, and throw- ing things around the apartment and my father would be laughing at her—just laughing at her like. . . . Whatever. Something like that. And there's kind of a crowd of people gathered, and I'm crying, my father is laughing, and Aunt Rosie is telling everybody that I had gotten lost. "No, no; he just got lost." And—oh—and I can—I can hear my mother; my mother is calling to my father's—calling out my father's name. "Marty! Marty!!" And she's really yelling, and she's obviously very angry. She sounds very angry. So, you know. It wasn't . . . it. . . . no; it

XIII

"NOW TELL ME WHAT IT MEANS"

THE LOMAN FAMILY PICNIC

BY DONALD MARGULIES

Stewie, thirteen, lives with his younger brother and parents in an apartment in Brooklyn in 1965. He's a week away from his bar mitzvah, a day his mother describes as "a gala affair starring me." After Hebrew school one day, he breaks the news to her.

STEWIE: I've had it. Cancel the bar mitzvah. □□□

Mr. Shlosh is a cretin. □□□ I don't care he's a rabbi, he's still a cretin. We're going over my Haftarah . . . □□□

I know almost all of it by heart. □□□

And I'm really singing it this time. Like Jerry Vale. Soft and sweet? It's so beautiful I'm embarrassing myself, I feel my cheeks getting hot. And I get through the whole thing perfectly, I sound just like the record, and he doesn't even compliment me! □□□

He's not human. □□□ I decided to have a conversation with him? □□□

Big mistake. I mean, I've been sitting in this room with this guy with bad breath for years, reading the same stuff over and over, preparing me for the big day, right?, and he never even talked to me! I don't mean Talmudic dialogue, I mean your basic chat. □□□

I gave up my boyhood to him, Ma! Hundreds of afternoons I'll never get back! I missed years of watching *You Don't Say* after school! That's irreplaceable, Ma. □□□

So I thought I was entitled to ask a question at least. I said to Shlosh, "Okay, so finally I can read all these little symbols right to left. Great. Now tell me what it means." Well, the guy looks like he's gonna go berserk. □□□ Like Ray Milland in *X—the Man with the X-Ray Eyes* right before he plucks his eyes out? □□□ "Tell me what I'm reading," I said, "tell me what the words mean." He looks at me like I'm not speaking any known language. "What does it mean?!," I said, "what am I saying?!" "What does it matter?," he says, "you can read it." "Yeah, but what does it mean?!" "It means you will be bar mitzvah!," he says. "But the words don't mean anything to me, they're just these funny, *chuchy* little sounds." "Those funny sounds," he says, "are what make a boy different from a Jew!" "So?! You taught me how to read but you didn't teach me how to understand! What kind of Jew is that?!" This does not go over big. His lips are turning blue. I think he's gonna have an angina attack. *(Beat)* All he cares about is rolling out bar mitzvah boys to repopulate the earth. We look the part and we can sing, but we don't know what we're saying! I have had it!

WHAT DID HE SEE?

BY RICHARD FOREMAN

Foreman's experimental theatre pieces are plays of ideas, bold phys-ical gestures, and dark, extravagant fun. He considers What Did He See, *although still nonrealistic, his most autobiographical play—"a kind of spiritual autobiography." Will, named after Will Patton, who originated the role, is a surrogate for Foreman, caught in a moment of philosophical reckoning: "how to deal with the realization that the goals you work toward aren't worth a candle, while nonetheless understanding that giving up is morally unacceptable." This dilemma means crisis for a man who's chosen a reclusive life of the spirit. Will's a Byronic type, "a recherché recluse, a romantic figure, who was also a little Lord Fauntleroy in a bathrobe."*

WILL:
Here's the truth:
Since I've been young
when confronted with a task
I've wanted to get through
that task as quickly as possible,
so that,
freed of the task,
I could again be in a state
of nonactivity.

Outside time? □□□
Resting in place.
Doing . . . Nothing.
Why?
Because perhaps I realized there was no value in producing
anything really
No value
in letting the impulse of a conditioned, hypnotized person such as
my representative self, COAGULATE . . . into an artifact, into a thing,
a task accomplished, or an adventure. □□□

Because the corruption of my own fallen, conditioned state would be
hidden in the center of that THING I would produce no matter how
beautiful and seductive that thing might seem. That hidden corrup-
tion would separate me, and others, from the true source inside the
self.
Alas.
How can I make that "alas" . . . more
believable. More heartrending.
Alas.
That's what's most seductive about me. Be careful. That "alas."
(Pause)
Alas.
(Pause, then he tries again with feeling)
Alas.
(He smiles)
That's another one of my little secrets—"Alas." □□□
By the way . . . what is the REAL TIME in which I claim to find myself
placed? And why this need to solidify such real time in the midst
of our shared experience? Turning it into some kind of . . . specta-
cle? Okay. Strike out irrelevant and foolish questions, because I've
already made a fool of myself in giving away my power. Except, giv-
ing away one's power is not making a fool of oneself. It depends
who's watching.

SLEEP DEPRIVATION CHAMBER

BY ADAM P. KENNEDY AND ADRIENNE KENNEDY

Teddy, son of a prominent African-American family, is a senior in college when police stop him outside his father's home for driving with a broken taillight. A policeman beats him, knocks him to the ground, and drags him across the driveway. The police then charge Teddy, who has never had any trouble with the law, with assault and battery. Here he describes his first meeting with the lawyer hired to defend him.

TEDDY: Her office was in a small brownstone in the black section of Alexandria and we must have easily waited twenty-five to thirty minutes before we were led downstairs into this gloomy basement office.

She was in her forties. After I told her what happened, she asked very few questions about the evening and acted like it was no big deal. Then she blurted out that for twelve-hundred dollars she could handle the case. But first, she needed some background information about me.

She asked me, had I ever been arrested before, and I responded, "No, of course no." She stared at me with this all-knowing eye and replied with a smirk on her face, "It's all right, you can tell me, even though your father's here, you can tell me if you have been arrested before. Come on!"

I was furious and ready to leave. What kind of help was she going to give me when she just assumed I had a police record and she didn't believe me. She painted a pretty bleak scenario of my chances of beating this assault charge. She said my best possible hope was to plead guilty and receive a suspended sentence.

As I sat in that chair, my mind filled with every graphic image of prison life. Every prison movie, prison documentary and prison story I had ever seen or heard blanketed my thoughts and sent absolute horror and fear to my heart.

I think at that point, everybody in the room was thinking the same thing, because they all just looked at me. I was afraid to ask. I feared what she might say but I had to know.

Am I going to jail for this?

THE MODERN LADIES OF GUANABACOA

BY EDUARDO MACHADO

Cuba, 1928. Oscar courts Manuela according to highly prescribed codes of behavior. Tonight is his first visit and he sits, as he will until they are married, surrounded by her family, which includes Manuela's mother and three brothers. A thirty-year-old taxi driver, Oscar will, within three years, run a thriving bus company, staffed by his new in-laws. He believes in himself and in his inevitable success; in a later scene he compares the meticulous blending of ingredients in business to the blending of "café."

OSCAR: It used to be a religious drink. □□□

It's still like a religious service. □□□

The name derives from the Arabic "Kahwah." □□□

Kahwah makes an aromatic beverage which is very valued which is made into brew with toasted and ground coffee seeds. In the thirteenth century a preaching Arabian mulatto observed how the cows after they ate the fruits of some trees became animated. He noticed a certain activity which departed from the norm and that it was a direct result from the trees and leaves they were eating. Well, the Arab, after noticing, prepared, with the grain of the before-mentioned kahwah, a brew which became a part of his religious ceremonies. The results were stupendous. His followers were able to stay awake through all the religious services. □□□

Since then, the use of coffee became generalized in Egypt's Pergia. It was introduced in Europe in 1660, passing through the French Antilles and later to South America. □□□

As the years passed, coffee began to become a habit according to the different customs of each different country. In each country, it had a special characteristic. In some countries, a small cup of coffee is used to welcome visitors. □□□

It's become more frequent an expression these days. To offer a small cup of aromatic café is to bring a note of courtesy to a reunion. □□□

In Europe as well as America, coffee shops became famous, where scholars and students seated around a table with their respective cups of aromatic café discussed very passionately, politics, literature, poetics and art. Some of these establishments, like . . . Merchants' Coffee House, have become a part of history. ☐☐☐

It was there in 1717, no 1774, a "Committee of Correspondence," started by New Yorkian patriots, sent a letter to a group of Bostonians proposing the union of American colonies. ☐☐☐

Well, today the producers of the fabulous bean are Colombia, Brazil, ☐☐☐ Guatemala, El Salvador, Mexico, Costa Rica, Honduras, Haiti, Santo Domingo, Puerto Rico, Cuba. ☐☐☐

Yes, today in the entire world, one always savors a small cup of the brown nectar from the white gods.

WOMBmanWARs

BY JUDITH ALEXA JACKSON

WOMBmanWARs, *a solo performance piece about sexual and racial politics, intercuts clips from the Clarence Thomas hearings with scenes from the Mike Tyson/Desiree Washington confrontation, stylized movement theatre, and stand-alone satirical monologues like the one below, in and around the more naturalistic story of a couple and their daughter. While Jackson, an African-American woman, played Senator Out-to-Lunch in a large white mask representing the white male establishment, other actors will find other ways.*

SENATOR OUT-TO-LUNCH: Please turn with me, Professor, to page 94 in the transcript of your testimony.

About halfway down the page, you will see the item in question. This morning I asked you if you intended to have lunch today. You answered, and I quote, "No, I won't be having lunch today."

Do you see that on your copy Professor? "No, I won't be having lunch today"? Is that a fair reading of your statement?

I'd like now to come to a consensus, an agreement, if you will, on the definition of lunch.

If there are no objections, I'd like to submit as evidence the definition of lunch as stated in Webster's Unabridged Dictionary. And I quote, "a light repast taken between breakfast and dinner; usually around noon." Would you agree, Professor, that that is a fair representation of the word "lunch"?

I want you to think before you answer this next question Professor. Is it fair to surmise that the sandwich I saw you eating at noon today was your lunch? Did you not state on page 94 of the transcript that you would not be having lunch. But, yet, as soon as our collective backs were turned you had lunch. LIAR. LIAR. PANTS. ON. FIRE. How can you expect us to believe anything you have to say about the honorable judge is beyond me. You . . . you . . . you Lunch EATER.

XIV
"IT'S TIME WE GO OUR SEPARATE WAYS"

THE MODEL APARTMENT

BY DONALD MARGULIES

In the middle of the night, Max and his wife, both Holocaust survivors in their sixties, run away to their retirement home in Florida, hoping to elude their "obese, unkempt, mentally disturbed" daughter Debby. Debby, however, chases after, tracking them to the model condominium in which they've been put up until their own unit is ready. When Debby turns on Max and tries to strangle him, her parents subdue her (with the help of Debby's teenage, mildly retarded boyfriend), gag her and tie her to a chair. She's in the chair now, and Max strokes her hair, as he explains.

MAX: Debby. *(Shrugs)* I pour everything I *got* into you. Nothing works. Special schools, special doctors. Hospitals. "Residences." In-patient, out-patient. My head spins from you. *(A small chuckle)* You're amazing! I never knew a person like you. You don't give up. You come after us no matter what. You're amazing! We don't sleep at night, worried what you might do. We live our *lives* worried what you might do. We gotta face the facts: You gotta help yourself. I can't make you get well. Your *mother* can't make you get well. You gotta get well your*self*. *(A beat)* It's time we go our separate ways I think. □□□

Shh shh shh. You think I en*joy* this? The way we have to live? Yelling and carrying on? No good. How many good years we got left, your mother and me? Think about it. *(Shrugs: "What am I supposed to do?")* I'm a simple man, nothing special. I walked out of the woods. For what? So I could come to America? Sell sportswear in Flatbush? For this I walked out of the woods? Where are the children? Where are the grandchildren? *(A beat)* Look, darling . . . all I want . . . I want to clip on my clip-on sunglasses, put up my feet, sit in the Florida sun, read my *Wall Street Journal*, see how my stocks are doing. *(A beat)* Sweetheart . . . *(Pause)* Debby . . . *(A very deep sigh)* Why can't we just shake hands, wish each other luck. Hm? Is that so terrible?

THE SUBSTANCE OF FIRE

BY JON ROBIN BAITZ

Isaac Geldhart, the director of the distinguished but increasingly unprofitable Kreeger/Geldhart Publishers, is confronted by his three children. Although Isaac hired his M.B.A. son Aaron to run the business end of the company, he addresses him with characteristic disdain and treats him like a lackey, refusing to credit or listen to him, especially now. Aaron wants to publish a novel he thinks will provide a life raft for the foundering company. Isaac dismisses it as a "trashy novel by a slicko-hipster." Their disagreement ignites a family crisis that has been mounting since the death of Mrs. Geldhart six years before. In that time, Isaac has grown steadily more isolated, intractable and financially self-destructive. He's publishing only the most esoteric books, such as a glossary of Anglo-Indian words and a six-volume study of Nazi medical experiments. Isaac wears "a dark suit of impeccable cut" and has "the slightest of accents—Belgian/ German, barely detectable."

ISAAC: I spent a couple of days, a little boy, wandering around after the liberation. I saw a particular kind of man—a wraith-like figure—who could only have been in the camps. But with a brown pinstripe suit, a fleur-de-lis on his tie and manicured nails, trying to pick up where he left off, as if you could. I never say anything about this. Why talk? Why bother? I wasn't in the camps. You know? They're busy throwing the Farbers and the Hirsches into the ovens, and I'm happily eating smoked eels in the basement, with my Stendahl, my Dumas. What did I know? I was protected, sheltered by my cousins. And then I got out of the basement and into the wrecked world. I came to this country. You reinvent yourself. Make it as a bon vivant in Manhattan. Meet this woman—this extraordinary woman. Marry. Have these kids. Go to so many cocktail parties, host so many more, but still . . . they haunt. *(Beat)* I have kept my eyes closed to the world outside the basement for so long. The wrecked world all around us. But I can no longer close my eyes. *(He turns to Aaron)* My son. You are fired. I will give you a week to clear your desk, and I will give you letters of recommendation. But I will not speak to you, I will not communicate with you, I will not . . . *(Pause)* . . . *give at all.* Kiddo. To the victor go the spoils.

THE SUBSTANCE OF FIRE

BY JON ROBIN BAITZ

Martin Geldhart's father, a distinguished publisher, has always been exacting, caustic and full of rage, but in the six years since his wife died, he's seemed hell-bent on hurting everyone, isolating himself from the world and destroying his business. When Martin, his brother Aaron and sister Sarah intervene to save the business, Isaac turns his venom on them. The conflict weighs heavily on Martin, who, having recovered from cancer as a teenager, staged a solitary retreat of his own to a quiet life teaching landscape architecture at Vassar. He wants out of the family drama and makes a first stab at it here by giving up his part of the business.

MARTIN: Publish *Hustler* or publish Proust. I don't want to have anything to do with it anymore. Your books. God. I am so tired of these books. And your endless posturing, position-taking, ranting, judging. □□□

You want to talk about poison? Look at what you've done. You've created a family of literary zombies. You know that people are afraid of you. It's why you've gotten so far. Yes. "Isaac Geldhart knows something, he came from some awful childhood in Europe that nobody knows about." He has a "seer-like standing in the book world." Blah-blah-blah—phooey. Let me tell you, we're fucked up by it. I grew up running around this building. When I was eight, you gave me the *Iliad* in Greek so that someday I could read it. Monster! People's lives are ruined by books and they're all you know how to relate to, Dad. You too, Aaron, for all your talk. You too, Sarah, pretending you hate to read. Sometimes I want to take a pruning shears and do an Oedipus on myself. I counted my books last week. Do you know how many I have? Want to take a guess? □□□

Fourteen thousand, three hundred, and eighty-six. The sixty crates of books that Mom left me. Well, I finally had them carted up the Hudson, but I had to have shelves built. The whole house. Every room. And instead of just guessing—I was, I mean—speechless. A wreck of a life. It just flashed before my eyes. No sex, no people, just books 'til I die. Dickens. In *French*. The bastard didn't write in French. What the fuck am I doing with *Dombey and Son* in French? The twelve-volume *Conquest of Mexico*. Two hundred cookbooks. The *Oxford World Classics*, the little ones with the blue bindings, you know? □□□

They're all just words. And this is life, and besides, I hear the book chains are now selling preemptive strike video games, so why bother anyway? I'm out.

FULL MOON

BY REYNOLDS PRICE

Walter Parker, in his mid-thirties, has been cook and butler to the Bascombs for years and, so, is "firmly aware" of his indispensability. He "enjoys alternating a refined white accent with his deeper native black. . . . His self-assurance and dignity are strong." So is his belief in dreams and spirits. The nineteen-year-old Kerney Bascomb, on the verge of a decision that will change her life, comes to Walter with a dream in which her dead mother appeared to point the way. Walter gives Kerney a gift: the story of her mother's last living moment.

WALTER: I held her the instant she left this world. □□□

Right at the end her face got young. She said "Walter Parker, here, set me up." Your pa had told me not to move her an inch; it hurt her that bad. So I told her I couldn't, and she warned me hard. *(Walter's voice lightens but no falsetto)* "If you don't set me up this instant, I'll claw my way back here from the grave and press you down."

So I raised her up. Turned out, that way she could finally breathe. She drew one breath about two minutes long and shot me a smile. Then she said "Walter Parker, give that frown a rest. I'm looking at things you can't even dream. Where I am now is all pure water with low trees smelling like white honeysuckle. Tell everybody I know, the grass is deep."

I said "Miss Christine, then you mow it for me"—she knew how much I hate to mow grass. She opened her mouth to say her answer. I could see she meant it to be another joke. The air moved in front of her face but no words came.

XV

"I CHOOSE NOT TO BE INCONSOLABLE"

DRINKS BEFORE DINNER

BY E. L. DOCTOROW

Joel, a successful doctor, is, with his wife, the host of a dinner party thrown in their "modern, well-appointed" New York City apartment for an old friend, a government secretary and Nobel Peace Prize winner. Before the guest of honor arrives, though, another guest, Edgar, hijacks the discussion with a diatribe against the meaninglessness of their lives. In elevated, literate conversational tones, the privileged partyers debate life-and-death principles. Here, Joel counters Edgar's desolation with his own sense of order and purpose in a difficult world.

JOEL: This evening Edgar is in great pain. We're trying to console him, but he's inconsolable. Today he went about his business as usual, and tomorrow he will go about his usual business, but this evening he finds himself inconsolable. Of course, by his own admission he doesn't know anything the rest of us don't know, nor perceive anything we can't perceive. We all know and perceive the same things. As a physician I probably have more of a reason than anyone to be inconsolable. I know of more disgusting and degrading means of dying than anyone else in this room could possibly know. Every day of the week I perform five or six operations of the same kind. I get up early in the morning to do that. Every day in the week thousands of physicians all over the country get up very early in the morning to do the same operations for the people who have come to us for the same conditions for which other people have come to us. The admissions officers of hospital emergency rooms can calculate by the week and month and year how many knifings they will get, how many shootings, how many cardiac arrests, how many ODs, how many car wrecks. They know in advance. Cars go up on sidewalks, through store windows, they skid into each other in the rain, they collide at intersections, they crash head-on on the highways. It is very farcical what cars do. They run into lampposts or hurtle off bridges. Trains derail, buckle, plow into the rear of other trains. Airplanes take off and crash, and they crash on landing. They hit other airplanes in the air, they turn on their wingtips on the runway, they skid off the runway, they miss the runway altogether. Everything disastrous that happens to people usually happens to many people at the same time. They even get sick in great numbers, as in epidemics. You would think that illness was a personal thing and a matter of individual character, but people are poisoned in great numbers by the food they eat at the same dinners, or they get cancer together from working in the same factories. There is very little that people can do disastrously by themselves. Neither crashing in airplanes nor burning to death in tenements. Most of the time, these things are done by groups of people. And of course, war is done by groups of people, and the dying in wars is comprised of enormous numbers of people. In fact, that is the meaning of dying in wars, that it be done by the greatest possible numbers of people. So it is all very painful. There's very little dignity possible and I find that quite painful. Nevertheless, nevertheless, I choose not to be inconsolable.

THE FILM SOCIETY

BY JON ROBIN BAITZ

The Blenheim School for Boys in Durban, South Africa, 1970. Hamish Fox is undergoing treatment for spinal cancer, a condition he compares to the "spread of decay and rot of our Africa." Before long, it will kill him. He is a hard-line British conservative and an exacting, even brutal, master in this academy for sons of the ruling class. This lecture will be his last.

FOX *(To class)*: When writing an essay, every thought must be crystal clear. Picture the sentence before you. Does it look correct? The comma in the right place? Spelling accurate? And the thought itself. How is that? Your penmanship must not waver because when it does, it weakens the idea. And, of equal importance, is that you do not let an inkblot foul the paper. Nothing is so damaging as an inkblot, like some vile black stain, occluding the light, breaking clarity. Make certain that the ink is running smoothly through the body of the pen to the nib which must never be bent. The nib must be as clean as the surgeon's scalpel—as vital an instrument. Imprint of the manufacturer must always be visible on the nib or blots will occur. Do not put red ink into a pen which has had blue or black. Rather, keep three pens. If you cannot afford three pens, then you must wash the one thoroughly before putting in the new color of ink. From the blue book, learn three new words a day. You must be able to convey the clarity of your intent under fire, in the office, on the field; clarity of expression equals success. Your privilege is this education which separates you from the savage and, in the years ahead, this will be a most formidable weapon. *(Pause)* I would also say, if I may be a bit more personal for a moment, that I would prefer it if nobody visited me in hospital—a strain on all parties that is best avoided. So, without further rigmarole, I shall see you, I'm certain, after Boxing Day when I shall tell you about the idiocy of the Maginot Line. And Douglas Bader, the war hero with no legs.

CHRISTMAS ON MARS

BY HARRY KONDOLEON

Nissim, a thirty-year-old "slightly pudgy" former airline steward, is a self-described "fruity" guy who chooses "to be frivolous." He'll go to the most exaggerated lengths to break up the romance between Bruno, his handsome roommate of ten years, and Bruno's fiancée Audrey. When Nissim finds out the couple is about to have a baby, he plops himself down in their new apartment to stay, determined to live only for the baby. The baby, he's certain, "will love me in the way no one and nothing has ever loved me." Audrey's mother, Ingrid, moves in, too, showing up years after abandoning her daughter to follow a man she loved. She's been Nissim's ally in this strange extended family. Now she's ready to walk out again—an abandonment he can't take. As Ingrid leaves the room, Nissim's credo—"We can brighten our own days can't we? We don't have to wake up in a

cloud depressed desperate, angry, and waiting to die"—is chal-
lenged. Nissim, practicing baby care on a plastic doll, responds in his
usual fashion: with desperate denial.

NISSIM: You've lost faith!—you can't lose faith! You haven't been reading the newspapers have you? I told you not to look at them, it's the same news over and over—they try to make you think it's some other news by making it more shocking on alternate days but it's the same thing and pieced together certainly to make us lose faith.
  (Ingrid exits)
  DON'T ABANDON ME! *(To himself, red alarm)* I mustn't collapse. I must think of presents and happiness. *(He picks up the practice doll)* Oh little play-baby, do you love me? I love you. You do, I know you do. Why don't we open some of our presents, wouldn't that be fun? It's naughty but oh let's. What would be in this pretty box, hard to tell. *(He opens it, using occasionally the forced help of the practice doll)* A brush and comb set for you, how nice, but we'll have to put those away for a while until you're a little less bald. What could be in this big box? Let's just see. Ooo! A coat with matching little shoes. Do you like them? Let's just try them on, okay? *(He puts the red baby coat and red shoes on the practice doll)* How dashing, how smart! You're a clever baby, ready for school already but I'll never send you to one of those public torture chambers don't worry or one of those schools named after saints that breed devils. I will teach you everything you need to know. Ask me a question. "Where do babies come from?" From God, little baby. "Who is God?" God is everything good and holy and pure and kind and healthy and growing and generous and good and good and good, that is God, little baby. "And where is he, where is God?" Why God is right above us, little baby, looking down on us. "Why then, tell me, why won't he help us, help us all, even just for a minute?" That's enough questions. We must get on our horse and ride away very fast from these questions, very fast because they will chase us, chase us through the day.

FURTHER READING

At TCG we have been honored to work with the following writers to provide a permanent home for their art in book form. We urge you to explore further these exceptional artists.

JON ROBIN BAITZ
The Film Society and *The Substance of Fire* from *The Substance of Fire and Other Plays*, copyright ©1993.

Three Hotels from *Three Hotels: Plays and Monologues*, copyright ©1994.

ERIC BOGOSIAN
Drinking in America from *The Essential Bogosian*, copyright ©1994.

Pounding Nails in the Floor with My Forehead, copyright ©1994.

LEE BREUER
The Gospel at Colonus, copyright ©1989.

CONSTANCE CONGDON
Casanova, *Losing Father's Body* and *No Mercy* from *Tales of the Lost Formicans and Other Plays*, copyright ©1994.

E. L. DOCTOROW
Drinks Before Dinner, copyright ©1978 and 1979.

RICHARD FOREMAN
Symphony of Rats and *What Did He See?* from *Unbalancing Acts: Foundations for a Theater*, copyright ©1992, published by arrangement with Random House, Inc.

MARIA IRENE FORNES
The Conduct of Life from *On New Ground: Contemporary Hispanic-American Plays*, copyright ©1986, published by arrangement with PAJ Publications.

MILCHA SANCHEZ-SCOTT
Roosters from *On New Ground: Contemporary Hispanic-American Plays*, copyright ©1987.

NICKY SILVER
Fat Men in Skirts, The Food Chain and *Free Will & Wanton Lust* from *Etiquette and Vitriol: The Food Chain and Other Plays*, copyright ©1996.

Raised in Captivity, copyright ©1995.

STEPHEN SONDHEIM AND JOHN WEIDMAN
Assassins, copyright ©1990 and 1991.

STEPHEN SONDHEIM, JOHN WEIDMAN AND HUGH WHEELER
Pacific Overtures, copyright ©1986.

PAULA VOGEL
Hot 'N' Throbbing from *The Baltimore Waltz and Other Plays*, copyright ©1996.

How I Learned to Drive from *The Mammary Plays*, copyright ©1998.

The following list provides contact information regarding performance rights to the works included in this volume:

Jon Robin Baitz c/o George Lane, William Morris Agency, 1325 Ave. of the Americas, NY NY 10019; Eric Bogosian c/o George Lane, William Morris Agency, 1325 Ave. of the Americas, NY NY 10019; Lee Breuer c/o TCG; Constance Congdon c/o William Morris Agency, 1325 Ave. of the Americas, NY NY 10019; E. L. Doctorow c/o Amanda Urban, International Creative Management, 40 W. 57th St., NY NY 10019; Richard Foreman c/o TCG; Maria Irene Fornes c/o PAJ Publications, Box 260 Village Station, NY NY 10014; Philip Kan Gotanda c/o Dramatists Play Service, Inc., 440 Park Ave. South, NY NY 10016; Spalding Gray c/o TCG; David Greenspan c/o TCG; William M. Hoffman c/o Random House, Inc., 201 E. 50th St., NY NY 10022; Tina Howe c/o Flora Roberts, Inc., 157 W. 57th St., NY NY 10019; Judith Alexis Jackson c/o TCG; John Jesurun c/o TCG; Adam P. Kennedy and Adrienne Kennedy c/o Joyce Ketay Agency, 1501 Broadway, Suite 1908, NY NY 10036; Harry Kondoleon c/o George Lane, William Morris Agency, 1325 Ave. of the Americas, NY NY 10019; Tony Kushner c/o Joyce Ketay Agency, 1501 Broadway, Suite 1908, NY NY 10036; Romulus Linney c/o Peregrine Whittlesey Agency, 345 E. 80th St., #31F, NY NY 10021; Eduardo Machado c/o TCG; Emily Mann c/o George Lane, William Morris Agency, 1325 Ave. of the Americas, NY NY 10019; Donald Margulies c/o Rosenstone / Wender, 3 E. 48th St., NY NY 10017; Marsha Norman c/o The Tantleff Agency, 375 Greenwich St., Suite 603, NY NY 10013; John O'Keefe c/o TCG; Suzan-Lori Parks c/o George Lane, William Morris Agency, 1325 Ave. of the Americas, NY NY 10019; Reynolds Price c/o TCG; Ronald Ribman c/o TCG; José Rivera c/o Joyce Ketay Agency, 1501 Broadway, Suite 1908, NY NY 10036; Milcha Sanchez-Scott c/o George Lane, William Morris Agency, 1325 Ave. of the Americas, NY NY 10019; Nicky Silver c/o George Lane, William Morris Agency, 1325 Ave. of the Americas, NY NY 10019; Stephen Sondheim c/o Flora Roberts, Inc., 157 W. 57th St., NY NY 10019; Paula Vogel c/o Peter Franklin, William Morris Agency, 1325 Ave. of the Americas, NY NY 10019; John Weidman c/o TCG.

TODD LONDON is the artistic director of New Dramatists, the country's oldest center for the support and development of playwrights. A former managing editor of *American Theatre* magazine and the author of *The Artistic Home*, published by Theatre Communications Group, he recently served as guest literary director of the American Repertory Theatre and visiting lecturer of dramatic arts at Harvard. He writes regularly about the arts for *American Theatre, The Village Voice*, and others. In 1993–94, he was senior writer on *Theatre in America*, a five-part documentary series in development for Great Performances, WNET/Thirteen in New York. He was an assistant professor of drama at New York University's Tisch School of the Arts from 1990–94. He has chaired the New York State Council on the Arts theatre panel and served as associate artistic director of New York's Classic Stage Company. In 1997, his writing for *American Theatre* magazine, including his three-part series "Open Call: A Year in the Lives of 15 Actors Starting Out in New York," garnered him the George Jean Nathan Award for dramatic criticism.

TCG Individual Membership

As a TCG book buyer, you're invited to become an Individual Member of **Theatre Communications Group**—the national organization for the American theatre and the publisher of **American Theatre** magazine.

As an Individual Member of TCG, you'll get inside information about theatre performances around the country, as well as substantial discounts on tickets to performances and publications about the theatre. Plus, as the primary advocate for not-for-profit professional theatre in America, TCG will ensure that your voice is heard in Washington. We invite you to join us today and receive all of TCG's benefits!

Members Receive These Special Benefits

- A FREE subscription to *American Theatre* magazine—10 issues . . . 5 complete playscripts . . . artist profiles . . . in-depth coverage of contemporary, classical and avant-garde performances . . . 3 special issues—including *Season Preview* (October), *Theatre Training* (January) and *Summer Festival Preview* (May).
- Discounts on tickets to performances at more than 230 participating theatres nationwide.
- 15% discount on resource materials including *Theatre Profiles, Theatre Directory, ArtSEARCH* and *Dramatists Sourcebook*—all musts for the theatre professional or the serious theatregoer.
- A FREE catalogue of publications.
- 10% discount on all books from TCG and other select theatre publishers.
- Your personalized Individual Membership card.

Take Advantage Now and Save!
Become a TCG Individual Member and
Receive Extraordinary Benefits!

❑ **YES,** I would like a one-year Individual Membership to TCG, which includes a subscription to *American Theatre*, among other extraordinary benefits.

> ❑ Individual Membership ~~$35.00~~ $30.00.
> ❑ Student Membership (enclose copy of ID) $20.

❑ **I prefer a two-year membership.**

> ❑ Individual Membership ~~$70.00~~ $55.00.

❑ **TOTAL ORDER** _____

To order, you may: Send this form to TCG Order Dept., 355 Lexington Ave, NY, NY 10017-0217; or Call (212) 697-5230, ext. 260; or Fax (212) 983-4847; or send E-mail to: orders@tcg.org.

❑ Check is enclosed. ❑ Please charge my credit card.
❑ VISA ❑ MC ❑ AMEX

NAME

ADDRESS

CITY	STATE	ZIP

* | PHONE/FAX/E-MAIL |

CARD #	EXP. DATE:

SIGNATURE

OCCUPATION/TITLE

* **all orders must have telephone number**

For Individual Memberships outside the U.S., please add $12 per year (U.S. currency only, drawn from U.S. Bank). Allow 6-8 weeks from receipt of order.